DANGER

Danger

Published by The Conrad Press in the United Kingdom 2020

Tel: +44(0)1227 472 874
www.theconradpress.com
info@theconradpress.com

ISBN 978-1-913567-33-0

Copyright © Robin Nye, 2020

The moral right of Robin Nye to be identified as author of this work has been asserted in accordance with the Copyright, Designs and Patents Act 1988.

All rights reserved.

Typesetting and Cover Design by:
Charlotte Mouncey, www.bookstyle.co.uk

The Conrad Press logo was designed by Maria Priestley.

Printed and bound in Great Britain by Clays Ltd, Elcograf S.p.A.

DANGER

Robin Nye

For Barbara

1
Tuesday 18 July

The path was rutted where muddy earth, squelched by hundreds of walkers in spring rainstorms, had become baked in the unusually hot summer weather.

Bushes and other woodland vegetation had grown uncontrolled since his last visit to this part of the estate so that he faced some potentially unpleasant hazards – a trip and a fall or a slap across the face from an unseen branch. Brambles were also growing out of control and their long tentacles pricked at his bare arms, occasionally succeeding in drawing pinpoints of blood. Stinging nettles waved serenely in what little breeze there was – just waiting for the faintest of touches to make life uncomfortable for unsuspecting victims.

Negotiating all these hazards, the man hurried on. He could see the water now and it wasn't long before the path dropped down to the edge of a lake which stretched out before him. He stopped to take in the scene on this hot summer afternoon. Staring off into the distance, he never failed to be surprised to see a lighthouse standing sentry-like in the middle of the lake. The building rose majestically towards the skies, its white walls showing signs of age and the ravages of the weather. The lamps had been removed a long time ago, and birds perched on the guard rail of the gallery which ran around the circumference of the boarded-up lantern room. They would have had an excellent view of the surrounding vegetation, the larger species perhaps lining up their next foray into the water below.

His mind flashed back to the last time he was here. With

only the faintest glimpses of the moon on an otherwise cloudy night, he had piloted the dinghy across the lake carrying its cargo – a zipped up black bag attached to four 25kg weights. Water had lapped over the sides of the dinghy and pooled around his feet. He had great difficulty mooring the small craft to the short wooden jetty which poked out from the entrance to the lighthouse, many of its timbers rotten with age. He had, however, eventually succeeded in getting a rope attached to one of the mooring points on the jetty, and then managed to get the bag over the side of the dinghy but not before he had almost gone into the water himself. The thought of drowning had always terrified him as a life-long non-swimmer.

Now he pushed these thoughts to the back of his mind as he negotiated the path round to the head of the lake where he rested on the wall overlooking a small weir, the water from the lake cascading down to a stream below. The stillness of the isolated location, the heat of the sun and the gentle sound of the water had a soporific effect on the man as he surveyed the scene of his darkest deeds. He stared at the sheer beauty of the woodland setting, trying to draw strength from his surroundings to help him overcome the severe misgivings he had about what he would be doing later tonight when he returned to this spot.

His reverie was rudely interrupted by the alarm on his phone which he had set to give himself time to get back to the hotel, have a shower, order room service, and be ready to greet his visitor for their 8.00 p.m. meeting. He continued around the top of the lake and then gingerly made his way back down the south bank which he found even harder going as the vegetation was very overgrown on the pathway.

Drawing level with the lighthouse once again, he stepped gingerly down to the lake's edge. Here, the dense undergrowth stretched out on to the water and provided an ideal shelter for the little dinghy. Even up close, it was difficult to make out the shape of the vessel, and he was satisfied that no one could have stumbled upon it.

Leaving the lake behind him, he climbed back up to the top path and trudged on towards the hotel. Negotiating a wooden stile and a kissing gate, he then followed a drystone wall up to the hotel's effluent plant. Although the stench was not quite as bad as when he was last here, he still reached for his hand-kerchief and held it over his nose until he reached the car park at the front of the hotel. He ascended the weather-worn stone steps which led into the grand hallway and closed the door quietly behind him. He then took the stairs two at a time on the way to his room, and hoped that he had managed to avoid being seen by anyone. However, the words "Good evening, sir!" meant that he had not been able to keep under the radar of one eagle-eyed receptionist.

Turning the key in the lock and pushing the door inwards, he encountered a wall of heat. The room was stifling hot. He went across to open the ancient windows in a vain attempt to attract even the very faintest zephyr of cooling air. He should have closed the curtains before venturing out but never even thought of it at the time. A bottle of sparkling water sitting on the small coffee table beckoned him over, and he drank greedily until its contents had all but been drained.

He called up reception and ordered a light snack and a couple more bottles of cold sparkling water. He also asked for a full bucket of ice. After taking a quick shower, he threw on a pair of shorts and a T-shirt and waited for room service to arrive. As he relaxed, he cast his mind back to the last time he was in this room. Although the layout and décor were the same, he thought how different the circumstances had been. Suddenly, his thoughts were interrupted by a knock at the door. He stood up and went across the room to open it.

2

One Year earlier

The sun shone brightly out of an azure blue sky. It looked a great day for a bicycle ride. Her parents had gone to work. Her two brothers were away at army camp. Her sister was staying with a friend in Plovdiv but everyone knew that this was really just a cover for getting some time between the sheets with her boyfriend. So, she had the house to herself and was making the most of some quality time on her own. The first priority had been to have a good lie-in which was never possible when her restless sister was in residence. It was lovely just lying in bed watching the shadows dancing around on the ceiling as the sun shone through the trees outside her bedroom window.

Once she had tired of this luxury, she got up and threw back the curtains so that the sunlight flooded into the bedroom. She looked at herself in the full-length mirror and pinched her bed shirt where her hips should be. She made a face at her reflection in the mirror and then stepped out of the bedroom towards the bathroom. On her way, she just checked in her parents' room to make sure that they had gone to work but the coast was clear – she was on her own!

Desislava had always enjoyed her own company and had never felt the need to socialise on quite the same scale as her sister who was never happier than when she was the centre of attention in a group – preferably of men. But now that she was well on the way towards her seventeenth birthday, she had been wondering if it was time to broaden her horizons. So, today she was cycling over to see a friend of hers who lived on a farm to the south of the village. Everyone cycled in the village since a new bicycle-producing factory had been opened nearby in 2007 producing half a million bicycles each year.

There were a lot of employment opportunities in the area in addition to the constant need for people to work on the traditional farms which coated the countryside. Her parents both worked for a company manufacturing a wide variety of equipment for churches such as church plates, furniture, accessories and icons. This was very much a family-run business and many of the employees had spent their entire working lives with the company, her parents included.

In the bathroom, she felt the tank of water and decided that there was enough hot water for a small but luxuriating bath. She ran the water and then padded back to the bedroom. She knew where her sister hid a small bottle of bubble bath which she then took into the bathroom and poured a liberal amount into the hot water. She slipped her bed shirt over her head and gave an involuntary shiver before stepping into the warm water. She quickly sat down and sponged water all over her young body. Using the bath gel which was a permanent fixture on the shelf beside the bath, she lathered herself up and then lay back whist gently coaxing ripples of water across her body using the sponge. Eventually, the water started to cool so she got out of the bath and wrapped herself in a towel. She brushed her teeth, had a poke about in her ears with a cotton bud, and then went back to the bedroom where she towelled herself dry.

What to wear?! As she had the bedroom to herself today, she could take as long as she liked trying clothes on in front of the mirror. Shorts or jeans? A loose top or a tight T-shirt? As she was going to be cycling, perhaps it should be jeans and a T-shirt. So, she tried on the shorts just to see whether she fancied them. The only problem she found with shorts was that they tended to ride up whilst cycling which made it rather uncomfortable, and she had to keep stopping to pull them back into place. She unzipped the shorts, slid them down her slender legs and tossed them behind her on to the bed.

She selected a pair of jeans from her half of the wardrobe and started to pull them on. She recalled buying these with her sister soon after her last birthday when they had both gone into Plovdiv on the bus. Her sister had bought a ridiculously tight pair of jeans which she could only just get buttoned up. But Desislava thought she looked so beautiful in them that she had to have a pair as well. Although she was still a couple of sizes smaller than her sister, the shop had had her size and, after a few intakes of breath, she got the jeans on and loved them. Both girls had been so pleased with their purchases that they had rushed home to give their parents a fashion show to remember.

When she had finally got the jeans done up, she rummaged in the chest of drawers that leant against the wall behind the bedroom door and pulled out a T-shirt which one of her school friends had brought back from a trip to England. It was plain blue with the words "Keep Calm and Get Inked" written across the front in white letters. She didn't know what the words meant but she felt so cool wearing a T-shirt from England – somewhere she had always dreamt of visiting but, in reality, she held out no prospect of doing so. The cotton material felt cosy against her skin and the T-shirt was just long enough to cover her bum which she was always quite particular about – not because she had a big bum but she always thought that that style looked so cool on other girls.

Her hair was next to come under scrutiny in the mirror and, having spent time brushing her long blonde tresses, she decided that a simple ponytail would be the order to the day today. Having her hair loose for a cycle ride was always a problem. She slipped her feet into an old but comfortable pair of trainers and squeezed some cash into the pocket at the back of her jeans.

She debated whether to take her mobile phone with her. Although her parents had provided mobiles for all their children as they were growing up, usage was quite expensive with only twenty minutes 'free' talk per month for around ten lev. After that, calls were charged at a slightly lower rate per minute if to the same network or at the same rate to other networks and landlines. As she only earned a few levs each week for helping out on one of the farms, she could only normally afford the twenty minutes 'free' talk and, in this particular month, the 'free' talk had been used up long ago. But she squeezed it into her other back pocket just in case of emergencies.

Finally, from under her bed she pulled out a small cardboard box which had seen better days but which contained her prized possessions. She pulled the lid off and rummaged around in all sorts of bits and pieces of jewellery which she had collected over the years. They all reminded her of special times in her life or special people. Today, she was looking for the necklace her grandmother had given her when she had become a teenager. A simple letter "D" encased in a heart shape. Once she had unravelled the chain which had got caught up with some of the other items, she put it round her neck and checked it in the mirror. Perfect! Placing the box back under the bed, she skipped down the stairs.

Turning into the kitchen, she headed for the fridge. She

pulled out the large plastic container from its customary position on the top shelf and took it over to the work surface by the window. Lifting the lid, she was pleased to see that there was plenty of *mesenitza* left so she cut a good-sized slice and returned the container to the fridge. The bread, stuffed as it always was with yoghurt and Sirene cheese, took away the hunger pangs she had endured earlier, and she was soon feeling full. Time for the bike ride, she thought.

Before he left for work this morning, her father had got her bike out of the shed and made sure the tyres were all pumped up. He had left it leaning against the side of the house. Desislava now collected the bike and, with her left foot in the nearside pedal, she eased her right leg through to the other pedal before pushing herself up onto the saddle. She headed south from the house towards the Citro fruit & veg store, before turning into its car park and skirting round the building towards a rough path which took her on towards the Yect factory where some of the tastiest olive oils were produced.

She was then looking for a gap in the hedgerow which hid the main road. She knew that the hedges grew in during the warmer months so she dismounted and walked along the path before spotting the break in the foliage. She pushed the bicycle through the gap until she was able to look both ways up and down the main road. Nothing coming, thank goodness. She ran across it, pushing the bicycle up a slight incline and then fairly skittering down the other side so that she was now a good two metres below the level of the road.

She remounted her bike and pedalled along the track which crossed the field until she came to another narrow track which took her on towards her friend's house. The track was very rutted and there were sharp stones littering the surface. The bike was juddering as she kept making minor directional corrections, wrenching the handlebars from side to side to avoid the sharpest of the stones. She had just reached a small wooded area when she suddenly saw an obstacle on the track which she instinctively knew she would be unable to avoid. The worn brakes on the bicycle were doing a poor job of slowing her down and, as she crossed over the obstacle, two audible pops signalled that both her tyres had been punctured. Eventually she stopped and dismounted.

She walked back to see what she had ridden over and, sure enough, there amongst the stones lay a metal strip with metal spikes like needles pointing upwards. She bent to take a closer look at what had caused her tyres to deflate. Desislava was so wrapped up in trying to work out why someone would put something like this on the track that she didn't see the two men who grabbed her from behind and mashed a cold damp rag into her face.

She barely had time to think about what was happening to her before a deep sleep overcame her and her whole body crumpled. Before she hit the ground, her frail body was swept up into the arms of a powerful man who quickly made off with her towards the woods. Another, shorter man released the metal strip and slung it away into the long grass which was swaying in the breeze. He picked up the bicycle and followed his accomplice into the woods.

They soon came across their cargo van which was well hidden amongst the shadows of the trees. The shorter of the two men unlocked the side door and slid it open. He pushed the bicycle into the van and followed it in, lashing it to the far wall. The girl was then pushed unceremoniously through the door and dumped on an old mattress on the floor of the van Her hands were tied behind her back and her ankles were lashed together. Duct tape was stuck across her mouth and a black cloth sack was placed over her head. Finally, a length of rope was fastened around her waist which was then secured to the partition panel. This would, hopefully, stop her moving around the back of the van whilst she was in transit. Making sure that all knots held fast, both men stepped out of the van and slid the door shut.

Jumping into the driver's seat, the taller of the two men waited for his colleague to get into the passenger's seat before reversing down the path leading out of the lane at the end of the wood. He then made his way to the main road, turned left and drove back past the shopping centre and the Avius factory. He indicated to drop down on to Route 805 before joining Highway Trakiya and the long journey to meet the next link in the transportation chain.

Meanwhile, the lovely Desislava was sleeping the sleep of the dead on an old moth-eaten mattress and, whilst she would eventually achieve her ambition of being in England, she could have no concept of the unimaginable hell she would be subjected to once she got there.

3
Wednesday 19 July

The waitress placed a huge oval plate on the table. It was piled high with bacon, sausages, mushrooms, tomatoes, hash browns, black pudding, baked beans, and a couple of kidneys for good measure. 'Any sauces?' she enquired.

Billy Woons surveyed the delights of his breakfast. 'Bit of ketchup, thanks luv. And another cup of coffee would hit the spot. You want anything, Trig?'

Trigger Harding sat opposite Woons, watching his boss settle down to do something which always came naturally to him – consuming huge plates of food. Harding's breakfast consisted of one anaemic-looking poached egg on toast which he would push around the plate while Woons stuffed his face with the largest "English" he had seen in a long time.

They were in a Beefeater on the B245 between Sevenoaks and Tonbridge, and had taken a table in a quiet alcove away from the few customers who were in for breakfast at early doors. Harding had been surprised to get a call from Woons at 6.00 a.m. that morning as he thought his boss was out of the country. But no, Woons had just arrived at Gatwick Airport and wanted picking up. 'Get your arse over here pronto!' he had been told so that was his day already off to a bad start.

At least the traffic hadn't been too bad although he had heard about a shunt on the anticlockwise carriageway of the M25 so decided to return from Gatwick across country. This always infuriated Woons who only ever seemed to be happy in a car travelling at high speed. The journey through winding country lanes on this particular morning had been a severe test for Woons' patience as they encountered farm vehicles, delivery vans and mothers taking children to school. However, Woons had been deep in contemplation or furiously texting on his mobile so the journey passed with barely a word spoken by either of them. Finally arriving at the Beefeater, Harding said a silent prayer of thanks to the Almighty – whoever he or she was!

Billy Woons was a time-served petty criminal who had longed to swim with the big fish and, one day, he got his opportunity.

As a scrawny ten-year-old, he had learnt his trade on the tourist-infested streets of London's West End. Nicking wallets and snatching handbags, he loved the excitement of zigzagging his way through crowded areas after making a "hit". However, he eventually became disenchanted by the few pennies he was given once he had surrendered his ill-gotten gains to minders who had little interest in helping him on to the next level of the criminal ladder. So, he branched out on his own. But the life of a pick-pocket was not quite as easy on his own and he missed the camaraderie of his mates and the protection he got from his minders.

Eventually, he managed to get in with a gang of house breakers in Wandsworth. He was still underdeveloped for his age which meant that he was able to climb through small windows and into confined spaces. He became a master at avoiding home security once inside houses, and then disabling alarms before letting his accomplices into the properties. The gang soon built up a bit of a reputation in the South London boroughs, but their increasing sense of invincibility was eventually their downfall when, one day, they were trapped by a very sophisticated police sting.

By this time, Woons was old enough to get a taste of life in a young offenders' institution, and he decided to use the experience to help plan his life once he got out. He was popular with some of his fellow inmates although he was careful in selecting those he wanted to associate with. Even at that age, there were those who were already hardened criminals, many already caught up in the misery of the drugs world. Woons believed that his future lay in more sophisticated criminality than simply ruining peoples' lives through the supply of drugs which they could ill afford and which would, more than likely, eventually kill them.

On his release, he got in touch with some of the contacts he had made whilst inside. He did a few jobs – nicking cars, burglary, fencing stolen goods – but still he came up against the same problem. He was not running the show and getting his hands on the real spoils of crime. He was always feeding from someone else's table which meant there was little left for him after everyone had had their share. He was also clearly mixing with a bunch of amateurs as he had not only been in and out of Wandsworth but also in and out of Brixton, Pentonville and Maidstone!

It was while he was on a nine month stretch at Maidstone that he shared a cell with Zurab, an inmate who hailed from Georgia and who was serving time for, among other things, the importation of child pornography. Woons was never quite sure exactly what Zurab's role in the operation had been, but he was intoxicated by the stories Zurab used to tell him about his homeland and the journeys he had made across eastern Europe to the UK, often in vehicles which were falling apart due to neglect.

If the truth be known, Zurab also saw something of himself in Woons and, as the day of Woons' release drew ever closer, Zurab confided in him the details of a covert operation being run by some of his fellow countrymen. He told Woons about a man he should contact but emphasised that any contact could only be face-to-face – the man didn't travel and didn't trust telephone communication. Zurab could set up a meeting if Woons was interested.

Woons was certainly interested so, on the day of his release, Zurab gave Woons the contact details of his brother who went by the name of Irakli. 'Zis man, he get you meeting with Mr Tsiklauri but you have to go see him in Tbilisi. Maybe he ask you to meet him in his town Kaspi – it is near Tbilisi. Irakli will help you and will take you to meeting. He can be trusted. I know him all my life of course!' And that was it. Woons had never seen or heard from Zurab since he walked out of HMP Maidstone although he often wondered what became of the likeable Georgian who had given him a ticket to riches he could only have dreamt of.

After several failed attempts at contacting Irakli, Woons finally managed to set up a meeting with the elusive Mr Tsiklauri and travelled from London Gatwick to Tbilisi. Irakli had met him at the airport and driven him to a deserted farmhouse off the main road between Tbilisi and Kaspi. There he had met Mr Tsiklauri who was a mountain of a man with angry red scars criss-crossing his face. In broken English, and with Irakli helping out with translation, he told Woons about a "project" which required an anchor man in the UK – someone to run the operation on his behalf. He would provide the raw materials – all Woons had to do was manage the day-to-day operation and collect the money. And he could keep sixty percent of everything he collected!

Woons was to make contact with a man called Tamaz Vashlili who was already set up in the south of England. Tamaz was a relation of Mr Tsiklauri although exactly what relation seemed to get lost in translation as Irakli had difficulty in understanding whether Tamaz was, in fact, actually related to Mr Tsiklauri. No matter! Woons was hooked on the business proposition which had been made to him, and he had spent a sleepless night in a rundown hotel in Kaspi waiting for Irakli to take him back to the airport for the morning flight to Gatwick. Once back in the UK, he drove straight down to Brighton to meet up with an old mucker he had last seen when they had been in Pentonville together.

Trigger Harding was a thief through and through. A weasily, nasally thief who was only interested in stealing. Nothing else in the criminal lexicon interested him, and he was never happier than when he had his hands on other peoples' possessions. He had established a network of fences throughout the south east of England, and was able to dispose of hot goods for the best prices at a moment's notice. The only thing Harding wasn't good at was looking after himself – he had the eating capacity of a hibernating dormouse and his personal hygiene left something to be desired.

His clothes hung off his thin emaciated frame as if from a cheap wooden coat hanger, and the skin on his face was so creased that it resembled a deflated plum left on the tree at the end of the summer. Woons often thought that one puff of wind on Brighton seafront would be enough to send him flying into the sea. In fact, Harding's careless approach to looking after himself had seen him undergo a couple of fairly major internal operations in the last eighteen months which had left him weak and needing time to recuperate. Thieving was, therefore, on hold for the time being.

But Harding had two things going for him – he was loyal to his mates, and Woons had a soft spot for him. They made a rather odd couple which Woons felt gave them a sort of cloak of invisibility as no one really expected that they could get up to much together. Neither of them was on the police radar and, indeed, why should they be unless Harding suddenly got back into thieving.

Woons had spent some time in Brighton with Harding, and had extensively briefed him on the opportunity offered by Mr Tsiklauri. At first, Harding was hesitant as this was work that he had never undertaken before, and he was worried that he was not fit enough for the long hours the job seemed to entail. But, after a couple of days of intense discussion, and after Woons agreed to increase the financial reward quite considerably, Harding was on board and the two of them shook hands on their new partnership. All Woons would have to do now was contact the seemingly elusive Tamaz Vashlili.

4
Wednesday 19 July

'Everything all right, Billy?'

Woons wiped a dribble of ketchup from the corner of his mouth and looked directly at Harding.

'We've got trouble with that fucker Vashlili,' Woons said, almost in a whisper. 'Not only has he failed to pick up the latest consignment of goods but he seems to have disappeared off the face of the fucking earth. Tsiklauri's doing cartwheels over in La La Land.' From what Harding had heard of Mr Tsiklauri, the idea of him being able to do anything remotely like a cartwheel drew a wry smile.

Woons droned on. 'I've just been at a meeting with a load of traffickers in Belgrade. Christ! They're a fucking scary lot! Bonkers, the lot of them! Anyway, this bloke came up to me - said he had a message for me from Tsiklauri. Basically, told me to get my arse back here and sort Vashlili out!'

Harding seemed to be daydreaming. 'Belgrade, eh? Never been there. What's it like?'

'Full of fucking Serbians if you must know!' snapped Woons. 'I wasn't there on a five-day fucking cultural visit so I haven't got a clue about the fucking place. Just for once in your life, concentrate on what I'm telling you!'

'Sorry, Billy.' Harding tried to sound contrite. 'So, where the fuck's this consignment then?' he enquired.

'Well, that's another problem Trig,' Woons replied as another slice of black pudding was slathered with ketchup before being forked up into the waiting Woons mouth. 'The Kaspi mob don't know what happened after it went into the tunnel at Calais. They've had no communication and no intel from the transponder on the wagon. For all we know, it could have been seized at Customs but that's probably unlikely given the fucking Georgians' track record of getting the paperwork spot on.' Woons returned to his breakfast, deep in thought.

Harding stared out of the window, watching the traffic build up as the morning rush intensified. It always comforted him to know that he was not, nor ever would be, part of that rat race. Everyone always looked so miserable – desperate to get from A to B with not a care for anyone else around them. His thoughts were interrupted when Woons' phone lit up like a Christmas tree on the table in front of him.

Woons answered it. 'Yeh?' he spat into the phone. 'Oh, it's you, Ems.' He looked across the table, pointed at the phone and mouthed 'It's Emma'. Harding nodded. He never really knew how Emma fitted into the Woons organisation apart from the fact that she was something to do with finding safe houses and ensuring there was always a bolt hole for Woons to run to if there was a problem.

'Yes, I know about the delay with the consignment, Ems,' Woons was saying. 'Yes, yes… yes, I can understand your frustration after all the trouble you've had getting that secluded property off the A26 up and running, but there's… yes, yes, but there's not much… no, no, I understand… yes… no… but there's not much I can do at the moment, Ems. I'm only just back from meetings with the powers that be.'

There was a further pause while Emma presumably had her say before Woons replied. 'OK, I do understand what you are saying… yes, OK! Leave it with me and I'll get back to you just as soon as I get more information. OK?' A further pause. 'OK, OK! I'll call you later.'

He was just about to end the call when he suddenly clamped the phone back to his ear. 'Ems – you still there? Good! One other thing – you haven't seen or heard from that idiot Vashlili have you?' Her reply seemed short and sweet. 'OK, Ems – speak later!' and the call ended.

'Jesus, Trig – what the fucks going on?' Woons whined, surveying what remained of his breakfast. 'Old Ems going into one because no one's turned up to play in her new house. What the hell am I supposed to do about that?' He rammed a last forkful of hash brown into his mouth and pushed the plate away. 'That's Vashlili's job but he seems to have fucked off at the same time the consignment's gone rogue. God, you don't think they're connected do you?'

Harding didn't really know what he thought or even what might have happened. But, in order to keep the peace with his boss, he said that he doubted the two incidents were connected.

'OK', said Woons dabbing his napkin at an imaginary spot of grease on his chin, 'we need a plan. First of all, we had better check that all our outlets are still fucking operating as normal. You can do that. Think you'd better eyeball the joints rather than doing it by phone so see if you can get round some of them today and report back as you go. I need to get to the office and send something off to Irakli just to get those crazy fuckers off my back for five minutes. You can drop me off on your way.'

'Shall I get Tricky along for the ride, Billy?' asked Harding. Tricky Dicky Spink was one of the most lethal club bouncers Woons had ever come across, and he had freelanced for Woons for the last twenty years on all matters to do with security

26

and health & safety. Spink had a very complicated private life so was always most grateful for the generous cash payments he received from Woons. His loyalty had been well and truly bought, and he would rather die a painful death than breathe a word of the Woons organisation to anyone.

'Good idea, Trig. Yeh, get Tricky along just in case there's something we're not seeing here.' Woons stared across the room, deep in thought. 'This Vashlili disappearance is beginning to worry me. I thought he was on side with everyone. I just can't think why he's suddenly gone off the grid!' And, with that, Woons got up from the table, took a twenty pound note out of his wallet, dropped it on the table and headed for the exit. Harding picked up the note, and handed it to the surprised-looking waitress. 'Keep the change, luv,' he smiled before following his boss to the car park.

5

Wednesday 19 July

'That was awesome!' The booming voice of an American guest resounded around the walled garden of the Meadowlands Hotel as two detectives from the Kent Police Force settled into a quiet corner of the gardens away from the other guests, some of whom were enjoying a leisurely morning coffee and a stroll in the sunshine.

Detective Inspector Sarah Hunter and Detective Sergeant Ted Selitto had been on the early shift at Tonbridge police station in Pembury Road, a modern brick-built edifice on three floors overlooking Tonbridge railway station and its surrounds. A blue 'Police' lamp hung from one of the corner walls at street level, and Kent Police shields adorned the brickwork on either side of the lamp. The building overlooked a busy roundabout bringing traffic into Tonbridge from the south, and feeding traffic to surrounding industrial estates and the sprawling town centre.

Hunter and Selitto had been trying to get on with coordinating paperwork on a car ringing gang which they had broken a couple of weeks earlier. The case seemed to be watertight but the paperwork still needed to be completed so that they could get it through the CPS. Paperwork had never been Hunter's strong point as she had a very low boredom threshold. She much preferred being on the road nicking criminals as her mother always told anyone who could be bothered to listen.

The call had come in from Meadowlands at around 7.30 a.m. The hotel was an exclusive country retreat with only 20 rooms where guests could enjoy the best pampering money could buy. That and food of Michelin star standard served up by a multi-Michelin starred chef. One of their rooms had been trashed and the occupying guest had seemingly disappeared without paying the bill or taking his car with him. Hunter said she'd take a look and bundled herself into Selitto's Megane for a drive into the Kent countryside.

On arrival at the hotel, Hunter and Selitto were met by a very flustered Duty Manager who had introduced herself as Sally Lancaster. She had made the call in the first instance, and took them straight up to the room so that they could see the devastation. Hands shaking slightly as she tried to unlock the room, Ms Lancaster explained that the housekeeper had gone into the room early as the *Please Make Up My Room* sign was hanging on the door.

Standing on the threshold of the room, the detectives surveyed a scene of some devastation although the room didn't seem to be quite as badly trashed as Hunter had been expecting. The contents of a room service tray had been upended onto the carpet, and some of the food had been trodden into the carpet. The mirror on the dressing table had a nasty crack in it, and the TV had clearly been thrown across the room and come to rest under the windowsill. The bed was still made up but the covers were crumpled, and a small occasional table was sitting at a jaunty angle minus one of its legs. The door of the mini bar had been wrenched off but the contents of the small fridge were nowhere to be seen. There appeared to be some broken glass on the bed, and an ice bucket sat proudly on one of the pillows. Hunter had poked her head into the bathroom but nothing had seemed out of place.

Sally Lancaster had explained that the general manager had been alerted and would be at the hotel later in the morning as he was currently in transit from Paris. In the meantime, they could have breakfast in the restaurant or just a coffee in the lounge. Hunter had opted for coffee but asked if it could be served outside. That appeared to be no trouble for the increasingly stressed Ms Lancaster so the detectives made their way outside.

The garden was in full bloom as the hot weather had boosted the colourful array of summer flowers. Hunter let her eyes wander over beds bursting with zinnias, daisies, peonies, marigolds, cosmos, hydrangeas. Sunflowers stood tall and proud along the York stone paths, waving gently in the warm breeze. A forest of enormous fir trees on a ridge to her right soared to the heavens, and a deep azure sky stretched as far as the eye could see above them. It was truly a view to die for.

'So, what have we got?' asked Hunter absent-mindedly, shading her eyes as she took in the magnificence of the garden.

Selitto consulted his notes for a moment or two before responding. 'Well, we have a trashed room and a guest who has disappeared although there appears to be no evidence of Mr Vashlili actually leaving the hotel.' He consulted his notes. 'He checked in yesterday afternoon at around 4.30 p.m. and seemed to spend most of the time in his room but I need to check this with the staff who were on duty at the time. Some of them are on the afternoon shift so they're not in at the moment. I'll have to catch up with them when their shifts start later.'

Hunter got up and shuffled over to a low wall where she could get a better view of one of the meadows which gave their name to the hotel, the grassland gently sloping down to a small oval-shaped lake. The scene reminded her of a visit to the Lake District a few years earlier when she had been fascinated by the number of small tarns which littered the green valleys. Everything appeared so serene – a pair of swans floating on the lake, birds singing in the trees, and the ever-present vapour trails writing their wispy codewords in the blue sky above.

'How much do we know about this man Vashlili?' she asked, turning back to face Selitto.

Selitto consulted his notebook. 'He doesn't seem to be on our radar but I've already heard that he might be a person of interest elsewhere.'

'Don't tell me! The Spooks are interested? Really?' exclaimed Hunter.

Selitto nodded. 'But I understand that they are not about to send in the troops. Vashlili seems to be of interest in the sense that they just want to keep an eye on his whereabouts. Sounds as if they might have mislaid him recently so they're happy to sit back and let us find him!'

'Terrific!' Hunter sighed. 'What time is Beth due here?' Bethany Dench was a CSI Manager attached to the Kent Forensics Team on a 2-year secondment from the Home Office. She was a well-liked member of the team, and Hunter had developed a certain respect for her analytical ability and all-round helpful attitude. Selitto had called her in to carry out a sweep of Vashlili's room in case there was anything they weren't seeing. She could also take a look at his car which had remained where it had been parked at the front of the hotel upon his arrival.

'She should be here in about half an hour – traffic will-ing,' Selitto said. 'In the meantime, I've arranged to meet

Dangerfield, the GM, just as soon as he gets in from Paris. He's coming on the mid-morning BA from Charles de Gaulle – a car has been sent to get him here. I'm also due to meet Leah Crawford who was duty manager yesterday evening and may have seen something. Hopefully, they'll both be able to provide us with a bit more information. Beth is going to call me once she gets through the gates from the road so we can meet her outside the front of the hotel.'

The driveway from the road to the gates of the hotel was over a mile long and wended its way through stunning countryside. On their arrival at the hotel, Selitto had commented that it was the smoothest piece of track in the whole of Kent, if not in the whole of the UK. They would have plenty of time to get to the front of the hotel to meet Beth when she arrived.

Hunter's phone sprang into life on the table. She swiped the screen to activate the call. 'Yes, Grace!' DS Grace Kendall was one of the best researchers a busy DI could wish for, and Hunter was ever-grateful that Kendall was on her team. She listened intently to what the DS had to say. 'And you're absolutely sure about that?' she said, getting Selitto's attention by raising her eyebrows in a quizzical look. 'OK, Grace, keep digging! I'll call you later.' She put the phone back on the table.

'Well, good old Grace has come up with something!' she said squinting in the sunshine and looking straight at Selitto. 'That car in the car park which hasn't disappeared, unlike its driver, is hot!'

6

Wednesday 19 July

Ted Selitto spent the next half hour prowling around the extensive gardens and around the rooms on the ground floor of the hotel just to get his bearings. He now skipped up the stairs from the reception desk and saw that Beth Dench had already arrived and was deep in conversation with Sarah Hunter along the corridor ahead of him. He caught them up as they were climbing the short staircase linking the corridor to Vashlili's room.

'G'day, Beth!' exclaimed Selitto from the foot of the staircase. 'Good journey?'

'Apart from potholes, speed bumps and moronic drivers, it was pretty average,' Beth replied. 'Sarah's just given me a quick heads-up on what we appear to have here so I assume that you just want me to check that there isn't anything you might have missed.'

'That's pretty much it,' Hunter replied. 'It looks like there's been a bit of a bun fight in there but hard to tell how many were involved. Could even have just been one person trashing the room whilst high on something plus the contents of the mini bar although we haven't seen any of the empties so that's another puzzle.'

She inserted the key into the door of Vashlili's room, and they all filed in. The room was already sauna-like, and there was now a noxious smell permeating the atmosphere which hadn't been noticeable earlier.

'God! What is that foul stench?' exclaimed Hunter.

'Smells to me as if someone has been having a good clean up in here,' said Beth, moving across the room and opening a door into the bathroom. 'Wow! It's even worse in here!' Hunter frowned and exchanged glances with Selitto as they moved towards the bathroom but hung back until Beth made a reappearance, deep in thought.

'Hmmm! Something's not quite right here!' she remarked, hands on hips. 'My first suspicion is that someone has made a very good attempt at forensically cleaning the bathroom hence the smell of what is probably some brand of industrial cleanser. So, let's have a look at what it is that they don't want us to see!' She crossed the room and picked up her equipment case before returning to the bathroom. 'You'd better tape this part of the hotel, and definitely no one coming up this staircase,' Beth called out from the bathroom.

Hunter looked at Selitto. 'Have we got some tape in the car?' she asked.

'Pretty sure there's some in the boot. I'll get it,' he said. 'I'll also have to do something with Vashlili's car. Probably just a "Police Aware" sticker rather than taping it. Hotel management will probably have a fit if there's a taped-up car sitting on the drive when the boss gets here,' Selitto chuckled. And, with that, he was off back down the stairs and away to their parked car.

While Beth Dench got on with her examination of the bathroom, Sarah Hunter made a closer inspection of the bedroom trying to avoid stepping on any of the food, crockery or broken glass which littered the floor. Pulling on a pair of nitrile gloves, she eased the wardrobe door open. A light was activated by the opening door, and Hunter found herself staring at a freshly ironed shirt and a pair of chinos on one hanger and a fleece hanging on another. A pair of walking boots rested beside a rucksack on the floor and, on the shelf above the hangers, there was a safe. Hunter tried its door – locked.

She lifted the rucksack and laid it on the bed. Initially, it seemed to be empty apart from some items of underwear and a paperback book. In one of the pockets, she found two Ordnance Survey maps. One covered the area around Meadowlands stretching up to Tunbridge Wells and Sevenoaks. The other covered an area to the north west of the hotel which stretched from Crawley up to the Reigate area and incorporated Gatwick Airport. There were no markings on the maps but they had been regularly used judging by the frayed creases and the dog-eared corners of the covers. Apart from thinking that paper maps were becoming a thing of the past, Hunter couldn't see that they were going to lead them to Vashlili so she put the maps back in the pocket and returned the rucksack to the wardrobe.

To the right of the clothes rail, there was a shelf with a kettle and a coffee machine on it. Under the shelf was a second small fridge which seemed to be struggling with the heat in the room, its contents feeling cool rather than cold. None of the drinks appeared to have been taken although there was a small jug of milk which was half empty.

Returning her attention to the shelf itself, Hunter noticed that there was one cup and saucer on a paper coaster next to the kettle. There was another coaster next to it, but there was no sign of another cup and saucer. Surely a double room would have two cups for making tea in the morning. As she stared at the empty coaster, there was something nagging in her mind – what else was missing?

She looked around the room and her gaze eventually focused on a tray sitting on top of a chest of drawers. On closer inspection, she saw that the tray had probably held a couple of glasses, each with its own paper coaster. There was also room for the ice bucket which now adorned the bed. The glasses were nowhere to be seen but one of them could be the broken glass on the bed. There was a half-empty glass bottle of water lying on the floor beside the bed. Hunter processed this information and began to wonder if they had a bigger problem here rather than just a guest trashing the room and then legging it without paying the bill.

There was a telephone on the bedside table so she called down to Reception. 'Hi, this is DI Hunter in Mr Vashlili's room. Could you send someone up to open the safe, please. As soon as possible would be good.' Replacing the receiver, she noticed that there was a small notepad which had become wedged under the phone. On its cover was a colourful photograph of the hotel after which there were about a dozen pages for notes. Taking the notepad to the window for better light, Hunter noticed that the top page showed indentations from writing on the page which had been torn off the pad. She briefly thought of trying the old pencil trick which they did at school as kids but, as she had a top forensics expert alongside her, she decided that she would let Beth Dench see what she could make of it.

Otherwise, the room showed little sign of having had anyone staying in it lately so Sarah went out onto the landing. When she had first come up the short staircase, she hadn't noticed that there was a narrow corridor leading off the landing. She had, however, seen it when she had come up the stairs with Beth, and she was now interested to see where it led.

Peering into the corridor, she realised that it was a fire escape – presumably for this one room or perhaps for other rooms below in the event that their escape route was blocked. She was just about to try to open the exit door when she heard someone politely clearing their throat behind her.

'Excuse me, madam, I understand that you would like the safe opened.' Hunter turned to find a smartly dressed young man who she had fleetingly noticed when they had arrived at the hotel earlier.

'Yes, that would be very helpful thank you.' Entering the room, the young man went into the wardrobe and soon reappeared. 'That's it opened for you,' he said. 'Just let us know if you require anything else.' And, with that, he was gone.

The safe was on a shelf above the hanging area so Hunter got a chair to stand on in order to eyeball the inside of the safe. She was, however, somewhat perplexed to find that the safe was empty. 'Why would someone lock an empty safe?' she muttered under her breath. She got off the chair and took a couple of steps back, her eyes never leaving the safe in the search for an answer to her own question.

In her reverie, she didn't notice that Ted Selitto had returned to the room. 'You OK, boss?' he said when he saw his boss seemingly staring into space.

'Yes, fine thanks Ted. Just another puzzle to solve. Tell me – why would someone lock a hotel safe if there was nothing in it?'

Selitto peered into the empty safe. 'No idea, I'm afraid. People do some very strange things in hotels,' he observed. 'Are we absolutely sure it's empty?'

'Be my guest,' said Hunter. 'I can't see anything.'

Being a good bit taller than Hunter, Selitto moved the chair to one side and stood in front of the safe. It was of a good size for a hotel – more than enough room for at least one laptop and other valuables such as a tablet, phone, passport and wallet. The safe did, indeed, appear to be empty. Selitto pulled a pair of nitrile gloves from his pocket before putting his hand into the safe. He carefully felt round the whole of the interior. Every surface seemed to be covered by a coarse dark blue material although he couldn't make out how it was attached to all the internal surfaces of the safe. He ran his hand across the floor and the roof of the safe, poked into the corners with his fingers and ran his knuckles along the narrow walls. Nothing.

He was about to agree with Hunter that the safe was empty when he noticed that a tiny part of the material attached to the roof of the safe did not appear to be stuck down properly. It had come away from the groove above the door. He carefully wriggled a finger into the small gap between the material and the frame of the safe. As he moved his finger along, he found that the material didn't seem to be stuck down and simply dropped out of the groove thereby exposing a pocket between the material and the frame of the safe. He pulled a small LED torch from his pocket and shone it into the gap he had created.

'Got something?' enquired Hunter.

'Looks like we might have a little hidey hole here,' replied Selitto as he prised more of the material from the groove. At first, it was difficult to see what he was looking at as the light from the torch seemed to just show up a dark void between the material and the roof of the safe. However, once he got his eyes more in line with the thin opening he had created, he realised that there was what looked like a piece of paper wedged into the space.

'Interesting!' he exclaimed to a surprised looking Hunter. 'There's definitely something in here but I'll need an implement to pull it out with if we are to preserve the scene. Any chance Beth might have a pair of tweezers?' Hunter was quickly back with the tweezers which she handed to Selitto. Clamping the torch between his teeth and holding the material back with his left hand, Selitto carefully manoeuvred the tweezers into the gap between the material and the outer shell of the safe and gently coaxed the piece of paper towards the opening. Finally, enough of the paper was exposed so that he could use his fingers to gently pull it out of its hiding place.

'Right! Let's see what we've got here,' said Selitto, turning to face Hunter. There were, in fact, two pieces of A4 paper. Both pages were covered in lines of numbers and letters which appeared to have been written in some sort of encrypted format. Selitto stared at the page and read off the first couple of lines.

010715 N1T1L91 4252/2520 7161847880 SHARKFIN 180420 3T6U2N VAS

001118 12Y21D13I12A 4226/2539 5283737880 BLACKMAMBA 180602 8C8N1T VAS

Hunter also stared at the page. 'Means nothing to me,' she observed, 'but someone obviously knew the whereabouts of this information. Could this be some sort of dead-letter box where this encrypted information was being passed between people who only stayed in this room?'

Selitto had been studying the lines of code, trying to see if there was a simple solution to the puzzle. 'That's an interesting proposition and rather changes the scope of our investigation. There could, of course, be nothing sinister in this at all but my hunch says that we've stumbled onto something.'

'Hmmm!' Hunter grunted. 'We might find out more by sending it all to the Codebreakers so, if you can get it ready for despatch, Beth can take it with her. Get an envelope from Reception so that we can at least see if there are any prints worth looking at.'

'I get the feeling that Mr Vashlili always asked for this room,' Selitto informed her. 'These sheets of paper could be the reason why. Or perhaps he was picking up information which had been left by another so-called guest. Perhaps they didn't even know each other! But why are these pages still in the safe?'

They both thought about this. If Vashlili breathed his last in this room, his killer obviously didn't know about the contents of the safe.

Selitto was the first to speak. 'We're going to have to have a look at all the bookings for this room around the same time as Vashlili's visits to see if we can identify any other guests who have always stayed before or after he has been here.'

'Agreed!' said Hunter, having another look at the encrypted pages. 'You'll have to get Mr Dangerfield onto this asap. Looks like this is going to elevate our investigation to another level if I'm not mistaken'

'So is this!' exclaimed Beth Dench from the doorway to the bathroom.

7

Wednesday 19 July

The CSI Manager stepped into the room and then turned to face Hunter and Selitto. She had put on a white Tyvek suit and had tucked her loosely clipped blonde hair into the hood of the suit. Her hazel eyes peered at the detectives over a white mask which covered most of her face. She wore nitrile gloves and protective overshoes.

Dench was frowning. 'It looks like we were right about an attempt being made to clean up the bathroom. The smell we got when we first came into the room appears to have been some industrial strength cleaning agent which has been so liberally used that I found it easy to get any number of samples. I can get this confirmed back at the lab.'

'That sounds ominous,' mused Hunter.

'I'm afraid it is because I've also managed to uncover evidence of blood splatter over the walls and in the bath. From what I can see of the spray pattern using the limited equipment I have with me, it looks as if a major artery was severed so it is very likely that one person didn't leave this room alive.'

'Shit!' exclaimed Hunter. 'So, we now have a possible murder on our hands but with no body, no name, no weapon, no motive — and no idea what this is all about!'

Dench continued. 'When I arrived, I thought it was strange that there were no towels in the bathroom but they were probably used in the clean-up operation. Also, there are traces of blood on the bathroom window but none on the blinds. I have, therefore, had to conclude that someone went to an awful lot of trouble to replace the blinds. This, in turn, would lead me to believe that someone had an extremely good knowledge of this room and had probably spent time planning what would be needed to cover their tracks. There is not much in the way of fingerprint evidence but you would probably get better info from studying the guest register for this room.'

'Assuming that someone didn't leave this room alive, is there any evidence to indicate how a body was spirited away from here?' asked Hunter realising that her missing person enquiry was almost certainly about to be upgraded to a full-scale murder investigation.

'Well it couldn't have been down the stairs and out through reception,' said Selitto. 'I checked with Claudine who confirmed that a night porter is in situ every night from 11.30 p.m. until 6.00 a.m. It seems that he doesn't do any patrolling as the hotel is locked up by that time, and he can pretty much see all the ground floor areas from the reception desk.'

'So, no one could have got in either,' said Hunter, more to herself. 'Beth's evidence rather suggests that Vashlili had a visitor in which case how did he – or she – get to the room?'

'I made a few enquiries while I was down getting the tape,' said Selitto, 'but no one seems to have noticed any strangers in the hotel yesterday. Apparently, it was only half full last night which meant around a dozen guests plus a few others who had come in for dinner. Claudine says that it would be possible for someone to slip past reception without being noticed but they would have had to wait for the receptionist to be distracted by something else. All in all, she thinks it unlikely that anyone could have got up here without being seen.'

'No, I agree!' replied Hunter. 'But I may just have the answer.'

With that, she pushed past Selitto and the CSI Manager, exited the room onto the landing and turned into the small corridor she had spotted earlier. The other two followed.

'This is one of the hotel's fire exits. Very handy for Vashlili's room and a most convenient entry point to the hotel if the objective was to avoid being seen. Vashlili gets a call or a text message, goes and pushes the door off its lock, and his accomplice gets almost straight into his room without being noticed by anyone. Let's see where it leads.' And, with that, Hunter depressed the bar and pushed the door open. Sunlight flooded into the dimly lit corridor as they focused on a huge area of lawn which stretched away on both sides of the exit. A small wooden bridge spanned the area from the fire exit to the lawn.

Selitto was first over the bridge, and he immediately turned right as his sense of direction told him that this was the way to the front of the hotel and the car park. He soon spotted a path which led down to the parking area so he retraced his steps to the fire exit.

'Certainly looks like a possible point of entry or exit,' he said catching up with Hunter who was now standing in the middle of the lawn gazing back at the hotel. 'Tarmac path leading gently down to the car park with trees and hedges providing a natural cover so that anyone using the path is unlikely to be seen.'

Hunter turned round and stared towards a wooded area on the far side of the lawn. 'What's up there?' she asked. Selitto followed her gaze and could just make out what appeared to be wrought iron railings. He was about to tell Hunter that he had not yet had a chance to explore that area of the gardens when a small tractor suddenly started up and rolled past their line of sight on the other side of the railings.

'Well, well, well!' exclaimed Selitto. 'Could that be another point of entry?'

Their thoughts were interrupted by an urgent call from Dench. 'Hey, guys. I've got something here you should see.' She was in the door way of the fire exit and had been examining the area around the push bar and the latch mechanism. Hunter and Selitto joined her in the doorway.

'You see here where the latch bolt is. It looks very much as if the bolt has been taped up.' Dench was pointing to the latch mechanism. 'Did you notice some slack on the bar when you pushed the door open just now?'

'Possibly!' Hunter replied although she had been keen to get the door open rather than noticing if there was anything unusual about the push-bar itself.

Dench continued. 'If the mechanism was taped up, then the door could be opened from the outside without the bar having to be released from the inside. This would allow someone to enter the hotel without having to go through the front entrance.'

'See what you mean!' Selitto said as he looked over towards Sarah Hunter who was nodding sagely.

Dench turned to re-enter the hotel. 'I'll be able to tell you more when we get more equipment here. The UV lamp has also shown evidence of a small blood smear but, again, I'll need better equipment to confirm this. But, if you want my opinion at this stage in the proceedings, I reckon that there is a strong chance that your Mr Vashlili didn't leave the bathroom alive!'

8

Wednesday 19 July

Peter Dangerfield had just returned from a few days in Paris with one of the owners of Meadowlands. Under the guise of developing a new 5-year strategic plan, the general manager had taken in the sights and sounds of the French capital as well as a couple of exceedingly good dinners in top class Michelin starred restaurants. He had also very much enjoyed the nightlife to the extent that he now felt rather jaded and in no mood to start talking to a couple of detectives about a missing guest. One of the porters, Bruce Appleyard, had collected Dangerfield from Gatwick Airport, and they had travelled back to Meadowlands with barely a word spoken between them.

Selitto eventually caught up with Dangerfield at the reception desk. He introduced himself and shook the hand of a tall man, smartly dressed in a dark suit, white shirt and tartan tie. Engaging eyes peered out from under bushy eyebrows and a full head of hair, slightly greying around the fringes. Selitto wondered for a moment whether he had met Dangerfield before, but he quickly put that thought to the back of his mind.

'DS Selitto, welcome to Meadowlands.' Dangerfield made a sweeping gesture with his right arm as if to indicate that all one could see of the hotel was, indeed, his. 'I'm only sorry that I am not welcoming you as a guest as I am sure that you would very much enjoy spending some time relaxing in the comfort of this lovely old building.'

'I'm sure I would, sir,' replied Selitto, 'but I'll probably need a few promotions before I can afford such luxury! But I'll bear it in mind for the future.'

He glanced over his shoulder to the open lounge behind and then turned back to Dangerfield. 'Unfortunately, on this occasion we have other matters to attend to so is there somewhere we could have a chat and won't be disturbed?'

Dangerfield leant over the reception desk and plucked a set of keys from an unseen peg under the desk. 'Follow me, sergeant.'

Selitto followed the general manager along a dimly lit corridor, the walls of which were covered in photographs and other memorabilia. Although Selitto couldn't see the pictures very clearly, they seemed to show famous guests visiting the hotel at various times during its history. Dangerfield unlocked a door at the end of the corridor and Selitto found himself in what appeared to be a private dining room with wood panelling and views out on to the gardens at the front of the hotel.

'Can I get you a drink, sergeant? Tea, coffee or something cool?' Dangerfield asked.

'No, I'm fine for the moment thank you,' replied Selitto. 'I'm sure that you have a very busy day so perhaps we can just get through the questions I have and then we can both get on.' He sat down at the table and invited Dangerfield to do the same.

Selitto opened his notebook and consulted his notes. 'Perhaps we could start with Mr Vashlili's arrival at Meadowlands. What time would that have been?'

Dangerfield consulted a card which he had taken from his jacket pocket. Well prepared, thought Selitto. 'It seems that our records show that he checked in at 4.31 p.m. yesterday afternoon. As he had stayed with us on previous occasions, the check-in formalities would have been very brief and informal. In fact, we only took a signature from him.'

Selitto frowned. 'Does that mean that you had automatically assumed that all his details such as address, phone numbers, car registration number were unchanged from his last visit – or even from a visit prior to that?' he asked.

'Many of our guests make frequent returns to Meadowlands, Detective Sergeant Selitto, so we get to know them quite well. Mr Vashlili had visited us on a number of occasions and he was known to us. When he arrived at reception, he would have been asked to check that the information printed on the registration form was correct before signing.'

'And did he go straight up to his room? Selitto enquired.

The Manager scanned the card and then gave this question some thought before replying. 'Well, I presume that he did although he must have returned downstairs pretty quickly because it seems that Leah Crawford, the Duty Manager, saw him walking through the lounge and into the walled garden whilst she was talking to one of the guests in the hall.'

'And that would have been at about ...?' Selitto let the question drift.

'I'm afraid that I don't have an exact time for that – you will have to ask her yourself. But I should think that it would have been around 4.45 p.m. as Leah goes on her break at around 5.00 p.m.' Dangerfield replied.

Selitto pressed on. 'Have you been informed of any other sightings?'

'Claudine, one of our receptionists, mentioned that she caught a fleeting glance of Mr Vashlili going upstairs at around 7.00 p.m.' Dangerfield replied. 'It was only a fleeting glance as he seemed to be in a tremendous hurry and was taking the stairs two at a time.'

'What about luggage?' asked Selitto. 'Did your porter help him in with any cases?'

'Not as far as we know,' replied Dangerfield. 'I have checked with Bruce who said that Mr Vashlili had a small sports bag with him on arrival. He was staying for only one night and was probably travelling light as a consequence.'

'And his car is still parked outside,' Selitto stated in an attempt to see how much Dangerfield actually knew about this increasingly shady guest.

'Yes, it's the BMW 320i. Probably a hire car. We are pretty sure that Mr Vashlili only drives hire cars as he seems to have a different vehicle every time he visits.'

'I bet he does,' Selitto mused to himself.

Dangerfield got up and wandered over to the window. Pointing to a vehicle neatly parked on the gravel drive he said 'That's it parked directly in front of us. I haven't seen him driving that one before, and it has a new registration plate.' Selitto made a note.

'You said that Mr Vashlili had visited you on a number of occasions. Would you describe him as a frequent visitor?' Selitto asked as he joined Dangerfield at the window.

'Yes, probably,' Dangerfield agreed. 'But it's nearly always a short-notice booking which seems to indicate that he had not previously planned for an overnight stay. Perhaps he meets people flying into Gatwick which is only about forty miles away – or he has other business interests in this area which suddenly require him to be here. He always asks to stay in the room he had last night. It's slightly isolated from the other rooms in the hotel so perhaps he likes that aspect of the accommodation which we can offer.'

'What about visitors?' Selitto enquired. 'If he was coming here at short-notice for business reasons, one might expect him to have had some visitors – business associates, clients, customers – that sort of thing.'

'I can only answer for myself,' replied Dangerfield, suddenly shooting his cuffs and showing off a pair of ornate gold cufflinks. 'I have never seen him with anyone else whilst in residence at Meadowlands and, in fact, I have never seen him in conversation with anyone at all. He never dines in our restaurant, preferring to order from room service, and he normally leaves before breakfast service has started. He keeps himself very much to himself – almost as if he doesn't want anyone to know he is here.'

Selitto turned to the general manager. 'Okay, Mr Dangerfield, that'll be all for the moment. You've been very helpful but do let me know if you think of anything else which might be of interest to us. You can contact me on this number.' Selitto pulled a business card from his jacket pocket and handed it to Dangerfield.

'Will you be here for much longer,' Dangerfield asked, searching Selitto's eyes for a clue as to what happened now.

'Well, sir, it really depends on what my colleagues from forensics come up with,' replied Selitto. 'They are going to carry out a rudimentary sweep of Vashlili's room so that we can see if anything more sinister has occurred there. Shouldn't take too long. Then we can be out of your hair. However, I will have to insist that the BMW is not moved or even touched by anyone as it appears to have been stolen in the last few days.'

Dangerfield looked aghast. 'Oh, my goodness!' he blurted out. 'Oh, my goodness!' he repeated. 'Could that mean that every time he came here, he arrived in a stolen car? My goodness!'

Selitto hadn't got round to thinking about this but Dangerfield could, indeed, be right. 'That is certainly a possibility, sir. But your records will not be of much assistance to us if you have never asked him for an update of the registration number of the car he drove on his first visit to Meadowlands. And, even if that was also stolen, it would have been too long ago for it to still be of any interest to us.'

Selitto returned to the window and looked down on the BMW. 'I'll send someone to collect it,' he said before turning and making for the door.

9

Two Months earlier

Shafts of bright sunlight pierced the tree cover overhead, lighting up the leaves and grasses which littered the woodland floor. Here and there, little groups of wild flowers swayed in the breeze offering a brightly coloured carpet of colour.

Daniela held her mother's hand tightly as they made their way along the narrow path on the banks of the River Lazovo. They were on their way to see her Uncle Nikolay, something she and her mother tried to do every Thursday. She had recently turned seventeen and had just started a foreign languages course at the local university. She had always wanted to travel and to see the world but realised the importance of being able to speak other languages. Thursday was her self-study day so she would cram her studies into the morning which then give her the time off in the afternoon to visit her uncle. It was always quicker to walk than go by car as their old car was becoming more and more unreliable. In any case, it was now without a front offside wheel which had been stolen by some enterprising thieves who had simply jacked the car up one night and removed the wheel.

Her uncle's house was on the other side of Interstate 55, an 8-lane highway which had been indiscriminately bulldozed through the community where she had lived all her short life. Many families had been split up, and it was difficult to look after elderly relatives who had suddenly found themselves cut off from their loved ones. The only way of crossing the highway was to follow the river or one of its many tributaries which had been allowed to flow under the highway through a network of narrow tunnels. Many of these were only the width of the water itself so using them as access meant trudging through the flowing water. Daniela and her mother were, however, taking the longer route via the main river as trudging through the water in one of the tributaries was often a hazardous task, what with slippery rocks under foot and the occasionally fast-flowing water.

The path widened as they came in sight of the river with the highway in the distance. A couple of unmade local farm access roads intersected with each other just ahead of them, and Daniela noticed a small van which seemed to have come to a halt at the intersection. The bonnet of the van was raised and two men were peering into the engine compartment. As they came closer, one of the men looked up and waved at them. 'Hi,' he called over. 'Are one of you ladies by any chance wearing stockings today?'

Daniela looked at her mother and giggled. 'No sir, it is far too warm today,' her mother replied. But she was intrigued as to why the men would ask such a question, and they both left the path and went over to look at the van.

'We have a problem with the fan belt,' the other man explained, 'and a lady's stocking is often a very good substitute.'

'And how does that work?' asked her mother getting ever closer to the van.

'Well, if you look here,' the man beckoned them over to the vehicle, 'you see the belt is wearing out so you tie a stocking round these two wheels.' The two women peered at where the man was pointing in the engine compartment but could not make out what he was talking about. Suddenly, powerful hands grabbed Daniela by the waist and dragged her to the back of the van. The doors were open and she was launched onto a pile of damp oily blankets. Before she could get her breath back, the doors were slammed shut and the engine started. The van lurched forward on the uneven ground. Daniela screamed as she lost her balance and her head smashed into the floor of the vehicle. There was a loud thump as the van bounced over an obstacle in its path. 'What was that?' she thought as a dread fear suddenly gripped her entire body. 'Oh no!' she whispered in disbelief. Where was her mother?

'Maiko!' she screamed. 'Maiko!'

Daniela sat bolt upright in bed, her thin vest soaked through with sweat. It stuck to her body which made her shiver.

A hand stroked her long hair. 'It's okay Dani, it's okay You're just having that dream again.' Daniela drew her legs up under her chin and buried her face in her hands. Tears came easily, huge sobs convulsing her body. She reached out for the hand that had stroked her hair. It was warm and tender to the touch, and belonged to Elena who she shared a room with. She grasped it tightly like she always did after this recurring nightmare.

Still holding on to Elena's hand, Daniela snuggled back down under the blanket, dried her tears on the sheet, and turned to face Elena.

'I'm sorry if I woke you,' she whispered.

'No problem. I wasn't even asleep,' replied Elena. 'I got called to go with that asshole with the dragonfly tattoo. He'd just done some big deal and fancied the whole nursing thing with internal investigation before he got home to his long-suffering wife. Belinda threatened me with a visit from Jax if I didn't do what he wanted. She is such a fucking cow.'

Elena reached under the covers for Daniela's other hand. 'I'm so desperate to get out of here. I just can't sleep for thinking of how to escape'.

Daniela strained to see her friend's face in the meagre light filtering in from the night sky outside. 'My dear Elena, how are we ever going to escape from here? We do not know where we are. We have no money, no identification. We are illegal immigrants in this country. We are mixed up with people who would have us killed in a heartbeat if we tried to escape. They are everywhere. They see everything. They torture, they kill. They are traffickers with no morals and certainly no heart. You don't ask them for any favours. You are just one bit of dog shit on their shoes.'

'I know,' Elena eventually sighed, and Daniela thought she caught sight of Elena's eyes glistening with tears in the half light. 'I just don't think I can take any more of this. My body aches all over and I have some wounds which are just not healing up properly. And the food's crap. You would have thought they might at least feed us better!'

10
Wednesday 19 July

Sarah Hunter had called for back-up, and there were now half a dozen uniforms gathered on the lawn where Selitto was briefing them on a search of the grounds. Beth Dench had also called for reinforcements, and the area around Vashlili's room and the fire exit was now an officially designated crime scene. Hunter sat on the low wall which surrounded the lawn and waited for Selitto to finish the briefing. Once the uniforms had been dispersed, he joined her on the wall.

'The grounds are much more extensive than I thought,' said Selitto, watching as two uniforms scaled a steep bank on the opposite side of the lawn and made their way towards the wrought iron fence.

'I know,' said Hunter. 'I just had a word with Dangerfield who told me that there are, in fact, two lakes here. There's the one we have seen from the terrace and then there's another in the woods to the north. Apparently, it's quite overgrown but it is all part of the hotel grounds so we will need to take a look at it as well.'

'They haven't been very generous with the back-up have they?' mused Selitto. 'At least the place doesn't seem to be too overgrown so it should be a fairly straightforward eyeball search but, even so, there's a lot of ground to cover – and that's based on what we can see from up here.'

'Well, there's not much more we can do for the moment,' observed Hunter, 'and I'm feeling hungry!' So, they went in search of Dangerfield with a request for sandwiches and a cooling drink.

Dangerfield joined the detectives as they sat in the garden enjoying some freshly made sandwiches under the increasing heat from the early afternoon sun.

'I hope you will forgive me for asking,' Dangerfield started, 'but can you give me any idea when that part of the hotel can be used again. Fortunately, we haven't got anyone booked into that room for tonight but tomorrow we are fully booked. If I can't use the room then I would rather like to issue a cancellation today so that the guests can make alternative arrangements.'

Hunter delicately dabbed the corners of her mouth with a napkin hoping to remove any remnants of the gorgeously fresh egg sandwich she was savouring. 'I imagine that we will be finished later today – perhaps early evening,' she surmised. 'You should then have time to carry out a deep clean of the room before welcoming tomorrow night's guests.'

Dangerfield seemed to relax now that he felt that he might be back to full capacity for the following night.

'One other thing you might like to bear in mind is that the blinds in the bathroom have probably been replaced,' Hunter informed him. 'So, you will probably want to get a new set of blinds made in due course. Anyway, you can decide what to do once you get the room back.'

'Thank you for letting me know.' Dangerfield moved as if to get up from his chair when Selitto caught his attention.

'I understand you mentioned to my colleague that there is another lake here in addition to the one we can see from the terrace. Is this correct?'

'Yes, that's correct,' replied Dangerfield. 'Unfortunately, it has become a bit overgrown this year which is partly because not many of our guests have ventured down there and partly because we just haven't got the resources to keep the undergrowth under control. We have to ensure that the extensive gardens here at Meadowlands are kept in tip top condition. This takes up so much time for our small team of gardeners that there's no available time to get down to the lake, so I took the decision to let the vegetation grow in this year.'

'How easy is it to access that area of the grounds?' asked Hunter, eyeing up a coronation chicken sandwich.

'Well, there's really only one point of entry and that's by way of a style and kissing gate which are located through the trees at the bottom left of meadow nearest to us.' Dangerfield got up and went over to the wall. 'You see, just down there in the corner of the grassland.' Hunter and Selitto also got up and followed the direction of his pointing finger. Retaking their seats, Dangerfield continued. 'That lake is much deeper than the one at the bottom of the meadow, and there is a weir at the far end of it which limits the water draining into a small stream. It is the furthest point which walkers reach before the path returns them round the other side of the lake and back towards the hotel.'

'So, you would only be able to get there on foot?' Hunter asked. 'There is no access for motorised vehicles – quad bikes for example?'

'No, you certainly couldn't get a quad bike in there,' mused Dangerfield. 'I suppose that you might be able to get around the lake on a motor bike or an ordinary bicycle but I'm not sure how you could get it through the gate to start with. I'd have to look at that.'

Hunter's phone erupted into life and she stepped away to take the call, taking her plate of sandwiches with her.

Meanwhile, Selitto finished up the crisps which had been sitting rather forlornly on the side of his plate. 'There's a track leading from the front gates of the hotel past a large house and then on down to some glass houses and what looks like a garden equipment storage area,' he said, squinting at Dangerfield in the bright sunshine.

'Yes, that's right. The house you refer to is in fact staff quarters. Because we are in quite a remote location, some of our staff stay in if they are on early or late shifts. We also have a couple of staff who have no other home to go to so they live on site. One of them has actually lived-in for nearly 20 years!'

'So, it would be possible for a vehicle to access the hotel grounds by using this track?' Selitto continued.

'Certainly,' confirmed Dangerfield. 'Down the drive from the main road and turn right just before the gates into the hotel grounds. There are normally quite a few cars parked up there but you could easily get a car or a van through there and then down towards the glass houses.'

'And beyond the glass houses?' Selitto pressed on. 'How much further could one go in, say, a van or some sort of off-road vehicle?'

Dangerfield shot his cuffs and gave this some thought. 'Difficult to say, really. You could probably get round to the gravel path at the top of the meadow, and I suppose that you could even get down to the bottom of the meadow by the lake. But I think that you would have to be in some sort of off-roader to do that without ripping out the underside of the vehicle.'

'But it would not be impossible to get a vehicle from the main drive down to the bottom of the meadow,' Selitto summarised.

'Not impossible, no. That could probably be done with the right sort of vehicle – not easily, but it could be done.' Dangerfield stared off into the distance.

'Talk to me more about the lakes', Selitto asked whilst watching Hunter who was still deep in conversation, her left arm conducting an imaginary orchestra.

'Well, the one that we can see from here isn't very deep,' replied Dangerfield, pointing aimlessly over the wall. 'We call it Swan Lake because there are a pair of swans living around it. It tends to dry up in the hot weather with more of the shoreline becoming exposed. We did try dredging it a couple of years ago in order to try and encourage more fish and general pondlife, but it was a thankless task and I just couldn't justify the cost.'

'But the other lake is a bit deeper you say.'

'Yes. The lake in the woods has always been thought to be deeper – mainly because it has a lighthouse sitting in the middle of it.'

'A lighthouse?' exclaimed Selitto.

'A lighthouse, indeed,' Dangerfield went on. 'No one knows why or even how but it is a fine example of late-1800s construction in a mixture of chalk and masonry. The light has been removed but the lantern room is still intact. There's no access, however, and the small wooden landing stage is rotting in the water. In any event, there is no way of getting to the structure because we don't allow boats on the lake. There are no fishing rights either.'

'And you're certain that it can't be accessed?' Selitto quizzed the general manager.

Dangerfield suddenly looked a bit awkward. 'Well, no one

has been inside it since I've been here, and there doesn't seem to be any folklore about people getting into the building. My understanding is that the only door has always been nailed shut making the structure inaccessible.'

At that moment, Selitto noticed that Hunter had finished her call and was on her way back to them having wandered off to the other side of the garden.

'Mr Dangerfield,' she began as she got closer. 'I am going to need to take a look at your register of guests staying in the hotel over, say, the last 6 to 9 months – possibly longer. How quickly can DS Selitto get started on this?' Selitto gave her a quizzical sideways glance but waited for Dangerfield's response.

This request didn't seem to faze Dangerfield. 'Probably best if I set DS Selitto up at the workstation in my office. I have various people I need to catch up with so I'll be out and about for the rest of the day. All our systems are fairly straightforward so you should be able to find whatever it is you are looking for.'

'By the way, sir, I'd be grateful if you didn't leave the premises until we have completed our search,' Hunter said, looking directly at Dangerfield. There was something about him which was arousing her suspicions and, once that started, she was like a dog with a bone.

'No problem!' replied Dangerfield. 'I had planned to stay over tonight so I would not have been leaving in any event.' Selitto noticed that a few beads of perspiration had formed on the general manager's forehead, and he was starting to look distinctly uneasy.

Hunter thanked him and said that they would get to his office a bit later on. In the meantime, there was something she wanted to check out. Dangerfield picked up the empty plates and glasses and took his leave, heading off down the path towards the entrance to the bar before being swallowed up by the shadows spreading their tentacles out from the ancient granite walls. The two detectives watched him go.

11

Wednesday 19 July

The CSI wagon had lurched into the car park at the front of the hotel, liberally spraying gravel in all directions as it slewed to a halt near the path up to the lawn. Two CSI officers climbed down on to the gravel and started to remove equipment via a door in the side of the van. Beth Dench appeared on the bank above them.

'Hi guys!' she called down. 'There's a pathway up here,' she said pointing to her left. 'You get to the scene this way without having to traipse through the hotel. Do you need a hand with anything?'

'No, I think we'll be okay Beth,' replied Donny Campbell, the taller of the two CSI Officers. 'Jimbo here can do the carrying!' he joked as James Carrigan lifted another heavy case out of the van.

'And what did your last slave die of?' Carrigan asked with a smile on his face.

'Come on you two! No time like the present.' And, with that, Dench turned on her heels and headed for the fire exit.

Campbell and Carrigan were not far behind her and, when they got to the platform leading to the open fire door, they stopped to put on Tyvek oversuits and plastic bootees.

'Will we need face masks?' Campbell asked.

'Doubt it,' replied Dench, 'but bring them with you just in case.' They followed her across the platform, through the fire exit and on into the room recently vacated by the elusive Mr Vashlili.

Selitto was having difficulty trying to make sense of the room booking records which Dangerfield had shown him. It took him some time to realise that Vashlili's room was classified as "Crocus" in the register. Once he had established this, he began to trawl through the bookings. But he soon realised that the hotel obviously used a code for identifying the names of guests so that, whilst he could see all the bookings, the names against the bookings made no sense whatsoever.

Looking at Vashlili's last booking, he tried to make out whether the code name was in some way connected to Vashlili – perhaps an anagram of his name. But he couldn't see anything in this approach. For his last booking, Vashlili was simply known as 488H18011. Selitto sat and scrutinised this code. The only part that made any sense was the 18 as probably being a reference to the year. The figure one at the end could also be the number of nights for the booking. Was 488 the reference given him by the hotel? He scrolled down until he came to another code beginning 488. This time he read 488G18012. So the number 488 was probably the reference for Vashlili, 18 was the year, and the last figure related to the number of nights. But what was the H and the G and the figures 01? He left the room and went in search of Dangerfield.

Meanwhile, Sarah Hunter had wandered down to the corner of the meadow. She had difficulty opening the tall metal gate in the wall which was on a very tight spring. Scrambling through before it slammed shut behind her, she wandered on into the shadows of the trees. She quickly came across the stile and the kissing gate which Dangerfield had mentioned, and peered into the distance to see if she could catch a glimpse of the lake.

Caught in two minds as to whether she should go on or get

back to see if Selitto had had any success with the register, she suddenly found herself clambering across the stile and through the kissing gate. A path wound its way in front of her and she started walking along its uneven surface, her face being brushed by leaves and ferns from the vegetation growing up alongside and sometimes over the path. She had an inclination that the lake would appear on her left so she kept peering off to the left to see if she could catch a glimpse.

Suddenly, there was a break in the curtain of vegetation which had grown up around the edges of the lake, and Hunter could see the water shimmering in the afternoon sun. She left the path and gingerly stepped down towards the water's edge. The closer she got, the more of the lake she could see. But nothing had prepared her for her first sight of the lighthouse.

Like a magnificent obelisk, the rounded white tower rose from the lake and seemed to brush the deep blue sky above. The lantern room on the top of the structure glinted in the sunshine, and several birds perched serenely on the rail which ran around the outside. That would be some view, she thought as she got out her phone and took a few shots to show Selitto.

The sound of a twig snapping interrupted her enjoyment of the scene, and she spun round expecting to see someone behind her. But there was no one. She peered into the shadows but couldn't detect any sign of movement. Feeling a cold shiver making its way from her neck to the base of her spine, she retraced her steps until she got back on to the path. Perhaps she would bring Selitto back here and they could make their way a bit further around the lake. But, for now, she was finding this whole experience a bit spooky and decided that it was time to get back to the safety of the hotel.

Selitto had discovered that Dangerfield was in a meeting with the Head of Household and couldn't be disturbed. However, he had noticed that one of the receptionists was on duty at the reception desk so he approached her.

'Hi Claudine,' he started, reading her name off the smart badge pinned to her left lapel. 'I understand that Mr Dangerfield is unavailable at the moment but I need some help understanding the way you code guest visits in your register.'

'Oh, I can help you with that,' Claudine smiled at him. 'What is the code you've got?'

Selitto took his notebook out and read off the code.

'OK', Claudine said after looking at the code. 'The 488 is Mr Vashlili's unique hotel number. Every guest is allocated a number the first time they stay with us, and that is used for every booking thereafter. The letter H you are having trouble with is the numbered visit during the year – in this instance, it tells us that this was the eighth time Mr Vashlili has visited us in the year as H is the eighth letter of the alphabet. The number 18 after the H denotes the year 2018. The number 01 is our code for the room, otherwise known as Crocus, and the final figure 1 is to denote the number of nights of his stay. It's probably not a perfect system for recording guest registrations but it's OK once you're used to it and it does help us get around some of the strict laws on data protection.' Claudine smiled at him.

'That's great!' Selitto thanked her for her help and retraced his steps to Dangerfield's office.

Sitting back at Dangerfield's desk, he reactivated the screen and started scrolling down the register. He picked out all the 488 codes since 1st January and made a record of the dates and the number of nights. There had, indeed, been eight visits this year and Vashlili had only ever stayed in the Crocus room. His stays had been mainly for one night although he had stayed for three nights around the beginning of April which Selitto noticed had been the Easter weekend. He had also stayed for two nights in mid-June.

As Selitto and Hunter were of the opinion that the hidden contents of the safe meant that it was some sort of dead-letter box, he concentrated on looking at all visitors to Crocus. He began by concentrating his search around the dates on which Guest 488 had stayed at the hotel, and soon found that 488's stays were often preceded by a one-night stay by Guest 627, also in Crocus. He then broadened his search to see if Guest 627 had stayed in any other rooms or on any other dates. But Guest 627 had only ever stayed in Crocus, and had never stayed on any other nights apart from those close to Vashlili's dates. In fact, the last entry in the register was for a booking only two nights before Vashlili's disappearance. This was coded as 627F18011. Now all he had to do was identify who Guest 627 was.

Sarah Hunter arrived back at the hotel, a little out of breath after climbing up from the bottom of the meadow. It was at times like this that she always promised herself that she would get back into the gym that Ted Selitto used opposite the Bat & Ball railway station in Sevenoaks. But something always seemed to derail these good intentions. She strode into reception, climbed the stairs to the first floor, and then sauntered along the corridor that led to another short staircase at the top of which was the Crocus room.

'Hi, Beth!' she called out from the dingey corridor outside the room. 'Anything to report?'

Dench appeared, pulling the hood of her Tyvek suit back off her mop of blonde hair which was loosely pinned up with a couple of fierce looking clips. She unclipped her facemask and smiled at her visitor.

'Not quite sure where to start,' she sighed. 'One thing is certain though: you are definitely looking for a body. Now that the boys have brought all the proper equipment, we have found evidence of considerable blood spatter which indicates that the bathroom is more than likely to be the scene of a murder. We can find very little evidence of blood in the bedroom – perhaps a couple of smears on the door frame but not much else. Jimbo has concentrated on the bedroom whilst Donny has been with me in the bathroom.'

Dench fiddled with the facemask. 'Jimbo has come up with an interesting assessment as well – he thinks that the so-called damage in the bedroom has been staged. He feels that items have either been broken and placed or simply placed to give the impression that a fight took place. He reckons that the fact the fridge door has been partially wrenched off is a bit of a giveaway as not only is that difficult to do but, in the heat of battle, would anyone really want to spend time trying to get a fridge door off its hinges?'

Hunter nodded. 'That's very interesting, Beth. But I wonder why someone would take the time and effort to stage manage the trashing of the room after they had already gone through the blood-letting in the bathroom? I mean, I have to assume that the trashing came after the killing – yes?'

'Yes, I think you're right, Sarah,' replied Beth, now reclipping her hair into a tighter mop. 'I doubt that your man Vashlili would trash his own room whilst waiting for someone he was then going to cut into little pieces in the bathroom. Doesn't really make sense to me. But an assailant coming into the room and killing Vashlili might think of trying to throw us off the scent by making us believe that there had been a fight. I don't know – sometimes it's difficult to see what goes on in people's minds in situations like that.'

'I suppose there are hundreds of prints in there,' Hunter surmised.

'Well, hardly any in the bathroom as you would expect after such a clean-up operation,' replied Beth, 'but there are some in the bedroom. Trouble is these will be from other guests who have used the room. If we run them through the data-base, we could waste valuable time trying to trace people who have absolutely nothing to do with this. I sincerely doubt that anyone who entered this room to kill Vashlili would have left any prints. If they have gone to the trouble of making a new set of blinds and swapping them with the hotel's blinds, then they are unlikely to leave any fingerprints behind!'

'Still happy that entry and exit was through the fire door?' Hunter asked.

'Yep. The tape on the lock mechanism was a bit of a give-away. They must have forgotten to remove that. There does appear to be a smear of blood on the door frame but that's all. So, it's likely that the body was carried out in some sort of container such as one of our body bags. There is no sign of anything being dragged across the floor or the grass so we have to assume that, whatever it was, it was carried. Have you any idea of Vashlili's build? Tall, short, thin, fat?'

'No idea!' Hunter hadn't a clue about Vashlili's build but made a mental note to ask Dangerfield. 'So, all we've got to do is find you a body?'

'That's about the measure of it,' Beth smiled, tucking another wisp of unruly hair behind her ear.

Hunter turned as if to go out through the fire exit on to the lawn. 'Just one other thing. I presume that the safe and its contents were clean?'

'As the proverbial whistle,' Beth responded. 'And I haven't had time to take a look at that sheet from the note pad which you gave me. I'll try and do that before we leave here but the equipment I need for that is probably back at base. Leave it with me though and I'll get it done just as soon as I can.'

'Okay Beth. What time do you reckon you'll be out of here?'

'Another couple of hours, tops. The boys will need feeding by then!' And, with that, the Crime Scene Manager retreated to the sanctuary of the bathroom and its darkest secrets.

12

Wednesday 19 July

Selitto had returned to the reception desk to find that Claudine had been replaced by someone whose name badge identified her as Mandy.

'Hello, Mandy,' he started, 'I was talking to Claudine earlier about your guest register. I'm trying to discover the identity of another guest who might be a friend of your guest Mr Vashlili.'

'Yes, sir. Mr Dangerfield mentioned the work you were doing,' Mandy replied, her big blue eyes glittering in the reflected light of the afternoon sun.

'Great!' Selitto exclaimed. 'Then I'd be grateful if you could provide me with the identity of Guest 627. A copy of the registration form for his latest visit which was three days ago would be most useful.'

'That should be fine, but I'll just check with the duty manager first. Just hang on there for a moment.' And she was gone through a door behind the reception desk.

Selitto looked around him, reviewing the geography of the entrance lobby and the lounge in front of reception. The huge fireplace which would no doubt have a burning log fire in the winter months. An elderly couple sitting on one of the deep settees with the remains of tea and scones on the table in front of them. She was wrestling with a broadsheet newspaper; his chin was on his chest as he gently surrendered to the delights of the cream tea.

He heard the door click behind him and turned to see Mandy returning to her desk.

'Yes, that's fine,' she said. 'Here is a copy of the registration form as requested. Please do let us know if you require any other information.'

Selitto thanked her and went off in search of DI Sarah Hunter.

The heat from the afternoon sun was oppressive so Hunter and Selitto headed for the shade of the open pavilion that overlooked one end of the long lawn. The tall trees sweeping along the west side of the lawn swayed gently in what little breeze there was but, otherwise, the scene was serenity personified.

'Borislav Zlatkov!' Selitto was reading from the copy of the register which he had been given by the receptionist. 'Showing an address in Enfield which is probably fake. I've already tried the mobile number and that's coming up as disconnected. His latest visit was on Sunday night, and the booking reference has the letter F in it which means that that was his sixth visit this year. On nearly every occasion, he has come in some two or three days before Vashlili, and always to the Crocus room and only for one night.'

'How does he get here,' asked Hunter looking off into the distance at two residents who were crossing the lawn, presumably on their way to another part of the Meadowlands estate.

'Looks like he comes in by taxi which could mean that he is arriving from outside the UK via Gatwick or he's coming by train from London.' Selitto folded the document and put it in his pocket. 'Name doesn't mean anything to me but I'll get Grace to run it through the system as well.'

'Okay! I'm thinking we're about done here,' Hunter summarised as she stood up and stepped back on to the lawn. 'Have you had time to look at the lighthouse on the lake yet?'

'Not yet, boss. Have you got anything else to do here before we get going?' Selitto asked.

'A couple of calls to make. And I'm curious about CCTV coverage. Haven't seen much evidence, have you?' Hunter looked around as if trying to spot the blinking eye of a camera.

'Good point!' conceded Selitto. 'Shouldn't take me too long to have a spin round the lake so I'll meet you back at the front door in, what, 30 minutes?'

Selitto was through the kissing gate and over the stile in no time and, brushing aside the overgrown vegetation which crisscrossed the path, he soon caught sight of the lighthouse sitting proudly in the centre of the lake. He continued along the path to a point where there seemed to be a break in the foliage surrounding the lake, and stopped to take in the view. It was certainly a spectacular setting with the sun glinting off the windows which surrounded the lantern room.

He decided to follow the path around the lake to its northern extremity just so that he could take in the magnificent view and get his bearings in the context of the location of the hotel. If anything, the lighthouse looked even more impressive from this angle against a background of tall trees and water stretching off into the distance.

Having negotiated a further kissing gate and stile, he found himself on a narrow, cobbled bridge which took him across the neck of the lake and on to the western bank. This looked even more overgrown than the path he had already followed. He paused on the bridge to take in the view, and watched as water from the lake flowed through a small weir before cascading over the edge of the lake and out of sight.

Turning away from the lake, he looked over the opposite wall which dropped steeply down to a small stream below. He could see the water crashing onto some rocks below him before it swirled downstream. His attention was also drawn to some rubbish which appeared to have been tossed away by people who clearly had no thought for preserving the countryside. He counted two plastic water bottles, a cardboard sandwich box and a couple of sweetie wrappers – there was even what looked like a black household refuse sack down there. The sack struck him as being rather out of place, but Selitto simply shook his head at the thoughtlessness of people leaving their rubbish behind in a beauty spot like this.

He turned his attention back to the lighthouse. From his new vantage point on the bridge, he was now able to see the steps leading up to a sheltered entrance. This presumably housed the door through which the lighthouse keepers would come and go in all weather conditions. He could imagine the storm waves crashing against the base of the structure, and he looked more closely to see if there was any sign of a jetty or landing stage. Surely, they didn't just sail up to the door and jump on to the bottom step? From this distance, it looked as if there might be some sort of wooden platform where a boat could be moored but he couldn't be sure. It might be interesting to take a closer look but Dangerfield had told him that no boats were allowed on the lake.

After having another look around, he continued across the bridge and joined the path leading back around the lake towards the original kissing gate and stile. The path was more overgrown on this side of the lake and he had difficulty navigating his way through the vegetation. On occasion, he had to leave the path to get around a particularly overgrown area, and he found himself being drawn closer and closer to the edge of the lake. Here, he found himself not only having to battle the branches and nettles but also midges and flies which buzzed all around him.

Selitto stopped to get his bearings. He sensed that he wasn't too far from the kissing gate at the entry/exit point and that, if all else failed, he could probably turn to his right and make his way through the undergrowth to the field he had caught a glimpse of when he was on the bridge. He was pretty sure that he could not make much more headway in a straight line, and was just about to take the easier option and head for the field when he stopped dead in his tracks. Something was glinting in the sunshine. The leafy vegetation seemed to be at its thickest along what he imagined must be the edge of the lake, but it hadn't prevented a shaft of reflected light catching his eye.

He instinctively turned to take a closer look at the source of the light. Taking great care to make sure that he did not accidentally step into the water, he inched forward until he had a better view. There, in front of him and covered in branches, leaves and creepers was what looked like a small rowing dinghy. The light was being reflected off a manufacturer's identity plate which was stuck on to one of the gunwales. Selitto was desperate to get a closer look at the boat but he was also acutely aware of how close he was getting to the edge of the lake. He finally stopped when he realised that he had reached the water's edge, and he peered through the overhanging vegetation to get a better look at the small vessel.

It seemed to be a run-of-the-mill rowing dinghy but there were no oars visible. He noticed that there was a plate at the stern of the boat for affixing a small outboard motor but no motor was attached. A rope was coiled up on a bench in the bow section. The boat was painted in a strange greenish-brown colour which meant that it was very well camouflaged in its location. Selitto doubted that he would have been able to see it if his attention had not been caught by the reflected light. He took his phone out and fired off a couple of pictures.

Retracing his steps away from the water's edge, Selitto headed up the bank towards the field and then on towards the kissing gate. He wondered what Hunter would make of his discovery.

Hunter was sitting on a bench at the top of the meadow. She was concentrating on her phone which she poked vigorously from time to time. She looked up at Selitto as he approached.

'I think we're done here,' she announced. 'I really need to get back to HQ and it's going to be a good hour at this time of the afternoon. I've spoken to the uniforms and they have nothing to report whatsoever. Told them to give it another half hour and then bugger off back to the station. Beth's already gone.' She looked back at her phone and then put it down beside her. 'Anyway, how did you get on? You seem to have been gone for ages.'

Selitto perched on the arm of the bench, and started fiddling with his phone. 'You'll never guess what I found?' he taunted her. Hunter just looked at him with a 'go-on-surprise-me' look in her eyes. He turned the screen of his phone so that she was looking at one of the pictures he had taken of the boat.

'What am I supposed to be looking at?' she asked, trying desperately to make out the subject matter of the photo in the afternoon sun.

Selitto expanded the picture on the screen so that the boat was now clearly visible, and passed the phone back to Hunter. 'If I'm not very much mistaken,' Selitto said, 'that's a boat on Mr Dangerfield's no-boats lake.'

'Wow!' Hunter exclaimed, peering at the photo. 'Doesn't look very seaworthy or, rather, lake-worthy but, if it's still afloat, it can't be letting the water in. Is it of interest to us?'

Selitto took another look at the photo. 'Not sure, boss. Dangerfield was at pains to tell us that no boats were allowed on the lake so he presumably has no knowledge of this boat. In which case it may well be used by poachers for fishing in the middle of the night although there is no evidence of how the boat is propelled – no oars or engine. Or maybe it's for the private use of our Mr Shooting Cuffs Dangerfield – perhaps for getting him to the lighthouse?'

Hunter laughed at Selitto's analogy of Dangerfield who did have the annoying habit of shooting his cuffs. But she could also see the relevance of the boat if it was used to access the lighthouse.

'Okay,' she said. 'Is it going anywhere? I doubt it from what you have said so let's leave it parked in the undergrowth. I'll get Beth to send Jimbo to have a look at it in the morning. Anything else?'

'Not really. Quite a lot of rubbish has been thrown off the bridge at the northern end of the lake. If the boat is an item of interest then I would probably want to just get a look at what has been discarded. But I doubt it will be of any interest.'

'OK, let's keep this to ourselves. I don't really have the stomach for starting another conversation with Dangerfield today, and I'm sure everything can wait until the morning.' She stood up from the bench. 'Let's get going – this place is starting to give me the creeps.'

Selitto followed Hunter along a gravel path, through and archway and into the car park. His precious Megane was still parked where he had left it when they had first arrived at the hotel. He looked across at the BMW in the car park which now had crime tape all around it. 'No Police Aware stickers then! Dangerfield must be delighted! Do we know when it's being collected?'

Hunter looked across the car park. 'Not for a day or two by all accounts. Grace mentioned something about our colleagues from Hampshire wanting to get their hands on it, but she's told them that it isn't going anywhere until Beth's had a good look at it!'

'That's my girl!' Selitto mumbled as he opened the door of the Megane and sank into the driver's seat. He pushed the start button.

13
Wednesday 19 July

They drove back to Tonbridge mainly in silence. Hunter was busy poking away at her phone, and Selitto periodically swore at other drivers, cyclists and pot holes in equal measure. Taking the back roads through Haxted Mill, Hever and Leigh, they seemed to miss much of the traffic and arrived back at Pembury Road with the sun still high in the sky.

'Grace is waiting for us upstairs so let's go and have a chat with her first,' Hunter said as she got out of the car and walked across the concrete floor of the underground car park to get to the lifts. Exiting the lift on the first floor, they both stopped to grab a cold bottle of water from the fridge and made their way over to DS Grace Kendall's desk which occupied a coveted corner spot in the large open-plan Operations Room.

'Hi guys!' Grace looked up as Hunter and Selitto approached. 'How's it going?'

There was a spare seat in front of Grace's desk and Hunter took it even though she had to peer round the desktop monitor to catch sight of Grace. Selitto stood to the side of the desk, leaning against the window sill.

'Thanks for getting some info on that car,' Hunter started.

'No problem!' Kendall replied. 'Almost as soon as I put it up on the countrywide board, Hampshire were on to claim it. 'They're quite keen to get it back but accept that it's part of an investigation at the moment. Chap I spoke to didn't know much about where it was nicked from so I'll try and get some more on that if it helps.'

Hunter nodded. 'The CSIs are going to take a good look at it tomorrow and then we can get someone to take it away. If we know it's from Hampshire then I'm sure we can pretty soon release it back into their tender care!'

Hunter's sarcastic tone brought a smile to Kendall's face just as her mobile pinged with an incoming message. She grabbed the device and had a quick look at the screen before jettisoning it and turning back to Hunter and Selitto.

'Yes, as I was saying – the guy I spoke to only seemed to know that it had been reported as nicked and seemed to have no information as to where it had been nicked from. So, I'll follow that up in case it gives us any other information. Quite often the location of the theft leads us to consider other lines of enquiry.'

'Okay! Good work.' Hunter was keen to get on. 'Now, we've got another name for you – Borislav Zlatkov.' She waited while Grace keyed this in. 'We know nothing about him other than that, on five occasions this year, he has stayed at Meadowlands a couple of nights before our man Vashlili – always in the same room that Vashlili would occupy a night or two later. This would probably be somewhat irrelevant if Ted hadn't found a couple of sheets of A4 hidden in the room safe. My hunch is that they are connected but that they don't necessarily know each other. I think that the safe was probably being used as some sort of dead-letter drop box with one man leaving infor-mation for the other to act upon. At the moment, we can't make head nor tail of the code being used although Beth Dench is going to try and get it looked at by one of her spook friends up in London.'

'Can I have a look?' Kendall asked.

Selitto rummaged around in his coat pocket and took out his notebook. 'Beth's taken the originals but I made a note of one of the lines of code.'

He passed his notebook over to Kendall who keyed the code in, and then sat back staring at the array of numbers and letters on her screen.

010715 N1T1L91 4252/2520 7161847880 SHARKFIN 180420 3T6U2N VAS

'Intriguing!' she exclaimed. 'Would you mind if I took a look at it as well as Beth's spook? It'll be on the back burner but I may come up with something.'

'That's fine!' Hunter got up from her uncomfortable chair and strolled over to the window. She looked out on to the bustling roundabout leading up to Tonbridge railway station where people were piling out from yet another commuter train arrival from London. She turned back to where Kendall and Selitto were staring at the code which was now highlighted on Grace's screen. 'Could you also have a good look at Meadowlands and our Mr Peter Dangerfield. You know – history, ownership, profitable or loss making, any scandals – that sort of thing. I doubt that Dangerfield will have ever been on our radar but just check and see where else he's been. I just get the feeling that he's keeping something back from us.'

'Yep, I can take a look at all that,' said Grace. 'Presumably ownership is somewhere on their website but we have other means of establishing that.'

'I get the impression it's the plaything of some financial whizz kids or something like that – investment funds maybe,' replied Hunter. 'Don't think it's owned by any rich Sheikh or international money launderer – but you never know!'

'Okay,' Kendall replied. 'I'll get on to that. Only one other question at the moment. What about CCTV? Any of that in place?'

'Another fairly blind alley, I'm afraid,' Hunter replied. 'Once I had had the lecture on discrete surveillance and data protection from Dangerfield, I had rather lost the will to live! Anyway, it seems that they have a bit of coverage in the lounge and bar but none upstairs where the guestrooms are. There is a camera on the car park at the front but it isn't working at the moment. Another is set up in the rear garden but is as good as useless as there is a branch of a tree in full leaf directly in front of it. That's pretty much it.'

'OK! Anything else you'd like me to be getting on with?' Grace tapped some more keys and then sat back in her chair.

'Let's re-group once Beth's team has been back to Meadowlands tomorrow.' Hunter suggested. 'Thanks, Grace. Most useful. And now my sergeant is going to buy me a well-deserved glass of something refreshing!' And, with that, Hunter strode across the room and disappeared into the corridor.

'The life of a sergeant, eh?' Selitto rolled his eyes at Kendall and then followed the trail of the whirlwind across the office.

14

Wednesday 19 July

Hunter had managed to get a corner table away from the hubbub of the early evening drinkers, and was nursing a pint of Guinness. Some of the light brown froth still stuck to her top lip, and she slowly licked it off savouring the mild taste. She liked this pretty country pub as it provided her with the sort of the anonymity she craved after finishing a day in a job which, she felt, exposed her to the extremes of public scrutiny. The locals were always very polite to her, and seemed totally respectful of her preference to sit on her own if she was in the pub unaccompanied.

Sarah Hunter had policing coursing through her veins. Her parents had met when they were both in the West Yorkshire Constabulary, later to become the West Yorkshire Metropolitan Police. In the days before computers, her mother was a Police Indexer and her father was a bobby on the beat. She was an only child, and was devastated when her father's life had been cut short by a hit & run driver who had never been caught. She managed to get a place at Liverpool University to study Law and, after graduation, she had eyes for no other job than a Graduate Entrant with the West Yorkshire Met. Naively, she had thought that, by having access to police records and detection techniques, she might be able to catch the person who had killed her father.

Over the years, and at times when things were quiet, she had tried to access the evidence which had been gathered about the incident in which her father had lost his life. But she had quickly found that doing this on her own was very difficult and fraught with danger. Misusing her position to obtain information which did not relate to current operational matters within her orbit was a very serious matter and, if she had been found out, she could have faced either demotion or dismissal from the force. However, she had never given up hope that the perpetrator would one day be charged, so identification of that person was still an unticked box on her 'to-do' list.

She quickly made her mark in Yorkshire, and was soon transferred to the bright lights of London where she became a detective constable in the corridors of power at New Scotland Yard. She loved the high-profile policing which London offered but, although she made it to detective sergeant, she became frustrated with the lack of opportunities for further promotion. It just seemed that obstacles to career advancement were always being strategically put in her way, so she decided to look for a change of job away from the Met.

Eventually, she managed to get a move to Kent Police and it wasn't long before she was promoted to detective inspector. She swapped her tiny flat in Stockwell for a little cottage deep in the Kent countryside which offered her the privacy and seclusion which she craved when she was not working. She immersed herself in country life, often walking for miles at weekends when time allowed. She loved stopping at small country pubs, and sitting in the gardens simply admiring the view or studying a map to see exactly where she was. She very occasionally engaged in conversation with locals at the bar but always made her polite excuses when conversations started to get round to the "and what do you do?" question.

· Ted Selitto had been her DS for coming up to two years now.

He was a few years older than Hunter, but had an excellent work ethic – much like herself. He was also single but was more of a townie and lived in a small apartment in Sevenoaks. Hunter enjoyed their relationship as there were no expectations on the part of either party and, although they very much enjoyed each other's company, there was no pressure to take things further. She had learned her lesson about workplace relationships right at the beginning of her time at Yorkshire when she started dating a young DC, kidding herself that she'd get to spend more time with him if they both worked on the force. She was quickly disabused of this idea when he started spending more time with his DS, and they had each gone their separate ways after she discovered his duplicity.

Just as she was getting lost in thought about the events of the day, Selitto appeared in the bar. She made a couple of hand signals to indicate that it was his round and she wanted a half, so he moved over to the bar to order the drinks. Juggling two glasses, a packet of crisps and his change, he eventually made it to the table without spilling a drop.

He plonked himself down on the threadbare banquette next to Hunter. At an early age, he had been taught to never sit with his back to a crowd – a lesson he had always tried to remember. He opened the bag of crisps down the seam so that he could spread the contents out, took a long slurp of his pint of Larkins bitter and sat back with a sigh.

'I like this pub – good choice!' he said staring off into the distance. 'Thought I'd treat you to dinner – it's cheese and onion flavoured!'

Hunter smiled and deftly poured her half pint of Guinness into her pint glass making the glass back up to about three quarters full with a good head of froth.

'Is Beth organised for tomorrow?' she asked, taking a quick squint at her phone which lay on the table beside her glass.

'Yep,' replied Selitto. 'She's sending the boys down to Meadowlands first thing. They're going to give the car the once over and then take a look at the boat. I think it's a good idea of yours not to mention the boat to Dangerfield for the time being. Must say I really would like to be there when he finds out that one of his golden rules has been broken!'

'Hmm!' Hunter took another gulp of her Guinness. 'I'll be interested to see what Grace dredges up about him. Good front-of-house man but I'm not sure he's got full control of what goes on behind the scenes. Also, I got the impression that he not only doesn't live on site but also lives quite a long way from the hotel so maybe doesn't go there every day. I know that lots of people can work from home these days but I would have thought that a hotel manager needs to be a bit more hands-on.'

'Yet the others didn't seem to be able to make decisions or offer information without his say so,' observed Selitto. They both appeared to give this some thought.

Selitto broke the silence. 'I'm also going to see if the boys can just give that rubbish at the top of the lake the once over. Just in case the lake has been used for some nefarious activity and someone tossed incriminating evidence off the bridge. Mind you, the amount of water cascading down the wall will probably have nullified any usable evidence but probably best to just take a look.'

Hunter nodded. 'In the meantime, we really must get on with that paperwork for the car ringing case. I'll try and get in for 7.30 a.m. in the morning – that OK for you?' Selitto nodded. 'What you got for dinner tonight?' she enquired.

'Think I'll pick up something with chicken in it from the local Chinese,' he replied. 'What about you?'

'It's a Moussaka for one plus salad followed by a nice hot bath and, hopefully, my fair share of zeds!' Hunter drained her glass and wiped the back of her hand across her mouth. 'Right! That's me done. You staying for another?'

'No fear!' replied Selitto. 'I'm starving! Seems ages since Dangerfield's sandwiches!' They both got up from the banquette and threaded their way through the increasing numbers of drinkers towards the door, Selitto making a detour to deposit the empty glasses on the bar. ''Night!' he called to the barmaid as he walked through the doorway and out into the car park. Hunter was already beside her car and waved to him as she got in and drove off into the encroaching dusk. Selitto smiled and, with his stomach rumbling, he drove off in search of a steaming plate of Szechaun Chicken and Singapore Noodles.

15
Wednesday 19 July

The girl climbed on and on up the ladder, up the ladder to the roof. What had Marijka told her? Never go up! Escape is only possible by going down. But going down hadn't been an option. She loved Marijka like a sister. Marijka would know what to do in a situation like this. Marijka always knew what to do. But Marijka wasn't here.

If she stopped now, she could possibly let the man catch her up and then stamp on his ugly greasy head. But he would probably just grab her by the ankles and yank her back down the ladder. She had to keep on moving, keep on getting as far away as possible.

She suddenly reached the platform at the top of the ladder which led on to the roof. From there, she leapt on to the flat asphalt surface and raced across a landscape populated with chimney stacks, aircon units and solar panels. Could she hide from him for long enough to get her breath back and find another escape route? If only Marijka hadn't been taken from her. Marijka would be able to assess the situation in an instant. Marijka would tell her what to do next. But all she could hear was heavy breathing as the man started his search of the rooftop.

She was also starting to feel cold. Her pathetically thin dress was totally inadequate for the drizzle which was now falling. Her teeth were chattering and she had to keep her mouth shut to avoid giving away her location. She had crouched behind one of the aircon units and now risked a quick look round its corner. She just caught a glimpse of the man sneaking behind one of the chimney stacks so she leapt across the open space to the next aircon unit.

Was she now heading back to the ladder? She seemed to have lost her sense of direction. Marijka would never lose her sense of direction. If Marijka was here, she would show her the way back to the ladder. But Marjka wasn't here.

The girl looked all around her, eyes wide with fear and desperation. The light had faded which was making it difficult to see exactly where she was on the roof. She chanced another furtive look around the corner of the aircon unit and, seeing nothing, she raced across another open space until she was snuggled behind one of the chimney stacks. By now, the cooler air was really getting to her and her body was beginning to shake with violent shivers. She was also terrified that the man was going to find her.

She crouched down and scuttled to the end of the stack. Just as she was about to take another risky peek round its corner, she caught sight of the top of the ladder with its platform stretching out towards her. Marijka was here after all! Marijka had guided her to this spot so that she could now escape. Marijka – the only person she had ever loved in her short, miserable life.

Taking a deep breath, she summoned up all her strength and courage, and leapt out of her hiding place towards the ladder and safety. But just as she thought that she was going to make it, the man appeared from nowhere and kicked out as she passed him. His boot connected with her thigh which sent her skittering across the wet roof. Pain shot through her whole body but she managed to get to her feet trying desperately to locate the platform at the top of the ladder. At the same time, she saw the silhouette of the man coming for her. She turned and ran blindly in the direction of the ladder. Surely it had just been over here? But the ladder wasn't here. Where had it gone? She suddenly realised that she had completely lost her sense of direction.

And, just as suddenly, she realised that she was no longer running. Instead, she was floating, floating downwards as if on some surreal fairground ride. She would soon reach the bottom and would then feel the G-force as she was whisked back into the air. Just like the time Marijka took her to the fair. Marijka had enjoyed all the rides as they had sat together holding hands and laughing until they cried. But this time she was not whisked back into the air. And her last thought as her frail body was smashed into a thousand pieces was that Marijka wasn't there.

16

Thursday 20 July

The call came in at around 11.30 a.m. Hunter and Selitto had got started on their car ringing paperwork at shortly after 07.30 a.m. as they had agreed the previous evening and, apart from a short break for a much-needed coffee, they had made good progress. Sarah didn't recognise the number on the screen so answered with an air of formality.

'DI Hunter,' she said.

'Good morning, ma'am,' a slightly breathless voice responded. 'It's Jimbo Carrigan here. CSI Unit. I think you know that I'm down at Meadowlands today with my colleague Donny Campbell.'

'Yes, yes! Beth told me,' Hunter was suddenly all ears. Surely Jimbo wouldn't be ringing her just to give her an update. His reporting line would be through his CSI Manager.

'Well, she's actually asked me to give you a call as she's out on another investigation,' he continued. 'The thing is that we seem to have a bit of a problem here.'

'OK, Jimbo,' Hunter replied. 'Just hold on while I try to get the speaker working on my phone so that DS Selitto can listen in.' She punched a couple of buttons on her phone and laid it on the desk. 'Can you still hear me?'

'Yes. And you can both hear me?' Carrigan asked. Selitto nodded his head and continued reading from the array of papers which covered the desk in front of him.

'Yep, perfect! Now, what have you got for us?' Hunter felt a small adrenaline rush as she always did when there was the possibility of a breakthrough in an investigation. She tried to keep her hopes in check.

'Well,' Carrigan started, 'the first thing is that we think the car has been tampered with. When we had a quick look at it yesterday, we were pretty certain it was all locked up. That's why we have come here today with a full tech kit to get us into it. However, this morning we found that the boot at the back of the car wasn't shut properly. I can't think that we wouldn't have noticed this yesterday so the only conclusion we can draw is that someone must have accessed the car during the night.'

'Okay', Hunter said, drawing the word out and looking across towards Selitto who had now stopped reading and was giving her a puzzled look.

'We've had a good look inside,' Carrigan continued. 'There's a strong smell of plastic, what you'd get from industrial strength packaging material, and it looks as if something might have been stored in there. We've identified a couple of very small smudges of what appears to be dried blood, and we've taken prints but they're probably all from the owner. Otherwise, it all seems pretty clean with only a minimum of dirt and grit in the driver's foot well. Don't think it's anything to get excited about but we'll keep a sample for testing.'

'Anything to tell us where it's been?' asked Hunter, remembering that Grace Kendall had mentioned that she thought there was some sort of journey recording system.

'Yep, there seems to be something that might tell us a bit more but we haven't got the gear here to get into it,' replied Carrigan. 'Donny's been fiddling about with it, and thinks he's got some data downloaded onto a memory stick so we'll have a look at that back at base.'

'OK, Jimbo, is that it?' Hunter got ready to end the call and, rising from the desk, was on the point of moving back to her office.

'No, ma'am,' Carrigan's voice rattled out of the phone in her hand. 'There have been other surprises down here.'

Hunter stopped in her tracks and spun round, frowning. She put the phone back on the top of the desk. 'Oh, yeah – and what might they be?'

'Well,' Carrigan coughed to clear his throat. 'We had the devil of a problem trying to find DS Selitto's boat. We trooped up and down the western edge of the lake peering into all the foliage and vegetation which hangs over the lake but there was no sign of it. It was Donny who eventually spotted the reflection of the maker's plate which had caught a shaft of sunlight. The problem was that the boat was under the water.'

'What? It had sunk?' exclaimed Selitto, looking incredulously at the phone. 'How on earth...?'

Carrigan's voice crackled through the ether. 'No, no, it hadn't sunk. It had been sunk!'

'What?' Selitto raised his voice. Hunter was staring at the phone in disbelief. 'Go on,' she said in a calming tone of voice, trying to hold back a frisson of excitement which was growing inside her.

'Fortunately, we had brought a pair of waders with us so Donny went into the water to see what was going on. The boat was completely under water but resting on the shallow bank beside the lake. The water is quite clear so he had a good look around. He found that half a dozen holes had been drilled in the bottom of the boat using a thick bradawl head so the boat would have sunk pretty quickly. It's now sitting in about four feet of water where it will have to stay pro-tem as we have no way of moving it.'

Selitto stared at the phone in disbelief. 'So that's screwed any evidence we might have got from the boat?' he added more as a statement than a question.

'Well, let's just say it's not going to help us,' Carrigan chipped in, 'and the longer it stays submerged the more the water is going to compromise the evidence. We'll need to get someone down here with the equipment to get it out of the water. It'll need to be manoeuvred away from the overgrown vegetation before we can start to raise it.'

'Okay, Jimbo,' Hunter chipped in, anxious to get on. 'See if you can find someone with the equipment you need, and keep us in the loop. Let me know if you hit any snags.' She looked at Selitto, her raised eyebrows asking if he wanted to say anything else. He shook his head.

There was further coughing from the phone before Carrigan's voice came back on. 'You still all there?' he asked warily, just in case he was just talking to himself.

'Yes, we're still here. Carry on,' Hunter responded, absent-mindedly repositioning the band of her ponytail. She normally wore her hair loose but the longer it went without being washed, the more likely it was to be tied in a ponytail.

'It's just something or it might be nothing,' Carrigan started, 'DS Selitto, did you mention a black bin bag at the bottom of the drop at the head of the lake?'

Selitto nodded at the phone. 'Yeah, there were some plastic water bottles, sandwich boxes, sweetie wrappers, that sort of thing. I thought I also saw a black refuse sack like the ones the councils give out for household waste. Just thought it was a strange place to toss some household waste.'

'We had a look over the side of the bridge,' Carrigan continued, 'but we couldn't see a black sack like you described. Donny spotted an easy access point for getting to the bottom of the wall so he went to take a closer look. Lots of rubbish as you described but definitely no bin bag. He had a look around away from the main drop site but couldn't see anything resembling the black sack. Unlikely to have been taken off by an animal as the whole area down there is fenced in. So, the only conclusion we can draw is that it was removed by a person or persons unknown.' Hunter looked across at Selitto, shrugged her shoulders and turned her palms upwards with a questioning look. When he didn't respond, she turned her attention back to the phone.

'OK, Jimbo, thanks for the update,' she said, bringing the call to an end. Then, as an afterthought, she asked Carrigan if he had seen Peter Dangerfield.

'Not today, ma'am. He's not on site. Get the feeling that he was supposed to be here but that one of his kids is unwell. Seems to lead a rather complicated personal life, and has left some of his colleagues in the mire today as they are already short-staffed. There's a few short fuses around at the moment!'

'Hmmm! There's a thing,' mused Hunter. 'OK, Jimbo. Thanks for the update – good work. Do you know if Beth's dropping in here later or has she got other things on her agenda?'

'No idea, I'm afraid,' came the reply.

'Okay, no probs. See you around.' Hunter disconnected the call and looked across at Selitto. 'Stranger and stranger!' she mused.

17

Thursday 20 July

Woons' phone was vibrating on the desk in front of him. He looked at the screen before swiping his thumb across it. 'Yeah, Trig. What you got?'

Woons was in his office, an old portacabin which had started its life on the Channel Tunnel project. He had picked it up for a song from a mate in the haulage industry in Faversham who had been on the dismantling team once construction of the tunnel was finished. He had originally been in discussion with a farmer about taking over some rundown outhouses at a location which was well off the beaten track but, when the offer of the portacabin came along, the farmer agreed that he could just put it alongside the dilapidated buildings. There was a track leading down to a country lane and, once Woons had done some work on creating a gravel-laid turning circle and parking area in front of the portacabin, he had all he needed to manage his day-to-day business. The farmer was happy with the rent Woons paid, and left him very much to his own devices.

Although he lived well, dressed smartly, liked to eat in posh restaurants and generally enjoyed an opulent lifestyle, Woons had never been keen on drawing attention to himself by having a swanky office at a posh address. What was the point? He never had any visitors to his office, he didn't employ anyone, and he did most of his work on the hoof. He was more than happy to divert the savings on extortionate office rents and rates into his own pockets, and he was canny with the way he organised his finances. Perhaps it was something he had learned in prison mixing with lags who just wanted people to recognise them as crooks. That wasn't Woons' style. He was much smarter than that.

'Yeah, Billy, I'm afraid that we've got a bit of a problem down at Wateringbury,' Harding reported. 'Seems one of the girls went off the roof yesterday evening. They managed to pick up the pieces before anyone noticed, mainly because it was pouring with rain and there was no one about. They then tried to get hold of Vashlili as per our procedures.'

'And I suppose the fucker couldn't be contacted,' Woons spat. 'What's going on with him? Where the fuck is he?'

'No idea, Billy,' Harding replied. 'But we've had to get our arses into gear to get the body off the premises and somewhere it can be stored for the time being. Thankfully, Tricky knows a mate who's got a mate who's got some freezers in a lock up near Paddock Wood so we've borrowed one of them. Tricky said he was calling in a favour so should be OK for a few days but not ideal.'

'No, you're right there!' Woons looked at his nails and flicked a speck of imaginary dust off the lapel of his jacket. 'And we can't afford to have no more accidents if our man from the Caucasus has gone AWOL. Otherwise, we're going to need more than one of Tricky's mate's freezers. Jesus, Trig – how did this Wateringbury thing happen?'

'Not sure of all the details,' Harding replied, 'but it sounds like one of the punters went out the fire door to have a smoke and the next thing the girl banged him on the head and leapt off up the fire ladder. He went after her and ended up on the roof. The story is rather vague after that but he seems to have tried to grab her just as she went over the edge. She ended up back on terra firma by the bins at the rear of the building so she wasn't actually in anyone's line of sight. Thankfully there was no screaming either so, all in all, we seemed to have been quite lucky.'

'Yeah!' Woons was thinking. Yeah!' he said absent-mindedly. 'See what you mean.' He got up from his chair and started pacing around the cramped office space. He stopped in front of a map of Kent and East Sussex.

'You still there, Billy?' Harding's voice suddenly interrupted the silence.

'Sorry, Trig – just thinking,' replied Woons. 'Do we know anything about what Vashlili gets up to once he gets an assignment or does he just turn up, take the goods away and that's that? Has anyone ever gone along with him or ever asked what he gets up to, where he goes? I mean, he does a very good job for us – don't get me wrong! But we seem to know fuck all about his method of disposal.'

'We don't have much intel, Billy,' said Harding, trying to think of anything he might have heard or seen which could throw some light on the murky world Tamaz Vashlili operated in. 'I did hear that he liked to get down to some place on the Kent/Sussex border but I thought that was more for some R&R. I think some of his cronies from the homeland fly into Gatwick from time to time, and he meets up with them for a bit of a lads' night out round the Crawley area. And he always seems to have a different set of wheels but I can appreciate that that's probably more of a necessity in his line of business.'

'OK!' Woons paused, still deep in thought. 'OK! Where else you been today?'

'Well, we did the farmhouse at Toys Hill, then on

to Hildenborough, then the woodland cottage back of Horsmonden, and we've just arrived at Fordcombe.' Harding was tapping the steering wheel of the Audi whilst he was talking to Woons. Spink was sitting in the passenger seat bashing out a lengthy text message on his phone. They were parked up a gravel driveway which led to a mock-Edwardian country house which had three expensive-looking vehicles parked in a row outside the front door.

Woons was surveying the map on the wall in his office, and mentally ticking off the locations as Harding mentioned them. 'Any problems anywhere else that I should know about?' he asked.

Harding looked across at Spink before replying. 'Not that we're aware of.' Spink grunted and nodded his head in agreement.

'So, what's-her-name at Wateringbury's okay with the clean-up operation but presumably pissed off that she's one girl down until we can get hold of that arsehole Vashlili,' Woons observed.

'Yeah! The punters seem to be quite understanding,' Harding replied, 'but some have had to be accommodated elsewhere which has caused one or two problems. That's why we really needed that fucking shipment. Any news on that, by the way?'

This question jolted Woons back to the here and now. 'No news of the shipment, and I'm getting pretty bloody hacked off with the way our Georgian friends are dealing with us. Not only has Vashlili disappeared but Irakli is now not responding to calls or emails and the emergency number for one of their contacts in the Dover area is coming up as unobtainable.' Woons glared at the map, almost willing it to tell him where

Vashlili was because, right now, he could quite happily throttle the good-for-nothing Georgian bastard.

'Tricky!' Woons suddenly raised his voice, presumably to make sure that Spink was listening in the car.

'Yes, Billy,' came the measured reply.

'Did you never follow Vashlili, see what he was up to, where he lived, that sort of thing?' Woons asked, now starting to question in his own mind who exactly this bloke was he had worked with all these years?

'Not really, Billy,' Spink replied. 'Following Tamaz is a very difficult gig. He floated in and out of this country without anyone really knowing much about it – including the Border Police! And when he was here, we never knew what to follow 'caus he always had a different set of wheels. Even when he went on the raz with his comrades over in the Crawley area, you could never find out nothing about what went down there. He's a fucking international criminal, Billy – pure and simple. And he's never likely to get caught. Would take a much better man than me to tail him to the level that he didn't know he was being followed.'

'Hmmm! Okay, Tricky. Thanks.' Woons lapsed into silence.

'Billy, we need to get on now,' Harding's voice stirred Woons' thoughts. 'We've got some more calls to make then we'll drop by the office later.'

'Okay, Trig,' Woons replied. There was a click on the phone and Woons' screen went blank. He looked at his watch. Blimey, it was already 2.30pm and he hadn't had any lunch!

18

Thursday 20 July

Late in the afternoon, Hunter got the call she had been dreading – and had hoped she wouldn't get today as she thought that Detective Chief Inspector Alan Iverson was over at the Force HQ in Maidstone for an all-dayer. But no, he was now in his office on the top floor with panoramic views over the car park at Tonbridge railway station, the rail lines stretching east towards Ashford and, beyond them, the local Sainsburys. On entering the office, Hunter saw that the DCI was sitting behind his desk with a face which clearly wanted to know what was going on!

In situations like this, Hunter always tried to give the impression of complete calmness so she now sat with legs crossed and her right armpit over the wing of the chair. She looked straight ahead at Iverson, knowing almost exactly what he was going to say before he had even opened his mouth.

'What on earth's going on Sarah?' he started in measured tones. 'There was I happy in the knowledge that you were preparing a watertight case for the CPS which will ensure that the bloody Hardwicks go away for a very long time. And then a little birdie pops up and tells me that you are crashing about on the Kent and Sussex border on some MisPer report which might or might not actually be a MisPer.'

'It was just a day yesterday,' Hunter blustered, trying to give a low-key impression of the case.

'Be that as it may,' Iverson continued, 'I cannot allow you to involve yourself in any other cases until we've put the lid firmly on the Hardwicks, turned the lock and thrown away the key. You know as well as I do that it's a complex case and the slightest error will put all our work in serious jeopardy of not coming out with a conviction. I can't have you being distracted by anything unless it's of such a magnitude that it constitutes a national emergency. A MisPer in leafy Kent or Sussex doesn't!'

'We're making good progress on the Hardwick case, sir,' she pleaded, 'and we still have five weeks to get it done. We got that extra time when DS Selitto uncovered those other witnesses. We're definitely on track. And this MisPer probably won't amount to much!'

'Tell me about it,' Iverson said, steepling his fingers under his chin.

'Sir?' Hunter was thrown by what Iverson had just said.

'Tell me about it!' he repeated. 'Tell me about the MisPer case!'

Hunter was knocked slightly off guard but she rallied quickly and gave her boss as much of the information as she herself had been able to garner.

'It does have the potential to either be a major case involving international criminals – or it could just be a damp squib when this mystery man Vashlili walks into a police station and gives himself up! At the moment, my money's on it becoming a major investigation as something definitely happened at that hotel, and I'm sure that there's more to it than a fight in a bathroom. Even if we don't have a body, my money would be on there being one somewhere!'

Iverson sat back and looked at Hunter. He had always admired her tenacity and her ability to get through mountains of work. She was dedicated with a capital 'D', and was the most reliable member of his team. She had a level of intellect which meant that she didn't miss much – she was always on the look-out for clues, and often found them through sheer persistence and hard graft, sifting and re-sifting all the evidence. She was an asset to any team, and he was just grateful to have her on his.

'Okay, listen up!' Hunter took her arm off the back of the chair and uncrossed her legs. 'Let's give it another 48 hours and see what else falls out of the tree. That takes us to Saturday pm so let's agree to talk again at that time when you can give me a full update. If there are no further developments on the MisPer then I must insist that it's 100% of your time on the Hardwick case until it's completed. If there are developments, then we will treat it as any other case and react accordingly. Just bear in mind our meagre resources. Just you and Ted for the time being. I know you're getting help from DS Kendall and the CSIs but that's all. If it escalates, I'll only be able to let you have a couple of 'green horns' but at least they'll be keen. And keep me fully in the loop. I need to know the second anything changes or there is a development. And tell DS Selitto that that goes for him as well. No heroics!'

Hunter was still slightly in shock as she found herself closing the door to Iverson's office and walking back down the corridor to the central stairway. That had gone well, she thought. But what had Iverson seen in the report she'd given that had changed his mind about letting her at least spend a bit more time on the MisPer? She clattered back down the stairs to the Ops Room on the first-floor, her eyes roaming over the office looking for Selitto.

19

Thursday 20 July

The ligature was tight around Rosica's neck, and she was having difficulty breathing. He had pulled the gag tightly across her mouth with the result that she could only get air into her lungs through her nose. Her hands were tied to two rings which hung from the wall at the top of the bed, and her ankles were secured to the tails at the foot of the bed. Her eyes focused only on the ceiling – she did not want him to have the satisfaction of thinking that she was looking at him while he was creeping around her body like some kind of perverted praying mantis.

She idly wondered how often this ritual was being played out. Must be at least two times a week although she had lost all sense of time in this hell hole. Her only memory of getting here had been the stranger who asked her for directions as she took a short cut from home to the High School she was attending in her beloved Karlovo nestled on the edge of the Central Balkan National Park. She had felt a cold, damp cloth being roughly placed over her mouth and nose and, although she had struggled and tried to kick out at her assailant, she was no match for his strength and she soon felt herself dropping, dropping, dropping like a stone into the abyss.

She remembered nothing until she awoke in a tiny room with no windows, a single bed and a solitary wash basin. She had no idea where she was or what fate lay before her. She was shivering with fear and was deeply traumatised by her desperate situation as she had never before been away from her home or her close-knit family. But things were about to get a whole lot worse when she encountered a huge woman who had what Rosica thought looked like a pile of snakes on her head.

The woman spoke in a language which Rosica recognised as English, but she did not understand what she was saying. The woman had grabbed Rosica by the arm and propelled her on to a landing which had several doors leading off it. They came to a halt in the middle of the landing whereupon the woman yelled a command. Her voice was deafening and Rosica's ears were ringing as the sound reverberated around the walls. But slowly, one by one, doors started to open and girls of Rosica's age started to appear. Rosica stared wide-eyed at the girls until it suddenly hit her that they were all prisoners in this place. And then the tears started to fall and she collapsed onto her knees, sobbing uncontrollably.

The huge woman had pushed Rosica roughly away so that she was sprawled on the floor. She had pulled her knees up so that she was in the foetal position to protect herself in the belief that she was about to get a good kicking. Her sobs rang out around the landing as the huge woman shouted out another command and stomped off down the stairs. At this, the other girls came out of their rooms and gathered round Rosica. One of them spoke and Rosica was astonished to hear her own language being spoken. Her eyelids flew open and she searched the sea of faces in a desperate attempt to discover who had said some words of welcome to her.

Over the next hour or so, Rosica had got to know the girls who would be her companions in what they described as a house of horrors. Amid much tearfulness and sobbing, she had heard terrible stories of men who would come to the house and the extraordinary acts of depravation in which the girls were required to partake.

It wasn't long before the huge woman was back, again grabbing her by the arm and this time pushing her down the stairs to the floor below. Here, she was shown into a room which had a double bed as its centrepiece with mirrors around the walls and on the ceiling. There were rows of sex aids and toys laid out on a table in one corner of the room, and a wardrobe full of clothes and uniforms. There was also a rolltop bath and a small cabinet crammed with oils and perfumes. Rosica stared wide-eyed at the layout of the room as tears began to again moisten her delicate young cheeks.

After that, she had been paired up with other girls as a way of showing her what she was expected to do but after that she was on her own. And on this particular evening she was with this crazy man who got his kicks from tying her up and then cutting the clothes away from her body. She stared fixedly at the ceiling, her mind wandering back to blissful days spent with her sisters skipping along the banks of the Stryama river at the southern end of the Balkan Mountains. The scent of roses was all around, and the municipality was getting ready for the annual rose oil festival when huge numbers of tourists descended on the area. All the while, mister crazy man snipped away, gradually revealing her nakedness and stripping away any decency which she still had.

She was just about to raise her head in order to see how close he was to being finished when her nerve ends started tingling out an urgent warning. The ligature was being tightened and now she really was having trouble with her breathing. She started to struggle but that only seemed to make things worse.

She was feeling light-headed as mister crazy man's face swam in and out of focus. She was terrified and tried to scream but the gag meant that the scream died in her throat. She pulled at the tethers which were holding her in place but they held fast. She felt as if she was drowning, her life flashing before her.

And then her whole body arched upwards as a searing pain engulfed her chest and she watched, mesmerised, as a fountain of blood shot up towards the ceiling. Some of it coming down to splatter her face. Mister crazy's face swam into her vision, dripping with her blood, its lips fashioned into a maniacal grin. She tried desperately to make sense of what she was seeing but her eyelids were getting heavier and heavier as life drained out of her. And just as the curtain came down on her pathetically short life, her lasting thought was of golden days in the sunshine of Karlovo.

20

Thursday 20 July

'Billy! It's Emma.'

Woons was reaching for the remote to turn down the TV and, at the same time, preparing himself for bad news. Emma never rang him on this number in the evening.

'Hey, Ems. What you doing calling me on this number?' he asked clearing his throat.

'Sorry, Billy, but sounds like we've got a mega problem out at Furnace Lane.' Emma sounded breathless, as if she had been running up a set of stairs. 'I've just picked up a garbled voice message from Belinda. Timed at 4.30pm this afternoon. I've been out with Lucy and didn't have my phone with me so only just picked up the message. Sounds like one of the punters has killed one of the girls. It's a mess, multiple stab wounds, blood all over the place. Seems like he totally lost it. Belinda was screaming down the phone – totally apeshit about the whole thing. I think she said that she's had to close the place down.'

'Shit!', exclaimed Woons. 'That's all we fucking need! Anyone else in the loop yet?'

'No, I thought I'd better get you involved straightaway as we don't seem to have access to Vashlili at the moment,' Emma continued. 'I've tried to call Belinda but her phone just keeps going straight to voicemail. Last time I called it came up as unobtainable which is really worrying.'

'Bloody hell! What does that mean?' Woons was not very tech-savvy so didn't appreciate the difference between a call going to voicemail and one which showed the number as unobtainable.

'I'm worried it means that something is very wrong,' Emma replied. 'Why would her phone suddenly stop working? Particularly at a time like this.'

'God knows!' Woons butted in. 'And fuck knows where that waster Vashlili has got to.' They lapsed into silence, Woons trying to quickly put together a plan of action in his head. 'Okay! Okay!' he finally said. 'I think I'd better go and take a look, try to pacify the Gorgon and get the place cleaned up. I'll get on to Tricky and meet him there. He lives in the area doesn't he?'

'Yeah, not sure exactly where but it should be easy for him to get there,' Emma replied. 'I'll give him a call if you like and tell him what's happened. He can then bring anything he needs to dispose of the body. You got any of those bags at your place?'

'No, I gave them to Tricky so you give him a call and tell him I'll meet him there – say in about 45 minutes. And tell him to bring one of them bags.' Woons got up from his chair and walked through to the bedroom. He would need to change into clothes which he could simply dispose of afterwards.

'OK, Billy,' Emma replied. 'I'll get all that organised.' There was a click on the line and she was gone.

The headlights from Woons' car searched out the small wooden post with the red arrow pointing to what looked like an over-grown track on the opposite side of the road. Very few people used this narrow lane, and none of them would have given a second glance at the arrow post or the track. Passing a five-bar gate which would have once prevented access to the track but was now standing rather forlornly open, he made his way through tall deciduous trees before the track skirted around the corner of a field. His headlights eventually picked out the huge gates at the entrance to Belinda's mansion which hung from enormous pillars, each with the head of a gorgon on the top of it. Rather alarmingly, the gates were standing open which did not bode well as Woons recalled that Belinda usually relied on a very sophisticated security system. He inched the car through the gateway and onto the gravel drive which swept round to the front of the house.

He recalled the first time he had visited this secluded property. It was an imposing but ultimately decaying mansion which had once been a secure home for mentally retarded children although it had been abandoned for some years. Woons and Emma had done well to find this property and, with the backing of their paymasters in Georgia, they had done a deal with its corporate owners to convert it into what Woons had described as a boarding house for local workers. All he had to do then was find someone to run it.

Just when he was beginning to get frustrated about being able to find anyone for what had become known as the 'Furnace Mansion', Emma had heard mention of a woman who had a fearsome reputation for her no-nonsense approach to organising events for discerning adults as they were known in the sex industry. And so Belinda had been parachuted into the Kent countryside to manage the Furnace Mansion.

Belinda was only ever known as Belinda. She went by no other name. Her past was a complete mystery. She had no family, and had spent the early part of her life roaming the countryside, sometimes living from hand to mouth. She was a formidable woman by any stretch of the imagination. Always dressed in black, her clumpy jet-black hair looked as if a pit of snakes had taken residence on the top of her head and, because of this, she was often referred to as the Gorgon. Tattoos adorned her arms and there was a chain of spiders making its way around her huge flabby neck. She had little beady eyes which never missed a trick, and their glacial blue colour was a good indicator of her explosive temper. She would never miss an opportunity of screaming at anyone who stepped out of line. She was a huge, powerful woman who only truly seemed to relax when she was stuffing her face with cake and chocolate.

If he was brutally honest with himself, Billy Woons was a trifle in awe of Belinda after their first meeting – and probably a little frightened of her in equal measure. From that day on, he had always sent Spink to see her on his behalf in the belief that she would show more respect for someone of Spink's physique and sheer presence. And, by all accounts, they got on well so everyone was happy.

The first thing Woons noticed once he was on the drive was that the mansion was in darkness. Had they had a power cut? There was also no sign of Spink's car. He thought of hanging back and waiting for Spink, but he was intrigued by the lack of lighting in the building so he nosed the Merc up to the front of the building and parked. He leant over and fished a torch out of the glove compartment before stepping out on to the drive. He turned the torch on and made his way over towards the front door. There was an entry phone with camera and screen to the right of the door. He pressed the bar under the screen, fully expecting to hear a buzzing sound. No sound. Nothing. He pressed the bar again and waited. Still nothing. Not working perhaps?

Woons was now starting to sweat. There was something not right here and he desperately needed Spink by his side. Where was he for Christ's sake? Abandoning the entry phone, Woons turned his attention to a huge ornate door knocker in the shape of a leaping salmon. He gave it a couple of hefty blows. Blimey! The noise would have been enough to wake the dead. However, to his utter surprise the door swung open. He shone his torch into the extensive hallway and stepped over the threshold.

Woons had not been to the mansion since before Belinda took it over so he was unsure as to the layout of the place. The first thing he tried was the light switch. Nothing. So, there was some kind of electrical failure going on here, he thought. But there was something else which was really worrying him – the lack of any sound. He stood absolutely still and listened intently but there was just an all-enveloping silence.

Across the hall, he saw a couple of doors. He crept over the carpeted floor and tried the first door. He shone the torch around the room which seemed to be kitted out as some sort of reception area. Door number two led into a small kitchen with a couple of fridges and a row of optics above a shelf crammed with drinks and cigarettes. The door on the other side of the hall led into an office which he assumed was where Belinda ran her operation from.

Still with no answers as to why the door had been left open, and with no sign of Spink, Woons climbed the staircase to the first floor. Here, there were several doors, all shut. The first door he tried led into a large room with a bed, a bath, wardrobe, mirrors on the wall and ceiling, and a large array of sex toys and aids. There didn't appear to be anyone inside the room so he retreated back on to the landing. The next door led into a smaller room with a similar layout to the first, and was similarly empty.

Woons was beginning to feel a little spooked by the whole experience but he pressed on. He turned the handle of the next door and then gasped as his torch lit up a huge curtain of blood adorning the wall immediately in front of him. He looked round the edge of the door and shone his torch on to a scene of utter carnage. Emma had not been wrong when she reported that someone had lost control.

A young girl lay on the bed. It looked as if her skimpy clothes had been cut while she was still wearing them so that she was, in fact, now naked. Her body was covered in lacerations and a pair of scissors had come to rest in a gaping hole where her heart would have been. She was soaked in blood which was all over the bed, the wall, the ceiling and the carpet. Woons backed away out of the room, horrified by what he had seen. Beads of sweat had formed on his forehead as he leant against the wall, staring into the darkness of the corridor in front of him.

Suddenly, something caught his eye and he crept back along the corridor to the top of the stairs, dowsing the torch light as he went. He peered over the bannister. He couldn't be sure but it looked like a light of some sort was coming towards the front door. He held his breath as the light got closer until someone entered the mansion and started shining a beam around the empty hallway.

'Tricky, where the fuck have you been?' Woons hoarsely whispered down from his elevated position.

Spink shone the torch up in Woons' direction and then took the stairs two at a time. 'Sorry, Billy. I wasn't at home when I got Em's call so have had rather a long drive to get here.

Anyway, what have we got?'

'Well, you'd better take a look in that room over there to see the extent of the problem we've already got,' said Woons, pointing off to his right. 'But I'm thinking that there's something a bit more sinister going on here.'

Spink stepped across the hallway and put his head round the door. 'Jeez, Billy. That's gross!' He returned to Woons' side. 'That'll take ages to clear up.'

Woons nodded and turned towards another door which was resolutely closed. He opened it gently and then pushed it wide so that Spink could also see into the room. There was a double bed in the centre of the room, a dressing table and a single, free-standing wardrobe. A couple of chairs lay on their sides, perhaps indicative of a struggle. But their eyes were drawn to the bed on which lay what appeared to be a huge mound of black material. Woons edged closer to the bed and shone his torch on to what remained of Belinda's face, her life blown away from point blank range.

'My God, we've got a problem here!' Woons groaned. Spink also moved into the room and took in the scene. He then shone his torch around the room before coming back to the grotesque sight on the bed.

'That looks more like a professional hit to me, Billy,' Spink surmised. 'What the hell are we going to do with her?'

Woons was shaking his head as he went back into the hall and headed for the stairwell. 'What are we going to find up here?' he asked no one in particular, as he started up to the next floor, Spink right behind him. On the top landing he was faced with five doors but, unlike on the floor below, all of them were open. After a full inspection, it was clear that all the rooms were empty.

Spink blew out his cheeks. 'Five rooms, five girls – or perhaps four if one of them is the one downstairs. The others could have been herded into another part of the mansion or maybe they've been taken away altogether. We better have an inspection of the rest of the building. We also need to find out why the lights don't work.'

They both went down the stairs to the entrance hall and searched the rest of the mansion but there was no sign of anyone else in the building. They also discovered that all the fuses had been removed from the fuse box in the cellar. This was looking more and more like a professional job and, even more worrying for Woons, it looked like someone was trying to muscle their way onto his manor.

Spink followed Woons back to the office near Bidborough Ridge. On the way, Woons had called Emma to say that they would all meet at the office in about half an hour.

Some forty minutes later, Woons' mood had not improved as they sat round a small table at one end of the portacabin. Spink had picked up three coffees and a packet of biscuits from a 24-hour petrol station. He laid them out on the table.

'Ems, I just want to get the sequence of events right in my head,' Woons started.

'OK, Billy,' she replied. 'Belinda must have called me at about 4.30 p.m. She was going mental on the phone, screaming and shouting. When I first listened to the message, I couldn't make out what she was talking about but, once it was clear that something major had happened, that's when I rang you.'

'Right. So, I got your call at around 8.45 p.m. 'caus that *Masterchef* was just finishing. I got changed and went straight down to the car and drove over to Furnace Lane. Must have got there for about quarter to ten. That means that, in that five-hour period, someone got into the mansion, bumped off Belinda, took all the girls and removed all the fuses from the fuse box. Two things spring to mind – it was well planned and someone had a knowledge of the building.'

'Could even have been the punter who wasted the girl,' suggested Spink, looking for support for his idea.

'Doubt it,' Emma replied. 'He would have been so high on adrenalin that he wouldn't have been able to think straight.

In any case, I'm sure that Belinda would have got him off the premises as fast as she could. She must have been quickly aware of what had happened through her CCTV system. I bet his feet didn't touch the ground. She probably slung everyone else out as well and went into lockdown with the girls.'

Woons had a slurp of his coffee and a chocolate biscuit. He was starving, having had very little to eat since a sandwich at lunchtime. He hated having to think on an empty stomach.

'What's her CCTV like up there, Tricky?' Woons asked.

'It's a bit archaic if truth be known and the picture's terrible,' Spink replied. 'I've been trying to get it either upgraded or replaced altogether but Belinda was in no hurry to get it done. Relied on her own way of doing business to deal with any problems. I'll have a look when I get back there but I doubt it's going to help us. And it doesn't work when the power's off!'

'You got any pearls of wisdom, Ems?' Woons turned to Emma who was busy studying the label on her coffee cup.

'Not really, Billy,' she replied. 'Because she was such a huge presence, I tended to leave Belinda to get on with it herself. As long as she had a full house of girls, she was fine. She always created when she didn't have enough to cater for all her punters but, otherwise, she pretty much managed the mansion on her own.'

They sat there, deep in thought.

'One thing I have been wondering,' Emma started, 'is whether there is a connection between Vashlili going off grid, our consignment going missing and the events of this evening. Or is it all just one huge coincidence?'

'Hmm!' sighed Woons. 'I was just wondering that myself. And I think I'm going to have to have a word with our boys in

Kaspi just in case they've got any intel which we are missing at this end. Vashlili's the key to all this, I'm sure. But, if I get in touch with Irakli, he's going to tell me that Mr Tsiklauri wants a meeting which means that I'll have to go all the way over there just to be told what I already know. It'll be a fucking waste of time.'

Spink suddenly got up from the table. 'OK guys, I've got a mountain of work to do. I'll get the girl into that freezer we're already borrowing. Don't know what I'm going to do with Belinda. You'd need a fucking crane to get her off the bed and down the stairs. You got anyone who can help with the clean-up, Em?'

'Think I better do it myself in the circumstances, but can't get started until the morning after Lucy's gone to school. I'll bring all the gear over if you like. Once we've got the worst of it off and it doesn't look like a crime scene, I can then get one or two others in to help. Probably need a lick of paint as well. Are you going to fix the fuses?'

'Ugh! Forgot about that.' Spink slammed a fist into the palm of his hand. 'Too late to do anything about it tonight. But I'll go over there now and collect the girl so at least that's out of the way. And I'll see you there at around 09.30 a.m. in the morning, Em.' And, with that, Spink was gone.

'Good old Tricky,' Woons ruminated. 'Always keen to get on and get things done.'

'Billy,' Emma started, 'you're going to have to make contact with the Georgians. I've just got this nasty feeling in the pit of my stomach that something's come up and we're not getting the full picture.'

'Yeah! Yeah! I hear what you're saying Ems.' Woons looked

her in the eye. 'I'll get on to it in the morning.'

22

Friday 21 July

Hunter and Selitto had agreed a 7.00 a.m. start so that they could get a couple of hours work done on the car ringing case before heading off to take another look at Meadowlands. Selitto had selected a country route from Tonbridge, and they were able to enjoy the dappled shades of sunlight as they made their way along largely unpopulated lanes.

They made a couple of stops on the long drive leading up to the hotel in an attempt to put more context into its surroundings. Hunter noted that the area was bordered by a ridge which rose up from the valley below. Was that called an escarpment, she wondered trying to recall her GCSE Geography course work. There appeared to be a line of houses along the top of the ridge in the distance so she assumed that this was probably a high point in the local area. The valley was a carpet of trees and, in the July sunshine, it looked a picture.

As they approached the hotel, they entered a forest of huge trees which came right to the edge of the drive. They slowed to look along a narrow driveway which led down to a couple of outbuildings with logs piled high around them. Eventually, they arrived at the gates into the hotel grounds and onto the gravel driveway. Selitto drove round to the front of the building and parked opposite the entrance. They noticed that the BMW was still parked in the corner so it obviously hadn't yet been released to the Hampshire boys.

Before he could get out of the car, the door was opened for him by one of the hotel's meeters & greeters. 'Good morning, sir, are you staying with us?'

Selitto eased himself out of the driver's door and reached for his warrant card.

'Oh, morning sir,' said the man who was sporting a badge with the name 'Stephen' on it. 'Have you got an appointment with anyone?'

Selitto noted that Hunter was still sitting in the car furiously bashing out a missive on her phone. 'No, Stephen,' he replied, 'no appointment but we'll probably have a chat with Mr Dangerfield if he's in.'

'Fraid not, sir,' Stephen replied. 'His kid's still poorly and he's not in again today. Young Sally's looking after things if you want to have a chat with her.'

'Okay. Thanks for the heads up. We'll probably just have a wander around the grounds first and then come in for a coffee.'

'That'll be fine, sir. I'll let Miss Lancaster know.' With that, Stephen turned and disappeared into the bowels of the hotel.

'I thought I told Dangerfield not to leave the hotel until we had finished our investigation,' Hunter said, getting out of the car.

Selitto stretched his legs. 'Presume he thought we'd finished when the CSI wagon drove off yesterday afternoon,' he replied.

'Even so, he's gone off a bit too quick for my liking!' Hunter noted, wandering over to the abandoned BMW. Selitto joined her and together they skirted round to the back of the vehicle and took a look at the boot. They could see the remnants of the fingerprint powder along the edge of the lid, and noted that it had still not been properly closed. Pulling his shirt sleeve down to cover his hand, Selitto gently pulled the lid up until they were looking into the empty boot space.

'Blimey!' Hunter remarked. 'That's certainly some smell of plastic. Are they sure it's not something else? Some sort of cleaning agent?'

Selitto had immediately noticed the smell of plastic which Jimbo Carrigan had reported but, other than that, he couldn't think of anything else it could be. He let the lid down gently just as he heard the sound of a car door closing as another guest arrived at the hotel. They crunched their way back across the gravel and climbed the steps to the entrance of the hotel.

At the top of the steps, Hunter turned to Selitto. 'Don't think there's much mileage in having another look at the room, but I would like to have another look at the lake, particularly the sunken boat if it's still there.'

Selitto nodded, and they both went back down the steps to the parking area. They then turned to walk under the arch and down the pathway which had been cut through the meadow grasses. It was another glorious day and they took the opportunity of having a closer look at the smaller lake once they had reached the bottom of the meadow. Eventually, they pushed through the ornate wrought iron gates with their intricate carvings, through the kissing gate and over the stile before taking the anticlockwise path around the lake.

The vegetation felt as if it had grown in the time since they were last here. They passed the wooden bench which was covered in yellow moss, and Hunter noticed another small pond behind the bench which contained some very murky water and a couple of boughs from the trees above. Eventually, they came upon a small wooden landing jetty which Hunter didn't recall seeing before. She tapped her foot on the first two boards to see if they were safe and then gingerly stepped on to the structure. It seemed incongruous to have a landing jetty if boats were no longer allowed on the lake. She could now see the lighthouse in all its glory and a very imposing sight it was. But it still left a question – did people really not go into it as Dangerfield had implied?

She jumped off the jetty back on to the path and they continued their walk, all the time taking in the environment surrounding them. There were numerous trees which had been subjected to some organised felling, and piles of sawdust were dotted around the area. An old red lifebuoy was propped up against a tree, upside down and mouldy. Hunter doubted it would be of much use if it were needed in an emergency. Apart from anything else, no one would be able to find it!!

They passed another sign – '*No boating, fishing or picnicking*' – before pushing through another kissing gate and onto the narrow path which ran across the top of the lake. Just before passing through the gate, Sarah had looked down and noticed two toads in an amorous embrace. Now another couple were hard at it. Must be the season, she thought with a smile. She leant against the wall and admired the lighthouse, the glass panels of the lantern-room glinting in the sunshine. She fired off some shots on her phone, mainly because it seemed to be so out of place and no one would believe her unless she could provide incontrovertible evidence.

Meanwhile, Selitto had stopped halfway across the path. 'This is where the water drains from the lake into the stream system below,' he said, pointing to where a semi-circular sink hole had been cut into the rock. The water cascaded all of thirty feet down into a frothing pool before tumbling through a gap in the wall and out towards the first stream. He indicated that

Hunter should move across the bridge and look over the other side. She looked down on a torrent of water crashing over what looked like a stone platform before pouring over another small wall into the stream.

Selitto was pointing downwards. 'That's where the black rubbish sack was. Just beside that pile of rubbish. No way it could have been swept downstream. And doubt it would have been taken by an animal because the whole area is fenced off.' He pointed to a fence which completely surrounded the area at the top of the lake. Hunter nodded, still peering over the wall at the water rushing to meet the stream.

Once on the other side of the lake, Selitto showed Hunter where he had found the boat. He was pleased to see that it was no longer there so the CSI boys must have taken it with them for closer inspection. 'Goodness only knows how they got it out of there,' he said, retreating back to the path. They continued onwards until they eventually returned to the ornate gate and wound their way back up the meadow to the hotel above. But, instead of climbing up to the garden, they walked along the top of the meadow which led them into the orchard before they found themselves standing in front of the glass houses. Hunter just wanted to see the lie of the land here so that she could picture it in her mind. She took some more shots to assist her memory but then succumbed to an overwhelming desire for a cup of coffee.

23

Friday 21 July

Following their visit to the lake, Hunter and Selitto had sat in the garden reviewing what they had learnt from their walk around it. They had also decided not to trouble Sally Lancaster who seemed to have enough on her plate judging by the passable impression of a windmill she was giving near the doorway into the hotel as she spoke to a couple of the waiting staff. And still no sight or sound of Dangerfield.

They had then driven back to Tonbridge, mainly in silence. Hunter was busy poking away at her phone; Selitto occupied the time by continuing his verbal onslaught on other drivers, cyclists and pot holes. He had opted to take some of the back roads through the lovely Kent countryside and, apart from the odd farm vehicle, they again seemed to miss much of the traffic and arrived at Pembury Road in the early afternoon heat. Hunter had rung ahead to warn DS Grace Kendall that they would like to have another chat with her, particularly as Hunter was now on DCI Iverson's radar, and she would have to provide more evidence to support her contention that this was a case she should be working on.

Grace was waiting for them at her desk in one of the corners of the Operations Room on the first floor. Hunter again took the seat in front of the desk, but this time moved it round until she could clearly see the monitor positioned on Kendall's desk. Selitto took his customary place by the window making sure that he could still see the monitor from where he stood.

'Hi guys!' Kendall greeted them in her usual informal manner. 'Sounds like you two have been busy!'

'You could say that, Grace,' Hunter commented once she had got comfortable. 'We've just had a quick visit to Meadowlands – another wander round the lake just to get it focussed in my mind. Have you managed to make any progress?'

'Well, we've been trying to do some tracking of the BMW through ANPR but it has not been particularly easy.' Kendall said, stroking some of the keys of the keyboard on her desk. 'We think that it spent some time in the Gatwick Airport area because we managed to pick it up at around 4.00 a.m. Tuesday morning around Pyecombe on the A23 travelling north from Brighton towards Gatwick. If it is wanted by our Hampshire colleagues then it probably travelled to Sussex via the M27/A27. It looks as if it left the M23 at Gatwick but its registration number is not showing for any of the onsite and offsite parking companies at the airport so we can probably rule out any connection there. There are plenty of hotels in the area so perhaps the driver took a day room at one of them. Anyway, that's not really of importance as it was picked up later in the day travelling north on the M23 and then on to the M25 travelling east. Off at Sevenoaks and on to the A21 but then off at Morley's which is where it was last seen. If the driver knew his way around, it would have been quite possible to drive around the area and eventually arrive at Meadowlands late Tuesday afternoon without being seen by another camera.'

'That fits nicely,' Hunter observed. 'As of a couple of hours ago, it was still at the hotel which is driving them a bit mental but there's not much we can do about it. The boot's still open which the CSIs discovered so it might have been tampered with while it was sitting outside the hotel on Tuesday night. Oh, and there might be another car for you to chase up but, so far, we haven't got a registration number for it which isn't much use. Looks like the guest information is pretty limited at Meadowlands which seems to classify itself as something of a discrete hideaway – no questions asked sort of thing.'

'What sort of discrete? You mean "naughty" discrete?' Kendall asked with a cheeky smile and a raised eyebrow.

'Doubt it!' Sarah replied. 'It just seems that they rely on regular guests to a large extent so the amount of information they collect at check-in is minimal – not even a car registration number. All they ask is whether the information shown on the check-in sheet is correct. Who's to say it isn't if the guest just signs the sheet?'

Hunter fished her phone out of her pocket and looked absent-mindedly at the screen. 'We might be able to tell you a bit more if Beth's people can download any information from a fancy on-board navigation gadget. Hopefully, it will have recorded journey information so at least we might be able to see where it originated from. We'll just have to wait and see.'

'OK! Anything else you'd like me to be getting on with?' Kendall tapped some more keys and then sat back in her chair.

Hunter got up and moved towards the windows as if seeking inspiration. She turned and faced Kendall. 'I know I told you it would be helpful to have some gen on Dangerfield and the ownership of Meadowlands, but it might also be interesting if you could find out how a bloody great lighthouse came to be stuck in the middle of a lake in the grounds!'

Kendall's eyes widened. 'A lighthouse?' she exclaimed. 'My God! That must be quite a spectacle!'

Hunter tapped the screen of her phone, bringing up a picture of the lighthouse. She passed the phone over to Kendall. 'Wow! What a sight!' enthused Kendall.

'Certainly is!' Hunter agreed with her. 'But what I've suddenly realised is that it doesn't appear in any of their promo material. I was having a look at their website on the way over here and there's not even a mention let alone a photo. You would have thought that, with something like a lighthouse in your garden, you might have put it in your logo or somewhere on your website!'

'Hmm! See what you mean,' said Kendall. 'Just imagine the interest you could create by opening it up and encouraging visitors. High tea in the room at the top with glorious views all around!'

'Quite!' replied Hunter. 'But nothing, not even a mention. Bet most of the guests don't even know it's there! Anyway, back to the here and now. I'll be getting some more info from Beth's team so I'll send that over to you and perhaps we can meet up again on Monday.' Hunter got up and turned as if to leave.

'That's good,' replied Kendall, 'as I'm not around this weekend. Wedding on the Isle of Wight so having to get down there tonight and back on Sunday. Can't say that I'm looking forward to the journey but it'll be nice once we get there.'

'OK, Grace, hope it goes well and we can re-group on Monday once Beth's team has reported back.' And, with that, Hunter swept out of the room and down the corridor in search of another cup of coffee. Selitto winked at Kendall, and followed in her wake.

24
Friday 21 July

Meandering through wooded terrain to the south of the hamlet of Basted in the countryside rolling down from the North Downs, the River Bourne was little more than a trickle at this time of the year although it did benefit from the shaded canopy above it. Bourne Lane wound its way down towards the river from the outskirts of Plaxtol, crossing fields and tunnelling through copses and more substantial woodland. When the trees finally gave way, there were fields and orchards to be seen on either side of the road.

Unless you were looking for it, or actually knew where it was, you would be forgiven for missing the turning which took you onto a long, pitted track leading from Bourne Lane to what was known to the locals as the Basted Heights Allotments. At the end of the track, a metal five-bar gate prevented further access by anyone not in possession of the 4-digit code for the combination lock. Those who were lucky enough to have the code were invariably the allotment plot holders, some of whom had spent months or years on a holding list just waiting for a plot to be given up so that they could take over.

Once through the five-bar gate, plot holders would drive onto an area of reinforced grass paving which had been specially laid so that vehicles would not tear up the grass in wet or wintery weather. It had been acquired using Big Lottery funding and all plot holders were unanimous in their praise of this recent addition to facilities at Basted Heights. Upon leaving their vehicles, they would make their way to their individual plots along the many grass paths which criss-crossed the area.

Set on a site of just over twelve acres, the Basted Heights Allotment Association had, in fact, been formed in 1918 and had just celebrated its centenary. The fertile sandy soil on top of chalk produced bountiful crops of fruit and vegetables all the year round. In a quaint link with the past, the allotments were still measured out in rods with one rod being roughly five metres in length. Rods had been first standardised in 1607 and were not, in fact, phased out until the start of metrication in 1965 but they were still used for the determination of plot sizes on many allotments throughout the country.

Although of uniform size, each allotment plot was unique to each tenant with some growing basic vegetables such as potatoes and runner beans, and others with greater ambition who grew sweetcorn, cabbages, brussels sprouts, carrots, parsnips and other root vegetables. Some had even planted fruit trees, raspberry canes and gooseberry bushes, or simply grew flowers for display at the many local garden society shows held throughout the summer. It really depended on the amount of time which each tenant had available to spend on their allotment. And, although not all the tenants knew each other, there was a certain camaraderie amongst them with everyone always willing to lend a hand or give advice. And there was always spare produce which was either exchanged or simply given away.

The only slight drawback with the location was that it was a long walk from the village so the plot holders tended to drive to the site which, on occasion, led to chaos when available parking spaces were all taken. But, in general, the plot holders welcomed the seclusion of the location which, although set among the trees, was blessed with its fair share of sunshine and shade in equal measure. They didn't take much notice of a large country house which stood in its own grounds on the other side of the parking area.

No one knew the history of the house although some of the older plot holders thought they recalled a member of the local landed gentry living there in the past. That was a time when children used to run about outside and even strayed into the allotments from time to time, particularly when the strawberries were at their reddest! Known as The Garden House, it was accessed from Sheet Hill along a bumpy and poorly maintained rough track. The house had probably been built between the wars on a slight rise in the ground so that it looked down on the allotments.

There was a ground floor and a first floor which comprised large day rooms and grand bedrooms. Canopies extended out from the walls above the first-floor windows which distorted the views of the windows. There was then a line of gabled windows in the roof space indicating more rooms which could have originally housed servants or children from a very large family. But, in general, it drew so little attention that very few people even knew of its existence. And it was unlikely that anyone was watching over what went on at the allotments as most of the windows at the front of the house appeared to have been boarded up. Anyone taking a close look at the house might notice that the two main windows with canopies on the first floor which overlooked the allotments were covered by shutters and net curtains on the insides but, in truth, no one was bothered. The house posed no threat and, to most people, it was empty.

What no one realised was that the back of the house was used as the main entrance with the track from Sheet Hill finally hitting a substantial set of electronic oak gates which marked the entrance to the grounds. An eight-foot high wooden fence surrounded the property, and stretched into dense woodland either side of the house. With the tree line running almost up to the back of the house, vehicles had to park where there were spaces between the trees.

The blinds at the back of the property were also permanently closed which, to the casual observer, would give the impression that the house was empty although the presence of a number of expensive vehicles might dictate otherwise. However, it would be difficult for a 'casual observer' to observe anything given the security equipment which guarded the area around the back of the house. Razor wire lined the top of the fence, and a motion-sensitive floodlighting system operated over an area of at least 25 metres leading up to the fence. CCTV also covered the area although anyone taking a close look at this would have quickly noticed that it was likely to be ineffective as the foliage around the cameras had been allowed to grow to such an extent that it obscured the view.

So, in harmony with their surroundings, those tending their allotments rarely gave The Garden House a second thought. As far as they were concerned, it had always been there and probably always would be – and it had always been empty. What they didn't know was that the house was an important part of the Billy Woons empire.

Originally from a small village in the countryside of Galicia in the north-west of Spain, Maria Travisedo was a feisty, fiery

Spanish matriarch who ruled The Garden House with a rod of iron. Woons had always admired her ferocious good looks, tending to overlook the crinkling of the skin around her dark eyes and the wisps of grey hair at her temples. She was, however, extraordinarily fit and, more than once, Woons had marvelled at her neck muscles and the biceps on her arms. She gave the impression of not being frightened of anything or anyone, and she always seemed to dominate any interaction she had ever had with Woons. He knew that Emma couldn't stand the woman but even Ems had to admire the amount of money which The Garden House raked in on an ongoing basis.

No one was quite sure why Travisedo was so successful. True, she did have some high rollers on her books who came from far and wide with wads of cash in their pockets, probably laundering like crazy. And, whenever possible, she liked to pick the girls who came to stay with her so that she could maintain the quality of what was on offer to those who were able and willing to pay in excess of top dollar. She also tried to pander to the depraved needs of her rich clientele by offering what she liked to call "treatment rooms". These were renewed from time to time if a new sexual deviation became fashionable and, in the past, she had kitted out a nursery room with a full range of baby products, a fully-equipped doctor's consulting room with an examination chair and couch, and a school classroom with desks, canes and other school equipment. There was also an enormous wet room with a full range of rubber clothing and other rubberised equipment.

Last but not least was Travisedo's pride and joy, an elaborately furnished dungeon in what was originally the double garage attached to the house. It was fully sound-proofed and boasted instruments of torture which some of her clients could only have dreamed about. Travisedo had searched high and low for the best and most unusual equipment, and she had attracted some of the very best clients who wanted to experience time in the dungeon. There was also an ornate double rolltop bath so that clients could cool off with the girls after a strenuous session. Some of the BDSM gadgetry she had collected was only for the more adventurous pervert and was only available for use by trusted clients. Otherwise, the dungeon remained locked up. Travisedo wasn't in the habit of inviting trouble.

Once through the elaborate security system which had been devised by one of Travisedo's Hispanic cronies, there were a couple of reception rooms where clients could relax and have a drink at the bar. A huge kitchen boasted a large farmhouse table as its centrepiece which was always lavishly covered with delicious tapas dishes as well as other buffet delights. Travisedo was keen to ensure that her clients were well fed and watered, and she would encourage her girls to head for the kitchen to mingle with the high rollers when they were not busy elsewhere in the house.

The top floor had been converted into a series of small rooms each with a bed, a chair and a hanging rail. This was where the girls slept, sometimes two to a bed. There was a communal bathroom at the end of the hall, and a small kitchen next to the bathroom. All the windows in these rooms had been boarded up so the girls virtually never set eyes on daylight. They had very little idea of time of day or even whether it was daytime or night time. Clients came and went at all times, many of them arriving from Gatwick or Heathrow after flying in from all corners of the world. The girls were always expected to be awake and ready for action whenever Travisedo demanded, sometimes dragging themselves from deep sleep. Sheer exhaustion was never far away.

Travisedo was sitting in her office peering out through the shutters at the allotments below and thinking that it was nearly time to close the blinds as the sun began to make its way below the tree line. All the allotment plot holders seemed to have gone home, and the view from her window was a picture of tranquillity.

It had been an exhausting day with some of her most valued clients all arriving on the same day from important overseas visits or simply just jetting into the UK in search of pleasure. And they were, of course, all keen to see the girls. Thank goodness she had sent her trusted assistant, Christina, on an extended food shop the day before. Christina had impeccable taste when it came to snacking food, and always knew where to get some of the classic Iberian foods. She always ensured that the fridges were crammed full of goodies which could be put on the table in an instant. She even kept a whole serrano ham on its own carving stand so that the cold meat was at its freshest. The bar was always fully stocked with the best spirits and two wine coolers kept the finest white wines at the best temperature for maximum enjoyment. There was also an excellent collection of reds which many of her clients enjoyed with plates of fresh serrano.

One of the keys to Travisedo's success was her eye for picking the very best girls. She was very particular about the sort of girls she wanted in her house, and she was continually making changes to the line-up so that her clients wouldn't get bored or want to go elsewhere. And Billy Woons was always the man who was able to provide her with top class girls whenever she had a need. As far as she was concerned, it was a great arrangement for both of them but more so for her as she was able to offer her clients fresh faces all the time. Constantly changing the girls also reduced the potential for two or three of them to get to know each other well enough to either gang up on the others or to collectively cause a problem for Travisedo.

The only problem Travisedo had with the Woons organisation was in the form of Tamaz Vashlili who she considered to be an obnoxious, self-important arsehole of the highest order. In fact, she often referred to him as a 'puto gilipollas', often shrieking the words down the phone after getting the disconnect signal once a call with him had ended. But, invariably, Vashlili eventually did what he was asked to do, mainly because he knew that to cross Travisedo would bring the wrath of Woons down on his head – and that was certainly worth avoiding.

She got up from her desk and walked stiffly over to the window. She could now see that there were no cars parked in the allotment car park and, if she looked to her right, she could see that the gate was shut and locked. She twiddled a thin wooden pole at the side of the blinds to close them up and then returned to her desk. It was busy this evening with all the girls in action. That meant no availability if any others of her high rolling clients chose to breeze in.

Daniela was with a client who had actually arrived already dressed up as a young schoolboy in shorts, an ill-fitting jacket and a school cap set at a jaunty angle. He was a regular and had more recently been with one of the other girls, Emilya, on several of his visits. Although she had no proof, Travisedo suspected that the client was secretly very fond of Emilya and had been paying her for 'extras' which was strictly against house rules. However, when she herself was picking up a fat fee for each visit, Travisedo was prepared to overlook this minor irregularity. But she wouldn't countenance clients becoming over-friendly with her girls, so she had decided to introduce Daniela to the client this evening.

Emilya had been moved to the dungeon where she was entertaining a new client who had put a few grand down for a no-holds barred session of BDSM. Travisedo never felt entirely comfortable when a new client arrived flashing the cash – even when he had been introduced by one of her regular clients from the East who was also here this evening – so she intended to keep a close eye on events in the dungeon. She hadn't invested much in covert surveillance inside the house but she did have an all-seeing eye in the dungeon just in case any of her girls got into difficulties with an over-zealous client. She opened a drawer at the front of her desk and pulled it out to its full extent. Reaching over a divide in the drawer, she pressed a green button and a panel opened in the bookcase on the wall to her left to reveal a screen. She then pressed another green button and toggled a small lever which was attached to a console in the drawer. A view of the room came up on the screen, and she could see that Emilya had the role play well worked out with her as the dominatrix. As far as she could tell, the client appeared to be already handcuffed, and he certainly seemed to be enjoying himself so there shouldn't be too much to worry about. She turned the camera off and closed the drawer. The panel on the wall slid back into place.

Her mobile buzzed on the desk in front of her. Travisedo

looked at the number and frowned. Why the hell was Vashlili ringing her? Fucking idiot! Didn't he know the protocol? She angrily thumbed the green blob on her screen.

'Hey, Tamaz! What the fuck you calling me for?' she shouted into the phone.

There was a pause and complete silence. She was just about to disconnect the call when she heard a click on the line. Had Vashlili just hung up on her? Imbecile! 'What the fuck's he playing at?' she swore under her breath, staring at the phone. And then it buzzed into life again in her hand. She angrily swiped the green blob. 'WHAT?' she shouted into the phone.

'Lady! Lady! Lady!' A mellow voice addressed her as if in an attempt to calm an irate schoolgirl. Travisedo didn't like the condescending tone.

'Who the fuck are you? Where's Tamaz?' Her voice oozed aggression.

'Hey! Hey! So many questions!' the voice of calmness continued. 'Now you listen to me, and listen good.'

Was that a threatening tone she detected? Travisedo was so busy trying to compute what was going on that she simply let the voice continue.

'Don't you worry your pretty little head about Tamaz. He's taking a well-earned break from working with people like you which means that you and me can get to know each other better and have a nice little talk about things', her tormentor went on.

Travisedo was frowning, deep furrows creasing her forehead. What on earth was this little shit talking about? And she suddenly realised that he had a foreign accent, a bit like Vashlili's but more pronounced. What was of more concern was that Vashlili had been the only person she had ever dealt with in the Woons organisation who was not British. So, who the hell was this man and how come he was in a position to tell her that Vashlili was taking a break? With all these thoughts crashing around in her head, she nearly missed his next words.

'But, first of all, you have to get rid of the punters and lock the girls in their rooms. Then we can talk.'

Travisedo took the phone away from her ear and stared at it. WHAT?? Was this guy totally off his head on something? Had he no comprehension of the type of business she was running here? Her clients were not to be messed with — they had paid top dollar to be here and she couldn't just go around knocking on doors asking them to leave. She was just about to declare that she had no intention of getting rid of her clients when she had another idea.

'You know I can't do that,' she began, 'and, in any case, there are no what you call punters here.' There was a moment of silence on the line.

'Hey! Hey!' That condescending tone again. 'Don't lie to me or we won't get off to a friendly start to our relationship.'

'What the fuck are you talking about,' Travisedo barked into the phone. 'What relationship? We're hardly likely to be going to have any re-lay-shon-ship the way you're going on. And, any case, who says I'm lying to you?' Again, she had to wait for a response.

'Dear lady, from where I'm standing, I can see the back of your property,' came the reply, cool and with a sense of amusement in the voice. 'There are five very expensive vehicles parked here, and I have observed men entering the property. One even has a school cap on and is wearing shorts — most strange! No one else has arrived or left in the last hour so all these men must still be in your house. Am I right?'

There was silence. Travisedo was so shocked by the realisation that she was being spied on that she was momentarily silenced.

The voice continued. 'I know that you have five girls in the house with you, and that your loyal friend Christina is away collecting supplies. She will not disturb us until we have finished our little – how you say in England – our little chat? Yes, I think that is it – a little chat!'

'For fuck's sake!' Travisedo exploded. 'What have you done to Christina?' Not Christina. Please, not Christina. Travisedo couldn't imagine life without Christina.

'Hey! Calm down! She is enjoying a little break from shopping and will be back later.' The voice was totally devoid of compassion, and Travisedo had a feeling in the pit of her stomach that her dear friend Christina was in trouble.

'I can't just chuck my high rollers out,' exclaimed Travisedo. 'They've paid good money! That's not the way we do things here.'

'Lady!' Was there a hint of frustration creeping into the voice? Travisedo was aghast at the prospect of having to ask clients to leave.

'Lady!' the voice continued. 'I am sure that you would not like to see what I can do if you make me angry. It would surely be bad for business if your girls were so broken that they couldn't perform for your punters. And then your punters would stop coming and your little business would go pop!' There it was again, that hint of amusement in the voice which Travisedo didn't like.

She suddenly got up from her desk and made her way through to Christina's room at the back of the house. She crept into the room. The curtains were partly drawn which was the way Christina kept them to avoid the brightness of the morning sun. As she had left early today, she had not drawn them fully back as she normally did in the early afternoon. Standing away from the window, Travisedo tried to see if she could see the man who was tormenting her on the phone.

'You will not be able to see me!' The voice suddenly erupted from the phone.

The hairs began to prickle on the back of Travisedo's neck, the same feeling of dread which she had experienced as a young girl when her father and his friends would try to touch her young body after a day of drinking in the hot Spanish sun.

Travisedo was now frightened, her bravado quickly fading, her mind thinking things through in a more practical, pragmatic way. She was clearly on a hiding to nothing unless she agreed to the man's demands so her best course of action seemed to be to comply. She could probably get rid of her clients with about 30 minutes' notice without losing too much face. Perhaps make up some story about getting a call from the gas people who were investigating a leak in the area, or something like that. She would give them all a hefty refund next time they came by but, for now, everyone had to leave.

'OK', she eventually said into the phone. 'Thirty minutes and I'll make sure my clients are gone. The girls will also be in their rooms. I do have other clients due in later so hopefully your visit won't take too long.'

'Just get the punters out and the girls in their rooms. I won't wait more than thirty minutes so you have been warned.' There was a loud click on the line as the call was disconnected.

Saturday 22 July

Borislav Zlatkov sat at what was left of Maria Travisedo's desk. It was late and the blackout blinds had been drawn across the windows. He poured a small measure of the best vodka he could find in the bar, and slugged it back feeling the warm tentacles prickle as they made their way down into his stomach. He had already tried some of the canapes which he had found on the table and in the fridges in the kitchen, and had found them quite acceptable. A few slices of Serrano ham had also been appreciated, and he now had a couple of quarters of Scotch Egg on his plate which he was saving as this peculiar British food reminded him of his favourite *Chiftele* from his beloved homeland.

By any stretch of the imagination, Zlatkov would be described as imposing. Well over six feet tall, his huge biceps were moulded into what appeared to be a tight-fitting jacket although the stretch qualities in the material allowed freedom of movement. His shaven head seemed to reflect overhead light, and a couple of scars around the corners of his eyes were testimony to a life which had seen him involved in plenty of fights. His pudgy, squint nose had also taken its fair share of knocks in times gone by. Bushy black eyebrows and a full covering of black stubble gave the impression of an enforcer - someone who didn't take lightly to being messed with. And, indeed, Borislav Zlatkov was a deeply repugnant character who lived life well on the other side of the tracks to humility and harmony.

The room gave a good impression of having been royally

ransacked – papers and books all over the floor, filing cabinet drawers hanging at angles, picture frames smashed, shards of glass littering the floor.

A mobile phone pinged an incoming message on the desk in front of him. Zlatkov screwed up his eyes and inspected the screen. He then punched out a response to the text message and tossed the phone back onto the desk. He stood up and stretched. How he hated inactivity although his team would have to take a rest soon. It had been a very busy few hours since he had entered The Garden House, and now his men were nearly finished with the clean-up operation. The odour of cleansing materials hung thick in the air although this did not affect Zlatkov who had lost his sense of smell years ago.

He took a walk around the desk and then picked up the phone again. He thumbed the screen until he got to the contact he wanted and poked the name to connect the call. He listened to the ringing tone, becoming more impatient every second that the phone went unanswered.

At last there was a click and a gruff male voice crackled in Zlatkov's ear. 'Boss? Is that you?'

Zlatkov wondered why Dracul always sounded so surprised when he answered phone calls. Perhaps he was just a cautious character, but it still annoyed him.

'Hey, Drax!' replied Zlatkov, knowing full well how Dracul hated being called Drax. He always called him Drax on the phone just to get him wound up, but never when Dracul was standing in front of him. Dracul was the one person in all the whole world who Zlatkov actually feared and, having seen him in action at close quarters, he knew what Dracul was capable of doing to his fellow human beings.

'Don't call me that!' came a guttural response.

'Okay,' Zlatkov sighed, 'but tell me what you and that pig Omar are doing.' He eyed the bottle of vodka standing sentry-like on the desk in front of him but then thought better of it.

'Yes, boss. Well, we got rid of the girl as you suggested and now we're taking the old woman and the man down to Vashlili's dumping ground like you said. The weather is very bad here with some of the roads flooded but we have sent a message to your contact so that he will be expecting us. We should get there in an hour or so.'

'Good! Good!' Zlatkov ran through all the arrangements in his head. Was there anything he had forgotten? The more he thought, the more an intriguing idea started to burrow its way into his brain. Hey! Was that an idea or what? His eyes glazed over at the thought of how he could really mess with that fucker Woons's mind.

'Drax! You still there?' Zlatkov was back in the zone.

'Don't call me that!' Dracul snarled.

'Okay! Okay! Listen! New orders. Do not, repeat do not take the woman's body to the dumping ground. I have had another idea for disposal. So just leave the man with Vashlili's contact. You understand that?'

There was a pause until Dracul's voice crackled through the ether. 'Yes, boss. I will keep the woman and bring her to you later after I have got rid of the man.'

'Okay!' Zlatkov replied. 'You call me when disposal of the man has been finished, and then you two disappear until I contact you about getting the woman's body later. Also, make plans to get rid of the van as soon as you can. They have tracking systems in this country that our police can only dream of.'

Zlatkov stared off towards the darkest corner of the room trying to think of any other orders for Dracul. He was pleased that this little episode would soon be over because there was still plenty to get done, and he had masters who did not like to be kept waiting. The rest of the girls were already on the road to a new location, and he would soon be reaping the financial benefits. Perhaps he would buy another house in the countryside in the homeland – one could never have too many properties and this one could have a full-sized snooker room and a swimming pool in the basement. Why not? He had earned it.

'You're cracking up, boss. What did…' The phone suddenly gave out a loud 'beep' and the call was disconnected. Zlatkov snatched the phone away from his ear and stared at the screen. No fucking signal!!

'Bloody country!' Zlatkov swore under his breath. 'They've got all the technology of a first world country and the phone coverage of a piss poor African republic.' Suddenly, the bottle of vodka regained its appeal and he poured another slug into the waiting glass. But, before he could get it to his mouth, Ladinas appeared at the door.

'What do you want?' Zlatkov's voice was laden with vitriol.

'We're done here, Boss,' Ladinas advanced into the room. 'I just need to get this room sorted when you have vacated it and then the hallway to the door.'

'Okay! Okay!' Zlatkov slugged the vodka and put the glass into his jacket pocket. He took one final look at the desk and then brushed past Ladinas and into the hall. 'Get a move on, can you? I'll be leaving in twenty minutes.'

He headed off down the hall towards the back door but then took a detour to take a quick look at the garage. When he had carried out his initial inspection of the house after the tiresome woman had been removed, he had found that the garage had been converted into some sort of dungeon with sophisticated items of punishment and torture. However, that wasn't all he had found.

Still trying to piece together the probable sequence of events in his head, Zlatkov stared into the garage which now appeared spotlessly clean. Some hours earlier, he had been looking at a scene of carnage. There was a naked girl floating head down in a bath of water, her long fair hair fanning out just under the water's surface as if she had been carefully laid out in death. On the floor beside the bath lay the body of a naked man. His hands were handcuffed in front of him, and his throat had been slashed from ear to ear. There was blood all over the walls and the ceiling, the water in the bath had turned a pale shade of scarlet and it was clear that the man had died where he lay as a huge pool of blood had run down the side of the bath and spread out across the floor.

Zlatkov had seen the aftermath of many killings during his life, and he had been responsible for most of them himself, but he had never seen anything quite so baffling as this. How could the girl and the man both die? Unless, of course, someone else intervened. Was it possible that the infuriating woman had killed the man because he had drowned one of her girls? Possible, he thought, but she hadn't given him the impression that she would get that involved. He also had a suspicion that the dead punter had remained on the premises despite his demands that all punters had to leave. If he had been a bit more on the ball, he might have checked this room first. In which case, the girl might not have died. He didn't care about the man. The girl was valuable – or, at least, she had been. Fuck it! He had cocked up there. Why had he listened to that bloody woman? Well, she won't be fucking with him again!

He closed the door to the garage and walked back into the kitchen where a number of black sacks had been piled up by the door. Ladinas was nothing if not thorough. His phone pinged in his jacket pocket. He looked at the screen and slid the green blob across to take the call.

'Hey, Stefan!' Zlatkov lifted his head and looked at the ceiling.

'Borislav my friend!' Stefan Popescu was perhaps Zlatkov's most trusted associate. They had worked together on many missions around Europe and, although they very rarely met, they got on well and made a very dependable team for whoever hired them. 'I am just calling to tell you that the delivery has been made so I am staying at the safe house tonight and will wait for your call tomorrow about where we go next.'

'Did you get any trouble about being short of one girl?' Zlatkov was concerned that questions might have been asked as he had promised to deliver six girls – and his masters usually came down very heavily on people who broke their promises.

'Not trouble exactly,' Popescu explained, 'and they were reasonably understanding when I told them about the girl being killed by the punter. I think I got them to believe that it was that woman's fault, but I also think they found the explanation just as weird as it seemed when you first got into the room.'

'Okay! Hopefully, we will hear no more about it.' The hand-over seemed to have gone well, and Zlatkov was relieved that not too many questions had been asked. In this game, losing one of the girls was a cardinal sin given the logistics of getting them to the UK in the first place and then the loss of earnings as a result. He knew of many of his fellow countrymen who had perished as a direct result of carelessness, and he didn't want to end up as just another such statistic.

'Anyway, Borislav,' Popescu continued, 'I am calling to say that I have another assignment to go to now so I will call you when I am finished with that. Good luck, my friend.'

'Okay, Stefan. Thank you. We will be in contact.' Zlatkov disconnected the call just as Ladinas walked into the kitchen with yet another black sack.

'You ready to go now?' Zlatkov asked as Ladinas tossed the bag on to the pile.

'Yes, boss. Are we taking these to the dumping place?' Ladinas asked.

'That's the plan,' Zlatkov replied. 'Dracul and Omar will wait for you. They say the weather is not good and that there is flooding on the road so be very careful – we don't want any accidents which might give the police an opportunity to search through these sacks.'

Ladinas ignored the remark and began collecting up the sacks. He pushed past Zlatkov and just about managed to open the door before barrelling through the porchway and out to the small white van which he had earlier reversed up to the entrance.

Zlatkov had another quick look around before switching off the lights and leaving the building. He stopped by the front of the white van just as Ladinas finished loading the last of the sacks. 'I will call you in the next few days, my friend, when we know details of the next house. Better get some more sacks!' He laughed as he turned and plipped the key in his hand. The side

147

lights on his car lit up the path in front of him as he sauntered across the uneven ground and away from this hell hole.

26

Saturday 22 July

Geoff Rawlings wrestled with the opening mechanism on the five-bar gate which guarded the entrance to the Basted Heights allotments. Although the so-called committee which ran the allotments was responsible for setting the combination on the lock, it was never a very memorable number and Rawlings nearly always had to have several goes before he got it right. Then he had to pull the spring-loaded opening mechanism in order to actually open the gate. He also found this difficult, and he wasn't helped by the fact that his arthritis was getting worse, particularly in his hands. Normally, he tried to get up to the allotment at a time when others would already have opened the gate, but today he had to be off early to see his son, Julian, and his lovely family. He wanted to take some of the fresh vegetables which were now growing in abundance.

Now within touching distance of his eightieth birthday, Rawlings had had an allotment on the Basted Heights site for nearly thirty years – a present from his wife on his 50th birthday when she had finally had enough of her flower borders being taken over as extensions to her husband's kitchen garden at home. He had worked feverishly to get his allotment up and running, and it soon became the envy of some of the other plot holders although they were always quick to praise the hard work which he continually put in, particularly during the lighter evenings of the summer months.

One of the first projects he had undertaken was to build a good-sized wooden shed at the end of his plot so that he could store all his gardening tools and the other detritus which gardeners seem to acquire over the years. Although he had tried desperately to maintain some form of order in the shed as more items found their way inside for storage, he knew he was always fighting a losing battle. But there was still room to shelter from the rain if a shower suddenly blew over on one of the prevailing westerlies, and he loved that horticultural smell which adorned most garden sheds – a heady mixture of fertilizer, two-stroke engine oil and freshly mown grass.

Rawlings headed off towards his allotment, taking a bit of a detour along the central pathway between the plots so that he could take a look at old Bill Moody's pumpkins and see how they were coming along. Although they were the best of friends, Rawlings and Moody always clashed for the 'Best Pumpkin in Show' prize at the village's Garden Society Autumn Show with the prize almost inevitably going to the biggest pumpkin in show rather than the judges considering which was the best specimen. Honours were fairly even over the years although both men had to enlist the help of sons and grandsons to help them lift the giants and get them to the village hall.

He was studying the Moody pumpkins when a thought struck him. There was something out of place on the site. In his determination to get to Bill Moody's plot, his eyes had alighted on something but his mind had not registered its significance. He now looked up and turned his attention to his own plot which was some forty metres in front of him. He screwed up his eyes in the early morning sun and tried to focus. What on earth was that standing proud beside his wigwam of runner beans?

He started off towards his plot and then stopped dead in his tracks. He could feel the hairs on the back of his neck start to rise as he slowly took another couple of paces forward until he could clearly see that, standing proud in the midst of his allotment was, of all things, a scarecrow!

'Bloody kids!' he muttered under his breath as he continued walking towards the plot. He knew that the village had an annual scarecrow competition but that was not for a couple of months yet so it couldn't be for that. Must be the local kids having a bit of a laugh. It was known that some of them came out here in the evenings to sit around drinking cheap cider and smoking dope or grass or whatever they called it these days. He often had to clear empty cans of cider or super strength lager from off his allotment which he didn't really mind doing as long as there was no damage done.

Now he was up to the path in front of his plot, he could see the scarecrow standing erect but with head bowed. His old eyes peered at the object, his mind processing the information. He knew there was something wrong but he just couldn't put his finger on it. And then it came to him in a flash and a cold shiver convulsed his body. There was no sign of straw. The arms were stretched out on each side horizontal to the ground but, instead of straw sticking out of the end of the shirt sleeves, there were tiny fingers – almost like you would see on a mannequin in a shop. Rawlings was rooted to the spot. The scarecrow's head was doubled over so that all he could see was the top of a broad brimmed denim hat. Was it straw that cascaded down from under the hat? 'Oh, my God!' he exclaimed. 'Oh, my God no! Surely not!'

Rawlings inched forward, carefully placing his feet between rows of vegetables. After a few paces, he was within reach of the scarecrow. Bending down as far as his stiff back would allow him, he tried to peer under the hat. He turned his neck and glanced up. The sight that greeted him was from his worst nightmares, and he recoiled in sheer horror. He sank down, gripping his knees with his hands, gulping breaths of fresh air, his heart pounding in his chest, blood coursing through his weakening arteries, the deafening sound of silence ringing in his ears.

After what seemed an eternity, he straightened his back and turned to face the scarecrow. Plucking up courage, he approached the scarecrow once more and peered up under the hat. The deathly pale face of a young girl seemed to look down at him in pity, the eyes bulging from their sunken sockets. Her long blonde hair covering the edges of her beautiful little face. A face that was now lost to this world.

Rawlings was shaking. Despite the increasing heat from the early morning sun, his body felt cold and clammy. He reached into his pocket and pulled out the mobile phone his daughter, Flora, had given him for use in emergencies. She didn't like the idea of her father being up at the allotment with no means of communicating with her if there was a problem. There was only one number in the phone's memory and he pressed the name on the screen. He eventually heard a ringing tone.

'Dad?' a questioning voice answered. 'Are you all right?'

Rawlings paused, trying to control his emotions. 'Hello, darling,' he stammered. 'Yes, I'm okay but there's a bit of a problem here at the allotment.'

'A problem? What sort of problem?' Flora was immediately in a state of heightened anxiety. Her father hadn't been in the best of health lately, and she hoped that he wasn't having a turn on the allotment.

'It's best you come and see for yourself. Can you get up here right now?' There was a sense of urgency in Rawlings' voice.

He could hear Flora's sigh, and he could picture her in the kitchen of her cottage with piles of washing which one husband and three teenage boys managed to generate on an almost daily basis. 'Okay, Dad. Give me five minutes.' And, with that, she disconnected the call. Rawlings stared at the phone and then slowly put it back in his pocket. He turned to look at the scarecrow again.

He could feel tears welling up in his old, hooded eyes. 'Who are you, my beautiful fair-haired child?' he found himself muttering. 'And what have they done to you?'

27

Saturday 22 July

Flora stared at the pile of dishes which she had still not managed to load into the dishwasher, and nearly tripped over the vacuum cleaner as she turned to get her car keys from the hook next to the fridge. 'What was up with Dad now?' she wondered. Her mother had been taken a few years before, ravaged by cancer, but her father had done well to look after himself without having to lean on Flora for too much help. But, just lately, she had begun to notice that he was getting a little forgetful and that he had started to imagine things. Not big things, but more flights of fancy. His call just now had made her feel uncomfortable and she had a frown on her face as she started up the old Land Rover which sat on the drive.

She negotiated her way through the narrow lanes leading to the allotments, not expecting to meet anything coming towards her at this time of day. She turned down the rutted path leading to the allotment gates and parked next to her father's car. She looked off into the distance where his plot was located, and saw him just standing there as if rooted to the spot. At least he was still standing and hadn't suffered a fall, she thought as she climbed down from the vehicle.

She made her way down the main path towards her father's plot, giving a little wave as she went but getting no response. Her father just seemed to be standing there staring. As she got a bit closer, she realised that he was staring at a scarecrow which had been erected at a jaunty angle in the middle of his patch. No doubt the over-exuberant youth of the village, she thought making a mental note to interrogate her three boys about names of possible culprits. She finally arrived at the plot.

'Hello, Dad!' she called as she moved closer to him. He turned, and she saw tears making their way down the greying stubble on his cheeks. 'What's the matter?' she asked, a sense of urgency creeping into her voice. Her father said nothing but simply turned and pointed at the scarecrow. She looked over his shoulder and then moved around him to get a better look. At first, it looked like any other scarecrow she had ever seen. Just like the ones her boys used to make for the village fair before they had discovered sport and girls.

But she soon realised that there was something wrong with this particular scarecrow as it seemed to be devoid of one of the main ingredients for any scarecrow – where was the straw? She took a couple of paces towards the object and then stopped dead in her tracks. The golden tresses tumbling from under the wide-brimmed hat were certainly not straw and, unless she was very much mistaken, she was looking at human hair. She turned back to look at her father but he was resolutely staring off into the distance so she took another couple of paces until she was within touching distance of the scarecrow. She suddenly noticed the tips of thin fingers sticking out from the sleeves, and a wave of nausea washed over her.

Trying desperately to subdue the fear and trepidation which was in danger of consuming her whole being, she bent down to peer under the hat and let out a stifled scream as the bulging eyes gazed sightlessly back at her. Flora staggered away from the horrific scene and threw up at the edge of the plot. Wiping away spittle and remnants of her morning porridge from around her mouth with the back of her hand, she just stood and stared at the scarecrow – a thousand thoughts buzzing around in her head like an angry swarm of bees. After what seemed an age but was probably no more than a few seconds, she pulled her phone out of her back pocket.

'We're going to have to report this, Dad,' she called over to her father who had now moved off up the main path. With trembling fingers, she punched in 999 and was almost immediately connected. Flora explained the situation, gave the location and was then asked to remain at the site until the emergency services arrived. With the call ended, she put the phone back in her pocket and looked around for her father who was still slowly trudging back up the main pathway. She took one last look at the scarecrow and then headed off to take the hand of an old man who had stared into the abyss of a horror from which he might never recover.

28

Saturday 22 July

From the Basted Heights allotments, the house looked like many of the other country properties in this area of west Kent. Many of them lay empty during the week when their high-flying owners resided in bijou London apartments before descending on the countryside for long, lazy weekends. On the way, they would often pick up their children from weekly boarding schools or from relieved grandparents.

Ted Selitto surveyed the house from his vantage point on the main pathway which wended its way through the allotments. The first thing he noticed was that all the windows were shuttered which probably meant that no one was at home. A huge wooden door was recessed into what looked like a stone portico and was presumably the main entrance to the house. However, it appeared not to have been used recently as leaves and other rubbish had collected in the corners of the area surrounding the front door. Letting his eyes wander to either side of the front door and then taking the façade in as a whole, it looked as if two large reception rooms flanked the front entrance with smaller rooms on the first floor and then a row of small gabled windows where the roof began.

There was a single storey extension adjoining the left side of the house which Selitto assumed was probably an integral garage. However, there were no garage doors on the front of the structure facing him which seemed a bit odd. There was also a high wooden fence stretching out on either side of the building which disappeared into the encroaching woodland giving the impression that some of the woodland belonged to the property.

Earlier, Selitto had got a call from one of his mates in the Maidstone Control Room to tip him off that the CSIs were on their way to a body discovered in the Sheet Hill area. No further details. Was he interested? Selitto was already at his desk putting in some extra hours on the Hardwick case so he was pleased to have a distraction even if it was potentially for only a couple of hours.

Now, as he made his way out of the allotment and past the initial response vehicles, he thought he'd have a quick look around the house and then get back to his desk. Once he got down onto the level ground in front of the house, the fence seemed higher than it had looked from the allotment, and he was now able to observe a thin string of razor wire running along the top of the panels. A need to keep people out was his first thought, but a little voice in his head asked whether it could also be a need to keep people in. He moved along to the front entrance.

The large front door looked as if it had been welded to its frame, and probably hadn't been opened in a long time. There were cobwebs in the corners of the portico and the amount of rubbish littering the floor in front of the door was even worse than it had looked when viewed from the allotment. An ornate horse's head door knocker took centre stage on the door. The brass had tarnished over time, no doubt due to lack of upkeep. There was also a central hexagonal door knob which was similarly tarnished. He fished a pair of nitrile gloves out of his pocket and put them on before stepping carefully into the portico. He raised the horse's head and let it thud back onto the brass plate. The sound seemed to echo around him, and reminded him of the sound a door knocker makes when a property is empty. A hollow sound which was bereft of warmth. He made a mental note that there was no letterbox or other receptacle for mail.

He wandered off along the front of the house, past the end of the single storey extension and then followed the fence as it disappeared into the encroaching woodland. He peered through the undergrowth and saw that the wooden panels didn't extend much further so, pulling some of the overgrown vegetation out of his way, he felt his way along the fence until he came to a corner. Turning the corner, he then followed the fence deeper into the wooded area although the branches from the trees above and the saplings growing up from the ground seemed to thin out a bit so his progress was a little less encumbered.

He eventually arrived at a doorway in the fence. The door was of solid construction with heavy duty wooden panels attached to the metal frame. A huge bolt was rammed into the staple attached to the upright metal post, and a very large padlock secured the bolt in place. But why would the gate be locked from the outside? This didn't seem to make sense to Selitto, and he was just about to continue on his way when a sixth sense made him take a closer look at the padlock. From a distance, the padlock was a clear barrier to entry but Selitto now noticed that its shackle had, in fact, been sawn through and then replaced to make it look as if it was locked. He gently twisted the shackle so that he could prise the padlock from its socket. He pulled back the bolt and pushed the gate open.

Although still under cover of the trees, Selitto found himself to the rear of the property. It looked as if someone had a deep-seated hatred of gardening as the entire area appeared to have been laid out as a gravel driveway. There was a weathered York stone path leading from the gate towards the back of the house. From this distance, Selitto could see that the extension to the side of the house had, in fact, been a double garage. Its entrance had been bricked up at some stage although the outline of the entrance was still in evidence. The garage had probably been converted to create another living space, he ruminated.

He also noted that the single storey garage extended well beyond the building line at the back of the property so Selitto had to walk almost past the end of the extension before he was able to see the rear entrance to the house. A smaller portico than the one at the front of the house jutted out into the gravel drive and was framed with glass panels. The path continued to the entrance but Selitto crunched his way across the gravel until he was up to the rear of the house. He tried to peer in through the windows either side of the portico but could see very little as the glass was tinted. So, he stepped into the portico where he was confronted by a solid oak door with a huge black ring handle. Above the door, the all-seeing eye of a CCTV camera looked down on the entrance and a sophisticated screen entry system was attached to the wall beside the door.

Selitto took a couple of steps back out onto the driveway and craned his neck upwards to survey the fenestration at the back of the house. Unsurprisingly, it was much the same as at the front with the size of windows diminishing floor by floor. As with those at the front, all the windows appeared to have shutters drawn apart from the ground floor. He stepped back into the portico and idly twiddled the door ring whilst contemplating what to do next. He gave the ring one final twist and, to his surprise, thought he heard a click. He held the ring in place and gently pushed as the door started to open in front of him.

He was instantly on his guard, hackles raised. Was the house actually occupied? Had someone been watching him on the CCTV? Were they lying in wait for him? He questioned whether he should step over the threshold without at least some back up let alone a warrant. The door had swung almost to its fullest extent, and Selitto peered into what seemed to be a cavernous kitchen area. He could see dust particles hanging in the shaft of light created by the open door which seemed to indicate that no one had been walking around in this room for some time. So, weighing his options up, he stepped through the doorway taking care to close the door behind him.

His eyes adjusted to the gloom inside the house, and he was quickly able to locate a light switch just inside the doorway. Thankfully, no one had turned the power off and, at the flick of the switch, an array of spotlights bathed the room in light. He now found himself in a large country kitchen with a huge oak table as its centrepiece. A farmhouse range cooker lined one of the walls next to a double ceramic kitchen sink. He noticed the Villeroy & Boch logo on the sink so concluded that someone must have lavished quite a lot of money on kitting this room out. Two American-style fridges took up much of another wall alongside a tall freezer. The doors of all these appliances hung open, their contents having been removed. There was nothing on any of the work surfaces or on the window sills, although Selitto noticed that the cupboards and drawers did contain plates, cutlery and a number of pots and pans which displayed signs of wear and tear so had probably been in daily use for cooking. He was, however, interested to note a line of optics attached to the wall above one of the kitchen dressers. Bottles of gin, whisky, vodka and other spirits stood sentry-like in the optic dispensers – some full, some half-empty.

Selitto wandered out of the kitchen and found himself in a dark hallway. He needed to get some light into the place and eventually found a switch on the wall but the quality of light provided by the two wall lights in the hallway was very poor. Was there a dimmer switch somewhere or was the lumen count just very low? He could just make out some doors off the hall-way but his attention had been drawn to the door at the end of the passage which, he presumed, would lead into the garage area. He approached this in full expectation that it would be locked and was, therefore, surprised when he turned the ornate knob on the door and he heard a click as the catch was released. He pushed the door open and immediately felt some resistance. There was obviously some sort of spring mechanism which ensured that it was always closed when not in use. He stood in the doorway and peered into what seemed like a large black void. Not a crack of light was coming in from anywhere, and the pale light from the hallway made no impression on the stygian gloom in front of him.

He reached into his jacket and took out the small LED torch which he invariably kept clipped to the inside pocket. More substantial than a normal pencil light, the beam provided excellent light in just the situation he now found himself, and he flicked the switch to 'on'.

He immediately realised the reason why it had seemed so dark. The door from the hallway had opened into a small ante-room, and he was now looking at three black walls. The walls to his left and right each contained a black door with a gold handle. Instinctively, he reached for the door to his right and found that it opened towards him. He now peered into another black void. Surely there were some lights in this place? He ran the beam round the ante-room and eventually spotted what looked like a control panel near the floor behind the door that he had originally walked through. Reaching down, he pushed the first in a line of buttons. Out of the corner of his eye, he caught sight of a dim glow of light beyond the door with the gold handle. He pressed the next two buttons and the amount of light intensified. He located a knob beside the panel and found that it dimmed the lights quite effectively. He returned the LED torch to his pocket and walked through the door.

29

Ten Months Earlier

An unusually hot summer had given way to a warm and balmy September. The sun still shone out of a bright azure sky, and there was a gentle breeze drifting across the extensive area of common land which covers the area between Ashdown Forest and Chelwood Gate.

Enjoying the warmth of the day, three men sat around a wooden table in the picturesque gardens of The Red Lion at Chelwood Gate. It was just after 12.30 p.m. and the pub already had a few customers in for lunch. In an attempt to get some privacy, the men had chosen a table which was well away from the rear doors of the pub and, although it was close to the children's play area, their thinking was that the number of children being taken to a pub on a Tuesday in term time was likely to be limited. The order had been two americano coffees and a glass of sparkling water with ice.

A huge man with a full-grown dark beard and wearing designer sunglasses was doing much of the talking. He gesticulated constantly, trying to emphasise the points he was making and, with each gesticulation, his huge biceps threatened to split the stylish shirt he was wearing. Occasionally, he looked menacingly into the eyes of his companions.

'Well, that is enough information on our operation and plans,' the huge man concluded, eventually sitting back and putting his hands flat in the table. 'Now you tell me what is going on in your world.'

Next to speak was a swarthy looking man with gleaming

white teeth. He was not quite as bulky as the man with the beard but, if anything, he was a little bit taller. He was probably of eastern Mediterranean origin and had close-cropped black hair. His sunglasses were wrapped round the dome of his head, and he wore a faded England rugby shirt.

'We already have the channels set up for transporting the goods to the UK,' he was saying. 'Our people are located at strategic points along the route to take care of matters if there is a problem, but we have been doing this for so many years that we can almost guarantee safe passage.'

'And who is this man?' the huge man pointed a stubby finger at a rather dapper-looking man who was sitting in the shadow of the faded rugby shirt. He wore a white shirt and tie under a navy-blue blazer, light blue slacks and highly polished black lace-up shoes. A picture of Englishness only a stone's throw from the Garden of England.

'He helps when we get problems,' the man in the rugby shirt replied. 'He has facilities which I use when the goods can no longer be used. He can also store the goods until we have use for them. He has large place in country some distance from here.'

The huge man looked the dapper Englishman up and down with a quizzical gaze. 'And you can trust him?' he growled.

'Yes, yes,' came the reply. 'We have worked together for some time. I can use him to pass information on to you.'

The two men then lapsed into a language which the dapper Englishman did not either recognise or understand. Every so often the huge man glared at him whilst rugby shirt occasionally put one of his huge hands on his shoulder and gave him a good shake. The thought of getting up from the table and walking out on these two oafs was appealing, but the Englishman knew that that was not an option. He was in too deep, and he valued his life which would no doubt come to an early end if he stepped out of line with either of these murdering bastards. So, he sat still, focused on a point in the middle distance and thought of all the work that was piling up on his desk back at the office.

Eventually, amidst much laughter and high-fiving, the two huge men seemed to have come to some sort of agreement and started to unfurl themselves from the constraints of the pub bench-table. They began ambling towards the car park, the Englishman in tow. After more shoulder slapping and high-fiving, they both turned to the Englishman and saluted. 'Goodbye my friend!' the huge man growled. 'I will see you again!'

Rugby shirt shook the Englishman roughly by the hand. 'I will see you very soon my friend,' he said in a whisper. He then turned towards his car, and both cars had soon left the car park. The Englishman walked over to his car, plipping the locks as he went. Before getting into the car, he smoothed a strand of hair back into place, brushed an imaginary piece of fluff from his lapels and shot his cuffs.

30

Saturday 22 July

As a general rule, Ted Selitto was rarely lost for words but, on this occasion, his jaw hit the proverbial floor almost as soon as he was through the door into the garage area. An array of different coloured lights lit up the space which he could now see was about one and a half times the size of a standard double garage. He noticed a small square of wood on the floor by the door so he jammed it between the door and the frame to prevent any chance of him getting locked in.

With the door closed, the effects of the down lighting as well as some up lighting gave the place an eeriness which made Selitto feel uncomfortable. He was also struck by how deathly quiet it was in the room. He ventured further into the vacant space and then suddenly stopped. It was as if all sound had been neutered. He coughed and then clapped his hands together. There was no reverberation – the sound had no prolongation; it just died. Was the room soundproofed? The flooring seemed to be of a material he had not come across before, and felt as if it had some give in it – not exactly bouncy but not as hard as concrete either. He tapped the wall nearest him with his knuckle. A dull thud indicated a layer of plasterboard but he reckoned that there was also soundproofing material between that and the brickwork.

But it was what was on the walls that really commanded his attention. There were racks and racks and racks of equipment which could only be used for bondage, dominance, discipline and other sadomasochistic pleasures. There were also clothes rails from which hung rubber suits, uniforms, and other items of clothing. He turned to a unit of drawers and found that each drawer contained more sex aids. There was a bath with a gold rolltop right next to a huge wardrobe. Other paraphernalia was stored on shelves around the room. As far as Selitto could make out, this was an extremely upmarket BDSM chamber which gave him a good idea of what he was going to find in the rest of the house.

He took another look around the room, and noticed two paintings on the wall of the anteroom which looked completely out of place. The first was a framed oil painting depicting an array of flower pots using subtle shades of light. The other was an unframed but colourful oil painting. Some children were fishing in a pond in a woodland setting while a picnic was underway on the river bank close by. He studied the two paintings. *Art in a torture chamber? Ridiculous!*

Shaking his head, Selitto walked over to the farthest recesses of the room, judging himself to now be by the wall which was where the garage door would once have been located. He gave it a tap with his knuckle and got the same dull thud on plasterboard. He got his torch out again and shone it up towards the ceiling of the room. In so doing, he realised that the ceiling was much higher than an average ceiling in a modern garage construction. He shone his torch into the corner above him where the walls met the flat ceiling, and noticed what appeared to be a smoke alarm. It was mounted on a small strut of wood which had been secured across the angle of the two walls. Selitto couldn't help thinking that a smoke alarm looked out of place in a room like this. Had he seen any others since he had entered the house? Surely, he would have noticed if there had been one in the kitchen? He made a mental note to check when he had finished here.

Meanwhile, his attention had again been grabbed by the very fashionable roll top bath with ornate taps which was positioned against the wall next to the wardrobe. He went over for a closer look and immediately thought he detected the same sort of smell he had first encountered in the bathroom at the Meadowlands hotel. Recoiling slightly, he noticed that the bath with its shower attachment and taps appeared as if brand new although his keen eye noticed a small drip of water hanging from the shower unit which rested in its cradle above the taps. On a hunch, he sank to his knees and shone the torch under the bath. Reaching out, he ran his hand over the floor. There was a definite dampness which, he surmised, could have either been caused by water splashing over the side of the bath or a fault with the plughole.

He bent right down until his face was resting on the floor, and shone the torch over the four legs of the bath unit. He noticed that each leg had made a slight indentation into the floor covering which made him think that the flooring might be some type of thick PU foam material. He craned his neck to get a better view as he played the spot beam from the torch over the two legs nearest the wall. After a couple of minutes of close examination, he was all but certain that he could see the faintest spots of what looked very much like blood spatter on one of the legs. He stayed in that position, his mind whirring, until the stiffness in his knees told him that it was time to get back into an upright position.

Stepping back into the centre of the room, he took time to have another look at his surroundings. He was undoubtedly standing in some sort of dungeon which had been expensively kitted out for sexual pleasure. What on earth was he going to find in the rest of the house?

Returning to the kitchen, he realised that the entrance hall was directly on his right so he walked through a passageway and took a look at the front door from the inside. Small shafts of light trickled into the hall through shards of coloured glass which formed a crown above the huge door. Their colours gently played across the walls around him. There seemed to be no means of opening the door from the inside, and it did not look as if it had been opened in a long time. He turned to retrace his steps and paused momentarily to look up the stairs into the gloom of the first-floor landing. He would be up there just as soon as he had finished with his search of the ground floor.

Turning to his left, he now opened the door into another room of stygian darkness. He quickly found a light switch and realised that he was in an opulently furnished sitting room. Two comfortable settees and a couple of easy chairs took up much of the space. There was also a large gate-legged table with two high backed chairs. A huge sideboard stretched almost the length of one of the walls, its glass doors hiding an array of expensive-looking drinking vessels. There was also a glass ice bucket and other bar equipment which were arranged on the surface above two small cupboards. On another wall hung an enormous television screen. Otherwise, the walls were bare and there were no ornaments or knick-knacks on any of the flat surfaces in the room. The only oddity which drew his attention was the two place settings which had been laid at the table complete with wine glasses and a wine cooler.

Selitto made his way over to the window where the curtains had been drawn tight shut. He drew them back but found that the shutters had also been closed up. In fact, on closer inspection, he found that they had been screwed into place so that opening them was not an option. He turned the light off and exited the room.

Across the hallway, he entered a second darkened room. Having located the light switch, Selitto drew back the curtains but found that the shutters had been similarly screwed into place. He was now in a spacious room which contained a double bed as well as a single bed which was jammed up against the wall under the window. A door led off the room and he found himself in an en-suite bathroom with bath and walk-in shower. The beds had been stripped to the mattress and the bathroom was completely empty – not even a bar of soap! There were no clothes in the built-in wardrobe, and nothing in the dresser which stood in the corner behind the door.

Selitto switched the light off and, returning to the entrance hallway, he climbed the stairs to the upstairs landing. He was just about to reach for his torch when he caught a glimpse of a light switch. The lighting in the corridor was as gloomy as it had been downstairs but at least he could see where he was going. There were five doors on this floor, all closed.

He decided to start to his left and found himself in a large room which he judged would have looked out onto the allotments at the front of the house if he had been able to get the shutters open. The room was lavishly furnished as a bedroom with mirrors all around the walls and on the ceiling. A copper bath stood in one corner and there was a huge dressing table in another corner next to a wardrobe which extended almost the entire length of one of the walls. Selitto had a look inside the wardrobe. There was a long clothes rail with dresses and uniforms of all different shapes and sizes. Nurses, school girls, St Trinians, waitresses. Selitto gave up trying to recognise them. There was also a slim set of drawers which contained piles of sexy underwear, sex toys, and one drawer which was solely devoted to oils and condoms.

The centrepiece of the room was an enormous round bed. A camera stand looked down on the bed, and various wires trailed off along the floor to a power socket in the corner. Although there was no bed linen on the bed, decorative drapes hung from the ceiling and the already luxurious carpet was covered in even more expensive looking rugs. Lights danced off the mirrors as a glitterball slowly rotated above the bed making it feel as if the bed was sitting in the middle of some sort of live sex nightclub.

Two of the rooms facing the back of the house were all similarly decorated although they were smaller and had more conventional king-sized beds. As with all the other rooms, the shutters had been screwed into their frames. The third room was a bathroom with fairly standard bathroom furniture including another walk-in shower. This left the final room at the front of the house.

On entering the room, Selitto noticed that light was seeping in around the area where he expected the window to be. There was enough light for him to make his way across the room, and he opened the curtains. He fiddled with the catch on the shutters which eventually came loose, and he opened them to allow the daylight to flood into the room. Outside, he could see the CSIs all dressed in their Tyvek suits on the allotment and a couple of his uniform colleagues enjoying a chat at the entrance to the site. Turning around, he looked back into the room.

He found himself standing behind what would originally have been a large leather-covered desk with a column of drawers on each side. A half-empty bottle of expensive Russian vodka stood rather forlornly on the top of the desk which appeared to have been subjected to a series of blows from a very heavy implement – either a sledge hammer or an axe. The structure with its drawer columns was just about intact but had been significantly damaged. A luxury leather executive chair on wheels had been shunted into a corner near the window as if it had been discarded by someone in a hurry to leave the room. There were a couple of filing cabinets against one of the walls with drawers hanging open, the contents spread around the room. A large bookcase took up much of the other wall, its books and other reading materials littering the floor on that side of the room.

He crouched down to look into the kneehole of the desk and noticed that the carpet had been disturbed. He hadn't noticed this when he entered the room, probably on account of the ornate modesty panel which covered the front of the desk. Now squatting down on his haunches, he saw that a flap of carpet had been ripped and pulled back. He shone his torch into the empty space and soon realised that the carpet had concealed a small underfloor safe. Down on his hands and knees now, he craned his neck over the top of the safe and found that there was no security lid attached to the safe. He was staring into an empty container.

He scrambled out of the kneehole, and then stood back from the desk. After a minute's reflection, he decided to try the desk drawers but found that they were all locked. Last of all, he took a look at the long drawer in the middle of the desk immediately above the kneehole. Taking hold of the ornate handles and fully expecting it to be similarly locked, he was surprised when it gently slid open. Inside, he could see that there were a few biros and pencils, a felt marker pen, a pair of scissors, a small jar of Nivea cream, a Black & White A4 notebook, and some paperclips.

On a hunch, he pulled the drawer out to its full extent and laid it on the top of the desk so that he could look at it more closely. Bingo! His hunch had paid off. A key had been taped to the wood on the outside of the back panel of the drawer. What he couldn't understand was why this drawer had been left in place when the rest of the desk had been subjected to such wanton destruction? He released the key and inserted it into the lock of the first drawer in the right-hand column. There was a satisfying click and he opened the drawer. But it was empty.

He was just about to close the drawer when he noticed its dimensions didn't seem to match those of the desk columns – particularly the depth of the drawer space. He gently pulled it further out beyond the rear panel and then just kept pulling to reveal a secret compartment at the back of the drawer. Nestling inside the compartment was a small control panel. There were two green buttons and a red button, and what looked like a small toggle lever. He pressed one of the green buttons but nothing seemed to happen. So, he pressed the other green button and heard a movement off to his left.

He turned his head just in time to see a panel in the bookcase start to slide back. Selitto watched as a screen came into view, fitting almost exactly into the gap in the bookcase. Assuming that the red button would close the panel around the screen, he pressed the other green button again. The screen flickered into life but, at first, it was difficult to see what he was looking at. The image was very grainy and the screen was constantly pixelating. Eventually, he realised that he was looking at the inside of the dungeon. The first thing he noticed was that the lights seemed to be on. Had he really forgotten to turn them off?

He looked back into the drawer and toggled the lever. The image moved and he found that he could view just about any part of the large room although with some difficulty due to the poor quality of the picture. He was just getting used to the grainy images, and how little he had to move the toggle in order to pan around the room, when he thought he caught a glimpse of something moving across the bottom left corner of the screen. He instinctively toggled the camera to his left to try to pick up the movement but nothing came into view. At the same time, he stared at the screen trying to remember where the camera was positioned. Had he really missed it? He slowly swept the room again, trying to picture what he had seen. Then he suddenly realised that the camera must be in the smoke alarm. Very clever, he thought. So, the person sitting at this desk was keeping an eye on things in that room but not, as far as he had so far discovered, in any of the other rooms.

He was just thinking of seeing whether the red button would close the screen up when he again caught sight of a shadow flashing across the bottom of the screen. This time there was no doubt in his mind that there was someone down there. A shiver ran down his spine. Surely no one had followed him into the house! The place appeared uninhabited. Could the owner or occupier have just returned? He toggled the camera with greater urgency in his haste to discover who else was in the house. But there was no further movement in the room. Looking down, he pressed the red button and the panel slid back across the screen, hiding it from view.

He got hold of his phone and set it up in camera mode. In situations like this, he often clipped the phone into the top pocket of his jacket which was not very deep so it didn't cover the top of the phone and the camera lens. An IT Tech had set it up so that the images and voice recording were automatically transmitted to Selitto's email. This meant that he could run it all back when he got to a workstation at the Tonbridge nick, and often saved an awful lot of time when confronting suspects who wanted to deny everything.

He crept down the stairs and stopped on the bottom step, listening. He peered around the corner and then inched his way down the passageway towards the kitchen. He then cast a glance towards the dungeon. The same block of wood was still preventing the door from shutting, and the doorway was silhouetted in the light from inside the room. Had he really left the lights on, he asked himself again. He crept along the corridor and took up position to the left of the door. Should he remove the wood and slam the door thus imprisoning the intruder, or should be just burst in and confront the person? Suppose the intruder was armed? He looked around but couldn't see anything he could use to defend himself. In any case, what defence could he have against an automatic weapon? No, it would have to be the closed-door option so that he could then get reinforcements to deal with whoever was in there.

Opening the door just a tiny fraction in order to release the piece of wood, he gripped it tightly and, in one swift move, he yanked the wood away from the door and pulled the handle towards him. The door slammed shut. Quickly turning the key in the lock, he breathed a huge sigh of relief and stood there, listening for any reaction from inside. Not a sound so he assumed that no one could make themselves heard through the sound proofing. He was just wondering what to do next when a voice came from behind him.

'What on earth are you doing, Detective Sergeant?' He spun round, a small bead of sweat detaching itself from his forehead and splashing on to the wall next to him.

31

Saturday 22 July

'Boss?' Selitto stammered, a mixture of surprise and relief in his voice. DI Sarah Hunter stood in the hall by the doorway into the kitchen. She was holding one of the heavy-duty copper pans he had spotted on the range in the kitchen and, he had to admit, she did look quite fearsome.

'Have...?' Selitto stammered, 'have you been here long?' He eventually managed to get his words out.

'Not too long,' Sarah replied. 'I kept getting calls from Beth so I thought I'd better come over and see it all for myself. One of the uniforms mentioned you might be in here but it took me a while to find my way in. How did you know I was here?'

'Saw you on TV,' Selitto smiled.

'That's interesting!' Hunter raised her eyebrows. 'I can't say that I've seen any cameras so they must be well hidden.'

'Well, I wouldn't have known if I hadn't seen it from the other end first so to speak.' Selitto squeezed past Hunter and walked off into the front hall. 'Come on up to what looks like an office on the first floor.' Hunter dutifully followed, still holding onto the pan which she then placed on a small table by the foot of the staircase.

Sunlight was still flooding the room when they entered. "I've left it exactly how I found it,' Selitto advised her. 'The chair looks as if it's away from the desk for a particular reason – perhaps a struggle? The shutters and blinds were all drawn but, unlike in the other rooms, they had not been screwed into place so I was able to get them open and see what sort of view there was.'

Hunter nodded and shuffled over to the window. She gazed out on the allotments across the parking area, staring at the blue and white crime scene tapes fluttering around Plot 44 where a white tent had been erected. No doubt there was still intense activity within the temporary structure where the well-drilled CSI team would be gathering evidence by the minute. She couldn't help thinking that the view from where she was standing afforded a perfect line of sight to where the body had been found. But she couldn't yet see a direct link between what she had so far seen in this house and the poor young girl whose life had been so tragically cut short in such a grotesque manner. But, with the sun still high in the sky, and the occasional zephyr of breeze bringing the leaves in the trees to life, it was indeed a picture of tranquillity.

Still wearing his nitriles, Selitto pulled open the drawer with the false back to uncover the buttons and the toggle lever. Hunter inspected the equipment. Selitto leaned over and pressed the left-hand green button whereupon the panel in the bookcase started to slide back. Hunter watched as the screen was revealed. Selitto pressed the second green button and the screen sprang to life giving a fuzzy picture of the dungeon. 'Looks like we've left the lights on in there!' he observed.

Hunter always kept a supply of nitrile gloves in the back pocket of her jeans, and she now snapped a pair on before touching anything on the desk. 'And this thing moves the camera does it?' she asked, moving her hand towards the toggle lever. She gently nudged it to the right and the camera swept around the room. She quickly got the hang of gently moving the lever and did a comprehensive sweep of the room. 'Not many places to hide from this all-seeing eye,' she remarked at last. 'Have you found the recording equipment yet?'

Selitto was over by the bookcase trying to see if he could spot any other false panels. 'No, but I reckon that it's hidden in here somewhere. Thought I'd leave it to the CSIs – they'll probably have more of an idea where to look. But there's no sign of any other equipment. No lap top or phones or documents – nothing! It looks as if whoever was here has just disappeared into thin air!'

He would have to get the CSI boys & girls to go over this room with a fine-toothed comb in the hope that they would find the CCTV footage. At the moment, it was not clear to Selitto where the recordings might be stored but he suspected there could be other equipment either hidden in the bookcase or behind another secret panel in the room. Best to leave it where it is and let the experts get to work, he thought.

Hunter pressed the red button and the panel slid across the screen. 'Anything else?'

Selitto drew her attention to the disturbed carpet under the desk where the safe had been placed in the floor space above the ceiling of the room below. 'There's a small safe under the carpet but it's now minus its lid and anything that might have been inside it. Probably mainly for money but could have been items of jewellery as well. Anyway, it's been cleaned out.'

'Okay.' Hunter straightened up from the crouching position she had adopted to take a look at the safe. 'Any more gems in here?'

'No, and I haven't got up to the second floor yet but it certainly looks as if this house was used as some sort of upmarket knocking shop,' Selitto reflected. 'Certainly an upmarket

BDSM dungeon which you've already seen, all sound proofed and fully equipped to satisfy just about any depraved kinky fantasy. Plenty there to get your teeth into if you'll excuse the pun! And no expense spared. The other rooms I've seen so far are exotically decorated and equipped with just about every sex toy you could imagine. And there are beds of all different shapes and sizes with mirrors on walls, ceilings, floors – you name it! But not one chink of daylight in any of the rooms – all shutters and blinds have been screwed into the frame and cannot be opened. And one other thing – I may be mistaken but I'm pretty sure that there is some blood spatter under the bath in the dungeon – if that's what we're going to call it. I'll make sure that Beth takes a look at that as soon as she gets over here.'

They left the room and walked back to the staircase. 'I'll have a quick shufty around the other rooms you've already been into and take a look under the bath. Then I'll get back across the road.' Sarah Hunter took out her phone and jabbed at the screen. 'Another three texts from Beth so I better find out what's getting her excited. Will you get over to the allotment when you've finished in here?'

'Yep, fine with me', replied Selitto.

Selitto wearily climbed a much narrower staircase and found himself in a darkened corridor on the second floor of the house. He took out his torch and played the beam along the walls looking for a light switch. Finding nothing, he looked back down the stairs and noticed that he had passed two switches on his way up. He went back down and flicked the one nearest the stairs. He glanced back up the stairs just as an overhead fluorescent tube sprang into life casting its cold, shadowless light around the hallway above him.

He reclimbed the stairs to the second floor and found himself in a narrow corridor with wooden doors on either side. He was also immediately aware of a huge barred metal gate which hung on runners so that it slid across the opening to the staircase. A large padlock hung from the bolt lock. It occurred to Selitto that this was more for keeping people in rather than keeping people out – although it could probably have worked both ways.

The first door he opened led into a small bathroom. He groped for a pull cord and harsh white light flooded down from LED bulbs embedded in the ceiling. There was no sign that the room was in regular use. Even the bathroom cabinet on the wall behind the door was completely empty. The bath with shower attachment was spotlessly clean as was the toilet. The whole room felt as if it had been recently subjected to a deep clean.

Selitto moved on to the next room which was clearly a bedroom. A double bed was jammed into one of the corners of the room which otherwise had a spartan look to it with a small chest of drawers and an old wooden chair. A clothes rail nestled up against another wall with a couple of bent and buck-led coat-hangers hanging forlornly from it. A second bedroom was similarly furnished although with a smaller double bed which seemed to have been made up. Both rooms had their small windows boarded up.

Out on the narrow landing, Selitto noticed that there was a panel in the ceiling directly above his head which was presumably the entrance to some loft space. He would leave others to search the loft once they had finished at the allotment. To his right was a sliding door which, at some point in time, had obviously been secured shut with a padlock. However, the hasp and staple which would have held the padlock were now hanging off the door, only held in place by a couple of loose screws.

Selitto slowly eased the sliding door to his left but only managed to open the gap to about a foot before the door seemed to become stuck. He closed the door and opened it again but this time with more intent. Still the door stuck. Taking hold of the edge of the door, he manoeuvred it until it was almost shut and then wrenched it as hard as he could to the left. This time he managed to dislodge whatever obstacle was preventing the door from opening to its full extent, and then stood back letting his eyes adjust to the dark interior. There was no light switch inside the door but he finally located a pull cord which activated some very dim lighting above a little built-in dressing table.

The room was very small, only really a box room, with a narrow wrought-iron bedstead down one side. It was this which had initially prevented him from opening the door. At the end of the bed was a small window which had been boarded up. However, on closer inspection, he noticed that the screws weren't as deeply embedded as they were in the boards across windows in the other bedrooms. He searched in his pockets for his trusty penknife and selected the screwdriver attachment. Right enough, the screws were very loose and he was able to quickly remove the board.

Sunlight flooded into the room, and he realised that this room enjoyed the same view of the allotments as he had seen from the office on the floor below. There were four panes of glass in the window, all very grimy through years of neglect. But what really drew his attention was the word "*HELP*" which had been painstakingly etched into the grime. He felt a lump in his throat when he realised that whoever had written the imploring word had no conception of what it might look like from the other side of the glass. Desperation had driven someone to use their ingenuity to find a way of unscrewing the board over the window but, in their moment of triumph, they had ultimately failed to convey the message to the outside world.

Looking around him, there appeared to be nothing else in the room apart from a small built-in wardrobe. Pulling the double doors open, he was confronted by narrow shelves and a hanging space laid out much as he expected. He was just about to close the doors when he noticed something glinting in a shaft of sunlight which had pierced a gap between the floorboards at the bottom of the wardrobe. He bent down to take a closer look but couldn't make out what the object was. He slid a thumbnail down between two of the floorboards to see if he could prise them apart but they wouldn't move. Looking more closely at each of the boards, he noticed that one of them was flush against the side of the wardrobe. So he gently pressed down on the opposite end of that board and was intrigued to find that the other end lifted up from its position next to the wardrobe.

He peered into the space under the floorboards and saw that the object glinting in the light was a small mobile phone. He reached into the space under the floorboards and carefully lifted the phone out of its hiding place. He sat back on his haunches staring at a silver Nokia C3. He lightly depressed the button that normally activated the phone but the screen remained blank - there was no life in it. He reached back into the space and felt around under the floorboards, his fingers suddenly brushing another object. He groped around and finally managed to grab hold of something that fitted neatly into the palm of his hand. Extricating himself from the wardrobe, he looked down to see that he was holding a bunch of fifty-pound notes. They had been carefully rolled up and were kept in place with a small rubber band. He flicked through the corners of the notes and counted up to fifteen – £750!

'Well, well, well!' he said to himself. 'If only someone had been able to see the desperate plea for help!' He decided to leave the phone and the wad of cash where they had been hidden and let Beth Dench and her team deal with them. He returned the board to its original position and got up from the floor.

Exiting the tiny bedroom, Selitto took another look at the hasp and bracket which were hanging limply from the sliding door. It was apparent that the room would have been secured with a padlock at some point in time although it did look as if the whole mechanism had been forced very recently. There were small flecks of paint on the threadbare carpet and some shavings of wood were still stuck to the hasp.

He had a quick look in the other rooms but they all seemed to be very simply furnished with a bed, a dresser, and somewhere to hang clothes.

Once back down on the ground floor, he had another quick look around the dungeon, turned the lights off and then went back outside onto the gravel drive. He looked off into the distance to see if he could locate an entrance to the driveway but it seemed to meander its way through the trees. He would get one of the uniforms to find out where the drive finally hit a road. For now, he should get back over to the allotment.

He retraced his steps across the gravel drive until he got to the door in the fence. Once through into the woods, he closed the door leaving the padlock as he had found it. He then followed the fence round to the front of the house, finally stepping back until he could see the windows on the top floor. He could just about make out a smudge on the window where he now knew the desperate plea for help had been etched. As he craned his neck to make out the word, he wondered how long someone had clung to the forlorn hope that rescue would one day be at hand.

32

Saturday 22 July

As he ducked under the crime scene tape, Selitto saw Sarah Hunter making her way towards him. He involuntarily turned and looked back at the house, his eyes straying towards the windows at the top of the building. No, he concluded, you definitely couldn't see anything from here.

'What's got your eye?' Hunter asked as she caught up with him.

'There's a message on one of the windows at the top but you can't even see the outline of it from here,' he replied, continuing to stare at the house.

Selitto filled her in on his search of the tiny room, how the board had obviously been removed by the room's occupant, the pathetic message for help, and the phone which had been hidden under the floorboards.

Hunter was now staring at the house as well. 'We'll have to get the CSIs to take a close look at this place.' It was a comment more than anything else. 'It's all far too clinical for my liking.'

'Agreed!' said Selitto, nodding. 'It was like that throughout the house, as if someone had been through the whole place sanitising it as they went. But there are some clues so even the best team of cleaners is not completely infallible.'

Hunter's mind went back to her first view of the kitchen. It reminded her of her early childhood when her mother used to take her to see Aunt Nibs. As a little girl, the bleakness of the Nibs' house frightened her – it was always so cold and devoid of life. Aunt Nibs was a strict authoritarian who had no truck with anyone who did not share her views on the need for harsh discipline both within the family and in the wider society. She kept no photographs or ornaments on any of the flat surfaces in the house, and there were no mirrors. The only decorative item was an ancient threadbare tapestry which adorned the wall over the fireplace in the sitting room. Hunter had had the same misgivings when she first walked into the kitchen.

'So, what are you thinking?' she eventually said, snapping out of her recollection of times past. She brushed past Selitto as she made her way to the car park area. 'Facts, Ted,' she said, looking back over her shoulder so that she could check that Selitto was following her. 'We need to consider the facts. We've got a dead girl, unidentified so far, who may or may not have been killed where she was found. And we've now got an empty house which certainly looks as if it's been in use as a very upmarket brothel, a load of expensive sex aids and furniture, some sort of CCTV surveillance system which we haven't yet managed to work out, and a mobile phone which might or might not give us some clues.'

Taking one final look at the house, she spun round to address Selitto. 'I'm getting the hell out of here! But I want the CSIs crawling all over this place the minute they've finished at the allotment. They can take the house to pieces brick by brick if necessary. My gut feeling is that there are clues here which someone has tried very hard to cover up. Get the allotment plot holders all interviewed. Let's try to get some idea of who lived here, comings and goings, cars, deliveries, things like that. They must have seen something over the years!' And then as an after-thought, 'Who's the pathologist likely to be?'

'Think I saw old man Partington up here earlier taking a

quick look at the body and its surroundings,' Selitto replied. 'Given that we probably won't get the body lifted until sometime this evening, it'll likely be done by the weekend team which he would normally lead.'

Norman Partington was a man of indeterminate age but probably nearer seventy than sixty. He had had a long and distinguished career with the Home Office Pathology Department but chose to retire to the country in his early sixties. After a year or two of tending his garden, improving his proficiency at solving The Times crossword, and trying (but failing) to lower his golf handicap, Partington had approached the local authorities to offer his services and was soon covering for weekends and other unsocial hours. This was a great help to what was left of the Pathology team which was stretched to breaking point after a number of swingeing cuts. Having quickly developed a fondness for Partington's quirky ways, Hunter had often described him as like "a pig in shit" in his new role but she highly respected the work he did and the thoroughness of the reports which he produced.

'Good', she replied. 'At least we should discover something useful by close of play tomorrow. Suggest you attend just to chivvy Partington along. He's a bit of a chatterbox in the cutting room.' Then, looking at her watch, she got into her car and started up the engine. The nearside window zoomed down and Hunter leaned across the passenger seat, shouting out to Selitto.

'I've got to report in to Iverson at 5.30 p.m. Now that we've got a body, it looks like he'll have to elevate this to an active case status so I'll have to find out what resources we might have at our disposal in terms of personnel.'

'Not many, I expect!' snorted Selitto. 'Can't think of anyone who's not already up to their eyeballs at Pembury Road.'

Hunter left the car idling as she looked off into the distance. Then, suddenly coming out of some sort of a mini daydream, she leant across the passenger seat again and addressed Selitto. 'I'll need a drink after all this excitement! Meet me down at The White Rock once you've checked on progress with the guys over the road. And make this place secure. I don't want to hear that any of the evidence has been tampered with, lost or otherwise abused. This is where something significant happened. I can almost taste it!' And, with that, she drove off into the late afternoon sun.

Selitto waited until she was out of sight and then beckoned to one of the uniforms who had been standing, sentry-like, at the entrance to the allotments. He recognised the man from the station quiz nights which he occasionally attended. 'How's it going, Dave?' he asked.

'Fairly quiet, Sarge,' PC Dave Fairbrother replied. 'Once word got round the plot holders, no one has come anywhere near here. And it's pretty much off the beaten track so I doubt that we'll see many ghouls. Any event, everything'll be packed up soon enough.' Dave was a time-served PC who had been round the block several times and probably just the person they needed on the gate here. Selitto was happy.

'Okay, Dave. Can I leave it to you and a couple of your mates to get the tape round the house? Make sure you get right round the fence as well. It goes into the woods on either side and there is a gate down the left-hand side. Suggest you run it across the entrance to the drive as well. Has anyone been down that track to find out where it comes out?'

'Yeah, one of them went down there,' Fairbrother replied. 'Said it didn't seem to come out on the lane which serves the track up to here, so could be Sheet Hill. I'll take a look later. Seems the track's covered by a five-bar farm gate which has been left open and there was a big padlock hanging off one of the bars. Whoever was last to leave obviously knew they weren't coming back!'

'Hmm! Interesting!' commented Selitto. 'Anyway, Sam-the-Lock should be round soon to secure the place. Could you make sure you get the keys or lock combos off him before he leaves and get them over to the CSIs – they're going to be back in the morning to look round the house.'

'Will do, Sarge. Anything else while I'm at it?' Fairbrother asked.

'Not that I can think of, Dave. Just make sure that no one can get into that house. That's my number one priority.' And, with that, Selitto turned and found the path leading into the allotments and went in search of Beth Dench. When he found her, she was deep in conversation with her two CSIs in the far corner of the tented area.

'How's it going, Beth,' asked Selitto carefully stepping over some of the CSI equipment which littered the ground around the body. Breaking off from her discussion, Dench took a few paces towards Selitto clutching an A4 note board.

'The Rottweiler's gone has she?' Beth enquired, smiling. Selitto hadn't known Beth Dench for long but he enjoyed the repartee which they had struck up. He was also impressed by her henchmen as he liked to think of them. Carrigan and Campbell seemed to get through a mountain of work which was more than some of his workshy colleagues back at base could ever dream of.

He'd heard on the grapevine that Beth Dench was regarded as one of the bright stars of the Home Office CSI set up, and Kent Police were very lucky to have got her for this secondment.

'Yep, she's shot off to kick some ass back at the station,' he replied. 'Fingers in so many pies as usual, and frothing at the mouth if people don't get on with things at the same frenetic pace that she adopts. Plus, she's got to persuade the old man that we've got a bona fide case going on here!'

'Thought so,' Dench replied. 'She was in and out of here like a whirling dervish and then spent the rest of her visit pacing up and down the central pathway issuing instructions on her mobile phone.'

That sounded like Hunter, Selitto thought. She was never happier than when organising people. Not a great one for dealing with the volume of paperwork which went hand in hand with all police work, she reasoned that, if she delegated everything, she wouldn't have to do the ensuing form filling. She had adopted a hot-desking policy for herself so that she didn't actually have a designated desk which could become cluttered with paper. And, if any paper did land on the desk she was sitting at, it was either quickly despatched on its way with a flourish of her red biro denoting the next recipient – or it was despatched to the shredding machine which she ensured was always within easy reach.

Beth smiled to herself. She'd only been in Kent for a couple of months but already knew of the reputation of DI Sarah Hunter – a fearless detective with an envied record of success in tackling and clearing up complex crimes. Always keen to learn from the very best, Beth had found working with Hunter was quite a revelation, and she enjoyed the challenge of keeping up with the way Sarah's mind operated.

Dench flipped over a couple of sheets of paper on her board. 'Should be wrapped up here by midnight with the body being delivered to the morgue early evening. I've organised the transport. At least it's now clear that this is not where she died. But I doubt that she was killed very far from here as there are no significant signs of the body having been transported any distance to this spot. Normally I might expect to see some evidence of ripped clothes or scratches on bare flesh if the body had been transported in the boot of a car for example. But there is no such evidence in this case.'

'Is there anything that would give us a clue as to how she got here?' asked Selitto.

'Well, we probably know more about the ways in which the body was not brought here than anything else,' Dench replied, consulting her notes and looking back towards the body. 'There's no mud or dried earth on the body so she was not dragged here. And her clothes show few signs of having been disturbed so it seems more than likely that she was carried to this location and then rather morbidly set up as a scarecrow.'

'Anything else to be going on with?' Selitto asked. 'Any idea of cause of death or even of time of death?'

'We'll have to wait for Norman's pronouncement on time of death but I would have thought that death occurred within the last twenty-four hours.' Dench consulted her notes again. 'As to cause of death, we have been slightly side-tracked by the fact that she looked and felt as if she may have been in water for some time before she was placed here. There doesn't seem to be any water round here so, if we are right in thinking that she wasn't transported here, we're at a bit of a loss to explain the connection with water.'

'Hmm!' Selitto cast his mind back to the bath in the dungeon and his discovery that the carpet around the bath had been damp. But kept his own counsel on this for the time being. Best to let Beth and the boys take a good look at the dungeon before suggesting a possible connection.

Dench was continuing. 'Identification isn't going to be easy as her face is quite distorted. We'll have to try and get some ID through her DNA, fingerprints and dental records although DNA and fingerprints will only be of use if she's already on the system. Clothes don't seem to have any labels in them and are totally unremarkable but smart – the sort of fashion you might find in M&S or somewhere like H&Ms perhaps? Or even by catalogue or via the Internet. They aren't, however, second-hand so she hasn't been shopping in charity shops or at boot fairs. There are no visible surgical scars as far as we can see although Norman will be able to give you more information on that.'

Selitto nodded as Dench continued. 'And her lower body appears quite unremarkable with all her clothes in place. No obvious sign that she has been in sunny climes – no bikini lines, just plain white skin. The only item of jewellery I can see is an ankle chain but, again, it is quite unremarkable and could have been bought almost anywhere in the world I should imagine.'

'That's it then?' asked Selitto.

'Pretty much,' replied Dench. She half turned away but then seemed to think of something else and turned back to face Selitto. 'There is one other thing but I don't know that I'm enough of an expert to make an informed comment or not.'

'Quite honestly, Beth,' Selitto began, 'we're going to need all the help we can get and if such help comes from the seemingly off-the-wall ideas of a CSI Manager then let's hear it!'

Dench turned over some more pages of notes. 'I'm not much of an expert when it comes to fashion but I just have a feeling about the way she is dressed. To me, her style of clothing seems to be more European. You know, girls in the UK these days seem to be wearing very loose-fitting clothes and several layers of them at that. But this girl is simply and fairly smartly dressed. She also seems to lack any body piercings or tattoos although I haven't been able to fully check that out. But, if there are no body piercings and no tattoos, then I would certainly start wondering if she is actually not from the UK.'

Selitto stared at Dench. 'So, let me get this straight. You're saying not only that identification is going to be extremely difficult but that we may also have the body of a girl who is not even British?'

'That's about the sum total of it,' replied Dench. 'And I'll also wager my next month's salary on the fact that she was dressed by someone else before she was placed here. Her vest and knickers seem to be on back to front. She's also wearing a pair of trousers with a zip fastener at the side. This will normally be on the left but, in her case, it's on the right which means that the garment is back to front and out of shape.'

They had been picking their way across the equipment laid out on the ground around the girl, and they now exited the tent. Selitto thought for a moment. 'So, it's possible that she was killed and then either kept in water or in a wet place. She may or may not have been wearing clothes but, if she was naked when she was killed, then at some point later she has been dressed and transported either a short distance or very carefully to here before she was set up as a scarecrow.'

'Yeah! That probably is what I'm saying,' Dench replied. 'It's the connection with water that's just puzzling me at the moment.'

Selitto turned his gaze away from Dench and looked over to the house which stood in splendid isolation just across from the allotments. 'I wonder!' he said under his breath.

'Sorry, did you say something?' enquired Dench following Selitto's gaze.

'I was just thinking,' he replied. 'Your lot will have to take a look at that house because, if I'm not mistaken, this girl is connected with what's been going on there. And, from what I've seen, I may well be able to pinpoint the connection with water. To carry a girl of her size and weight from that house to here would present little problem for a muscle-bound enforcer or, indeed, any fit and strong individual.'

'Sounds interesting! When do we get started?' asked Dench, smiling.

33

Saturday 22 July

Hunter had thought of taking the scenic route back to Tonbridge but, in the end, she doubled back to Bewley Lane before turning left onto the Ightham Road, following the road through the Fairlawn Estate, across Shipbourne Common and eventually into the north of Tonbridge past Towngate Wood Park and Whistler Road. The closer she got to the town centre, the more of the Saturday afternoon traffic she encountered so it was pretty slow-going as she passed the Dry Hill Park roundabout and made her way down the Shipbourne Road to the lights by The George & Dragon. She inched past the pub as she waited for the lights to change and noticed that the door to the bar was open. 'That's a first', she thought. 'Don't think I've ever seen that pub open!' Finally, she got through on a green light and then slowly progressed past the front of Tonbridge School. Once through another set of lights at Bordyke, she picked up a bit of speed but then slowed down when she reached the bridge over the River Medway, in the shadow of the impressive Tonbridge Castle. Finally, she was through the High Street, up past Tonbridge railway station and then hung a left into the car park under the police station.

She just about had time for a quick toilet stop on the way up to the Operations Room and then, armed with a cold bottle of sparkling water and a notepad, she presented herself at the door of Iverson's office.

DCI Alan Iversen was standing by the window, looking down at the endless stream of traffic as it wound its way around the roundabout immediately below him. He was dressed casually but smartly in dark brown slacks and a salmon pink long-sleeved shirt with sleeves folded up so they sat just under his elbows. A light brown jacket hung from the coat-hanger on the back of his office door. It was difficult to know if he was just back from a lunchtime function or he was just on his way out to an evening function. Hunter took the seat that was directly in front of the desk, placing her notepad and bottle of water on the desk.

'Never ceases to amaze me the number of people this town attracts on a Saturday afternoon,' Iversen commented as he turned back from the window. 'All these people crammed into the town and we ain't got the numbers to afford them a completely safe shopping experience!'

Hunter watched Iversen as he took a slug of water from a bottle on his desk. She knew that he had made his way up through the ranks right from uniform, and that he was well respected in the Kent Force as a safe pair of hands, a copper's copper as she had heard him described. Although Hunter occasionally found his attention to detail unbearable, she always listened to what he had to say and liked the freedom he gave her to just get on with things. But, when he called her to account, she knew that she had to be meticulously prepared and completely honest with him.

Iversen was now sitting across the desk from her. 'So, Sarah,' he began, 'how's your MisPer case going? I hear on the QT that there's been some activity and things have moved on since we last spoke.'

Hunter took a couple of seconds to compose her reply. 'Well, it has and it hasn't, sir,' she began. Iversen frowned. 'What I mean is that we haven't actually progressed much with find-ing the missing person or, in fact, determining if it is actually a genuine MisPer at all. But we have found the body of a young girl.'

Iversen raised an eyebrow. 'Was this out at Sheet Hill?' Hunter nodded. 'On an allotment or some other public place?' Hunter nodded again.

'The body of a young girl had been placed on an allot-ment plot and made to look like a scarecrow,' Hunter went on. 'Some poor plot holder found it first thing this morning and almost had a seizure. The body will be in the mortuary later this evening. Seems there's no clue as to who she is and nothing to ID her until we put the DNA and prints through the system. We may get a bit more info tomorrow when old man Partington opens her up but, for now, pretty much all we know is that she is probably around seventeen years old and that cause of death would appear to be drowning.'

Iversen frowned again. 'Drowning?' It was a question which might also have been a statement. 'Has the allotment got a lake?'

'Not as far as we are aware,' Hunter replied, 'although there are any number of water butts so she could have been dunked in one of them. Problem with that theory is that her whole body shows signs of having been totally immersed in water for some time so it is doubtful that anyone could have squeezed her into one of the butts. So, we think that she was drowned elsewhere and brought to the allotment site.'

'Hmmm! Any idea of time of death or are we waiting for Partington to do his stuff?' Iversen enquired.

'Crime Scene Manager reckons within the last twenty-four

hours but that's pretty broad brush,' Hunter replied.

'Who've you got over there from the CSI lot?' Iversen asked.

'Beth Dench is leading the team,' Hunter replied. 'She's good – very thorough. Leads the team well. They're all very motivated which is a good sign.'

'Good!' Iversen sat back in his chair. 'I was keen that she should come to Kent for her secondment from the Home Office so I am very pleased to hear that she is getting on well. Good! So how are we going to find out where this poor girl was drowned?'

'Well, sir,' Hunter began, 'there's a huge house overlooking the allotments. We think it's known as The Garden House. DS Selitto thought that it appeared to be empty so took a look around the outside of it. He soon discovered that the entrance to the property is on the other side of the building so any comings and goings could not be viewed from the allotments. Although you get to the allotments along a track leading from Bourne Lane, the back of the house is accessed via a lengthy track leading from Sheet Hill. Anyway, DS Selitto discovered that the main entrance door was open so he went into the house to see what was going on.'

'Was that wise? Not telling anyone where he was or calling for back-up?' Iversen was displaying his cautious approach.

'Ted can be a bit impulsive at times,' Hunter agreed, 'but, in this instance, he quickly concluded that the house was empty so I think he probably made the right call.'

'Okay!' Iversen didn't seem too convinced but invited Hunter to carry on.

'After I had spent time with the CSI team, I went over to join Ted in the house,' Hunter began. 'What we appear to have uncovered is a very up-market gentlemen's club, a house of pleasure, a bordello, or perhaps simply a plain old-fashioned brothel – I don't know what it would be described as. But it's got the best equipped BDSM dungeon you are ever likely to see, and all the guest rooms are decorated and equipped to a very high standard. Someone has spent a small fortune putting it all together – and now it's deserted. But, and this is the interesting thing, it doesn't look as if its occupants went willingly. There is quite a lot of destruction inside the house, and there is the overpowering smell of cleaning fluids and sanitisers.'

'Hmmm!' Iversen was scribbling a note to himself on his pad. 'Remind me what BDSM stands for – bondage, what and sado-masochism?'

Hunter gave him a sideways glance. 'Well, I think the D can stand for either discipline or dominance as in dominance and submission but it's not something about which I am hugely knowledgeable, sir!' she replied with a wry smile and emphasising the word 'sir'.

Iversen scribbled himself another note and then sat back. 'Christ, Sarah!' he exclaimed. 'What on earth have you uncovered this time?' He was shaking his head, looking down at his notes.

'What I really need to do is put the girl inside the house so that we then have a connection between the two,' Hunter surmised. 'If we can get that connection, then we might find out where she was killed which would be a start. But I have to say that the discovery of a house of sin deep in the Kent countryside is a bit of a puzzle and begs the question as to whether there are any more?'

Iversen was looking idly at his pad, shaking his head. 'Please don't say that, Sarah! We haven't got the manpower to be chasing down organised crime on that sort of scale. Let's just see where this one leads us. If you can put the girl inside the house, and you can establish how she came to be drowned, then we may have a clearer picture of what we are up against here.'

'Agreed, sir,' Hunter replied.

'And the original MisPer?' asked Iversen. 'What's going on with that?'

Hunter flipped her mind back to Meadowlands and what had been going on there. 'DS Selitto and I were back at Meadowlands yesterday to have a look around again. We also met up with DS Kendall who has discovered that the BMW parked there by the MisPer was lifted from somewhere in Hampshire. We're waiting for the exact location to be advised. Otherwise, we are awaiting a full briefing from the CSI team on Monday. At present, if the MisPer is actually this chap Vashlili then we have no idea who he is, where he is, where he came from or even if he's still alive. So, the short answer to your original question is that we are no further forward at this point in time.'

Hunter paused while Iversen appeared to consider the update she had just given him. She, therefore, decided that this was the best moment to ask the sixty-four-thousand-dollar question. 'So, going back to the scarecrow girl case, do we have the go-ahead to set up an official murder investigation team?'

'Looks like I'll have to sanction a small Major Incident Team but we really haven't got the resources,' Iversen was saying as Hunter ran through in her mind the numbers she would need. 'We could probably raid the trainees' room and get a couple from there. I've also heard that there's an officer from Traffic who's desperate to move into CID – done all the exams and is ready to fly so this could be her first opportunity. Not sure where else I can trawl for support but those three should at least get you started.'

'No, that's fine, sir!' Hunter was genuinely happy with the resources he was offering. She had never backed away from taking trainees because she had always found them to be keen and committed. It was only once they got older and had developed chips on shoulders that they became a problem. At least the officer from Traffic would have experience of how things worked in Kent Police and should be keen to impress.

'OK, I'll get that authorised,' Iversen said, starting to get up from his chair. However, he then seemed to have second thoughts and sat down again. 'And, before you go, a progress report on the Hardwicks.'

Hunter had been ready for this. 'DS Selitto and I are getting in at around 07.00 a.m. every day and trying to give at least three hours to the case, sir. I wouldn't say that we have quite broken the back of it but we're getting there. We should be able to maintain this level of commitment even while involved in the scarecrow girl murder so I don't see too much of a problem.'

'OK! But I want to be kept up to date,' Iversen said, this time rising fully from his chair. 'Let's meet again for a full debrief on Monday at 5.00 p.m.' He put his pad back into the desk drawer, locked the desk and then locked the filing cabinet behind him. 'In the meantime, you must let me know the minute anything changes or you make any significant discoveries. I can sense that those looking down on us from on high will be taking an interest in this case.' He collected his jacket from the hanger on the back of the door and slung it over his shoulder.

'And one more thing, Sarah. The press. Have we got any involvement from them yet?' Iversen was always highly critical of journalists, believing them to be far from helpful in the battle to fight crime, but he also had to acknowledge that, if handled astutely, they could also help in that battle. There was a fine balance to be had.

'Nothing so far,' Hunter replied. 'The story of scarecrow girl is probably not going to get out just yet and, with tomorrow being Sunday, I doubt anyone will be standing outside the morgue trying to find out what's going on!'

'Yes, point taken,' agreed Iversen, 'but if you do start to get hounded, make sure you contact that Margot woman at HQ. You know, the one that fronts all the press briefings. She's supposed to be shit hot at dealing with arrogant journos so, rather than you wasting your precious time, get her to sort them out.'

'Will do, sir,' Hunter gathered up her notepad and bottle of water.

'Right, better go,' Iversen said looking at his watch. 'Got tickets to a concert at Great Comp this evening. Part of the Great Comp Music Festival. Ever heard of it?' Hunter shook her head. 'Quite fun really. You take your own picnic and sit in the garden before moving into the old barn for the concert. They normally have great musicians there and it's a really intimate setting. You should try it one day.' Hunter nodded and smiled.

Iversen held the door open for her. 'Right! I'll see you here at 5.00 p.m. on Monday. Your team will report for duty at around 07.30 a.m. tomorrow morning! Good night!' He turned towards the stairs and she heard him clattering down the stairwell, the noise of his footsteps gradually fading as he made his way to the car park.

Hunter turned and made her way back to the Operations Room. There was an array of post-it notes stuck to the screen of the workstation she had been working at earlier in the day. She scanned them but none looked urgent. She suddenly felt very weary. It had been a long day and tomorrow was shaping up to be the same. A nice pint of cold Guinness and an early night seemed far more appealing than dealing with any of the post-it notes so she left the room and returned down the stairs to the basement. She remembered that her phone had vibrated in her pocket towards the end of her meeting with Iversen. She now looked at the screen and saw a text message from Selitto that he was just leaving the allotment and heading for The White Rock at Underriver. Smiling, she got into her car and drove off into the Kent countryside.

34

Saturday 22 July

Selitto started his car and negotiated the pot holes that sprinkled the poorly maintained track linking the allotments with the outside world. When he eventually got to Bourne Lane, he sat for a moment trying to remember how to get to The White Rock from here. His mind was still processing all the information Beth Dench had provided about the young girl who had been so cruelly propped up as a scarecrow on the allotment site. The revelation that she might have spent time immersed in water, and the proposition that she had been dressed post mortem were intriguing. The possibility that she was not from the UK cast a long shadow over his investigation as he knew just how difficult it could be to get an identification for the girl, particularly if (as he privately suspected) she had entered the country illegally.

He checked both ways and turned right taking the road towards the village of Plaxtol. Still deep in thought, he instinctively turned right when he got to Plaxtol Parish Church and then took a left onto the Ightham Road. He passed The Chaser on Shipbourne Common before bearing right onto the Hildenborough Road. The road got progressively narrower with a few twists and turns. The pot holes were difficult to see in the shadows cast by the trees and Selitto shouted frequent oaths in the general direction of Kent County Council who were responsible for the state of the roads, although he wondered if anyone at the Council offices really cared – they'd certainly never driven their own cars down this track!

Eventually, he came to the turning onto Carters Hill and, after passing Underriver Church and the village hall, The White Rock crept into view on his right. He came to a halt next to Hunter's car which was parked at such an angle that it looked as if it had just landed from outer space.

The sun still had some warmth in it, and he spotted Hunter sitting in a shaft of sunlight at a table in the garden. She made hand signals at him which basically meant that she hadn't got anything for him and could he get her a half. Selitto knew these signals well.

Inside, the pub was busy with the usual gang of early evening drinkers crowding round the bar. Selitto made his way to one end of the bar and ordered a half of Guinness and a foaming pint of White Rock bitter from the Westerham Brewery. He also asked for a bag of Salt & Vinegar crisps which Hunter always euphemistically referred to as 'dinner'. Whilst the drinks were being poured, he looked round to see if he recognised anyone. Old habits die hard in the force, he thought. He paid up and went out into the warm evening air.

Sliding on to the bench opposite Hunter, Selitto clinked glasses with her half-empty pint and took a good gulp of the local brew. 'Good crowd in this evening,' he observed. 'You been here long?'

'Not too long. Managed to get out fairly unscathed. The old man either had a picnic or concert to go to – I wasn't quite sure which!' Hunter deftly added the half-pint of Guinness to her pint glass and tore open the bag of crisps. 'He's still pretty agitated about the fact that we haven't completed the car ring-ing paperwork yet but has at least assigned the scarecrow girl as a case for MIT and has told us to get on with it.'

Selitto didn't know much about Detective Inspector Alan Iversen apart from the fact he was in his early fifties, and was a stalwart of the Kent force. There wasn't much about crime in Kent that Iversen didn't know, and he was generally well respected. Selitto knew that Hunter occasionally got frustrated with Iversen's constant 'need to know' attitude but he felt that this was more borne out of a general frustration amongst her colleagues about the amount of paperwork required these days in order to conclude the most basic of criminal cases. She was always banging on about this whenever Iversen started questioning her about why investigations were taking so long to complete. And, although they now had the car ringers locked up having been refused bail, Hunter seemed to have been seduced by the challenge of finding Vashlili and the killer of the little girl at the allotment. Were they in some way connected? This type of case never failed to hold a fascination for both Hunter and Selitto.

'How're Beth and the boys getting on at the allotment?' Hunter enquired. 'Hopefully, they won't be too late tonight.'

'No, they're probably packing up as we speak,' Selitto replied, taking another draught of the local brew. 'Preliminary findings are that the girl had probably been lying in water for some time before she made it to the allotment. She was also dressed by someone without much finesse as her vest, knickers and trousers were on back to front. Setting her up as a scarecrow seems to be unexplained or unexplainable as all it has done is draw our attention to the house. I just can't see the point. Is it some sort of machismo thing? You know, here I am – free to wander in and murder whoever I want to right under your noses! But you can't catch me! Or was someone really trying to give us a clue?'

'Hmm. Hadn't thought of it quite like that,' said Hunter, wiping a Guinness moustache off her top lip. 'I particularly hadn't thought that it might be someone giving us a clue. That really is an off-the-wall thought.'

They sat in silence for a while, Selitto watching some wispy white clouds turn crimson in the evening sun, Hunter picking at her nails.

'If the girl had been in the house,' Hunter mused, 'she surely wasn't the only person there, so where's everyone else? And you're right, why would they leave her behind? Leaving her to rot in the house would make more sense, particularly if she was submerged in water like in a bath…' Hunter trailed off, concentrating instead on plucking a sliver of skin from the cuticle area of one of her fingernails.

'The bath!' Selitto almost whispered the word. 'That dungeon needs a thorough going over from the CSI boys. Someone's obviously done a first-class job of cleaning up whatever went on in that room, but I'm absolutely sure that I could see some flecks of blood on the legs of the bath. And we need to find the recording from that camera. It must be somewhere in the office.'

Hunter had now finished with her nails and was looking at Selitto. 'Did you find any more evidence of CCTV? Only having one room on camera seems a bit light if this was the sort of up-market knocking shop we're now thinking it was.' Hunter took a slurp of her drink, getting another Guinness moustache which she wiped away with the back of her hand.

'Well, I didn't inspect all the light fittings,' said Selitto somewhat defensively, 'and God knows what might lie behind all the mirrors in the bedrooms. I didn't really have time to take a look around outside either. Anyway, let's see what Beth and the boys come up with.'

Selitto, dared to pinch a crisp from under Hunter's stern gaze, and got a sharp rap on the back of the hand for his troubles.

'So, if the old man's sanctioned a small MIT to take on this case,' Selitto reasoned, 'have we any idea who might be available given our overall lack of resources?'

'No doubt it'll be a small unit to start with,' she replied. 'Iversen was talking about a couple of trainees plus someone from Traffic who's just transferred into CID. I think we only have two trainees at Tonbridge anyway so we'll no doubt get them. Elaine Jennings and Stuart Crosby if I recall. Good reports from what I've been hearing. I think the incoming from Traffic is Pennant – can't remember her first name.'

'Think it's Carolyn,' Selitto offered.

'Yes, that's it – Carolyn Pennant,' Hunter confirmed as the name suddenly came to her. 'Yes, she has come to us from Traffic and I got a bit of gen on the QT that they were quite glad to get shot of her. Bit of a fiery one if my information is correct. Also, got a bit of a smell under her nose or something like that. I'd probably like to see her under a bit of pressure early on so perhaps you should take her with you to the PM tomorrow – might knock her down a peg or two. Probably quite capable but I would hate to think that we'd been sold a pup by Traffic!'

'OK, I'll take her with me and see what she's made of.' Selitto just hoped that she wasn't going to be someone who spent the whole PM throwing up in the corner. 'We've got the opportunity of giving Jennings and Crosby a good grounding in CID, and these two cases should give them something to get their teeth into. Perhaps put Elaine on to Vashlili and let Stuart see what he can make of the house of horrors at the allotment. Talking of which, did you persuade Beth to put in a Sunday for us?'

'Out of the kindness of her heart, she said, and I owe her one!' Hunter smiled. 'Then she let on that her sister had invited her round for lunch which meant that she would have had to put up with the demands of three boys under five! So, she was more than happy to get the gig at the house by the allotment instead. Apparently, Donny's already going to the PM to collect the clothing so he'll pick up Jimbo on his way through to the house. I've asked the Desk Sergeant to tell the others to get to Pembury Road by 08.00 a.m. and, even if there's nothing for them to do, they can familiarise themselves with the Procedures Manual.'

Hunter drained the last vestiges of the Guinness and screwed up the empty crisp packet before stuffing it into the glass. 'That you off, then?' Selitto enquired.

'I think so,' Hunter replied, searching in her handbag for car keys. 'I think I'll stop off and see Pippa on the way home – see what she's been up to and if she needs anything. Might get an Indian from Cinnamon if she hasn't already eaten.'

Selitto would never let it show, but he did have feelings for Sarah Hunter although they were purely from a platonic standpoint. He did, however, harbour an almost overwhelming desire to look after her, to protect her. He was never quite sure who the mysterious Pippa was, and Hunter very rarely mentioned her. Selitto had certainly never met her. All that he had managed to find out over the two years they had been working together was that Pippa lived on her own. He also thought that she might have a disability as Hunter had once had to excuse herself from a meeting in order to take Pippa to an assessment at a hospital. He didn't think that she saw that much of Pippa, but he always felt a bit of a twinge in the pit of his stomach when he heard that Hunter was going to see her. Was that a jealousy thing? Anyway, this evening was one of those occasions.

'Yep! A takeaway will probably do for me as well,' said Selitto, putting a brave face on things as he contemplated an evening slumped in front of the TV. 'Might try that Malaysian place in Riverhead. A nice plate of something in chilli and black bean sauce with ginger should do the trick!'

'Yuck!' Hunter snorted, getting up from the table. 'So, you'll stop by the station in the morning and collect Pennant, and I'll see you when you get back from the PM?' Selitto nodded.

She untangled herself from the bench table. 'You doing the honours?' she asked, pointing to the empty glasses. Selitto picked up the empties, wished Hunter a cheery goodnight, and made his way back to the bar.

35
Sunday 23 July

'Come in! Come in! Don't be shy!' Norman Partington's voice boomed across the cutting room as Selitto crept through the door from the scrubs room.

They were in the mortuary at Tunbridge Wells which mainly carried out forensic post mortems, and was also a teaching centre which accounted for the raised circular viewing gallery that stretched around the periphery of the lab. There were three stainless steel autopsy tables lined up across the lab, each with a flexible hose snaking away to a drainage channel which was out of sight of the visitors. There was also a dissection table off to the left. Harsh overhead lighting reflected off stainless steel mortuary washing units which were arranged along one wall comprising a combination sink, an embalming sink and a wash hand basin. Various dispensers hung from the wall containing an array of liquids and thicker cleansing substances. A couple of mortuary trollies were parked against another wall next to a small mortuary chamber with a huge lock keeping its contents safe from any unauthorised prying eyes.

Selitto had been up early this Sunday morning so that he could drop into the Pembury Road station to check on the arrival of their young, inexperienced Murder Investigation Team. The two trainee detective constables were already at their desks although with little to do at the moment. Selitto also discovered that DC Carolyn Pennant had already taken herself off to the mortuary to meet up with Donny Campbell so that she could be there when the CSI officer and the Pathologist bagged up the clothing.

Selitto quickly explained to DC Elaine Jennings and DC Stuart Crosby that the investigation was in its very early stages but that DI Hunter would soon be in to give them both a fuller briefing. Both were young, bright-eyed and enthusiastic, and he was glad to have them on the team. Making sure that they had his contact details, he had then headed off to Tunbridge Wells but had got caught up in traffic attending a boot fair.

He had finally arrived at the mortuary and now, kitted out in his surgical green gown, hairnet, mask, gloves and booties, Selitto waddled over to where Partington was standing. He stole a glance at the tiny figure lying on the table in front of him. Under the harsh lights, she appeared to have the sheen of one of the waxworks from Madam Tussauds. Pale as pale can be.

He spotted DC Pennant and the CSI Officer standing beside one of the trollies where they were looking through the contents of two paper evidence bags. So, he'd obviously missed the start of proceedings. Terrific!

'Morning Ted,' Partington came towards Selitto with his hand outstretched for a handshake. 'Sorry but I had to start a bit earlier than the advertised time. I've got a golf match this afternoon over at Knole Park and they've pulled the tee time forward by an hour so that's rather thrown my plans for the day. Hope you don't mind and, in any case, you haven't missed much – just dealt with the bloods and saliva, and the alcohol and drugs testing. Your two over there have got the clothing all bagged up so I think we are pretty much ready for the main event.' And, with that, he reached up to where a microphone was suspended across the table and pulled it down towards him.

As Partington started talking into the microphone, setting

the scene for the autopsy, introducing the cast around him, Selitto moved across to where DC Pennant and CSI Campbell were deep in whispered conversation.

'Morning you two,' he whispered, 'have I missed anything?'

'Morning, sarge,' DC Pennant replied. 'The main activity has been the removal of the clothing which we have now bagged and labelled. As I think you know, some of the clothing was on back to front, and we can now confirm that her vest, panties and trousers had been incorrectly put on. We also found that her bra had simply been fastened at the back; the shoulder straps were hanging loose at the sides. Anyway, it all seems to point to the fact that she was dressed by someone else.'

'You OK with that, Donny?' asked Selitto turning towards the Crime Scenes man.

'Yep, total agreement with that,' replied Campbell. 'I would even go as far as to venture that she was dressed after death as, whoever put the clothes on, simply didn't care how they looked because he or she was dressing a lifeless body. But that will be in my report'

Selitto turned back to where Partington was leaning over the body, pushing and prodding unresponsive flesh and, all the time, giving a running commentary for the microphone hanging above his head. There was something particularly clinical about the sight of a naked body bathed in harsh LED light lying on what resembled a stainless-steel altar, all dignity drained away like the water constantly sluicing along the gutters built into the floor of the lab.

Partington was continuing with his examination so Selitto turned back to the DC and the CSI man. 'Any other worthwhile clues from yesterday, Donny?' he asked.

'Not much more than you already know,' Campbell replied. 'We were frustrated not to find more clues on the allotment plot but it looked like whoever set her up as a scarecrow used a rake to obliterate all traces of their footprints. There was an old rake in Mr Rawlings' shed which had some fresh earth attached to it. As he doesn't keep the shed locked, we have to assume that this was the rake used. But it was impossible to get any prints from it as it had probably been wiped clean by the gloves used by the scarecrow maker. We couldn't get anything from the grass paths and none of the other plots looked to have been touched.'

'When are you due at the house?' Selitto asked.

'Leaving at about 11.00 a.m. if Beth's got all the paperwork done by then,' he replied. 'That's why I'd quite like to get away now if that's OK with you.'

'No problem for me,' said Selitto. 'What about you, Carolyn? Did you two come here together?'

'Yes, we did,' Pennant asserted. 'But I'm happy to stay if you need me here, sir. I've never attended a post mortem before so it would be a useful learning experience.'

Selitto looked at her, one eyebrow raised to the heavens. 'Yeah! It'll certainly be an experience!' he muttered. 'OK, I think it would be good for you to stay and watch what goes on here so I'll take you back to Tonbridge later.' Donny Campbell then took his leave of them with a wave in the direction of the Pathologist who was still talking away into his microphone.

A few minutes after Campbell had left, Partington suddenly looked up and summoned them over to the table. Close up, the girl looked even more frail than she had when Selitto had last seen her on the allotment. Her eyes still bulged out of their sockets and her skin was deathly white. Her small breasts lay flat against her chest, a triangle of fair pubic hair caressed the lowest part of her torso and brushed the tops of two thin legs where the skin had become translucent in death.

'Right!', Partington began. 'We have a white female aged around seventeen or eighteen. I'll have a better idea of age once I have conducted an internal examination. She's one metre fifty-seven centimetres tall – that's five foot two inches in old money, Ted!' He looked over towards Selitto, a broad grin on his face. 'And, as you can see, she is of slim build. If we were allowed to go on supposition, I would say that she was probably malnourished but I have no concrete evidence of this. She has no external markings such as tattoos or scars from invasive surgery and no piercings apart from ear piercings.'

Partington then beckoned them closer. Turning the girl's head to one side, he pointed to the back of the cranium and carefully parted the fair hair to reveal what looked like an indentation of the skull and an ugly contusion. 'She's clearly suffered some sort of blunt trauma injury here which is most likely to have occurred if she had been hit from behind or had fallen backwards onto something with an edge. But that is not what killed her.'

He straightened the girl's head, and looked across the body at the two detectives. 'Unless I'm very much mistaken, I think that the cause of death was drowning! I'm pretty sure that when we open her up, we are going to find that her lungs are full of water.'

Selitto nodded. 'The CSI team said that her body seemed to be damp and clammy, as if it had been submerged in water for a long period of time. Would the force of the blunt trauma have rendered her unconscious?' he asked.

'What, you mean could she have been knocked unconscious and then fallen into, say, a swimming pool and drowned?' Partington sought clarification of the question.

'Yes, that sort of thing,' said Selitto looking down at the body.

'That could be a scenario, but probably not in this case,' the Pathologist replied. 'I'm not certain that the force of the blunt trauma caused her to lose consciousness. It is more likely that she suffered the blunt trauma before entering the water and was then held under water until she drowned. Although I can find no evidence of any bruising which you would normally expect to see in a drowning of that nature. And, if the body had remained in the water for a long time before it was pulled out and dressed, that would probably explain why there were no superficial injuries synonymous with the body being manhandled.'

Selitto turned to Pennant who was staring agog at the body on the slab. 'Anything from you, Carolyn?'

'No, sir. Just trying to get my head around the probable sequence of events,' she replied sheepishly, unable to take her eyes off the body.

Partington turned and walked off to a bench in the corner which was bristling with medical implements of all shapes and sizes. Talking over his shoulder, he said 'I'll let Carolyn off lightly on her first PM by saving the use of the Stryker saw until after you've both gone! But I would like you both to stay for the internal examination as I have a feeling in my water that we might find something which may help your investigations.'

The detectives looked at each other, both frowning. But they turned their attention back to the table as the pathologist returned with a tray of implements. He snapped on a fresh pair of surgical gloves and gently eased the girl's young legs apart. Pennant gave an involuntary shudder, her squeamishness showing in her deepening red face. Selitto tried to look calm but his guts were churning inside him.

Partington selected a speculum and gently inserted it into the young girl's vagina. He picked up a small torch from the tray and shone the beam into the opening he had created. Peering through thick horn-rimmed glasses, he reached for another implement. 'I'm now inserting a tenaculum which will allow me to gently hold the cervix and uterus steady so that I can get a better view of the uterus.'

Everyone seemed to be holding their breath as Partington gently manipulated the implements he had at his disposal. Eventually, he removed the tenaculum and picked up what Selitto thought looked like a giant pair of forceps. He carefully inserted these through the speculum and, after a bit of what appeared to be trial-and-error, he finally pulled the forceps out with something attached to them.

'Well! Well! Well!' the pathologist exclaimed. 'For the uninitiated, this is an intrauterine device otherwise known as an IUD. These are basically contraceptive devices which were invented about a hundred years ago by a German physician. They are reasonably simple to insert although this one was obviously inserted by an amateur and the poor girl would have suffered a great deal of pain as a result. Let me just get it cleaned up then I can tell you more about it.'

Partington shuffled off to the sink area and subjected the device to a jet of warm water. The detectives exchanged glances, each feeling embarrassment at being present at such an intimate examination even though the girl was no longer alive. Meanwhile, Partington returned to the table having put the IUD into a stainless-steel dish.

'Right, let's have a close look at this.' He pulled out a drawer under the table and extracted a large magnifying glass. Holding the IUD with the forceps and looking at it through the glass, Partington turned it slowly making sure that he hadn't missed anything. Finally, he returned the device to the dish and put the forceps on the table next to the girl's body.

'Okay,' he said removing his glasses. 'This might be a crucial bit of evidence for you. The IUD is not one that is manufactured in the UK and, indeed, you would very rarely see it being used in UK clinics. It is made by a company called Venus which is located in Bulgaria. So, the chances are that this girl is Bulgarian and that the device was inserted by an amateur in the back streets of Sofia.'

Selitto looked across at the girl. DC Pennant stared at the floor, her faced flushed red.

'I will give more detail in my report,' Partington continued, 'but, from what I have observed in retrieving the IUD, the girl has been very sexually active in the recent past which would lead me to believe that it is more than likely that she has been involved in the sex trade. And, with the Bulgarian connection and the fact that someone has gone to a great deal of trouble to avoid her being identified, she may well have been illegally trafficked into the UK. But that's something for you to find out, Detective Sergeant.'

He shuffled off back to the sink area. 'Oh, by the way,' he continued, talking over his shoulder, 'I should think that time of death was around 10.00 p.m. on Friday. But it'll all be in my report. Now, away with you unless you really are keen to see what we can get up to with a Stryker saw!'

Selitto finally found his voice. 'No thanks, Norman. We'll be going! Many thanks for the heads up on what we're looking at here, and I'll look forward to receiving your report as soon as.'

'OK, my boy,' replied Partington, snapping on yet another new pair of gloves. 'And remember me to the lovely Sarah. Tell her I'm missing her. She never seems to get down here to see me anymore!'

'Will do!' Selitto said as he and Pennant exited the lab to the safety of the scrubs room. They were just getting out of their gowns when the whine of the Stryker saw split the air. 'Let's get the hell out of here!' Selitto urged as they dropped their protective clothing into a clinical waste bin. Taking a healthy squirt from the container of hand sanitiser which was screwed to the wall near the waste bin, they bolted for the door.

36

Sunday 23 July

Back at the Pembury Road, Hunter called a meeting in the newly-acquired Major Incident Room. The two young DCs had had a busy morning commandeering white boards and other items of furniture to make the room more functional. DC Stuart Crosby had done sterling work in hooking up four computers to the server so they had access to internet and email, and DC Elaine Jennings had shown her skills as a telephone engineer by hooking up all the phones to the outside world. She had also procured a bundle of stationery and a couple of desktop printers. It was a start, and Hunter showed her appreciation by thanking the two DCs at the outset of the meeting.

Hunter then turned to address Selitto's newly-acquired acolyte who stood rather awkwardly beside him. 'And how did we get on at the PM, DC Pennant?'

'It was a bit of an eye opener, ma'am,' Pennant replied. 'I can't say that I enjoyed it and I was relieved that we left before the pathologist got to work with his Stryker saw. But it gave me a good insight into how much we can learn from a PM examination – I suppose I'd never really thought about it before. I need to be a bit more detached. When I was standing there next to this poor little girl who had been stripped of all her dignity, I just felt very uncomfortable so I need to toughen up a bit.'

'You'll never get fully comfortable at a PM,' Hunter assured her. 'In fact, it just gets more and more difficult trying to understand the depths to which human beings will stoop to inflict pain and suffering on fellow human beings. In this job, you will see things that you wouldn't want to see in your own worst nightmares.' Hunter caught Pennant's eye, and a frisson of understanding passed between them.

'Good!' Hunter clapped her hands together. 'Now let's see what else is going on. Ted, can you just get us up to speed on Vashlili.'

For the next five minutes, Selitto filled the team in on the disappearance of Vashlili from Meadowlands and the suspicion they had that he may have been murdered on the premises and the body disposed of. He described the grounds of the hotel with its two lakes, and referred to the information they had found in the room safe. This was now with DS Grace Kendall for analysis, and he was hoping for an update tomorrow.

'At the moment, we don't think that the disappearance of Vashlili is linked to the death of the girl at the allotment,' Hunter interjected, 'but we should probably keep an open mind on this. Anyway, Elaine, I'd like you to get involved with the Vashlili case so you'll need to get up to speed with Grace when she's back tomorrow, and spend time looking through the CSI report. Ted, are we still looking to do an underwater search of the big lake?'

Selitto was perched on the corner of one of the desks, arms folded. 'Given that the row boat was sunk in suspicious circumstances, and that some other potential evidence may have been removed after we started looking around, I think that we should get the lake searched. But that's easier said than done! I've been on to the Marine Unit and have been told that our request will not be at the top of their list for some days yet.'

'Blimey!' exclaimed Hunter. 'How many other lakes in Kent

can they possibly be searching for fuck's sake!'

'Don't know, boss, but it's probably something to do with the fabled budget cuts!' replied Selitto, making a note in his notebook. 'I think they've also got a problem dealing with all the little boats full of illegals that keep peppering the shores around Kent. But I'll have another go tomorrow.'

Irritated by the very mention of the words "budget cuts", Hunter strode towards the white boards and, taking hold of a black marker pen, wrote "Meadowands" and "Vashlili" at the top of the left-hand board. Turning back to the team, she pointed the marker pen at DC Jennings. 'It will be your responsibility, Elaine, to keep this board updated throughout our enquiries so that we have an up-to-date and accurate analysis of progress at all times.' She now turned her head towards Selitto. 'Okay, Ted. What have we got for the scarecrow girl?'

Glancing at his notebook from time to time, Selitto gave the team an overview of the findings at the house and the likelihood that it had been used as some sort of upmarket brothel. In particular, his suspicions that there was evidence of blood spatter in the dungeon. He also mentioned the discovery of a CCTV camera in the dungeon and told them that the CSIs should be on site right now. Finally, he gave them the initial findings from the post mortem, and introduced the possibility that the scarecrow girl was more than likely to be an illegal who had been trafficked into the country from Bulgaria. They would, however, have to wait for old man Partington's report.

'So, Stuart,' Hunter said, returning to the white boards, 'this is your board.' Pointing to the two boards at the right-hand side, she wrote "Scarecrow Girl" at the top of the nearest one. 'It's absolutely vital that you keep this up to date throughout the investigation.'

She looked at her small team. Such a lot of inexperience, she thought, surveying their young and expectant faces. But it was her job to mould them into the professional detectives of the future. It always gave her a buzz when she was put in a position of influencing a young person's career.

'Carolyn,' Hunter continued, looking directly at DC Pennant, 'I want you to liaise closely with DS Selitto and support your two colleagues whenever they have a need. Our ultimate success will be as a team so I don't want anyone here to think of going for individual glory. We will all meet twice a day for briefing meetings at 7.30 a.m. and at 6.00 p.m. in order to share information. I want you all to understand the discipline needed in a successful Murder Investigation Team, how it operates, and how we can become an effective group in the shortest time possible. Hopefully, the envy of Kent CID!'

Selitto's phone buzzed on the desk beside him. He looked at the screen and then across the room at Hunter. 'I'd better take this, boss. It's Beth Dench.' Hunter nodded her agreement and Selitto left the room.

He paced up and down the corridor while Beth Dench gave him an update on her progress. At the end of the corridor, he stopped to look out of the window, watching cars weave their way through endless roadworks which seemed to permanently cover the entrance to Tonbridge railway station. To his left, he caught sight of the majestic steeple of St Stephens Church. He suddenly stiffened up. 'Say that again, Beth!'

He listened intently, the view out of the window becoming fuzzy and ill-defined as his mind cast back to the interior of the office in the house where the CCTV recorder had been found. Dench continued with her debriefing as Selitto turned away from the window and headed back to the MIR. 'Okay, Beth. I'll just brief the others and then I'll come straight over.' With that, he disconnected the call and pushed through the door and faced his fellow team members.

'Hey, guys, listen up!' He caught their attention, faces turned in expectation of further information. And Selitto wasn't going to disappoint.

'Just had a bit of a debrief from Beth Dench,' Selitto started. 'Seems it could be the proverbial house of treasures! The most important find so far is that there is far more CCTV than we first thought. One of the CSIs has found other cameras and he says that there are any number of covert listening devices located all over the house, many of them hidden in light fittings. They've carried out a detailed search of the dungeon and have found traces of blood but it's difficult to tell how recent they are. Some of the torture implements might be good for DNA but, again, it's difficult to tell how recently they've been used. It'll be interesting to see if we get any matches. Beth thinks that the rooms on the top floor were where the girls were kept and that the sliding metal gate was used to keep them locked away when they were not working. The phone I found there has already gone for analysis and the roll of banknotes is being screened for any evidence.'

'Well, it's a start.' Hunter sounded cautious but Selitto detected a tiny note of excitement in her voice. 'Okay, Ted you get over there and take Stuart with you. Let me know if there are any other significant developments. The rest of us will get on with organising things here and we'll all meet up again at 6.00 p.m. Off you go!'

Selitto looked across to where DC Crosby was studying the empty white boards. He caught Crosby's eye and flicked his head towards the door. Crosby immediately straightened up, marched across the room and out into the corridor in pursuit of Selitto. Hunter watched them go with just a hint of a smile.

DCs Pennant and Jennings remained in the room. 'Okay, you two,' Hunter addressed them. 'Your first bit of field work on this case! Get yourselves down to Meadowlands and get familiarised with the lie of the land there. Take a good look at the lake and try to get someone to show you the room Vashlili stayed in. Also, take a look at the escape route through the fire exit. See if Dangerfield, the manager, is there. I just want to keep a little pressure on him – I'd hate him to think that we had gone away!' The two DCs looked at each other with raised eyebrows as they slid off the desks they had been sitting on and gathered up their belongings. 'And see if you can get a pool car. Don't want all this mileage coming out of our expenses budget!' Hunter added as they turned towards the door.

37

Sunday 23 July

Selitto couldn't stand pool cars because of the lingering smell of fast food and body odour. In any event, getting a pool car out on a Sunday was a chore because none of the skeleton admin staff ever seemed to know what paperwork was required. His vehicle of choice on this Sunday morning was, therefore, his trusty Renault Megane. Crosby gingerly lowered himself into the passenger seat as Selitto pressed the start button and the engine sprang into life. Although the car was nearly ten years old, it had only done around 50,000 miles, and Selitto was still very happy with its performance.

Crosby still seemed to be in a state of shock that he was finally going to visit a crime scene which would be his responsibility. He'd be the person the team would rely on for information and up-to-the-minute analysis. On one hand, he was excited beyond belief. On the other, he was terrified in case he cocked up.

'You OK?' Selitto asked as they drove through winding country lanes in the early afternoon sun.

'Yeah, fine thanks,' Crosby replied. 'Just a little nervous, that's all.'

'Nothing to worry about!' exclaimed Selitto trying to brighten the young DC's mood. 'Got to start somewhere, and you might as well start at this house which has got plenty to offer us if my hunch is correct.'

Selitto didn't bother looking for the entrance via Sheet Hill and took the track up to the allotments from Bourne Lane instead. He parked facing the house and got out of the car. DC Crosby did the same once he had finished wrestling with the seat belt. The Megane plipped itself locked once they had moved away from the car, and Selitto led the way round to the side of the house.

They walked down the length of the fence until they came to the gate. This time it was well and truly locked with one of Sam-the-Lock's specials so he continued along the fence, occasionally ducking to avoid overhanging branches. The fence soon turned right so that he assumed that he was now walking along the back of the house. And then, all of a sudden, the wooden fence came to an end and they found themselves at the entrance to the driveway at the rear of the house, the track from Sheet Hill stretching out behind them. Blue and white 'Do Not Cross' police tape was strung across the entrance and fluttered in the breeze.

They walked up the drive, crunching over the gravel which echoed around the enclosed space. The CSI wagon stood by the back door. Selitto imagined that it had made a hell of a noise when it turned up earlier. The door was slightly ajar so he pushed on through with DC Crosby in hot pursuit.

Crime Scene Manager Beth Dench met them as soon as they entered the kitchen with a cheery 'Hello!' She gave each of them a Tyvek suit to put on, covers for their shoes, hats and nitrile gloves. She also offered them bottles of water and explained that they weren't yet able to use any of the kitchen facilities.

'Okay, Beth. Thanks.' Selitto introduced Stuart Crosby to Dench who shook him warmly by the hand. 'Stuart's going to be your liaison with the MIT on this one although I'll be overseeing him for the time being. Sarah is keen that he gets as much exposure to the workings of the Crime Scenes team as part of his development.'

'Good! Good!' replied Dench. 'Always good to have young, enthusiastic DCs on the team. I'll have to introduce you to my two!' She smiled across at Selitto as he struggled into the Tyvek suit and had even more trouble pulling the covers over his shoes. Once they were both fully kitted out to the satisfaction of the Crime Scenes Manager, she asked them where they would like to start.

Selitto thought for a moment. 'I'm really keen to see where you've got to with the CCTV. You mentioned that you've found more cameras and listening devices. Is all this information recorded somewhere?'

'Let's go up to the office,' Dench suggested, leading the way into the hall by the front door and then turning up the staircase. DC Crosby's eyes swivelled around on stalks, taking in every detail of his surroundings. Once in the office, Dench introduced Crosby to Jimbo Carrigan before joining him by the desk. She beckoned the two detectives to follow her.

'Right!' she said as they gathered beside her. 'For starters, this is no ordinary desk! Ted, you found the false back in the top drawer and managed to get the screen up in the bookcase. But all the other drawers were locked. We have now managed to open these and, in each drawer there is the same false plate which hides a set of red and green buttons and a toggle lever. But not all of them operate a screen. Jimbo will explain.'

'Yes,' Carrigan started, 'in most of the drawers, the green button on the left activates a panel in the bookcase and the green button on the right activates the camera so that whoever is sitting at the desk will be able to see what is going on around the premises. The green buttons in a couple of the drawers don't seem to operate panels in the bookcase so they may be something to do with the listening devices which I have found around the house. I think that I have accounted for most of the cameras although there is one outside which I haven't looked for yet. In general, the quality of the direct feed from the CCTV is poor. It lacks sharpness and is constantly pixelating – all the usual problems associated with modern surveillance equipment purchased online or through other cheap suppliers. Certainly not like those perfect images you always see in films and on the TV!'

Beth Dench took over. 'We've yet to discover where all these images are stored but it's more than likely to be onsite as it seems to be a fairly amateurish surveillance system. Jimbo also thinks that the cameras are motion-sensitive so the actual usage is quite limited which, in turn, means that the surveillance records will not need a huge storage space. But, until we can find the storage device, we cannot speculate any further.'

Dench turned as if to leave the room and then turned back. 'Oh, and you might like to know that we found traces of blood around the safe under the desk. Looks like someone wasn't keen to give up the combination of the locking device. Once we've finished dealing with that, we'll probably move the desk to make sure there are no other hidden treasures. You okay showing the DC round the rest of the house, Ted?'

'Yep, fine with that. Think we'll start off downstairs,' Selitto suggested. 'Are you finished in the dungeon?'

'Are we ever likely to be finished in there?' Dench asked mischievously. 'Have you any idea how many items there are in that room? Hundreds! Poor old Donny drew the short straw but he's doing a sterling job. Also broadening his knowledge of the BDSM world so who says that you can't learn anything new as a forensic scientist?'

'Okay, Beth, we'll remember you to him!' Selitto smiled at her as he left the room closely followed by Crosby. 'Next stop, the dungeon. This should open your eyes!'

They made their way down the stairs and soon found themselves stepping over the threshold into the dungeon. It was much brighter than when Selitto had been here before which was all down to the CSI lighting units which had been erected strategically around the room. He thought he detected an audible gasp as DC Crosby finally made it into the room.

'Hi Donny', Selitto said once he had located Campbell who was on his knees in a corner of the room. 'Like you to meet DC Stuart Crosby. Stuart, this is Donny Campbell – the other half of the Carrigan & Campbell Roadshow!' Campbell scrambled to his feet and the two young officers shook hands. Selitto went on. 'Stuart's just starting out with us as part of the Murder Investigation Team, and DI Hunter has assigned him to the scarecrow case so you'll probably be seeing quite a lot of each other. Anyway, got anything for us yet?'

Removing the face mask he had been wearing, Campbell looked around him. 'Well, as you can imagine, this is probably a Crime Scene Officer's worst nightmare! I've never seen so much gear – hanging on every wall, propped up on shelves around the room, and every drawer you open is crammed full of stuff. I mean, look at this rack over here.' The detectives moved over to one wall and studied a rack from which hung just about every conceivable type of leather collar you could imagine as well as leather cuffs in all different shapes and sizes.

'I've detected spots of blood on a number of these collars and there are many traces of dried skin which have obviously not been cleaned off after use. Some of the whips have traces of what seems to be flesh stuck between the strands but, again, it doesn't look very recent.

The CSI Officer pushed past the detectives and drew their attention to a shelf on the far wall. 'The range of equipment is quite staggering, and some of it defies belief!' He pointed to what looked to Selitto like a gas mask which had been placed on a mannequin's head. There were two large glass windows for the eyes, and a long tube protruding from the nose of the mask. It looked like some sort of elongated appendage, a proboscis, and gave the mask quite an alarming aura. 'For the life of me, I can't think what that could be used for!' exclaimed Campbell.

'And look down here,' he continued, pointing to what appeared to be an ordinary briefcase. He bent down and opened the case up. Inside was an array of medical instruments all housed in their own padded insets within the top and bottom of the case. 'Even I have rarely seen so many medical instruments gathered together in one place!'

He moved along the wall. 'Mind your head on that,' he warned as they passed what appeared to be a metal cage in the shape of a head which was suspended from the ceiling. Selitto shot Campbell an enquiring glance. 'Don't ask! Looks like some sort of head cage. Perhaps you have your head in it while you're being whipped,' he mused.

Continuing with their tour around the room, they found themselves staring at a wooden structure the likes of which none of them could recall ever having seen before. Four square wooden posts stood at each corner with what looked like a medical examination couch attached to crossbars between the posts about a metre off the floor. The posts themselves were over two metres high and two further crossbars were positioned near the top of the posts, and a single wooden bar was attached to these running the length of the couch underneath it. Four small steel mooring rings hung equidistantly along the bar and, at one end, a length of galvanised metal chain was draped between the posts. Further mooring rings had been attached to the wooden frame at either end of the couch. Tucked underneath the couch, was a stainless-steel frame with what looked like a toilet seat suspended from it on springs.

Next to the wooden structure was an examination table which wouldn't have looked out of place in a gynaecologist's consulting room. 'To be honest,' Cambell was saying, 'I expected the corner cupboard next to the examination table to be full of medical equipment but,' he continued, opening the door, 'you'll see that it contains an array of whips, masks, cuffs, gags and other material commonly associated with bondage.'

They passed another rack from which blindfolds hung limply. Some ropes also hung from the hooks, and there was a range of wooden and leather paddles as well as a selection of canes. Finally, they arrived at what appeared to be a built-in wardrobe which had been recessed into the end wall of the garage. Campbell pulled open the two central doors to reveal a huge range of rubber clothing of all colours, shapes and sizes. A flight of shelves to the left of the clothes rail contained an array of dildoes, vibrators, strap-ons and what could only be described as gags, one with something resembling a golf ball attached to the middle of the gag. There was even a pair of boxing gloves.

Closing up the wardrobe, Campbell pointed over to the far corner. 'Obviously keen on health and safety as well. There's a couple of first-aid boxes over there and one of the drawers is full of surgical gloves, condoms, Dettol wipes, tubes of lubricant, and disinfectant.'

Selitto nodded sagely although he was still trying to take in a human being's capacity for getting pleasure out of harming another human being or from actually being harmed. He certainly didn't have an answer to his own question – why?

'I do see what you mean about the room being well equipped,' he said staring at a particularly nasty looking pair of cuffs. 'When I was here yesterday, I thought it looked like there was some blood on the legs of the bath, and I just got the feeling that someone had tried to clean up around there. Have you had a look at that yet?'

'All done,' Campbell replied, 'and I think you're right. The carpet was actually quite damp and smelled of some sort of cleaning agent. Not too dissimilar to what we found at Meadowlands. There are spots of blood on the legs of the bath and some on the underside where the cleaner obviously couldn't see them. I've taken all that evidence away for analysis. I haven't yet had time to look at some of the larger items of equipment but I expect that I'll have the same problem of assessing what's recent and what's not. We've also got a huge problem with cross-contamination as you can probably appreciate so I'm not really expecting to get much out of this room.'

Selitto wandered over to the bath. He had recently been helping a friend to redesign a bathroom so he had spent some time researching baths on the internet. His friend's partner had wanted a roll top bath but one that she and her man could both sit in and drink champagne! He knew that the bath he was now looking at was a double-ended roll top slipper bath which had four chrome claw feet supporting it. The shower attachment was affixed to the wall behind but overhung the side of the bath itself. The bath had been embellished with what looked like a gold rope which snaked its way around the extremity of the roll-top. Not really to Selitto's taste, he decided, but a germ of an idea suddenly forced its way into his head.

Turning back, he saw that Campbell and Crosby were engaged in conversation. 'Donny!' Selitto called over. 'Have you had a good look at the gold embellishment around the top of the bath?'

Campbell and Crosby ambled over to where Selitto was standing. 'I have, yes,' said Campbell somewhat defensively. 'Couldn't find anything of note. Why? Could there be a link?'

Selitto ran his gloved hand along the gold rope and felt some areas of roughness along its predominately smooth surface. 'Suppose – just suppose that the girl hit the back of her head on this raised surface, knocked herself out and collapsed into a bath full of water. Would she drown?'

Campbell stared at the bath, clearly trying to conjure up an image of the girl's head coming into contact with the gold rope. 'Well, I would say that that would be possible,' he said after a moment's reflection, 'but then I would expect her to have been lying across the width of the bath with her legs over the front side in which case it is unlikely that her head would have been in the water. Someone would have had to reposition the body so that she was lying in the bath full length, and even then she would probably have had to be held under water to effect the drowning.'

They all stood there staring at the bath. 'That would certainly explain the gash in the back of her head,' Campbell offered. 'This raised surface is clearly intended to be ornamental but I'm sure you've already found that there are some rough patches. If her head hit one of those, then I would expect the skin to have been broken. In which case she would have bled, perhaps over the back of the bath. Hmmm!' Campbell was deep in thought. 'I'll have another look,' he said, turning away to collect some of his equipment.

'We'll leave you to it,' Selitto said, beckoning Crosby to follow him out of the dungeon.

Selitto showed Crosby the two downstairs rooms – the one in which the table had apparently been set for two people, and the bedroom with en-suite. Upstairs, Crosby's mouth hung open as he went from one mirror-panelled room to another, occasionally stopping to examine the range of sex aids which seemed to adorn shelves and dressing tables, and to inspect wardrobes full of just about every uniform he could think of.

They eventually made it to the top floor where the opulence of the rest of the house immediately ceased. Selitto made for the room where he had found the phone, and bumped into Beth Dench coming out of it.

'I've collected the phone,' she said, 'and have asked for it to be opened up as soon as. We can have the cash looked at back at the ranch. It's probably not going to tell us much, but we're getting some good prints from the window so, even if it's only for the purpose of elimination, we might learn something.'

'Good!' Selitto replied. 'Did you find anything else in the hidey hole?'

'Well, I did explore as far as I could feel with my fingers. I was trying to see if anything was hidden in the insulation wool when I eventually found this.' She held up a sealed evidence bag in which she had placed a silver necklace. 'It's a standard identity necklace with the initial 'E' hanging from it. We'll get it tested to see if it belongs to Scarecrow Girl. If it does, chances are her name begins with an 'E' which might help. Doubt it's worth taking any more of the floor up because the access point was so limited. But I'll have one final look before we go.'

Just then, a slightly breathless and flushed Jimbo Carrigan appeared at the top of the stairs. 'I think you'll all want to come and have a look at this before I process it,' he informed them.

They all filed downstairs behind Carrigan who headed straight for the office which looked even more like a bomb had hit it. The top of the desk was propped up against one of the walls along with the modesty panel. The two columns of drawers had been moved to the side of where the desk had been so that the area around the floor safe had been fully revealed. What they hadn't been able to see before were two other areas where the carpet had been cut away. Cables protruded from each hole in the floor and disappeared under the two columns. What appeared to be recording devices had been placed into each hole which had its own power supply.

'Aha!' exclaimed Selitto. 'I presume these are what I think they are?'

'Well, they look like recording devices to me,' said Carrigan. 'The one on the left looks like the CCTV recorder of some sort and I have to assume that the one on the right is a voice recorder given the number of listening devices I have found. I'll know more when I get them back to the tech boys at the lab.'

'But presumably there's some sort of playback device in this room.' Selitto pressed on, looking around him.

'You would think so, wouldn't you!' Dench interjected, similarly looking around the room. 'What I can't quite get my head around is that this seems to be the control point for the recording devices yet recording is only activated when the Controller is in situ. So, you open a drawer, press the green button and a panel opens up in the bookcase to reveal a screen. You then have to press another green button to activate the camera in the room although this is motion-sensitive so it may not show anything apart from an empty space. And once you press the red button everything stops. So, it looks as if the device buried in the floor only records the CCTV feed monitored from this desk whenever the Controller is actually sitting here monitoring.'

'Not necessarily,' came a voice from behind them. They both turned to look at Crosby who's face was turning a deep shade of red. 'Sir!' he added. Selitto nodded to Crosby, inviting him to continue. 'I've seen something like this before. You're right - these are simply devices for storing selected recorded material; they will not hold all the recordings. There must be somewhere else that collects all the feeds from the CCTV system. This may or may not have a bank of screens round a central console with an operator who selects which film or voice recordings should be retained and which can be discarded. Those that are retained could be edited and sent wirelessly to the equipment we are looking at here. This sort of set-up is used extensively by criminals operating extortion rackets.'

Selitto looked at Beth. 'I thought I'd been all over this house but haven't seen any sign of a monitoring station,' he said at last.

'Me neither!' commented Dench. 'We haven't looked in the loft space yet but I can't see it being in there as it's not very accessible. The only other thing we'll have to look out for are false panels or walls. Perhaps I need to take another look at the house from the outside to see if anything doesn't quite fit with what I know of the inside layout. But thank you, Stuart, that's a good steer for us. Very helpful.'

'Yes, very interesting Stuart. Thanks.' Selitto was keen to move on. 'So, what's the plan, Beth?' he asked the Crime Scenes Manager.

'We'll probably finish up here soon and then get back to base,' she surmised. 'We've still got masses to do on the evidence we took away from Meadowlands, and we've still got Vashlili's car parked in the car park. You can guess that that's put a few noses out of joint, and I don't really want to keep it longer than we have to. My priority is to put Scarecrow Girl inside this house, and to get hold of the CCTV feeds. I just have a feeling in my water that this is the tip of a much bigger iceberg, and that there will be more casualties along the way.'

'Great!' sighed Selitto. 'No rest for the wicked then!' Turning as if to leave, he beckoned to Crosby. 'Just going to take Stuart over to the allotment, then we'll be heading back to Tonbridge. Let me know if you find a CCTV console!'

38

Sunday 23 July

Woons sat at his desk staring at his phone. He jabbed at the screen, punching in numbers he'd never had to use before. He wondered what the word 'emergency' meant to those lazy good-for-nothings in the Caucasus. Perhaps they might get off their fat backsides when they had heard the news he had for them about their brother Tamaz who'd gone AWOL and left Woons up the creek without a fucking paddle.

He looked at the screen and then at the scrap of paper on his desk, checking to make sure that he had got the numbers right. He looked up at the ceiling and then at the clock on the wall directly in front of him. He hit the green button and then sat back. The single ringing tone signifying a call was being made to a country outside the UK eventually wormed its way into his ear. Suddenly, there was a loud click followed by silence. Had he been cut off? He was about to disconnect the call when he thought he heard breathing. He jammed the phone to his ear.

'Aloo!' came a deep voice, more a growl that anything else. Questioning but defensive. Very defensive.

'Irakli?' asked Woons, not really recognising the voice which seemed to be at least an octave lower than he remembered Irakli's voice to be.

'He no here. Who want him?' Don't tell me I'm not going to be able to speak to the bastard, thought Woons.

'It's Billy Woons in the UK. Irakli told me to call him on this number if there was an emergency.'

'He no here!' the voice replied.

For God's sake! Woons was trying to control his temper, but he was never very patient when he was having to communicate with arseholes. He tried another tack.

'Can I speak to Mr Tsiklauri, then?'

'He no here! They both no here!' Well that was typical, Woons thought. In his hour of need, the fucking Georgians had disappeared. It wasn't as if he'd contacted them on many occasions over the years, and they'd done very well, thank you, from the proceeds which Woons had raked in from his little operation in the south-east of England.

'Do you know when they are coming back?' Woons tried again to see if he could get this guy to say anything more than that Irakli and Tsiklauri weren't there.

'No,' came the one-word response. Woons nearly hit the roof of his portacabin. 'They no tell me. They go in car to airport. Fly in big machine to somewhere secret. They no tell me, just say no speak to persons who phone.' The next thing Woons heard was the dialling tone. He sat in his chair staring at his phone, incandescent with rage. How dare they treat him like this after all he'd done for them. He'd remained loyal to Tsiklauri and his mob, mainly because they tended not to interfere with his operation so he could pretty much get on with business without being forever called to account.

The Georgians also provided good quality girls. He'd had very few complaints over the years, and they were always willing and able to provide new girls if there were any problems. But, just lately, he had detected a change in attitude. They were really starting to wind him up, and the way he'd just been treated by some phone-minder back in Kaspi seemed to indicate that his association with the people from east of the

Black Sea may be coming to an end.

The sound of a car making its way up the track to the office interrupted his thoughts. He sprang out of the chair and inched the blinds open so that he could see who was coming. Harding's car was bumping along the track. Good! He could unburden his anger with Tsiklauri and his mob on Trigger and then make a plan as to how to deal with the Georgians. He sat back down and waited for Harding to make his way into the office.

'Hello, Billy,' Harding said as he entered the office. 'All right?'

'No, I'm not all right if you must know!' Woons snapped. 'I'm having trouble with that fucking Kaspi mob.'

Harding raised his eyes to the ceiling and then fixed Woons with a steely look. 'Well, that'll have to wait, Billy.' There was an urgency in Harding's voice, and Woons was immediately on his guard. 'I've just come round by Sheet Hill and was going to see how old mother Travisedo was getting on at The Garden House. You know, the one with the lavish BDSM dungeon?'

'Yes, yes, I know where you are!' Woons' patience was wearing thin and he always got agitated when Harding started on one of his long preambles before getting to the point of what he wanted to say. He knew all about the dungeon and had even seen photos of it but he had never visited. As for Travisedo, she had a fearsome reputation for running a very strict house but, at the same time, she was probably the most successful of his managers. She always demanded the brightest and prettiest of the girls, and would often change them out if they didn't provide her clients with exactly what they were paying for. But she was worth the trouble as her earnings were truly remarkable.

Harding finally came to the point. 'Well, the property is surrounded by police crime scene tape and there's a bloody great

Crime Scenes van parked outside the back door!' He looked over at his boss for a reaction. He didn't have to wait long.

'For fuck's sake, Trigger, what the fucking hell is going on?' Woons exclaimed, his face turning a deep shade of crimson. 'Where's Travisedo? She ran that place with an iron fist or whatever. And what the fuck are the cops doing there? Blimey! If they've got that tape round the place, it means that something's happened. And they don't just get the CSI van out if they're popping in for a chat about Neighbourhood Watch! Jesus! Surely one of her customers hasn't gone rogue on her? She wouldn't be that stupid!' He launched himself from his chair and paced to the door of the office, turned and looked directly at Harding. 'What's going on, Trigger?'

'Afraid I haven't got a fucking clue, Billy,' confessed Harding. 'I fairly high-tailed it out of there once I'd seen the van. Came straight here!'

Woons looked up at the ceiling in search of inspiration just as his phone started thrumming on his desk. He reached out and picked it up, squinting at the screen. Recognising the name, he accepted the call. 'Tricky! What the fuck's going on?'

There was a slight pause on the line. 'It's Emma, Billy. Tricky's driving.'

'Ems? What the hell's going on? Why're you two out together? I thought you didn't do Sundays! Blimey! This is getting too much for me to cope with!' Woons looked at Harding and shrugged his shoulders, a deep frown etched on his forehead.

'Billy, listen!' Emma commanded. Woons was taken aback by the tone of her voice, a sharpness to it that he had rarely detected before. 'We have a mega problem over at The Garden House at Sheet Hill.'

Woons cut in. 'Yeah, yeah! I know all about that. Trig's just told me that there's a CSI van there. God knows what that Travisedo woman's been up to.' He was trying to make light of the news about a problem at The Garden House, but in the back of his mind he couldn't stop wondering why the fuck the cops had got a CSI van up there?

Emma was back on. 'Listen, Billy, and listen good. Tricky was talking to one of his mates earlier who mentioned that he had heard from someone in Kent Police that a dead girl turned up dressed as a scarecrow on the allotments opposite the house. The cops are trying to link the girl to the house. The worrying thing is that they just walked into Travisedo's place – it was completely fucking empty of people. No one! Nada personas! Whichever way you look at it, Travisedo, her helper and all the girls have disappeared. Gone! So now the Crime Scenes geeks are crawling all over the place with their fingerprint powder and infrared tech equipment. God knows what they are going to find in there!' She paused for breath.

Woons sat down on his squeaky chair. Harding had never seen his boss look quite so pale. 'Bloody hell, Ems. This is a fucking disaster!'

'You said it, Billy!' Emma replied. 'We've just taken a look and the CSI van's still there so they're obviously taking the place apart. Not quite sure what sort of CCTV she had there but that could be a real worry if they started taking a close look at that! Anyway, we're on the way over to see you at the office so that we can decide what we're going to do – specially if the cops get interested after having had a good look through the Garden House. You just stay there and we should be with you in ten.' The dialling tone followed as she disconnected the call.

Woons put the phone down on the desk and just stared at it. 'Blimey, Trigger, we've got a problem here! You get the gist of what that Ems was saying?'

Harding shook his head. 'Not much of it, no. Why are the police there in the first place? Have they had a tip off from an aggrieved punter or something of that sort?'

So Woons told him about the scarecrow body and the fact that there was no one in the house. 'Those fucking cops are going to have a field day in that house. Let's hope the old woman's CCTV wasn't working otherwise there could be a number of very worried high rollers out there once the news gets out.'

Woons sat at his desk staring off towards the door. How he wished he still smoked. He would have lit a large Havana and sat back with his feet on the desk to concentrate on how to prevent the potential unravelling of his business empire.

'Supposing this is linked to the clearing out of Belinda's gaffe at Furnace Lane!' he said to no one in particular. 'Where else have we had problems?' He got up from the desk and went over to look at the map on the wall, studying it carefully. 'Yeah! Hildenborough wasn't it Trig? Where they had all that food poisoning from something a punter brought in? And we lost that girl off the roof at Wateringbury but I think that was more of an accident – a little game which ended in disaster. But we've definitely now had two houses cleaned out.'

There was a rap at the door. Harding instinctively crept over to the window and inched a blind up. He saw Spink's car parked next to his and nodded to Woons who went over and opened the door. Emma swept into the room in front of Spink who was carrying a tray of four coffees and a packet of biscuits.

Obviously never goes anywhere without sustenance, Woons thought. Spink put the coffees down on the table, pulled out a chair, and sat down to open the biscuits.

Woons took one of the coffees and went to sit behind his desk. He looked over at the other three who were now seated around the table.

'Right!' he began. 'Has anyone got a fucking clue about what's going on here?' They looked at each other and then back at Woons as if awaiting his next pronouncement. When it wasn't forthcoming, Emma broke the silence.

'Have you been able to speak to those Georgians yet because my feeling is that there is a problem right at the very top of their organisation. At least with Belinda's gaffe at Furnace Lane, we were able to clear the place out although we don't really know what happened. But to lose another complete operation like at Sheet Hill...' Her voice trailed off for a moment as she took a sip of coffee. 'Strikes me that someone's trying to muscle in on our manor or else they're hell bent on closing us down.'

'Hmm. Hear what you say, Ems.' Woons had his elbows on the desk resting his chin on the backs of his hands. He picked up his phone and looked blankly at the screen. 'I tried to get hold of our friends from the Caucuses earlier on, using the emergency number they gave us. Got some fucking gobshite who didn't know where Irakli or Tsiklauri were and seemed to be saying that they had left the country. So, the answer to your question is no, I haven't been able to speak to the Georgians.' He got up from his desk and again went over to look at the map on the wall and stared at it as if hoping that it would provide answers to the many questions that were spinning around in his head.

'I reckon this all stems from the disappearance of Vashlili.' It was Spink who broke the silence. 'He's a key player in the operation. He sources the girls, gets them into the country, holds them somewhere if they can't be used immediately, and clears up any nasty incidents of which there have been quite a few lately. He has a direct link into Kaspi, he speaks their lingo – he's one of them! Suddenly, he fucks off and we get all this aggro starting. Must be a connection!'

A further period of silence hung in the portacabin while they each gave this some thought. 'Blimey! Don't tell me he's gone rogue and all!' Woons turned away from the map. 'Surely not! He's one of them for fucks sake! One of the family – the bretheren, the band of brothers! Nah! Can't be having that! But I have to accept Tricky's point that all this aggro has started since the bastard disappeared so we shouldn't rule out a connection.'

'Makes you wonder if the incident with the dodgy curries was a deliberate attempt to destabilise the Hildenborough operation,' observed Spink. 'You heard any more from them on that Ems?'

'Nope,' she replied. 'So, I've assumed that Candice is back to normal. I called her a couple of times yesterday but the calls went to voicemail. She's not very good with voicemail so I'm not surprised she hasn't called back. But I haven't tried her again today so I suppose I'd better just check.' She thumbed the screen of her phone. Poked it a couple of times and then held the device to her ear. All eyes were on her as she suddenly pulled the phone away from her ear and stared at the screen. 'Fucking number's unobtainable! That can't be right. Candice has had this number for years! Must be a connection error. I'll have another go.' Emma went through the same procedure again before tossing the phone onto the table and looking over at Spink. 'I've got a horrible feeling that we're going to have to pay Candice a visit – and soon!'

'What's that then, Ems,' Woons interrupted. 'Don't tell me that Candice has fucked off and all? Jeez! Give me strength!'

'Yeah, Billy. I think we better get over there pronto.'

39

Sunday 23 July

The Team reassembled in the Major Incident Room at 6.30pm which was slightly later than Hunter had intended. Selitto and Crosby had arrived back from the Basted Heights Allotments in good time, and were busily updating the white board which had been assigned to 'Scarecrow Girl'. Selitto was showing Crosby how to put key information up on the board, and both of them had their heads down referring to notes which they had taken earlier in the afternoon.

Meanwhile, Jennings and Pennant had only just made it back to Tonbridge to get to the meeting on time, and had arrived in the MIR rather breathless having run up the stairs from the car park. They had spent several hours at Meadowlands familiarising themselves with the layout of the hotel and its grounds including the lakes. Hunter had thought that this would be a good idea, and it would also afford them an opportunity to get to know each other a bit better.

Seeing that everyone was now present, Hunter clapped her hands together and called for attention. 'Okay!' she started, 'I'm sure that we don't want to stay any longer than we have to so let's have the two reports from this afternoon's activities. Stuart, you and Ted have been to the allotments. What's been going on there?'

Crosby filled the team in on the meeting with the Crime Scene Investigators, and identified the CCTV system as being a possible source of information for the investigation. He also mentioned the bath in the dungeon as being an item of interest in connection with the drowning of the young girl, and that the CSIs would be taking a further look at that.

'Good! That's interesting!' Hunter summarised. 'As it's unlikely that she would have been brought far before being propped up on the allotment, the bath would seem to be as good as anywhere to concentrate on at the moment. Have you got a de-brief planned with the CSIs?'

Selitto said that they were hoping to do so tomorrow (Monday) once they had got back to the lab. Might be a bit soon, he surmised, but at least it would keep the ideas flowing. He also hoped that the PM report might be ready by lunch-time Monday.

'Okay! Good! Good!' Hunter was enjoying the keenness being shown by her team. 'Elaine! You and Carolyn took yourselves off to look at Meadowlands. Anything to report from there?'

Elaine had her notepad in hand and flipped over a few sheets. 'Well, we got there at a particularly busy time – Sunday lunch was in full swing with every table taken in the restaurant so we weren't exactly welcomed with open arms. Anyway, we had a look round the grounds to familiarise ourselves with the layout and then walked around the large lake. We were most impressed with the lighthouse – what a setting! We were allowed to have a look at the area outside the Crocus room but couldn't get inside as there was a guest occupying it. But we were able to have a good look at the fire exit nearby and also the potential escape points from there. The BMW is still there and is now a source of annoyance to the hotel management! It's already got a heavy sheen of dust on it and, of course, it still has the blue & white tape round it! Thankfully, it's parked in a corner of the car park but the duty manager still made a plea for it to be removed as soon as possible.'

'Duty manager?' asked Hunter. 'Wasn't Dangerfield there?'

'No, ma'am, he wasn't,' replied Pennant. 'It doesn't seem that he has been there for a few days – possibly not since you met him on Wednesday. Seems to be some problem with his children being ill but we got the distinct feeling that the duty manager wasn't impressed. She seemed to imply that this wasn't the first time that he had effectively gone AWOL, and that members of staff were beginning to tire of his absence because it was causing more work for others.'

'Who was the duty manager you spoke to?' Hunter asked.

Pennant looked at her notes. 'We spoke to Sally Lancaster, ma'am. I think she mentioned that she had met you when you were there. Seemed to have everything under control but you could just feel that there was tension amongst the staff. We got the impression that Dangerfield was not very well liked but, at the same time, the team needed his guidance so his absence for days at a time creates a problem.'

'Hmmm! Interesting observation, Carolyn!' Hunter's interest had been piqued. Was Dangerfield becoming more of a person of interest as the days went by? And the reaction of the staff to his absences was interesting. She recalled that he had been in France immediately before they had met at Meadowlands on Wednesday. Who had he been visiting? He'd been there for five days hadn't he? Had he spent all five days actually in Paris? Or had he gone elsewhere in Europe – perhaps travelling by train so he couldn't be traced. She made a note in her book to follow this up. Perhaps Grace could get some information on the French trip when she returned on Monday.

'Okay! Well done everyone!' Hunter called the meeting to a close. 'There's not much more we can do this evening so let's just get the boards updated and have an early night. Elaine, could you also put a question mark on your board about Dangerfield. We need to decide whether he is a person of interest as his recent absences seem to have been largely unexplained and have coincided with a major incident at his hotel.'

'Yes, Guv,' Elaine replied, busily getting to work on updating her board with the help of Pennant who was referring to her notes.

Hunter nodded towards Selitto and slipped out of the room. 'I'm getting a bad vibe about Dangerfield,' she told Selitto as he joined her in the corridor. 'Can't quite put my finger on it at the moment but his absences, if you include the French trip, look suspicious. Let's get Grace on it in the morning and see if she can pull up any other information. Who he actually visited in France would be nice to know rather than just a bland statement that he went on a jolly organised by the hotel group which Meadowlands belongs to.'

'Agreed!' Selitto nodded. 'We also need to have a closer look at his movements from the time we left there on Wednesday. When you told him to stay at the hotel, his response was that he would be staying the night in any event but then he wasn't there when the CSIs turned up on Thursday. By which time the boat had been sunk and the black rubbish sack had disappeared.'

'Yep!' Hunter agreed. 'Our Mr Dangerfield certainly warrants a much closer examination!'

40
Sunday 23 July

Given that it was a Sunday evening, Spink decided not to risk continuing too far up the A21 towards the dreaded M25 so took the Tonbridge slip road and then hung a left into Pembury Road. He passed the Vauxhall pub which was teeming with drinkers sitting at tables, on the grass, leaning against cars. He took a right at the roundabout outside the Tonbridge police station and then up the High Street trying desperately to observe the 20mph speed restriction in very light traffic. On past the castle and Tonbridge School before taking the left-hand fork onto London Road.

Emma sat in silence in the passenger seat, her hands in her lap clutching her phone. She stared ahead keeping her eyes firmly on the road. She was tormented by what seemed to be happening to the Woons empire, and her stomach was in knots. She had met Billy Woons more by luck than good judgment. A friend had asked her if she would like a small cleaning job to help her get by. She had only just got Lucy off the breast-feeding so she said that she could provide a few hours of assistance every week as long as her mother was able to baby sit for the hours she was working. The father had fucked off almost as soon as she had announced that she was pregnant so funds were very limited, and this little job paid quite well for the minimal number of hours it involved. She liked the people she worked with but soon realised that the houses she visited were not your ordinary family homes. So, she kept her head down and just did what she was told to do. She didn't talk to anyone when she was in the houses, and didn't have any contact with her fellow cleaners outside work. In return, she was paid very well so that she could afford nice things for Lucy.

One day, news came through that her boss had decided to return to her native Australia and was leaving her job. Emma had thought nothing of this until her boss introduced her to Billy Woons who was visiting one of the houses she was working at that day. She sat in his car for about half an hour while he spoke mainly to her about his plans for the future. He had then offered her a job as part of his team at an eye-watering rate of pay. She had rushed home and told her mother who insisted that she must take the job – they could work the childcare arrangements out as long as there was some flexibility in the hours she was required to work. Billy Woons had been an understanding boss, and she soon discovered that he was extremely loyal as long as she was always singing out of his songbook. As time went by, the job grew and so did the financial rewards. She soon had enough to put a deposit down on a small cottage in the Kent countryside near Tunbridge Wells which had plenty of room for her mother as well. Over time, she became quite close to Woons – they were easy in each other's company but they both knew that that was as far as it was ever likely to go. Her job was everything to her. She had very little time for any socialising as all her spare time was taken up with looking after Lucy.

As they weaved their way through the countryside, she looked out at the passing hedgerows and houses, and tried to make sense of the events of the last 72 hours. Was her idyllic lifestyle about to hit the buffers? What if there was something going on which they had no control over. Some sort of turf war? Someone else trying to muscle in on Woons's business interests? Both possibilities filled her with dread fear.

As Spink took a right, she registered that they were now in Stocks Green Road. 'Never quite sure from here, Ems.' Spink looked over at her for guidance. 'Second opening on the left after the second bridge,' she instructed. Spink drove on.

He found the second opening on the left after the second bridge and swung the car into what could only be described as a narrow farm track pitted with pot holes. He soon came to a halt in front of a metal five-bar field gate.

'Shit! This looks ominous,' observed Emma. 'That gate's never been closed as long as I've been coming here!' Spink got out of the car and went to take a look. The gate had a lockable sliding latch but there was no padlock in sight so he eased the latch back on its spring and pushed the gate open to its full extent. He then got back in the car and drove on.

'I don't like the feel of this, Tricky,' Emma said, sitting forward in her seat and looking all around her. They continued along the track as they advanced deeper into the lush countryside. Eventually, the house hove into view. Spink dropped the revs to cut the noise from the engine, and they approached with extreme caution.

The track gave way to a gravel driveway which wound its way around a circular lawn in front of the main entrance into the house. In the centre of the lawn was a piece of sculpture but Emma had never had any idea what is was supposed to depict. There were other stone sculptures arranged around the front gardens including a very ornate birdbath which they passed as Spink drove slowly round the circular driveway, carefully eyeballing the house and the grounds as he passed. Eventually, he brought the car to a halt at the point where the gravel drive re-joined the track so that he was facing in the right direction if he had to make a hasty exit.

They both got out of the car and, in the fading evening light, stood there looking at the house. 'Looks ominously quiet to me, and no sign of any lights,' Spink observed.

Grabbing his torch from the storage pocket in the driver's door, Spink joined up with Emma and, together, they walked towards the house. Emma's heart was racing. She could easily picture the inside of the house and would know in an instant if anything was wrong. Spink spotted a CCTV camera which presumably was meant to be focused on the front door. Only it was now pointing to the heavens. He pointed it out to Emma. She grimaced. They got to the door which looked as if it was closed. But a gentle push from Spink and it swung back on well-oiled hinges. They stood on the doorstep and stared into an ever-darkening interior. Not a sound apart from the distant rumble of traffic on the busy A21.

'What's the layout of this place?' Spink whispered to Emma as they both stepped over the threshold and into the main hallway.

'The client rooms are on this floor and upstairs,' she replied. 'Candice has her quarters upstairs, and the girls live in an annexe out the back. There's also a kitchen and entertainment room on the ground floor. I think she's got a small BDSM dungeon downstairs in what used to be a cellar but it's pretty basic. Nearly all the rooms have en-suite. There's quite a lot of CCTV in here if I recall but I can't see any tell-tale flashing red lights. Is the power on?'

Spink got his torch out and shone it around the walls. There was a light switch at the foot of a grand-looking staircase. He went over and flicked the switch. Nothing! They both looked at each other in the stark realisation that something was very wrong here. Even in the grainy light coming through the doorway, Spink could see the colour draining from Emma's face.

'OK, Ems,' he said, taking charge. 'Where to first?' He let the torch beam shine down onto the lush hall carpet.

'Better check on Candice's office,' she replied. 'Up these stairs to the left.' They climbed the stairs with Emma leading the way down a dark corridor off the landing. Spink's torch provided enough light for Emma to see her way, and she soon stopped outside an ornately decorated door. She depressed the gold lever handle, as she had done on many occasions, and they entered a large airy room which would have had plenty of light during the day judging by the size of the windows. Even in the gloaming, Spink could see that the view went on forever, a line of red lights in the far distance providing more evidence of heavy Sunday evening traffic on the A21. But his reverie was cut short by a gasp from Emma who had stopped in her tracks just inside the doorway.

Spink shone his torch around the room. It was a scene of devastation with papers, books, files and what appeared to be ledgers covering the floor. Paintings hung at drunken angles on the walls, their canvasses torn and mutilated, shards of glass all over the carpet. Lights had been smashed, and a two-seater settee had been slashed – its padding had been roughly extracted from the frame and now lay all over the floor as if it had been removed by a crazed maniac. It seemed that nothing had been left intact.

'Bloody hell!' exclaimed Spink. 'This looks like some frenzied attack by a madman!'

'Come on, Tricky,' Emma tugged at his sleeve. 'Candice is obviously not here. Maybe she's been locked up with the girls in the annexe. Let's get over there and take a look.'

Emma led the way down the main staircase, Spink trying and mainly failing to light her path from behind. At the bottom of the stairs, she doubled round to the back of the staircase and found a plain door. This led into a narrow corridor. They both followed its path until they came to another door which was locked with a Yale lock. Emma turned the knob and flicked the button down securing the lock open. They both walked out into a courtyard area which had a couple of washing lines criss-crossing it.

Emma pointed to the far corner of the courtyard where Spink could just make out another door. They approached this and then stopped in their tracks. The smell that greeted them was horrendous, unlike anything that either of them had ever come across before. Spink rated it even worse than what he had to put up with in the piggery he'd worked in after leaving school with one GCSE. Emma was gagging, frantically covering her mouth and nose with her hands. She turned and scurried back towards the other side of the courtyard. Spink followed.

'My God!' Emma panted, trying desperately to suck in some fresh air. 'What the fuck's that smell?' She bent over, hands on knees, breathing heavily.

Spink looked back across the courtyard. 'I don't know for sure, Ems, but I reckon it's probably human excrement,' he said. 'What's the layout in the annexe? Can you remember?'

'Yeah,' she replied. 'Candice wanted it to be like a communal dormitory with a large bathroom at the far end. But the girls wanted some privacy, especially as they were on call twenty-four seven so she put up some drapes which could be let down or rolled up. Worked well as far as I understand.'

'Okay. I'm just going to take a quick recce in there. I'll be right back. You stay here for the moment.' Spink took a handkerchief out of his pocket and held it up to his nose and mouth. He made his way back across the courtyard and sidled up to the door. Emma saw him give the door a nudge and then hang his head back before turning and entering the room. Through the cracks in the doorway, she could see the torch strobing round the room before Spink reappeared and legged it back across the courtyard.

'Jesus H Christ!', he whispered, breathing hard. 'I have never seen anything like it in my life! It's the most revolting sight. Just about every surface is covered in shit and vomit. A lot of it is just liquid which has pooled in various areas on the floor. The flies are finding it difficult to find anywhere to lay the eggs. There's a girl in there curled up in the foetal position on one of the beds but she's not showing any sign of life – I couldn't find a pulse, and the flies are definitely getting interested.'

Emma stared off across the courtyard. 'No other girls then?' Spink shook his head. 'Jeez! Candice normally has six or seven regulars.' She turned her gaze back to Spink. 'This is a fucking disaster! Let's get back inside the house.'

They retraced their steps along the narrow passageway and re-entered the hall under the stairs. Knowing the layout of the house, Emma led them through all the ground floor rooms and then through the other rooms on the first floor. Mirrors were smashed, bedding was slashed, furniture was overturned, curtains and blinds ripped and left in tatters. Devastation in every room. Every bottle in the drinks bar located just off the kitchen had been smashed, the floor a sticky pool of alcohol. And still no sign of any of the girls or of Candice. The other problem they had was that Spink's torch was running out of battery, its light dimming with each new room they looked into.

'We'll have to take a look in the cellar,' whispered Spink. 'How do we get down there?' Emma pointed to her right and Spink flashed his torch into the darkness. He could just make out a door at the end of the hallway, and they made their way towards it. The door had a hasp & staple locking mechanism on the outside, and a padlock hung redundantly from the staple. Spink slipped the padlock into his pocket and pulled the grab handle which had been crudely attached to the door. The fading light of the torch showed a set of steps leading down into a dark abyss. There was an ominous smell wafting up from below, not as bad as in the annexe but unmistakably of human excrement. Emma's body gave an involuntary shiver as she slowly descended the steps behind Spink. She had never been down here so didn't know what to expect.

Spink stopped at the bottom of the steps and shone the torch around the cellar area. BDSM material hung from numerous racks along the walls, and other equipment was strewn around the floor. In the middle of the room, Spink's torch just picked out what looked like a punishment chair, its back facing towards them. Chains and leather straps snaked their way across the back of the chair. Emma suddenly grabbed Spink's arm and let out an audible gasp as she saw a mane of blonde hair hanging over one of the arms of the chair.

'Quick!' she urged and pushed past Spink towards the chair. The yellowing beam from the torch lent a rather ghostly appearance to the figure strapped into the chair, head bowed, wrists lashed to the arms of the chair, legs secured with chains. Having little doubt that this was Candice, Emma carefully lifted the head up and then wished that she had left that job to Spink. Candice's face was almost unrecognisable. One eye was bulging out of its socket, the other was so badly bruised that it was firmly shut. Her nose was just a mass of blood and gristle, and there was a deep gash across one of her cheeks. But the worst sight was her bottom lip which hung limply over her chin having been cut from each corner of her mouth. Emma felt the bile rise in her throat, and she had to look away to overcome the desire to throw up.

'There's a very faint pulse,' Spink whispered after feeling Candice's carotid artery. 'She needs urgent medical attention but how the hell are we going to organise that? Vashlili used to organise all the medical people – I've no idea who to contact. And we can't really hand her over to the emergency services or the police will be crawling over this place in seconds. Any ideas?'

Emma took her phone out of her pocket and was just about to call Woons when Candice gave a sigh and moved her head slightly. Emma sank to her haunches so that she could look up into Candice's face. 'It's okay Candy,' she said reassuringly. 'It's Ems here. Me and Tricky are here to help you.' There was a faint nod of the head. 'We're going to get you out of here and get you properly cared for,' Emma continued.

At this, Candice seemed to summon her last ounce of strength. 'Camerash', she muttered.

'Cameras?' Emma asked, leaning in closer. But, stealing a glance at her face, it looked as if Candice had lost conscious- ness. Emma looked up at Spink. 'Cameras? I wonder what she means.'

She was just about to stand up when Candice let out what sounded like a low growl. 'They ne'er 'ound 'em!' she whispered. 'You go – ar'en hed, under loor.' Her head drooped again as she seemed to lapse into unconsciousness. Spink looked down at Emma who was still crouched in front of the chair. 'Candice!' she spoke directly to the bowed head. 'Candice! Hang on! We're going to get you out of here!' No reaction. Spink again felt around Candice's neck for a pulse, his movements becoming increasingly frantic. Finally, he looked at Emma and shook his head. Emma just stared at the figure sitting limply in the chair. She couldn't believe that Candice had just died right in front of her. She felt her eyes moistening but now was not a good time to start crying. That could come later.

Spink was trying to shine his torch into the far corners of the cellar but he couldn't see anything else to detain them down here. He motioned Emma to follow him back up the steps, and he pushed the door closed once they had reached the main hallway. He fished the padlock out of his pocket and replaced it in the staple of the locking mechanism.

'Christ!' Spink exclaimed, looking back towards the front door. 'What the hell are we going to do now? What do you make of what Candice was saying?'

'She seemed to be telling us about cameras, presumably around the house, and then something about under a floor. But what floor?' Emma looked off into the distance where she could almost detect a faint shaft of moonlight framing the front door. They both stood there playing Candice's last mutterings over in their minds.

'I've got it!' Spink suddenly grabbed Emma's arm. 'Ar'en hed.

Garden shed! She was trying to tell us to look in the garden shed. How do we get into the garden?' he asked looking around him to see if there was a doorway they had missed. 'Didn't see any way out of that courtyard.'

'There is a back door into the garden but Candice always kept it locked and bolted. I think it will be easier to walk back out onto the driveway and then round the side of the house,' said Emma, trying to remember the layout of the back garden at Candice's house. 'Let's go and take a look.'

They made their way out of the front door and, in the ambient light given by a rising full moon and the reflective headlights from the traffic on the A21, they found their way around the side of the house. There was no fence so they simply walked on into an extensive back garden. Spink shone his weakening torch beam around the area which appeared to have been mainly laid to lawn. There were a couple of what looked like fruit trees cut into the lawn, and the patio immediately adjoining the house sported a number of pots of different shapes and sizes, their contents waving in the slight breeze which had sprung up now that night was drawing on.

Away to their left and a good distance from the house stood a standard size wooden garden shed. As they walked towards it, they could see that it had one long window along the front of the structure which would give a good view back across the lawn to the house. The pitched roof was covered in felt and had a gutter running its length to a downpipe feeding a water butt. The door to the shed was at one end, and was secured by way of a small padlock. Spink took a look at the padlock in the fading torch light and then pulled a set of implements out of his pocket. He selected one of them which looked to

Emma like one of her hairclips and inserted it into the padlock. With a couple of swift movements, the lock sprang open and he pushed on into the shed. Emma followed, closing the door behind her.

A workbench ran the entire length of the shed underneath the window, and a set of blinds covered the window from end to end. The blinds were well fitted and clearly designed to not let any light or prying eyes into the shed. The workbench itself was covered in various flowerpots and seed trays. Small garden implements were scattered around – trowels, dibbers, secateurs – and there was earth and compost all over the work surface which indicated that the shed was probably in constant use. On the other side of the shed, there were a number of bags of compost and farm manure, all with their labels facing to the front for easy identification. Larger garden implements were arraigned along the wall – hoes, shears, rakes, hedge cutters, forks, spades. A wheelbarrow was parked at the far end of the shed, and contained yet more bags of compost. Next to that sat a pile of empty garden waste sacks.

Spink and Emma both looked down at the concrete floor of the shed. Spink was the first to speak. 'This is either going to be very easy or impossible!'

'What do you mean?' Emma asked, frowning.

'Well, either we are going to find an easy-to-reach secret compartment under these bags of shite or we are going to have to find some way of smashing up the concrete!' He continued to shine the torch around what they could see of the floor. 'Come on, let's move some of those sacks.'

To begin with, they pulled the sacks away from the wall and then they manoeuvred more of them away from the end walls.

Nothing. Not even a crack in the concrete. Spink was getting frustrated. He pulled the wheelbarrow out of its slot with such force that he scattered the garden waste sacks all over the floor under the workbench. He bent down to retrieve them and saw that they had fallen onto trays and trays of young plants which were growing there. He tried to carefully pull the sacks off the plants but a corner of one of the sacks snagged on one of the pots and pulled it over. The young plant and some of the topsoil spilled out of the pot onto what he now realised was a piece of board which covered the floor under the workbench. He squatted down to clear up the mess he had made. He righted the pot and put back some of the soil. He then picked up the plant.

'What the fuck...?' he exclaimed. Just at that moment, the torch finally gave up the ghost and they were plunged into darkness. 'Hold on!' Emma's voice came out of the darkness. Spink thought he could hear a rustling of clothing and then a small light lit up the area under the workbench. Emma's phone light would have to do for the time being.

'Well done, Ems. Give that a shine down here can you?' Emma did as she was asked and squatted down beside Spink.

He held up the pot he had knocked over. 'You see this little plant or seedling or whatever you want to call it?' Emma nodded. 'It's plastic! It's not a real plant.' He put it back onto the floor and picked up another pot. Holding it up to the light, he pulled a plastic plant out of the pot. 'All these plants in pots are plastic!'

'Bloody hell!' Emma reached out and touched the plant in the pot nearest to her. Plastic!

'You thinking what I'm thinking?' Spink asked her. Emma

266

cast her eyes along the floor under the workbench, looking at all the plastic plants sitting in their own pots. 'Let's do it!' she finally replied.

They both got to work moving all the plants off the board under the workbench. Spink had thought of simply chucking them into one of the garden waste sacks but thought better of it in case they didn't find what they were looking for and wanted to put everything back as they had found it. Once they had cleared the pots, they sat back and stared at the wooden panel they had revealed. Spink wondered how they were going to remove the panel in order to look underneath it as the bench supports were in the way. It was Emma who suggested that they simply flip it up under the bench which they finally managed to do, leaning it against the wall of the shed.

'Aha!' exclaimed Spink under his breath. In the light of the beam from Emma's phone, they found themselves looking at two ring pulls inlaid into a block of concrete. He pulled one end up to test the weight of the concrete and was relieved to find that it wasn't too thick. He adjusted his position so that he was now kneeling on the concrete floor, and gently lifted the panel. He then slid it to his left until it was completely away from the hole. Grabbing the phone from Emma, he looked into the space he had discovered.

'Christ Almighty!' Emma whispered. 'Where the fuck do we start with all that lot?'

Spink had been studying the equipment in its hiding place. There were five laptops laid out next to each other along the length of the hole. All were positioned side on so that cables led from each laptop to a plug-in point for electrical power which was set into the concrete. There were no other cables which confirmed to Spink that he was dealing with a wireless system.

Motioning Emma to get down on the floor next to him so that she could shine the phone light on what he was doing, he took one of the laptops out of its concrete tomb and flipped it over. He got out the set of implements he had used to break the shed padlock, and selected one. 'Hopefully, this little chappie will do the job,' he said, holding up what looked to Emma like a spindly bent screwdriver. He then removed the cable and the battery from the laptop before setting to work on unscrewing the plate on the back of the machine. Once he'd got the plate unscrewed, he quickly removed the hard drive and then simply pushed the plate back onto the laptop before returning it to its resting place. He wasn't going to waste precious time screwing the plates back on to the laptops.

Emma had craned her neck over his shoulder to look at what he was doing, and it hadn't been long before she had heard a click and a satisfied grunt from Spink. He had passed the hard drive to her for safe keeping. 'One down, four to go!' he said as he moved on to laptop number two. He then did the same with the other laptops before sitting back to survey his handiwork. Emma sat there with five hard drives in one hand and her mobile phone with its tiny beam of light in the other.

'OK, let's put this lot back as we found it!' Spink said as he covered the hole with the concrete blocks and pulled the false wooden floor back into place. They then placed all the pots with their plastic flowers back onto the wooden board so that, to the casual observer, there were just a load of seedlings in pots under the workbench. Spink had put the hard drives into his jacket pockets, and had taken over control of the phone light.

'Right! Let's get out of here!' He looked over to Emma but

noticed that she was frowning and looking around her. Spink suddenly realised that something had changed. He could now see Emma more clearly than when they had been relying on the light from her mobile phone to see anything. But the extra light which was now coming into the shed was not constant, and it was not white light either. Red shadows danced across the garden implements hanging from the wall behind him and, with a dread fear, he suddenly realised what was going on. He signalled Emma to stay down whilst he slowly changed his position and gradually put his head above the workbench and lifted one of the blinds so that he could see out of the window.

To his horror, Spink saw that the annexe to the side of the house was well alight with flames already coming through the roof of the single storey extension. He looked at the rest of the house which was bathed in darkness. He felt Emma beside him – looking over the bench, her mouth wide open in dismay.

'Come on, Ems! We're going to have to make a run for it. We can't stay here and we certainly can't leave the car here!' Spink pulled the shed door open and they spilled out into the cool night air. He just had time to replace the padlock before they made a run for it across the lawn. Smoke was swirling around the fire and they could hear the crackling of wooden joists as the fire swept remorselessly through the annexe. All of a sudden there was a sound like a small explosion and Spink felt something whistle past his head. They were almost at the house now and collapsed into the darkness of the eastern wall.

'For fuck's sake! Someone's firing at us!' he yelled at Emma to make himself heard above the noise from the fire. They inched along the wall and peered around the corner to the front of the house but it was pitch dark. Spink could just make out the shape of his car on the driveway. 'We'll have to make a run for it, Ems. When we get to the car, jump in the back and get as far down as you can. Try to run on the grass. You can just see that it's the darker area, okay?' She nodded then realised that he couldn't see her so she uttered a timid 'Yes!' He took one more look around the corner towards the front door. 'Let's go!' and they both sprang out of the shelter by the side of the house.

Although they would have to cover more distance to the car, keeping to the grass meant that they would not make any noise crunching on the gravel which might give away their position. But they had forgotten about the number of elaborate garden sculptures which littered the front garden. Emma was the first to realise this as she cannoned into the ornate bird-bath which she had noticed on their arrival. Having hit the structure almost full on, she then lost her footing and hit the ground just as a bullet ricocheted off the bath itself showering her with fragments of stonework as she desperately scrambled away from the structure.

She finally managed to get to her feet and, ducking her head down, she set off in the direction of the car although finding her progress hampered by the evening dew which was now covering the grass. She slipped and slithered around another of the sculptures as the noise of another shot caused her heart to leap in her chest but she just kept on running as fast as she could in the direction of the car.

Spink was almost at the BMW when another shot rang out. Bits of gravel exploded from the drive and clattered against the side of car. He activated the door release and was relieved when Emma suddenly appeared beside him. As he opened the back door, Spink was horrified to see the interior light come on – they must look like sitting ducks now, he thought. Emma threw herself across the back seats, and Spink slammed the door behind her. He instinctively crouched down, keeping as low a profile as he could. Another shot boomed out in the confined space of the driveway, this time the bullet skimming off the roof of the car. He yanked the door open and threw himself into the driver's seat. He started the engine and, with wheels spinning which sent a cloud of gravel skywards, he shot off down the track, door still open.

He was just picking up speed when the rear window exploded, showering fragments of glass all over the interior of the car. At the same time, he felt a searing pain in his left shoulder but managed to keep hold of the steering wheel as the car sped down the rough track. He finally managed to get the door closed and continued driving without the lights on to avoid presenting even more of a target to the gunman, but he soon realised that he was putting them in danger of losing their way in the dark thereby greatly reducing their options for escaping. He reluctantly turned the lights on just as another bullet zinged through the car and straight out through the front windscreen on the passenger side. Miraculously, the screen didn't shatter and he was relieved to see that the track was now veering round to the right so that they were at last out of direct line of sight of the house.

Spink felt a trickle of something warm running down his arm and he instinctively reached across to try and assess the damage. Surely no more than a flesh wound, he thought, although his shoulder felt as if it was on fire. 'You OK Ems?' he shouted, trying to catch sight of her in the rear-view mirror.

A faint voice came from the back seat. 'Think so, but covered in glass so daren't move at the moment.'

They soon passed the open gate and bounced down onto the Hildenborough Road. Spink turned right and then took a left onto Rings Hill, another left onto the London Road and up to the Morleys roundabout before dropping down onto the A21 going south. By now, there was very little traffic around so he opened up the engine and sped down the dual carriageway, taking the Tonbridge exit and joining the A26 towards Southborough before taking a rather circuitous route back to Woons' office.

41

Monday 24 July

Spink slewed to a halt outside the office and leapt out of the car. He immediately opened the rear door and saw Emma lying under a thin layer of glass shards which glinted in the light coming from the single floodlight above the office door. 'Okay, Ems. Hang on. I'll be right back.'

He banged on the office door which was immediately opened by Harding. 'God Almighty!' he exclaimed, 'where the fuck have you two been?'

Spink squeezed past him and into the office where Woons was sitting at his desk. 'It's a long story but right now we need to help Ems out of the car.'

Woons shot up from his chair. 'Hey!' he shouted. 'Hey! Is she okay? What's happened to her?' He came toward Spink and then stopped dead in his tracks. 'What the fuck's going on, Tricky? What the fuck have you two been up to? Look at you!'

Spink looked to where Woons was pointing and realised that the shoulder on his jacket had been shredded and there was a dark stain around the top of the sleeve. 'Just a flesh wound, Billy. Our priority right now is to help Ems as she's lying on the back seat under a pile of glass. You still got that old Henry in here?'

Woons pointed at a cupboard by the door. Spink retrieved the Henry vacuum cleaner and roughly pulled the cable out of the old vacuum's innards to its full extent. He plugged it into the socket just inside the door and then took it out to the car. Tapping the Henry on the head, it roared into life and he started to carefully hoover the glass off Emma's back and around her legs. He also removed the glass from around the back seat and on the floor. After giving her the all clear, Emma rather gingerly raised her head and then pushed herself up with her hands before manoeuvring herself into a sitting position so that she could clamber out of the car.

She carefully shook her hair to try and get rid of the glass which had crashed down on her head. Miraculously, Woons appeared beside the car clutching a wide-toothed comb. Spink wondered where on earth he had got that from. Emma, on the other hand, grabbed it and started frantically pulling it through her hair, releasing a cascade of glass and stone particles which glinted in the light from the floodlight.

'Right, that's me done!' she announced after she had given her hair a thorough combing. 'Better get that shoulder looked at now!' And, with that, she turned and walked into the office – clearly expecting them all to follow her.

For the next thirty minutes, Spink briefed Woons and Harding about the evening's events out at the Hildenborough house. Emma had busied herself cleaning up Spink's flesh wound. The bullet had, indeed, grazed the flesh at the top of his left arm but had not made contact with a bone. He would have some muscle pain for a few days but was expected to make a full recovery. She did the best she could with a bandage from a rather dated first aid kit which Woons had bought from Amazon, possibly in its first year of trading if the state of it was anything to go by.

Harding had sat passively through the briefing but Woons had looked increasingly uncomfortable after every revelation. By the time Spink reached the point where someone had opened fire on them from the darkened house, Woons was pacing round the room.

'Fuck me!' Woons exclaimed when Spink had finished. 'So, there was obviously more to this food poisoning than we originally thought. Sounds as if the girls were deliberately poisoned by eating the food that geezer took in the other evening. Not just a case of Delhi-Belly but a deliberate poisoning. So that when he and his mates came back, they knew that there would probably be no punters there and the girls would be so weak that there'd be little resistance to just taking them away. But they left one of the girls because she was either already dead or very close to it. What about dear old Candice? She'd clearly not eaten the food so presumably she was trying to protect her girls and got a right hiding in return.'

'I think they were looking for something, Billy.' Emma had been sitting quietly at the table since she had finished patching Spink up. She looked pale, her hair dishevelled, tiny scratches on the back of her hands. 'Her office had been ransacked. In fact, more than ransacked. It looked like someone had been looking for something specific and had then gone apeshit when they couldn't find what they were looking for. Candice looked as if she had been tortured for information but had held out. The cutting out of her bottom lip and chin was grotesque – the work of a madman.' She held her head in her hands staring at the table, an involuntary tear splashing onto its surface. Her thoughts were back in that dungeon, a sight she would never be able to strike from her memory.

The ensuing silence was too much for Woons. 'So, Tricky, you and Ems got those drives or whatever – well done for that. What's your thinking on them?'

Spink absent-mindedly felt his pockets to make sure that the hard drives were still there. 'My understanding of what Candice was trying to tell us was that there were secret cameras which she had set up around the place, and that they were linked in some way to equipment in the garden shed. We saw some of the cameras which she had around the house but they were either pointing skywards or had been trashed altogether. So, our theory is that the five laptops are linked to five secret cameras that no one knew about except Candice.'

'Perhaps some sort of insurance policy in case she got rolled over by one of her Clients,' mused Woons, again wishing that he still smoked those large Havanas. Lungs full of sickly cigar smoke right now would do wonders for his powers of concentration, he thought. 'Or perhaps she was running the same sort of extortion racket that we've always thought old mother Travisedo was up to.'

'Whatever!' Spink interrupted Woons' train of thought. 'We need to get a look at these hard drives like now! You got your laptop here, Billy?'

Woons opened the bottom drawer of his desk and removed a smart silver laptop with the HP logo embossed on the lid. He placed the device on the desk in front of Spink who drew his chair up so that he was sitting in front of it. Harding shuffled round so that he was looking over Spink's right shoulder; Emma got up from the table and came to stand just to Spink's left. Woons stayed where he was, staring back at his team, wondering what the fuck was going to happen next.

Spink removed one of the hard drives from his pocket, connected it up to the laptop and tried to fire up the machine. Nothing happened – the screen remained blank.

'You got a direct charge cable, Billy?' Spink asked. Woons delved back into the drawer and brought out a cable which Spink slotted into the laptop. The plug just reached to the socket behind Woons' desk. The screen brightened up immediately which confirmed his suspicion that the battery was completely flat. The laptop hadn't been used for months.

Once the laptop had come to life and he had a smattering of icons on the screen, Spink was surprised to find that he was not asked for a password to get into the drive. He looked at the screen trying to understand the short cuts and then hit on one which was labelled "Driveway". Eventually, an image of the Hildenborough house came up on the screen and they found themselves looking at the circular driveway and front entrance. A car suddenly appeared from underneath where the camera was positioned and made its was round to the front door. Spink froze the image.

'This camera must be positioned in a tree by the drive,' he said. 'So that Candice could keep a record of all the comings and goings.' He unfroze the image and watched as the driver got out of the car, looked all around him and then walked up to the front door. He appeared to be speaking into an intercom before returning to the drive and driving the car to a parking place beside the house. The car was now in full view of the camera which was able to record make and registration plate. The driver then had to return to the front door, his face in full display for the camera lens as he walked across the drive. No doubt he was one of the punters.

Spink exited the program and disconnected the hard drive before replacing it with another which he pulled from his pocket. This time there was a short cut headed "Hallway".

Eventually an image of the entrance hallway and the main staircase came into view. The camera had been positioned centrally at the top of the staircase. Spink couldn't remember what was there as he and Emma hadn't been able to see much in the darkness. But he assumed that the camera had been somehow secreted away in the staircase. As they watched the screen, a man entered the front door, crossed the hallway, and climbed the staircase before veering off to the left and out of shot. But by then, they had all had a good look at his face so, again, Candice had been ensuring that she had a lasting record of her visitors.

'Okay! So where does this get us?' asked Woons. The others continued looking at the view of the staircase, each with their own thoughts. But no one was prepared to commit to answering Woons' catch-all question.

Eventually Spink broke the silence. 'Well, I don't know about you guys but I'm shattered. I'm sure Ems will want to be getting home as well so perhaps we should wind things up for now and get back together in the morning. If we all brought our own laptops we could get through these drives and find out if there's anything there of interest. Candice must have thought so otherwise she wouldn't have told us about the garden shed. Also, the cops'll be all over that fire. If it didn't spread to the house, or if the fire people got there in time, they may well have found Candice so that'll start a murder hunt. Probably good that someone torched the annexe so they can't make a connection with Travisedo's scarecrow girl. Anyway, let's see what's on the news in the morning, and I'll contact my mate to see if he's got any intel.'

'Okay, Tricky. You and Ems get going,' said Woons. 'You'd better take the spare car. I'll get your windows fixed up in the morning. And you, Trig, off you go – get some shut eye. I'll just finish up here. Let's get back here for eight shall we?' Woons tossed a set of car keys to Spink and waved them towards the door. They all nodded and slowly filed out of the portacabin.

42
Monday 23 July

The sun was already climbing into the sky as DI Sarah Hunter arrived at Pembury Road. The team's first briefing meeting of the week was due to start at 7.30 a.m. but she had given herself 30 minutes to prepare and get that all important first coffee fix. She walked up the stairs to the MIR, and was pleasantly surprised to see that everyone else had also decided to get in early. Hunter was particularly pleased to see that Grace Kendall was there. She was deep in conversation with Carolyn Pennant, both studying something on Grace's laptop. The two young DCs, Stuart Crosby and Elaine Jennings, seemed to be discussing the weekend's Tonbridge Angels friendly against Folkestone Invicta – both of them despairing of the Angels' current lack of a striker. Selitto was leaning against one of the windows thumbing through his phone and occasionally jabbing at the screen. The two large white boards stood sentry-like at the end of the room, hand written information starting to cascade down the pristine white surface of each board

She nodded a general 'good morning' to them all and went and sat at a desk in the corner of the room. Although she could have a small office in another part of the building, Hunter liked to be with her team as it gave her a far better idea of how the team was moulding itself into an effective unit. And, in any event, she was a devotee of hot-desking.

She took out her laptop and scrolled through all the emails that had come in overnight. She was particularly keen to get up to speed on the fire in suspicious circumstances at a house in the Hildenborough area. Kent Fire & Rescue had tweeted that it had taken over three hours to bring the fire under control, mainly due to a shortage of fire crews who had all been engaged on other incidents. Naturally, the press would have a field day with that comment in their belief that any delay was probably more to do with cuts in manpower rather than the number of incidents the service was dealing with. She found out that uniform had got the place taped up and that the CSIs were already busy at work on site. She hoped that that was not another assignment for Beth Dench and her team as she rather wanted Beth's full attention on the Scarecrow Girl investigation. There was precious little other information about the fire so she moved on to the rest of her emails but there was nothing else of note.

Sarah looked at the clock on the bottom right of her screen and, realising that time had ticked up to 7.30 a.m. she got up from the desk and moved over towards the white boards. Clapping her hands together to get everyone's attention, she detected an intensity among those who were gathered around her. This was always a good sign as it meant that everyone was up for whatever challenges the day would throw at them.

'Good morning everyone!' she started. 'This is our third official progress meeting in the investigation of the murder at The Garden House, Sheet Hill. For those of you who haven't yet met Grace, this is DS Grace Kendall who is one of our techie wizzkids, and I'm personally super-excited that she has been assigned to us. So, a very warm welcome, Grace.' The two young DCs nodded an acknowledgement to Grace. As Pennant and Kendall had been in conversation with each other when she arrived, Hunter assumed that their paths must have crossed when Pennant was in Traffic. She noted a familiarity between them.

Selitto waved across at Grace. 'Welcome to the Team, Grace.' She smiled demurely and turned back to look towards Hunter.

'Right,' Hunter started. 'Let's just deal with this fire first. I have little other news apart from the fact that there are suspicious circumstances. We obviously won't know what these are until the CSIs have taken a look. They're on site now but I imagine that KFR are still waiting for the structure to cool down so that they can declare it safe. So, there's nothing that immediately involves us.' She let this sink in before continuing.

'Okay,' Hunter turned to look at Selitto. 'What's the plan for today, Ted?'

Selitto was perched in his usual position by the window. He picked up his notebook from the desk beside him and flipped over a couple of pages. 'Well, as you know Stuart and I carried out an extensive search of The Garden House whilst the Crime Scene boys were on site. It was generally agreed that there is a possibility that the girl was killed in the dungeon and then placed on the allotment. The CSI team had found a CCTV system but had not yet discovered how it was activated. I'm hoping that Jim Carrigan will be able to break into it today so that we can take a look at events leading up to the time that the house was evacuated.'

'What's the problem with the CCTV?' It was a question from DC Elaine Jennings.

Out of habit, Selitto consulted his notes before answering. 'Well, it seems that what we had so far found was a sort of edited version of a full CCTV coverage. Stuart here,' he said, pointing at Crosby, 'felt that there should be a console with multi screens where the input was monitored all the time. But Carrigan had been unable to locate such a system by the time we left. At the moment, our best thinking is that there was an ulterior motive for the CCTV which is linked to blackmail and extortion but we're a long way from being able to take that forward. So, our objective today will be to try and squeeze further information out of the CSIs in the hope that we can at least establish how the girl was killed.'

'Okay, Ted. Thanks,' Hunter said surveying the team. 'I agree that we should get over to the lab later and sit on the CSIs until we get some worthwhile intel so that we can at least start trying to find out exactly what was going on at Sheet Hill. Stuart and Carolyn – looks like a task for you as Stuart knows the house and you, Carolyn, were at the PM. Probably best to let the CSI team finish their breakfast before piling in there!'

'Right!' Hunter continued, regaining their attention. 'We still need to concentrate on looking for Vashlili. She looked over to where DC Elaine Jennings was sitting at one of the desks fiddling with a computer mouse. 'Elaine! I'd like you to sit with Grace for at least this morning and get a handle on the sort of work she does for us. Should be more than interesting bearing in mind the sort of puzzles we have passed her way in the last seventy-two hours!' Grace smiled at Hunter and beckoned Jennings to join her. 'I'd also like you to start processing the information you picked up yesterday down at Meadowlands. Particularly, you should concentrate on getting as much intel on Dangerfield as you can. I still can't help thinking that he is a person of interest to us.'

She looked around the room at her young team. 'Okay! De-briefing back here at 6.00pm this evening!' Hunter called out as she crossed the floor as if going to leave the room. On the way, she caught Selitto's eye and nodded towards the corridor. He followed her out of the MIR as she made her way to the drinks area at the end of the corridor.

She turned to face him. 'I fancy a run out to Hildenborough. What about you?' she asked as she filled a cup with hot water from the wall unit, spooning in some coffee. 'I just can't help wondering whether this fire is linked to our other investigations. You know? Isolated pile of bricks, outhouses, no one's sure who the owner is, apparently uninhabited. Lots of similarities - but no bodies as far as I am aware. Coffee?'

Selitto declined another caffeine fix having already picked up a strong Costa on the way into the station earlier. 'Okay,' he replied, 'I can see your thinking but they might still be damping everything down. Besides, haven't we got enough on our plate to be going on with at the moment?'

Hunter shovelled some sugar into black coffee and gave it a stir. 'Yeah, probably, but I'd just like to eyeball it all the same – just so I've got the picture in my mind. Can't do any harm to have a poke around out there and be back in time for an afternoon visit to see dear old Beth and her boys!'

'Fine by me,' Selitto replied. They chatted some more about the dynamics of the team while Hunter drank her coffee, and then took the stairs down to the car park.

The traffic seemed to be particularly bad in Tonbridge High Street today. Millions had been spent on widening the pavements a couple of years ago so the road width had been narrowed thus preventing anyone from overtaking buses that had stopped to pick up passengers. An increased number of pedestrian crossings had also been put in place, and the lights seemed to change to red every time Selitto approached. He could feel Hunter's impatience rising as they continued their stop-start progress along the road. They eventually popped out of the top of the High Street like a cork out of a bottle and took the left fork towards Hildenborough.

'You know where this place is?' Selitto asked as he carefully negotiated the speed camera outside the Orchard Theatre.

'Think so,' replied Hunter. 'Either find Stocks Green Road or get on to Rings Hill and down past The Cinnamon. Then under the A21 and second left according to the chap I spoke to at KFR.'

'Okay,' said Selitto. 'Not sure how to get to Stocks Green from here so I'll go on to Rings Hill.' They drove in silence until they had exited Rings Hill and passed under the A21.

Hunter was looking off to the left. 'KFR said second left after the bridge. Hard to find.' Selitto slowed right down much to the annoyance of the car behind. Hunter suddenly shouted 'Left here!' and he yanked the wheel over, no indication. He received a prolonged hoot from the car behind as it sped off into the distance.

They found themselves on a very uneven and rutted farm track and soon came to a farm gate which was manned by a young WPC. 'Morning Susie,' Selitto said as he wound his window down. WPC Susie Maxwell was another member of the Tonbridge Quiz Team who Selitto had met on a number of occasions at quiz nights. She always struck him as a bubbly, carefree spirit who loved her job but didn't seem to have much ambition to progress further.

'Oh, good morning Sarge,' she replied. 'Didn't expect to see you here today.' She bent down to look across to the passenger seat. 'Oh, good morning ma'am!' she said, her face reddening.

'We're just going to take a quick look around,' Selitto told her. 'Who's up there?'

'We've got the CSI team, a couple of my colleagues and KFR have left a couple of their blokes there for the morning.'

'Thanks,' said Selitto. 'See you on our way out!' As the car moved forward, WPC Maxwell made a note of the names of DI Hunter and DS Selitto on her clipboard and inserted the time of arrival beside each name. She then put the clipboard under her arm and turned to face the sun.

Meanwhile, Selitto was gently crunching through some sizeable potholes as he crisscrossed his way along the farm track, trying to avoid craters of all shapes and sizes but not doing a very good job. Eventually they rounded the corner and, for the first time, laid eyes on a magnificent country house which had obviously been built with the intention of enjoying wonderful views of the rolling countryside – and the A21. He parked on the grass verge just short of the start of the gravel drive where a line of police tape had been erected. They ducked under the tape, walked past the large CSI van and a smaller KFR vehicle, and made their way towards the front door where they were met by another PC who neither of them recognised.

'Morning, Constable. I'm DI Hunter and this is DS Selitto. Who's in charge here?' Hunter tried to sound as informal as she possibly could but Selitto could still detect an air of superiority.

'Ma'am!' the PC replied, looking at a clipboard and failing to spot their names on his list of expected visitors. Frowning, he went on. 'You don't seem to be on my list for this location.'

'No,' replied Hunter. 'We're investigating a murder not far

from here and heard about the fire. We were just passing so thought we'd drop in and take a look to see if there is any potential crossover with our case. So, who's running the show here?'

The PC looked down at his clipboard. 'We have Crime Scenes Manager, Julian French, and he has two CSI officers with him. We also have two fire officers from KFR. Just to let you know that the KFR officers have not declared the whole structure of the building safe yet so the CSIs are confined to the front hall and staircase.'

'Okay,' said Hunter. 'We'll just pop our heads round the door and have a word with the CSIs.' With that, she pushed past him, up the steps and into the cavernous entrance hall where arc lights lit up the staircase in front of them.

'Walk no further!' boomed a voice from the shadows at the back of the stairs. They stopped in their tracks as a tall individual in a white suit, white hat, white booties and face mask appeared at the side of the staircase.

'Morning Jools!' Hunter called over to him. 'Just came over for a bit of a nose. Would you like us suited and booted?'

French made his way over to the two detectives, taking off his gloves as he walked and then shaking them warmly by the hand. 'Hello, Sarah! Haven't seen you in ages – and hello Ted. Don't think I've seen you since Kit's leaving party!' Selitto recalled a dreary night at the Vauxhall pub when one of the desk sergeants had retired. More people had turned up than had been expected and the food had gone before he even got there. So, he ended up having to get a fish supper from a local chippy on the way home.

'In answer to your question,' French continued, 'yes please if you want to walk any further into the house, and no if you just want to stand here. But there's not really much to see from here. You'd be better off taking a look out the back. You'll see far more of the fire damage from the garden at the rear of the house.'

'When are you hoping to get access to all areas?' Hunter asked, looking around the entrance hallway and craning her neck to see upstairs.

'Not sure at the moment,' came the reply. 'The fire seems to have started in an annexe which was joined on to the house by way of a courtyard. Access to that is from behind this staircase but that's off limits for us at the moment. The fire doesn't seem to have done much damage to the house itself but the annexe looks pretty gutted. We're hoping to get upstairs soon, and we think there's a cellar down that corridor so we'll get in there once it's safe to do so.'

'Okay!' Hunter had seen all she was going to from this vantage point, and she couldn't be bothered to get all togged up in a Tyvek suit if there wasn't much to see. 'Let's go and have a look around outside. Thanks, Jools. We'll look in before we go.' The detectives retraced their steps back on to the gravel drive and headed off to the side of the house.

Once they got round to the back of the house, it was clear to see where the fire had raged. There was little left of the annexe as a building, just a pile of twisted metal and other charred building materials that had collapsed into the inferno. Two KFR officers stood close to the back of the house, yellow helmets tucked under their arms, having a smoke and drinking from bottles of water.

'Morning, Officers,' Hunter called over as they approached. 'DI Hunter and this is DS Selitto from Tonbridge nick.' The

KFR officers turned to face them, instinctively discarding their cigarettes and grinding them into the grass under their fire boots.

'Good morning, ma'am,' one of the officers said. 'Fire Officer Phil Green and this is Fire Officer Ben Ryan. We're just keeping an eye on things until it's safe for the CSIs to get fully involved. Shouldn't be too long now.'

Hunter looked over to the smouldering ruins. 'Not much of that building left. Must have been quite a fire,' she surmised.

'Likely to have been deliberately started,' this from FO Phil Green. 'One of the lads found traces of an accelerant in the courtyard which links the house with the annexe. I think it's entirely likely that the whole lot would have gone up if we hadn't got to it fairly quickly. Luckily, some eagle-eyed motorist on the A21 called it in and we were on the scene soon after.'

'Any idea what might have been inside the building?' Selitto asked. 'Was it just an outhouse used for storage or was it used for some other purpose perhaps?'

FO Ben Ryan took over. 'Well, we haven't been able to have a good look but it seems that there are what look like a number of metal bed frames under all the other twisted metal so it could have been used as some sort of dormitory.'

Hunter had been looking off down the pretty garden but mention of the word 'dormitory' really got her attention, and she spun round to face the two fire officers.

'Could you be a bit more specific?' she asked. 'Did the beds look as if they had been spaced out, possibly with partitions between them or were they just all arranged along the walls like in a hospital?'

The fire officers looked at each other. Ryan took the initiative.

'Well, it's hard to say, ma'am. The contents of the building would have been moved around by the jets of water but, judging by the amount of debris we have, it doesn't look as if there was much partitioning in the area apart from one retaining wall which separated what was probably a bathroom. You can still just about make out the facilities.' He pointed over to an area furthest from the house. 'The bathroom area was over there.'

FO Phil Green suddenly seemed to remember something. 'One thing you might be interested in is the windows. Unless we're very much mistaken, they all had bars on them. And not just those thin bars that you used to get in the toilets at school, but really thick heavy-duty metal. Hardly damaged by the fire. You can pick them out quite easily.'

'I'm getting more interested in this place,' Hunter murmured to herself. 'How much longer did you say?' She addressed the fire officers.

'I think we're about ready to hand over to the CSIs so we'll go and have a word with them,' FO Ryan replied.

'Okay, thanks. Coming Ted?' she said and wandered off to look at a flower border which stretched the length of one side of the garden. Selitto nodded at the Fire Officers and followed Hunter down the garden. When he caught up with her, she turned around to look back at the house.

'Beds? Bars on windows? Communal bathroom? Remind you of anywhere?' she asked him. 'I may be barking up the wrong fucking tree but I can't help thinking that there are some similarities with that house next to the allotment. And, if we're able to find another scarecrow girl, I'd say that we would have a perfect match.' They wandered on to the end of the grassed area, all the time looking back to the house. Hunter pointed to

290

a shed which stood in the other corner of the garden and they walked over to it. As they approached, Selitto noticed that a padlock hung redundantly from the staple of the lock.

'Hmm!' Selitto grunted. 'Why would someone leave a padlock unlocked?' he questioned before pushing the door open.

43

Monday 24 July

Woons was at the office early. He sat at his desk, once again wishing that he still had that large box of havanas on the desk like he always had in the good old days. He would have lit one now and sat back to do some very serious thinking. But, a few years ago, he had quit the habit of a lifetime after bumping into some quack in a pub who had offered to do some tests on his lungs. These resulted in Woons being given a little jar of liquid tar which had allegedly been extracted from his lungs. He was so revolted by the sight of what was surely going to cost him his life that he tossed the box of havanas away and had never smoked anything from that day to this. But that didn't mean that he didn't still have the craving – such as right now.

Today, his primary objective was to work out what to do about Tsiklauri and his bunch of good-for-nothing fuckers who had dumped him right in the S H One T. He tried the emergency number in Georgia once more but this time it didn't even ring through. He fired up the computer on his desk and accessed the Georgian Airlines website. He knew that there were flights on Mondays, Wednesdays and Saturdays from Gatwick so he could go as early as tonight he thought. He twiddled his pen through the fingers of his right hand trying to work out the best strategy. Should he just turn up unannounced and demand to see Tsiklauri? What other option did he have if he couldn't get hold of them by phone?

He clicked on the Monday night flight and waited. And

waited. Why was the Georgian Airways website always so bloody slow? Finally, the flight times appeared. Flights to Georgia were always overnight which Woons found very tiresome as the seats they had on their planes had long ago lost their padding and, in any case, he just couldn't sleep sitting upright. Plus, the in-flight refreshments were shit so he would arrive at Tbilisi tired and hungry which would just make him even more pissed off with his paymasters than he usually was. Seats were available on the 11.00 p.m. flight – no wonder, he thought, who in their right mind would be wanting to go to that fucking country at that time of night? He clicked for a return arriving back at Gatwick on Wednesday evening, and found that there were also seats available on that flight too. He clicked to buy and then paid using a euro account from his bank in Madrid.

Feeling better now that he had a plan, plan, he took out his now powered-up laptop and googled the local news pages and found that the fire at Hildenborough was headline news on a number of the sites. Sketchy details but Kent Fire & Rescue would be making a statement soon. Police also there but no statement yet. Suppose they'll have to take poor old Candice to the cutting room so that she can be diced up, he surmised. She had been a great find and had made him a pile of money over the years. Despite her often fiery temper, he had a bit of a soft spot for her but hadn't seen her for a year or two.

His reverie was broken by the sound of a car pulling up outside the portacabin, the door slamming and a brisk knock on the office door. He flicked the blind up a couple of centimetres and saw that Spink was already back with the firm's car. Woons let him in and indicated a chair at the table by the door.

'I would offer you a coffee but I see you've already got one,' said Woons as Spink placed a huge beaker of Costa coffee on the table.

'Thanks, Billy, but I just picked this up at the Shell place up the road. Didn't know they did Costa so that'll be useful to know in future.' He sat down at the table and started rummaging around in a smart holdall he had carried in with him. He took out a laptop and plugged it into a socket in the wall behind him. The screen came to life as soon as he opened the lid.

'Okay, Billy,' he said, looking at the screen, 'I've had a go at looking through these drives. Two things. One, there's masses of stuff on them. And two, the quality's not too good.' He looked up at Woons. 'It's also been quite difficult finding the most recent stuff so we could at least see who might have caused all the damage. It looks like whoever came in and wrecked the place managed to find some of the cameras but not others which I have assumed are so well hidden or disguised that they can't be found. So, we do have some CCTV of the raid before the power was turned off but it's not particularly good.'

'Are you saying that the tapes are a load of rubbish and not worth nearly getting killed for?' Woons was now pacing the tiny space between his desk and the table.

'Not completely!' There was a trace of optimism in Spink's voice. 'Come and take a look at this.'

Woons did a detour around his desk and pulled a chair up so that he was sitting next to Spink who moved the laptop slightly so that Woons could see the screen. 'Here, take a look at this sequence. I'm not sure where the camera is hidden but you can see the front door and the lower part of the staircase.

I'll run the sequence and see what you make of it.'

Spink tapped the advance key and the time-lapsed images began to run stiltedly across the screen. Woons watched as two men in either balaclavas or ski masks came through the front door and rushed up the stairs. Another man then entered the house, his face similarly covered by something. He soon disappeared from view. 'I reckon he went behind the stairs and out through the passageway we found leading to the courtyard.' Woons kept watching the screen. Finally, another figure entered the house. Woons craned his neck to get a better view.

'That fucker's not got a mask on,' he observed. His eyes stayed glued to the screen as the figure crossed the hall and then took the stairs two at a time, quickly passing the camera's line of sight. Spink ran the tape back.

'Difficult to make out, Billy,' he said manipulating the touchpad on the laptop, 'but this seems to be the best I can get.' He stopped the image as the figure was about to start up the staircase. This was a muscular, powerfully built man with huge shoulders and biceps. The face was difficult to see as it appeared to be in shadow or was it a beard? Woons was straining to make out the facial features.

Spink sat back in his chair. He steepled his fingers and looked at the image on the screen, trying desperately to think where he had seen that face before. After what seemed like an age, Woons sat back, still staring at the screen.

The only sound they could hear was the faint whirring of a small fan deep inside the laptop. Otherwise, the silence was oppressive.

Spink eventually spoke. 'I've seen him somewhere before, Billy,' he said.

'I know, Tricky,' Woons almost whispered. 'So have I. So have I. But I can't for the fucking life of me think where. Foreign, that's for sure. And obviously in charge. Looks a hell of a beast. Where would I have seen him? Why would I have seen him? God! This is going to start to annoy me! Have we seen him together – you and me somewhere?'

They lapsed into silence again, still staring at the screen, wracking their collective brains, coming up with no answers to the number one question. Who the fuck was this guy?

44

Monday 24 July

It looked like any other garden shed Sarah Hunter had been in although, if she was brutally honest with herself, she hadn't been in many. Gardening wasn't really her thing and, although she now had a pretty little garden to go with her chocolate-boxy country cottage, she had chosen to delegate its upkeep to a lovely retired gentleman living a bit further down her lane.

'Doesn't look like there's much for us here,' she said scanning the walls and the workbench, subconsciously noting that all the implements seemed to be in their place. Sarah had learnt her lesson about observation at an early stage in her career in CID when she had failed to spot that a scythe was missing from its peg in a garage. There was an outline of the scythe on the white painted wall but the implement was missing. As this had turned out to be the murder weapon, she had missed a vital piece of evidence early in the investigation. It had taken a long time for her to live down the embarrassment and, to this day, some of her old colleagues still recalled the tale if they were all out together for a few drinks in London.

Hunter backed out of the shed. 'Can't explain the unlocked padlock but we have to assume that someone just didn't lock up properly. Probably expecting to come back but then got side-tracked. Sort of thing I'd do – phone rings, you answer it or look at the screen – distracted – can't remember what you were doing...' she trailed off. They both walked back up the garden in silence.

As if to order, Sarah's phone rang. She thumbed the screen.

'Hi, Beth. How's it going?' She stopped walking and concentrated on the phone call. Selitto assumed that Dench was giving her an update on progress as Hunter frowned, raised her eyebrows, frowned again and then squeezed her eyes tightly shut before opening them and staring off into the distance. 'Okay, Beth. Keep going. Shall I get Grace to liaise with Jimbo with regard to getting those tapes looked at?' She nodded, nodded again, wished Dench good luck and disconnected the call.

She was just about to relate Dench's news to Selitto when a shout came from across the lawn. It was FO Ryan. 'DI Hunter,' he called out. 'Something you should see over here!' The detectives hurried over to the scene of the blaze where FO Ryan was standing. 'We're trying not to move anything until the CSIs have done their work but it looks like there might be the remains of a human body in here. Over there!' he said, pointing to one of the twisted metal bedsteads which had a couple of blackened and burnt rafters strewn across the top of it. 'Looking at the remains, we can probably say it was quite a smallish person. Anyway, Phil's just gone off to alert the CSI people so they should be able to arrange to get it down to the morgue this afternoon.'

Hunter and Selitto stood outside the ring of crime scene tape which surrounded the area where the annexe had once stood, and stared into the morass of twisted metal. 'Thanks for the heads up,' Hunter said to the fire officer. 'Not sure it'll help us much if the body's been severely burned. But you never know what these pathologists can make of even the most damaged corpses these days!' Turning to Selitto, she added 'Think we'd better go and find Jools', and walked off across the patio at the back of the house and round to the front drive.

She skipped up the steps into the front hallway. 'Jools!' she called out, 'Can we just help ourselves to the Tyvek suits?'

A voice came from somewhere behind the staircase. 'Yes, okay, they're in the back of the van. The PC's got the keys. Sorry, can't remember his name!'

Once they were both suited up with covers on their feet and wearing hats and face masks, the two detectives returned to the main entrance and took their first steps into the hallway. French was still behind the staircase and, having propped a door open, he was looking at the walls of a narrow passageway with a UV lamp. He caught sight of them out of the corner of his eye.

'This passageway leads out into a courtyard which seems to have been the way to get to the annexe. As far as we can see, anyone using the annexe would have had to come through this corridor and out across the courtyard.' French continued to scan the walls with the lamp. 'Looks like it was well used. Lots of scuffing and marks on the wall. Finger-trailing. Dirt on the floor probably picked up walking across the courtyard. Food crumbs on the floor. Food stains on the walls – probably soup. But nothing of particular interest. Perhaps we will be able to tell more when we get into the burnt-out annexe.'

'One of the FO's reckons they've found remains of a human body out there,' Hunter chipped in, retracing her steps to the main hall.

'Have they, by jove!' exclaimed French. 'Better get out there and see what they're on about. Last time I had an FO telling me he'd found human remains, it turned out to be a badger which had got caught up in a fire. Poor bloke didn't notice that it had two too many legs!' And, with that, French shuffled off down the passageway and through the door into the courtyard.

'Come on, let's have a look upstairs!' Hunter suggested as they looked up at the impressive main staircase. Once at the top of the stairs, they turned to their left and were looking down a corridor which had two doors on either side and one at the end. Selitto ambled to the end of the corridor and tried the door. It opened into an ornately equipped bathroom with luxury roll-top bath, walk-in double shower, double wash-hand basin, bidet and toilet. Mirrors on all the walls. Candles on numerous shelves dotted around the walls. Two light settings – subtle or stark. The best toiletries. Lots of fluffy towels. Deep pile wall-to-wall carpet. Luxurious.

'Wow! You could spend some time in here!' he purred, particularly eyeing up the walk-in shower.

'Speak for yourself!' groaned Hunter who had craned her neck over his shoulder for a quick squint at the bathroom before turning back into the corridor. Pampering was not really her thing. She tried one of the plain doors just up from the bathroom, pushed into the room, turned to flick the light switch, and then stood back with her mouth half open. 'Good grief!' she whispered.

Selitto eased his way into the room and stood beside her. 'Good grief, indeed!' he began. The room wasn't dissimilar to one he had seen at The Garden House but it was much more expensively furnished. There was also a considerable amount of BDSM equipment arranged around the room as well as two movie cameras on tripods. Two huge screens were built into the wall at the end of one of the biggest beds Selitto had ever seen. Some lighting equipment had been stored in one corner of the room, and a huge wardrobe was built into one of the other walls.

Sarah Hunter walked into the room and did a 360-degree twirl. 'Hmmm!' she sighed. 'If I'm not very much mistaken, it looks like we've got two rooms knocked into one here. Better make sure Jools takes a good look at those cameras. Doubt that there'll be anything stored on them here but it would be handy to know how content was transmitted to a host receiver – and where that might be!'

Retracing her steps, Hunter returned to the corridor and went across to inspect an ornately decorated door. An abstract pattern had been carved across two central panels which had been inlaid into the wooden door. In the centre of the design was a black iron ring door knocker which had two grey serpents twisting their bodies around each curve of the ring. Their heads jutted out from the top of the knocker on either side. An interesting effect, Hunter thought, and totally in keeping with the other opulence she had so far seen along this corridor.

'Shall we knock and go in or do we already know there's no one at home?' she joked as Selitto finally managed to take his eyes off the bedroom and had come across the corridor to stand beside her. In the end, she simply depressed the ornate gold lever handle and the door swung open until its progress was halted when it crunched into what sounded like a piece of furniture. The floor in front of them was strewn with papers, files of every size and description, record books, magazines.

Drawers from a centrally-positioned desk had been emptied and slung away to the far corners of the room. A large office chair had been unceremoniously launched across the room and it was this that was preventing the door from fully opening. Paintings on the walls had been slashed, canvasses hanging forlornly from their wooden frames. Glass which had once covered the artworks was now smashed to smithereens all over the carpet. A TV monitor on the far wall had been completely smashed. A photocopier next to the desk looked as if it had been attacked with a sledgehammer, its innards hanging pathetically from its frame. The desk had two deep craters in its top with splinters of wood pointing to the ceiling at the point at which either an axe or a sledgehammer had impacted.

'Wow!', Hunter exhaled. 'Someone really lost their rag in here! I'm surprised that the desk hasn't gone over!' Selitto got down on his haunches and shone his torch into the knee hole.

'I can answer that,' he said from under the desk. 'It's been screwed to the floor!' He pulled his head out of the knee hole and remained squatting beside the desk, looking around to see if there was any sign of a break in the plush carpet which covered the floor of the room. When nothing caught his eye, he grabbed hold of the desktop and levered himself up.

He looked around at the devastation in the room. 'You know what? I'm almost getting a feeling of deja-vu in here. The room at the house by the allotments which was obviously an office was trashed in the same way as this room. In both cases, it looks as if someone was looking for something, couldn't find it, so went berserk. In the allotment house, we think they were looking for the tapes from the recorders. Could be the same motive here. And this is clearly another very upmarket knocking shop so that's another connection. But, again, a complete lack of people.'

Before Hunter had a chance to answer, there were raised voices from down in the entrance hall. They retraced their steps to the landing in time to see French scuttling round the foot of the staircase and off down another dark corridor.

'Come on!' Hunter beckoned as she sped down the stairs in pursuit of French. They both came to a halt just inside a door at the end of the corridor where they found themselves standing at the top of a steep flight of concrete steps leading down into what would have been a dark and cool cellar. Only it most certainly wasn't dark as at least three powerful torches played their beams around the room, and onto what the detectives quickly realised was a body slumped into a high-backed chair. Huge studs surrounded the chair's frame, and an array of chains and leather straps criss-crossed its back.

French and his two colleagues were standing around the chair as Hunter and Selitto inched their way down the steps. 'That's far enough for the moment, Sarah.' French had caught sight of them out of the corner of his eye. 'We'll need a little time just to set up in here and get the photos done then you can have a look. Not a pretty sight I'm afraid, and it's definitely a homicide so it'll be over to you soon enough.'

'Okay, Jules!' replied Hunter. 'Thanks for that! We've got to be going anyway. We can catch up with the body at the PM. Any clues for identification?'

'White, female. Probably late forties early fifties,' French said as he stood back from the seated corpse. 'A few tattoos from what I can see so they may give you some help. But you'll probably require a facial reconstruction if you want to go for a publicity shot. As I said, not a pretty sight!'

'And I won't ask the sixty-four thousand dollar question,' said Hunter, jokingly.

'And I won't answer it!' replied French. 'Might see you at the PM?' he asked as Hunter and Selitto climbed back into the hall and made their way to the front door. Taking off their Tyvek gear, they dropped it into the waste sack provided by the PC on the door. Walking out into the fresh air, Hunter turned to look up at the house whilst walking backwards towards the car.

'Quite a building,' she remarked. 'I'm glad the fire didn't spread to the main part of the house.' She then turned to get into the car and waited for Selitto to drive her back to Pembury Road.

45

Monday 24 July

It started as a low growl that grew louder. The sound of a throaty exhaust on a vehicle motoring at speed interrupted the silence in Woons' office. Spink looked across at Woons and then at the window where the blind still shut out much of the daylight. The blast from a triple airhorn split the serenity of the sunny morning and they both instinctively dived for the window. Woons was first to get there and yanked the blind up just in time to see a black van sliding into a handbrake turn in the small turning circle at the front of the office, dirt and small stones flying everywhere.

Just as the vehicle was coming out of the turn, one of the back doors flew open and what looked like a black sack was propelled out of the van to roll in the dust which was now forming a cloud around the portacabin. With another blast from the airhorn, the van then accelerated away back down the track.

'Fuck's going on, Tricky?' Woons muttered under his breath, staring at the black sack which had come to rest just in front of Spink's wrecked car.

Spink was already out of the office and was gingerly approaching what he had originally thought was a black sack. But, now that he was closer to it, he recognised it as a body bag which could only mean one thing. The way it had come to rest, its shape reminded him more of a sack of potatoes than of the body of a human being. He bent down, pulling a couple of the handles so that he could straighten the bag out and get hold of the main zip fastener. And then he stopped as a feeling a dread fear coursed through his veins. Whatever's inside this bag, he thought, doesn't seem to be in one piece!

He took hold of the zipper and gently tugged it down. A mass of dark, wiry hair, strands of grey, more strands of grey, an older person. He tugged further. A deathly white forehead came up to meet the hairline. Spink held his breath; his heart was thumping against his rib cage. He took hold of the zipper and gently tugged it down further and then sat back on his haunches. Dark eyes stared sightlessly at him from a face which had lost none of its vivaciousness in older age. Despite cuts and bruises and an obviously broken nose, the face that looked back at him from within the bag was unmistakably of Hispanic origin. As he continued to inch the zipper downwards, an uncontrollable shiver suddenly coursed through Spink's entire body as a stark realisation overwhelmed him. The head was not attached to anything; it had been severed at the neck. The head of Maria Travisedo stared back at him almost as if in a gesture of supplication.

Spink was squatting by the body bag with his back to Woons who was now creeping across the driveway, trying to see what Spink was up to. 'You all right, Tricky?' Woons whispered. Before Spink had a chance to pull the zipper back up, he heard a sharp intake of breath and an audible gasp from behind his left ear. He quickly closed the bag and stood up. Woons was transfixed to the spot, his eyes boring into the black sack. Spink edged away and took up a position between Woons and the portacabin.

Eventually, Woons turned to face Spink. 'We're fucked, Tricky!' he whispered. 'We're well and truly fucked!' And, with that, he slowly picked his way across the driveway and stepped back into his office. He sat in his chair behind the desk, hardly daring to breathe. He could see Spink through the window where the blind had not yet been returned to its normal setting of completely closed. Spink was on the phone, extravagant arm signals indicating that he was having difficulty getting his message across. Eventually, he went out of Woons' line of sight before appearing back in the office.

'OK, Billy,' he said closing the door and sitting down at the table, 'think I've got that sorted. Had to call in another favour but Mickey should be here soon to take that away. He's got a mate who's got a contact on a big development over near Crawley.'

They sat in silence.

Spink spent most of the morning running through the CCTV material which he had collected from the Hildenborough house the night before. The overall quality wasn't that good and he'd spent a lot of time toggling the picture backwards and forwards to see if he could make out any of the faces of the people who flitted across the screen. He also found that the cameras had been poorly positioned – either too far away as with the one which covered the drive and the front entrance, or too close as with the one which only covered the bottom few steps of the staircase.

Harding had arrived and taken the BMW away to have the rear window repaired, and Emma had stopped by briefly to replace the dressing on Spink's shoulder wound. She looked tired and drawn after their escapade of the night before, and she had announced that she was going home to get some rest.

Woons had disappeared altogether which was a common occurrence when he was troubled – he always made out that he needed time to think on his own. A weasely little man had turned up in a battered four-by-four to collect the body bag, and Spink had handed over the cash demanded. He now had the office to himself and was concentrating on the mystery man they had identified earlier.

The picture moved forward, frame by frame. Once the man was out of shot, Spink toggled the picture back, frame by frame. Was it a beard or just shadow? What was mystery man's actual size? He looked enormous. Or was that just the camera angle playing tricks? Maybe Spink hadn't seen him before – maybe it was just someone Woons had met on his trips to Georgia. Or could he be one of Vashlili's cronies? He had met a couple of them – right headcases he had thought. But, try as he might, he just couldn't get any further than just thinking that he had seen the man before.

He had another look at the tape from the outdoor camera, saw the car drive up to the front door and the three men get out. Too far away to get any sort of I/D on them, and the quality was so poor that he couldn't even read the registration plate – just on the off chance that he recognised it. He wasn't even sure what make and model of car it was! He did, however, notice that there were no other vehicles parked outside the house which would seem to indicate that there were no punters in residence at the time of the raid.

Spink recalled that Candice had had to close things down because of an outbreak of what Harding had politely described as the screaming abdabs. He disconnected the hard drive he had been looking at and rifled through the others until he came to the one which he recalled was from a camera overlooking the courtyard between the house and the annexe. He connected it to the laptop and ran the sequence back until it showed Friday's date. He then ran it forward and soon realised that this wasn't a motion-sensitive feed. Absolutely nothing was going on and he speeded up the feed until, sometime on Friday afternoon, he noticed what looked like Candice crossing the courtyard from the house. She was very soon on her way back and that was that until the tape cut out at around 9.00pm.

He sat back and tried to recall Harding's report on the Hildenborough house. Something about a client bringing in a dodgy curry and Candice having to shove punters off to other houses. So, when did the dodgy curry arrive? He wracked his brains to try and recall the sequence of events. Was it the day after the girl went off the roof at Wateringbury? In which case, the dodgy curry must have arrived on Thursday. He rewound the tape until Thursday's date came up. There was quite a lot of activity – girls frequently crossed the courtyard to where they were quartered, and Candice also made several visits to the annexe. He stopped the tape, thinking about what he had just seen. Lots of activity on Thursday – no activity on Friday. Presumably that was the day the girls were out of action.

With this thought in mind, he started the tape again. It was now later in the afternoon, and the activity seemed to have lessened so Spink decided to move the tape on.

In doing so, he nearly missed the man sneaking around the walls of the courtyard clutching the tell-tale brown bags which are the stock-in-trade of takeaways. He looked at the clock in the bottom right hand corner of the screen. 5.47 p.m. Nearly ten to six in the afternoon. He continued to watch, and it wasn't long before the man crept out of the annexe and quickly crossed the courtyard, head down in an effort to avoid the all-seeing eye of the camera.

Spink stopped the tape and stared at the retreating figure, frozen in time as the clock read 5.53 p.m. He sat back in his chair, a look of disbelief on his face. Even without a good look at the face of the visitor, Spink would have recognised him any day. It was just that he couldn't put the whole thing into context. He just sat there staring at the screen. What the fuck was Vashlili doing delivering a dodgy curry to the girls at the Hildenborough House?

46
Monday 24 July

When they got back to Pembury Road, Sarah Hunter went straight to the MIR in search of DS Grace Kendall. When she couldn't find her there, she toured the first floor looking in all the offices. She eventually found her and DC Jennings in conversation with a couple of DCs from another team in one of the small meeting rooms.

'Hi, Grace,' she called from the doorway. 'Any chance of a bit of a debrief?'

'No problem!' replied Kendall. 'I've got my laptop so we can do it here.' The two DCs took the hint and left the room. Hunter sat down next to Kendall so that she could look at the screen. Elaine Jennings took another chair and positioned herself on the other side of Kendall so that she could also see the screen.

Grace Kendall had been one of the first detectives Sarah Hunter had met when she moved to Tonbridge, and the two women had quickly formed considerable personal respect for each other. Whereas Hunter was impatient and was always looking for ways of getting things done in the shortest time possible, Kendall took a far more measured approach, preferring to check and check again and, if necessary, to make sure that the information she was providing was as accurate as it could possibly be. She had started her professional life in the Spooks Service but, after several years of field support work, she decided that she wasn't getting the work/life balance which had become important to her. Wanting to get back to her childhood

311

roots in Kent, she had approached the Chief Constable and offered her all-round services as a desk investigator (as she had called it), code breaker, profiler and an extra pair of hands in any murder investigation team.

To her great surprise, the Chief could see certain advantages in having someone of Grace's calibre and experience in one of his busier Major Investigation Teams so he had assigned her to Tonbridge for six months to see what sort of impact she could make. To begin with, her colleagues were slightly suspicious of her, particularly as the Chief had put her in as a DS. But Grace was soon showing her credentials as a supremely talented desk investigator. She was not only impressing her colleagues with the quality of her research work but also with the quantity of work that she was able to get through. She also had a network of contacts which went well outside the boundaries of Kent Police and, indeed, of the police force in general. Her ability to tap into old contacts in the other services and into other key sources of information such as the Border Agency and the Foreign Office was of considerable benefit to Kent Police which, apart from anything else, was engaged in a never-ending front-line fight against illegal immigration.

Grace was also the ultimate team player and was universally liked at Pembury Road. Although she was ferociously protective of her private life, she took part in various social activities and was an avid touchline supporter of the Tonbridge Police Football XI, happy to come out in all weathers dressed in a myriad of colourful jumpers, scarves, coats and woolly hats.

In the early days of her tenure at Pembury Road, Sarah Hunter had quickly recognised what the Chief Constable had clearly seen in Grace Kendall. They became firm friends and had, on occasion, stolen the odd evening together in a dark corner of a country pub where they feasted on steak & chips and the odd glass of wine, talking non-stop about work-related matters. If the truth be known, Hunter knew very little about Grace Kendall, the attractive mid-30s woman with long auburn hair, other than the fact that she was bloody good at her job and was a godsend for all the MITs at Tonbridge. They laughed a lot when they met socially but their relationship at work was always thoroughly professional.

'Right! This is what we've got so far,' Hunter started. 'We've got someone who has disappeared from a posh country hotel, a dead girl dressed up as a scarecrow, an empty house with signs of blood spattering in one room, another empty house where fire has destroyed an annexe, and a dead middle-aged woman who had her face rearranged ante mortem. And probably another dead girl burnt to a cinder in the fire. At the moment, I am struggling to see a connection always assuming that there actually is a connection.'

'Agreed', said Kendall, nodding. 'It's hard to see how they can be connected but I do have something for you on that sheet of codes you got from the safe in the hotel room.' Her fingers whistled over the laptop keypad and two of the lines of code came up on the screen. She turned the screen more towards Hunter so that the DI had a better view. The following appeared on the screen –

010715 N1T1L91 4252/2520 7161847880 SHARKFIN
180420 3T6U2N VAS

001118 12Y21D13I12A 4226/2539 5283737880

BLACKMAMBA 180602 8C8N1T VAS

'Some of this seems to be fairly straightforward code work,' Kendall said, turning towards Hunter. 'Like reversing numbers and letters. Some of the other numbers and letters had me stumped for a while as they seemed to make no sense at all. So, let's look at the first line.' She highlighted it on the screen and used the arrow to point to each section of the line of code.

'The first numbers are quite obviously a date. It could be 1st July 2015 which could be a date of some significance. But my bet is that it has been reversed so that it's actually 15th July 2001. That would make more sense on the basis that I think the next set of numbers and letters is a name. In this line, the code is straightforward using numbers of letters in the alphabet so 1 is A, 2 is B, etcetera. The name in this line is, therefore, Natalia.'

Hunter peered at the screen. 'Can that really be right?' she asked. 'Looking at the next line, I'm having trouble applying that theory as we'd have a name like ABYBADACAABA. Can't think of anywhere you'd get a name like that. Sounds more like the name of a Genesis LP!'

'That was ABACAB', replied Kendall with a smirk. Hunter raised an eyebrow but soon focused back on the screen. 'No, of course you're right,' Kendall continued, 'and this did have me stumped for a while until I realised that the single numbers only went as far as the letter I. Since nothing was making sense, I started looking at double figure numbers. So that the first letter is actually the 12th letter of the alphabet which is L. The third letter is the 21st letter which is U and the fifth letter is the 13th letter which is M. The seventh letter is another L so the name we have is LYUDMILA.'

314

Sarah Hunter sat back, thinking. 'What are those names — Eastern Europe?'

'Well, I've done a little research and, yes, Eastern Europe is favourite. Could be Bulgarian, Romanian, perhaps even from Georgia. Difficult to be precise. I'll need to do a bit more research.' Kendall moved the pointer to the next set of numbers.

'The next sets of numbers have caused the most problem and, to be honest, I'm not sure I've quite got it sorted.' She sat back in her chair. 'I contacted an officer from the Border Force who I met at a conference earlier this year. He's had a good look at these numbers and has come up with the possibility that they are co-ordinates of some sort. I haven't been able to take this theory much further but he did call me this morning to say that he thought the numbers ending in 7880 were Bulgarian mobile phone numbers. He says that mobile numbers in Bulgaria start with 0887 so that would mean that these numbers have been simply reversed.'

'So that's twice I have heard Bulgaria mentioned,' observed Hunter.

'Yes,' Kendall agreed, 'but then the trail goes a bit cold as I've been unable to break the code of SHARKFIN or BLACKMAMBA or any of the other words inserted in this column. It is, of course, always possible that they are simply aliases which would mean something to the person reading the list. This would make sense as the words are often repeated so perhaps these are aliases used by people who have responsibility for something or someone.'

'Hmm!', Hunter grunted. 'What about the last set of numbers? Looks like more dates to me.'

'Yep,' agreed Kendall. 'Again, reversed to give us 20th April and 2nd June. The last set of numbers and letters took me ages and was eventually solved by a friend who is a crossword fanatic. She thinks they are anagrams of postcodes. So, assuming that she was looking for local postcodes, and knowing that all Kent postcodes can only start with the letters C, D, M or T, my friend eventually came up with a postcode for Bethersden and one for Etchinghill, both of which are not far from the Dover area or the Eurotunnel terminal. Looks straightforward once you know what you're looking at!'

'What about the VAS?' asked Hunter.

'Well, I reckon that's your man Vashlili, don't you?' Kendall looked across at Hunter as if she was stating the blindingly obvious.

'So, what have you made of these co-ordinates?' Sarah asked, getting a bit restless as she felt that they were on the edge of a mini breakthrough given all the information that Grace was now turning up.

'My best guess is that they are map co-ordinates but without knowing if they are north, south, east or west it's difficult to work out where they pinpoint. Plus, we don't know if they have been reversed or whether they're as is. My guy at the Border Force is getting a pal of his to have a look at them so we may know more later.'

Hunter sat back, still staring at the laptop, willing a solution to the puzzle to suddenly pop out of her head. At the same time, her mind was frantically processing the information which Grace Kendall had just presented to her. Eventually, a thought crossed her mind.

'If we are dealing with people trafficking or illegal immigrants or something else related to these activities,' Hunter started in a hypothesising tone, 'this might be some sort of register of people who have already been trafficked into the UK or who are currently being trafficked to the UK. If you're right and the first set of numbers is a date for the year 2001, then these could be the dates of birth of two young girls aged around seventeen. The dates towards the end of the sequence are in the here & now so could perhaps be dates of delivery or expected arrival in the UK. I agree that Sharkfin and Blackmamba and all the other names are probably aliases of people who are in the network of the traffickers, and the mobile numbers are probably the means by which to contact them although I doubt that the numbers remain active for very long. If we continue this train of thought, the Kent postcodes could either relate to where the girls are being kept following arrival in the UK or they could denote the end delivery point. Have you got the full list there?'

Kendall tapped a few keys on the laptop and a pdf file opened up showing the two pages of information which had been taken from the safe at the hotel. Hunter squinted at the screen, looking for inspiration. After a while, she pointed at the penultimate column.

'Yep, I'm right!' she murmured. 'There are only about half a dozen different postcodes on this list so these must relate to either delivery points or safe houses where the illegals are kept until they're moved to their final destinations. So, it looks like trafficking in its purest form. And not just the trafficking of illegal immigrants. If I was a betting person, I'd put my shirt on each line on this list relating to a girl who is being trafficked specifically for the sex trade.'

'Steady on!' quipped Kendall.

Hunter smiled, but she knew she was on to something. She stared at the mystery numbers which someone thought were co-ordinates. She cast her mind back to training at Hendon when she had first joined the Met. Had she learned map reading as part of her training? She couldn't recall but, casting her mind back even further to her Duke of Edinburgh Award days she most certainly had. She remembered cold days and nights trying to navigate her way around the Yorkshire Dales with just a map and a compass to help her. And then she saw what had been missing.

'If these are map co-ordinates, aren't they normally expressed in degrees and minutes?' she asked no one in particular. Kendall shrugged and returned her gaze to the screen. 'In which case these numbers would need to be split up into pairs.'

Hunter rummaged in the drawer of the desk they were sitting at and pulled out a dog-eared pad of paper and a biro which looked as if it had been chewed within an inch of its life. She scribbled down the numbers in pairs, leaving gaps between each pair. So, she now had 42 52 / 25 20. She held the biro over the numbers and then inserted the symbol denoting degrees after the first pair of numbers in each sequence. She couldn't remember how you annotated minutes so she just sat back in her chair.

Kendall leaned across and looked at what Hunter had come up with. 'Shall we try that in Google Maps?' she asked. Hunter nodded.

After a few keystrokes to save the pdfs they had been looking at, Kendall had got on to the Google Maps landing page and now keyed in one of the newly-written co-ordinates. She pressed the return key and the screen immediately changed so that they were now looking at a map of a foreign country where the place names were written in letters she recognised as being more like Russian Cyrillic script. The information box on the left of the screen indicted that these were the coordinates for the town on Gabrovo in Bulgaria. She then clicked on the 'satellite' box and found that they were looking at a large, well-developed town spanning the Yantra River.

'Wow!' Hunter exclaimed. She was clearly excited by this discovery and suggested that Grace try the other set of coordinates which they had. Kendall's fingers caressed the keys once again, repeating the exercise to access Google Maps. This time, the information box on the left of the screen showed that they were looking at a map of Stara Zagora, the satellite pictures showing that this was another large town in Bulgaria.

'Bingo!' Sarah's voice was barely above a whisper as she drank in the information on the screen. 'Now at least we know that there's a connection with an Eastern European country!' This was a breakthrough!

Sarah Hunter and Grace Kendall agreed to meet up again in an hour's time to review other seemingly unconnected parts of what could now be a major case in the making. Leaving Kendall's office, she strode along the corridor, keen to get back to the team. She barrelled through the door into the MIR and was surprised to see everyone hard at work. No doubt checking and double-checking the sparse information which they had already accumulated.

She stopped at Stuart Crosby's desk. 'Not at the CSIs yet, Stuart?' she asked.

'No, ma'am,' he replied. 'They weren't ready for us first thing so we're doing a bit more desk-work and then we'll get over there in about half an hour.' Hunter nodded, and made her way over to the white boards.

'Right! Listen up!' She clapped her hands to get their attention. 'Okay! We may have just got ourselves a mini breakthrough although, at the moment, it is just a theory we are working on.' Selitto, who had taken up his customary position beside the window, shot her a quizzical look.

'As you know, Grace Kendall has been trying to unscramble the data contained in the documents which we recovered from the safe in the room at Meadowlands. It now looks like we have managed to access important information which opens up new lines of enquiry for us and gives us a clearer picture of what we are probably looking at here.'

Hunter had their attention now. Every member of the team

had turned to look at her and no one was idly staring at a screen with half an ear on what she was saying.

Sarah continued. 'The data itself probably relates to young girls who have been, or are in the process of being, trafficked to the UK illegally – and probably for the sex industry although we have no cast iron proof of that right at this moment.'

The team members shuffled in their seats and looked around at each other. For such a young and relatively inexperienced team, this case was potentially a baptism of fire and they were probably all experiencing the same emotions – excitement tinged with sadness and a great deal of apprehension about what the investigation might uncover.

'It looks like the girls are mainly aged around seventeen. Grace is unravelling the complete list now but the ones we looked at were predominately from areas around towns and cities in Bulgaria. It is, therefore, more than likely that Scarecrow Girl was Bulgarian.' There was an audible intake of collective breath as Hunter passed on this information. 'We think that they are probably entering the UK through Dover or the Channel Tunnel and are then being kept at holding points in East Kent until they're moved to their final destinations.'

DC Pennant wanted to say something. 'Yes, Carolyn,' Hunter encouraged.

'The IUD which the Pathologist removed from Scarecrow Girl was apparently of Bulgarian origin,' she said. 'So that would seem to fit with the theory that the girls are being sourced from Bulgaria.'

'Yes, good point!' Hunter replied. 'Have we got Partington's report yet?' Pennant shook her head. 'Okay! Who's in charge of the Scarecrow Girl board?' DC Crosby put his hand up.

'Right, Stuart,' Hunter began, 'suggest you start by putting in the location where the body was found. Get hold of a picture of the body in situ on the allotment. You can get one of these from the CSIs. Also get hold of a picture of the girl's face. You'll probably find one in the Pathologist's report when it arrives. You can also write down time and date of death and stated cause of death. Then add any critical information such as the Bulgarian IUD being found inside her. That should get you started anyway.'

Hunter turned back to the team. 'Right, the fire at Hildenborough.' She was just about to give them an update when there was a knock at the door. 'Yes,' Hunter called over, sounding slightly irate that she had been interrupted whilst in full flow.

The door opened and a young man of Asian origin stepped into the room. Hunter raised her eyebrows, questioning who this might be.

'Hello, ma'am, I'm DC Azzar Mishraz,' the young man said, introducing himself. 'The DCI has suggested that you might need another pair of hands so I have been assigned to your team.'

Hunter was very rarely stuck for words but this was one occasion when she was transfixed to the spot, open-mouthed. She caught a glimpse of Selitto out of the corner of her eye, shoulders pumping, trying not to laugh. She quickly gathered herself together and went over to shake the young man's hand.

'Welcome to the team, Azzar!' she said, deciding against following up with a comment that she'd take whoever she could get. 'We're in the middle of a short briefing but you can meet the team members and get up to speed on what's been going on when we've finished.' DC Mishraz shuffled along the wall of the MIR until he was close to Selitto whilst the others turned back to face Hunter.

'Right! Back to the fire at Hildenborough,' she continued. 'We know that there is at least one body at the house and that cause of death will be nothing to do with the fire. We also think that there might be another body where cause of death is likely to be on account of the fire. Crime Scene Investigators are all over it but I think we should have a presence there so that we can then follow through to the post mortem. So, let's see...' Hunter scanned the collection of fresh faces in front of her. 'Elaine, you take DC Mishraz with you and get over to Hildenborough. Sit on the CSIs if you have to but make sure that you collect all the information you can so that we don't have to actually wait for their report. Also, you should both attend the PM – it may be a bit gruesome but we need to know time, date and cause as soon as possible. Uniform are guarding the site and you should introduce yourselves to Julian French who is the Crime Scene Manager – tell him I sent you! Any questions?'

Jennings looked over at Mishraz and raised her eyebrows. He shrugged and looked towards the door. 'No, that's all understood,' she said to Hunter.

'Good!' Hunter exclaimed. 'Right! Carolyn and Stuart – you're responsible for leaning on Beth Dench's team for all they can give us on the allotment house and the location of Scarecrow Girl's body. Even if they haven't finished the formal report, lean on them and get as much information as possible. Also, chase up the PM report. Partington must have done it by now but I haven't seen it yet.'

She looked around the room, and sought out Selitto. 'Ted, you and I will spend some time with Grace as she continues to debrief on information we got from Meadowlands. We'll also need to speak to Beth Dench but will try to avoid getting in your way, Carolyn.'

'What time would you like us back?' one of the team asked.

'Oh, yes, listen up!' Hunter raised her voice. 'All back here for a further briefing meeting at 18.30 but keep in touch if there is any progress or you hit any problems. Okay! Let's get to it.'

48
Monday 24 July

'The BMW 320i was lifted from Southampton Airport.' Hunter and Selitto had joined Grace Kendall in one of the cubby holes which were euphemistically referred to as meeting rooms on the station's floor plan. Hunter plonked herself down on the only other chair leaving Selitto to lean against the window in his customary pose. There always seemed to be a chronic lack of chairs at Pembury Road.

'Southampton?' queried Hunter. 'That seems a rather out-of-the-way place to nick a car for a visit to Kent!'

'Agreed,' Kendall nodded, 'but it's an up-and-coming regional airport with connections to the European mainland, so I did a bit of digging to identify the airlines flying routes between Europe and Southampton. Turns out that there is only one carrier which predominately serves smaller cities like Nantes and Bordeaux but they also have daily flights to Paris and Amsterdam. Thankfully, we have a good track record with them so I was able to ask if Vashlili's name appeared on any passenger lists around the date when we first spotted the car. Turns out that he flew to Southampton from Amsterdam two days earlier and that he was travelling on a Bulgarian passport. But we have no way of knowing where he might have started his journey as the airline's records show Amsterdam as being the starting point. This means that his journey didn't include a transfer from one flight to another at Schiphol.'

'Hmmm!' Hunter was looking towards the window as if in search of inspiration. 'So, he lands at Southampton, nicks a car and sets off for the Kent countryside to meet someone or, at least, to get information from his dead-letter box.'

'Well, he doesn't go straightaway.' Kendall Interjected. 'The car wasn't nicked until the day after he landed so he presumably spent some time in the Southampton area.'

'Okay,' Hunter agreed. 'You also suggested that someone else was interested in our Mr Vashlili and that it was fortunate for them that we had found him.'

Kendall's fingers flew over the keyboard, screens changing in the blink of an eye. 'Yes', she eventually said. 'He seems to have been on the periphery vision of MI5, mainly because he is suspected of having committed crimes in Eastern Europe – but has never been tried or even arrested. He travels on a Bulgarian passport but that doesn't seem to count for much as no one is quite sure if he is bona fide Bulgarian or whether he has his roots in Romania or even Georgia. As he is not on record as a criminal, and as he has a current passport from a country affiliated to the EU, he can come and go to the UK as he pleases. Although MI5 likes to keep an eye on these people, there are so many of them that it is not always possible to follow their every movement.'

'Is there any indication of what sort of criminal activities Vashlili was suspected of being involved in?' Selitto asked from his position by the window.

'Not specifically,' Kendall replied. 'Most of the crimes committed in that part of the world are connected with kidnapping, trafficking, extortion and racketeering in general. Although we don't yet have enough information about Vashlili's movements, it looks as if he came into the UK at will but that he didn't stay here for very long once he got here. This would lead me to believe that he was supervising some sort of pipeline where the UK was the ultimate destination so he's probably into trafficking and racketeering.'

'Tell me about the other guy with the long name,' Hunter asked. 'He's the other guest of interest from Meadowlands.'

Kendall carried out a few more keystrokes and then looked at her screen. 'Well, this is a bit of a puzzle,' she started. 'The register at Meadowlands refers to a Borislav Zlatkov who checked into the Crocus room a couple of days before Vashlili got there, and who had similarly taken the room before Vashlili on a number of other occasions. As far as I have been able to establish, Zlatkov is Romanian and is considered to be a very dangerous international gangster. However, he very rarely travels outside his orbit of activity which is around the Black Sea so countries such as Bulgaria, Romania, Turkey and Georgia. It is virtually unheard of that he would travel to a country such as the UK or, indeed, any Western European country. So, we either have someone else called Borislav Zlatkov or we have an imposter who is passing himself off as a Romanian hard man who has entered this country with another identity.'

Hunter stared at the scruffy carpet tiles surrounding her feet, continually searching for inspiration. Who, exactly, were they looking for? Were Vashlili, and whoever was passing himself off as Zlatkov, in cahoots with one another – or were they deadly enemies? Had Vashlili been killed by the person pretending to be Zlatkov at the behest of some other powerful figure giving orders from the relative safety of Eastern Europe? No, wait a minute! Had Vashlili actually been killed? Did Scarecrow Girl relate to Hildenborough in any way, and were there other yet undiscovered sexual pleasure houses elsewhere in the Kent area?

'Oh, Grace, this is doing my head in!' Hunter exclaimed. 'I just feel that we're only scratching the surface of what's going on here. And it's been going on right under our noses for some time!' Kendall nodded; Selitto did the same but he wasn't in Hunter's line of sight so she didn't notice his acquiescence.

'So, let me recap – mainly for my own benefit. From your intel, Grace, it seems that we may have had a couple of Eastern European criminals operating in this area for a while – probably working together for a Mr Big based in the Black Sea area. But they have recently either had a bust up or one of them has gone rogue and joined another gang. Whatever happened has possibly resulted in the execution of one of them. These guys are involved in people trafficking, more particularly in the trafficking of young girls from Eastern Europe into the sex trade – and probably right here in Kent.'

'Excuse me, boss, sorry to interrupt.' Selitto had moved his position so that he was now leaning against the wall right in front of Hunter. 'If the house at the allotment where we found Scarecrow Girl and the house at Hildenborough are both linked to the sex trade, are you inferring that these guys are or were responsible for these places?'

Hunter looked at Grace in the hope that she might like to answer that one. And she wasn't disappointed. 'I think it would be highly unlikely that they had anything to do with the houses. These sorts of people only tend to have one mission at a time, and it is reasonably clear from the intel that they are traffickers. It would be unlikely that Vashlili would make such short visits to the UK if he was controlling a number of upmarket brothels. If he was the controller, he would be more likely to be resident here. And I doubt that the guy masquerading as

Zlatkov lives here or has even been to the UK more than a few times. So, no. I think that they're traffickers – pure and simple.'

Silence reigned once more in the stuffy little office apart from the low hum of traffic negotiating the roundabout outside the Pembury Road building. Eventually, Hunter slid off the desk and walked over to the window.

'Thanks, Grace,' she began. 'I have to agree with you that these guys are traffickers and are controlled by someone who is hundreds if not thousands of miles away from here. Judging by all the evidence we have so far gathered Bulgaria looks favourite but we can't rule out other countries in that area. However, there is a bigger question. If these guys are the traffickers, who the hell is running these sex houses which we are coming across? Even if they are standalones, you would still have a Mr Big here in the UK to organise the operation, order the girls from the traffickers, deal with any problems – all that sort of shit. So, are we thinking that there are other accomplices from Eastern Europe who are here in the UK providing this sort of support or do we have our own homegrown Mr Big controlling a huge slice of the sex trade in this area of the UK?'

Kendall looked at her screen as if searching for an answer to the question. 'I have to agree with you, Sarah,' she began, 'I cannot see that anyone is going to be putting any more of their countrymen into the UK than they absolutely have to so there must be a UK connection out there – probably right under our noses!!'

'Okay, agreed!' said Hunter. 'That means that we really do need to get the CSI findings like yesterday so that we can see what clues they might hold for us. Ted, who'd we send to see Beth?'

'DCs Pennant and Crosby, boss. Shall I get down there and chivvy them all long just in case Beth's giving one of her long CSI lectures?'

'Yes, good idea. We could do with some fresh intel this afternoon,' Hunter said, turning to Kendall. 'Many thanks, Grace. 'Let me know if you come across anything else which might be useful.' And, with that, she and Selitto exited the room and made their way back to the MIR.

49
Monday 24 July

'VASHLILI?' Woons screamed.

'Vash-fucking-Lili?' His face had turned a nasty shade of crimson and there were tiny specks of spittle forming on his lower lip. His eyes darted around the office as if he was watching balls in a pinball machine. He started pacing – always a bad sign.

Spink remained silent, his laptop screen showing a moment frozen in time. He knew that Woons normally calmed down once he had had a good rant but this one seemed to be taking longer to pass over. Suddenly he felt Woons leaning over his right shoulder, a porky finger jabbing at the screen where the unmistakable image of Vashlili was caught in mid-step, trying desperately to avoid being picked up by the camera.

Woons had returned in good spirits from wherever he had gone to think things through, and Spink had fleetingly wondered if he should perhaps delay giving Woons the heads up on Vashlili. But the more he thought about it, the more he reasoned that he had to tell Woons sooner rather than later – particularly as he knew that Woons was planning to meet up with the Kaspi brethren tomorrow. He hadn't, however, thought that his revelation would get quite such a reaction.

Woons strode over to the door, opened it and marched outside. He did a couple of circuits of the small car park, strutting around like a marionette on speed, stamping his feet as if trying to dislodge a giant turd. He finally barrelled back through the door of the office and slammed it with such venom that the whole portacabin gave a passable impression of being struck by an earthquake. He took up a position by the window, fixing Spink with a demonic stare.

'You're telling me that that tosser Vash-fucking-Lili delivered something that completely bolloxed the whole operation out at Hildenborough so that it was shut down.' Woons was recapping the sequence of events that Spink had so far been able to gather from the CCTV he had watched. 'Then some arseholes just roll up out of nowhere without a how's your father and stroll in to nick all our girls and hack Candice to death before shooting you and Ems up and setting fire to some of the evidence?'

Spink had to conclude that Woons had got it pretty much spot on from what he had been able to gather from the tapes. 'Looks that way, Billy,' he replied. They both stared at the screen until Woons swung away and stomped over to his desk and sat in the chair. Where were those Havanas when he had the craving like he had at this moment? Silence reigned in the portacabin.

Eventually, Spink decided that Woons had probably calmed down to a point where he could have a reasonable discussion.

'I've been looking at the time lines, Billy,' he started. Woons looked up and fixed him with a quizzical stare. 'You know, the clock on the bottom right of the screen which is always whizzing round?' Woons nodded. 'Well, unless I'm very much mistaken, these guys cleared Hildenborough out on the Saturday afternoon which seems to be when the cameras stopped rolling. We already know that they cleared Belinda's house out on Thursday, and we suspect that they cleared out Travisedo's house on Friday as the cops were there on Saturday.

So, this begs the question…' He was unable to finish before Woons butted in.

'Who the fuck was in the house shooting you and Ems up on the Sunday night – last night?' Woons sat back in his chair, steepling his fingers under his chin. Silence again descended on the office as both men considered the recent chain of events.

Always the businessman, Woons was already counting the cost in financial terms. He had now lost three trusted operators in Belinda, old woman Travisedo and Candice. He had also lost God knows how many young girls and, even after only three or four days, his net cashflow must be shot to pieces. He'd never really considered how he would replace any of his businesses should one of them go down for whatever reason and, although he could always order up a new consignment of girls, the thought of finding another house manager of the quality of, say, Travisedo, filled him with trepidation.

'Right!' Woons suddenly seemed energised. He launched himself out of his chair and strode across the office to the map on the wall. 'Right, Tricky! We need a plan!'

Spink closed his laptop and put it to one side. He leant on the table and watched Woons who was now pointing to little flags which had been stuck on to the map. They denoted all the business enterprises in the Woons stable. 'My thinking is that all the hits so far have been in the west of Kent. Now, we still have quite a lot of business going on in the east of the county which may not be as well known to the real high rollers who are presumably flying into the country through Gatwick, Heathrow possibly, and even Biggin Hill. And then there are the guys coming down from London. It's been easy for them to get to somewhere like Hildenborough or Sheet Hill 'caus it's just a hop, skip and a jump from the M25. The wrecking crew have probably also come in by plane from some god forsaken country so they probably aren't planning on staying for long or travelling too far from an airport which offers them a quick means of escape.'

'So, Tricky,' Woons said, pointing at some of the flags on the map, 'my thinking is that we should get some discrete security at some of our other west Kent houses. I'm particularly thinking of Toys Hill and Wateringbury, and probably that Kilndown place which no one can ever find. What's the name of that crap road you have to drive along to get there?'

'Rogers Rough Road,' Spink replied.

'Yeah, that's it! Rogers Rough Road – and it is fucking rough!' Woons smirked at his own joke. 'God knows how anyone ever finds their way there but good old Cassandra must have a warm welcome for them as they seem to keep coming back!'

Woons made his way back to his desk and sat in his chair. 'And, apart from anything else, I can't afford to lose any more girls. Do you know how much the Georgian bastards charge me? Fucking thousands! It's a bloody rip off!' Woons was getting agitated again so Spink took his time before answering.

'Okay, Billy,' he eventually started. 'I'll get on to it. But, in the meantime, it looks like Vashlili is very much alive and kicking – and seems to have gone rogue. You'll have to put that to the band of brothers when you get over to Kaspi. They'll have to get someone to come over here and take care of him but that'll still leave us without a contact point for the traffickers so you'd better ask them about that as well. Ems says that she can get Furnace Lane back up and running soon but it won't be much bloody use without any girls so getting the Kaspi boys to sort that out is a major priority.'

'Yes! Yes! I understand Tricky,' Woons replied, testily. 'I didn't realise that Ems was already on the case down at Furnace Lane. Has she got someone in mind for looking after it?'

'On a temporary basis to start with, I think,' Spink replied. He didn't really know much more than that. Emma had called him earlier in the day when she had been on the treadmill which she had set up in her garage. The combination of the sound created by her running on the moving walkway and her breathlessness meant that it had been difficult to make out what she was talking about but they had agreed to meet this evening so at least he should get some clearer information then. 'I'll get some more info about the woman later and do all my usual checks. Think it's someone Ems has known for ages so should be okay for us even if it's only on a temporary basis. Should have it sorted by the time you get back so we'll definitely need the girls pronto.'

Woons looked at his watch. All of a sudden, four hours on a Georgian Airlines flight seemed an attractive option to the shit he was having to deal with here. He sat back in his chair.

50
Monday 24 July

Selitto made the journey over to Maidstone in double quick time, the lunchtime traffic being light for a Monday. He parked in the only space left in the small car park behind the CSI's building, swiped his card through the reader and entered through the rear door. Using the phone on the desk just inside the door, he called up to Beth Dench to announce his arrival. Almost immediately, Jimbo Carrigan appeared on the other side of the complex glass entry system which controlled entry to the inner sanctum of the CSI HQ. A glass panel slid back in front of Selitto, and Carrigan motioned him to enter the glass bubble. The panel closed behind him and, once he had been photographed, another panel slid back in front of him. He stepped out of the bubble and shook hands with Carrigan.

'How're you doing, Jimbo?' Selitto asked casually as they set off along a brightly lit corridor with doors at regular intervals on either side.

'OK, thanks,' Carrigan replied. 'Relieved to be away from that house – gave me the proper creeps, all that equipment. And some of it in a disgusting state – urgh!'

'Hope our green horns haven't been preventing progress today?' Selitto asked.

'Nope, good as gold,' replied Carrigan. 'Mind you, they have been getting the Auntie Beth introduction to crime scene investigation spiel so they may be asleep when you reach them!' They were now in a lift heading for the third floor, and Selitto had a chuckle to himself.

The lift opened out into a small reception area. Carrigan swiped his card through the reader on the wall opposite and a panel slid back revealing an extensive laboratory area. Over to his right, he spotted Pennant and Crosby sitting round a small table with Beth Dench. A huge screen adorned the wall in front of them, and he could see Dench pointing to it as she continued talking. 'Thanks, Jim,' he whispered as he sidled across the room to join his colleagues.

'Hello, Ted,' Beth Dench said by way of welcome. 'Have a seat. I've just been taking Carolyn and Stuart through some of our initial findings. We're at the hotel to start with. Just to get you up to speed, our conclusion is that someone probably suffered a fatal injury in the bathroom of the Crocus room. The amount of blood spatter would probably indicate that a knife was the weapon of choice. It is possible that the victim was shot but we can find no trace of a bullet in either the bathroom or the bedroom. So, it's probably a knife.'

Beth let this information sink in before continuing. 'A significant effort has been made to clean up the bathroom and, for a moment, we were thrown by the fact that there were absolutely no traces of blood on the window until we realised that the blind had been removed. It is virtually impossible to clean every blood spot after an event such as the one which took place in that room so they were bound to leave plenty of spots for us to find. As I expected, there were virtually no usable fingerprints in the bathroom as the surfaces had been rigorously wiped down. In any case, surfaces in bathrooms are often smeared with toiletries and other body creams which tends to give smudged prints.'

'We then took a look at the bedroom. I think I mentioned to

you, Ted, that Jimbo thought that the damage there had been staged. And I tend to agree with him. Why would someone try to wrench the door off a minibar fridge during a fight? Doesn't seem to make sense. And I happen to think that throwing TVs around a room is a bit dated – in any case, it wasn't even damaged! There were a couple of oddities. The phone was still perfectly in place on the bedside table, and none of the lights had been smashed. There was also the mystery of the missing glass tumbler. There would have been two glass tumblers on the tray in the room but we could only find pieces of glass to account for one of them.' As she talked, Dench flicked through photographs on the screen which provided evidence of everything she was telling them.

'Next, we come to the fire-door. Leaving the lock mechanism taped up would seem to have been a mistake. But perhaps they were disturbed and had to get off the premises pronto. Or perhaps the last guy in the room simply forgot to take the tape off. I've seen some gangland assassinations in the past and there's always a small team with pre-assigned jobs. Last to leave is usually the cleaner who, whilst being quite thorough at the main crime scene, is less thorough elsewhere as he or she doesn't know how the "hit" has played out. In this case, it seems to me that the cleaner missed the fire exit door altogether which explains how we found more blood on the door frame. From our tests so far, all blood spots and spatter have come from the same person so we have to assume that that person was the victim.'

DC Crosby coughed to clear his throat. 'So, we're looking at more than one person being involved with this murder – if it was a murder?' he asked.

'Definitely!' exclaimed Dench. 'The main man would be the killer, and he would then contact one or two others if, as was the case here, they wanted to transport the body elsewhere. Once they had done their bit, the cleaner would be summoned and the others would get away. Somewhere like this, they'd have to have a couple of vehicles. I reckon that the cleaner arrived just as the others were leaving with the body. He would have been let in by the others but when he came to leave, he probably just let the door slam shut. We found that we could open the fire door from the outside with the locking mechanism taped up so it is possible that it was originally taped up by Vashlili to give his visitor access to the hotel building without being seen. In which case, the cleaner may not have realised that there was tape which needed to be removed. We are testing the tape for prints but I'm not very hopeful.'

'Obviously no idea of what time this all happened?' Selitto thought it was probably a silly question but asked it all the same.

'Not without a body, no!' replied Dench. 'If the TV had been properly damaged, the clock on it might have stopped but that wasn't the case. There weren't many guests staying that night – particularly in the rooms around Crocus, and the hotel staff didn't have any complaints of noise. I'm only guessing but a possible scenario is that the assault took place mid-evening and that the clean-up guy arrived around a couple of hours after midnight. I'm also prepared to stick my neck out and say that they departed by way of the service track which leads from the main drive down to the glass houses. CCTV up there hasn't been working for months according to one of the people we spoke to so no luck in testing my theory. Anyway, they're unlikely to have gone out via the front of the building as the noise of vehicles on gravel might have alerted someone's curiosity.' DC Pennant had caught Dench's eye. 'Yes, Carolyn?'

Pennant was looking at one of the photographs which had been left randomly on the table in front of her. 'If the body was transported to a waiting vehicle on the service track, would the vehicle have had to leave by the main driveway or is there another way out it could have taken? It's just that this photo shows very limited space for turning so they would either have had to drive on towards the greenhouses to find a suitable turning point or they could have carried on past the glass houses to another yet unidentified exit.'

'Hmm! Fair point, Carolyn,' Dench responded. Turning to Selitto, 'Did you get as far as the glass houses, Ted?'

'Not really,' he replied. 'I came at them rather from the other end. I could see them on my right from the end of the main lawn in the raised garden and there was a track of sorts which ran past the garden and into the meadow. But it's only a track for garden equipment - sit-on mowers, that sort of thing.' He paused to picture the scene in his mind, suddenly remembering something. 'Wait a minute! I've just remembered that there's a gravel path under the south-facing wall. It runs along the top of the meadow and, if I remember rightly, it eventually leads through an arch into the main car park.'

'Let's have a look,' suggested Dench as she pressed a few keys and put up an aerial view of Meadowlands on the giant screen. They all gathered round. 'Well-remembered, Ted! Yes, there is quite a substantial path on that side of the garden. Do I remember rightly that it was gravel?' Selitto nodded.

Dench studied the screen. 'As it's below the wall then the noise of wheels on gravel would be marginalised. They could

340

also have driven along the top of the meadow thus probably eliminating noise altogether.'

Looking at the screen, Selitto informed Crosby and Pennant that the tracks on the righthand side of the meadow led down to the lower lake. 'If you scroll across to the right you should be able to see this piece of water with its lighthouse.' Dench did as he suggested and the extensive lower lake filled the screen with its folly clearly visible in the sunshine. 'You took a spin round the lake, didn't you Ted?' she asked

'Yes, I did,' he replied, 'and it's probably somewhere we need to take another look at after Jim's report the following day.' Selitto explained the discovery of the rowing boat and its sinking, and the apparent removal of a black household refuse sack from an area under the bridge at the head of the lake. Fiddling with the mouse, he managed to zoom in on the bridge and then scrolled back to where the rowing boat had been located. 'Anything to add, Jim?'

'Not really,' Carrigan started. 'There is actually a landing stage on the lake – did you see it?' Selitto nodded his head. 'It's complete with a set of gates, and looks in reasonable repair. Interestingly, there is a sign next to it indicating that the lake is for private fishing and that poachers will be prosecuted.' He leaned across the desk, bashed out a few key strokes, and a picture of the landing stage appeared on the screen. He clicked the left side of the screen and a picture appeared showing the sign giving notice of private fishing which was wedged into some of the woodland vegetation by the water's edge. 'Interestingly, it's not far to the lighthouse from here.' They all stared at the screen, each with their own thoughts.

'Have you got any pictures of the bridge?' Selitto asked.

Carrigan flicked a few more keys and Selitto found himself looking at the bridge at the head of the lake. 'Hmm! I'd forgotten there was another kissing gate there,' he said under his breath. The next picture showed the lake water spilling over a ten-metre drop where it passed under the bridge. Then there was a shot of the water reappearing on the other side of the drop as it made its way into a stream and off to goodness knew where.

'See that picture there,' Selitto said. 'That's where I saw the black sack just in amongst all that rubbish that you can see.'

Carrigan looked at the photograph. 'Well, that was what it looked like when we got there and before Donny went down. No sign of your bag. And it couldn't have been swept away by the water because of the netting which is over the water here.' He pointed to the screen. Selitto bitterly regretted not having made a closer inspection when he had originally spotted the bag but he recalled that they were up against the clock and he had assumed it would still be there the following day when the CSIs were due to take a look.

Carrigan tapped a few more keys and a picture of the sunken boat appeared on the screen. Taken from the woodland path, it was very difficult to make out the boat amongst the reeds and silver birch trees which flanked the lakeside, some of the dense foliage touching the water. The next picture was right up at the water's edge and, even then, it was difficult to make out the sunken boat. But with a bit of techno wizardry, Carrigan managed to strip away the reeds and trees and then zoom in on the holes in the bottom of the boat. Selitto was impressed.

'Well, that looks like a professional job.' Selitto commented. 'Someone didn't intend that craft to float again! Is it on its way here?'

'Hopefully!' Dench interjected. 'Our colleagues in marine are a bit under the cosh at the moment but I'm hopeful of it arriving by the end of the week. Not sure what it might tell us but at least we will know rather than be forever wondering.'

'Okay,' said Selitto, 'is that it for Meadowlands?'

'Not quite,' Dench replied. 'You asked me to have a look at a notepad you found in the room.' Selitto nodded. 'Well, there are some indentations but it's likely that the writer tore off more than one sheet of paper so probably knew what he was doing in terms of leaving a trace. Not sure why he didn't take the whole pad but then that probably never occurred to him. Anyway… there is some trace which I have managed to extract and this is it.' She flicked a couple of keys and the sheet of paper came up on the screen.

Selitto stared at the screen, trying to make sense of what he was looking at. From what he could make out, it seemed to be a list of place names. 'Just place names?' he asked no one in particular.

'That's what it looks like to us,' replied Dench. 'With the use of our enhancing gear, we have made out Horsmonden, Sheet Hill, Wateringbury, Kilndown, Toys Hill and Hildenborough.'

Crosby suddenly became animated. 'Sheet Hill is near where Scarecrow Girl was found,' he observed, 'and there was that fire at a house in Hildenborough. Do you think there's a connection?'

'Well spotted, DC Crosby! We'll make an ace detective out of you yet!' Selitto replied, smiling. Crosby's cheeks started to redden but his gaze remained fixed on the screen.

DC Pennant wanted her turn. 'So, are we looking at a list

of sex houses or brothels or dungeons or whatever you want to call them?' she asked no one in particular.

'Well, I don't think we should get ahead of ourselves Carolyn but it's certainly a possibility,' Selitto said in response to her question. He liked it when the youngsters were using their imagination but had to keep them to the basic principles regarding all the evidence – what does it actually tell you? In this case, there was a huge potential for surmise.

'Okay, let's park that for the moment,' Dench suggested. 'It's just that I have another meeting at 2.00 p.m. and I wanted to cover Scarecrow Girl before I go.' They all nodded and waited for her to start. She keyed in some other commands and then directed their attention back to the screen on the wall in front of them. A picture of the girl hanging like a scarecrow immediately transported Selitto and Crosby back to the allotment. This was Pennant's first view of the girl in the position she was found, and she immediately turned away preferring to concentrate her gaze on Dench.

'Right!' Dench began. 'This is who we have euphemistically referred to as Scarecrow Girl. She was found on Saturday morning on the allotments at Sleet Hill, and her PM was done on Sunday by dear old Norman. He's nearly finished his report but I had a quick word with him this morning and he confirmed what we all believed. That the cause of death was drowning. There is a blunt trauma wound at the back of her head but this would not have caused her death according to Norman, although it may have rendered her unconscious. Anyway, you'll be pleased to know that we've made good progress on two fronts – one through standard practice and one through a huge slice of luck.'

The three police officers looked at each other with Selitto picking up the thread. 'Sounds intriguing, Beth. We're all ears!'

Dench made a few more keystrokes and brought up a picture of a small room with a grubby window at the end of a metal bedstead. Selitto leaned forward. 'I recognise that', he said. 'That's the room where we found that stuff under a floorboard.'

'That's right,' Dench continued. 'There was plenty for us to lift prints from and I can now confirm that Scarecrow Girl was more than likely the owner of the artefacts found in this room. It is also probable that she fashioned the word HELP in the gunge on the window as we found her prints on the sill and on the black-out panel which was removed. Unfortunately, we don't know much more about her other than that her name probably starts with the letter E. But all the evidence of the clothing and the IUD which Norman found would suggest that she is of Bulgarian extraction. We've charged up the phone but there's no SIM card in it so it's as good as useless in its current state. She may have hidden the SIM card somewhere else in the room so I'm going to send one of the boys back to have another look.'

'Excellent!' exclaimed Selitto. 'And the outrageous slice of luck?'

'Yes, Ted,' Dench began. 'Remember standing in that office with all those wires, false drawers, hidden screens and bits of desk all over the floor?' Selitto nodded. 'Well, Jimbo spent hours pulling it all together so that he could understand how the CCTV surveillance system worked. Not the most modern system, and the equipment hadn't been well maintained so the images tend to be a bit grainy plus the lighting in the rooms was not always conducive to making a Hollywood blockbuster.

But not a complete write-off, eh Jim? He'll give you a quick rundown while I just nip to the loo.'

Jim Carrigan took over the keypad as Dench left the room and then took them through the CCTV equipment, how it worked, where it was located. 'As you know, the non-working smoke alarm in the dungeon had a wifi spy camera concealed within it, and this allowed live remote video to be viewed in the office upstairs. It also seems to have allowed motion-activated recording for later viewing. The rest of the cameras were fairly standard equipment, mainly hidden behind two-way mirrors.'

Selitto was intrigued to discover that he had been right to wonder if there was a hidden room somewhere and that its location at the far end of the corridor on the second floor had housed the sort of console they had been looking for. Dench returned and re-took her seat.

'Right,' she said, looking at each of the officers in turn. 'I'm going to show you a sequence of grainy film from the camera in the dungeon. Although it is not particularly clear, I would say that it's not for the faint-hearted so do feel free to look away at any time. I won't make it count against you!' There was an uneasy shuffling of feet and three sets of eyes focused on the screen in front of them. 'Okay, Jimbo – let's run the tape.'

Dench was right! It was difficult to see exactly what was going on but Selitto's eyes quickly adjusted to the gloom of the picture. He found himself looking at a young girl in a skimpy nurse's outfit running water into the rolltop bath in the dungeon. He recognised the gold braid inlaid around the top of the bath. A man wearing chains, a black mask and very little else was massaging the girl's buttocks as she leant over the bath. All of a sudden, he rammed his hand between her legs. She shot up, turning round in one move and delivering a powerful slap across the man's face. Selitto wondered if this was just part of the act but the man reacted angrily to the slap and grabbed the girl's wrist, forcing her arm roughly up her back. But the girl was a feisty fighter and was soon free of the man's grasp. She then tried to deliver a kick between the man's legs but he managed to get hold of her foot before leaning forward and pulling her by her long hair. Her arms flailed around him but didn't seem to be making much contact.

All of a sudden, she jerked downwards and then sprang back up as if she was playing Jack-in-the-Box. This seemed to catch the man by surprise as he seemed to loosen his grip on her hair. Selitto stared at the screen as the girl now leapt at the man, mesmerised by the realisation that she held a knife in her hand. And, in one seamless movement, she slashed his neck slicing through the carotid artery and sending a spray of blood raining down on everything around her. The man grabbed the girl round the throat and pushed her so hard that she fell across the top of the bath smashing her head on the rolltop. It was difficult to tell if she was still conscious because the man had collapsed on top of her. And, in fact, Selitto could just make out the girl's whole body being pushed under the water by the weight of the man on top of her.

There was no further movement on the screen. There was no movement in the lab. Everyone was just staring at the screen. DC Pennant had gone very pale and was looking at her finger-nails; there were little spots of perspiration on DC Crosby's forehead despite the fact that the aircon kept the lab very cool. Dench hit a couple of keys and the screen went blank.

'So, there you have it,' said Dench. 'Death by drowning

is the most probable cause. The bang on the head obviously knocked her out and she must have remained unconscious while her body slipped under the water only to be held there by the weight of the dying man on top of her. The image fades out eventually because there is no motion to keep the camera active.'

'Difficult to see where she got the knife from,' commented Selitto.

'Under the bath,' came Carrigan's reply. 'We found a loose piece of material which probably hid the knife from general view. It's difficult to see on the CCTV but she was definitely in the right place to be able to access the knife. The incredible thing was the speed with which she got hold of the knife and delivered a pinpoint accurate slash across the artery. It clearly surprised the punter as well although he was strong enough to exact some retribution by grabbing the girl and, almost with his last breath, smashing her head on the bath.'

They all looked at the blank screen.

'Okay, that's me done!' said Dench, gathering her papers together. 'I must away to another briefing. Jim'll take you through the other CCTV findings although there is precious little of any interest unless you have a particular penchant for tits and bums – and a bit of whipping on the side!' And, with that, she wandered off to the other side of the lab.

Selitto wanted to know a bit more about the recordings. 'Thanks for putting that together, Jim. It certainly helps us to get a handle on how the girl died. But wouldn't we have CCTV showing the clear-up operation?'

'Can't find anything on that,' Carrigan replied. 'The whole CCTV system is a bit dated and, as we know, it's motion-sensitive so there would have been no more recording in the dungeon until someone went into the room. We're working on the theory that some sort of catastrophic incident took place in the house which resulted in the immediate close down of the recording system. We did find a camera set up in one of the trees overlooking the doorway into the house at the back but, when I finally got up there, I found that it hadn't been maintained for months and was covered in bird shit – no chance of it recording anything.'

'Okay!' Selitto was conscious that time was ticking on and he had a mountain of stuff to get through this afternoon. 'So, we can put Scarecrow Girl in the house through the prints you took in that room. Presumably, we can put that into AFIS and see if we get a match elsewhere?' Carrigan nodded but DC Crosby looked puzzled. 'It's the Automated Fingerprint Identification System,' Selitto clarified. 'All European Police Agencies are now required to open their AFISs to each other, primarily for fighting terrorism but we may find a match with another agency which is looking for this girl by way of her fingerprints. Perhaps even DNA, Jimbo?'

Carrigan nodded. 'Yep, we've got that stored. And you could probably do no worse than have a chat with someone in the Bulgarian missing persons department bearing in mind what we discovered at the PM.'

'Okay! Thanks for the advice, Jimbo.' Selitto was out of his chair and ready to move on. 'Anything else?'

'Only that I think we could actually put a name to this poor girl rather than simply calling her Scarecrow Girl.' replied Carrigan. 'I found a name carved in tiny letters on the reverse of that wooden window panel in the room where we found the necklace with the letter E. Now, I realise that it might not be her but perhaps we should just refer to her by this name?'

'Good idea, Jim,' Selitto mused, 'and the name is?'

'Elisaveta.'

DI Sarah Hunter sat in the MIR all on her own. The sun was streaming through the windows, the traffic was uncommonly quiet for this time of the day, so she had the perfect opportunity to reflect on what they knew about this rather odd case in which they had at least two bodies but no tangible means of connecting them. From time to time, her gaze wandered to the white boards but it was still early days and they had yet to hold enough information to make any sense of anything. She was also running through the post mortem report which had been delivered about half an hour ago. Not much in it that she didn't already know but it would be useful when it came to writing up her case reports after the team meeting later. She was just reading through Partington's conclusions when there was a knock on the door.

Hunter turned just as a head popped round the door which she instantly recognised. 'Ursula!' she exclaimed. 'How lovely to see you! Come in! Come in!'

WPC Ursula Johnson did as she was asked, and threaded her way through the desks to where Hunter was gathering up the papers around her. Johnson had helped Hunter enormously when she first arrived at the Tonbridge police station. The young WPC had taken her under her wing showing her round all the nooks and crannies of the building and making sure that she was properly welcomed by everyone.

'Hello, ma'am!' Johnson said as she approached Hunter's desk. 'Everything okay in here? At least you've got some desks and equipment!'

'Yes,' Hunter replied. 'The youngsters on the team seemed to know how to magic stuff out of other offices!'

'Very good!' the WPC said, admiringly. And then almost apologetically, she went on. 'Anyway, sorry it's not a social visit, but we've just had an urgent message from Control about an accident out at Fordcombe. On the bend near Chilstone Pots I think. Golf November 66 is on the scene and reports not much damage although both vehicles will need to be towed away. One of the drivers has a fractured wrist and the other is badly shaken up. The ambulance is on the scene. But we do have a problem as one of the PCs has discovered a body bag in the back of one of the vehicles. And there is apparently a body in it!'

'What?' Sarah butted in. 'Someone's driving around the leafy lanes of Kent not only with a body bag in the back of the vehicle but also with a real body in it?' She sounded incredulous.

'Seems that way, ma'am,' Johnson said as she continued. 'We've had to send another crew to the scene as the PC passed out when he opened up the body bag and discovered the body was minus its head. I thought you would want to be aware.'

'Yes, Ursula, well done! I think I'd better swing by and see what's going on.' Hunter was rolling her eyes. 'Let's hope it's not another young Eastern European girl.'

Sarah Hunter sped over Bidborough Ridge, down through Penshurst before the climb up to Fordcombe, past The Chafford Arms and then she was at the scene of the accident. Two PCs were controlling the traffic, one was standing at the back of the ambulance and the other was nowhere to be seen. The vehicles looked as if they had been pushed to the side of the road, but she couldn't be sure. One was a silver Clio and the other was a small Ford van with a pair of doors at the rear which stood open. She walked towards the PC standing by the ambulance who soon recognised her and came over to meet her.

'Ma'am!' he said, nodding to her. 'Constable Rayner from Traffic.'

'Thank you, constable,' she replied. 'So, what have we got here?'

'Well, these two have had a coming together on this bend although goodness knows how because visibility is quite good here. Perhaps lack of concentration, phone call, cat, dog, lemur – you know how it is!' Hunter smiled. 'Anyway, my colleague Constable Tyler had a look in the back of the van because the doors had sprung open and that's when he found the body in the bag. Fairly knocked him out. He's now in the ambulance – compos mentis but might be a few sleepless nights coming up.'

Without seeming to pause for breath, Rayner continued. 'Van driver's got a fractured wrist so he's not going anywhere. I've had a word with him and he says he knows nothing of the bag apart from the fact that he picked it up in a layby near Haysden Country Park. Says he does odd jobs for a bloke who rings him up from time to time.'

'How does he know this man who contacts him?' Hunter asked.

'Says he doesn't know the geezer but always seems to trouser five hundred quid for his troubles. Never gets told where to make the drop off until he is almost there. Thinks it's creepy that they seem to know exactly where he is but the money's good so he's not too concerned. For this pick up, he was to take the bag to a lock up in Crawley but would be given further directions once he left the M23 at Junction 10. Always seems to pick up from a layby and deliver to a lock-up. The lock-up's always open so he just dumps the stuff in it then scarpers. Today's not the first time he's moved one of these bags but says that he's never known what was inside.'

'Okay, thanks!' Hunter said once she was sure that Constable Rayner had nothing else to add. 'Have you arrested him?'

'Yes, ma'am!' came the response. 'I'll be taking him back to the Wells to be bailed and then on to Pembury to get the wrist set. He's got a temporary dressing on it at the moment but seems to be in a great deal of pain so best to get the plasterers to weave their magic before he gets to sit down in front of the tape.'

'And what are you going to do with the body?' she asked, expecting a blank face and a questioning look from the young traffic cop.

'I've got the undertakers on their way to take it to the mortuary at Pembury. Should be here any minute. Hope you don't mind but I haven't actually looked inside. Couldn't pluck up the courage I'm afraid. But I can confirm by feeling the bag that the head is not attached to the body. I'm also not sure that any of the limbs are even attached – feels like the proverbial bag of bones to me!'

Hunter was becoming more drawn to Rayner by the minute. She always felt good when she came across intelligent, competent, keen, enthusiastic young officers. She thought Rayner would go far.

'Right, constable, here's what we're going to do,' she said in a conspiratorial tone. Rayner gave her his full attention.

Selitto had sent Crosby and Pennant back to Tonbridge to prepare for the evening briefing, and then diverted to Hildenborough to see how DCs Jennings and Mishraz were getting on with Julian French and his CSI team.

He parked just to the left of the CSI van and watched as the same PC who had accosted him and Sarah Hunter earlier reappeared at the front door. Selitto climbed out of the Megane and called over. 'Have you seen a couple of my DCs? One blonde and one of Asian origin?'

The PC looked askance at Selitto's description of his two colleagues but pointed him round to the back of the house.

Finding his way round the side of the house, and taking in the view over to the A21 which seemed to be busy no matter what time of the day, Selitto spotted the DCs by the burnt-out shell of the annexe. He made his way across the patio at the back of the house and joined them.

'How're you two getting on?' he asked as he got up to them. DC Jennings looked as if she had taken charge and brandished a note pad on which she had clearly scribbled pages of notes.

'Well, Sarge, I'm not really sure where to start,' she said, scrolling back pages of the notebook. 'The CSI Manager, Julian French, has been very accommodating and has allowed us to see pretty much everything. He told us that he had excluded you and DI Hunter from seeing one of the bodies this morning, but we were invited to see it in situ before it was moved to the morgue.'

'We were excluded from seeing both of the bodies!' grumbled Selitto.

'Yes, Sarge, so I heard,' Jennings continued. 'They found the badly burned body of a young girl here in the annexe. She was lying curled up in the foetal position on one of the beds over there,' she said pointing into the annexe. 'She's already been taken to the morgue.'

'What about the body in the cellar?' Selitto asked.

'All I can say is that both Azzar and I were glad that we hadn't had any lunch!' Jennings reported. 'It was quite the most revolting thing I have ever seen. The woman was tied to a chair but had probably suffered a severe beating before being put in the chair. Her face was a mass of bruises, both eyes were swollen beyond recognition. Her cheeks had been slashed and her lower lip and the skin underneath it had been cut in such a way that it hung down like some sort of grotesque flap. She had also suffered other lacerations and a slash across her throat which may have been fatal although there is no sign that she actually bled to death. As I said, she's now in the morgue, and they're hoping to get a PM for tomorrow afternoon.'

'Okay,' said Selitto wanting to move on. 'We saw quite a lot of crazed destruction in the rooms upstairs. What did the CSIs make of that?'

'I think they're still sifting through all that'. DC Mishraz had suddenly found his voice. 'All the rooms had been systematically trashed, almost as if someone was looking for something specific, and they then became increasingly frustrated when they couldn't find it.'

'Yes,' agreed Elaine Jennings, 'and we think we know what it was they were looking for!' Selitto looked from her to Mishraz as if seeking a clue. 'If you look behind you, Sarge, you'll see a shed at the bottom of the garden.' Selitto remembered the shed from his visit earlier, and the unlocked padlock on the door. Nothing much in there, he recalled, so he was quite taken aback when Jennings continued.

'If we're not very much mistaken, that shed holds a major clue as to why the house was so badly trashed,' Jennings stated, 'and probably why that poor woman was made to suffer quite such a horrendous death. We can take a look because CSIs have finished with it.'

'DI Hunter and I had a look in there earlier,' Selitto said, 'and we couldn't see anything to get excited about. But happy to take another look.'

Jennings led the way down the garden. Selitto followed, looking at the flower beds around him and turning to look back at the house and the burnt-out shell of the annexe. When they got to the shed, Jennings pushed the door open and disappeared inside. Mishraz motioned Selitto to follow Jennings. 'I'll stay outside,' he said, 'not really room for three in there.'

Inside the shed, Selitto stood next to Jennings in the cramped and stifling space. 'CSIs think that this is probably what whoever ransacked the house was looking for,' Jennings said. Selitto looked around him. All he could see was a workbench with flowerpots and seed trays spread out on it. There was a range of garden tools hanging from the wall behind him, and a number of bags of garden soil and manure on the floor behind his feet. A wheelbarrow stuffed full of half used bags of compost sat rather forlornly at the far end of the shed. Cobwebs decorated the corners of the wooden structure, and a window ran the whole length of the workbench. Interestingly, a venetian blind ran the whole width of the window, presumably to control the amount of light coming into the shed. At the moment, the slats were fully open allowing copious amounts of daylight into the cramped space.

Jennings pointed to the floor under the workbench. 'CSIs think that this was the control room, if you can call it that, for the CCTV system operating in the house.' Selitto bent down to take a look but all he could see where rows and rows of what looked like seedlings growing in small pots. 'That's what we thought!' she continued, noting his puzzled look. 'Pick up one of the pots and pull the plant out of it!' Selitto picked up one of the pots, stood up straight and put it on the workbench. Looking at it with some suspicion, he did as she suggested and plucked out a plastic plant.

'It's plastic!' he exclaimed. 'What the…?'

Jennings was trying to hide a smile. 'Took everyone by surprise, CSIs and all,' she informed Selitto. 'Best explanation we've got is that anyone looking for the equipment would see a floor covered in little flower pots and wouldn't either have the time or the inclination to move them on the off chance that there was anything underneath them.'

Selitto was still peering down at the rows and rows of seedlings which crammed the space under the workbench. 'Very clever!' he commented. 'So, on the basis that these plants have presumably been put back in place for a reason, perhaps you could tell me what was underneath.'

Azzar Mishraz, who had been observing from the doorway, took over from Jennings. 'The decoy plants are on a board that goes the length of the floor under the workbench. It's not easy to move but with a bit of wiggling, you can lift it up so that it leans against the side of the shed. Underneath is what can best be described as a hollowed-out concrete tomb. It's got a two-inch thick lid which is lifted by ring pulls. Inside, there were five laptops which the SOCOs removed. They're sure these are the receptors for the CCTV images so quite a neat little set up. Only problem we have is that it seems from first examination that all the data has been removed!'

'You saw the destruction in the house didn't you, Sarge?' Jennings asked. Selitto nodded. 'Seems that whoever did that probably didn't find this little set-up otherwise the shed might have resembled a pile of kindling wood by the time they had finished. So, the question is – who else might have wanted to get their hands on all this data? And how would they know to look here?'

Selitto gazed out of the window across the lawn to the house and its burnt-out annexe. This had the feeling of the allotment house to him; Hunter had had the same feeling earlier on. But were they really connected? The wreckers at both premises had obviously been desperate to get their hands on the CCTV feeds but had been frustrated at each venue. The set up at this house near Hildenborough appeared to be much more sophisticated but, at the end of the day, it still took on the appearance of an up-market brothel for high rollers. If they were connected, were there others? What other clues were to be had here?

'Can we get into the annexe yet?' he asked no one in particular. 'Yes,' replied Mishraz, 'but we'll have to approach through the house, and pick up some covers for our shoes.'

The three police officers trudged back across the lawn, round to the front of the house, and then across the hall to the door behind the stairs. They could hear the CSI team working through the rooms on the first floor, their arc lights casting shadows down the great staircase even though it was a bright sunny day.

They donned the shoe covers which were by the door that led into the courtyard and entered the annexe. Despite the fact that the building had no roof, a couple of its walls were still reasonably intact. There was still the overriding stench of faeces and death now intermingled with the smell of the burnt and charred building. The twisted metal of an unknown number of bedsteads formed incongruous sculptures around the room, and pipework littered the floor where it had fallen once the ceiling had caved in.

A blackened toilet bowl stood like a large ornament at the far end of the room with more twisted pipework lying around it. Selitto guessed that this was probably the bathroom area and the pipework was what remained of the shower. He looked around for a sink but couldn't see one although there were other pieces of blackened porcelain lying around the floor. The heat of the fire must have been so intense that nothing of any use to the investigation had survived. They would just have to see if the CSI report turned up anything of interest, and it would be important to try and get some clues from the PMs on the two bodies they had found here.

He turned to DC Jennings. 'Remind me which bed the girl was found on.' Jennings briefly consulted her notes and then turned and pointed to one of the bedsteads which was located close to one of the walls. Selitto moved across to take a closer look at what was left of the metal frame. He got down on his haunches to have a look at the area around the bed but eventually rocked back on his heels, shaking his head at the seemingly impossible task of finding any evidence which was going to help them. 'Anything else about this room?' he asked no one in particular.

DC Mishraz had been giving his attention to something on the other side of the room, and he now coughed to clear his throat. 'This gap in the wall over here was presumably a window,' he observed. 'Looks like a serious set of metal bars was in place across it to make escape from this room all but impossible.' The detectives could see that the heat of the fire had caused the bars to buckle, but they were still firmly in place across what had been a window.

Selitto went over to make a closer inspection. He found that the end of each bar was embedded in concrete lintels at the top and bottom of the window. This dramatically reduced the options for anyone wanting to break out. You'd either need a good hacksaw or a couple of pounds of a reputable explosive, he thought.

'Well, the bars are definitely for keeping people in!' he commented. 'Presumably there was a hefty door leading onto the courtyard but there's not much of that left now.' He wandered back to where they had entered the room, but all he could see was a mass of twisted metal and burnt detritus littering the floor. 'And, by the way, have either of you come up with any ideas about this dreadful stench around here?'

'I was thinking it was a drain problem,' Jennings suggested. 'A dead rodent in a drain? Something like that?'

Mishraz had other ideas. 'I'm afraid that my sense of smell is not the best,' he began, 'but the stench in this place just reminds me of the open sewers they still have in my grandparents' village back in the homeland. So, I would go for human excrement rather than drains.'

Selitto smiled. 'Very graphically put,' he commented. 'And you could be right. It hasn't quite got the aura of drains for me but either suggestion is worth taking forward. Okay, anything else we should be seeing in here?'

The two DCs looked at each other and shook their heads. 'Okay,' Selitto repeated, 'let's get back into the house. I want to have a quick look in the dungeon and then we should probably get back to the station.'

While Selitto went off to look at the dungeon, the two young DCs went out into the front garden, having a quick chat with the duty PC on their way. Jennings had spotted a rather ornate birdbath which was certainly one of the biggest she had ever seen. The stonework was perfect in every way, and all self-respecting members of the avian fraternity would want to be seen bathing in the luxury offered by this beautifully crafted structure – especially if it had any water in it!

Her reverie was, however, interrupted when she reached the bath and realised that one of its corners had been crudely gouged out leaving a jagged crater in the stonework. She took a closer look at the imperfection and a frown suddenly creased her forehead. She looked up and saw that Mishraz was still chatting to the PC as Selitto brushed past the two of them and made his way towards his car.

'Sarge!' she called out, 'over here a minute?' Selitto diverted towards where Jennings was standing. 'I think you should have a look at this,' she said pointing to the corner of the damaged birdbath. Selitto ambled over to the birdbath and looked at what Jennings was pointing out. When he looked up at her, he was also frowning.

'I've done some ballistics training,' Jennings informed him, 'and, unless I'm very much mistaken, that looks like it's been caused by a bullet. And recently, too.' Selitto was slowly nodding his agreement. His ballistics knowledge wasn't brilliant but he was pretty sure that he could identify the damage done by gunfire, and it certainly looked as if a bullet had hit the birdbath fair and square.

'CSIs see this?' he asked. Jennings shrugged her shoulders before bending down and making a closer inspection of the grass around the garden ornament.

'There's some trace from the stonework just lying in the grass here,' Jennings alerted Selitto. 'Could mean it's quite recent – you know, since the last time the grass was cut.'

Selitto looked around him but there was nothing else for a bullet to hit unless it hit the gravel – but how would he find any evidence on a gravel drive? Lost in thought, he crunched across the gravel and then turned to take a look back at the house. He noticed that one of the upstairs windows was open. Had it been open when he arrived? Or had the CSI boys opened it? The window offered a great view of the drive, and the birdbath would also be in a clear line of sight. He turned back to the drive and continued crunching through the gravel until he came to the point where the driveway met the track from the road.

His eye caught something glinting in the sun, just off the gravel area and to the side of the track. He crouched down to take a closer look and found himself looking at a small piece of glass. Pretty soon he realised that there were other tiny pieces of glass over the area in front of him. He stood up and returned to where DC Jennings was still circling the birdbath looking for other clues.

'We need to get the CSIs out here,' she said as Selitto caught up with her.

'Sure do!' he replied. 'Looks like some glass on the track up there, but it would be interesting to get their opinion. If there were bullets flying around, then chances are the glass is from a car – probably as it was leaving.'

At that point, Julian French appeared at the front door and walked over to the CSI van. Selitto called over to him. 'Got a minute, Jools? Couple of things here for you to look at.'

'No problems, Ted,' French called back as he crunched over the gravel to where Jennings and Selitto were standing. When he reached them, Selitto pointed to the damage to the birdbath. 'First thoughts as to what that is?' he asked.

French peered at the spot where the stone had been gouged out of the ornate upper level of the ornament. 'Hmmm!' he sighed. 'Looks like a bullet to me but I'll probably have to get that corroborated by Ballistics.'

'There's trace from the stonework on the grass around the bath,' Jennings added.

'Something else up here for you to have a quick look at.' Selitto turned and headed up the gravel drive towards the track. After having a quick look at the trace which Jennings had been referring to, French followed Selitto who was now down on his haunches looking at the glass he had discovered. French joined him, pulling a pair of tweezers from his coat pocket. Plucking up a piece of the glass with the tweezers, he rotated it in the sunlight before reaching into another pocket for a small magnifying glass. He carefully studied the glass through the magnifier, looking for clues.

'Pretty certain that's from a car,' he said after putting it back on the ground. 'Doubt its headlights though. More likely to be from a window judging by its thickness. We'll get it tested but looks like there could be a membrane through it which might indicate a back window with a heating element in the glass. Presume you think the shots came from the house?'

Selitto nodded. 'And there's a window open up there which I hadn't noticed before. Gives a good view of this area.' He turned and pointed for French's benefit. The CSI chief turned and eventually nodded his agreement to Selitto.

'We've been in that room but there wasn't too much damage so it was probably more of a cursory inspection,' he said. 'I don't recall that we would have had any reason to open the window so it was probably already open. I'll get the team to take a closer look for residue around it though. If there is some, then it's certainly going to complicate things as we haven't so far got any evidence of a shooter being on the premises.'

Both men stood looking back at the house. 'It's the level of wanton destruction which is confusing things, Ted,' French began. 'As if someone just went berserk in there. Perhaps they did have a shooter and started firing off rounds. Perhaps they were high on something, unable to focus but pointing in the general direction of whoever or whatever they thought was out here. The birdbath looks like a completely random hit and, if it was a car on that track, then it obviously got away so the damage could have been superficial meaning the aim was poor. Somewhat unusual to find someone hacked to death, another burnt alive and another possibly shot – all under the same roof! Glad I haven't got your job of trying to piece it all together.'

Monday 24 July

Hunter was sitting in her car in the underground car park at Pembury Road. The radio was blaring out Odyssey's 'Native New Yorker' and, although she hadn't been born at the time it was released in the UK, she felt that the music had transcended the years since its first release in 1977. The song had always been a big disco hit, and she fondly remembered it being played at a zillion decibels in clubs she used to visit as a gangly teenager at seaside towns along the Yorkshire coast. Even now, she was tapping the steering wheel with her fingers, nodding her head from side to side in time with the beat. She almost didn't hear the rapping on her window which was most definitely not in time to the beat.

She quickly extracted the key fob from its position on the control panel which cancelled the radio, and opened the car door. 'Hello, sir,' she said as she got out of the car. 'Just reliving some of my misspent youth!'

'So I see!' said DCI Iversen, standing to one side to let Hunter reach into the back of the car to get a couple of files. 'We were due to meet in a quarter of an hour. Do you just want to come up to the office now or do you need to go via the MIR?'

'No, I'll just come up now,' Hunter replied. 'It'll save a bit of time as I'll only get caught on something else if I catch up with the team in the MIR first.'

They both set off up the stairs to Iversen's office on the first floor. 'Just been down to Maidstone,' he said over his shoulder as he climbed the stairs. 'All they ever talk about is cuts. Cuts! Cuts! Cuts! Nothing about what we're going to do about the rising crime rate. What about all the illegals that are being washed up on our shores and dropped off on our roads almost daily? Not a dickey bird about the real world. Just numbers, finances and budget cuts! If I'd wanted a job that involved all that, I would have become an Accountant!'

Iversen pushed the door open when they got to the first floor, and Hunter followed him down the corridor to his office. She didn't really want to get into a discussion about public funds and the seemingly constant need to reduce costs so she kept her own counsel. Iversen waved her to the seat in front of his desk and took up position by the window where he briefly gazed down on the traffic – much of it leaving town at the end of another working day. 'So, things have moved on I see!' he said, turning to face Hunter. This was clearly an invitation to provide him with an update.

'You could say that, sir!' Hunter replied, crossing her legs and making herself comfortable. She had placed the files on Iversen's desk which always seemed to be bereft of any paperwork, and she had now draped her customary arm over the corner of the chair so that she was, in effect, adopting a sideways profile.

'Facts are that we now have two premises which, on the face of it, appear to have been high-class brothels. The quality of gear we have found in the houses is of a very high calibre and would certainly have cost a fortune. Plus, the houses themselves could probably go for well over a million in the locations they're set in. At the moment, we cannot connect them but I'm hoping that we'll be able to find that connection soon. We have the body of Scarecrow Girl who is still unidentified, and we found two bodies at the house near Hildenborough, both of which are unidentified and awaiting a PM. This afternoon, we collected another body which was in a body bag in the back of a van involved in an RTA out near Fordcombe. That's on its way to the morgue but we suspect that the contents are not all in one piece.'

Iversen frowned and raised one eyebrow at the same time. 'How come?' he asked.

Hunter explained how the body bag was found and how the initial inspection carried out by the Traffic PCs had led to the conclusion that the bag probably contained multiple body parts. 'We won't know any more until we can get some fingerprints and DNA to see if there is any connection with the two houses. I have asked if we could have another pathologist and, glory be, someone's coming down from London tomorrow so, with luck, we can get more information once these three bodies have been posted.'

'Okay!' Iversen eventually sat down at his desk and pulled a notebook from one of the drawers. 'What about the original MisPer?' he asked.

Hunter explained that they had no further information on the whereabouts of Vashlili but that they had discovered that he entered the UK via Southampton Airport a couple of days before he disappeared. She also related the findings of both Grace Kendall and the CSIs, and the conclusion that Vashlili was involved in trafficking young girls from Eastern Europe. She told Iversen about the findings of the post mortem on Scarecrow Girl and the fact that she was probably of Bulgarian extraction.

'I think it would be fair to say at this stage of the investigation that we are dealing with trafficking of young girls for the sex trade,' Hunter summarised. 'However, we can't quite knit it all together – nothing concrete links the sum parts of the puzzle. But it does seem as if the girls are being sourced in Bulgaria and taken into the UK where they are delivered to order. We suspect that Vashlili is part of that chain and probably rocks up in the UK when a shipment is due in. He then supervises the distribution and then buggers off back to the Black Sea.'

Iversen had steepled his fingers under his nose with both elbows on the desk. He appeared to be deep in thought so Hunter let the silence develop in the room.

Eventually, Iversen sat back in his chair and looked across the desk. 'And how are the trainees getting on? Sorry I couldn't get Mishraz to you earlier.'

'They're fine,' Hunter replied, reaching up to reset a clip which was helping to hold her hair in place at the back of her head. 'Keen, enthusiastic – quite bright as well. I'm particularly drawn to Jennings and Crosby. Haven't seen enough of Mishraz yet and Pennant is gradually getting rid of that smell under her nose. Don't know where Traffic cops get the idea that they're the bees' knees! She'll be okay but I just need to work on her. But, overall, a good team so thank you for organising it.'

'Good!' Iversen exclaimed. 'As you know, I'm always very keen to identify young talent so it appears that we might be recruiting the right people at last!' He got up from his desk and resumed his position leaning against the wall by the window.

'You might like to know that I mentioned this case to Superintendent Eaves whilst I was at Maidstone,' Iversen started. Hunter groaned inwardly. Detective Superintendent Hannah Eaves was a stickler for protocol and getting things done by the book, so Sarah had a pretty good idea of what was coming next. 'She had heard a rumour about this case,' Iversen continued, 'and wondered whether we should involve the boys from Serious Crimes?'

He looked over at Hunter to get a reaction, but didn't have to wait for long. She was ready with her response. 'I don't think we have enough yet to package it up as a serious crime,' she replied. 'If we could link the two houses, put the bodies in them and then find another house, then maybe. But, at the moment, I think we can handle it.'

'Yes, I thought you'd say that,' Iversen replied, pushing himself away from the wall, 'and I tend to agree with you. Admittedly, the body count is mounting but we can't prove that they are all related so, for all we know, there could be a number of different cases to investigate here.' Hunter nodded and took to inspecting her fingernails. 'Anyway,' Iversen continued, 'I told Eaves that we would get on with it for the time being and that I would get back in touch with her if things escalated to the point where we had concrete evidence of large-scale serious crime. But we'll have to keep things under constant review in case this thing runs away from us and we find ourselves up to our necks.'

'Okay, sir. That's understood.' Hunter stood up and walked behind the chair. Leaning down to rest her hands on the back of the chair, she fixed her eyes on Iversen. 'Anything else?'

'Afraid so,' Iversen looked uneasy. 'I was collared by that infernal Press Liaison Officer. Margot somebody. Never can remember her surname. Anyway, she's a right pain in the arse whatever her name is! Says that she's had a call from a journo asking questions about the fire up at Hildenborough.

Apparently KFR have published the incident on their website but newspaper boy can't seem to find where the fire was so called the Press Office at Maidstone. The PLO says that she kicked the enquiry into the long grass but just be aware in case the journo decides that he might be better served by asking someone at Tonbridge nick seeing as we're just around the corner from Hildenborough.'

'I'll talk to the team and keep a look out myself,' replied Hunter, knowing what a hindrance a reporter could be to an investigation. Although they had their uses in certain circumstances, one always had to judge what information could be divulged whilst at the same time avoiding the potential for sensationalist reporting. And, in most cases, there was information which could not and should not be divulged as, in doing so, the integrity of the investigation would be compromised. Hunter hated having to liaise with the Press, but it came with the territory, and she just had to deal with each situation and enquiry as it arose.

'Okay, I'll let you deal with any approaches but maybe best if you let me know if anyone from the Press starts getting a bit too keen for information,' Iversen replied. 'I'll see what strings I can pull.'

'Thanks, sir.' Hunter pushed herself off the chair and stood upright. 'That it?'

'Nothing apart from my usual rhetorical question!' Iversen was trying not to smile.

'Yup, coming on sir,' Hunter replied as she headed for the door and off towards the safety of the MIR.

'Daily meetings at 5.00 p.m. from now on, DI Hunter!' Iversen called after her.

54

Monday 24 July

Everyone was back in plenty of time for the evening briefing so Hunter decided to start early as she suspected that there was going to be a lot to get through.

'Okay everyone! Listen up!' Hunter called the room to order. 'Ten-minute warning! We'll start the evening briefing in ten minutes.' There was an air of excitement in the room, and she wanted to harness the collective energy of her team.

Once she had made the announcement, she caught Selitto's eye and nodded towards the door. He followed her out of the MIR and they wandered down to the kitchen area at the end of the corridor. 'How's your day been?' she asked leaning into the fridge and extracting a cold bottle of fizzy water.

'Certainly an interesting one,' he replied looking out of the window down on to the never-ending queues of traffic as they snaked their way around the roundabout in front of him. 'And I think I'm rapidly coming to the conclusion that the allotment house and Hildenborough are linked in some way. There are a number of similarities which we are going to have to concentrate on. And I wouldn't be surprised if we then discovered an organised crime syndicate on a huge scale.'

'Yep!' Hunter agreed. 'I had been thinking about that myself because of my suspicion that our friend, Vashlili, is also linked into this organisation. I'll also be letting the team know about another development this afternoon with the discovery of a body in a bag at the scene of an RTA out at Fordcombe.'

Selitto raised his eyebrows at this news. 'Tell me more,'

he enthused.

'Seems like some little toerag picked up a bodybag from the Haysden Lakes area and was taking it to Crawley when he was hit by a pensioner coming round a bend on the wrong side. One of the Traffic boys discovered the bag in the back of his van. When he looked inside it, a woman's head was staring back at him but it was unattached to a body! Thankfully, the body was also in the bag but it gave him a bit of a shock to start with!'

Selitto nodded sagely. He had long admired the Traffic boys for the resilience they always showed when confronted with the most grotesque scenes imaginable after man and machine had come together. 'And where is this upstanding member of the public now?' Selitto enquired sarcastically.

'What? The body or the van driver?' Hunter played along.

'Ha! Ha!' retorted Selitto. 'I'm assuming that the body's on one of the shiny steel gurneys down at TW. No, I meant the scruff who was arrested. Presumably we get first go at him?'

'Hopefully, he's still attached to the PC who has taken him down to Pembury to get his fractured wrist sorted out. Sounds like a bad break so they might have to do some surgery later today which means we won't get to him until later tomorrow. Meantime, I've got another pathologist coming down from London tomorrow so that we can get a speedy PM for the body in the bag. At least we should be able to get the finger-prints checked.'

'How'd you get on with Iversen?' Selitto ventured, never quite sure whether Hunter saw eye to eye with her boss or not.

'Came away fairly unscathed,' she replied. 'That bloody woman Eaves had been bending his ear about getting the Serious Crime boys and girls involved in our investigation but, fortunately, he wasn't having any of that so he's put her back in her box for the time being. But we really do need to establish an indisputable link between these seemingly separate incidents.'

Selitto shrugged his shoulders and followed as Hunter turned and started wandering back along the corridor to the MIR. 'Not quite sure how that body bag fits in with everything else we've got, but I sure as hell think it does!' she said to no one in particular. She opened the door to the MIR and was pleased to see that the young DCs were getting used to their roles with Crosby and Jennings writing up notes on their white boards. She walked up to the boards and turned to face her team, clapping her hands for attention.

55

Monday 24 July

If there was one thing Billy Woons had never mastered, it was the art of queuing. He hated queuing with a vengeance. He hated the people in front of him, and he hated the people behind him in equal measure. Why couldn't they just all fuck off and leave him on his own?

It was just coming up to 7.00 p.m. on a Monday evening when he found himself in one of the many queues which snaked its way around the check-in hall in the North Terminal at Gatwick Airport. Everyone eagerly awaiting their flights or, in Woons' case, simply waiting for the Georgian Airlines check-in desk to open. Why did they insist that you get to the airport two or three hours in advance of the flight if no bastard from the fucking airline could be bothered to turn up? And the only reason he was here in the first place was because the airline's poxy website was down so he couldn't print his boarding card. And he couldn't get his booking up on his phone so he was royally stuffed. He'd just have to put up with it, queue and all.

To try and pass the time, he assessed his fellow passengers. A right shady bunch if ever there was one. Perhaps he should avoid making eye contact with anyone so he stared resolutely at the floor. He was also acutely aware of a pungent smell all around him which seemed to be a mixture of body odour and bad breath. He'd noticed the same smell when he had been in Kaspi visiting Tsiklauri, and had always put it down to the mountains of marinated vegetables they ate every day. It made his stomach turn just thinking about it, and he suddenly realised that he hadn't had anything to eat. He'd just have to get a burger once he'd got through Security.

Come! On! Where were these lazy sods?

At the top of one of the escalators which carries passengers up to the check-in hall from the inter-terminal shuttle station and shopping area, a man casually leant against an unmanned movable information desk which had been parked away from the check-in desks. He was dressed in very similar fashion to Gatwick's own staff who patrolled the hall looking for any passengers who required help or information. He had a lanyard with a swipe card draped around his neck, the card bearing a fictitious name and barcode. From a distance, he looked like any other airport employee.

Woons would never have noticed the man in a million years, but the man had noticed Woons as soon as he had walked into the airport. He had his orders to follow Woons until he was certain that he was getting on flight A9-752 to Tbilisi. After a while, the man slid a hand inside his jacket and extracted a phone from his shirt pocket. He held it to his ear, listened, nodded curtly a couple of times, said very little, never took his eyes off Woons. Eventually, he returned the phone to his shirt pocket. From his vantage point, he had a clear line of sight to Woons who was still standing, head bowed, in the queue of passengers awaiting the arrival of the check-in staff. At the moment, it looked certain that the person he had been ordered to maintain close surveillance on would, indeed, be on flight A9-752.

A risible cheer greeted the arrival of two airline staff to start the check-in process, and sporadic applause made its way down the queue towards Woons who was certainly not going to participate in such childish antics.

Over the next thirty minutes, Woons shuffled forward until he was almost at the front of the queue. Meanwhile, the man was still leaning against the information desk, his jet-black hair caressing his shirt collar, dark glasses perched just behind a prominent and luxurious quiff. He still had his eyes set firmly on Woons although he had to slightly alter his position as Woons stepped forward to the check-in desk.

As Woons wasn't travelling with any luggage, he was checked-in quickly and issued with his boarding pass. No apologies for the website failure earlier, and he didn't bother to bring up the subject as he noticed that the check-in clerk was wearing a badge showing that she was working for an airport service company. His pent-up anger and frustration would have been wasted on the poor girl.

He left the check-in desk and headed straight for the security check. The man pushed off from the information desk and made his way around several luggage trollies, keeping his eyes fixed on Woons. He watched as Woons showed his passport and boarding card to a security guard, and then he disappeared behind a partition and entered the screening area.

The man walked on past the door through which Woons had disappeared, peering discretely to make sure that he had not somehow and improbably returned to the check-in hall. He continued on to the end of the hall and then doubled back to his position at the top of the escalator. On the way, he checked one of the many information screens and noted that flight A9-752 was currently on time for a 10.50 p.m. departure.

He reached for his phone again, punched in a number and

spoke briefly. He then pocketed the phone and took the escalator down to the next level and the inter-terminal shuttle to the South Terminal.

56

Monday 24 July

Sarah Hunter closed the door to her cottage, picked up the post, kicked off her flatties, and went in search of the fridge for a glass of cold white wine. She was gradually working her way through a bottle of Bianco Salento from the Amastuola vineyard in Southern Italy. Her friend, Heidi, had recommended the wine after visiting the Amastuola Masseria near the town of Martina Franca. Eventually Hunter had tracked down a UK importer and had extravagantly ordered half a dozen bottles. She had not been disappointed, and was really enjoying the wine's smooth and fresh taste.

She reached for her favoured glass and poured herself a decent slug of the wine. Leaning against the kitchen unit, she flicked through the post which mainly consisted of unsolicited junk mail assiduously delivered by Royal Mail. Car insurance from the Co-Op, 50% off Hillary's Blinds, sale at the Mobility Furniture Company, "Become an RHS Member Today!", save on personal alarms, half-price sale at Oak Tree Mobility, great offers at your local Budgens. Taking care to remove her contact details from any of the junk mail which had been personally addressed to her, she dropped the leaflets into the recycling bin. She walked over to the small bureau which was located next to the settee and dropped the pages bearing her contact details into the shredder.

Returning to her glass of wine, she again rested herself against the kitchen unit and took in the view from the kitchen window which looked across a small terrace and a postage stamp lawn toward an area of woodland which became a sea of bluebells in late spring. There were footpaths covering much of the surrounding area and, just as the light was starting to go, the colours of her surroundings started to go out of focus with the onset of twilight and eventual darkness. She loved this time of the day and often sat or stood watching until it was difficult to make out any shapes in the gloaming.

The cottage had been tastefully decorated by the previous owners, and much of the ground floor consisted of a spacious open plan kitchen, dining and lounge area which had plenty of seating space. One of Hunter's absolute prerequisites was that the kitchen should be modern and well equipped so she had invested in a dishwasher and washing machine, an electric oven and a hob. Her pride and joy was a huge refectory table which sat in the middle of the kitchen and dining area. There were rustic benches on either side and a high-backed carver chair at either end. Two patio doors led out onto the small terrace which had a private seating area on which she had placed an old garden bench which she had found in the undergrowth soon after moving in. Some lovely walks could be embarked upon straight from the cottage which she much enjoyed – either on her own or when the occasional friend visited from London.

Finishing her wine, she padded upstairs where there was only one bedroom covering much of the floor space. A king-sized double bed was its main feature with two contemporary bedside tables. An ornate dressing table was positioned in front of one of the windows looking out onto the wooded area, and a large built-in wardrobe ran almost the entire length of one of the walls. However, as Hunter only had enough clothes to fill half of the hanging space, the rest was used as storage for suitcases and a large collection of shoe boxes. There was also a vertical chest of small drawers most of which were bursting at the seams with T-shirts, sweaters, underwear, and other clothing that she never wore but couldn't face throwing out. A door led off the bedroom into an en-suite shower room. Soon after moving in, she had got a local plumber to install a large walk-in shower and "his-and-hers" basins which she knew were an extravagance but she had always found it rather opulent to have two basins when she stayed at swanky hotels. "Little things…" she had thought at the time.

She quickly changed out of her work clothes and flung them on the bed. She pulled on a baggy pair of kimono shorts and a Ken Bruce "One Year Out" T-shirt which she had seen in the window of one of the charity shops that littered Tonbridge High Street. It was her pride and joy as she had heard a lot about the famous Popmaster quiz on Radio 2, and now she had the T-shirt which would be the envy of millions of listeners. She went into the bathroom and splashed water on her face before heading off back downstairs in search of some food.

She had just reached the freezer when her phone sprang into life on the refectory table. She picked it up, thumbed the red disk across the screen and answered.

57

Monday 24 July

Woons always travelled light when flying, and he had already put his watch, phone, wallet and cash in his holdall before arriving at Security. His belt was also in the bag and he now added his passport and boarding card. He wore a pair of cheap flat shoes which normally allowed him to get through without being asked to remove them. Tonight was no exception and, having completed all the security checks at the airport, Woons found himself in the cavernous departures lounge at Gatwick's North Terminal.

Apart from the thousands of passengers sprawled on the seats that were spread as far as the eye could see, there were thousands more mooching around the rows of retail outlets which clung to the very edges of the floor space. Woons now stopped by one of the shop fronts, fished his belt out of the holdall and threaded it through the loops on his trousers. He also retrieved his money, passport, watch and phone. Feeling human again, he turned to face the departing throng.

He quickly realised that his number one priority now was to feed himself. He was famished! Woons knew from bitter experience that visits to Kaspi could not in any way be described as gourmet adventures so he usually bulked up in one of the many eateries crammed into the gallery on the upper floor of the departures lounge. So, he made his way to the end of the lounge and rode the escalator up to the next level. He wandered through the foodie outlets on this level to see what was on offer and what might satisfy his palate tonight. He passed wholesome food outlets, a sushi bar, Asian noodles, Italian pasta & pizza, kebabs of all shapes and sizes – it was all here. But, in the end, he decided on an outlet serving wholesome Californian food which had the added attraction that they cooked the food in a kitchen located in the centre of the restaurant. This should give him some entertainment, he thought.

Sitting down at a small table for two, Woons suddenly realised just how hungry he was. A young girl dressed in ripped jeans, a plain T-shirt with the name of the restaurant emblazoned all over its front, came over and plonked a menu down on the table. In a faltering American accent which was more downtown Crawley than west coast USA, she asked him what he wanted to drink. He had been thinking of having a pint of local beer but, at nearly £6 for a pint, he decided on a smoothie which combined passion fruit with pineapple, mango and apple. It sounded delicious. And, in any case, he had to keep his wits about him. The girl scuttled away and Woons was left to study the simplified menu.

With one eye on the meagre rations of edible food he was likely to get over the next forty-eight hours, Woons decided on the biggest Club Burger they had on the menu with a side of sweet potato fries. He gave the girl his order when she returned with the smoothie, and then sat back to take in his surroundings. He was fascinated by the work going on in the kitchen at the centre of the restaurant as the chefs darted this way and that, whizzing around the confined space in orderly chaos. It reminded him of watching the dodgem cars at the fair.

For their part, the waiting staff flew around the floor between tables, chairs, bags, prams and the occasional pair of crutches. Backwards and forwards to the serving point – plates of food going out, empty plates coming back in.

Woons quickly tired of watching this never-ending panto-mime and turned his attention to his fellow diners. A mixed bunch if ever there was one, he thought. And how many differ-ent nationalities must there be in this small space? Couples, families, elderlies, singletons like himself, children, babies. Women wearing saris, hijabs, flowing robes – some in shorts and skimpy tops, ready to hit the beach as soon as the plane landed. Men wearing a fascinating range of international head-wear – there were kippahs, Jewish Orthodox fedoras, hundreds of baseball hats all sporting different logos, the odd fez, a few yorubas. It was all here.

He spotted the girl making her way through the maze of tables, one arm raised with splayed fingers balancing a tray of food. She eventually made it to his table and placed the tray in front of him. 'Any sauces?' she asked. Woons surveyed the plate of food and wondered if the chips could do with something. 'Ketchup?' he asked. The girl looked at the plate and then at him. 'Tomato okay?' she asked. Was there any other type of ketchup, Woons wondered but simply replied that tomato ketchup would be fine. The girl shot off in search of the ketchup and he had a good look at the plate of food in front of him, trying to work out where to start.

Woons had never been a pretty eater. He was now attacking the burger with gusto, flecks of the avocado smash already smeared around his mouth in the company of the smoky peach bbq sauce. As he continued munching into the burger, clear drops of calorie-infested grease dripped from his chin and formed a viscous pool under the tired iceberg lettuce leaf which was forlornly trying to cover the plate on which the burger had been presented. He slathered the ketchup the girl had brought him all over the sweet potato chips, and was using his fingers to cram these into his mouth when it was not actively engaged in taking another bite of the burger.

Amidst all his chomping and licking of lips, Woons suddenly had a thought. Not a light bulb moment but just a little irritating rumination. What if the Kaspi brethren really had fucked off into the sunset or been wiped out in some vicious, cold-blooded turf war?

As he munched on, he stared idly at the crowd around him with unseeing eyes. Had he, perhaps, been a bit hasty in getting himself onto this flight and across Europe to find out from Tsiklauri just exactly what was going on. Apart from the President of the country himself, Tsiklauri was probably one of the most powerful men in Georgia with fingers in any pie you might care to mention. No! Tsiklauri would be there, Woons reasoned, because he had too much to lose in the UK if his operation was smashed. Although he had never considered Tsiklauri as a true mate, they had been good for the fortunes of each other so there was a mutual respect. No, he'd be there! Nothing to worry about!

It wasn't long before the plate of food was clear and his napkin resembled the flag of one of the rainbow nations. The girl came and took his tray away, asked him if he wanted a dessert and then brought him a large cup of strong coffee.

Replete for the moment, Woons sat back and continued scanning his fellow diners, now trying to match which destination each traveller might be going to based on what they were wearing. There was, however, one traveller he couldn't actually see from where he was sitting. And, in any event, the man at one of the tables outside Starbucks opposite would not have attracted his attention. Short and stocky, and wearing a black shirt and dark suit, the man sat hunched over a tabloid newspaper, one hairy hand grasping a huge beaker of coffee. He had perfect sight of Woons' back as he sipped his coffee and looked down at his paper. When Woons moved on from the restaurant, he would follow and, when Woons was settled in seat 14F, the man would be sitting across the aisle and one row behind him. And when Woons had cleared passport control at Tbilisi airport, the short stocky man would make his move. But, for now, he released his phone from its holder attached to his belt and punched in the country code 0995 followed by the area code 371 followed by the number which was imprinted on his brain. The people of Kaspi would want to know that the Englishman would soon be on his way.

58

Monday 24 July

'Hello, Mum!' Hunter's mother often called at about this time of the evening just to check that her little girl was all right. Carol Hunter had never quite understood why her daughter had joined the police which had become a far more dangerous occupation since her days in the force. Why couldn't she have followed a more sensible career path as a Solicitor or an Accountant or even something in the Charity Sector? But the police! Carol knew all about the long hours, rubbing shoulders with all those very dangerous men and women from the criminal underworld, all the death and degradation! How could she?

'Hello, Darling!' her mother's voice sounded as if she was talking from a sunken wreck at the bottom of the sea instead of from her beautiful bungalow in the North Devon countryside. Hunter could picture her sitting by the huge picture window looking across scattered houses to the moors beyond.

Although she had lost her husband quite young, Carol Hunter had never remarried although she led quite a busy social life. She had learnt how to play bridge and had joined a couple of local groups who played on two afternoons a week. She enjoyed the social interaction although she wasn't much good at the game itself. Possessing a bit of artistic flair, Carol also helped out with painting scenery for the local amateur dramatic society where she had met lots of interesting and talented would-be thespians. On Mondays and Tuesdays, she pulled the pints at The Old Market Inn at lunchtime, and she helped out in the kitchen on Thursday evenings. She lived within easy reach of her sister, and they both did quite a lot together. Although she would have dearly loved to become a grandmother, she seemed fairly resigned to the fact that that was unlikely to happen, certainly not at the moment with the way Sarah's career was going. But she lived in hope.

'I was just wondering how you were,' Carol Hunter carried on. 'Just that I thought you sounded a bit throaty last time I spoke to you. Is everything all right now?'

Hunter stared longingly in the direction of the freezer. Wouldn't it be wonderful to just wave a magic wand and have a plate of steaming hot food suddenly appear on the table in front of her. 'All okay now, Mum – just a bit of a tickle. It's been very dry and quite dusty here. Anyway, how's you?'

Hunter listened as her mother went through everything she had done over the last fortnight and made her usual barbed comments about some of the people she had associated with. Then she dropped the proverbial bombshell.

'Oh, and I'm thinking of coming up to see Gracie at that new place they've opened somewhere near Tunbridge Wells – I forget what it's called. You know, the one with the expensive rooms.' Gracie was Carol Hunter's one remaining aunt who was in her nineties and, as an only child, had inherited a fortune when her father had died. Not only had she been left a 10-bedroom Georgian mansion in the leafy Berkshire countryside, but she had also inherited his controlling shareholding in a small technology business. Soon after his death, the company was bought for an undisclosed amount by a leading European conglomerate making all its shareholders millionaires many times over. For a while, Gracie had lived in the mansion but, when it got too big for her, she took to travelling the world on the largest ocean-going liners – always checking into the most luxurious suites where she would be waited on hand and foot around the clock. But the onset of Parkinsons disease and the increasing pain caused by her arthritis meant that Gracie found it more difficult to cope at sea so she had moved into a five-star hotel in the Kent countryside.

Hunter certainly knew the place her mother was referring to – very luxurious and very expensive. And she knew exactly what was coming next!

'Oh darling, would you be able to put me up for a couple of nights?' her mother enquired, a slight tremor in her voice. 'I won't get in the way and you won't need to feed me as they do lovely lunches at Gracie's place – and we'll probably have the high tea as well.' Hunter's heart sank. The way she had laid out her house suited single occupancy. On the infrequent occasions when her mother came to stay, she found that her private space became overcrowded. Although Hunter loved her mother dearly, she just wished that she could find another accommodation option. Couldn't Gracie put her up somewhere?

Gritting her teeth and trying to sound welcoming, Hunter replied. 'No problem, Mum. Just give me about forty-eight hours' notice so that I can get things organised.'

There was a pause at the other end of the line, followed by a small cough as if her mother was clearing her throat. 'Well, I was actually thinking of arriving late on Thursday so that I could see Gracie on Friday, darling. I hope that will be okay. Promise not to get in the way and I'll be off early on Saturday so you can have the weekend to yourself!'

Chance would be a fine thing, Hunter thought. God! This

Thursday! Aaargh! 'Yes, that should be fine!' she stammered, just managing to pull herself together before saying something to her mother which she might later live to regret. 'Just let me know what time you're getting here so that I can get away from work and let you in.'

'Oh darling, thank you so much!' enthused her mother. 'And it'll be lovely to see you again. I do so miss seeing you, you know! It can get very lonely rattling around in this house on my own.'

'Okay, Mum! Okay.' Hunter had had enough of this phone call. 'Let's catch up on Thursday. Must get off now as I haven't had anything to eat yet.' A few more expressions of gratitude from her mother and then she was gone. Hunter put the phone down, gripped the edge of the cold marble work surface and stretched out her arms, staring at the floor. This Thursday! Aarrgh!

59

Monday 24 July

An hour later, feet tucked under her to keep warm, Hunter was snuggled into the corner of her settee watching the news on a small TV screen perched precariously on the top of the bureau which she had inherited from her grandparents. These days she tended to watch most of the news with the sound turned down as she couldn't bear to listen to reporters and presenters with egos which were much greater than the sum total of their knowledge of the subjects they were talking about. It also provided her with a little game as she had to try and guess what each news story was about just by looking at the pictures. She often thought that, when you lived alone, you sometimes needed these little distractions to pass the time.

She was on to the third news story of the bulletin when her mobile phone spluttered into life on the small coffee table in front of her. She picked it up, looked at the caller number and swiped the bottom of the screen. 'DI Hunter.'

'Oh, good evening ma'am,' a voice replied. 'Sorry to trouble you at this time of the evening. It's Sergeant Arnold, Trevor Arnold, on the desk at Tonbridge tonight.'

Hunter thought for a moment. 'Yes, Trevor,' she said, suddenly recalling his animated face with its engaging smile. 'How can I help you?'

'As I said, ma'am, sorry to trouble you but there's been a hit and run which you might be interested in.' Arnold sounded almost apologetic but had the courage of his convictions to contact Hunter at this time of night as he knew of her reputation for dealing with those who didn't at least offer to keep her in the loop as situations developed.

'Go on,' said Hunter, now focusing her attention away from the television.

'Well, details are quite sketchy at the moment but Golf November 88 attended a triple nine which was called in by a member of the public who thought he had hit something on the Pilgrims Way between Kemsing and Wrotham.' Arnold paused, presumably to look at his notes. 'Yes, he then stopped and walked back to where he thought the hit had been, and found a young girl lying in the ditch at the side of the road. She is now in Pembury but in a very bad way – touch and go they say. She'll probably be moved to a London hospital before the night's out. Thought you'd like to know.'

'Thanks, Trevor,' Hunter said, deep in thought. 'What about the driver, have we got his details?'

'Yes, ma'am. He's also in Pembury suffering from a bit of shock. I get the impression that the girl may have been hit more than once and was not a pretty sight.'

'Have you got troops at the scene?' Hunter asked.

'Golf November 88's still there and has been joined by Golf November 59,' Arnold said, reading from his notes. 'The FCR's up to speed with this and the Roads Policing SIO has been notified.' FCR was the Force Control Room which was informed of any and all incidents attended by Kent Police.

'Have we got a duty RSM on tonight?' Hunter asked.

'Yes,' replied Arnold. 'The Road Scene Manager's on the way to the location, and a Forensic Collision Investigator will be allocated in the morning as they've had a bit of sickness in that unit.'

Hunter was impressed that Trevor Arnold had already got on to the FCI unit. 'Sounds like everything's under control,' she commented. 'As a matter of interest, what made you think I might be interested?'

'Only that one of the ambulance crew apparently mentioned that he thought the girl was a foreigner.' Arnold paused for a moment, possibly again consulting his notes. 'Ah, yes,' he continued, 'she apparently came to as they were getting her into the ambulance and started shouting the odds but not in a language anyone understood. Even the driver of the car said he hadn't a clue. I heard that you were looking at a couple of incidents involving foreign girls so thought I'd give you the heads up first.'

'Okay, thanks Trevor,' Hunter said, appreciating the early notification she had been given. 'Suggest you keep tabs on the driver as we'll want to get a statement from him in the morning.'

'Well he's not going anywhere,' Arnold responded. 'Just had a message flash up on my screen to say he's being kept in over-night for observation. I'll make sure he doesn't go anywhere until one of yours gets down to statement him in the morning.'

'Thanks, Trevor. We'll pick this up in the morning.' Hunter ended the call and tossed the phone back on to the table. A weather presenter was giving a very good impression of a semaphore operator on the TV screen as Hunter reached for the remote and zapped the off button. She stayed tucked up into the corner of the settee, trying to make some sense of the seemingly unconnected incidents of the last few days. But what if they were, in fact, connected? And, if they were connected, what on earth was going on?

She glanced at the clock and saw that it was well past the

time when she should be in bed given the early start she had promised herself for the following day. She unfolded her legs from underneath her and padded over to the kitchen sink. One plate, one cup, one glass and some cutlery. The washing up could wait until tomorrow evening. She crossed to the stairs, flicked a couple of light switches so that the downstairs lights went off and light flooded down from the upstairs landing. She wearily climbed the stairs and got underway with her nightly preparations for bed.

An hour later, nicely tucked up under the duvet, Hunter was still wondering if there might be a connection between Scarecrow Girl and the girl just discovered by the Pilgrims Way. She also needed concrete proof of a connection between the abandoned house next to the allotment where the girl was discovered, and the fire damaged property at Hildenborough. And what about the disappearance of the hotel guest – what was his name? Something foreign. Was that all connected? She needed some answers and, as she finally drifted off to sleep, she determined to speak to Grace Kendall first thing in the morning.

As her eyelids became heavier with the onset of some much-needed sleep, she caught the sound of an aircraft as it continued its climb from Gatwick Airport, no doubt tracking its way to some exotic location, she thought, as the curtains of sleep slowly drifted across her brain.

Little did Sarah Hunter know that the man sitting uncomfortably by the window in row 14 of the jet as it soared over the Kent countryside held the answers to many of the questions which were swimming around inside her head.

60
Tuesday 25 July

Despite some hold-ups while taxiing at Gatwick, the flight was only about 25 minutes late into Tbilisi landing at just after 7.00 a.m. on a bright, sunny but cool Georgian morning. During the flight, Woons had slept fitfully sitting upright. The seats in the Embraer 190 didn't seem to have as much padding as he remembered from the old Boeing 737s they used to run on this route, and the seat frame seemed more restricting which made the whole experience rather uncomfortable. He hadn't understood most of the announcements made by the cabin crew during the flight. They were in a local Georgian dialect before being translated into an approximation of the English language which was spoken with a thick, eastern European accent. He had, at least, been able to establish that he was now three hours ahead of UK time so he put his watch right as the plane taxied from the runway to the terminal building.

The aircraft eventually came to a halt beside the airbridge leading out from gate 101 of the Arrivals Terminal at Tbilisi International Airport. The engines were switched off and passengers started to scramble for their bags in the overhead lockers. Woons always stayed in his seat whilst this pantomime took place, biding his time by looking out of the window and watching the local airport staff rather lazily attending to the offloading of suitcases and other effects which had been loaded on board at Gatwick. The short stocky man in row 15 also bided his time.

Eventually, there was movement from the front of the aircraft and people started to disembark. Woons rose from his seat and stretched. Boy, did he need to stretch! He got out into the aisle, lifted his holdall out of the overhead locker and ambled up the narrow passageway before disembarking onto the airbridge. His short, stocky follower had waited to get two passengers between himself and his quarry, and soon followed onto the airbridge.

The line of passengers snaked its way into the airport and followed the signs to passport control. There was a short queue for EU passports, a longer queue for other internationals and no queue for Georgian nationals. The short, stocky man now faced a dilemma – if he went through the Georgian nationals' channel, he would get in front of Woons so he hung back in the EU passports queue.

An officious immigration officer urgently waved Woons towards his desk and almost snatched the passport from Woons' hand. He quickly scanned the details page and held it up to a machine under the counter which Woons couldn't see. He then flicked through the remaining pages of the passport before slapping it back on top of the counter for Woons to pick up. No smiles, no nodding, not even a 'Welcome to Tbilisi'. Woons knew he was in Georgia.

Gripping the handles of his holdall, he made his way downstairs to the baggage reclaim area and thankfully saw a sign for the toilets. He never knew quite what to expect in the men's toilets at international airports, so he slung the long strap of the holdall round his neck and hitched up his trousers before entering. Sure enough, there were some wet patches on the floor so he gingerly picked his way across to the urinals, uncertain as to whether he was trying to avoid water or piss or a mixture of both! Thankfully, the place was nearly empty so he was in and out of there in the shortest possible time. He made his way back to the baggage reclaim area and noticed that many of his fellow passengers were leaning on trollies waiting for the carousel to start. He smirked in the knowledge that they had a long wait ahead of them.

Woons breezed through customs trying not to attract attention to himself, finally exiting into the main Arrivals Hall through two heavily frosted automatic glass doors. This was where his problems would start because, as far as he was aware, no one knew that he was travelling to Georgia. But he had known the crowd from Kaspi for a long time, and he knew that there was very little that they didn't know about when it came to keeping an eye on their empire, and who came in and went out of their country.

He turned right, walking past a line of people waving placards with names scrawled on them or just standing there looking excited about meeting a long-lost friend or relative. He didn't notice a short, stocky man exit the customs area just behind him and turn left towards the other side of the hall, a wireless blue tooth device wrapped round his left ear. Taxi drivers had been banned to an area outside the hall so the arrivals area itself was sparsely populated with people who were genuinely engaged in meeting up with inbound travellers.

The short, stocky man now took refuge behind a display of special offers outside a food store, his eyes glued to the Englishman who was standing in the middle of the hall staring up at an arrivals information screen as if looking for inspiration. He continued a whispered commentary, relaying details of the Englishman's movements until he suddenly caught sight of two men entering the hall through the main doors from the car park. Abruptly ending his call, he watched as the two men approached Woons. After a brief conversation, they accompanied the Englishman across the concourse and exited through the doors to the car park. The short, stocky man followed at a distance and also entered the car park. Crouching behind a row of parked cars, he watched as Woons got into a car which then roared towards the exit barrier and off into the morning sunshine. The short, stocky man returned to the Arrivals Hall urgently relaying the news of Woons' departure into his phone. He breathed a big sigh of relief when his call was finished, unwrapped the blue tooth from around his ear, picked up a bag of donuts from the stand to his left and started munching one as he went in search of the pay desk.

Woons sat in the back of the black Mercedes E Class, his two minders in the front as they negotiated their way out of Tbilisi Airport soon picking up the Kakheti Highway which would take them to the west of the city. Although he hadn't made this journey for a while, Woons remembered some of the landmarks on the route and started to tick them off in his mind. But, as the speed picked up once they were on the highway, and as the warmth inside the vehicle started to take effect, his eyelids began to droop and he found himself nodding off only to come to when the car hit a rough patch of road which was all too frequently.

After one particular crunch when he thought that a tyre might have shredded, he found that they had left the confines of Tbilisi behind them and he was now looking out on the mighty River Mtkvari. On an early visit to Georgia, Irakli had explained to him how the river had its source in Turkey and flowed through the Greater Caucasus and Lesser Caucasus ranges before emptying out into the Caspian Sea. The road offered unparalleled views of the river and Woons sat back to enjoy the scenery.

Soon he caught sight of the Jvari Monastery of Mtskheta perched on a rocky mountaintop in the Lower Caucasus range at the confluence of the Mtkvari and Aragvi Rivers. He remembered Irakli telling him that the monastery had stood for fifteen hundred years and overlooked the town of Mtskheta which had formerly been the capital of Georgia. Although the building had been listed as a World Heritage site by UNESCO, erosion was doing its best to deteriorate the monastery with its stone blocks being degraded by wind and acidic rain. Woons had always been fascinated by this structure and would have dearly liked to have had the opportunity of wandering about inside the ancient building.

The car sped on, his two minders staring unflinchingly at the road ahead. He allowed his eyelids to droop once more and enjoyed a further nap before resurfacing as he subconsciously felt the speed drop. He looked ahead and saw that they were approaching the Pirveli Market which was where they would turn off on to the Kaspi-Kavtiskhevi Road. The quality of the road surface was now considerably diminished from the highway they had just left and was not conducive to napping. So Woons just watched the scenery go by. Soon, they were travelling across the Mtkvari River and to the north of a town called Mikeltsqaro where, he recalled, some of Irakli's distant cousins lived.

Before much longer, they were entering Kaspi and Woons recognised the Central Market and the railway station where they would turn right onto M Kostava St. Woons was always amused by this choice of route as it took them right past the police HQ – there was surely some sort of irony in a bunch of international gangsters passing within a road's width of those who would dearly like to have them locked up! They carried on past the local Green Area and then out into the countryside where the slopes of the Lower Caucasus came down to meet the dense forestation of the area.

Eventually, Woons spotted a petrol station ahead on the left and the car slowed once more to make a right turn on to a rough track. Up ahead, Woons could see the wooden wicket fence which surrounded the Restaurant Palakhuri which was perched on the banks of the Lekhura River. The Mercedes passed through an entrance in the fence and under an ornate arch before wheeling away to the right and down a short drive to a car park where two other cars were already parked. As it was still early in the day, Woons assumed that these cars either belonged to Tsiklauri and Irakli or to others of their group.

Once the car came to a halt, Woons heard the locks click open and he climbed out into the fresh morning air. He stretched and then leaned back into the car to collect his holdall. His two minders were standing at the back of the car already lighting cigarettes and chatting in low voices. Woons looked around him and spotted the wicket gate which he knew led to a short bridge over a stream and then onto the restaurant's veranda with its numerous tables and chairs – probably already set for lunch. He looked at his minders and nodded his head towards the gate. They nodded back which he took as meaning that it was OK to walk up to the restaurant. He was desperate for something to drink even if it had to be the lousy Georgian tea.

He crossed the car park, through the wicket gate, across the bridge glancing down to see if there were any fish in the stream, through another wicket gate and then across a grassed area and up a couple of steps onto the veranda. The tables had, indeed, been laid for lunch but there was no other sign that the restaurant was even open. He threaded his way through the tables towards the doorway into the inner sanctum of the building. The door itself had been wedged open against the wall so he stepped into a darkened room in which he could just about make out other tables and chairs. There seemed to be no lights on anywhere in the building and no sound was coming from the kitchen.

He was about to turn round and go and sit at a table on the veranda when a heavily accented voice came out of the darkness in front of him. 'Yes, what can I do for you my friend?'

Woons peered into the gloom. Was that Irakli's voice? It was a while since he had spoken to Irakli so he couldn't be sure. If it was Irakli, why had he not come forward and shaken his hand as he normally did when they met? Well, if it wasn't Irakli at least it might be someone who could get him a drink.

'Hello, there,' he started. 'Some tea, please.' Then realising that he was absolutely starving, he added 'and some bread. Thank you.' He heard what sounded like someone getting off a stool and shuffling towards the back of the room. He saw the silhouette of a door opening and a buzz followed by two flashes as the strip lighting fired up in the kitchen and the door swung shut.

Woons retraced his steps onto the veranda and found his way to the far corner where he took a seat at a table which offered him a clear view of the whole area around him.

He was feeling tired, the effects of a night on a Georgian Airlines jet starting to take its toll. Whilst he knew that this was the place that he had always met Irakli and Tsiklauri, why were they not here today? After all, they had sent a car to meet him so, surely, they would know that he had been delivered to the Palakhuri. Just as he was replaying the events of the last twenty-four hours in his mind, a slightly dishevelled man in ill-fitting clothes shuffled across the veranda with a tray on which was his tea and a plate with two slices of bread. He laid these items on the table in front of Woons and turned to leave.

'Wait!' Woons commanded. The man stopped in his tracks and turned to face Woons. 'What's your name?'

'I am Grigol,' the man replied.

'Okay Grigol,' Woons continued. 'I have come here to see Mr Tsiklauri. Where is he? Is he coming here today? Where's Irakli?'

So many questions. Poor Grigol looked as if he under-stood about half of what Woons was saying. But he obviously recognised the names. 'Tsiklauri, he no here in Kaspi. I no know Irakli.'

Woons felt as if he had been kicked in the stomach by a bucking bronco. He was speechless. Had he really come all this way to find out that the two men he wanted to talk to were out of town? Should he have, perhaps, listened to the insolent bastard who had spoken rudely to him on the phone? And how could he not know Irakli? When Woons had been in Kaspi in the past, everyone knew Irakli – he was a son of Kaspi for God's sake!

He stared at the man in disbelief just as a rather more sinister thought started to fester in his overcrowded brain. If Tsiklauri wasn't here and, by the sound of it, neither was Irakli, who the fuck were the two goons who had collected him from the airport? Without touching his tea, Woons jumped down from the veranda and ran across the little bridge to the car park. But the Mercedes had gone.

'Fuck! Fuck! And fuck again!' he shouted at the space where the car had been parked. How had he been so gullible? And how had he missed the Mercedes driving off? Probably when he was in the restaurant asking for the tea. 'Stupid! Stupid! Stupid!' he castigated himself as he once again crossed the bridge and climbed back on to the veranda. He was about to head for his table when he noticed that the door into the restaurant was now closed. He strode over to it and turned the handle. Locked! He stared at the door in disbelief and tried the handle again, a sense of desperation creeping into his actions. He slammed his fists into the closed door, pummelling the woodwork. No response.

He moved to the edge of the veranda and jumped down onto the grass. 'There must be another way into this godforsaken place,' he thought as he strode along the wall towards the back of the building. There was, indeed, another door but it was firmly locked. Around the other side of the building was a hatch which was either used for deliveries or for transferring waste to the bins lined up along the wall. He tried to push it open but it wouldn't budge.

Moving further along the wall, Woons found that he was back at the veranda where his tea was now stone cold. He sat down at the table and drank it anyway. He also crammed the two slices of bread into his mouth and eagerly consumed them. He was ravenous. Then he sat back and tried to make some sense of his predicament.

61
Tuesday 25 July

For the first time in over a week it dawned cloudy and wet. The summer had, so far, been a mostly sunny affair so digging out the wet weather gear at silly o'clock in the morning had been tiresome. Damp coats were now slung over the backs of chairs, and Sarah Hunter noticed that there were one or two bedraggled looking hairstyles around the room as she surveyed her team. Computer screens were all blinking away, coffee cups sat bolt upright on most of the desks, and there was a general air of expectation in the MIR.

'Okay! Morning everyone!' Sarah called her group together from her customary position in front of the white boards. 'Sorry about the weather but it had to break sooner or later!' The team looked less than impressed with this generalisation since most of them had had to trudge some ten minutes in the rain from the public car park. But they paid attention nevertheless.

'Right!' she continued, 'we've got a busy day ahead of us so let's just run through where we're at.' She looked over at Selitto who was in his customary position, leaning on the window sill, casting occasional glances down to the roundabout below as the morning traffic built up. He had been in very early so was aware of overnight developments which Hunter was about to report to the team.

'The first thing to deal with is the van driver from the RTA out at Fordcombe when the body in the bag was discovered. The body's at the morgue and awaiting the attention of the sainted Professor Ilona Jenkyns who is on her way from London to help out. She's been here before and I can assure you that she is one of the very best in the business. I'd like you, Elaine, to progress this one. The van driver seems to have required some attention to his broken wrist and has been kept in overnight at Pembury. No doubt they'll want the bed by the end of the day so suggest that you get over there straight after this briefing and find out what he was up to. Name's Kevin Bland and claims he just picked the bag up near Haysden Lakes. Got five hundred quid for his troubles in cash and was taking it to Crawley. Says he's done something similar a number of times – some bloke rings him up and tells him where to pick up. He then gets further info about the drop-off on the way but always seems to get directed to some lock-up or piece of wasteland so never sees anyone. Five hundred quid seems to be the going rate each time he does the job. That's a monkey isn't it, Ted?'

'Yep!' Selitto adjusted his position and addressed the turning heads. 'It seems that soldiers returning from India introduced the word monkey meaning 500 pounds sterling. Comes from the 500 rupee note in India which used to have a drawing of a monkey on it. I also think the twenty-five rupee note is said to have had a drawing of a pony on it thus introducing the slang word 'Pony' meaning twenty-five pounds but I'm less sure about that derivation.'

'Whatever!' sighed Hunter, wishing she'd never asked the question. 'Still, a reasonable bung in this day and age. Probably more than a week's wage for our Mr Bland! Anyway, Elaine I want you to get down to Pembury and take a statement from him. Also find out whether Traffic processed him here at Tonbridge. As he was taken in the ambulance directly to Pembury and kept in overnight, I doubt that he's been either arrested or charged. In fact, he probably doesn't even know what was in the bag so won't know that he's in the shit!' DC Jennings nodded, and went back to furiously scribbling notes in her book. 'Then get over to the PM on the body in the bag – hopefully Professor Jenkyns will be doing that so you can watch and learn. She's well worth the entrance money alone!' A peal of sniggering went around the room.

'Next, and this will be new to you,' Hunter teased them. 'I got a call late last night from the desk here at Tonbridge. A girl was run over on Pilgrims Way between Kemsing and Wrotham. Seems she had probably already been knocked down by a hit-and-run and then this guy came along and ran her over. Anyway, the driver called it in and was eventually taken to Pembury suffering from severe shock, and I understand that he's still there. The girl was also taken to Pembury but was in a very bad way so she may not have survived. Carolyn, can you get on to that? Get over to Pilgrims Way and have a look at the scene of the incident. I think CSIs are still poking about there. And see if you can find out how she got to Pilgrims Way. I can't recall there being much property around that area so had she run across fields from elsewhere or could she have just been dumped from a moving vehicle and then run over while she was still on the ground? We need to know if she was another of these girls like Scarecrow Girl so you'd better then get down to Pembury to see if they know anything about her like who she is.' DC Pennant looked energised and signalled that she was happy with her assignment.

'Right, Azzar, you're next.' Hunter looked over to where Mishraz was sitting tapping information into a small tablet which he had set up on the desk. 'I'd like you to split your time between the morgue and the CSI Unit so that you can get as much information as you can about the Hildenborough house. It'll mean a bit of travelling between Maidstone and the Wells but it shouldn't be too difficult to keep one foot in each camp. We particularly need to know more about the incinerated girl and the woman in the dungeon so try to be there for their PMs. Julian French's team ran the scene at Hildenborough so get in to see him – tell him I sent you if he asks! And drop in to see Beth Dench's team while you're there – see if they've got any more information for us.'

'Yes, ma'am!' Mishraz replied. 'I make that at least three PMs today. Are they normally done one after the other or could two be done at the same time?'

Hunter hadn't given this much consideration so, after some thought, she responded. 'With the arrival of Professor Jenkyns, they may well schedule two to take place at the same time, particularly as one is the burnt remains of a body. So, you and Elaine will just have to talk to the guys down there and find out what sort of time you need to arrive.' Mishraz nodded and entered more data into his tablet.

'Okay,' she continued. 'Ted, I want you and Stuart to act as a kind of roving support for the team. You should both circulate round to make sure that we are getting as much intel as we can. By the end of today, I want to be able to tell Iversen that all these incidents are inextricably linked. If possible, it would be good to have some ID on some of the bodies – or, at least, more information about them than we currently have. So, team, keep in contact with Ted if you turn up a nugget of information or you need help in some way.' They all nodded and started collecting their things together.

'Good luck, everyone! Back here for a 6.30 p.m. briefing, and let's see if we can marry up these boards,' Hunter said, thrusting out her left hand and pointing at the white boards behind her.

62

Tuesday 25 July

'No fucking signal!'

Woons tossed his mobile onto the table. What else did he expect? How had he ever got involved with people from this godforsaken country? Okay, they had led him to unimagined riches but that wasn't the point. Well, not right at this minute anyway. He sat back in the chair, trying to make some sense of the last few hours.

He had been met by those two guys at the airport. They didn't have much English between them but they asked him his name and led him to believe that Mr Tsiklauri had been expecting him. They would drive him to Kaspi where Mr Tsiklauri would be waiting to meet him. When he had asked if Irakli would also be there, they had simply nodded. He had been tired – the thought of an hour's kip in the back of a nice comfortable Merc was enticing.

The journey had passed without incident – as far as he was concerned, they had followed the same route that other drivers had followed when he had been collected from the airport in the past. Yet, he had now been told that Mr Tsiklauri wasn't here and the idiot at the restaurant had never heard of Irakli. Unbelievable!! But the merest germ of an idea started to worm its way into his brain like the tentacles of a sea anemone, and he focussed on a point in the middle distance whilst he let it develop.

This was the second time that he had been told that Mr Tsiklauri wasn't here although the goons in the car had given the impression that he was here. The same went for Irakli although of more concern was the fact that the man here at the restaurant had never heard of Irakli. How could that be possible? Irakli was Kaspi – Kaspi was Irakli. This place was one of Tsiklauri's strongholds – Irakli was one of their band of brothers. Unless, unless…

Woons suddenly shot forward in his chair and gripped the table in front of him. Suppose the guy in the restaurant wasn't from Kaspi. Suppose he had just been put in here to keep an eye on Woons until it was time for him to leave. Woons knew that the restaurant was in the countryside and he wouldn't have a hope of finding his way back into town on foot. But, at the same time, if these guys really weren't part of the Kaspi brethren, then who the fuck were they?

He picked up his phone, rose from the table, and climbed down from the veranda. There were no outbuildings apart from one which housed the toilets, and that was definitely not to be visited unless you really fancied a few days in bed with a debilitating illness. There was one lawn covered in bench-tables like the ones he had seen in some of the gastro pubs back in Kent. There was another small veranda with more formal tables and chairs, and there was a large barbeque area which could be accessed from all directions. He crossed the little bridge to the car park and noticed that the two cars were still there. He had seen them when he arrived but had paid little attention to them since then. He now crossed the car park to take a closer look but he soon realised that neither car would be travelling very far any time soon. Quite apart from a couple of flat tyres, neither of them had a steering wheel.

He turned back towards the restaurant and had just re-crossed the little bridge when he heard the roar of an engine as a vehicle sped down the driveway and careered into the car park, churning up dust and small bits of gravel. Woons turned to watch as the vehicle slewed to a halt not far from the two abandoned cars. Trying not to be noticed, he crept backwards towards the veranda and felt his way around to the side where he had been sitting, his eyes never leaving the vehicle.

After what seemed like an age, the two front doors of the vehicle opened and two men got out each dressed in a black suit, white shirt and black tie. They each wore trademark dark glasses even though it was now quite overcast. They both walked towards the little bridge and, before Woons had a chance to make a move, the taller of the two men called out to him.

'Ah, Mr Woons! Welcome! I heard that you flew in this morning. Did you have a good flight?' They started walking towards the wicket gate and the little bridge. 'And were my men there to meet you? I hope that they looked after you.' All the time getting closer. Woons was stuck to the spot, unable to assess his options, slightly mesmerised by the calm voice which was speaking directly to him. Getting closer and closer.

Eventually, the two men stopped just short of the veranda and peered through a sea of table legs to where Woons was cowering. The tall man continued in the same patronising voice.

'Now, Mr Woons. We would like to have a little chat with you! But not here, I'm afraid. So, we would like you to come with us to a place where you can get a shower and some food – you are hungry, yes? And when you have enjoyed our hospitality, we will have our little chat. We can also get you back to the airport for your flight home. What is there not to like about our little plan?'

411

A sinister smile crept across the tall man's face which sent a shiver down Woons' spine. But what options did he have? He guessed that refusal was out of the question. Or would at least result in a hell of a beating, a journey in the boot of the vehicle to God knows where before a bullet to his forehead brought his nightmare to an end. So, he raised the palms of his hands to shoulder height and moved out from his position beside the veranda.

'OK, guys!' he started, 'Doesn't seem that I have much choice so let's do it your way. I'll just get my holdall.' Woons pointed to the holdall which was slung over a chair next to the table where he had been sitting. The tall man flicked his fingers and his partner leapt on to the veranda and collected the holdall. He passed it down to Woons and then jumped back down to the grassed area.

'Follow me,' the tall man ordered, leading the way towards the little bridge. The other man signalled for Woons to follow the tall man and then brought up the rear as the three of them filed across the bridge and through the wicket gate into the car park.

Once they reached the vehicle, the tall man turned to face Woons. 'We have to take precautions my friend,' as he pulled a set of plastic cuffs from his jacket pocket. The other man pulled what looked like a black hood from his pocket. 'You have a choice. Either you allow us to tie your hands and put the black hood on you and you can sit in a comfortable seat for our journey – or you can make it difficult for us in which case we will use force to cuff you and throw you in the trunk of the vehicle.'

Woons meekly proffered his wrists to the tall man. 'A sensible decision, my friend,' he smiled as he tied Woons' wrists together in front of him. 'Now, please get into the car.' Woons climbed into the back of the vehicle behind the front passenger seat and sat facing forward. The other man leaned in and placed the hood over Woons' head which cut out all but the merest glint of daylight and consigned him to a dark world punctuated by the sounds around him. He heard the door slam beside him, and then the front doors opening and closing once the two men had got in. The throaty roar of the engine then took over and he was soon aware that they were moving across the bumpy track out of the car park and away from the restaurant.

Woons had always thought that he had a good sense of direction so he decided to try and concentrate on the direction of travel. He soon heard the clicking of the indicator and felt the vehicle turn right which meant that it was turning away from the town of Kaspi. This set alarm bells ringing in his head. Where the fuck were they taking him? The vehicle picked up speed, the driver paying scarce attention to the pot holes which made for an uncomfortable ride in the back seat. After a while, Woons heard the indicator again and felt the car drifting to the left. He had also found that he could see a shaft of light on the floor of the vehicle and, as this gently moved across his vision, it confirmed the move to the left.

The vehicle was now picking up speed, and he was aware of greater traffic noise all around him. With his limited knowledge of the geography of Georgia, he decided that they had travelled north of Kaspi and were now on one of the country's highways travelling in a vaguely westward direction away from Tbilisi. This was a serious worry, and his stomach started churning at the thought that he would not make it back to the airport for his return flight some thirty hours from now. They drove on, maintaining a relentless speed which was putting tens of kilometres between him and the sanctuary of the departures lounge at Tbilisi Airport.

Suddenly, a phone rang. Although Woons couldn't see who answered it, the voice didn't sound like the tall man who had spoken to him at the restaurant. He concentrated on listening to the voice. If it was the shorter of the two men who had taken the call then he didn't have much to say for himself. There were long periods of silence interspersed by the odd grunt, as if the man was listening to a series of instructions. Eventually, the call was ended whereupon the two men started talking to each other, the shorter one presumably telling his colleague about the call.

Woons tuned into their conversation as the car sped on, a deep feeling of unease creeping over him the more he listened. When he had previously been with Tsiklauri and Irakli, they had always spoken to him in English. Yes, he had heard them speak in the Georgian dialect but he hadn't really bothered to listen that closely as he knew that he would never be required to understand the language. However, he had picked up on some of the accents and the way that the locals spoke to each other.

He was now listening intently to the conversation between the two men at the front of the vehicle, aware that he was sitting forward in his seat. And, with every word spoken, it became increasingly apparent that he didn't recognise the language these two were speaking. The way they spoke to each other, the way they accentuated words at the end of sentences, the nuances in the local dialect. Everything was wrong!

By 8.00 a.m. the MIR was empty and Sarah Hunter was sitting behind one of the desks in the centre of the room staring at the white boards, desperate for inspiration. It seemed that the more her investigation progressed, the more bodies were piling up in the morgue. How many were there now – four? Maybe five if the hit-&-run girl didn't survive. No wonder they had had to ask London for help – and thank goodness it was Ilona Jenkyns who was on her way. Sarah had formed a close friendship with Ilona during her time with the Met. They had the same interests, had a similar sense of humour and generally enjoyed each other's company. She had a great respect for Jenkyns as one of the emerging stars in the world of pathology, and she had learnt so much simply by attending autopsies carried out by Jenkyns and lectures given by her.

In her mind, she replayed the information Grace Kendall had provided yesterday. It did look as if there were two distinct parts to the puzzle which she had been charged with solving. There were the criminals from Eastern Europe who seemed to be able to come and go with impunity, and who were presumably the masterminds behind whatever was going on in this part of the UK. But as Grace specifically pointed out, these guys are hardened international gangsters connected with kidnapping, trafficking, extortion and racketeering. They would have someone local on the ground in the UK who, although also undoubtedly a hardened criminal, was more into the fortune to be made at the high end of the sex trade which seemed to go hand-in-hand with blackmail and extortion on a large scale.

Was she right to separate the two so that, on the one hand she was looking for Vashlili and this Zlatkov character – if it was, indeed, him? Or should she concentrate on looking for the Mr Big in the UK and hope that Vashlili and Zlatkov were served up to her on a plate once she had found the person running the UK end of the operation? It was a conundrum which she felt she was still far from solving.

Sarah had returned her gaze to the white boards and was so deep in thought that she almost failed to notice that her phone had lit up and was thrumming its mute tone on top of the desk beside her. She grabbed it and swiped the bottom of the screen. 'DI Hunter,' she growled.

'Oh, hello ma'am. It's DC Jennings.'

'Yes, Elaine,' replied Hunter. 'How're you getting on?'

'Well, I thought I'd better call you because I've found out that they've discharged Kevin Bland already!' Jennings sounded slightly breathless. Hunter looked to the heavens. Surely, he hadn't just walked out of the hospital and disappeared!

'And?' Hunter wondered if she really wanted to hear Jennings' reply. Bland was the only person they had managed to get hold of who could possibly help them with their enquiries, and that was more by luck than good judgment. Although he probably wasn't going to be of much use to the case, she would be furious if he had now disappeared.

'No, no, it's okay ma'am,' came Jennings' reassuring tones. 'I've got him locked in the car. Fortunately, I got here just as he was about to leave the ward. Sister pointed him out to me so I chased after him. He's in no fit state for heroics so came quietly. Shall I get him over to Tonbridge and book him in for a statement?'

'Yes, Elaine,' replied Hunter. 'That would be the best plan then you and I can have a little chat with him once he's settled in here.'

'Okay, ma'am,' Jennings was finishing. 'While I'm on, I've tried to find out about the girl from the RTA on Pilgrims Way. Apparently, she's in theatre at the moment but it's doubtful that she will make it. Fingers crossed that she proves them wrong!'

Hunter grimaced. Another blind alley for them. DC Pennant would have to spend more time with the traffic investigation team as it was now a priority to find out where the girl had come from.

'Sorry to hear that, Elaine,' Hunter replied. There was silence on the line for a few seconds before Hunter thought of something else. 'Have you been able to find out anything about the bloke that ran her over? Is he still in the hospital or did he go home straight from A&E?'

'Not sure, ma'am. I'll find out.' Jennings sounded keen which was always a good thing as far as Hunter was concerned. It always meant that a job would be done well. 'I can leave matey in the car for a few more minutes while I just go and ask someone. I'll call you straight back.'

The call was disconnected, and Hunter put her phone back on the desk. Just as she did so, she heard the door open behind her. 'Have you got a minute?' It was the voice of DS Grace Kendall.

'Sure!' Sarah replied, raising a hand above her head and waving it in a forward motion. Kendall eventually came into view and took a seat behind one of the desks facing Hunter. She was carrying a couple of big files which she placed on the desk in front of her. Just at that point, Jennings called back to confirm that the car driver, a Mr Ollie Dolman, had been kept in the hospital for further cardio tests and wouldn't be fit to be questioned for a while yet. Hunter thanked her for the call and placed the phone back on the desk beside her empty coffee cup.

'How're you getting on?' Kendall enquired, peering over the top of the spectacles which were perched on the end of her nose.

'To be perfectly honest with you, Grace, I am lacking inspiration,' Hunter sighed. 'And, the longer my lack of inspiration goes on, the more bodies are piling up in the morgue. Probably another today already and it's not even 9 o'clock in the morning! I'm sure they're all linked but I just can't seem to get the connection. Frustrating or what!'

Kendall opened one of her files at a page which had been marked by a post-it note stuck to the page. 'Well, I might have something for you,' she said. Sarah suddenly focused her full attention on her colleague for the first time since she had entered the room, her eyes boring into the file which Grace Kendall was now consulting.

'I've been doing a bit of digging through my contacts in London,' she began, 'and I managed to persuade one of them to give me an intro to an officer at Europol in The Hague. Not just any old officer, but one in Europol's European Migrant Smuggling Centre – known as the EMSC – which supports member states in targeting and dismantling the complex and sophisticated criminal networks involved in smuggling migrants across the world. Listen to this!'

Kendall started reading from a page in her file. 'Tackling this multi-billion-euro trafficking trade became an essential part of the EU's response to the migrant crisis. Indeed, the EU's Agenda on Migration (2015) identifies the fight against migrant smuggling as a key priority. Supporting police and border authorities to coordinate highly complex cross-border anti-smuggling operations, therefore, became the primary objective of the EMSC, which brought together some of the best investigators in Europe. The EMSC closely cooperates with its partner EU Agencies dealing with judicial cooperation and border management.'

When she had finished, she looked up at Hunter. 'I told this guy about our suspicions that there was a sophisticated operation involving the trafficking of young girls from Eastern Europe for exploitation in the upmarket sex trade in the UK. He gave the impression that, whilst they were aware that there were gangs who were controlling the trafficking of people from Eastern Europe, they spent more of their time trying to shut down the movement of immigrants from Africa and other countries outside Europe. He was, however, interested to hear about what we seem to be uncovering here in Kent so I tried him out on the two names we have.'

Hunter was all ears. Could this be the bit of inspiration she needed to kickstart her brain? She'd never heard of the EMSC or whatever Kendall had called it, but it sounded the sort of organisation which could give them vital information about the people who were causing mayhem in her part of the Garden of England.

Grace continued. 'I began with Vashlili but that wasn't a name that started any bells ringing. When I told him that we knew that Vashlili had arrived at Southampton Airport from Schipol and had been travelling on a Bulgarian passport, he explained in the nicest possible way that they would probably not be interested in someone who was able to travel in and out of the UK without attracting any attention.'

Hunter's spirits took a dip. 'So, why have we been getting all excited about an upstanding citizen of Bulgaria who just happens to have disappeared from a hotel room without paying? Should we not be thinking that he is a man of mystery and is somehow involved in the deaths of god knows how many people?' Hunter was at her sarcastic best!

Kendall waited for Hunter's frustration to dissipate before continuing. 'I did, however, get a completely different reaction when I mentioned Borislav Zlatkov. The guy was straight on it – where had I got this name from? How did I know he was in the UK? Has he been seen? Did we know who we were dealing with? Question after question. Most of which I couldn't answer bearing in mind that we have very little information about the man other than that he had registered at Meadowlands a couple of days before Vashlili.'

'Hmmm!' Hunter was wrapped in thought. 'So Zlatkov is a person of some considerable interest and he's right here on our patch?' Kendall wasn't quite sure if this was meant as a statement or a question, so she continued.

'Well, not necessarily! From what I could gather, the EMSC also has evidence to support MI5's theory that there is more than one Borislav Zlatkov.' She paused to let this sink in. 'Wasn't it always thought that there was more than one Colonel Gaddafi so that any would-be assassin was never quite sure whether they would be killing the right person?' Hunter nodded absent-mindedly, trying to weigh up the significance of this information to her investigation.

Kendall continued. 'Anyway, the EMSC guy told me that the real Zlatkov is apparently a big man, about six foot five and weighing around twenty stone. He is very fit which is the result of a punishing training regime. He sports a very full black beard and also a full head of black hair, and he always wears dark glasses. So, as long as his double has the right physique, it would be very difficult to spot that it isn't Zlatkov. The guy at the EMSC says that their intel indicates that the only way of identifying the real Zlatkov is the fact that he is missing about an inch off the top of the pinkie on his right hand.'

Sarah Hunter was furiously twirling a pencil through her fingers, alternating her gaze between the white boards and the files on Kendall's desk. Suddenly, she had an idea.

'So, the only place where we have evidence of a sighting of Zlatkov is at Meadowlands,' she said, now looking directly at Kendall. 'He, or someone pretending to be him, signed the register there a couple of nights before Vashlili checked in. How long ago would that be now?' There was a calendar hanging on the wall beside the white boards and she got up to take a look at it. 'If Vashlili checked in on Tuesday and we were there on Wednesday because he had disappeared, Zlatkov must have come in on the Sunday. That's only nine days ago so someone at the hotel must be able to remember if they saw a six foot five fully bearded hulk wandering around the place.'

Kendall was nodding as Hunter returned to the desk and scooped up her phone. 'Right! Let's see how observant they are!' She returned to the white boards where one of the DCs had helpfully pinned a picture of Meadowlands with its phone number written underneath. She poked the number into her phone and waited for the ringing tone. She was slightly miffed to immediately get soporific music and the dulcet tones of a voice giving her a set of options to follow. She chose to be put through to reception and stabbed the number two. Eventually, a real person answered the call.

Hunter found herself talking to Claudine at Reception. Had she met her when they had been at the hotel last week? She couldn't remember. She introduced herself anyway and asked if she could be put through to the general manager, Peter Dangerfield.

'Oh, I'm sorry madam, Mr Dangerfield is not in today,' Claudine said, cheerily. 'Can I put you through to Miss Lancaster who is on duty this morning?' The hairs on the back of Hunter's neck were beginning to rise. Dangerfield not there again? When had she last tried to contact him? Had he actually been in since they saw him nearly a week ago?

'Okay, thank you,' Hunter replied, and waited while the phone seemed to go dead. Almost immediately, there was what sounded like a crash and a rather breathless voice announced that Hunter was now speaking to Sally Lancaster and how could she help. Hunter started by saying that she had hoped to speak to the general manager, no offence to Miss Lancaster intended.

'I'm very sorry, Inspector, but Mr Dangerfield will not be at the hotel today,' Sally Lancaster replied.

'When I spoke to Mr Dangerfield on Wednesday last week,' Hunter said, moving over to the calendar to make sure that she had the right day in her mind, 'I suggested to Mr Dangerfield that it would be helpful if he did not leave the hotel until the following day, Thursday, as we would have some more questions for him. When talking to the Crime Scene Investigators on Thursday, I discovered that Mr Dangerfield was not at the hotel on account of an illness in the family.'

'Oh, yes Inspector,' Lancaster intervened. 'One of his daughters had been taken ill at school so he had gone home at the request of his wife.'

'And then one of my team called to speak to him on Friday and he was still absent,' Hunter ploughed on. 'Tell me, has he been back to work since last Wednesday?'

There was a pause on the line. 'Well, no – we haven't seen him since last Wednesday,' Lancaster eventually replied. 'It's become a real problem for us because we can't seem to get hold of him, and the owners are starting to ask questions about his whereabouts. We are aware that he has a complicated home life. His wife has mental health problems and two of his children are disabled, but he normally always answers our calls or replies to emails if he is delayed at home for whatever reason. It's as if he has just disappeared.'

Lancaster seemed to stop to take a breath. Hunter got in quickly. 'So, you're telling me that Mr Dangerfield hasn't been at the hotel for the last six days and is not answering phone calls or emails? Has anyone tried ringing his landline at home?'

'Yes, Inspector,' Lancaster continued. 'But there's no answer and it keeps going to voicemail. That's not unusual as his wife is sometimes admitted to a care home for periods of therapy to relieve the pressure. He then looks after the children but he normally gets his wife's parents to look after the two disabled children and the older girl stays with her school best friend. That frees him up to come here. But he's normally always in contact or contactable.'

Hunter's mind was whirring at the news that Dangerfield hadn't been seen for nearly a week. She thanked Lancaster for the information but indicated that that wasn't why she had called in the first place.

'The reason for my call is actually to do with one of the guests who had stayed in the Crocus room. When we were at Meadowlands, my colleague DS Selitto found out that the same person had stayed in Crocus almost immediately before Mr Vashlili on each occasion that Mr Vashlili had stayed with you over the last year or so. I now have some information about this person so it would be very helpful if I could speak to whoever it was that was on the desk at the time that the guest registered.'

'Okay, Inspector.' Hunter could hear some tapping on a keyboard in the background. 'And the name of the other guest is?' she asked.

'We think he registered in the name of Borislav Zlatkov.' Hunter spelled out the name.

'Okay!' More tapping. 'Ah, yes – that's right,' Lancaster continued. 'Mr Zlatkov is a regular guest at Meadowlands and seems to always have that room. Did you say that you wanted to speak to the person who saw him when he arrived? In which case, that would be Francesca. She has been with us for a couple of years and may well have seen Mr Zlatkov on more than one occasion.'

'Great!' exclaimed Hunter, her spirits rising. 'Is she there now?'

'I think so,' replied Lancaster. 'I'll just call reception and get her to come down to my office now. I'll put you on hold for a minute or so.' The soporific music returned.

Kendall raised an eyebrow. 'Problem?' she whispered. Hunter shrugged her shoulders and turned down the corners of her mouth in an I'm-not-sure gesture. 'Dangerfield's disappeared,' she whispered back. Kendall's other eyebrow joined its mate. At which point a new voice came on the line.

'Hello, Inspector. This is Francesca speaking.' The receptionist sounded alert and intelligent. 'Miss Lancaster said that you have a question for me.'

'Yes, hello Francesca,' Hunter replied. 'I wanted you to cast your mind back to the last time Mr Borislav Zlatkov checked in to the hotel. I understand that you were on duty at that time.'

'Oh, yes Inspector!' the Receptionist exclaimed. 'I remember him very well. He had a problem with his car. One of the tyres had had a puncture on the long drive from the main road and he was blaming us. I managed to sort the situation out, and Stephen changed the tyre for him. I think we gave him a bit of a discount on his account as well so he was happy in the end.'

Too much information, Hunter thought. She pressed on. 'What I really want you to do is describe Mr Zlatkov to me.'

'Sure!' Francesca began. 'Well he's very tall. Most people are taller than me as I'm only just over five feet but he was very tall – well over six feet I would say. He was wearing a designer sports T-shirt and seemed to have a good physique – quite athletic. What else? He had short-cropped black hair with quite a high hairline. Very dark almost jet-black eyes.'

'He wasn't wearing dark glasses?' Hunter butted in. 'You could clearly see his eyes?'

'Yes, Inspector,' Francesca continued, 'although he may have had some shades wrapped around the top of his head. Can't be sure about that, I'm afraid. But I do remember thinking that he looked quite menacing and didn't seem to smile a lot. He also had all that stubble which seems to be all the fashion these days. I suppose it's okay for men if they've got a good covering all over the face but it's not for me really. I prefer my men clean-shaven!' Hunter raised her eyes to the ceiling.

'So, no sunglasses on but perhaps wraparounds on his head, short-cropped hair and stubble but no beard,' Hunter summarised. 'Nothing else you noted or can remember?'

'No, not apart from the jewellery,' the Receptionist replied. 'I remember he placed both his hands flat on the desk while I was printing the registration document and I was mesmerised by the sight of the rings on his fingers. I don't normally like jewellery on men but these rings were stunning. They must have cost a fortune.'

Hunter was thinking fast now. 'Was there anything about his hands you noticed? Any scars? What about his fingers? Manicured nails perhaps?' She tried to be deliberately vague.

'Oh yes,' sighed the Receptionist. 'His nails were beautifully manicured and were just gorgeous!'

'Okay, Francesca, thank you very much.' Hunter needed to wrap this up. 'Can you put Miss Lancaster back on.' There was a pause before the duty manager came back on the line. 'Okay, Miss Lancaster, thank you for allowing me to speak to Francesca – she was very helpful. Could I now ask you to keep me informed about Mr Dangerfield, particularly if you hear anything from him. If you still haven't heard from him by, say, Thursday then give me a call. I seem to recall that he lives in the Brighton area which is out of our area so we may have to arrange for our friends in Sussex to pay him a visit.' Hunter gave Lancaster her contact number and then disconnected the call.

She had been pacing the office while talking to Francesca, and had now found herself by the window looking down on the bustling streets of Tonbridge. A train passed along the track in the middle distance on its way to Ashford and beyond.

'Well,' she looked at Kendall. 'We now know that the real Borislav Zlatkov did not visit Meadowlands - and has probably never even heard of it!'

64

Tuesday 25 July

The vehicle roared on.

How long had they been on the road? Two hours? Three hours? Woons wasn't sure. The cuffs were biting into his wrists, the dull pain preventing Woons from doing the one thing he really wanted to do – sleep! He was also finding the hood somewhat claustrophobic although he had been able to raise his hands to extend the gap at the bottom of the hood so he could see more of the daylight that pervaded the footwell of the empty seat beside him. He had resigned himself to the fact that he could do nothing until the journey came to an end and he was released from his restraints. The tall man had seemed very civil towards him so Woons had no reason to believe that he would not be afforded the hospitality which had been promised.

However, the language spoken by the two men continued to gnaw away at his brain and, unless they were speaking in some western Georgian dialect which he had never heard before, Woons' only other thought was that they weren't Georgian at all. And, if they weren't Georgian, where the fuck had they come from?

Why the hell had he come here? He'd been told that neither Tsiklauri nor Irakli were here. Why not just accept that they had disappeared and just keep trying to call them. It wasn't as if he hadn't got plenty of his own mess to clear up. But no, headstrong as ever, he had dived into this cesspit of a place and now he was being driven to an unknown destination by two men who clearly had nothing to do with the Kaspi brethren. 'Idiot!' he castigated himself under his breath.

He was going in for more mental self-flagellation when he felt the vehicle slowing down, the two men once again talking to each other.

'OK, Mr Woons!' It was the tall man speaking. 'We have to get some gas so this is how it's going to work. When we stop at the gas station, my friend here will remove the hood so we don't cause any alarm to the other customers. Don't try to do anything stupid, and we can then move on to our destination which is very close by. Understand?'

Woons nodded but then thought that they may not have noticed the nod so he answered with a rather croaky 'Yes!' He really did need something to drink.

Very soon he felt the vehicle come to a halt and heard the handbrake being applied. All of a sudden, the hood was off his head and the daylight almost blinded him. The tall man exited the car and Woons heard him unlocking the petrol cap. He looked ahead but all he could see was the layout of the petrol station. They were universally similar these days, he thought, just different names of international conglomerates above and around the petrol pumps.

The tall man was soon back in the driving seat, and instructed Woons to lean forward so that the hood could be put back on his head. 'Okay my friend. Not far now.'

Woons detected that they were now in a town as the vehicle was stopping and starting as if in heavy traffic or perhaps because of traffic lights. There seemed to be some debate amongst the two men as to which road to take which didn't help. Woons' sense of smell was also working overtime, and he suddenly realised that he was picking up the same aroma as when he used to go down to places like Eastbourne and Hastings. It was the smell of the sea! So, they had travelled west! Because Woons knew that the only coastal area in Georgia was on its western border with the Black Sea.

Soon, the vehicle came to a halt. There was a pause before he felt a blast of fresh air. Someone must have opened a window. He then heard the tall man speaking although it was difficult to make out if there was a response. Perhaps he was announcing their arrival into an intercom. The vehicle then moved forward, bouncing over what were probably speed bumps before coming to a halt once more. The engine idled for a few seconds and was then cut. The two men exchanged some words before he heard a door open as one of them got out. Woons sat forward in the seat trying to work out what was happening when the hood was suddenly removed from his head, and he found himself looking directly into the eyes of the tall man.

'We have reached our destination, Mr Woons!' the tall man said. 'And, since you have co-operated with us, we are pleased to offer you the hospitality we promised. My colleague has just gone to get things ready.' He then produced what looked to Woons like some sort of hunting knife, and cut the plastic cuffs. The relief was instant. Woons flexed his fingers, urgently trying to get some feeling back into them. He looked through the side windows but could only see other vehicles around him so they were probably in a car park.

He was just about to ask the tall man where they were when the door next to him opened and the other man beckoned him to get out of the vehicle. Stepping down onto the tarmac, he stretched his legs and bent over to stretch his back. The other man had leaned into the vehicle to retrieve Woons' holdall then took him by the arm and marched him towards a doorway leading into the building in front of them. The man keyed a number into the entry system and then pushed through the doorway.

Woons found himself in a vast changing room with huge upright lockers lining most of the walls. Wooden benches were arranged haphazardly around a set of lockers in the middle of the floor space, and storage chests of various shapes and sizes were arraigned around the walls of the room. There was a distinct smell of the sea fighting for supremacy in the aroma stakes against a strong smell of disinfectant and a much weaker whiff of male cologne. The man propelled Woons across the room and around the benches before passing through an open doorway which led into a huge wet room. He put the holdall on a shelf which ran the entire length of one wall and pulled out a deep storage drawer from under the shelf. He made some hand signals which Woons interpreted as telling him to put his holdall and clothes in the drawer and then take a shower and freshen up. The man collected a couple of towels from a shelf to the right of the doorway, and pointed to his watch raising both hands twice to indicate that Woons had twenty minutes. He then turned and left the room.

Having no appetite for a fight with these guys, and no thought of bolting for it as he hadn't the faintest clue where he was, Woons slowly undressed, put his dry clothes into the drawer, picked up a towel, and walked into the shower.

When the man re-entered the room, Woons was ready and dressed in the fresh set of clothes which he always brought with him on these trips. The man looked him up and down and then smirked before beckoning Woons to follow him. They walked down a dimly lit corridor before stopping at a set of lift doors. The man pressed the illuminated button and they waited. On entering the lift, Woons checked his appearance in the mirror on the back wall and was then surprised to feel the lift descend – he had automatically assumed that they would be ascending. He could feel the tension in his stomach tighten, and his mouth suddenly felt dry.

It wasn't the fastest lift he had ever been in but the doors soon opened onto another dimly lit corridor. The man led the way across a lobby area and through a swing door. Woons now found himself in a brightly-lit but deserted kitchen, pots & pans and other cooking paraphernalia spread across every surface in the room. They crossed the chequered floor and then through another swing door. This led into a small anteroom which had, for its centrepiece, a square table with six chairs around it. There was a dining place set for one person and, opposite this, sat the tall man.

'Ah, Mr Woons. We meet again! Sit! Sit!' he said, clearly indicating that Woons was expected to sit at the place setting. 'We have prepared some good food for you, and then we can have our little chat. You must be very hungry so it would not be good to have our chat when all you were thinking about was food.' The tall man flicked his fingers and his companion disappeared through the swing door. Woons took his seat at the table.

Almost immediately, the door swung open again and a squat woman in a white chef's jacket with her hair in a hairnet bustled into the room carrying two dishes. She put both down on the table in front of Woons. She quickly left the room but was soon back with a clean plate and what appeared to be a large soup bowl. Woons looked suspiciously at the food but had to admit that the aromas were exciting his taste buds. The woman left the room again.

The tall man leant over the table and pointed to the first dish. 'Here we have what is called *Khachapuri* which is a flatbread flavoured with cheese. It is very nice on its own or with the other dish which is *Kharcho*. This is a slow-cooked spicy beef stew which you will like. Enjoy the food my friend, and then we will have our talk.' He got up from the table and exited the room through the swing door.

Woons now realised that he was ravenous. He spooned some of the stew into the soup bowl, and then tore off a piece of the cheesy bread. He took a mouthful of the stew. Delicious! Just the right amount of spice, and the meat was surprisingly tender. He shovelled more of the stew into his mouth and tore off another corner of the bread. It didn't take him long to finish the stew and the bread, and he sat back with a satisfied feeling in his stomach.

But his mind still continued to struggle with the situation he now found himself in. On the long journey from Kaspi, he had developed so many theories as to what was going on that he had become more and more confused. The most popular theory, and the one that he kept coming back to, was that Tsiklauri had offloaded part of his empire which had been picked up by a gang on the Black Sea coast. Perhaps Tsiklauri had died and his empire had been ceded to a distant relative. Or perhaps he had been murdered in some grisly gang warfare. Whatever had happened, the tall man seemed to now be in charge although Woons was still puzzled by his accent and the way he spoke. He just couldn't put his finger on what was wrong but his gut feeling was that he was going to be in for a nasty shock before too long.

65

Tuesday 25 July

The rest of the morning had gone by in a maelstrom of activity. The EMSC contact had emailed some other information about Borislav Zlatkov which Hunter and Kendall had reviewed to the point that they could confidently conclude that he had never been to Meadowlands and had probably never even met Vashlili. But someone had been masquerading as Zlatkov and this person was now of considerable interest to Kent Police – whoever he was.

Sarah Hunter had had to pause her session with Kendall upon the arrival of Kevin Bland in the company of DC Jennings who had him cautioned and then put in Interview Room One to await the arrival of the duty solicitor. Thankfully, the solicitor only had to come from up the High Street so the interview hadn't taken too long to set up. But Hunter was frustrated by just how little Bland knew about the people he was dealing with and the jobs he had been doing. Yes, the bags and sacks he had picked up from laybys and hedgerows had been heavy but he had never once thought they might contain bodies or, worse still, body parts. As far as he could tell, it always seemed to be the same voice on the phone telling him where to make the pick-up, the money was always in an envelope under whatever package he was picking up, and he always received two or three calls directing him to the drop-off location. Although he seemed to be initially directed towards a town centre, by the time the last instructions were received, he was invariably at a remote out-of-town lock-up. Occasionally, he ended up in the countryside dropping off in some remote wooded area or on rough pathways leading to derelict farm buildings.

On Hunter's suggestion, Jennings had rushed Bland's mobile phone to the tech boys upstairs but the phone number which had been used to summon Bland to the pick up at Haysden Lakes was no longer in operation – a burner phone or whatever. Hunter soon tired of the whole charade and suggested that Jennings bail him for the time being so that they could get him back if anything new came up once the PM had been done. In any event, Bland wouldn't be going anywhere far due to the complex restructuring his wrist had required, and he was clearly in considerable pain so the best place for him was home for some rest.

DS Selitto had also called in to say that he was at the mortuary with DC Mishraz and DC Crosby. Mishraz was observing the post mortem being conducted on the woman found in the basement at the Hildenborough house, and Crosby and Selitto had joined Ilona Jenkyns who was carrying out an autopsy on the burnt remains of the girl.

'Pleased to have my face mask on,' he had informed Hunter. 'The smell of burnt flesh in this enclosed space is nauseous.' He told her that Jenkyns was being exceptionally careful in order to avoid any of the really crispy parts of the body just snapping off, but he wondered just what conclusion she was going to reach apart from the fact that death was likely to be as a result of smoke inhalation and incineration. As far as the other PM was concerned, the cause of death seemed to be largely due to the severe beating the woman had received. It appeared that a garotte of some sort had been applied to her neck but strangulation was not the cause of death. She would have suffered severe shock with the laceration to her mouth and chin but that had also probably not killed her. However, the pathologist considered that a significant amount of time had elapsed from the time of the beating until time of death so her already severely damaged internal organs had just packed up one by one – plus the fact that blood had haemorrhaged inside her body which eventually had caused her heart to stop. Selitto told Hunter that the boy Mishraz was doing well and had, so far, managed to keep his breakfast down!

Hunter wanted to know who was doing the PM on the woman. 'We've got the top man here today,' Selitto replied. 'Toby Swartzman himself! Presumably he's come along because of the imperial presence of La Jenkyns,' Selitto joked.

'Very funny – and probably true!' Hunter was quick with her riposte.

Swartzman was the Clinical Head of Pathology for Kent Police and, although Hunter held him in high esteem as far as his medical skills were concerned, she had always found him to be someone who couldn't help preening himself in front of influential movers & shakers. She could just imagine him gushing over a meeting with Professor Jenkyns. 'Do you know if Ilona is staying over tonight?' she asked Selitto.

'Not one hundred percent but I think I heard her mention something about Chilston Park so perhaps she's staying down there tonight,' Selitto replied.

'Okay! Keep me up to speed with developments.' Hunter cut the call and returned to the desk in front of the white boards. DS Kendall had gone back to her own office with the brief to find out all she could about Peter Dangerfield. Something wasn't right about his apparent disappearance, and

Hunter wanted to get some more information on his background before pressing any buttons with the Sussex force. She had just put her phone back on the desk when it sprang into life again.

'DC Pennant, ma'am. Just to let you know that I'm still at the RTA scene on Pilgrims Way with the CSIs.' Hunter invited her to continue. 'Well, the actual scene is on a sharp bend where Pilgrims Way technically becomes Kemsing Road although everyone just calls it Pilgrims Way.'

Sarah Hunter had walked some of the Pilgrims Way and knew that it was an historical route taken by pilgrims from Winchester in Hampshire to Canterbury in east Kent. The route runs the whole way along the North Downs, and much of the traditional route is now part of the modern road network. Having walked the route between Otford and Wrotham, Hunter could picture roughly where Pennant was calling from.

'Anyway,' Pennant continued, 'there seem to be three sites of interest which all show traces of what CSIs have presumed to be the girl.'

'Three sites?' Hunter interrupted. 'How come?'

'Well, they worked back along the road until they came to some blood both on the road surface and the grass verge. There were also bloody handprints on the pole of a road sign which looks like she probably used the sign to lever herself upright. There is then a trail of blood leading along the road to the bend and then a larger pooling of blood about ten metres from the bend itself. CSIs reckon that she probably collapsed here in the road after which she was hit by the guy who called it in.'

'Okay, that all makes sense,' Hunter replied. 'But I thought you mentioned three sites?'

'Yes, ma'am', Pennant went on. 'One of the CSIs decided to go further back up the road and found minute flecks of bloodied skin stuck to the road surface about three hundred metres from the other sites, close to a rough entrance to a field. If tests prove that this skin is from the same girl then, due to the evidence at this site, the CSIs have suggested that she may have either jumped out of a vehicle as it travelled along the road, or that she was deliberately pushed out. She then staggered down the road until she was catapulted off the tarmac by a hit-and-run driver. She eventually managed to get herself upright by holding onto a road sign and then staggered on before collapsing by the side of the road. She was then hit by our man who probably couldn't see her or only just saw her at the last minute as he prepared to negotiate a ninety-degree bend in the road.'

'Okay! Nice work, Carolyn,' Hunter replied. 'Not sure where it gets us but at least we now know what happened to the girl.'

'Yes, ma'am,' Pennant continued, getting ready to cut the call. 'Oh, and by the way, you may already know this but I've just been told that the girl died on the operating table earlier.'

66

Tuesday 25 July

The tall man's colleague collected Woons from the kitchen and took him back to ground floor level by way of the slow lift. He then led the way down another dimly lit corridor until they came to what appeared to be a dead end. The man turned to a small black box on the wall to his left and lifted the lid. He pushed a button inside the box whereupon a section of the wall retracted into itself. They stepped through the gap and out into bright sunlight. The wall closed behind them.

Once Woons' eyes had become accustomed to the light, he found himself on a quayside with the sound of waves gently slapping against the seawall. He took in the fresh air offered by the stiff breeze which was blowing in from what he assumed was the Black Sea, and looked up at a cluster of gulls circling above a fishing boat which was disgorging its catch of the day onto another quay across from where they were standing. In the distance, he could also see a line of cranes standing sentry-like beside the sea busily unloading cargo vessels which were docked along the quayside. Other vessels were biding their time, no doubt using satellite navigation systems to hold their positions while waiting for an unloading bay to become free. This was certainly a working port with vessels coming and going across the busy shipping lanes of the Black Sea. He could also see some storage tanks in the distance, and caught sight of a freight train threading its way through them towards the line of cranes.

As they rounded the corner of the building, another blast of cool air caused Woons to momentarily turn his head away.

He then caught sight of a marina with a flotilla of yachts moored alongside pontoons which snaked out into the sea, their halyards thrashing out a deafening tuneless beat in the wind. Stealing a look to his left, he suddenly realised that the building he had just exited must be the port's Yacht Club or some sort of Seafarers Mission building. The tall man must be well connected if he had the run of a place like this, he thought.

He felt the grip tightening on his upper arm as he was propelled along the front of the building towards the marina. They stepped down on to one of the pontoons and took the second avenue which had boats of all shapes and sizes moored on each side of it. They continued along towards the end of the pontoon until Woons felt the pace slowing. They eventually stopped in front of a motor yacht which Woons estimated must have been about 30 to 40 metres in length. A line of small portholes ran along the side of the yacht just above the waterline. The main deck was virtually all enclosed except for a seating area at the rear, and the upper deck appeared to be open to the elements but with a hood covering part of the seating area. It looked as if there was a pool at the rear of the upper deck, but Woons couldn't see whether it was just a jacuzzi or something more substantial.

As they stood there, the door at the rear of the main deck opened and the tall man appeared. He beckoned to the two men. 'Come aboard!' he called out. 'Come! Come!'

Woons made his way gingerly across a narrow gangway which linked the yacht to the pontoon. He then climbed a couple of steps and found himself in an open seating area at the back of the main deck. 'Welcome aboard, Mr Woons,' the tall man greeted him from the doorway into the main salon.

'Come in! Come in!'

Woons stepped through the doorway and into a spacious and opulently furnished salon. Floor to ceiling windows ran down each side of the deck. A semi-circular settee was positioned on one side of the salon, freshly plumped cushions liberally spread across it. An ornate coffee table filled the space in front of the settee. On the opposite side of the salon, two enormous armchairs flanked what looked to Woons like a TV and video centre. In the distance he could see a dining table with chairs around it and, beyond that, what he assumed was the galley area. The whole deck was bright and airy.

Woons was just beginning to get used to the movement of the yacht which was being buffeted by the strong breeze coming in off the Black Sea when he saw another man entering the salon from the dining area. As he walked towards Woons, the tall man came over and made the introductions. 'Mr Woons,' he began, 'Mr Vasile Lupescu has heard so much about you and would like to meet you.' Lupescu walked up to Woons and offered his hand. The handshake was firm without being crushing, and it gave Woons an early opportunity of assessing the man close up. Was he a friend or an adversary? What could he see in his eyes? Mr Lupescu looked as if he had probably not led an angelic life thus far judging by the two scars on his face, one running from the corner of his right eye to the corner of his mouth. The other looked as if it had been caused by a slash across the left cheek. He had short cropped jet-black hair and dark eyes which exuded charm and sophistication – but also menace in equal proportions. He was immaculately dressed in a light blue jacket, white shirt and navy blue chinos. He wore a diamond stud in his right ear, and some expensive jewellery on his fingers, a standard Rolex adorning his left wrist. Even his deck shoes looked expensive, Woons thought.

Making a sweeping gesture with his right arm, Lupescu indicated that Woons should sit on the settee whilst he made himself comfortable in one of the armchairs. The tall man perched on the front of the other armchair. 'Mr Lupescu has asked to see you today because he has a proposition for you. He has good use of the English language but I am here in case of any misunderstandings,' the tall man said. Lupescu smiled across at Woons.

'First of all,' continued the tall man, 'can we get you something to drink?' Woons shook his head. Lupescu appeared to indicate that he wanted a drink so the tall man pressed a button on the armrest of the chair. A young girl suddenly appeared from the galley. Lupescu said something to her out of the corner of his mouth, and she scurried away. Without further ado, Lupescu addressed Woons.

'Okay Mr Woons,' he began. 'I'm thanking you for meeting me today.' He paused. 'I'm sure your mind is, how you say, confused by what has happened. So, I am going to tell you a story.'

Woons sat back on the settee, transfixed. What on earth was this bloke on about? The girl returned with a mug of some herbal concoction judging by the aroma now permeating the salon. Lupescu took a sip of the drink and then put the mug back down on a small table beside his chair.

'Once upon a time,' Lupescu started, 'there was a Georgian gang boss and he had the idea to take young girls to Northern Europe and sell them for sex. But he didn't take pretty little Georgian girls. Oh no! He didn't want to hurt the young girls

443

of his homeland. So, he and his men went across this sea here.'
He pointed in the general direction of the sea behind him. 'He
took girls from other peoples' lands and trafficked them for sex.
And he became very rich. And then he found people like you,
Mr Woons, who had sex businesses and who needed to buy
lots of girls to keep up a constant supply of young sex slaves.
The more girls he could lay his hands on, the more money
he could make – and the fat Georgian got even fatter. And
everybody was happy if the girls kept coming and the punters
kept getting what their depraved minds wanted. Are you with
me so far, Mr Woons?'

Woons found himself nodding involuntarily. He had a
barrage of questions spinning round in his head but decided
to let this guy carry on. What on earth was the point he was
trying to make?

'So, Mr Woons,' Lupescu continued, 'I have, how you say,
acquired this fat Georgian's business interests which makes you
and me business partners!' A big smile creased Lupescu's face
but Woons could see only coldness in his eyes.

He leaned forward on the settee, forearms resting on his
knees. 'Where is Mr Tsiklauri?'

'The man Tsiklauri, he has run away to Bulgaria to see why
his business is not working. He will soon find out that he has
no business as his supply chain has been broken up. My people
are now in charge.'

'And where are you from, Mr Lupescu?' Woons asked,
sounding relaxed although his churning stomach belied this
mask of confidence.

'I am from Romania, Mr Woons,' Lupescu proudly declared.
'You will find that we do things differently than you have been

used to with these lazy Georgian bastards. For a start, we understand more about business than they do, and we know how to screw every last cent out of every deal we do. So, you will have to get used to smaller, how do you say in economics, profit margins? Yes, profit margins! Your profit margins will be slashed. You have been making millions over the years because these Georgian nonces know nothing about business.'

Lupescu focused his eyes on Woons across the room. The Englishman stared back but he felt his mask of confidence slipping under the intense gaze of the Romanian. Then Lupescu dropped another bombshell. 'We will also be changing our supply of girls and the way we transport them so you will have to take more responsibility for getting them into your country through the ports. In short, Mr Woons, this is what you English call a wake-up call, n'est ce pas?' Woons wasn't quite sure why the smiling assassin facing him across the salon had lapsed into French, but he certainly got the message. And several pieces of a puzzling jigsaw were starting to fall into place.

It became deathly quiet in the salon, both men eyeing each other up like prize fighters at a weigh-in. There were so many thoughts crashing about in Woons' head that he had difficulty selecting one to concentrate on. 'Does the name Tamaz Vashlili mean anything to you?' he eventually asked. Lupescu looked slightly puzzled and glanced over at the tall man. They had a brief conversation in their own language and then Lupescu turned back to face Woons.

'Ah yes, Mr Vashlili.' He looked away into the distance and steepled his hands under his chin, elbows on the arms of the chair. 'Our friend Tamaz, he began to get a bit too big for his boots – is that how you say it? He was a prima donna who thought that he could boss my people around. He insisted on being paid more for joining us but one of my people found that the quality of the information he was trying to offload was shit. He is now resting and will not be troubling any of us again any time soon – you can be sure of that Mr Woons.'

What the fuck did that mean? Had Vashlili been quietly disposed of? Since he was last spotted on the CCTV at Candice's house last Thursday? Had he been taken somewhere no one was ever likely to find him? One thing was certain, Woons doubted that he would ever clap eyes on Vashlili again. Well, at least that solved that puzzle and explained why no one had been able to get hold of Vashlili over the last week or so. But what about everything else that'd been going on? Had Lupescu's bunch of murderers been rampaging their way through the Kent countryside killing people such as Candice, Belinda and that old woman Travisedo? Had he been responsible for kidnapping Woons' girls and setting fire to buildings? In effect, had he already brought the Woons empire to its knees?

'You look worried, my friend!' Lupescu interrupted his train of thought.

Worried? Yes, I am fucking worried, Woons thought. Very worried! But he needed to know more detail about what Lupescu was up to. He was also starting to doubt that Lupescu knew what was actually going on the UK. As he reviewed Lupescu's comments about Vashlili in his mind, he became less convinced that his host was as in-charge as he was trying to make out. He finally decided that there was no point just sitting here and listening to this arsehole wittering on. Woons just had to know what was going on.

He locked eyes on Lupescu who sat back in his chair, one

long leg crossed over the other. 'Tell me, Mr Lupescu, have your people been responsible for the murders of three of my most trusted colleagues and the kidnapping of some of my girls?' There – he'd said it. It was a question which demanded an answer. But the answer, when it came, was far from what he had expected.

A darkness descended over Lupescu's face, and his black bushy eyebrows knotted together in a deep frown. He fixed Woons with a quizzical look, absent-mindedly tracing a finger down the scar on his left cheek. Eventually he spoke in hushed tones.

'Do you know, Mr Woons, I honestly wish that I could tell you that all that was my work, and that all I wanted to do was fuck up your business. But then, what good would you be to me if I had done that? So, there you have your answer.'

Was that it, Woons wondered. But Lupescu wasn't finished. He slowly leant forward in his chair and pointed a bony finger at Woons.

'Which means that you and I share a common problem, Mr Woons. We are both being fucked by someone else!'

447

67

Tuesday 25 July

Ted Selitto had decided that he could leave DC Jennings to keep an eye on both post mortems at the mortuary, and had taken DC Mishraz with him as he made his way to the CSI labs at Maidstone. They had been escorted through the elaborate entry system by Donny Campbell and up to the lab on the first floor.

'We've had a bit of a problem processing the fingerprinting we carried out at the house by the allotment,' Cambell was saying as he showed the detectives into a small room which had a screen across one wall and a central table with four chairs. He pulled two of the chairs out so that Selitto and Mishraz could sit at the table, and then sat across the table from them. 'Anyway, we've sorted out the glitch and have come up with some information which should hopefully be of help to you.'

Campbell pressed a few buttons on a small console which was on the table in front of him and the screen sprang into life. A short introduction to AFIS appeared on the screen.

'We always put this slide up first to remind everyone of what the automated fingerprinting identification system is all about. It is basically the process of using a computer to match fingerprints against a database of known and unknown prints.' Selitto felt that this was a bit like the proverbial grandmother sucking eggs scenario, but Mishraz was studying the words on the screen intently.

'The reason I'm just reminding you of this,' Campbell continued, 'is that there were a great number of fingerprints lifted from the house but many were damaged through smudging and the effects of what appears to have been a frantic clean-up operation. We have, therefore, been unable to get many prints which can help us identify people at the house. Although there are some usable prints, these appear to be mainly related to people who are not on the AFIS database.'

Selitto looked glum. He could see another blind alley opening up. God, this job could be frustrating at times, particularly when you already had so little to go on. His unfocused eyes looked at the screen waiting for some little spark to rejuvenate his skills of detection. He didn't have to wait long.

'However,' Campbell pushed another button on his console, 'we do seem to have a match!' At this point, two fingerprints appeared alongside each other on the screen which, even to Selitto's untrained eye, looked pretty similar. 'These were taken from the room which looked as if it was an office where the desk had been badly smashed up. I think that they were probably lifted from the desk itself. Anyway, they match a set of prints which is held on the database and which belongs to a woman by the name of Maria Travisedo.'

Campbell pressed another button on the console and a photograph of the woman, Maria Travisedo, flashed up on the screen. For a long time, Selitto stared at the screen taking in this Hispanic beauty who was probably little more than mid-twenties. She had the classic facial bone structure of a Latin American woman with a full head of jet-black hair resting on her shoulders and probably cascading down her back, dark eyebrows and dark eyes, the shapes of which were drawing him in to her. Her full lips seemed to be set in a smirk, and there was a haughtiness in the look she was giving to the camera.

Her looks reminded Selitto of a flamenco dancer he had seen perform in one of the late-night bars in the back streets of Seville when he was there a couple of years ago.

'I'm afraid we don't have all her details but you'll be able to get those from your own database. That headshot looks a bit dated so she is probably quite a bit older by now.'

Mishraz was scribbling in his notebook. Selitto was transfixed by the photograph on the screen. Was this their first real breakthrough? Had they at last got a name that they could work on in this increasingly complex case? He needed to get back to the station and start a search of the database.

'Finally,' Campbell continued, 'just to let you know that we do have some prints which we have put on AFIS but they are all listed as unknown at the moment. That may change if you find us any more sites which are connected with your investigation. You may also want to circulate these around your colleagues in Europe on Eurodac. Although that's principally the EU fingerprint database for identifying asylum seekers, they may also be interested in the prints of people who are being trafficked. You never know, you might get a hit somewhere, particularly with the prints we took from the girl's room.'

'Thanks, Donny, that's really helpful and we'll follow all that up.' Selitto got up from the table but then seemed to have a second thought. 'Are we in the right part of the building for Julian French's team?'

'Yep! I can take you there if you like. Follow me!' Campbell led them out of the room and they threaded their way across the floor between workbenches and desks. They took the lift to the next floor and found French sitting at his desk in one corner of another huge area with technicians working at benches festooned with powerful microscopes and other paraphernalia which only Crime Scene Investigators would know how to use.

Selitto had forgotten that French had already met DC Mishraz and was just in the process of introducing him again when both men smiled and informed Selitto that they already knew each other. The detectives then spent the next half hour listening to the information French had gleaned from the Hildenborough house. Eventually, French came to the subject which interested Selitto the most.

'It was fortunate that DC Jennings spotted the considerable damage to the birdbath,' French continued, shuffling the papers on his desk. 'The evidence points to it being caused by a shot from a powerful handgun as opposed to a rifle. Possibly something in the Sig Sauer range or an S&W 500 Magnum or any other similar type of weapon. You were right to point out the open window, Ted – don't think we had made a note of that. There were traces of residue on the windowsill and on one of the panes of glass. A powerful handgun would have the range to hit a vehicle trying to make a getaway, and the glass you spotted on the driveway is from the rear window of a car as it has the heating element running through it. Not easy to identify the make of car but probably an Audi or BMW.'

French pushed a couple of photographs across the desk – one was a magnification of the traces of residue on the windowsill and the other showed the view from the window taking in the birdbath and the area where the circular gravel drive joined the track which led down to the main road.

Selitto had a good look at these before sitting back in his chair. 'So, it's not beyond the bounds of possibility that someone was trying to run away from this building and had a car as a means of escape?'

French nodded. 'That's the sort of scenario I have in my mind. But we can't find any trace of blood so we would have to assume that whoever was running managed to get away unscathed. Either that or the gunman was simply a lousy shot!' That got a smile from Mishraz who was still frantically jotting down notes in his book.

'The other thing to bear in mind,' French continued, 'is that it may have been dark in which case it would have been very difficult to accurately locate a target. We noticed that there were no external lights at the front of the house so the only source of light would probably have been that thrown up by the headlights of the cars on the distant A21. A sort of ambient light which wouldn't have amounted to much.'

'Hmmm!' Selitto was deep in thought. 'What about the shed?' he eventually asked.

'Ah! The shed!' French exclaimed. 'What fun we had with that! I've never seen anything like it!' He opened another file and placed three photographs on the desk in front of Selitto and Mishraz. 'We have to assume that the five laptops concealed in their concrete chamber under the workbench were connected to the CCTV system or to some other recording system which we haven't yet found. It is entirely possible that voice recordings from the rooms and any footage shot by the standalone cameras in the rooms may have also been stored here. But as we now know, all the hard drives have been removed. So, we are faced with a simple question – who removed them?'

'Agreed!' Selitto was nodding his head. 'And it's likely that it wasn't anyone who was involved in tearing apart the house in view of the wanton destruction they left behind. No, my guess is that this was done by someone else connected with the house, someone who knew what they were looking for but didn't want anyone to know that they'd found it. And someone who had the time and the patience to put everything back to the way it was.

French put the photographs back in the file and reached across to a stack of documents which were in a metal tray positioned at the corner of his desk. 'Have you seen the report from KFR,' he asked Selitto, holding up a bunch of papers.

'Briefly skimmed it,' Selitto replied. 'Accelerant used to get the fire going in the annexe. Can't decide if the sole purpose was to get rid of the annexe or whether it was hoped that the flames would eventually take hold of the entire house. Initial thoughts are that this was where the girls lived, and that they were all taken away apart from one who died in the fire. Or perhaps she was the reason the annexe was torched – get rid of the evidence. But the evidence of what? Hopefully, the PM might turn something up but I wouldn't have thought there was much evidence to be had on a body as burnt as that one.'

'Yes, certainly a problem for the pathologists,' French echoed Selitto's words. 'From our perspective, it does look as if it was a dormitory for the girls. Some of the ash contained material which could be attributed to clothing, and we found a couple of small items of jewellery which had miraculously not been completely melted down. There were also the remains of shoes which were too small to be considered as men's footwear. The only other thing of note was that, even after being ravaged by fire, there was still a residual smell of drains or excrement. Wasn't it you, Azzer, who likened the smell to the stench of open sewers in your grandparents' village back home?' DC

Mishraz nodded. 'I think we'll probably have to settle for excrement which is another little puzzle in itself!'

'Fingerprints? DNA? Anything useful?' Selitto was desperate to find something that might help them with identification.

French flicked through the files on his desk and finally found the one he was looking for. He flipped the cover over. 'Ah, yes! Fingerprints and DNA. I'm afraid not much in the way of fingerprints as most of the surfaces were smudged – looked as if someone had been trying to clean them up. Not quite sure why but I understand that the allotment house was also subject to a good deal of cleaning. As for DNA, where to start! We've brought a lot of the bedding back to the lab and some of our Techies are working on it as I speak – should have some results in a day or two.'

Although disappointed, Selitto was aware that a lot of the techie stuff took time to complete as there was no room for error. He just had to content himself with the fact that his cases were being worked on.

French closed the file he had been consulting and tossed it to one side. 'On a brighter note,' he said, peering over his glasses at Selitto, 'we do have a positive match on the prints taken from the dead woman in the cellar. She is on file as Candice Lombardi.'

Selitto's mouth fell open, his eyes wide. He felt the urge to punch the air but managed to control himself.

'No photo at the moment.' French continued, 'but you should be able to get her full history from your database. Otherwise, that's about it for the moment. I'll get the full report completed, hopefully with some DNA input, and send it over the wire to you.'

Selitto was ecstatic that they now had a second name. Surely, this was the sort of breakthrough the team had been looking for. The two detectives thanked French for his time and made their way out of the labyrinthine security system which surrounded the CSI operations centre. At last, Selitto had a spring in his step. They now had two names which should be on the database.

68

Tuesday 25 July

Woons was sitting in the covered alfresco dining area on what he had been told by the tall man was the yacht's 'flybridge'. All fucking gobbledygook sailing jargon to him. He hated boats and pretty much all who sailed in them. He always traced this aversion back to a time when he was a spotty teenager on holiday with his parents. Someone had a canoe and invited him to sit in it. Woons had descended a set of steps, and put one foot in the canoe. Next thing he knew, he had shot straight over the other side of the poxy canoe and into the freezing cold waters of the English Channel. Everyone had thought it very funny apart from a young master Woons who swore that he'd never get in another boat ever again!

Now, here he was perched on a sun-lounger next to a jacuzzi on a luxury yacht which was being buffeted by a strong westerly coming off the Black Sea. Lupescu had made his apologies and gone off to a meeting in the Yacht Club. The tall man had offered him something to eat but he wasn't hungry. He was, however, thirsty and the young girl had brought him a Diet Coke. She looked terribly young to Woons and, even though he had summoned up the broadest smile he could manage, her face remained expressionless – as if she was on autopilot.

But that was the least of his worries. He had already spotted the two cameras mounted at strategic points on the flybridge, and had tested them out by moving from his seat to the stern of the yacht. One of the cameras followed his every move so someone was obviously watching him closely. He had returned to the table where he now sat, pushing the glass of Diet Coke around the table top and staring off into the distance. The Black Sea stretched out as far as the eye could see, although he had difficulty seeing too much because his eyes kept watering as the cool wind got ever keener.

And he was thinking! Thinking! Thinking! Thinking! Trying to make sense of what was going on. Everything had been so straightforward with Tsiklauri. Woons never asked any questions. He simply ordered the girls, Vashlili dealt with the logistics of getting them to the UK, and the likes of Belinda, Candice and old woman Travisedo were able to carry on their businesses with little interference from anyone. Now, Tsiklauri was apparently gone and a new gang had taken over.

Woons was not stupid enough to underestimate the Romanians, and he was more than aware that they would be a lot more street savvy than the Georgians. He also knew that, if he was going to stay in this game, he was going to have to work harder for the sort of financial rewards he had been used to. But the biggest concern was the fact that neither he nor Lupescu knew the identity of the gang which was doing its best to completely fuck up his operation in the UK.

It was doubtful that it was another Georgian set up, and surely Lupescu's intel would be good enough to know if it was another bunch of Romanians. Or was it the Bulgarians coming to take their girls home? Woons sat back and thought about this. Surely not, he concluded. No, it had to be someone who was intent on disrupting Lupescu's organisation and taking down the Woons operation as collateral.

He fished his phone out of his pocket. He'd dearly love to call Tricky to find out what was going on at home. Any further catastrophes? But its blank screen stared forlornly back at him, sadly bereft of all power. The early evening air was beginning to turn decidedly chilly and he was just starting to wonder if he should go back to the salon on the main deck when the tall man appeared. He sat down at the table opposite Woons.

'I have some news from Mr Lupescu,' he began. 'He regrets that he has been detained for longer than he expected and will not be able to meet up with you again before you leave.'

Woons raised his eyebrows. 'I am leaving?' he questioned the tall man. 'Where am I leaving to?'

'We will be taking you to Tbilisi Airport, my friend,' replied the tall man. 'Mr Lupescu has arranged for you to stay at a hotel nearby so that you can get your flight back to London tomorrow. You will be leaving soon.'

69

Tuesday 25 July

'Hello, boss – can you hear me?' Selitto had decided to call Hunter from his car as he and Mishraz arrived at the mortuary in Tunbridge Wells. Almost as soon as they got parked, the heavens had opened and the noise of the rain mixed with hail stotting off the roof of the car was deafening.

'Yes, Ted – just about,' came Hunter's reply. 'What on earth's going on?'

'Well, it's chucking it down here. Isn't it raining with you in Tonbridge?' Selitto sounded incredulous.

Hunter got up to look out of the window. It was certainly getting darker outside with huge black clouds to the south of the police station but no rain yet. 'Not at the moment but could be on its way', she replied.

'Okay!' Selitto paused. 'Just to let you know that Azzar and I ducked out of the PMs and have spent some time catching up with the CSIs. Probably a better use of our time as we now have two names for you!'

Hunter had been scribbling notes to herself on the pad on the desk in front of her, but she was now fully tuned into what Selitto was saying. 'Two names?' she said, trying not to sound too surprised. 'What? Through prints or DNA?'

'Both prints,' Selitto replied. 'It seems that a woman by the name of Maria Travisedo was at the house out at Sheet Hill. She must have a record because CSIs had been able to get a photograph of her although it had probably been taken quite a long time ago. Anyway, she is definitely a person of interest!'

'Okay!' Hunter said as she scribbled Travisedo's name down on her pad. 'And the other name?'

'Julian French printed the woman found in the cellar at Hildenborough,' Selitto informed her, 'and he's come up with the name of Candice Lombardi. Says she's on the database but no photo for verification. We've just got back to the mortuary to see how they're getting on so I'll give the name to Swartzman and see if he has drawn the same conclusions from his examination.'

'Excellent! Well done the both of you!' Hunter exclaimed. 'I'll get Grace to run these names through and see what we get. It would be good to get some info about the body in the bag before close of play today. I'm not that interested in the incinerated girl as she was probably an illegal like Scarecrow Girl so perhaps you could get someone to look at the headless body as soon as possible – like yesterday!'

'Right! Will do! Call you later', and Selitto disconnected the call. The rain continued to pound on the roof of the car so he and Mishraz just sat where they were, peering out through the rivers of water flowing down the windscreen of the car.

Hunter got up from the desk, went over to the white boards and wrote the name Candice Lombardi on the Hildenborough board. The woman must have been in charge of that house but why had she been despatched in such a sickening way? By all accounts, she had been severely beaten, almost garrotted, and had had half her face torn away. But why? Was it some sort of turf war? And this woman, Travisedo, was she running the Sheet Hill house? In which case, where was she? God, so many questions. She slipped her phone into her pocket, had another look out at the still rainless street below, and went off to find DS Kendall.

Once the rain had eased off, Selitto and Mishraz made a dash for the mortuary and got there largely unscathed apart from Mishraz who had a soggy right foot after he didn't see a large puddle on the surface of the car park. Once kitted out in their protective clothing, they walked into the cutting room with Mishraz desperately trying to avoid making the squelching noise which followed every step of his right foot.

DC Jennings immediately sidled over to them and indicated that they should go back into the scrubs room for a quick update. Once they were all in there, she briefed them on the progress made by Professor Jenkyns and Dr Swartzman. Apparently, Jenkyns had decided that the body from the fire was a young girl, probably in her late teens. Even with the considerable damage done by the fire, it looked as if she had been strangled but Jenkyns had reserved judgment on this until she could have a closer look using equipment which hadn't yet been installed in Tunbridge Wells.

'Dr Swartzman is finishing off with the woman from the Hildenborough house,' Jennings continued. 'Professor Jenkyns has started on the body in the bag which wasn't quite as badly dismembered as was originally feared although we seem to have one hand missing. It also appears that someone had tried very hard to obliterate the fingerprints on the other hand but only partially succeeded. The Professor spent some time questioning why anyone would chop one hand off and then leave the other in place but spend time trying to cut off the fingerprints unless they were into carrying out surgical lacerations. It didn't make sense to her and it doesn't make a lot of sense to me either!'

Selitto filled Jennings in on the information from the CSIs and that the woman from the Hildenborough House was probably Candice Lombardi. Jennings knew that Swartzman had processed her prints at the beginning of his autopsy so he would no doubt be hoping for a confirmation at any time. 'So, she's got form then?' Jennings asked.

'Probably,' Selitto replied. 'The boss is on the case.'

Selitto peered through the round window in one of the doors and noted that both pathologists were still bent over the cadavers in front of them, dictating notes into tiny microphones pinned to their lab suits. The Lab Technicians scurried around carrying implements and stainless-steel dishes. One was using one of the weighing machines which were placed at intervals along the main workbench, making notes in a register which would later be transferred into the main report. The technician working with Jenkyns was being particularly attentive but Selitto wasn't sure if that was because he was star-struck in the presence of pathology royalty or because he was terrified that one of the body parts might tumble off the table and onto the floor. He turned back to the two DCs.

'Is there much more we can gain from being here, Elaine?' Selitto looked across to DC Jennings who thought for a moment and then shook her head. 'Okay,' he continued, 'let's get out of this gear and get back to the station. We'll probably be more use there.'

70

Tuesday 25 July

Woons was eventually taken back to the car park at the Yacht Club where the tall man introduced him to Vlad and Marko who would be driving him back to Tbilisi. He noted that one of the men was clutching his holdall. He instinctively patted his pockets and was relieved to find that he still had his passport with him.

He turned to the tall man. 'This accommodation,' he began, 'Mr Lupescu has paid for it?'

The tall man smiled. 'Of course!' he replied. 'He has an arrangement with the owner. Anyway, he wants to welcome you to his organisation so providing accommodation is the least he can do.' Woons smirked. What a load of fucking tosh, he thought.

He turned to face Vlad and Marko who by now had got the rear passenger door open. The holdall had been tossed into the vehicle and Woons was being invited to get in. The vehicle was some kind of Subaru 4 x 4, and Woons found himself sitting in a comfortable bucket seat behind the front passenger seat. The two Romanians got in with Marko driving – or was it Vlad? Woons hadn't been paying attention at the time of the introductions so hadn't a clue who was who. The vehicle swept out of the car park into the town, and Woons soon recognised the petrol station they had stopped at on the way into the port area. But the scenery from thereon was new to him.

After a while, the light started to show signs of fading, and many vehicles already had headlights on. Their speed began to pick up as they got to the edge of the town where the road became a dual carriageway. Woons spotted a road sign which indicated that they were on the E60. He also recognised the word 'Tbilisi' and began to relax a bit. As they drove on, he concluded that this was some sort of motorway as junctions started appearing with signage showing various place names along the way.

He sat back in his seat and tried to chill out. Traditional folk music was playing in the background, and the two Romanians up front were enjoying quite an animated conversation. The tall man had told him that it was around five hours to the airport so there was not much he could do apart from sit it out. It was now pretty dark outside and the only light in the vehicle came from the control panels in front of the driver. He had got himself into a comfortable position by leaning to his left and using the armrest to take his weight. He was now able to see the road ahead and all the road signs as they were picked out by the Subaru's headlights. Although he could not really understand what they meant, he did occasionally see a sign which seemed to show the number of kilometres to Tbilisi, and he was relieved to see that this was gradually reducing.

They motored on with Vlad or Marko – Woons still didn't know which was which – keeping up a steady 140 kph. Woons was keeping one eye on the speedometer and the other on the road ahead but, as there was so little traffic, he felt quite safe being driven at this speed. He turned his mind to thoughts of home and all the problems that he faced there. No doubt there would be someone knocking his door down as soon as he got back – some of Lupescu's henchmen seeking to impose their authority on his operation – or what was left of it. And what the fuck was he going to have to do if he was to take over more of the responsibility for the actual trafficking operation? Was that something Spink could do? Doubtful. You'd need someone with the lingo and the detailed knowledge of how all this trafficking lark worked. He pondered on this. Was it all worth it? Had the time come to get out while he could? Was he starting to get soft? Was he starting to actually have feelings for these girls? And was he starting to sicken of living off the money generated by some of the most depraved humans on the planet? He was so confused by the fact that he was even having these thoughts that he almost missed the ringing tone of a phone.

Vlad or Marko – or whoever was driving – cut the folk music and pressed a button on the steering wheel. '*Gamarjoba!*' said Vlad or Marko. Woons hadn't heard that word before so assumed that it meant 'Hello'. A voice boomed through the car's speaker system. The man in the passenger seat leaned forward and twiddled a knob to reduce the volume. Woons listened as both Vlad and Marko entered into a conversation with whoever had called them, but he had no idea what they were talking about. The Subaru sped on as the conversation became somewhat heated, or at least that was the impression that Woons got. All of a sudden, the call was disconnected and the man in the passenger seat turned to face Woons.

'We have little problem,' he said. 'This Subaru, it no go Tbilisi. We change to another car, Toyota. In some minutes, we meet our friends near Agara. They have new car. Then we go Tbilisi.' Woons couldn't really understand what was wrong with the car he had been sitting in for the last two hours, but resigned himself to the fact there could be any number of reasons why this Subaru wasn't going much further. Anyway, it wasn't as if he was in a hurry. He nodded at Vlad or Marko, shrugged his shoulders and sat back in his seat as the Subaru continued to eat up the miles to Tbilisi.

71

Tuesday 25 July

The pot holes along the track leading to Woons' office had quickly filled with rain water and were now all but invisible. Spink tried to remember where the worst of them were located but was failing dismally as the car lurched from one crater to another. He eventually made it to the gravel area in front of the office and was relieved to see Harding's car parked to the left of the portacabin. He parked next to the Lexus and waited for the rain to ease off but it only seemed to intensify, the noise on the roof of the car becoming increasingly deafening. Eventually, he decided that he couldn't wait any longer and made the short dash to the office door, turning the handle to get in out of the rain. Locked!

'For fuck's sake, Trigger, open the fucking door!' he shouted while at the same time banging a fist on the steel plating. Eventually, the door opened a little way while Harding peered at the man standing outside. Once he had recognised his visitor, the door was fully opened so that Spink could get in out of the rain. 'God's sake!' Spink continued muttering under his breath as he brushed rainwater from his sleeves. Harding meanwhile had scurried across the office and installed himself in Woons' chair, both elbows on the desk in front of him. He looked grey with huge black rings under his eyes, as if he hadn't slept for a week.

'How's it going, Tricky?' Harding asked as Spink continued to pat himself dry and check his appearance in the vanity mirror Woons had nailed to the wall by the door. Eventually, he turned to face Harding.

'IT'S not going very well, is IT Trig?' Spink replied. 'We're two houses down, another is out of commission. The cops are getting a sniff, we're fighting an unknown enemy, cash is haemorrhaging out of the business – do you want me to go on?'

'No, no it's all right. I know we're in the shit!' Harding made a patting motion with his right hand as if to calm the conversation down. Spink noticed that Harding's hand was shaking and his eyes had adopted a desolate stare, the pupils darkening into unseeing orbs. He seemed to be having difficulty with his breathing.

'You heard from Billy?' Spink wanted to know if there was anything going on in Georgia which might help them. Harding shook his head before reaching into his shirt pocket and extracting his phone. He looked at the screen and shook his head again.

'Nope,' he replied. 'I've tried him a few times but just goes straight to voicemail as if it's been turned off.' He sat back in the chair and ran his hands through his mane of greying hair which he had recently allowed to grow so that it now reached his shoulders. It would be better to at least keep his hair clean if he was going to have it that length, thought Spink, but kept his own counsel on the subject. Harding was a naturally scruffy individual so his unkempt hair pretty much went with the territory. Whatever! Harding's sartorial elegance was the least of their worries, and certainly wasn't what Spink was here to discuss.

'Or the battery's run down more like!' Spink commented, trying to make light of their dire situation by referring to Woons' annoying habit of forgetting to keep his phone charged up. 'Anyway, as if we haven't got enough problems, I've heard through a contact that the body bag with the Travisedo woman in it got lifted by the Panda boys – or are they the Skoda boys these days?' He looked over at Harding, trying to get a reaction to his little joke – nothing! No matter! He continued. 'The arsehole who got the job of taking it to its final destination managed to hit another car up at Fordcombe and the cops found the body bag on board. It's in the morgue as we speak.'

Harding had stopped combing his hair with his fingers and was now sitting up in the chair and paying attention. 'Fuck's sake Tricky! Who the fuck did you give that job to?'

'One of my most trusted ex-cons but he normally offloads as quick as he can,' Spink said by way of explanation. 'The bloke who picked it up is well known to my guy and has carried stuff for us on a number of occasions. Just in the wrong place at the wrong time.'

'So, what's going to be the fall-out for us?' Harding looked particularly spooked by this development, and his greyness seemed to now be tinged with yellow. Spink watched him carefully, hoping that this wasn't the prelude to a heart attack or a stroke or something equally as sinister. Perhaps he should tread carefully.

'Well, I imagine they'll eventually be able to match her with the house at Sheet Hill so that's one house truly fucked. There's no way we're ever going to get that back up and running.' Spink walked over to the map and looked at Woons' little flags strewn across the map of Kent. 'I'd be tempted to take that one out,' he said, pointing to the flag sticking out of the area between Ightham and Plaxtol. 'And I really can't see that we'll ever get back to Candice's place,' he continued, pointing to the flag positioned on the Hildenborough place name.

Harding shifted in the chair and leant over the desk holding his head in his hands. 'And I've heard a rumour down at Furnace Lane that some busybody's got all hoity toity about the house there,' he said, gazing down at the top of the desk his eyes boring into the wood. 'Not sure what it's all about but I think it all started before Belinda copped it. Possibly something about cars arriving all hours of the night. Then all the clearing up work, which seems to have taken place at night, has also ruffled her feathers to the extent that she's now been to the cops but they don't seem to have picked up on it yet.' He let out a long sigh and continued staring at the desk.

'Shit! That's all we need!' Spink remarked as he surveyed the map, particularly noting that their coverage in West Kent was becoming somewhat marginalised. He turned back to Harding, and found himself looking at a shadow of the former ex-con – all the stuffing seemed to have been knocked out of him. He was as deflated as a party balloon which had been lost behind the sofa for a week or two. He changed tack. 'You been out to see Cassandra at Kilndown lately?'

'Nope!' came the monosyllabic reply. 'But I did have a run out to Toys Hill earlier and saw that Annette woman,' Harding continued, taking his head out of his hands and looking up at Spink. 'Blimey, she's a fearsome creature! God knows where Billy got her from. Anyway, she's got some bloody security system up there. Could swear that she picked me up as soon as I got onto that fucking Puddledock Lane. God, that's narrow – nearly went into the ditch twice! By the time I got to her gaff, the registration and car details had been fed into some sort of recognition system on the gate which opened when I got to it. She's got a biometrics system on the door – camera and fingerprint reader. Once you've got through all that shit, you're finally allowed in!'

Spink was encouraged by Harding's report, and by the fact that he'd actually been out today. 'Okay, Trig, seems that Toys Hill's in good shape,' he summarised. 'So, it looks like we probably need to get a handle on Kilndown. Ems doesn't think that Cassandra's security's up to much so we're going to take a run out there this evening. Anything I should know?'

'Not that I can think of,' Harding replied. 'You been there before?' Spink shook his head. 'All she has is massage rooms. What the punters get up to before, during or after the massage is entirely up to them but there are no dungeons or kinky sex rooms or any facilities for any other deviant activity. She spends time training her girls in massage techniques so the punters are getting the very best in massages. Whatever else goes on between the punters and the girls depends how deep the punters' pockets are.'

Spink eased a couple of the shutters open and saw that the rain had eased off. In fact, the sun was in danger of coming out and there were little clouds of steam starting to lift off the grass around the gravel driveway. He wandered over to the table by the door and sat on one of its corners, now facing Harding. He needed to engage with him as the apparent flakiness which he was displaying was starting to worry Spink.

'Trig, we need to have a little chat,' he began. Harding seemed to be listening so he carried on. 'I need you to be honest with me, Trig, 'coz we're in a fucking deep hole and someone seems to have pulled up the ladder!' Harding gave a very slight nod. 'What're you thinking Billy's hoping to get out of the Georgians?'

Spink had worked with Woons for a long time but was finding the current state of inertia increasingly stressful because no one seemed to know what was going on. It was easier when you knew who the enemy was so that you could plan accordingly, he had told himself. But the raids on the houses, the huge amount of destruction, the random killings – even the fact that he and Emma had come under fire. They had lost over twenty of the girls, and they had also lost Mr Fixit himself, Vashlili, who seemed to have just disappeared off the face of the earth or had simply joined the enemy – whoever they were.

'To be honest with you, Tricky, I'm not sure why he's gone hotfooting it out there!' Harding was now sitting back in the chair, hands fiddling with his hair, absent-mindedly twirling strands of it around his index finger. Just looking at Harding's state of disarray, Spink realised that the potential for the imminent destruction of the Woons empire had now become far too much for Harding to cope with. But he continued listening.

'What's he going say to the Kaspi brethren?' Harding asked, his voice faltering, sweat forming on his brow. 'Is he going to get them to fight his battles for him? They'll laugh in his face if he asks for their help. All they do is provide the meat in the Woons sandwich. The girls are all they're interested in. They can source the best, they can get them across Europe, they can get them into the UK, and they can serve them up to Billy on a plate - pretty much to order and at a price of their determination. If someone's trying to take over the Woons empire, the girls are the only thing of any value. Take the girls away, and your business is fucked. Murder a few key people along the way, burn a few buildings down – hey, that's just collateral damage! It's the girls that really matter and, right now, our stocks are running low.'

72

Tuesday 25 July

Keeping his eyes open and straining to decipher the road signs, Woons was aware that they were either very near Agara or, indeed, they had passed the town which Vlad or Marko had mentioned. He could see virtually nothing but darkness out of the side windows, and the headlights only picked out a tongue of black tarmacadam stretching for miles into the distance. The occasional car passed them on the other side of the road. But he had sensed a deceleration and, sure enough, the Subaru was now slowing down. The indicator was ticking as they turned off the main highway onto a slip road at the end of which was a small roundabout. The man in the passenger seat grunted and then pointed at one of the exits.

Peering through the gap in the seats, Woons saw that they were now driving along a narrow road which was in desperate need of some repair judging by the almost constant jolting as the Subaru negotiated one pothole only to be caught by the next. A high fence ran along the left-hand side of the road. Behind the fence were rows of low-level buildings which reminded Woons of run-down manufacturing units which he had seen on a previous trip to Georgia. The whole place looked as if it had been abandoned – it seemed to be dark and unin-habited. Eventually the fence ended and the Subaru turned left. The fence continued on the passenger side of the car but he now noticed some forestation on the driver's side of the road. There were occasional clearings in the tree line and it was into one of these clearings that the Subaru turned. By now, the tarmacked road had run out completely and they were on a rough path.

On they trundled until, out of almost nowhere, they drove into what looked like an abandoned farmyard. There were a couple of barns with huge wooden doors standing open. The wood was rotten and crumbling away, and the metal holding the panels together was seriously corroded. As the Subaru did a circuit of the yard before coming to a halt, Woons spotted what would have been the farmhouse except there wasn't a pane of glass left in it and half the roof appeared to have fallen in on itself. Off to his left was a single storey building with two five bar gates in front of it – perhaps a milking shed back in the day when this was a working farm, but not now Woons thought.

The Subaru's engine was quietly idling, the light from the headlamps reflecting back into the vehicle from the walls of the stricken farmhouse. From the comfort of his seat, Woons saw the shadow of the Subaru suddenly picked out in the light from another set of headlamps before he heard the vehicle screaming into the abandoned farmyard and barrelling into the rear of the Subaru. The vehicle leaped forward and crashed into the wall of the farmhouse. Woons was catapulted into the back of the seat in front of him. He then bounced back into the bucket seat with blood flowing from his nose and a gash across the middle of his forehead. He wavered on the edges of consciousness as he tried to turn around to see what was going on behind him.

He suddenly heard a small explosion and the front passenger's window disintegrated as did the side of Vlad or Marko's head. Woons was covered by a fine spray of blood and fragments of bone. In a desperate effort to avoid the same fate, he launched himself across the back seat in a vain effort to hide himself. He heard the driver's door being opened. There were raised voices as Vlad or Marko was unceremoniously dragged from his seat. There were two further explosions and then more animated chatter. He hung on to his holdall, face buried in the seat. Eventually, after some more shouting the door next to where his head rested was opened. Woons held his breath, his life flashing before him as he thought of all the things he had done – and all the things he still wanted to do. Like get out of this sodding country for one thing!

A pair of hands came through the doorway and roughly turned him over so that he was looking up at a face covered in a balaclava mask, two dark eyes staring down at him. The man spoke to him in a language Woons didn't understand and then obviously made a joke as he started laughing. Through a hole in the mask, Woons could see a row of yellow and black teeth, some of them missing. The man then barked an order and, after a bit of a scuffle outside the vehicle which Woons couldn't see, the man pushed his head back into the car. Woons wondered what was going to happen now. He hadn't yet been shot so perhaps that was not in their plans. He clearly needed some medical attention to deal with the blood which was still pouring from the gash over his eye. His nose was still bleeding and was probably broken, and he seemed to be in a general catatonic state after crashing into the back of the driver's seat.

Balaclava man, however, had other ideas. He roughly grabbed Woons' wrists and threaded some flex wire around them so that Woons once again found himself unable to move his arms. He was then pulled up into a sitting position, revealing his holdall in the process. The man looked at it, picked it up, unzipped it and rummaged around inside. Satisfied that it held no weapons, he zipped it back up and held it up to Woons. With his other hand, he pointed at the holdall and then pointed at Woons who nodded. The man then backed out of the doorway and tossed the holdall to someone who was out of Woons line of sight. What happened next made the hairs on every inch of Woons body stand on end as balaclava man pulled a needle and syringe from his pocket. Almost before Woons could react, he felt a pin prick in the side of his neck, and he fell headlong into the abyss of unconsciousness.

73
Tuesday 25 July

DI Sarah Hunter was geed-up by the fact that new information was starting to flow into her investigation, and she had spent much of the afternoon in further discussion with DS Grace Kendall. They had been doing a bit of brainstorming, or 'blue sky thinking' as those with silver braid on their hats at the force HQ in Maidstone liked to call it. Hunter hated both descriptions with a passion although she had to grudgingly accept that they quite accurately described what she and Kendall had been up to.

To start with, they decided to look into ownership of the two properties at Hildenborough and Sheet Hill. Kendall had already done some work on this but had largely drawn a blank. Mainly because the owner of both properties seemed to be some sort of shell company based in the Cayman Islands, and information about its set up and ownership was simply unavailable. All documentation was in order with the Land Registry, and there were no outstanding loans or other debts which were guaranteed on the properties. In short, there was nothing suspicious about the ownership of the properties other than the fact that no one knew who actually owned them.

Upon receiving news about the identity of Maria Travisedo, Kendall had obtained her records through the police archive system. These showed that, some thirty years ago, Travisedo had been arrested and cautioned on a number of occasions for importuning. Eventually, tiring of her persistent offending, a judge decided that perhaps a short stretch in the slammer might bring her to her senses and gave her nine months in Holloway. Nothing had been heard of Travisedo from that day to this. As far as anyone knew or even cared to know, she was living the life of a model citizen having learnt her lesson in the cesspool of iniquity offered by a few months in the company of the inmates of what was, at that time, one of the country's most notorious women's prisons.

Notification about the identification of Candice Lombardi had come in around mid-afternoon, and Kendall had quickly accessed the records system to see what Lombardi had been up to in a previous life. It turned out that she had been known to the Met's Vice Squad and, by all accounts, had been working in the capital's sex industry for many years. At some stage, she had served a short sentence for unlicensed prostitution but had then, like Travisedo, disappeared off the radar.

Sarah and Grace were now sitting in the MIR with Kendall's laptop open on the desk between them. Kendall was manipulating the cursor as it scurried around the screen trying to dig up more information about the two ex-cons. What had they been up to in the intervening years? Hunter had started exhaling deep breaths which she blew upwards over her face so that they disturbed her fringe which stopped just short of her eyeline. A sure sign that she was bored and frustrated! Every now and then she glanced at the white boards but decided against putting any new information on them until her troops got back with the day's findings.

Her phone suddenly buzzed into life on the desk beside her, its bright light demanding attention. It was a number she didn't recognise. 'DI Hunter,' she answered cautiously.

'Good afternoon, Sarah!' A voice Hunter had no difficulty

in recognising.

'Hey, Ilona! Great to hear from you!' Hunter gushed. 'I knew you were coming but I haven't had the time to get down to see you today. Hope my guys didn't interrupt too much!'

'No, good as gold!' Jenkyns assured her. 'In fact, I'd go as far as to say that you've got the makings of a good team there. I mean, I am right in thinking that they're a bunch of green horns aren't I?'

'Pretty much,' Hunter replied, 'but they are showing themselves to be quick learners! Anyway, how have you been getting on?'

'Well, you've certainly given me something out of the ordinary to look at, that's for sure! Do you want a heads-up now or would you like me to come over later and brief you more fully?' Hunter wanted a get any new information as soon as it was available but she also wanted to meet up with Jenkyns who she hadn't seen for many months – it might even be a year or two since they were last in each other's company.

'Both would be good,' Hunter replied, her mind wrestling with all the things she still had to do before she could even think of meeting up with her friend. 'Where are you staying this evening?'

'Hah!' came the exclamation from Jenkyns. 'They originally put me in Chilston Manor but I vetoed that on the grounds that it was too far away and too expensive! So, I'm now in the Hotel du Vin in the Wells which is much more sensible, and Dr Swartzman can drop me there on his way home. Do you want to stop by for some dinner on your way home?'

Hunter thought this arrangement would kill two birds with one stone so she agreed to meet up at around eight o'clock.

'That's great!' enthused Jenkyns. 'Just one piece of information before I go. When your guys were here, I was still trying to get fingerprints from the one hand we have for the woman in the bag. Someone had kindly hacked the other hand off and had clearly forgotten to put it in the bag! They'd also tried hard to obliterate the fingerprints of the other hand which is still attached to the woman's arm – although the arm isn't attached to the torso. Looks like they have used a range of tools in the process but I did manage to get some partials which I thought we could use until I get some more sophisticated equipment on the case. I've run them through the system and amazingly we do seem to have one hit.'

In trying not to miss a word Jenkyns was saying, Hunter had jammed the phone so close to her ear that the stem of her tiny stud earring was starting to pierce the skin behind her ear. 'And?' Hunter asked, almost a whisper.

'Well,' Jenkyns replied, 'the vic may well be a person who is already of interest to you as it looks like someone from Kent accessed her records earlier today. I will have to confirm my identification once I can get her back to the Home Office but, for the moment, I think that we probably have a lady by the name of Maria Travisedo locked up in the mortuary here at Pembury.'

Hunter's heart missed a beat as she let out a stifled 'Yesss!' before raising her right fist and shaking it in the direction of Kendall. 'That is great news, Ilona, and takes our investigation to the next level. I'll let the team know when they all get back, and then I can talk through the ramifications with you when we meet up later.'

Jenkyns and Hunter exchanged a couple of pleasantries

before the call was disconnected. Kendall, who had been listening in, was keen to know what it was that Jenkyns had said that had got such a reaction from Hunter. She didn't have to wait long.

'The body in the bag is probably this Travisedo woman!' she exclaimed. 'So, we now have the bodies of two older women with backgrounds in the sex industry who appear to have been involved in the running of up-market brothels located within about a ten-mile radius of each other. Surely, it would be churlish not to conclude that they were connected – probably as part of a bigger organisation?'

74

Tuesday 25th July

Sarah Hunter had just left the MIR and was on her way upstairs when her phone rang. DCI Iversen had been detained at Maidstone for yet another planning meeting so they wouldn't be able to meet today. Did Hunter have any updates he should know about? She had come to a halt in the stairwell so stayed where she was while she briefed him on the identities of the two women in the mortuary and her conclusion that not only were the two houses linked but that they may be part of something bigger.

Iversen seemed pleased that things were moving on apace but warned her that the Press Officer at Maidstone had received a number of calls from local journos who had started to sniff a possible major story. She should be careful who comes calling to see her at Tonbridge. Hunter kept her dislike of the press in check, and told Iversen that she would take his warning seriously. She would remain vigilant. He had to get back to his meeting but, before he disconnected the call, he indicated that he would expect a full briefing tomorrow evening.

On returning to the MIR, she found that most of the team were back in the office and there was a general buzz of activity around the room. Jennings and Crosby were updating information on their white boards, and had aligned them with each other as it became clear that both properties were linked. The others were sitting at the desks in front of the boards tossing in snippets of information, and rifling through the ever-increasing amount of paperwork which was already being generated by this investigation. They had also managed to acquire the help of a couple of civilian indexers who were trying to get all the information fed into the HOLMES 2 information technology system used by all UK Police Forces for the investigation of major incidents.

Hunter was just thinking about starting the briefing meeting early so that she would have plenty of time to get over to Tunbridge Wells for her dinner with Professor Jenkyns when her phone spluttered into life. She swiped the screen to answer it. 'DI Hunter'.

'Oh, hello ma'am, sorry to bother you. It's Sergeant Arnold here, down at the front desk.'

'Yes, Trevor, what can I do for you?' Sarah replied in a jocular tone. She was on a high.

'Well, we've got a lady down here who's not very keen to leave until she's spoken to someone about a house in the countryside which has been causing her a lot of bother and now seems to have been abandoned. Says she's rung it in on numerous occasions but no one takes any notice so she has come in here to speak to someone in authority – her words not mine I hasten to add. I thought that you being involved in the investigation of those other two houses in the countryside, you might want to have a word with her just in case there's any connection.'

Hunter thought for a moment. 'Hmmm!' she replied. 'Where does she come from?'

'Says she lives in the country to the north of Horsmonden,' Arnold replied. 'Mentioned something about Furnace Pond so she must be up Furnace Lane between Horsmonden and Brenchley. I think she does a lot of walking in the woods and obviously comes across this house quite often in her travels.

I've put her in Room One to make her think that we're taking an interest but can get rid of her if it's a no-go for you.'

What harm could five minutes with this woman do, thought Hunter. 'Okay, I'll be down shortly, Trevor. Have you got a big map I can refer her to?'

'Yes, ma'am, I'll put one up on the screen in the room and tell her you'll be down in a moment,' he replied and disconnected the call.

Hunter looked over to where Selitto was in conversation with DC Pennant. She eventually caught his eye and nodded her head towards the door. He followed her out into the corridor. 'We've got someone downstairs who has suspicions about a big house hidden away in the countryside near Horsmonden. Ring any bells?'

Selitto's eyes lit up. 'In-ter-est-ing!' he exclaimed as they turned to head down the stairs to the front desk.

Once inside Room One, Hunter made the introductions as she and Selitto took their seats opposite Renie Johnson. To Hunter, she appeared to be a woman of indeterminate age but probably nearer seventy than sixty. She was definitely wearing well, and looked fit. Despite the warmth of the day, she was dressed in what looked like jodhpurs and a hacking jacket although both items of clothing had seen better days and bore some serious stains. Perhaps the horse was tied up outside, Hunter thought, rather uncharitably. Johnson's hair was a mess – an unsightly tangle of gingery-grey tresses which could have done with a good comb through. There was no sign that she was wearing any make-up, and Hunter noticed that her fingernails were cracked and dirty.

'So, Miss Johnson,' Hunter started.

'It's Mrs Johnson. I'm married, or at least I was until the silly sod went and had a heart attack and left me to manage everything on me own.' Well that saved a few questions, Hunter thought.

'Mrs Johnson,' Hunter corrected herself. 'So, Mrs Johnson, you believe that there is a house which you pass regularly and which is now causing you concern?'

'No, no! You don't understand!' Mrs Johnson replied. 'You see, I don't pass the house, I live next door to it. Me and Norman, bless him, took a caravan into the woods off Furnace Lane one summer all those years ago and enjoyed living in it so much that we stayed. And it's still my home. I remember when the leaves started falling off the trees that first year we were there, we found we could see a huge house not far from our caravan. Lovely looking house with a big wall round it and all. Them who's in it obviously didn't want the likes of us nosing around so we never bothered with them.' Selitto sat back in his chair, crossed his legs and folded his arms. Where was this going, he wondered.

'Anyways,' Mrs Johnson continued, 'more lately than not, there's been lots of noise going on there – sounds like every night is party night. Lots of music, girls laughing and screaming, cars coming and going all the time. I went round once to complain and had to speak into one of those thingummys on the wall by the gate. Told me I wasn't welcome there and to bugger off. That was when I started ringing you lot. But, of course, no one was interested. Much bigger fish to fry no doubt!' Hunter shot a sideways glance at Selitto, one eyebrow raised.

'Then, the strangest of things,' Mrs Johnson paused and

stared at the two Detectives. 'The noise completely stopped one evening – when was it?' She paused again, clearly trying to get her thoughts in order. 'Yes, last Thursday. That's it! Last Thursday. I was just getting me dinner and I suddenly thought to myself – Renie, I thought, that noise 'as stopped! A nice summery evening with the last of the sunshine coming down through the trees, and I could 'ear the birds tweeting. Lovely!' Mrs Johnson leaned forward to rest her arms on the table in front of her.

'Anyway,' she continued, 'I usually go for a little walk before bed, just to check that the chickens are all tucked up in bed away from nasty Mr Fox, and that evening I decided to walk on 'til I come to the gates of the house 'caus I was still trying to get used to the silence. Just as I was getting there, a car came up the track from the road and drove straight through the gates. You see, they weren't closed – they had been left open. I had never known that in all the time I'd been there. So, I went and had a peek but couldn't really see anything 'caus the whole place was dark. But I could see a faint light bobbing around inside the house which looked more like someone with a torch. Well it were getting late by then so I started to walk back but then another car drove up and went into the house. I went back for another peek but still couldn't see nothing in the darkness so I just went back to the caravan.'

Hunter wasn't quite sure what to make of all this. So, she walked Mrs Johnson over to the screen which was showing the map of the area and asked her to point out where her caravan was located. After a minute in which she seemed to be trying to get her bearings, she pointed to a wood in an area off Furnace Lane, close to Furnace Pond. 'We're 'ere in these woods somewhere. The people going to the house come on a track from here,' she said pointing to Furnace Lane. Hunter pressed a button at the bottom of the screen and then drew a circle around the wood on the map. She looked at the area surrounding the wood and saw Furnace Pond which Mrs Johnson had mentioned. She also noticed the village of Horsmonden nearby with Brenchley in the distance. Eventually, she stood back from the screen.

'And you haven't heard any more noise since?' she asked, indicating that Mrs Johnson should return to her seat at the table.

'Nope!' replied Mrs Johnson, retaking her seat. 'Well not all that party stuff anyway. I was up early the next morning with the chickens and heard some noise going on so thought I'd have another look through the gate if it was still open. Anyway, there were about two or three white vans there. The voices I'd heard were four blokes trying to get a huge bag of something into the back of one of the vans. It seemed ever so heavy and they were having a lot of trouble. The language! Oh, my good God – haven't heard swearing like that since my Norman was still with us!' The detectives turned to each other, stifling a laugh. 'Anyway, I had things to attend to so I went back to the caravan. But later in the day I got to thinking so I rang you lot again but still no interest. I've rung a couple of times every day since then but no interest so today I decided to come in on the bus 'caus I'm just thinking that there's something not right in that house. And someone's now shut the gates again.'

Hunter told Mrs Johnson to stay where she was whilst she took Selitto into the viewing room next door. 'Well?' she asked him as she closed the door. They watched Mrs Johnson sitting at the table, looking at her surroundings.

'Hmmm!' came the reply. 'May be something and nothing. Similarities to our case? A big house in the middle of nowhere, has been used for lots of parties involving girls, now empty, possibly been cleaned out, nothing known about the occupants. Yep! There are some similarities. Worth a visit? Probably!'

'My own feeling is that we might be missing something if we don't take a look so I agree – probably worth a visit,' Hunter said. 'But when?'

'I could go now, take the old girl home and have a quick shufti while I'm there,' Selitto volunteered. 'Don't need to be in the briefing as I've been shadowing the troops all day so I know what they've been up to. If it looks interesting, you and I could get over there in the morning.'

'Okay! Sounds like a plan,' Sarah replied. 'You take her home, I'll get on with the briefing, and you call me later once you've had a look around the house.' With that, Hunter disappeared up the staircase on her way back to the MIR for the 6.30 p.m. briefing.

75

Tuesday 25 July

Selitto wondered whether Mrs Johnson had ever been in a car before! Although she had eventually managed to get herself comfortable in the passenger seat, she had been completely incapable of putting her seatbelt on. After a lot of delicate stretching across her, Selitto had managed to get hold of the tongue of the belt before finally managing to persuade it to click into the buckle. During the drive over to Horsmonden, he had had to endure a monologue from his passenger about living in the woods, her dear husband Norman, and the noisy people who lived – or had lived – next door. Selitto had tuned out most of this and instead enjoyed the views of the picturesque Kent countryside as the sun started to cast long shadows over the highways and byways.

He had taken the back roads from Tonbridge through Tudeley and then skirting round to the north of Matfield past The Poet and on towards Brenchley before dropping down towards Horsmonden. The entrance to Furnace Lane was on a bend just a couple of hundred metres before one of his favourite eateries, The Gun & Spit Roast Inn and, as he turned into the lane, he caught site of what looked like ANPR cameras attached to a lamp post a bit further along the road. He frowned, asking himself why they would have set up automatic number plate recognition at a location which was essentially in the countryside. Perhaps it was something to do with the proximity to the A21 Hastings road which was a main thoroughfare in these parts. He filed this information away in his mind as they drove on along Furnace Lane, Mrs Johnson providing a running commentary as they went.

Eventually, Mrs Johnson pointed out the entrance to the track leading to the house but insisted on being dropped further along the road so that she was nearer to her caravan. Selitto dropped her off as requested and, after declining numerous requests to come in for a cup of tea, he turned the car round and doubled back to the break in the trees which Mrs Johnson had pointed out. Leaving the road, he passed through a gateway and noticed that a five-bar gate had been rammed into the long grass beside the track. He gingerly made his way through the trees along an uneven, uncared for dusty track before finding himself in the open and skirting around the corner of a ploughed field before disappearing back into the trees. Eventually, he drove into a clearing and arrived at a set of huge black metal gates which hung from two enormous stone pillars. The gates themselves must have been getting on for five metres high. A complex sculpture was set on the top of each pillar which reminded Selitto of a picture he had once seen of Medusa, one of the Gorgons who had a pile of snakes for her hair and was considered as the "Guardian" in Greek Mythology. Very appropriate, he thought. A high solid stone wall spread out on either side of the gates and stretched into the woods surrounding the property.

He got out of the car and crossed over to the gates. They were certainly built to keep the great unwanted out – and perhaps to keep other people in. There was a sophisticated entry phone system with cameras and lights, and he spotted two other cameras set up on the top of the wall either side of the gate – one directed at where he was standing now and the other focused on the track he had driven up. A lot of security then, Selitto thought. He took a closer look at the entry phone, but couldn't see any tell-tale signs that it was actually working. He pressed the button and then waited – but nothing happened. He leant his shoulder against one of the gates and gave it a nudge. It moved slightly but ultimately remained in position. So, he pushed a bit harder. This time, a gap appeared between the two gates. He continued pushing the gate until there was enough room for him to walk through. He inspected the other side of the entrance and noticed that there were electro-mechanical operating arms holding the gates in place on either side. He would have to wedge the gate open otherwise he would be unable to open it from the inside if the power in the house had been disconnected.

He went back outside and hunted around in the undergrowth, looking for something to wedge the gate open with. He soon came across a surprising amount of discarded building material which appeared to have simply been tossed into the bushes, and it didn't take him long to find an old paving slab which he placed in the gap between the two gates. He then re-parked his car so that it was facing back towards the track and off to the left of the gates. He squeezed through the gap in the gates, carefully ensuring that the paving slab kept them from closing, and made his way around a circular driveway. He passed an ornate fountain which was adorned by more Gorgons heads, and continued on up to the front door.

There was another sophisticated entry system beside the door, and more cameras trained onto the porch around the main entrance. But he wouldn't have need of the entry system or, indeed, of the huge door knocker in the shape of a leaping salmon as it was clear that the door was not quite closed. So, pulling on a pair of nitriles, he pushed the door open and entered the house.

Immediately, two things hit his senses. One was the deafening silence – not a murmur nor any sound that would indicate that anyone was in residence. It was as if the air had been sucked out of the building. The other was the smell. The smell of cleaning, of disinfectant, of someone trying to eradicate traces of having been there. And it was a smell he had come across very recently. The same smell that had pervaded the air in the house at Sheet Hill.

'Hello, boss. Are you good to speak?' Selitto was back in his car, fingers tapping on the steering wheel as Hunter answered his call.

'Okay, Ted!' she replied. 'Briefing's just finished so I've got a few minutes before I have to get off to the Wells. What you got from Mrs Johnson's neighbours?'

'Looks like we've uncovered another of those expensive knocking shops, boss. Large pile of bricks, complex security system, cameras all over the place, rooms full of sex paraphernalia, a top floor with small rooms and single beds, lavish entertainment facilities, out in the middle of nowhere. All seems to have been left just as it was. Almost as if the inhabitants had been vapourised. Only difference this time seems to be that the clean-up operation didn't go according to plan and hasn't been completed yet.'

'How do you mean not yet completed?' Hunter enquired, phone nestling between her ear and her shoulder, hands pulling together the papers on her desk and shovelling them

493

unceremoniously into a folder.

'Well, even with the naked eye it looks like there's traces of blood on the walls of at least two of the rooms which even I could see just using a torch. God knows what the CSIs will find with their arc lights!' Selitto was staring through the windscreen towards the area of the forest where Mrs Johnson's caravan was located, the lengthening shadow of the huge black gates creeping over the ground in front of him. He glanced over to see that the paving stone was still propped up against the wall beside the entrance. 'One of the rooms has traces of extensive blood spatter on the walls, the ceiling and the carpet. It would have taken a superhuman effort to have cleared all that up in one go so I suspect that the cleaner is either planning another visit or hoping the decorators will get there first. There's another room of interest although I can't quite determine what happened in there. Some minute spots of blood on one of the walls, and it looks like something very heavy was dragged from that room along the corridor to the stairs. The carpet is black and there's a furrow in the pile where the item has been dragged. Possibly a body but would have been a massive person.'

'So, are you thinking that the cleaners will be back to finish off the job?' Hunter asked. She knew roughly how clean-up operations worked in the underworld, but just wanted to see what Selitto thought.

'Looks to me like the cleaners themselves have probably done the best they can,' he continued. 'I reckon it's the painters and decorators who haven't been in yet. No smell of paint, and the place looks as if it has only been superficially cleaned.'

'Okay,' said Hunter looking at the clock. 'I'm going to have to shoot. Suggest that you get some uniforms to secure the house so that we can get CSI's in there first thing in the morning. If anyone does come back to do some painting, then we may well find that he or she is just a local jobbing decorator who doesn't know who he's working for but at least we might get a little bit of information. So, get the site secure and we can then have another look in the morning.'

'OK, boss. Will do. Have a good evening with Professor Jenkyns.' But Hunter had already disconnected the call. Selitto's fingers were still tapping the steering wheel. This was going to be another late one, he thought.

76

Tuesday 25 July

'Are we getting close yet, Ems?'

Spink was driving, Emma sat in the passenger seat straining her eyes to see a break in the hedges and the young trees which lined each side of Rogers Rough Road. But it was not easy with the rapidly fading light creating black shadows across any breaks in the hedgerow. They had decided to take a look at the house near Kilndown to make sure that everything was okay with Cassandra who had run the house for just coming up to ten years. Emma's recollection was that the security wasn't up to much but, as it was simply a glorified massage parlour, she had never thought that it required the sophisticated entry software which had been installed at some of the other houses. The punters it attracted were mainly local Kent businessmen out for a good time rather than the high rollers jetting in from around the world for the sort of thrills and spills offered by Maria Travisedo and Candice Lombardi.

'Trouble is, Tricky,' Emma said, staring into the gloom in front of her, 'I normally come at it from the other end of the road so it's all arse about face for me coming this way.' Spink knew that she was having difficulty with the light and the resulting dark shadows, and he would have slowed down if he hadn't had a poxy red Toyota Aygo up his backside. And there were no passing places so Sunny Jim would just have to wait.

'Here!' Emma suddenly shouted. Luckily, Spink saw the opening in the hedgerow at the same time, and he wrenched the steering wheel to the left as the Toyota sped by, hand on horn.

'Fucking idiot!' he cursed under his breath as they bounced over a couple of huge ruts in the track before coming to a halt in front of a metal farm gate.

'I'll get that!' Emma exclaimed as she got out of the car to open the gate.

'Leave it open, Ems,' he called after her, 'in case we need to make a quick exit!' She waited, standing to one side and giving a mock salute as Spink drove through the opening. She then scampered round the back of the car before getting back into the passenger seat. 'Have you been here recently?' she enquired.

'Not for a few years,' Spink replied, as they lurched from one pot hole to another. 'Cassie's low maintenance as far as I can tell. Don't know that Billy's even clapped eyes on her more than once. No point in him wasting his time if everything's running tickety-boo and the bills are being paid on time.

'Well, you'll notice a difference in the driveway soon because Cassie has had some work done on it,' Emma told him. 'She's also upgraded the entrance to the house.' Very soon the ground started to level out, and the back-jarring craters and pot holes disappeared. 'See?'

'Hmmm! Great improvement!' Spink commented. 'By the way, I presume Cassie knows we're coming?'

'Sure does. Said to come by at a time to suit us.' They lapsed into silence as the drive seemed to go on forever, deeper and deeper into the woods with a leafy canopy preventing any remaining daylight from breaking through to the ground. The BMW's headlights had come on, picking out the track in front of the car as Spink drove on.

Eventually, Emma announced that the house was round the next corner. Spink had already instinctively slowed the car down as they had approached the bend but, as the corner of the house came into view, he suddenly slammed on the brakes whilst at the same time shutting off the lights and the engine. Emma gave him a sideways look as if to ask him what the fuck he was doing but quickly followed his gaze towards the house which was some 200 metres in the distance. Her mouth dropped open.

'You see what I see?' Spink whispered to her. Emma nodded, not daring to speak as she focused on the scene unfolding in front of her.

Spink had reversed back along the track until he was once again out of sight of the front of the house. He had then executed a three-point turn, which Emma thought was closer to eight points, and eventually brought the BMW to a halt facing back towards the road and off the track in a small clearing. On leaving the car, Spink had placed the key on the top of the rear nearside wheel, and they were now creeping towards the house, hugging the tree line at the side of the track, trying to stay in the shadows. Once they got within about fifty metres of the house, Spink thrust his arm out to hold Emma back, and they both retreated behind the trunk of one of the trees.

'I've definitely seen that van before,' he whispered as Emma peered past Spink's shoulder and concentrated her gaze on the entrance to the house. A black van was backed up to the front door although, from where they were standing, it looked as if the back doors were closed at the moment.

'Hildenborough?' Emma questioned, her mind racing back to the grim discoveries they had made at Candice's house just forty-eight hours earlier.

'Possibly,' Spink replied, 'but it also looks horribly like the van that delivered Maria Travisedo to Billy's office yesterday. Don't tell me we've actually stumbled on them, whoever they are, in the process of clearing out another of our houses?'

Spink kept his eyes glued to the front of the house, trying to plot a course to the door so that they wouldn't be seen. Fortunately, it looked as if blinds had been drawn in all the rooms and there was only one rather dim light which hung from the wall to the left of the doorway. There was no one standing around outside as far he could see.

'Is there any other entry point?' Spink whispered turning towards Emma. She was staring wide-eyed at the house, a look of considerable apprehension etched on her face.

'Afraid not,' she replied. 'All the other entry doors are round the back, and there's a high wall between the front and back to keep unwanted guests out when Cassandra throws her legendary parties.'

'Okay!' Spink paused. 'Let's get up to the house and see what's going on. Looks like the door isn't closed properly so let's see if I can get in and have a look around.' Emma nodded and crept after Spink as he made his way through the shadows towards the front door which he could now see was slightly ajar. As they passed the van, Spink had a quick look through the driver's window but there wasn't anyone in the cab of the vehicle. Emma thought that she heard a faint tapping from inside it but eventually decided that it was just the sound of the engine cooling down. They were both struck by the eerie silence which pervaded the building and the area around it. Spink finally reached the wall to the right of the door and flattened himself against it. Emma followed suit and they stayed like that for a matter of seconds, breathing deeply.

'Right! Let's split!' Spink turned to Emma. 'You get out of the light in the shadows over there,' he said, pointing to an area of lawn to the right of the house, 'and wait for my signal. I'll either text you or I'll come out and wave to you. Now go!' She scuttled off, and he waited until she was buried in the shadows before he turned, climbed the three steps up to the door and carefully eased it open until he could see what lay beyond it.

Easing himself through the narrow gap he had created, he found himself in a vestibule which looked like a three-sided box surrounding the main entrance, the lower parts of which were wood panelled. Above the panels were panes of frosted glass, and he looked up to see a sophisticated array of cameras and lights trained on the doorway. This was presumably the security system which Emma had spoken about although it must have been a recent addition to the house as he didn't think it had been here when he last visited. But Spink's attention was immediately drawn to the smashed glass and twisted wood panels which had once been the door from the vestibule into the hallway.

He gingerly stepped across the broken glass, a crunching sound echoing across the cavernous empty space beyond the vestibule. He peered into the all-encompassing gloom in the hallway and, looking both ways, he could just about pick out the doors that lined the soft pile deep blue carpet which stretched before him in either direction. He couldn't see any sign of a staircase which he found rather odd until he suddenly remembered that Cassandra had boarded it in. This meant that it was behind one of the doors. Using logic, he tried the door directly in front of him and was relieved to see that he had made the right choice. But the light was even poorer here so he reached into his jacket pocket and took out his LED torch .

He quickly realised that the main reason for the poor light was the fact that all the ornate wall-light fittings which caressed the walls around the circular staircase had all been smashed. The only source of light was a flush ceiling unit high up in the apex of the stairwell, and its effectiveness was all but useless. He sprinted up the stairs and arrived on the landing just as he heard a door open along the corridor immediately to his left. He took a couple of steps back down the staircase and crouched behind the balustrade which formed an ornamental parapet at the top of the staircase. He found that he could see through the balusters and down the corridor to the open door. Light streamed out into the corridor and a powerfully built man had one foot in the corridor as if preparing to leave the room but seemed to be giving orders to someone else in the room.

Try as he might, Spink could not make head nor tail of the language other than that it didn't sound as if it was Western European. Eventually, the man exited the room and sauntered off further down the corridor. Spink leaned around the corner of the balustrade to get a better view of where the man was going. Suddenly, a shaft of light split the gloom and the man entered another room and closed the door behind him. The corridor returned to darkness.

Spink got to his feet and skipped back down the stairs. His instinct told him that there were probably two or three men here, and he knew that they were probably all upstairs. So, he decided to do a quick search of the rooms on the ground floor. On exiting the stairwell, he turned right past the smashed door of the vestibule and came to a door on his right. He opened the door, trying to make as little noise as possible, and shone his flashlight into the room. He saw that it was laid out with a massage table as its centrepiece, and work surfaces adorned with various items of equipment were arranged along the walls. There was a camera on a stand in one corner, and he noted the mirror tiles in the ceiling.

Quietly closing the door, Spink moved on to the next room which looked much the same as the one before. Back in the hallway, he decided to look at the rooms on the other side of the vestibule. The first room he came to was yet another massage room so he moved quickly on. He gently opened the next door and suddenly recoiled at the stench of urine and human faeces which greeted him. Another massage table stood serenely in the middle of the room but, as he swung the flashlight around the room, its beam picked out two pairs of eyes blinking in the sudden brightness, desperation etched on two mournful faces. Two girls who were so petrified that they had soiled themselves. Duct tape covering their mouths, hands tied behind their backs, flexi-cord binding their ankles together. Someone had made sure that they weren't going anywhere in a hurry.

There was nothing he could do for them just now so he quietly closed the door and moved on to the next room. He found two more girls in this room and, although the stench wasn't quite so bad, one of the girls looked as if she had passed out as her head was almost touching her knees. His natural instinct was to help these girls, but he knew that he couldn't do anything for them until he had a better idea of what else was going on in the house. It would be counter-productive to simply untie the girls and tell them to get the hell out of there as the whole point of the Woons empire was to keep these girls at work in the houses. Letting them go would compound the problem which they already had with girls being taken from Hildenborough and Sheet Hill.

He crossed the hallway and gently opened the last door on that side. His flashlight picked out a wooden staircase which led down to what looked like some sort of dungeon. He would make a closer inspection of this once he had looked at the rest of the rooms. He closed the door and then stood stock still, listening. He thought he could hear the two men talking upstairs but perhaps it was his imagination so he moved on to the next door.

He noticed that this door was slightly ajar. He pushed it open far enough to allow him to step into the room. His eyes instinctively fell to the floor, his flashlight following the perimeter of the room, searching for more of the girls.

He was concentrating so hard on searching for girls on the floor that he didn't see the hand which brushed him lightly on the shoulder, the fingers caressing his ear. Recoiling in sheer terror, he brought the flashlight up and found himself staring at a grotesquely distorted face, eyes dangling out of their sockets, slices of skin carved off ample jowls, slash marks all over a bare torso, mutilated breasts hanging loosely down over milk-white shoulders, arms hanging limply, one severed hand lying on the floor under the body. On closer inspection, he could make out the handle of a vicious-looking knife which protruded from the ribcage, undoubtedly embedded in the heart. As if in a trance, he moved his gaze upward to take in a pair of long, slim legs which disappeared into the gloom. He stood back and, looking up, he shone the flashlight upwards into the ceiling recess and saw that a rope had been lashed to one of the wooden beams which crossed the ceiling. Two bare feet poked out from a complex knot in the rope. Crude but effective.

He just stood there, rooted to the spot, finding it difficult to take his eyes off the abject horror of what he saw before him. Cassandra would never again welcome guests to this house.

Spink was so deep in thought that he failed to notice that someone else had slid into the room behind him. Just as his senses were alerted to the fact that he had company, and he started to turn around to see who else was in the room, a crowbar crashed into the side of his head and he collapsed to the floor.

77

Tuesday 25 July

Sarah Hunter placed her spoon into the empty shallow bowl in front of her and sat back in her chair, dabbing the corners of her mouth with the nicely starched napkin which had been resting on her lap. She had managed to scrape up every last grain of arborio rice from an excellent seafood risotto which, in turn, had complimented the heavenly chicken liver parfait she had ordered as a starter. Ilona Jenkyns was similarly using a spoon to finish off her bowl of cassoulet which, to Hunter, had looked and smelled divine. She, too, sat back in her chair and wiped an imaginary droplet of the rich sauce from her lips.

'Excellent!' Jenkyns purred. 'Nothing beats a good, solid plate of tasty food after a hard day spent peering into dead bodies!'

Hunter smiled. She was enjoying some down time with her old buddy from the dark days of the Met when they were lucky if they got the time to grab a cheeseburger together. Now they sat in the opulence of a Grade II - listed Georgian mansion enjoying fine food, fine wine and each other's company. They both declined the offer of a dessert although Sarah had wondered if she had room for a crème brulee. Instead, they settled on Americano coffees.

'So,' Jenkyns said before taking a sip of her coffee. 'Let's just get back to your investigation for a minute or two.' During the meal, they had chatted away about their own personal lives, bringing each other up to date with any developments or, in Hunter's case, non-developments, talking about Jenkyns' escapades as a Home Office Pathologist travelling the length and breadth of the country when and wherever needed. Hunter had been royally entertained by some of the stories which her friend had come out with and, in return, Ilona Jenkyns had laughed out loud at some of the comparisons which Hunter had drawn between policing Central London and doing the same job in leafy Kent. It had been an enjoyable evening, but Hunter knew that she had to grab this opportunity to get whatever information Jenkyns could give her about the work she had done earlier in the day.

'Where we've got to,' Hunter began, 'is that we have uncovered a people trafficking operation which we believe is entirely linked to the sex trade. Girls are being trafficked into the country from Eastern Europe – possibly Bulgaria – and are then being put to work in what can only be described as high-end brothels. From the little information we have to go on, it looks like the punters are mainly very wealthy men from all over the world. The houses used for these activities tend to be hidden away in the countryside well away from public scrutiny, and it's likely that the punters would only know about their whereabouts if they had been introduced by someone already in the know.'

Ilona Jenkyns topped up her coffee as Sarah continued. 'We are only getting to these houses after an event has been flagged to us. But, based on the information we have been gathering, it looks like there might have been some sort of bust up between the gangs involved in the operation as we now have three dead girls and what looks like two dead Madams or whatever you want to call them. We've so far uncovered two houses with another one being looked at as we speak.'

'Hmm!' Jenkyns had been listening intently. 'Well, the body

from the fire is definitely a young girl, probably late teens. Difficult to tell exactly what killed her. The back of her skull appears to have been caved in but she also has a fracture of the hyoid bone which would indicate the possibility that she might have died as a result of manual strangulation. But I think you're correct about making a link to Bulgaria because I found the remains of an IUD inside the body which would seem to be of Bulgarian origin. I could just make out the maker's name, Venus, which manufactures these products in the old Eastern Bloc country.'

'Okay, that's good to know because that ties her in with our Scarecrow Girl.' It was a small step but Sarah Hunter was relieved that she was almost in a position to irrefutably tie the two houses to each other. 'So, what did you make of the body in the bag?'

'Again, not easy to exactly pinpoint the cause of death,' Jenkyns said, looking off into the distance over Hunter's shoulder as if in a trance. 'She suffered a blunt trauma to the back of the head which might not have killed her but would have certainly rendered her unconscious. I'm not yet sure whether her head was removed post mortem or whether she was still alive when the deed was done. Either way, I doubt that she knew anything about it due to the severity of the blow to the back of her head. It's likely that the limbs were cut off after she was dead as there was virtually no bleeding from the wounds. I didn't really see what Toby was up to although he did mention that Ms Lombardi had taken a very severe beating culminating in the slashing of her mouth. I think he mentioned to your guys that Lombardi probably died of heart failure after the rest of her organs packed up.' Hunter nodded.

'Anyway,' Jenkyns continued, 'it will be interesting to have a look at your third girl tomorrow, always assuming that she is connected to your case.'

'What time do you have to get away?' Sarah asked, hoping that Ilona Jenkyns would have time to post the third girl and take a look at Lombardi even though Swartzman had completed the PM on her.

'There's a train around 1.30 p.m. that'll get me back to the office for around four which will be just fine. I'll then get all the reports finished and send them down to you as soon as I can.' And with that, Jenkyns summoned one of the serving staff to their table. Sarah Hunter instinctively bent down to pick her bag off the floor to look for her purse but Jenkyns waved her away.

'My treat!' she said and smiled. 'I'm sure the Home Secretary would be pleased to pay for our dinner tonight so I'll just sign it on to the room bill and that'll get sent off to Whitehall in due course.

'Well, thank you Home Secretary!' Hunter exclaimed. In no time at all, the bill arrived and Ilona Jenkyns signed it with a flourish. The waitress collected her part of the document and her pen before scurrying off to the safety of the kitchen.

They got up from the table and made their way across the restaurant towards the lounge where some of the hotel guests were sitting up at the bar enjoying a nightcap.

Jenkyns turned to Hunter as they wandered through the lounge. 'Think I'll call it a day, Sarah. It's a long time since I got out of my bed this morning and I'm definitely feeling in need of some shut eye. Will I see you tomorrow?'

'Probably not,' Hunter replied, 'unless something truly

earth-shattering happens overnight and we have a morgue full of bodies!'

Jenkyns rolled her eyes. 'Heaven forbid! Okay, it's your turn to come and see me next time, and don't leave it too long!'

As they reached the reception area, Ilona Jenkyns turned to her friend. 'Look after yourself, Sarah. They speak highly of what you're doing down here in Kent so I hope it all continues to go well for you.' She reached out to Hunter and the two women warmly embraced each other.

Eventually, they parted. 'Thanks, Ilona.' Hunter said. 'Lovely to catch up – and thank the Home Secretary for the lovely dinner! See you soon!' She turned and made for the revolving door, waving a goodbye over her shoulder just before the door swallowed her up. Ilona Jenkyns turned and climbed the stairs to her room on the first floor.

78

Tuesday 25 July

DCs Elaine Jennings and Stuart Crosby had remained in the MIR following the evening briefing, reviewing all the information which was being crunched through the HOLMES 2 information system. They were principally looking for connections between the women they had now managed to identify, and any other similar incidents of trafficking and exploitation. It was dreary work at the best of times – and, after a long day of post mortems and interviews, it seemed even more wearisome. It had, therefore, been a blessing when DS Grace Kendall had breezed into the office and suggested that they all retire to The Carpenters Arms for some refreshments. She had offered to drive so the young DCs had piled into her Mini and they had made their way out of Tonbridge along the Hadlow Road before hanging a right into Three Elms Lane and then sharp left into the pub car park.

It had been a warm evening and the pub had been reasonably busy with drinkers and diners so they had decided to sit outside at a table in the pub's garden which gave them a bit more privacy. Grace had bought the drinks – a pint of Larkins bitter for Crosby, a small white wine for Jennings, and a tonic water with Angostura Bitters for herself – and carried them out to the table on a battered old tin tray which had seen better days. After some chat about the pub, and a quick assessment of the clientele sitting in the bar and in the garden, the officers' conversation returned to the investigation and the work they had been doing that day.

Elaine Jennings had filled them in on the interview she had attended with Kevin Bland, and Stuart Crosby had recounted some of the grisly features of the post mortems he had witnessed earlier. They had all had a laugh about Ted Selitto's remark that at least Azzar had kept his breakfast down, but all agreed that he had the makings of a good detective – an obvious asset for the team. Grace had given them a bit more information about the mysterious man, Zlatkov, and the possibility that someone was impersonating him here in the UK. The young DCs had found this most interesting, not least because they wanted to know how she had made this discovery.

As their conversation meandered, and the sun's rays were replaced by gentle flood lighting dispensed by lamps positioned in the eaves of the pub, their conversation had turned to the use of technology and the fact that they had only come across the houses as a result of something happening – an event. None of the houses had been identified as a result of any specific detective work which seemed to be a cause of concern for Stuart Crosby. He and Jennings had questioned Kendall about the use of CCTV and the ANPR system, and had wondered why this had not been made more use of. She had explained how the systems worked, the constraints regarding use of information, the costs involved, and the difficulties of identification solely by means of technology. They had had a lively debate about how this technology might actually help their investigation, and Grace Kendall had been invigorated by the enthusiasm which the young DCs were showing for an area of investigation work which had more or less taken over her life.

They had been so wrapped up in their discussions that they hadn't noticed the oncoming evening chill or even the fact that most of the other customers who had been drinking in the spacious garden had now made for the relative warmth of the bar as night drew in. On a whim, Kendall had offered to give the young DCs a demonstration of the technology and its application to the case they were working on. Both Jennings and Crosby had jumped at the idea so they had all piled back into Kendall's Mini and hot-footed it back to the Tonbridge police station.

On arrival at Pembury Road, they had found that the MIR was not as quiet as they had expected, particularly when they had bumped into DS Selitto wandering back from the kitchen area, a cup of steaming coffee in hand.

'Whoa! Who called the cavalry?' he joked as he placed his coffee on the desk he had clearly requisitioned for the evening.

'Might say the same of you, Ted,' Kendall riposted. 'What brings you from your bed at this time of night?'

'Not been there yet, Grace,' he said, sitting at the desk and pulling a keyboard towards him. 'Looks like we've stumbled on another house so I'm just getting some of my report done while it's fresh in my mind. Same MO as Sheet Hill and Hildenborough, in fact almost the same layout. Lots of sex aids and equipment but this time the clean-up operation either hasn't been completed yet or hasn't been done very well. There'll be a lot for the CSI boys and girls to get their teeth into – metaphorically speaking of course!'

Not even trying to supress a smile, Elaine Jennings was the first to ask a question. 'Was that a follow-up to that lady who came in earlier?'

'Yep!' replied Selitto. 'Good old Mrs Johnson seems to have

been living right next to one of these knocking shops for years! She'll be mortified when she finds out! Anyway, I've got a small team of uniforms keeping the place secure overnight, and I've reported it to the duty CSI Manager in Maidstone. As the electricity's all still connected up, he said they might get a team out tonight. That'll be good if we can get some initial feedback for the morning.' He took a slurp of the steaming coffee. 'So, what have you guys been up to?'

'We're looking at whether we can get anywhere with CCTV and ANPR,' replied Kendall. 'Elaine and Stuart have been expanding their knowledge of these areas, and we were just going to see if there was any chance of picking up any clues via these two mediums.'

Selitto thought for a moment. 'Hmm! That could be difficult as far as this case is concerned. Doubt there's any CCTV within miles of any of the sites we have so far located. A bit like looking for the proverbial needle in the haystack. And ANPR's mainly used in or near major towns isn't it, Grace?'

Kendall was logging into one of the workstations on a desk in front of the white boards. 'That's probably a fair summary. I think we've got just over 100 ANPRs now and a few more on order but they're all destined for towns like Sevenoaks, Tunbridge Wells, Dover, Sittingbourne. And the majority are for use on major routes so you wouldn't expect to find one on Sheet Hill or on the road round from Hildenborough to Leigh. Or wherever it is you've just been to near Horsmonden.'

'Ah well, that's where you might be wrong!' Selitto's eyes lit up as he recalled seeing what he thought was an ANPR camera in Horsmonden. 'Because on the way to Ma Johnson's caravan, I passed something that looked like an ANPR camera at the junction where Furnace Lane joins Brenchley Road in Horsmonden. I have to say that it looked a little out of place there because it's not a particularly busy junction but I suppose it's close to the Lamberhurst/Maidstone Road. Could it be ANPR, Grace, or is it just an empty box to deter anyone thinking of speeding on that road?'

'Well, we could take a look,' replied Kendall, settling herself in front of the work station and adjusting the height of the screen to reduce the glare from the overhead lights. 'Let's see what sort of camera it is to start with.' And, with that, she went to work on the keyboard, scrolling through screens of data until she found what she was looking for.

'Here we are!' she paused while she read through some of the data on the screen. 'Yes, you're right Ted,' she eventually announced, still looking at the screen. 'There is a camera there – in fact, there are two cameras there. Something to do with monitoring the traffic coming from Paddock Wood and trying to find a quicker route out of the area without using the A21. It doesn't look as if they're actual ANPR cameras but they seem to be feeding information into the ANPR database. If I can just find out who's doing the monitoring...' Her voice trailed off as she concentrated on interrogating the information system. Eventually, she sat back in her chair, still looking at the screen. 'Right! Well, my colleagues at Maidstone seem to be testing a new CCTV system which is designed to also enhance number plate recognition. The value seems to be that you get a moving picture rather than a static snapshot so it would be ideal for gathering traffic information as well as following any vehicles of interest.'

Selitto had got up from his desk and taken up a position

behind Kendall's left shoulder as the young DCs also gathered around. 'That's interesting, Grace. So, we can look at all the vehicles using that junction and get some idea where they have either come from or where they are going to,' he noted. 'Are you able to access the data from those cameras in Horsmonden? Maybe just run a sequence and we can see if anything jumps out of the screen which we can then concentrate on?'

'Not sure,' Kendall said as she spun the mouse around on its mat, trying to see what she could do with the data. After about a minute, she announced that she was ready.

'As we know, there are two cameras at that location, one for the Brenchley Road and one that seems to be focussed on Furnace Lane. The next question is – what date do you want me to input?'

Selitto thought back to what Mrs Johnson had said. 'Well, from the info given by Mrs Johnson, it seems that the noise stopped last Thursday which was the twentieth. So, perhaps we need to run something for the Thursday evening?'

Kendall continued manoeuvring the mouse, and eventually announced that she was ready to go. They all crowded in closer, looking intently at the screen. 'I'll start around 7.00 p.m. and see how we go from there. I'll be fast-forwarding in quiet periods so do shout if you see something you want to go back to.'

The first three hours saw the traffic gradually diminish so that, by the time the clock at the bottom right of the screen showed 10.00 p.m. there was virtually no traffic to be seen. Jennings had been trying to keep a note of vehicles turning into Furnace Lane which had then exited at the same junction later on but her list only comprised two cars. That meant that most of the traffic was either using the road to go home or to go elsewhere. There seemed to be little traffic coming down the lane and exiting onto the Lamberhurst/Maidstone Road. By this time, Kendall was fast-forwarding almost with abandon as the clock on the screen ticked past midnight and into the early hours.

'Stop!' Elaine Jennings suddenly blurted out, and then felt embarrassed. 'Sorry, didn't mean to raise my voice! Go back to the last vehicle to leave Furnace Lane.' Kendall did as she was asked. 'There,' said Jennings, staring at the screen and then looking at her notes. 'That car went up Furnace Lane at 10.43 p.m. and is now returning at 00.50 a.m. Worth making a note of.' Grace Kendall found that it was easy to read the registration number off the screen, and they moved on. Almost immediately, Jennings asked her to stop the playback again. 'That car turned up Furnace Lane at 11.12 p.m. and is now returning at 00.53 a.m. almost at the same time as the other vehicle. Coincidence?'

Jennings made a note of the registration number as Kendall continued fast-forwarding through the early hours of the morning. They all took note of a white Mercedes Vito van that turned up Furnace Lane at 01.47 a.m. and then reappeared at 03.22 a.m. Otherwise, there was virtually no traffic until the sun started to rise and another day was dawning in West Kent.

79

Wednesday 26 July

Woons was on one of his favourite walks. Along the foot-paths of the Pilgrims Way, under the local landmark known as 'Treacle Towers', and up on to the summit of Green Hill. As he crested the top of the hill, he heard some music and then set eyes upon a grotesque sight. He stopped dead in his tracks but found that the weird music was drawing him in, and he started edging ever closer until he realised that he was looking at Belinda and Candice. They were both nailed to crosses which were set against the skyline at the top of the hill. Turning his head, he saw that Vashlili was nailed to another cross slightly down from the summit of the hill but right in front of the women. They were looking out across the valley to a brown hazy smudge under which lay the M26 motorway. Beside them, Eric Idle was jauntily singing his 'Brightside of Life' song, and young teenage girls in summer dresses with posies in their hair threaded a dance through the monstrous structures. Woons couldn't believe his eyes and started slapping his face in an attempt to wipe this terrible spectacle from his sight. Then it began to rain. He was getting wet. He kept slapping his face. Rainwater was cascading off his face. His hair was plastered to his scalp. The slapping continued. He closed his eyes, desperate to blot out the hideousness all around him.

And then he heard different sounds. Were they voices? They most certainly were! Where were they coming from? The tableau of crosses and dancing girls was gradually disappearing, and he was no longer on Green Hill. He was no longer slapping his face and it had stopped raining. But his face was still being slapped, and he was still wet. Summoning up all his strength, Woons opened his eyes.

Suddenly, all went quiet. The face-slapping stopped. It was dark although he could detect a dim light coming from an area away to his right. And he knew that he was not alone. All around him, there were sounds of breathing and the air smelled rank with the heady odour of garlic, onions and spicy cooking. He had a raging headache, he couldn't breathe through his nose, and his mouth was parched dry. He moved his head slightly and a searing pain erupted in his neck. He let out an involuntary gasp, and screwed up his face. That was when he realised there was something on his forehead which felt like a cloth or a flannel. He screwed up his eyes before managing to raise his eyelids to take in his surroundings.

He found himself staring up into a dark pair of sunken eyes which he vaguely recognised but his mind was too confused to allow him to pull a name out of his befuddled brain. He felt as if he was lying on bare floorboards although his head seemed to be resting on a soaking wet pillow which stank of stale sweat and God knows what else. Part of his vision was obscured by a piece of material which hung from his forehead and wasn't helping him to understand his surroundings.

The corners of the dark eyes started to crease, their owner obviously smiling. "Hey, Billy!' He was taken aback at the sound of his name. He peered harder at the eyes. 'It is me, Irakli, your friend, no?'

Blimey, this was hard, Woons thought as his mind tried desperately to process what was happening to him. Where was he? Where had he been in the last twenty-four hours? Could he remember anything? He closed his eyes and tried to think. And immediately shot up from the pillow, almost delivering a Glasgow kiss to the man who was still leaning over him.

'Irakli?' Woons shouted. 'Irakli? Let me see you.' Some of it was coming back to him. He had been told that Irakli had left Kaspi, and probably the country. He had also been told by the waiter at the restaurant that he had never heard of Irakli which Woons had found puzzling at the time. 'Irakli? My friend Irakli?' he spluttered.

The man sat back on his haunches. 'It is me, Billy!' He pulled his phone out of a pocket in his jeans and shone the torch onto his face. Woons immediately recognised the Georgian man he had known all these years, and held out his hand. They shook hands and then Woons scrambled to his feet.

'Woah!' he exclaimed suddenly feeling extremely light-headed. In the dim light, he could make out that he was standing next to a table with some chairs around it so he promptly sat on one of them. Irakli moved to sit on the chair next to Woons, and two other men who he hadn't noticed before took the seats on the other side of the table.

'Grigol,' Irakli called over his shoulder. Almost at once, the young waiter appeared with a jug of water and some glasses. He also brought a bowl of steaming water and what looked like wipes of some sort. Woons' vision was still not quite back to normal so he couldn't be sure what they were. Irakli poured a glass of water and pushed it across the table to Woons. 'Drink!' he commanded. Woons hungrily guzzled the water down his throat, stopping for a moment to rinse it around his mouth to get rid of the foul bitterness of what he now recognised was the metallic taste of blood.

'We need to clean your face, Billy,' said Irakli, pulling the bowl of water towards him. 'You have been in crash and your nose broken. Nothing we can do for that but to clean off blood.' He dunked one of the wipes into the bowl of water and started to clean the area around Woons' nose. He then unwound a rather tatty-looking bandage from around Woons' head to reveal a nasty deep gash across his forehead. 'You have bad injury, Billy. We can only help to keep it clean. You must see doctor when you get home.' He pulled Woons' head towards him and started to clean the wound with the hot water.

Woons screwed up his face in pain as Irakli went about the business of dabbing away the detritus from the open wound. When he was satisfied that he could do no more, he dried Woons' forehead and applied some ointment to a large sticking plaster which he then placed across the wound. Woons sucked air in through his clenched teeth as the ointment stung the exposed nerve ends on his forehead. It was not very elegant but would have to do. 'You will wear black cap when you travel, Billy, which will provide cover, stop questions. Then you see doctor in England.'

Once Irakli had finished, he pushed the bowl away whereupon one of the men who had been sitting patiently on the other side of the table leaned across and proffered his hand. Irakli spoke by way of introduction. 'You remember Mr Tsiklauri, Billy?' Woons stared across the table at the man whose face was predominately in shadow. He had cursed this man on many, many occasions over the years but, now that he was sitting in front of him, he meekly accepted the handshake and sat back.

'Billy Woons!' the man said in a deep, gruff voice. 'We have known each other for many years, yes?' Woons nodded. 'And we have done some good business together, yes?' Woons nodded again, although each nod seemed to exacerbate the stinging pain he was feeling as the ointment went to work on his split forehead. 'But now you must forgive me,' Tsiklauri continued, 'because our operation is under serious threat from the Romanian scum who think that they control Eastern Europe and who are right now trying to take over our trafficking routes and businesses such as yours in UK. But they will not succeed!'

Tsiklauri paused and, in the dim light, Woons thought he could see a glistening in the old man's eyes. 'They have killed some of my most trusted friends – all sons of the Kaspi brothers. There is much hate in our town. And the bastards have been fucking with you guys and killing your women. This Lupescu, for many weeks we have been trying to get close enough to him so that we can kill him but he is very well guarded. Also, we have difficulty keeping track of where he is – he moves around like a panther and we do not have enough men to follow him everywhere and report his position.'

Woons interjected with a question which was at the forefront of his mind. 'How did you know I was coming to Kaspi when I hadn't been able to contact any of you?'

Tsiklauri looked across the table at Woons. 'Luckily, a brother at Georgian Airlines saw that you were on the passenger list. He contact Irakli so we send two men to airport to meet you. But when they get there, they see two other men talking to you and then taking you to car. They call Irakli. If this is the Romanians then they could take you to meet Lupescu, so Irakli told them to follow you. But the car then brings you here to the Palakhuri which we did not expect. But it was a clever thing because you would not be suspicious because we have always met here.'

Woons nodded, beginning to think that he had been played like a proverbial fiddle. Tsiklauri continued. 'We were watching but didn't know what to do. So, I sent Grigol to get you a drink. He was a very frightened young man and, if you asked him any questions, he was to say that he did not know me and Irakli. Then the other car came in so we decided to lock up the restaurant. We were hiding inside and watching you through the curtains. Then you went in the Romanian's car which caused us a problem as it took us time to get to our vehicle. Luckily, one of my men spotted the car leaving the restaurant and followed it until we were able to take over the chase. And it was all okay until we got to the port. Oh, my friend, that was a frustrating time. We didn't see you go into the gas station and it was only with luck that Irakli saw you going inside the yacht club. We could not get in there – they have the best security so we had to stay outside and wait.'

Woons was finding all this hard to believe. 'How the fuck did you know when I'd be leaving and which vehicle I'd be in?'

'Ah, my friend, our intelligence is good and we have people in Lupescu's organisation to help us. They all hate the Romanians for many reasons.' Tsiklauri looked pleased with himself. 'The girl who serve you drinks on the boat? She is one of our very best, how you say, agents? She keep us informed and give us phone number of the driver so that we can call and set up the ambush. We know Lupescu, he uses shit men who don't know nobody in his organisation. If you call one of his men and say it's Dimitri and Mr Lupescu told me to tell you to go somewhere, they would just go there. They wouldn't know if this Dimitri was good, bad, on their side or enemy. They would just do what they're told. So, we set them up and then we killed two of Lupescu's people which gave me a lot of satisfaction.'

Woons felt a shiver travel down his spine. These really were desperate men he was dealing with here and, but for the grace of God, etcetera etcetera! The room had gone quiet, everyone waiting for someone else to speak. Woons eventually broke the silence.

'Lupescu gave me the impression that Vashlili had been wasted. He also said that he had not been responsible for destroying three of my operations in the UK. He suggested that someone else was doing that so, on the assumption that your organisation has not been involved, should we assume that there is another band of brothers trying to take over?'

Tsiklauri leaned forward and placed his elbows on the table, the palms of his hands pointing upwards almost in an act of supplication. 'I know of Lupescu over many years. He is a good talker, he likes the nice things – boats, fast cars, girls, jewellery – but he doesn't know what's going on in his own back yard. My guess is that there is someone trashing your business who Lupescu thinks of as one of his own. But he doesn't know what damage his brother is doing. You guys have good English word for it – he has gone rogue!' Tsiklauri looked pleased with his knowledge of the English language. 'This man, he is creating fear so that he can get more protection money once Lupescu and his men have taken over. And Lupescu will never need to know because it will be a private deal. And, anyway, Lupescu would never dare to travel to the UK so he will only know what he is told.'

Woons wasn't quite sure that he believed what Tsiklauri was

saying but he let it go for the moment. He was more interested to see what Tsiklauri was going to do about the Romanians infiltrating his operation.

'We have a little – how you say? – local difficulty in Bulgaria but our people, they been with us a long time and are very loyal. We are sorting that, my friend. You need not worry.' Tsiklauri smiled, looking directly into Woons' eyes. 'We have also sent one of our very best men to your country. You will meet him soon. He is the most loyal of loyal brothers, and his name is Nikoloz Meshki. I will give you contact details when he gets there. I have also sent two of my best people to deal with the people who are causing you trouble. You will never meet them or even see them. They answer only to me, and their mission is to get rid of the Romanian scum.' In the dim light, it looked as if Tsiklauri's eyes were two fiery orbs staring deeply into Woons' soul, a feeling which he found most disturbing.

Tsiklauri suddenly looked at his watch. 'Now we must go. It is too dangerous to stay here. Lupescu might be stupid but he is not so stupid that he doesn't notice that none of his men have contacted him about delivering you to the airport. So, you must leave our country as soon as possible.'

The big man got up from his chair and moved behind Irakli, placing his large hands on the man's shoulders. 'Irakli here will take you to Tbilisi. It is too dangerous for you to be on the direct flight to London. The Romanian scum will be looking out for you. So, we have arranged for you to be on an early flight to Riga in Latvia. Here, you will change onto a flight to London. My people will look after you all the way so don't worry when someone makes contact with you at Riga and guides you through the airport. It is all part of our service,

Billy. You are one of our brothers!'

The two men regarded each other across the table, a frisson of understanding lighting the void between them although Woons wasn't quite sure that he actually wanted to be one of the brothers. He was dog-tired but not so tired that he didn't pick up the vibes which Tsiklauri was transmitting across the stygian gloom of the restaurant. Despite everything, he was a man of principle who looked after his people and, right now, Woons was glad to be considered one of Tsiklauri's people.

At Irakli's beckoning, Woons rose from the table and made his way unsteadily towards the door, following Irakli out of the restaurant. Once on the verandah, Tsiklauri turned to Woons and gave him a huge bear hug. 'I have to leave you now, my friend,' he whispered. 'Contact me when you are back in UK.' And, with that, he turned and walked back into the restaurant.

80

Wednesday 26 July

Spink pushed himself up from the cold stone floor and, after a good deal of trouble, he managed to twist his body so that he could now rest his back against the nearest wall. He had the mother and father of all headaches and his vision felt as if it was blurred even though he couldn't see much in the darkness. A shaft of light appeared to be coming from under a door but this was well above his eyeline. So, perhaps he was in the cellar he had peered into earlier in which case there would be a set of steps in front of him.

Had he been pushed down these steps? He quickly checked to make sure that all his joints were in working order. Apart from a few tender spots which would no doubt sprout deep crimson bruises in the next day or so, he seemed to be in one piece apart from the throbbing pain in the side of his head which was now accompanied by a buzzing in his ears. He reached up and felt the side of his head, his fingers scraping along a crusty ridge of dried blood where the skin had been broken. But he hadn't been tied up, gagged or hooded which made him wonder what his captors had in mind for him.

He carried out a quick reconnaissance of his pockets and was not surprised to find that he was without his phone. He had no doubt dropped it when that bastard had smacked him on the head so that was that. Thank God he had left the key on the wheel of the car although the value of that would only be known if the vehicle was still there when he got out of this hellhole. So, he sat there trying to figure out how he was going to make contact with Emma. How long had it been since he had left her outside the front of the building?

He was just thinking of trying to stand up when he heard a great commotion above him. There was shouting in a language he didn't understand and the occasional scream of a girl – or was it a woman? Was it Ems? Fuck! Had they got hold of her? How long had he been down here? Had she come looking for him because he hadn't contacted her? Fuck! What a mess!

As the shouting and screaming got closer, Spink saw shadows dancing across the shaft of light coming from under the door. All of a sudden, the door flew open and a body was unceremoniously propelled into the cellar, tumbling down the steps in front of him, a yelp and a squeal as flesh and bone came into contact with the unrelenting hardness of the cold stone floor. The door was slammed shut, and Spink could hear a key turning in the lock. Pushing his hands against the wall, he gently got to his feet and stood for a minute trying to regain his balance. He took a couple of paces in the direction of where he thought the steps were and then crouched down, patting the ground in front of him with his hands. Eventually, his hands brushed what felt like a leg so he edged closer feeling up the leg towards the hip joint. He immediately got a gentle whiff of a cologne that Emma often wore so he sat back on his haunches.

'Ems? Is that you?' he finally whispered. There was no immediate response so he remained where he was, wondering what their options were for getting out of here. He was also worried that any thought of escape might be hindered if Emma had any broken bones as a result of her fall down the steps.

After a while, he felt a little hand touching his knee, and a small voice came out of the darkness. 'Tricky? Is that you? Are you here an' all?' Emma groaned as she pushed herself into a sitting position. Spink caught sight of her outline in the meagre light which was trickling in from under the door.

'Sorry, Tricky,' she said, her voice barely audible even in the all-pervading silence. 'When I hadn't heard from you for so long, I decided to come into the house to see if you were in any trouble. They picked me up at the door, slapped me about a bit and then shoved me in here. I'll get over it – nothing broken I don't think. How long you been here?'

Spink quickly told her about his discovery of the girls and the grotesque sight of Cassandra before he was struck on the head and woke up in the cellar. 'Oh my God!' Emma exclaimed. 'How could they do that to Cassie? The bastards! They're fucking animals! What the fuck are we dealing with here, Tricky?'

That was what Spink was starting to wonder, but he kept his thoughts to himself. 'They must have taken my phone when they whacked me on the head,' he said instead. 'Or perhaps I just dropped it. Anyway, it's not in any of my pockets so it's gone,' he continued dejectedly.

'They took mine as well,' said Emma, 'but I think I might know a way of getting out of here if we're in the cellar I think we're in. There are two cellars in the house – one at the back and one at the front of the house. Cassie used the one at the back for small scale BDSM and the one at the front was simply used as a store room. I can't smell any of the BDSM stuff in here so I have to assume that we are at the front of the house. In which case...'

She started to move, every muscle and joint in her body screaming out in pain. 'Oh my God! I can hardly move!' she exclaimed. 'Here, help me up, Tricky!'

Spink helped her up into a sitting position as best he could but he was still feeling very dizzy and almost lost his balance. After a few minutes, they helped each other to stand up, and then stumbled around in the dark trying to find a flat wall so that they could lean against it. Meanwhile, Emma was trying desperately to get her bearings in a store room she had visited perhaps once before. She eventually found her way to the wall beside the steps and, dragging Spink across the uneven floor behind her, she followed it around the cellar area tapping her knuckles on the surface as she went. Spink sheepishly held her other hand but, in the circumstances, he had little option if they were to get out of there. Soon, the sound of the tapping changed to a hollow note and they realised that she was knocking on wood. Emma immediately stopped moving. Spink cannoned into her back. 'Sorry!' he whispered.

'If we're where I think we are, this is Cassie's secret door!' Emma sounded breathless. 'Now all we have to do is try to open the damned thing!' Emma exclaimed as she continued tapping and feeling around the black area in front of her. Spink stood behind her so as not to get in the way. 'Somewhere there's a latch and a couple of bolts.' Another pause, more groping in the dark. 'Here we are. One bolt. Let's see if it'll slide back.'

Spink was holding his breath in anticipation of getting out of the cellar, but he was not at all sure what they would find once they were outside. He also hadn't got a plan of what they should do once they were out. The men who had taken over the house and butchered Cassandra would no doubt come for him and Emma very soon so it was probably best to get as far away as they could and as quickly as possible. It would take him a few hours to get some firepower together before returning to the house by which time it was more than likely to be empty. But that was about the only option if they wanted to stay alive and take the fight to these murderous bastards.

With all these thoughts spinning around in his head, he was mightily relieved when Emma eventually managed to pull both bolts back. She quickly depressed the latch and he felt a zephyr of cool air filter into the cellar as Emma pushed the door outwards.

'This should be to the side of the house and in front of the wall if I remember rightly,' she said as she pulled aside a curtain of ivy which Cassandra had grown to cover the secret entrance. She stepped out on to an area of lawn. The moon was already up and almost full so there was reasonable visibility which was just as well as it meant that they both avoided falling over a garden bench which had been placed almost directly in front of the door. Hugging the exterior wall, they moved towards the front of the house. Spink inched his head around the corner so that he could take a look at the front entrance, and then immediately withdrew back behind the wall.

'Shit!' exclaimed Spink. 'They're loading the van!' Emma leaned past him so that she could see round to the front of the house. In the dim light by the front door, she counted a line of five girls all with sacks over their heads being unceremoniously manhandled into the back of the van by two huge men. One girl who seemed to be dawdling was actually scooped up by one of the men and hurled into the van. Their screams were muffled by a combination of the head sacks and the no doubt liberal use of duct tape.

'They're going to be looking for us soon,' Spink observed, 'and we need to follow that van!' There was now a sense of urgency, even though he still felt decidedly groggy. 'Get that door shut,' he instructed Emma,' and then we'll see if we can get back to the car under cover of these woods.' He pointed to the darkness to their left. Emma scurried back to the cellar door and pushed it shut, making sure the latch was engaged. She then returned to Spink's side. They both ducked down and then set out across the lawn and into the trees which surrounded most of the property.

Once they had reached the relative safety of the treeline, they made their way as best they could through the darkness, twigs occasionally snapping, the sound no doubt being carried on the breeze. But Spink was keeping an eye on proceedings at the front of the house, and was pleased to see that they didn't seem to have caught anyone's attention so far. Very soon they reached a point where they were adjacent to the BMW which was still off the track and out of sight of the house. The temptation was to get in, start the engine and wait for the van to drive off but that was likely to draw unwanted attention so they decided to wait until the van left.

They didn't have to wait long. Spink heard the sound of doors being slammed and, through a gap in the branches, he could see the beam of headlights starting to move. Eventually, the van came into view and passed them on its way down the track to Rogers Rough Road. He let it get around the next bend in the track and then pulled Emma through the undergrowth to the car. Spink retrieved the key from its hiding place, and they jumped in. He was relieved when the engine started first time having previously feared that someone might have immobilised it whilst they had been incarcerated in the cellar. He decided not to switch the headlights on so he negotiated his way back on to the track by the ambient light from the almost-full moon and gingerly drove down to the next bend. In the distance, he could see the van's brake lights as the driver negotiated the rough track, getting ever closer to the road.

Spink hung back, trying to stay out of sight but desperate to see which way the van turned at the bottom of the track. He watched as the rear lights of the van danced down the track before the brakes were applied whereupon the van suddenly lurched to the left and disappeared. He now picked up a bit of speed down the track and turned the sidelights on as he got closer to the entrance to the field, lurching from one pothole to the next. Eventually, he arrived at the tarmacked road where he spun the wheel to the left and set off in pursuit of the van. He was still only using the sidelights but soon decided to turn the headlights on as he really couldn't make out the road. The heavy tree cover was obviously blocking out all the moonlight. He just hoped that he would find it easier to judge when to hold back and when to accelerate once he had picked up the van's lights through the trees in front of him. But there was no sign of it yet so he increased his speed a fraction.

Around the next bend, they passed a red Toyota Aygo which looked as if it had spun off the road and crashed into the trees. Spink was concentrating so hard on following the road that he almost didn't register the significance of the little red car. But then an alarm bell suddenly went off in his head. A red Toyota Aygo. A poxy red Toyota Aygo. He instinctively hit the brakes. The BMW immediately slowed and Spink leaned forward in his seat as the car rounded the next bend in the road. But he was too late. The van had come to a halt in front of the BMW and now covered the width of the road. Spink and Emma were almost blinded by their own headlights which reflected back at them off the shiny doors of the van. 'Shit!' he cursed under his breath. His mind was racing, trying to work out the best option for getting the hell out of there. But he was still feeling the effects of the knockout blow which meant that he lost vital seconds before deciding to just ram the gearstick into reverse and try to get back round the last bend. He was conscious of Emma looking anxiously across at him, willing him to do something, anything to get them out of this place. But, as he finally managed to slide the gear stick into reverse, one of the doors of the van swung open.

The noise of the machine pistol split the night air as it dispensed instant death in a five second burst. The occupants of the BMW jumped about in their seats as each slug of metal coursed through their fragile bodies, all life being extinguished in a nanosecond. By the time the doors of the van had been secured shut, and the van had continued on its way, the BMW looked as if it was ready for the crusher's yard – its occupants' souls long since departed this life.

In the quietness that followed, a man dressed head to toe in black emerged from the Toyota. By the light of a torch attached to his headband, he made his way to the stricken BMW. Uncapping a plastic green container, he poured liquid all over the car and its occupants until there was not a drop left. He then turned and took up position a few feet behind the car and tossed a lighted rag towards it. He was always fascinated by the whooshing sound petrol made when it was ignited, and he was not disappointed with the whoosh as the BMW went up in flames. He quickly retreated to the Toyota and managed to reverse it out of the trees. He was well on his way down the narrow road before the BMW's petrol tank went up. The flames he could see in his rear-view mirror were spectacular. He smiled at a job well done!

81

Wednesday 26 July

Selitto and the two young DCs were sitting at their work-stations when Grace Kendall breezed back into the MIR. 'Well, that was an interesting exercise,' she said as she retook her seat at the desk in front of the white boards. They each turned to face her. 'Information we have is that the white van is running on false plates – the registration is a work of pure fiction, not even stolen or taken off a scrapped vehicle. But the BMW is using the registration number of a car which was scrapped in 2009 under the Government's scrappage scheme. The Lexus is, however, taxed and insured. It's registered to a Mr William Woons.' The detectives looked blankly at each other. The name didn't ring any bells with any of them. 'The address given is over in the Penshurst area. Sounds like it's either at a farm or on some agricultural farm land. You know how some of these farmers are pleased to rent off areas of their land just to get some extra income when the future for farming's so uncertain.'

They all nodded then lapsed into a further period of silence with everyone deep in thought about what to do with the information they had just uncovered and, indeed, whether it was at all relevant to their case. DC Stuart Crosby was first to break the silence.

'Perhaps we should pay Mr Woons a visit later this morning to see what he was doing up Furnace Lane last Thursday. Can't do any harm. But, Grace, my question is – what are the chances of being able to find out if any of these vehicles had ever been in the locations around either the Sheet Hill or the

Hildenborough houses?'

All eyes were on DS Grace Kendall as she scrolled through various pages of data on her computer, and eventually turned her chair to face her colleagues. 'There's not much CCTV that's going to help us, I'm afraid, and there seems to be even less ANPR coverage. So, I'd say that we've pretty much got zero chance. We've been extremely lucky to pick these vehicles up on a camera in Horsmonden. But what we've seen doesn't prove that the BMW and the Lexus have been involved in any criminal activity – apart from the false number plates on the BMW. Our information also doesn't prove that they were visiting the house. Personally, I think the van is a much more interesting prospect even if it has got rogue registration plates which may well have been changed by now! Even so, we might as well get an APB out for it as soon as we can just in case they try one more journey on the old plates.'

She turned back to her screen just as there was a rap on the door to the office. They all looked at each other, Crosby also looking at his watch and being astonished to see that it was getting on for 01.00 a.m. Jennings got up and opened the door. She immediately recognised WPC Yolanda Sugden who had joined the force at much the same time as Jennings, and they had both been fresh-faced trainees together. Yolanda had, however, soon left to start a family, and had only recently returned from her second period of maternity leave.

'Hello, Yolanda,' she said by way of a greeting. 'Come in! Come in!'

WPC Sugden rather sheepishly stepped into the MIR, probably not expecting to see quite so many people at this time of the night. 'Thanks,' she said as she stood before them.

'Hey, guys, this is Yolanda Sugden,' Jennings said by way of introduction. 'She and I joined up at around the same time and trained together. Then we rather went our separate ways, didn't we Yolanda.' Sugden nodded, the hint of a red embarrassment line creeping up her neck. 'How are the family, anyway?'

'Oh, they're fine thank you, now that we've got a routine going. Means I can work nights so I'm currently splitting my time working on the Desk and I'm also helping out in the Control Room tonight. Anyway, the reason I came up is that I thought you might be interested in an incident out to the east of Lamberhurst. We have a report of a car on fire on Roger's Rough Road, a narrow lane which links Kilndown with Bedgebury. KFR are on the scene after a motorist called it in. Information we have at the moment is that two bodies have been found in the car still with their seat belts on. The car's a complete wreck. Report says that it is, or was, a BMW.'

Four pairs of eyebrows rose towards the ceiling, and the detectives gave each other quizzical looks.

'Presumably the road's closed?' It was more of a statement from Selitto. 'In which case, which end should we approach it from?'

WPC Sugden said that she didn't have that information yet but would immediately try to find out if it was their intention to visit the site straightaway. She turned and left the room while Jennings re-took her seat.

'A BMW? Well, now, that really would be a coincidence!' said Kendall, laughing and turning back to look at her screen.

Ted Selitto was initially keen to take a look at the scene in Kilndown but was eventually persuaded to leave it until the morning. The others were now feeling the oncoming rush of tiredness after they had put in something like an 18-hour shift. So, they all decided to call it a day – or a night, as Crosby joked – and gathered up their papers. Empty coffee cups were jettisoned into the recycling bin, and they were just preparing to leave the office when a somewhat breathless WPC Sugden reappeared in the doorway.

'Sorry to take so long,' she said, apologetically, 'but I've spoken to KFR and they say that you should approach from Bedgebury Cross. I've also been told that a CSI team has already been despatched from Maidstone on account of KFR's discovery that the vehicle appears to have been extensively damaged by gunfire. The updated information I have is that the two occupants are most likely to have been shot dead before the fire took hold.' There was complete silence in the room.

82

Wednesday 26 July

They drove back to Tbilisi in the pitch dark; with very few vehicles on the roads at this hour of the morning, they were able to eat up the kilometres in quick time. Woons sat in the back of the SUV with Irakli while two of Tsiklauri's henchmen sat up front. Woons was still feeling the effects of the knock-out drops he had been given at the ambush, and drifted in and out of sleep as the journey went on. No one spoke a word, each man left with his own thoughts.

Eventually, they arrived on the outskirts of Tbilisi and made their way around the ring road to the airport complex which lies to the south-east of the city. Eschewing the signs directing traffic into the terminal buildings, the SUV made its way around the perimeter of the airfield to the cargo area.

The SUV passed through the security gate with the minimum of fuss and came to a halt amongst low loaders and other assorted transportation vehicles in the cargo area. Irakli got out of the SUV and motioned for Woons to follow him. They were soon met by two men who Irakli embraced before turning to Woons. 'These guys are my friends. They look after you and get you on aircraft. When you get to Riga, go through passport check as normal and get into arrivals hall. One of our people will meet you and take you to London flight. They will make contact with you so you just wait by exit door from customs. Just so there is no mistake, they will ask you name of my son. He is called Aleksandre so you must remember that. You have one and half hour in Riga airport, and arrive in London around nine o'clock this morning. That is okay?'

All Woons could do was nod. His head was swimming. 'Aleksandre,' he repeated. 'Okay! I've got that. So, we say good-bye now?'

'Yes,' Irakli replied. 'You go now with my friends. Here is your bag.' He passed the holdall to Woons and then embraced him. Standing back, he looked Woons up and down before gripping both his arms. 'Take care, my friend. We will be in contact to help you. Have a good flight!' Irakli eventually let go of his arms and joined the two men as they all got back into the SUV. They drove away back towards the airport perimeter, Woons watching until the lights disappeared. He then turned to the two men he had been left with. One of them produced a bright yellow high viz jacket, a black cap and a pair of head-phones which they indicated Woons should immediately put on. They sat Woons between them in the cabin area of a luggage truck which one of them then drove out onto the airfield apron.

Soon they were motoring towards a brightly coloured aircraft which was attached to one of the airbridges linking it with the departures lounge. Woons noted that the name of the airline, Air Baltic, was emblazoned on the engine casing, and that the words 'Airbus 220-300' were painted on the fuselage to the rear of the aft passenger door.

The luggage truck pulled up alongside the aircraft and the men signalled that Woons should follow them. They ducked round the tailplane of the Airbus and then sprinted up the steps which led to the rear passenger door. At the top of the steps, they were met by another of the ground crew, a rather attrac-tive but officious-sounding woman clutching a clipboard and barking instructions to one of the cabin crew. Woons followed and, once he was through the door and into the aircraft, one of the men removed the high viz jacket and headphones. The man then indicated that Woons should keep the black cap pulled down over the bandage on his forehead. He also thrust the holdall into Woons' hands which he had inadvertently left in the luggage truck. The woman pointed Woons to a window seat in the very last row of the cabin and indicated that he was to sit there. He sat down as he was told and then turned to take a look out of the window just in time to see the two men and the woman reach the bottom of the steps and turn away in the direction of the luggage truck. He turned back to find that the cabin crew were now in the process of welcoming the rest of the passengers aboard the aircraft.

As the seats began to fill up, Woons paid little attention to the short stocky man who slid into the window seat across the aisle in the row in front of him. In fact, Woons paid very little attention to anything. He was so exhausted that even the seats on the Latvian aircraft suddenly felt comfortable. As the aircraft taxied out to the runway, Woons' eyes started to droop and, by the time they were in the climb, Woons was fast asleep.

83

Wednesday 26 July

The flight to Riga took nearly three-and-a-half hours, and landed at around 07.00 a.m. local time. As he had been sitting at the back of the aircraft, Woons had to wait patiently to disembark. What time had they told him his next flight was due to take off? Eight something, he thought. Should have time to get to the London flight.

He made his way through passport control without any problem, the Immigration Officer smiling at him and wishing him a 'nice day' in broken English. There was the usual melee of people in the luggage reclaim area but Woons just walked on into what he assumed was the customs area before passing through a set of frosted glass doors and into a compact and airy Arrivals Hall. There was the customary line up of meeters and greeters, some with crudely fashioned name boards, some just waiting with faces full of excited anticipation. He instinctively turned left and walked along the line of people until it petered out and he was more or less alone. God, he could do with a strong cup of coffee right now.

He was just eying up one of the café bars across the Arrivals Hall when he felt a hand on his right elbow. He looked round and found he was looking into the eyes of a young woman with dip-dyed flattish brown hair gathered in a hair claw at the back of her head. She looked up at him with mesmerising dark eyes, the corners of her full lips turned upwards in an engaging and welcoming smile.

Without any introduction, she asked her question. 'Tell me

name of Irakli's son.'

Woons stared down at her. 'He is called Aleksandre,' he stammered. He had repeated the name to himself on a number of occasions since he had said goodbye to Irakli just to make sure that he got it right when he got to Riga.

'Good! Good!' the young woman exclaimed moving round so that she was now facing him. She held out her right hand. 'Welcome to Riga, Mr Woons. My name is Eleonora Smirnova.'

For once in his life, Woons was completely speechless. He stared at the young woman, open-mouthed as he shook her hand. He just about managed to mumble a 'hello' under his breath. He was immediately struck by Eleonora's beauty and the bright innocence she exuded. He was also finding it hard to believe that she was in the pay of an international gangster like Tsiklauri. Surely there were better opportunities both inside and outside Latvia for someone like Eleonora? He tried to pull himself together but he couldn't take his eyes off her.

'We don't have much time, Mr Woons,' Eleonora continued, not seeming to be phased by Woons' catatonic state. 'I have to take you to London flight. It will take us ten minutes to walk there. Do you want coffee now?' She had obviously noted that he had been eyeing up the café bar. Woons nodded. 'Come!' she commanded as she set off across the concourse to the café where she ordered two coffees, and then guided Woons to a quiet table away from a group of travellers who were tucking into plates of food while tapping away at mobile phones. She sat on a banquette against the wall, keeping an eye on the comings and goings in the bar area. She rested her arms on the table, her phone cupped between her hands, her thumbs urgently tapping out a text message which, he presumed, would be to let someone know that the pick-up had been a success. Keeping her eyes on the phone, she absent-mindedly unclipped the hair claw and allowed her hair to cascade over her shoulders.

Sitting directly opposite Eleonora, Woons watched her every move. He watched her eyes which were fixed on her phone as her fingers sped around its tiny screen. He was intoxicated with the heady mixture of beauty and innocence which he saw before him. Her manicured hands gave the impression of someone who took pride in their appearance, and her fresh complexion was accentuated by a dusting of rouge on both cheeks. While texting, she occasionally looked up at him with wide hazel eyes under long dark eyelashes. Her smile was warm and inviting. She palmed a strand of hair behind her right ear, and went back to her texting.

A surge of self-consciousness suddenly enveloped Woons. What on earth must he look like? He realised that he hadn't seen his reflection in a mirror since the ambush and, whilst he could feel the bandage wrapped around his head, and knew that this was covered by the hat Irakli's men had given him, what must his face with its broken nose look like? No doubt the bruising was now coming out, and he pictured himself with purple wheals under his eyes and a bent nose. He instinctively reached up to gently touch his nose but recoiled as a searing pain shot across his face. So, he just sat back in his chair and watched the girl texting as if her life depended on it.

As he was sitting there, Woons allowed his thoughts to drift. He was fascinated by Eleonora, even though he had only met her a few short minutes ago. Her youthful innocence seemed to belie a self-assured, fiercely independent young woman with an inner strength which signalled that she was not to be messed with. Woons found this quite engaging as it reminded him a lot of himself in his youthful pomp and, in some ways, he was beginning to empathise with the girl – a feeling he did not recall having ever had before. Her approachability might well put others on their guard, he thought. In turn, this might be part of an elaborate plan to give away as little of her inner soul as possible when meeting strangers. Whilst he felt that she demanded his respect and would not be taken for just another silly college girl, he also concluded that she would not allow him to exploit her in the same way as he had coldly exploited other young girls for much of his life.

He continued to rest his arms on the table, hands cupped around the steaming mug of dark coffee, deep in thought. In fact, he was so far away in his own thoughts that he had not realised that Eleonora was now addressing him. On noticing a slightly quizzical look on her face, he came out of his reverie and concentrated on what she was saying.

Her English was pretty good, Woons thought, and she briefed him on what was going to happen once they left the café. He was already checked in for the Gatwick flight so all he had to do was turn up at the departure gate thirty minutes before the flight departed. She handed over a boarding pass and circled the seat number with a pen she had fished out of her back pack. The flight was on time and normally took about two hours forty-five. Arrival time should be around 10.00 a.m. UK time.

Woons listened intently to what she was telling him, watching her sensuous lips as she spoke to him. He desperately wanted this fleeting moment with her to last longer than the few minutes that they were destined to have together. He wanted to know if she had another job away from working for Tsiklauri? What was it like living in Riga? Had she been to the UK? How old was she for God's sake? What was her home life like? Did she have any boyfriends? Girlfriends? There was so much to learn about her.

As Eleonora carried on talking to him in her lilting Latvian accent, Woons was suddenly so overwhelmed by a tidal wave of emotions for this young woman that he instinctively reached out and grasped one of her hands. He leant forward in his seat, looking deeply into her beautiful eyes, seeing an overt kindness tinged with an aura of fear and aggression. For she was surely only a young woman with her whole life before her. What on earth was she doing here helping someone like Billy Woons escape through Riga Airport?

Eleonora looked slightly taken aback by the suddenness with which Woons had grabbed her hand, but she retained her composure. She again gave him a quizzical stare, her head slightly tilted, its angle posing an unspoken question. They remained like this for what to Woons seemed like an age but, in real time, was no more than four or five seconds.

Woons slowly released his grasp of Eleonora's hand. 'How old are you, Eleonora?' he asked in a faltering voice. He didn't want to offend her by asking the question, but he just had to know.

'I had my nineteenth birthday just one month past,' she said brightly without taking her eyes off him.

Woons let out a long sigh and drew his hands up to cover his face, elbows on the table. 'And who asked you to meet me here at the airport?' he asked, tentatively rubbing the front of his hat with both hands, almost afraid to hear her answer. Her eyes left his and roamed around the area of the bar behind him as if looking for the person who had sent her, eventually returning to gaze at him again.

'My grandfather told me to come to airport to meet British man,' she eventually replied. 'He gave me photo of you and 100 Euros. It's good money for me. I can buy clothes. I give some to my mom.'

Woons was struggling to hold his emotions together as wave after wave of regret started to wash over his brain. His emotions were becoming submerged with feelings for this girl. And she was just a girl, not much older than the girls he had exploited for so many years. The girls whose lives he had systematically ruined to the extent that they would never be able to lead normal lives. And then there were the girls whose lives had been brutally brought to an end in sickening and unimaginably horrific ways. Girls who also had grandfathers who would send them on errands for pocket money. Girls who liked clothes and home cooking. Girls who had fresh faces, bright eyes and lots of hope for their futures. Only for all those hopes to come to nought, dashed by the sickening greed of one man, Billy Woons, who had made a fortune living off their immoral earnings for years.

A frown spread across Eleonora's forehead as she noticed Woons' eyes glistening in the harsh overhead lighting in the café. 'Are you okay, sir?' she gently asked.

His eyes were now so misted up that the girl had become a bit blurred. He dragged the backs of his hands across his eyes to clear the moisture and then leaned forward in his chair, placing his hands on top of the small hands that had remained flat on the table throughout.

'My dear Eleonora,' he began, his voice barely audible above the background noise of coffee machines and the clattering of plates as the bar got busier. 'You will never know how much of a pleasure it has been to meet you.' He paused, again staring deeply into those dark eyes. 'Although you will never know what you have done for me in the short time we have known each other, I can assure you that our meeting like this has been a life-changing experience for me.' He let go of her hands and sat back in his chair, never once taking his eyes off her. 'I hope that you have a long and wonderful life, and that you get the chance to fulfil all your dreams. My only advice to you is to not run any more errands for your grandfather! There are better ways of earning money to buy clothes and have a happy life!'

Although Eleonora didn't appear to understand some of what Woons was saying to her, a smile started to spread across her face, her lush lips parting to reveal her beautiful white teeth. Woons noticed that there was a slight reddening of her cheeks as she eventually turned away to activate the clock on her phone.

'We have to go now,' she said, quickly returning her phone to her back pack and getting to her feet. She looked over Woons shoulder, and focused on an information screen above the bar. 'Your flight is on time so you must get to the gate now.' She stood, sentry-like, and waited for Woons to get up from his seat. He bent down and picked up his holdall before they both walked out of the bar. Eleonora steered him to the left and they began the long walk towards the departure gates. Nothing more was said as they threaded their way through the melee of other passengers, each locked in their own thoughts.

Eventually, the gate number loomed in the distance. Eleonora tapped Woons on the arm. 'This is where I have to leave you,' she said. Woons turned and looked at her. Instinctively, he reached out and pulled Eleonora to him in an all-embracing hug, his chin coming to rest on her shoulder, his senses luxuriating in a heady mix of her fresh complexion and the perfume of youth which was all-pervading.

Stepping back, he held her at arms' length. 'Thank you!' he said. 'You will truly never know what a difference you have made to my life.' He leant forward again and kissed her on both cheeks. 'Goodbye, Eleonora.' As he turned to walk away, he felt his eyes moistening up again, and he determined not to look back. Someone had once told him that you only looked back if you had an intention of returning. Woons had no intention of returning to Riga. So he walked on.

84

Wednesday 26 July

Ted Selitto was so pumped up by the speed with which the case was developing that he found it very difficult to sleep at all. After tossing and turning for a few hours, he got up, grabbed his gym kit out of the cupboard by the front door of his flat, and sped over to the Better Body gym opposite Bat & Ball railway station in Sevenoaks. He was just in time to find George, his occasional personal trainer, opening up at 05.30 a.m. on what was going to be a sunny morning. A quick fifty-minute workout followed by a hot shower and he was ready for whatever the day would throw at him.

The southbound A21 was quietish at that time in the morning so he arrived in the MIR before 07.00 a.m. and in plenty of time for the morning briefing. He was pleased to see that Sarah Hunter was already there, and she beckoned him over as soon as he had poked his head into the room.

'Morning, boss!' he said, placing his cup of coffee on the edge of Hunter's desk and wheeling a chair over from an adjacent workstation.

'What on earth's been going on over at Kilndown?' she hissed, keeping her voice low. 'I understand that you were here when the news came in. Why wasn't I told straightaway rather than having to find out via the Desk Sergeant on my way in this morning?'

Selitto was a bit taken aback with Hunter's tone of voice. She sounded genuinely annoyed that she had only just found out about the incident which had occurred whilst she had been asleep. Perhaps he should have called her but, he had reasoned, there wasn't much that either of them would have been able to do if the CSIs were already setting up. In any case, he felt that she should be getting some rest time – even if he wasn't.

'And what the fuck was going on here anyway?' She clearly hadn't finished, and Selitto was beginning to feel a bit uncomfortable. 'What on earth was Grace doing accessing information generated by two cameras which are on loan to Kent for testing? I've had Iversen in my ear already this morning because he's getting an ear-full himself from those in authority at Maidstone. God's sake, hadn't you all got homes to go to?'

Hunter finally turned her eyes from the screen, and Selitto could see a fire which was burning deep within her. 'Sorry, boss, we were just trying to move things on a bit,' he said with a hint of an apology. 'I happened to have seen these cameras out at Horsmonden, and Grace was able to access the pictures. At least it's given us a name of someone we could usefully go and see if only to exclude him from our enquiries. But we never thought that there would be problems with accessing the information. Why hadn't Maidstone restricted access to the cameras?'

Hunter swept her hair behind her head with both hands and fiddled with an elasticated band until she had got it into a ponytail. 'God knows!' She sounded increasingly irritated, eyes darting around the room as the others started gathering for the morning briefing. 'So, who's the person of interest anyway?'

Selitto told her about the three vehicles they had observed and the fact that the Lexus was the only one with current tax and insurance. The name William Woons didn't register anything with her, but she was interested in the fact that both his Lexus and a BMW had used that same junction late at night within a few minutes of each other.

'If that BMW is connected to the Lexus, then Mr Woons should be a person worth talking to at the earliest opportunity. But I'm not holding my breath!' She looked across at Selitto. 'Right! Let's get this show on the road! I'm going over to Kilndown and then probably to the mortuary so you take the briefing meeting. After the meeting, I want you and DC Pennant to go find Mr Woons and see what he's got to say for himself. If necessary, bring him down here and keep him until I get back. The others can get on with trying to find out more about our Mr Woons, and you can send one of them out to the house next to Mrs Johnson to see how the CSIs are getting on.'

'Right, boss! I'll keep you updated with any developments,' Selitto replied as Hunter logged herself off the computer and made her way out of the MIR.

On her way to Kilndown, Hunter answered a call from Iversen. At least he seemed to have calmed down since his previous call so she spent some time updating him on the information Selitto had given her. He appeared to be happy that they now had the name of someone who was at least alive, and agreed that they should get Woons interviewed as soon as possible.

'You'll have to get your Press hard hat on when you get there,' Iversen was telling her as she negotiated her way along the Lamberhurst bypass. 'They're out in force and asking lots of questions. If this links in to everything else that's been going on, then it will be a massive story so we're considering a major press conference either later today or tomorrow. In the meantime, try to keep the lid on it until we can take a more structured view of what we can tell them.' Whatever that means, thought

Hunter. Anyway, she got the gist of what he was saying.

Hunter had never been very good at dealing with the Press, and was often hassled into saying something she hadn't intended. Because of this, her preferred option was to say nothing but she knew that this didn't go down well with the top brass who seemed to think that the scribblers had a role to play in the crime-solving process. This non-relationship had been more difficult when she had first arrived in Kent but the regular reporters had slowly come to the realisation that they weren't going to get much out of DI Hunter so had concentrated on looking elsewhere for crumbs of information to fill acres of space in little-read newspapers. And, with the advent of rolling twenty-four-hour news on the internet, the ladies and gentlemen of the press were even more desperate for news so tended to exert additional pressure on the likes of Hunter. She knew that the only way to combat this was to be even more defensive – and so the game went on.

She exited the A21 onto Lady Oak Lane and then continued on past the Bedgebury Pinetum before slowing to pass a number of cars which were parked on the side of the road. Realising that Roger's Rough Road was up ahead, she started looking for somewhere to park and ended up about ten metres past its junction with Lady Oak Lane. She noticed that the entrance was sealed off with crime scene tape, and that a number of journos were milling around beside the other parked cars. She had a look in her mirror to see whether she recognised anyone, and then took a deep breath before climbing out of the car.

As she strode towards the crime scene tape fluttering in the breeze, a small group of journos broke up and came scampering over to her. She now recognised a couple of them but couldn't recall their names. Perhaps it would be better if she got to know their names so that she could at least address them directly rather than doing what she was doing now which was waving her arms around and saying that she had no comment to make at this juncture. She showed her warrant card to the uniformed PC who was guarding the entrance to the crime scene and ducked under the tape, glad to be in the relative safety of the leafy lane.

She walked on up the lane and soon came to the entrance to a field. A sturdy five-bar gate stood open, a track running away into the distance. It looked well used and there was a fair amount of mud from the track which had been freshly deposited on the road surface. She noticed that muddy tyre tracks led off in the direction towards the burnt-out car. She stood there for a moment, taking in the scene. She pulled her phone out and punched in a name.

'Elaine, it's DI Hunter,' she said as soon as DC Jennings answered. 'I want you and Azzar over here at Roger's Rough Road as soon as you can. Take the B2079 from the A21, past the Pinetum and then look out for my car – park there and come into the lane. If you start walking towards the crime scene you'll come to a muddy entrance to a field. I want you to take a look up the track which leads from the road. We're specifically looking for another of these houses. Report back as soon as you've had a look. And bring wellies!'

'Will do, ma'am,' Jennings replied, 'and thanks for the tip about the wellies!'

'Oh, and one other thing,' Hunter remembered, 'try not to talk to the bunch of journos who are camped out at the end of the lane.' She disconnected the call, pocketed the phone and continued towards the crime scene.

A cluster of response vehicles which had been there for some hours soon came into sight as she rounded the next bend, and she could see the CSI screens in the middle of the lane. Dr Toby Swartzman was leaning on the roof of his car speaking into his phone as she made her way towards him. He finished the call as soon as he caught sight of her.

'Morning, Sarah,' he said brightly. 'As they say, the bodies are piling up! At this rate, I'll have to put in for more staff!' As usual, his smile was infectious, and the two of them had often shared a joke in the cold light of the cutting room. But, on this occasion, Hunter was not up to it – she just wanted to get a handle on what had taken place. Swartzman seemed to get the message.

'So, what have we got, Toby?' she asked, still looking off up the lane towards the screens.

'Okay,' he began, also looking back towards the screens. 'We have a white male and a white female. Not sure about age yet but probably in their forties. Their bodies have been raked by gunfire so it's likely that death occurred as soon as the shooting started. Likely to have been killed right here as the bodies are still both strapped into the car. The male was the driver and one of his hands is still attached to the gear stick which could indicate that he was trying to execute some sort of manoeuvre when the shooting started. Cause of death is likely to be physical trauma caused by shots from an automatic weapon. Once I get them on the table, we'll likely find extensive damage to the internal organs and a number of broken bones. It's not a pretty sight but at least the fire seems to have sanitised the scene so that there is very little evidence of bleeding.

This could, of course, also be a further indicator that death was instantaneous.'

'Hmm! I'd better take a look,' Hunter replied. 'When are you moving the bodies?'

'CSIs are going to move the car as it is with the bodies in situ,' Swartzman reported, 'so that they can do some more analysis in the lab. That should be as soon as they can get the low-loader down here. Then they'll release the bodies so we should get them this afternoon if you want to send someone along.'

'Okay! I'll think about that,' Hunter said, starting to walk towards the screens. 'Who's CSI Manager this morning?'

'That'll be the lovely Beth with her two faithful lapdogs!' he replied, a smile from ear to ear. Hunter smiled back as best she could in the circumstances and then went off to take a look at the carnage hidden behind the screens.

85

Wednesday 26 July

'William Woons you say? Sorry, don't think I've ever heard of him round these parts!'

DS Selitto and DC Pennant were standing outside the front door to Threepenny Cottage, a lovely eighteenth century farmhouse situated at the end of a long lane leading into the agricultural hinterland around Penshurst. Its owner seemed to be Derek Rodgers who now stood before them, scratching his head and giving the impression that he was trying hard to recall if he could remember someone who had what sounded to him like a Chinese name.

Selitto couldn't help thinking that, if he put a couple of wheat sheaves behind his ears and a flat cap on his head, Mr Rodgers would be a shoo-in for *Last of the Summer Wine!* He had another attempt at jogging a memory which seemed to be stuck in first gear. 'Perhaps you've seen his car, Mr Rodgers. It's a Lexus. White one.'

More head-scratching. 'Nope, sorry about that Sergeant. I'm not really a car person myself but it sounds quite an upmarket vehicle so I'd have to say NO on the grounds that no one comes down here in anything smart.' Selitto noted that Rodgers made this statement whilst casting a glance towards the Megane parked on the drive. Bloody cheek, he thought.

'You see, Mr Rodgers,' Selitto began, thinking he'd have one more attempt to see if Rodgers knew anything at all, 'Mr Woons has registered his car – his Lexus – as being kept at Threepenny Cottage which seems to be your house. So, logically, we have concluded that you would either know Mr Woons personally or would have seen the Lexus which has been registered as being kept at this address.' He shot a sideways look at Pennant who had her arms folded, head at an angle, patience wearing thin, waiting for an answer.

Rodgers looked around him and then focused back on the police officers who stood in front of him. 'I'm really sorry but I don't know any Mr Woons and I've never seen a Nexus in these parts. Sorry!' He turned as if to go back into the house.

'Before you go, Mr Rodgers!' It was Pennant now trying her charm to see if they could at least get something out of this seemingly fruitless visit. 'Could we just have a quick look inside your garage over there?'

'Yeah, sure – be my guest!' Rodgers replied. 'I'll just get the keys.' And he scuttled off inside. Pennant looked at Selitto and hunched her shoulders as they exchanged blank looks. Selitto took a walk along the front of the house and peered down a passageway between the house and a wall which ran along the perimeter of the property. Over this wall were fields as far as the eye could see. He meandered back to the front door.

'Taking his time, isn't he?' Pennant commented. Selitto aimlessly looked at his watch, quite aware of Pennant's mounting impatience. It wasn't as if he had been timing Rodgers but it must have been three or four minutes since he had gone off to get the key. Maybe he had mislaid it. Probably hadn't been put back on its peg. Sort of thing Selitto himself would do. Give him a few more minutes. Pennant, however, wasn't having any of that. 'Come on, Sarge, where the fuck is he?'

Selitto gave in and stepped through the front door. 'Mr Rodgers!' he called out. There was a deathly silence only broken by the sound of an aircraft decelerating on its way into Gatwick Airport. 'Mr Rodgers!' A bit more forceful this time. 'Where are you, Mr Rodgers?' He took a couple of steps further into the house and found himself in a hallway with stairs leading up to the next floor and various doors leading to rooms on the ground floor. However, what caught his eye was the door at the end of the hall which was open and lead into the kitchen. Beyond that, he could see another door which led into the garden behind the house. This also stood open.

'Shit!' Selitto muttered under his breath, now increasing his pace so that he was across the hall and into the kitchen in a flash, Pennant close behind him. Just as they arrived at the door into the back garden, they could hear the throaty roar of a motorbike starting up and then quickly fading as the machine ate up the distance back to the main road. 'Bastard!'

Pennant started looking around the kitchen and, when she couldn't find any sign of a key or a bunch of keys, she retraced her steps to the front of the house. The garage was a stand-alone building with an up-and-over door. She tried the handle but it was definitely locked. She wandered round to the back of the structure, looking for another way in, and eventually found a door but it was also locked. She carried on round to the front of the garage where she met up with Selitto.

'There's a door on this side wall which could probably benefit from your size tens, Sarge!' She pointed Selitto to the far side of the garage. His first effort with the boot wasn't successful but, after another couple of hefty flat-footed kicks, the door submitted and they were in. After the bright sunshine outside, the light in the garage was distinctly gloomy but there was no mistaking the fact that a gleaming white Lexus stood centre stage in the large garage.

'Bingo!' Selitto turned to high-five Pennant as they stood on the threshold of the garage. 'Better not contaminate the scene in case there's evidence here,' he warned her. The detectives returned to the front of the house where the door still stood open.

'I think we'd better get a warrant for this place,' he said looking up at the gables hanging from the front of the building. 'CSIs will also need to take a look at the Lexus. I'll let DI Hunter know that we've got the car – but no sign of Mr Woons. Better get a couple of uniforms out to keep an eye on the place in case Mr Rodgers returns for his toothbrush!' Pennant smiled and walked off to make her calls.

Selitto plucked his phone from his shirt pocket and punched in Hunter's code. Neither he nor DC Pennant noticed what looked like a flashing light in the woods which encroached onto the driveway leading in from the main road. With branches gently swaying in the breeze, the sun kept reflecting off the lenses of the binoculars as Trigger Harding tried desperately to get to grips with what was going on.

86

Wednesday 26 July

Billy Woons had had something of a cathartic release on his Air Baltic flight from Riga to London Gatwick. To start with, he had been starving hungry and, as soon as the trolley appeared in the aisle, he had ordered a croissant with ham, cheese and pickled cucumber. Having bolted that down, he then ordered a Scandinavian style salmon sandwich and a packet of olives. A couple of small cans of coke had washed the food down nicely, and the onboard crew had been most attentive. In an idle moment, he wondered if any of them were known to Eleonora's grandfather or, indeed, to Tsiklauri's mob. Was he getting preferential treatment? Probably not as he'd still had to pay for his food. But the real saving grace had been that he was able to recharge his phone so he would be back in contact with the world as soon as he landed at Gatwick.

His mind had then turned to the events of the last couple of hours, and he had spent much of the flight staring aimlessly out of the window as the aircraft crossed over the southern tip of Sweden, on towards the Kiel Canal and the northern coast of the Netherlands. His brain was playing and replaying his meeting with the lovely Eleonora at Riga Airport. Her elegance, her poise, her beauty, her eyes – oh, those eyes! He was wallowing in emotional feelings for this young woman which he had never experienced before. The heady cocktail of youthful innocence and self-assured independence had blown his mind, and he craved more time with her. He needed to know how she lived her life, her innermost secrets, the emotions which drove her very existence, her plans for the future, her desires.

And he knew that the tension in his stomach which had been gnawing away at him ever since he set eyes on Eleonora was a sign of the upheaval which their meeting had created within the deepest recesses of his soul. Although he kept trying to banish the thought from his mind, he couldn't help feeling a rising tide of guilt over the way in which he had selfishly exploited girls just like Eleonora. He had systematically ruined their lives and, in some cases, he had been the catalyst for the deaths of young girls before they had even had a chance to blossom into young women. He had lived off the riches which he had effectively plundered from these poor, defenceless human beings. They had once had the same hopes and aspirations as Eleonora before all chance of a normal life had been dashed on the jagged rocks of Woons's exploitative greed. His eyes had misted over, and he had turned even further into the window so that no one would see the glistening tears which he allowed to flow freely down his face.

He couldn't go on. He couldn't damage any more lives. In the very briefest of meetings, Eleonora had made him realise the value of life to a young woman. He found that he had respect for her, a respect which he had never had for any young woman before. What had he done to all those girls? What was he still doing? No, this couldn't go on. He had to get out of it. Suddenly, he didn't care what Tsiklauri and Irakli and all their crowd could do for him in the face of a take-over bid from a bunch of Romanian thugs. He was out of it! Away! Gone!

The aircraft started its descent when they were still well out in the North Sea. Woons had been planning what he needed to do as soon as he hit UK soil, his mind working overtime to evaluate all his options as the coastline came into view. He recognised Margate and Broadstairs as East Kent rushed by at around 12,000 feet. He then spotted Tunbridge Wells as the aircraft continued its descent, and he was sure that he had passed over Penshurst Place before the seat belt signs came on and everyone braced themselves for the landing at Gatwick.

Once the aircraft had come to a halt and the engines had been switched off, Woons reached for his phone and switched it on. He entered his pin number and then waited. Phones around him were all either pinging or ringing as his fellow passengers were immediately connected to the UK's mobile networks. His own phone eventually started pinging with a barrage of text and voicemail messages. He listened to the voicemail messages as he shuffled up the aisle to the front of the aircraft then onto the airbridge and into the South Terminal. By the time he was in the terminal itself, he took himself to one side and started to thumb through the text messages.

What on earth was going on? Most of his incoming messages had been from Harding who had sounded progressively more desperate and deranged as he implored Woons to get in touch with him. 'What the fuck's going on?' Woons whispered to himself. Looking up, he noticed that the last of the passengers from the Riga flight had disappeared into the distance. Woons never liked standing alone anywhere in an airport with its wall-to-wall CCTV coverage as he knew that a solitary person standing anywhere within the vast building would stick out like a sore thumb to any over-zealous operator. So, he decided to get to the Arrivals Hall before stopping to make any calls.

Cursing and swearing at the automated passport control

system, he finally managed to get through the glass doors. Why did it always take so fucking long to get into his own country when he seemed to be able to swan in and out of other countries with very little trouble. He was still chuntering to himself as he walked into the baggage reclaim area, through the 'Nothing to Declare' channel and out into the terminal building. He passed an endless throng of people from all walks of life and, by the look of it, from many different nationalities – each person with the sole purpose of meeting someone else. There was an air of expectancy, a low buzz of excitement.

Woons knew there was no one to meet him because no one knew he was arriving so he found a quiet corner to the side of one of the car hire desks and punched Harding's details into his phone.

'Trig!' he barked when the call was answered. 'What the fuck's going on?' Looking up, he realised that a small group of tourists had come to a halt a few metres from him and were now staring quizzically in his direction. Woons turned away from them and lowered his voice. 'You still there?' he wheezed into the phone, thinking that Harding had cut him off.

'Yes! Yes, Billy, still here!' came the breathless reply. 'You back at Gatwick now?' A sense of urgency in his voice.

'Yeah! Waiting for you!' Woons snapped. 'So, where the hell are you?' He was so annoyed that Harding wasn't there to meet him that he had completely forgotten that his original schedule had him landing at 8.00 p.m. that evening.

'Billy! Listen to me!' Woons could detect a sense of urgency in Harding's voice which was unusual so he clamped the phone even closer to his ear. And then Harding told him that Spink and Emma were probably dead – he'd heard that a BMW with one male and one female on board had been found burnt out near Kilndown during the night. He didn't know for certain that it was them, but he knew that they had been going to visit Cassandra's house in the BMW so he'd put two and two together. The colour was draining from Woons' face as Harding related this news to him. He was utterly distraught at the thought that Emma might have lost her life on his account, that his mate Tricky would no longer be at his side taking care of problems. And little Lucy would be growing up without the mother who had loved her and cared for her as doting mothers do.

'And that's not all, Billy,' Harding continued, 'the filth have found the Lexus – God knows how but they turned up on old man Rodgers' doorstep and found it in the garage after the old boy did a bunk on his bike. Can't be long until they get to the office and then we'll be in the real shit! I've now got the Merc and just changed course so that I can come and get you at the airport. Should be there in about fifteen minutes.'

For once in his life, Woons was truly lost for words – he simply couldn't think of anything to say in reply to the news Harding had just given him. His body was numb, his feet felt like lead weights, his brain was sinking in the quicksand of despair. He looked up just as a couple of heavily armed airport security officers moved across his line of vision. This suddenly jerked him back into the here and now. If they'd found his car, they must be looking for him. Shit! He turned his back on the officers and spoke urgently into the phone, making arrangements for meeting Harding when he got to the airport and what they would do then. He was well aware that, once the security people got a name and description these days, they would be on high alert. So, his priority now was to get out of the terminal building immediately and try to keep clear of the CCTV although he knew that that would be a big ask in a place like Gatwick Airport.

His rendezvous place of choice was outside the Hilton Hotel at the South Terminal so he made his way through the car park and across the link bridge to the hotel. Walking through the spacious reception area, he took the escalator to the ground floor and exited the hotel through the revolving doors. Harding was there in a couple of minutes, and they drove out of the hotel car park and off towards the M23, Woons hunkering down in the back seat, his black cap pulled low over his face.

87

Wednesday 26 July

DS Grace Kendall put the phone down, and blew her cheeks out, trying to get rid of some of the tension which she felt in her facial muscles after what had seemed like hours on the phone. But it had been worth it, and she was keen to get hold of Sarah Hunter to give her the news. She got up from her desk, stretched her back and walked down to the kitchen area. A few minutes later, a strong mug of coffee sitting on the desk in front of her, she dialled up the DI's number. Hunter answered on the second ring.

'Morning, Grace.' Hunter sounded distracted so Kendall decided to do without the chit chat that they normally indulged in on the phone.

'Sorry, Sarah, am I interrupting? Are you okay to speak?' Kendall asked. She knew that Hunter would be very interested in the information she had but wanted to make sure that she was in a position to take it on board as time was now of the essence.

'No, you're fine Grace,' Hunter replied. 'I'm just out at Kilndown looking at the victims of our double shooting. Not very pleasant, and we'll know more when they get them on the table but, from where I'm standing, it looks a hell of a lot like an execution. Anyway, enough about me – what you got?'

'Well, I've been on to a couple of contacts in the Home Office who can tap into the Border Force, and I might have some intel on William Woons who was mentioned in this morning's briefing as potentially being a person of interest.'

Kendall flipped the pages on her notepad and got to the notes she had made during one of her earlier telephone conversations. 'But, before that, we got confirmation that this man Woons has a record for theft. In his early life, he served a few minor sentences for burglary until one of the Judiciary got tough with him and stuck him in Maidstone for a couple of years. No one's ever heard of him since!'

'Okay, that's good background, Grace,' Hunter interjected. 'So, there's something more recent we should be interested in?'

'Yep,' Kendall replied. 'As I said, my guy at the Home Office decided to push his name across the bows of a mate of his in the Border Force, and it seems that Mr Woons has been travelling. He left Gatwick on Monday night and flew Georgian Airways to Tbilisi in Georgia. He then arrived back at Gatwick this morning on an Air Baltic flight from Riga in Latvia. I did ask them to keep an eye out for him at the airport but it was probably far too late as he would no doubt have got out of Gatwick as quickly as he could. I also found out that Mr Woons seems to be fond of travelling to Tbilisi although this seems to have been his first trip for a while. The return from Riga is, however, a first and is clearly unexplainable based on our current information.'

'Good work, Grace,' Hunter replied. 'Not sure what that's telling us but I've no doubt that it is significant. We'll have to get on with a search for Mr Woons. Anything else?'

'Only that Woons has been the only name on the DVLA records for the Lexus which DS Selitto has found so it's all above board,' Kendall reported. 'But I've been unable to establish who owns Threepenny Cottage yet. Land Registry are being a bit slow today. And I'm hoping to have something on that

Peter Dangerfield later. Remember him?'

'Sure do, although he's slipped down the list of people of importance in my mind,' Hunter confessed. 'But keep on him – I just have a feeling!' They chatted for a bit longer before she cut the call. Almost immediately, her phone buzzed into life and, seeing that it was DC Mishraz, she swiped the screen to take the call.

'Hello, ma'am,' he began. 'We took the track which you mentioned and we're now standing outside a large house with what looks like a sophisticated entry system. No sign of anyone. Elaine's had a look round the side but all seems very quiet – no vehicles.'

A tingle of excitement made its way down Hunter's spine. Had they just found another of these houses? 'Okay, hang on there,' she replied, 'I'm just down the lane by the wrecked BMW so I'll meet you at the house. Does it look as if we'll be able to get in?'

'That's probably affirmative,' Mishraz responded, 'as the door doesn't look as if it has been properly closed.'

'Okay, wait until I get there!' Hunter swiped her thumb across the screen to end the call and sidled over to where Beth Dench was giving instructions for getting the BMW ready for transportation to her lab. 'I'm going to have to get off, Beth. What's your timeframe on this?'

Dench looked up from the tablet which she had been using to input information. 'Still hoping to get the bodies to Toby this afternoon then we can get going on the vehicle without having to tread too carefully. Looks like the gunfire was from some sort of machine pistol so we'll have to spend time scrabbling about in the undergrowth to see if we can find any more evidence. Interestingly, we haven't found any spent casings yet which in itself is puzzling bearing in mind the number of shots which appear to have been fired – but we'll keep looking. Number one priority is to get this vehicle moved which should happen soon now that the low-loader is here.'

'Okay, I'll catch up with you later,' Hunter said as she turned to walk back down the lane. She replayed Dench's last remark in her mind. Why was there no sign of any casings? With the number of shots which must have been fired, there had to be some casings. Surely someone hadn't taken the trouble to pick them all up? It was certainly a puzzle, and she was so deep in thought that she almost missed the muddy track she had passed earlier.

Hunter couldn't immediately see Mishraz or Jennings when she arrived at the front of the house, but eventually heard some voices off to her right. 'Hey, guys, are you there,' she called out, making her way towards a small lawn which caressed the edge of the gravel drive and stretched round the side of the house. The two DCs suddenly appeared and walked over to meet her.

'Sorry, ma'am,' Jennings said as she clapped her hands together to get rid of some detritus which appeared to be attached to her fingers. 'There's a huge amount of ivy hanging down on the side wall which Azzar discovered was hiding a door. Can't get it open but it looks as if the entrance has been used recently as there are strands of the ivy lying on the grass around the door.'

'Okay, we can come back to that,' said Hunter, turning and walking back round the front of the house. 'Let's concentrate on the main entrance.' She walked up to the door and surveyed the security panel. 'Certainly looks like the door's open so let's see what we can find inside.'

She pushed the door open, and they all stepped into what remained of the vestibule. Glass and splinters of wood covered the area in front of them, and they had to pick their way very carefully across the floor until they reached the relative safety of the carpeted hall. 'Well, someone didn't like having to wait in there,' Hunter quipped as she peered into the gloom along the corridor. 'Okay, let's just have a quick look in here. Something tells me that we've hit on another house so the sooner we can get the CSIs in here the better. You two have a look at the rooms on that side, and I'll put my head round the doors along this side. Nitriles on and try not to touch anything. Is the electricity on?'

Mishraz noticed a switch on the wall and, pulling on his nitriles, he flicked the switch. Lighting came on in the hall but it was very superficial. Opening the first door they came to, Mishraz and Jennings recoiled from the smell of vomit and human faeces which hit them as soon as they had pushed the door open. They quickly eyeballed the room but could only see a massage table and a sideboard which was over-laden with equipment. Mirrors on the ceiling and along one of the walls. A camera tripod without the camera. No one appeared to be in the room - just a terrible stench of human excrement. So, they closed the door and moved on. The lights didn't seem to work in either of the two rooms which Hunter had looked in so she had used the torch on her phone. She had noted the massage tables and all the sex aids and other paraphernalia which adorned each room, but there was no sign of occupancy. The same was true for the next two rooms which Mishraz and

Jennings looked in. As they exited the room, they heard a stifled shriek coming from the room opposite.

'Oh, my good God!' Hunter exclaimed. 'What the...? Jesus!' The others crossed the hallway and looked into the room. Hunter's torchlight was playing over a body hanging by the legs from the rafters, a grotesque face peering at them. 'Fuck's sake! How many more of these are we going to find?' she asked as she retraced her steps into the hallway, furiously dusting some imaginary detritus off her shoulder. The two young DCs simply stood there, gawping, unbelieving eyes staring at the horror before them. 'Come on you two,' Hunter chivvied, 'let's just get round the rest of the house before we call it in just in case there are any other surprises.' Jennings and Mishraz eventually crept out of the room, still gobsmacked by what they had just witnessed.

'There's one more door down here!' Mishraz pointed along the hall just as Hunter was turning to make her way towards the staircase located by the vestibule. The door was already partially open so he pushed it until it was fully open. The light switch didn't work so he shone his torch into the darkness. It was a cellar with a set of stone steps leading down to what looked like a storage area. He was just about to close the door when he saw something on the floor which looked like a pile of dirty clothes. Only, he could see what looked like a pair of feet sticking out of it. 'Shit!' he muttered to himself as he descended the steps. He scampered over the uneven floor and got down on his knees, gently pulling back the material to reveal a young girl lying in the foetal position. His torch played over her face which was badly bruised, her jaw probably broken, one eye peering sightlessly, almost out of its socket. He felt for a pulse – very faint but it was there wasn't it? Wasn't it? He adjusted his grip and felt again. Yes, there it was!

'Quick!' he said turning to the others. 'She's still alive but only just. Can we get an ambulance – top priority!' Hunter didn't need to say anything to Jennings who was straight back up the steps and running down the hallway to make the call to the emergency services. They looked around the cellar and eventually found an old blanket which they shook and then folded over the girl.

'You'd better stay with her until the medics arrive,' Hunter told Mishraz. 'I'm just going to take a quick look upstairs and then call the whole thing in so that we can lock the place down. Don't want the scribblers thinking there are any more news stories up this lane.' And, with that, she left the cellar and sprinted up the hallway towards the stairs, her mind in a maelstrom of conflicting thoughts.

88

Wednesday 26 July

Under instruction from the passenger cowering in the back of the Mercedes, Trigger Harding turned onto the north-bound carriageway of the M23. Soon after getting onto the motorway, Woons' face swam into sight in the rear-view mirror giving Harding a bit of a shock as he looked at the huge black bruises spreading out either side of Woons' crumpled nose. His grip on the wheel tightened, his knuckles white. Harding always got anxious when driving Woons around as he was one of the worst back-seat drivers you could ever have the misfor-tune to meet. Today was even more tortuous as he simply didn't know what Woons was planning.

He drove on, fully expecting to exit onto the M25 going east back towards Kent. But, about half a mile from the junction, he was given instructions to continue on towards the west following signs for the M3. Woons was sitting in the middle of the back seat so that he could make sure that Harding was in the correct lane, and then sat back once they were on the M25 and travelling up Reigate Hill.

'We'll stop at that new service place past Leatherhead,' he told Harding. 'We need to sit down and make some plans.' He sat back in the seat, staring out of the window at cars they were passing and that were passing them. He was looking at the occupants, the drivers – did any of them have the same shed-load of problems as he had right now? He doubted it – they all looked far too bloody happy!

His eyes glazed over and he pictured Emma laughing politely

at his awful jokes, Spink arriving at the office with a fresh cup of coffee in hand, and little Lucy who would now have to grow up without the guiding hand of her mother. And, crashing into all these thoughts was the electrifying image of Eleonora who seemed to float tantalisingly before him but who was always just out of reach.

The sound of the car slowing brought him abruptly out of his daydreams as Harding moved across into the inside lane in preparation for entering the Cobham Services area. Once parked up, they made their way into the sprawling public area and found a couple of seats in one of several coffee shops. Woons had pulled his cap down so low that it almost covered his eyes, and he was trying desperately to ignore the strange looks he was getting from people around him. Goodness only knows what I look like, he thought, as he sub-consciously prodded the area around his nose.

Harding was despatched to get the coffees while Woons again fiddled around with the angle of his cap so that he could more clearly see what was going on around him. In doing this, he set off a searing pain across his forehead which reminded him that he really ought to try and find a hospital to get the wound washed and dressed. But, if the police were looking for him, would they have alerted A&E Departments? Surely not! Anyway, they didn't know that he had an injury so why would they think he'd visit A&E?

All this was going through his mind as he focused on a TV screen which was tuned into a rolling twenty-four-hour news station. Headlines were skimming across the bottom of the screen. Woons was idly reading the subtitles and wondering why they were always running about ten seconds after the words had been spoken by the news reporter when he suddenly realised that the story being covered was the shooting of a man and a woman in a car between Kilndown and Bedgebury in Kent. He was concentrating so hard on trying to read the subtitles that he almost didn't notice that Harding had returned to the table with two cups of coffee.

'Trig,' he whispered, a pudgy finger pointing at the screen. 'Watch!' Harding turned his attention to the screen, his mouth involuntarily falling open as he read the words being printed across the screen. Soon, the reporter handed back to the studio and the news anchor moved on to another story about a threatened hospital closure. Woons and Harding looked at each other – a mixture of horror, disbelief and fear etched on their faces.

'Jesus, Billy, what the fuck are we going to do?' Harding asked, despairingly. 'If they did that to Tricky and Ems, then they're certainly going to be out looking for the likes of you and me. And we won't last long once they find us!' Harding took a sip of his coffee, and Woons noticed that he was holding the mug with both hands because they were shaking so much.

Woons looked round the coffee shop. Was anyone watching him? How could he tell? There was a mass of people here. Perhaps if he got away from Kent for a while, things might quieten down. But would he ever be able to return to live a life safe from the threat of this unknown enemy. If only he knew who they were, he could probably do a deal with them. He wanted out anyway so he could just hand over the keys to the office and let whoever they were get on with it.

He had been wondering whether he should speak to someone from the Kent Police Force – just to spec out the lie of the land and see if they might be able to offer some protection in return for handing them the info on all the houses in his diminishing organisation. Tricky had once got him the number of one of the cops at the Tonbridge station – what was his fucking name? He sat back and scrolled through his phone's directory. Come on! Come on! Suddenly it was there on the screen. DS Selitto. No first name. Typical Tricky! Never dealt with detail.

All of a sudden, Eleonora's smiling face drifted across his thoughts as if to remind him that she was the catalyst for his decision to jack the whole operation in. She was driving him on to get out while he could. He had metaphorically sold his soul to her. He couldn't let her down.

'Billy? Did you hear me?' An urgency in Harding's tone brought Eleonora's brief appearance to an end. Woons thought that Trigger's voice seemed to have gone up an octave, and he was clearly finding it difficult to keep a lid on his emotions.

'Yes, Trig, loud and clear,' Woons replied. 'All I know is that we've got to get away from here and lie low for a week or two. We can't go back to Kent right now because someone will be waiting for us. And they'll either have shooters or handcuffs. So, if we value our arses, it looks like we'll have to hit the road and stay away until I can think of how we can get out of this shit.'

'Why don't you just call the cops and tell them what's going on?' Harding asked as he finished his coffee.

Woons was still looking up at the TV screen in case they replayed the news item. 'That's one of my options, Trig. But we need to keep away from them as well so it'll have to be just a phone call – don't want any fucking visits with warrants and dogs. Got to be on our terms or not at all. Perhaps once they know what we suspect happened to Tricky and Ems, they might want to talk without the rattling of cuffs and the slamming of cell doors.'

Looking around the coffee shop once again, and doing his best to categorise everyone he saw, Woons suddenly got to his feet. 'Come on, Trig, we've gotta get moving. Have a piss before you get in the car – don't want to have to keep stopping.' He headed for the door and then veered off to the toilets, Harding following a few paces behind him.

Once back at the car, Woons again sat in the back while Harding drove out of the car park and took the filter lane to rejoin the M25 travelling westwards. Where the fuck were they going to go? Woons needed to have a plan, a goal, a destination, somewhere they would be safe for a few days which could give them a chance to take stock of their situation. And, as they headed for the M3, he had something of a lightbulb moment which brought some clarity to his plans.

89

Wednesday 26 July

Selitto and Pennant made it back to Pembury Road soon after a couple of uniforms had arrived to babysit Threepenny Cottage. Pennant immediately went off to organise the warrant and the ensuing search of the property, and Selitto settled himself at a workstation in the MIR to get up to date with some of his reporting. He had just started to recall the events of the previous evening when he became aware of someone drawing up a chair beside him.

'Hello, Grace,' he said, turning to face DS Kendall who was flicking through her notebook as she made herself comfortable. 'What can I do you for?'

'Did Sarah mention that I had found out that this man Woons had just arrived back in the UK this morning?' she asked, not really sure how much of an opportunity DI Hunter might have had to brief her team on the information Kendall had given her earlier.

'Not to me,' Selitto replied. 'Haven't seen her since before the briefing this morning, and only spoke to her about going to see if we could find the Lexus at Threepenny Cottage.'

'Okay,' continued Kendall, thinking that she needed to update Selitto on where she had got to with the intel on Woons. 'Well, I've just received news that our man Woons flew into Gatwick this morning from Riga.'

Sellitto frowned. Geography wasn't his strong point but he was sure that he had heard of Riga before. 'Latvia?'

'Correct!' Kendall replied, referring back to her notes.

'Anyway, a contact of mine managed to persuade a colleague of theirs on the airport security team to get me a shot of Mr Woons going through Passport Control, and it's just come through. Pass the keyboard over here and I'll show you.'

After a few key strokes, Kendall managed to get the picture of Woons up on the screen and they both sat there staring at it. Eventually, she clicked on the 'print' icon and requested six copies.

'Well, at least we now know what Woons looks like!' Selitto let out a sigh. 'Although you can't see much of his face. Is that a shadow under his eyes or something a bit more sinister?'

Kendall looked at the picture again. 'Doubt there are any shadows in those passport cubicles so it looks like he's probably been in the wars. The cap's pulled down low as well. Wonder what it's hiding?'

Selitto had another long look at the image of Woons on the screen in front of him. 'Has he come up on any of your other searches?'

'Not apart from his criminal record which related to petty theft and was a good thirty years ago. Haven't had time to do too much of an in-depth search but I'll get on to that now.' She closed down the image on the screen, went and got the copies from the printer. Keeping one for herself, she placed the others on the desk in front of Selitto. 'Sarah also asked me to get some more intel on our friend, Dangerfield, from Meadowlands – remember him?' Selitto nodded. 'He seems to do quite a lot of travelling out of the UK – often to Paris where he then goes off the radar. However, I've been tipped the wink that he passed through Bucharest earlier this year – he's come up on an airline passenger record but it's not clear if he was travelling into or out of the city.'

'Hmm! I wonder what he was doing in Romania?' Selitto commented, sitting upright in his chair. 'Doesn't sound the sort of place the general manager of a British five-star luxury hotel would go to in order to get ideas for improving his hotel. Does Sarah know this yet?' Kendall shook her head just at the same moment that the door to the MIR opened and Sarah Hunter strode into the office, making a beeline for Selitto and Kendall.

'You two all right?' she asked as she placed a cup of steaming coffee on the desk and wheeled a chair over. 'Right! What have we got, Grace?'

Kendall showed her the picture of Woons and then filled her in on the travel history for Dangerfield. Hunter just nodded as Kendall spoke, all the time staring at the picture of Woons.

'So, we now know that Woons has just been to Georgia and perhaps to Latvia, and that Dangerfield has been to Romania. You'll also recall that Bulgarian IUDs have been found inside the dead girls so Eastern Europe seems to be well represented in our investigation! Anything else on Dangerfield, Grace?'

'Not that's coming up on the searches,' Kendall replied, consulting her notes. 'He's 53 years old, spent nearly all his working life in the hospitality sector both in the UK and in France. Speaks French and has spent a good deal of time working in hotels that are part of a French hotel group. No criminal record here or in France, and not wanted anywhere else as far as I can tell – certainly not in Europe. Meadowlands seems to be managed at arms-length by the owners who are offshore so he seems to be able to do pretty much as he pleases as long as they keep stumping up the money. I don't get the impression that Meadowlands is anything other than a vehicle for pouring cash into. Having said all that, Dangerfield seems to have been the driving force behind developing it to the status it now enjoys as one of the premier country hotels in the south of England. Oh, and I checked in with our friend, Sally Lancaster – still no sign of Dangerfield. I get the impression that things are running quite smoothly without him but that the owners have found out about his absence and are getting tetchy. Anyway, not our problem but Dangerfield might be.'

'Okay, Grace. Good work!' Hunter sought to wind that discussion up because she felt that there were other more important matters to deal with, so she turned her attention to Selitto. Kendall took the hint, got up from the desk and returned to her own working area.

'Right, Ted, we've definitely found another house – is that the fourth?' she asked, looking towards the white boards which she noticed had now been replaced by four very smart glass panels on which information about the case had been written with lines linking relevant parts to each other. There were pictures of the first three houses, and grainy photos of the likes of Travisedo and Lombardi. There were also facial close ups of the girls they had so far found plus location maps and other location photos. 'That's an improvement!' she declared, 'who's responsible?'

'I think Stuart got it organised,' Selitto said, looking at what Crosby had christened "the Crime Wall". 'It's certainly a step in the right direction!'

'Yes, very good. Right, where are all the troops?' Hunter was getting restless. She sensed that things were now happening at a fast pace, and she knew that she had limited resources to stay on top of the investigation so she was desperate to allocate tasks which would bring results quickly. 'I've brought Elaine back with me from Kilndown – Azzar's still there until we can get the house locked down. Where's Stuart and Caroline?'

'Stuart's at the morgue and Caroline's getting a warrant to search Threepenny Cottage, and will then be organising the search,' Selitto replied.

'Okay!' Sarah Hunter sounded frustrated by the lack of numbers to carry out all the actions she had in mind. 'I really want someone staying close to whatever headway we are making on the BMW. It's important that we identify the two bodies and see if that gets us any closer to understanding what's going on. In fact, if that does get us closer to this Woons character then we might be getting somewhere. Now we've got an up-to-date photo, we can put out an APB for him but ideally we also need to find out where he's operating from.'

'Yeah, that would be good,' Selitto commented. 'Unfortunately, he probably left Gatwick in another vehicle which is unknown to us so no chance of following him using ANPR. Flying in and out of Gatwick would normally be the preference of someone who is based in Kent or Sussex – or perhaps east Surrey. Would he need a base? Hard to tell really. If he's our main man then he's undoubtedly providing girls and collecting the rent, but I bet he's not involved in any of the transportation. Far too dangerous.'

Selitto shuffled some papers on the desk and scooped up the picture of Woons. 'He'll probably need a small office. These guys always like to have a base, don't they? They don't like operating from home or a car. Just somewhere with a desk and a coffee machine - nothing too posh which might draw attention to themselves. Something off the beaten track somewhere – a bit like that Threepenny Cottage but not so twee. Perhaps even an old portacabin or even an old container. What about getting the Kent & Essex chopper up and having a scout around the Tunbridge Wells area?'

Hunter gave him a steely look. 'You are joking aren't you?' she blustered. 'On our budget? Can you imagine what Iversen would say? Anyway, what would they be looking for, and how would they know if they had found it? It – whatever it is – is hardly likely to have a great big white cross painted on its roof with "*Come and get me*" written out in white boulders on the land around it! Sorry, Ted, great idea but a non-starter as far as I'm concerned.'

Selitto thought for a minute. 'Okay! So, if you're saying that using the Force helicopter was out of the question,' he began, 'what about one of our drones? Aren't they used for surveillance or observation work? All we'd have to do is identify a few possible sites and then get the pilot to get the thing in the air so that we could have a quick look at what's on the ground around us. On the assumption that what we're looking for is probably out in the country, we'd hardly be encroaching on the privacy of members of the public.'

They lapsed into silence with Selitto thinking that Sarah was ignoring him. Eventually, he heard what sounded like a sigh. 'A remote possibility is how I would rate that idea, Detective Sergeant. But not a completely daft one. I'll see if I can find anyone to talk to about that. Perhaps Grace can get me an intro. Only problem I see is that we really don't have a clue what we're looking for or where to start looking so just turning up at odd spots in the countryside and flying a drone is going to be spectacularly unproductive and, no doubt, very expensive.

And then it's highly likely that we would eventually draw the attention of the press!'

They lapsed into silence again, both staring vacantly at Crosby's Crime Wall. They almost didn't see or hear Selitto's mobile phone vibrating on the desk in front of them. Eventually, Selitto reached over and picked it up. 'Incoming call? Who the fuck's this?' he wondered aloud. He was tempted to just let it ring out and then see if he got a voicemail but then decided to see who the hell was calling him. He swiped the screen and announced his name and rank.

'Ah, DS Selitto, this is Billy Woons!' Selitto stared at Hunter, a deep frown on his forehead. He pulled a notepad towards him and scribbled the name "Woons" on it – then pointed to the phone. Hunter's eyebrows shot up behind her fringe before she also frowned, turning her palms up and shrugging her shoulders in an expression which said "What the fuck?" Selitto also shrugged his shoulders but jammed the phone to his ear.

'How the hell did you get this number, Mr Woons?' Selitto enquired, his tone of voice clearly implying that he was pissed off that a criminal of Woons calibre had the wherewithal to find out his mobile number.

'Never you mind about that, Sergeant. We've more important things to discuss than simply how I've managed to get your sodding number,' Woons continued. 'I know you're looking for me so just listen. Those houses you've been going over at Sleet Hill and Hildenborough, they're just two of many similar properties which I've got hidden in this beautiful county of ours. But I'm afraid that they are now being systematically ransacked by a gang of marauding thugs from Eastern Europe. If I knew who these bastards were, I'd tell you but, unfortunately, I haven't a clue. All I do know is that they are a bunch of murderous savages who will simply kill anyone who gets in their way. No doubt you're all over the shoot-up at Bedgebury? That was two of my most loyal people. I'm absolutely gutted about that, particularly as it will leave one little girl an orphan. So, I've decided to give you all the information you will ever need to bust a sophisticated trafficking network plus the locations of all these other properties so that you can close the whole fucking lot down before the murdering scum from Eastern Europe can get their blood-soaked hands on them!'

Selitto cleared his throat. 'And how do you propose to do that, Mr Woons?' he asked.

'I can't give it to you on the phone,' Woons replied. 'I shouldn't even be talking to you on this phone in case they're listening in. So, we're going to have to meet because they're out there looking for me. If they get to me before you do, then you'll only have a corpse to talk to. So, we need to have a chat soonest. And we can also discuss what you're going to do about my safety in exchange for the info I've got for you. Know what I mean? Safe houses and all that. I'm sure you can arrange all that.'

'But, Mr Woons, arranging safe houses is not that straight-forward,' Selitto blustered.

'Yeah, yeah! Heard all that before!' Woons mocked Selitto's bluster. 'You can do it! You know you can do it if the quality of the intel is good enough. And, believe me, the quality of my intel is off the fucking scale! So, get your arse into your car and get yourself down to Cornwall pronto. We'll meet this evening. I'll call you again from a different phone with a place and time. But you must be there or the deal is off.' There was a click and the line went dead.

Selitto stared at the phone before putting it back on the desk. He looked across at Hunter who still had a quizzical look on her face. 'Looks like our Mr Woons thinks that we'll want to do some sort of deal with him!'

90

Wednesday 26 July

'Right! That's given Kent's finest something to think about,' Woons declared as he pocketed his phone and reclined in the comfortable leather seat in the back of the Mercedes. Harding searched for Woons' face in the rear-view mirror but, because he had slid so far down in the back seat, he could now only see the top of his cap.

They had turned on to the M3 going south, and then continued towards Junction 8 where they joined the A303 going west. The traffic hadn't been too bad, and they had managed to negotiate their way past Stonehenge without too much difficulty. They had then made some good progress westwards until Woons' stomach began making a deep gurgling noise which meant a stop for a Bacon Double Cheeseburger at a Burger King near Ilchester. Harding had a mug of tea and a slice of cake before they had continued on their way. They were now passing Exeter Airport, and would soon turn on to the M5 going south before taking the A38 through to Plymouth.

Harding eventually plucked up courage to ask the question which had been on the tip of his tongue for the last seventy odd miles as they had sped ever further away from Kent. 'You sure this is a good idea, Billy?' There was no reply. 'Don't tell me the bastard's asleep,' he muttered under his breath. He sat further up in his seat and craned his neck to see Woons in the mirror. No, he wasn't asleep – just looking out of the window, deep in thought. Harding cleared his throat and made to ask his question again.

'Save your breath, Trig,' Woons pre-empted him with a sigh. 'Save your breath.'

Harding took this to be a polite way of telling him to shut up so he concentrated on his driving instead. He was soon having to make a few gear changes as he negotiated his way from the M5 onto the A38 Devon Expressway. Woons kept staring out of the window, watching the green countryside flashing by as they sped inexorably towards Cornwall. Eventually, he seemed ready to talk.

'You see, Trig, this is what it looks like from where I'm sitting,' Woons started. 'You and me? We are totally and royally fucked! We go back to Kent now, we're dead meat. These bastards, whoever they fucking are, will be waiting for us. They know where all the houses are, and they're systematically clearing them out. Tricky and Ems were obviously in the wrong place at the wrong time and must have driven into some sort of ambush, the way I'm hearing it. We go anywhere near any of the other houses, we go anywhere near the office, they'll be there to meet us – and they don't take fucking prisoners. We haven't got any protection. That mob in Georgia won't help us despite everything they said. So, we're on our own – you and me. Best thing we can do is lie low for a while, try to negotiate something with the cops, and then get away under the radar. That's why we're coming down here because them Romanians - or whatever the fuck they are - won't be arsed to follow us here. What's the point? We're out of the way here.' He paused, continuing to watch the countryside slip past as they motored on.

After a while, Woons shifted in his seat and bent forward so that he was leaning through the gap between the two front seats, staring straight ahead. Harding got a whiff of onions on Woons' breath – probably from the burger. Urgh! He felt slightly nauseous. 'There's another thing, Trig,' he said as they passed a sign showing twenty-six miles to Plymouth. 'I'm not in this whole game anymore. Not only is there no future in it but I've suddenly realised that people like us are destroying other people's lives – and I'm not just talking about the girls themselves. They all have families – mums and dads, brothers and sisters, grannies and grandads. The desolation felt by these people just so that we can exploit the apples of their eyes. And the hopelessness of their vigils – keeping a light on for their daughter, sister, granddaughter – or whatever – when there's not a chance in hell that they are ever going to show up.' He paused to watch some crazy overtaking manoeuvre ahead which almost ended in disaster for the driver of an Audi. Harding had instinctively braked, projecting Woons a little further between the gap in the seats.

Once they were back to cruising speed, Woons continued. 'You see, Trig, I've had my eyes opened. I've had one of those moments, whatever they're fucking called. I've met someone who quite innocently and unknowingly has taken over my mind, my thoughts and my emotions. I can't explain how it happened but it just did. I feel like I've been enveloped by an emotional tsunami of feelings for a nineteen year old girl. I'm thinking of her constantly, all the time imagining what she's doing, what she's thinking. I'm fascinated by her outlook on life, captivated by her looks, intrigued to know her innermost secrets, desperate to see her again.'

Harding was finding it difficult to concentrate on his driving. In all their years together, he had never heard Billy Woons talk about emotions. For all he knew, Woons had had every sinew of emotion cut out of his body at birth. Yet, here he was talking like a spotty teenager who had just been on his first date with a girl. He knew that Woons had a soft spot for Emma although that had taken quite a long time to manifest itself. But that was it. He had always seemed to lack emotion, a real cold fish and, dare he say it, a proper 'Billy No Mates'.

'So, that's me done with all that bollocks that we've been involved with over the years,' Woons droned on. 'I ain't got the stomach for it no more. It all used to be so straightforward – worked like clockwork with the Georgians doing their bit and Vashlili organising everything at this end. We just sat back and counted the cash. But that's all changed now, and I just don't want to be involved in all that trafficking shit – too many extremely violent Eastern European dickheads involved for my liking. It's probably OK if you're from that neck of the woods but they're suspicious of us Brits – sooner slit our throats than work with us. That's where Vashlili came in – he was the jam in the old sandwich.'

Woons sat back in the comfort of the car seat, contemplating what he had just said. 'Wonder what happened to Vashlili. Strange him just disappearing like that. You heard anything, Trig?'

Harding hadn't heard anything about Vashlili's whereabouts, and they motored on in silence. In the back seat, Woons was now engaged in changing the SIM card in his phone. Never an easy task for someone with pudgy fingers and, with the movement of the car making it difficult anyway, he was having a bit of trouble trying to extract the old card. But he persevered and eventually managed to insert another card which he only used when he was in Cornwall. He turned the phone back on and started scrolling through the phone directory. Having found what he was looking for, he pressed the call button.

'Hello, Siobhan, it's Billy Woons,' he said as the call was answered. 'You made the arrangements yet that I asked for?' He listened to the reply. 'Okay. That sounds good. We're about 45 miles away so if you can leave the key in the usual place. Everything else as normal?' He listened again before cutting the call. He always liked to plan ahead.

91

Wednesday 26 July

DC Stuart Crosby had been rather kicking his heels at the mortuary. Professor Jenkyns had completed her assessment of the girl found on Pilgrims Way and had also taken a look at Candice Lombardi. They were in the little office which was located just off the scrubs room where Jenkyns was putting the finishing touches to her reports.

'Were you at the PM when Norman discovered the IUD?' she was asking Crosby as she retrieved some sheets of typed paper from the printer.

'No, but I have read his report,' Crosby replied, feeling pleased that he was at least on the same page as Jenkyns with regard to the IUD evidence.

'So, you'll know that the IUD he found appeared to originate from Bulgaria,' she continued. 'The young girl I've just posted also had a Bulgarian IUD inserted inside her – made by the same manufacturer, Venus. So, I think that we can safely say that there is a connection there. However, I cannot detect any recent sexual activity which might indicate that she had only recently been trafficked into the UK. Perhaps she hadn't reached her intended destination before she was found.'

Crosby consulted his own notes. 'The CSIs reported that there was evidence on the road surface that she had possibly fallen from a vehicle which was travelling at speed.'

'Yes,' agreed Jenkyns, referring to her own recently typed-up notes. 'There are abrasions on her hands and knees and on her face which would support that theory. It is also probable that she was then winged by a car as there is extensive bruising down her right leg and a gash on her left temple which would have bled considerably and would explain the blood on the road sign. The trauma she would have suffered then probably led to her losing consciousness which is when the car hit her – doubt the driver would have had a chance of seeing her until he was right on top of the body. The impact of the car's wheels across her body ruptured several of her vital organs and she didn't really have a chance after that. She may not even have survived the previous impact but that is too difficult to call. It was certainly a contributing factor.'

Crosby scribbled a couple of notes on his pad. 'That's very useful, Professor. Thank you!' he said as Jenkyns reached for her document folder. She slipped the typed notes into the folder and then turned to Crosby.

'You might also like to tell your DI that I have had a look at the Lombardi woman,' she said, turning to face Crosby. 'There are certain similarities between her and Maria Travisedo who I saw yesterday. Most notably that both killings seem to have been carried out by someone who takes great delight in inflicting unimaginable pain and suffering on his victims. Both victims would have undergone a ferocious, frenzied attack before life was gradually sucked out of them. As you know, the perpetrator even went to the lengths of carving up Travisedo's body. He would be likely to have got off on this so must be considered as a highly dangerous individual. Sarah Hunter might be well-served by getting on to the Kent Profiling Unit to try to get some sort of profile about the person you are looking for. If Kent hasn't got anyone on profiling, tell her to give me a call and I'll try to get her a meeting with one of the

Home Office Profilers.'

Crosby was frowning. 'I'm afraid we didn't really cover profiling when I was at the training college,' he said, 'so I'm not really sure I know enough about what I would be recommending to DI Hunter. Is this more to do with the psychological state of the person or people we are looking for?'

Jenkyns smiled. She loved it when she was in the company of a young, enthusiastic officer who actually wanted to learn from her. 'Yes, you're correct on that. It's often referred to as psychological profiling which is a method of identifying a suspect not by way of DNA, fingerprints or other physical characteristics but by considering the mental, emotional and personality characteristics of a suspect simply by looking at what he or she has done or left behind at the crime scene. You should probably read up on a man called Labuschagne – can't remember his first name – but he defined what he called linkage analysis which is used to determine the possibility that a series of crimes has been committed by one perpetrator. He looks at modus operandi and similarities in other killings and tries to link them together when physical evidence such as DNA can't be collected. Basically, it's another means of identifying killers. However, profiling is still viewed with a great deal of suspicion by some of the older members of the force! Personally, I think it's an interesting development and should be used more if only to properly assess the contribution it can make to an investigation.'

Crosby scribbled some more notes on his pad. 'Many thanks for that! I'll certainly pass the message on to DI Hunter.'

Jenkyns looked at her watch and then at the clock on the wall as if to check that that really was the time. 'Do you know what time the double shooting is due in?' she asked Crosby who was still scribbling notes on his pad. 'Only I've got to decide whether to get back to London now or hang on to give Dr Swartzman a hand with a double autopsy.'

Just then, there was the sound of voices in the corridor and of rubber wheels squeaking across the flooring on the way into the cutting room. Jenkyns looked at Crosby. 'Looks like I might be staying for a bit longer!'

92

Wednesday 26 July

The call from Billy Woons had come as a bit of a bomb-shell to the team at Pembury Road, and to the Senior Investigating Officer, Sarah Hunter, in particular. On the face of it, the offer of extensive intel on the case was too good to turn down. But, at the same time, it came with strings attached and she knew that the powers-that-be would never sanction a safe house for a known criminal like Woons. She had, however, spent some time in discussion with Selitto since the call from Billy Woons and, in the end, they had decided that the DS should make the journey to Cornwall so that he could at least assess the quality of the intel on offer. After that, they could decide whether to formalise a request for temporary protection. Selitto had then made his way out of Tonbridge via the Shell petrol station where he filled up the Megane and picked up a sandwich and a bottle of Diet Pepsi for the long journey west. Should take him about five hours he thought, so an early evening arrival was probably on the cards.

Hunter had remained at the desk in the MIR, reading through reports and other information which was coming in almost by the minute. She pulled a strand of hair away from her eyes and tucked it behind an ear, and was now watching her phone which was vibrating on the desk next to her. IVERSEN! What the hell did he want now? But then, she thought, they hadn't spoken for at least 24 hours so perhaps he deserved an update.

She answered and found that Iversen was yet again at

Maidstone engaged in meetings with the top brass. Honestly, what on earth did these people find to talk about all the time? They were supposed to be catching criminals – not just talking about it. Nevertheless, she proceeded to brief him on the significant progress they were now making, particularly in the identification of Billy Woons. Iversen seemed to be happy that things were finally moving in a positive direction.

'There's something else that's just come up which I've got to brief you on,' he said just as Hunter was thinking of winding up the call. She detected a change in his tone of voice and gritted her teeth, waiting for what she was sure was going to be bad news. 'I'm afraid that the Super over here who I mentioned to you before, Hannah Eaves, she's decided that this case should now be referred to SOC, and is making the appropriate arrangements herself.'

This was worse than bad news and something Sarah Hunter hadn't contemplated! She was furious. The Serious & Organised Crime Unit was involved in breaking down organised crime groups which were responsible for serious offences not only in Kent but also across its borders and further afield. SOC worked with partners and other law enforcement agencies to disrupt and dismantle organised crime groups. Hunter had heard that the Unit was stretched to breaking point with the greatly increased numbers of illegal immigrants landing on the shores of Kent in little boats and other small craft, at Kent ports in the backs of lorries, and through Eurotunnel. Surely there was little they could bring to her investigation which would be of much help.

'I suppose that that's non-negotiable, sir?' Hunter questioned, face like thunder.

'Afraid so, Sarah,' Iversen replied, a placatory tone in his voice. 'But so far they plan to just send one of the SOC officers over to have an initial chat with you so that they can get an idea of how you can all work together. Chap called Jack Pennington – just been promoted to DCI. Have a chat with him and then get back to me with any comments. I would be prepared to go back to the Super if you have any well-grounded reasons for objecting to their involvement but you'll have to persuade me first. He'll make contact with you.'

Hunter grunted some almost unintelligible words accepting the situation before Iversen cut the call and she was left staring at the screen. SOC! For fuck's sake! Hadn't they got better things to do?

93

Wednesday 26 July

The Mercedes slowed as Harding negotiated his way past the roundabout leading onto the impressive Tamar Bridge. Woons immediately sat up in his seat. He always loved the view from the bridge, looking down on the Royal Albert Rail Bridge which had been constructed by Brunel all those years ago, and further afield to Plymouth itself and the English Channel beyond. On the other side, he could see hundreds of sailing boats moored close to the western shore of the river. He just caught sight of the Cornish Cross (indicating that they had at last arrived in Cornwall) before they entered the Saltash Tunnel where the Merc's headlights lit up the road ahead.

On leaving the tunnel, Harding followed the A38 until they got to the Trerulefoot Roundabout near Saltash. Woons leant forward in his seat instructing Harding to turn into the car park at the Route 38 roadside restaurant which adjoined a Shell petrol station. He was aiming to kill two birds with one stone – perhaps a Piri Piri Wrap for himself and some fuel for the car. That should keep them both going until they hit their destination!

Once Harding had got the car parked, Woons decided that it was time to make another call to Detective Sergeant Selitto. Harding was, therefore, despatched to find a quiet corner table while Woons once again changed the SIM card in his phone and made the call. When Selitto answered, Woons was pleased to hear that he was already on the road heading west so he gave him the location of their meeting place and the time he would be there. The DS sounded as if he roughly knew the location anyway which meant that Woons didn't have to start giving directions which he always hated doing. The call was short and sweet which was a bonus as it gave Woons longer to savour the treats awaiting him in Route 38.

Selitto wasn't really relishing the long drive to Cornwall, and wished that he had taken one of the young DCs for company if nothing else. But they had all been out on various missions so, as time was now of the essence, he had decided to just go it alone. Thankfully, the M25 had been free-flowing although it had slowed down by the time he got to the M3 junction but, once he had passed Farnborough and the Fleet Services, he was able to get some speed up. The first part of the A303 with its dual carriageway allowed him to make up any time lost at the M25/M3 junction and, despite some hold ups around Stonehenge, he was making good progress.

After taking the call from Woons, he called Hunter to relay the instructions for the meeting that evening.

'Be very careful, Ted,' she warned. 'I don't want us having to start explaining why we're operating on Devon & Cornwall's patch without telling them first. As far as I'm concerned, this is simply an information gathering exercise – pure and simple. We can't put him up in a safe house down there anyway so he'll just have to kick his heels in Cornwall while we decide what we can do for him – if anything!'

'Agreed, boss!' Selitto had no intention of discussing protection and safe houses with Woons anyway, but would probably have to string him along in order to extract as much information as he could at this stage. It would also be a long way to go if he came away empty-handed so he would have to draw on all his skills of interrogation once he was sitting in front of Woons.

He motored on, passing through the Blackdown Hills which he could see on either side of the road as the A303 wended its way through the Somerset countryside. After Exeter, he joined the A38 and continued towards Plymouth.

After leaving the Route 38 Restaurant, and having filled the Merc up at the Shell petrol station, Harding had continued on the A38 to Dobwalls where he turned onto the A390 towards Lostwithiel. He was keeping a beady eye out for a signpost just outside East Taphouse which would point him in the direction of his final destination. Once he had spotted the sign, he immediately indicated left and turned on the road which ultimately led to Polperro Beach. After about four miles, he turned right and they continued across a high plain passing through villages with interesting names such as St Veep and Lanteglos Highway – no doubt steeped in history, thought Woons. He always liked this part of the journey as he felt that he was almost home. Taking a left just before the road started to descend to the shoreline, Harding piloted the car down another steep incline into the tiny village of Bodinnick and stopped outside a stone-built bungalow just up the road from The Olde Ferry Inn.

'You know where to park this heap, Trig?' Woons said as he reached for the door handle. 'Just up to the right there,' he pointed to a turning just past the pub. 'The car park's on the right. Should be a space for you.' He gathered up his hold-all, exited the car and watched as Harding headed round the corner. He then walked through the gate of the bungalow and retrieved the key from under a flowerpot by the front door.

He walked into the house and just stood in the hallway, drinking in the slightly musty smell which always greeted him. Had always greeted him when he was a young boy as well. It was a special place which held fond memories of his childhood. He was home. He smiled to himself and walked through to the kitchen to put the kettle on.

94

Wednesday 24 July

From the terrace of the Old Quay Hotel, Selitto looked out across the Fowey estuary towards the small town of Polruan, resplendent in the early evening sunshine. Houses and cottages in all shapes and sizes and in every colour of the rainbow appeared to have been carefully pinned to the hillside, creating a fabulous vista of a quintessentially English landscape. The Polruan Ferry chugged across the estuary, threading its way between banks of sailing boats that were tied up to the myriad of bright yellow mooring buoys which dotted the estuary.

Selitto had made good time on his long journey from Kent, and was now just having a bit of a break before his planned meeting with Billy Woons. He was also taking the opportunity of having a luxurious Cornish cream tea with two huge scones and lashings of clotted cream. It had been a few hours since the solitary bacon sandwich he had munched his way through as he sat in the slow-moving traffic chugging its way past the Clacket Lane Services on the M25. He greedily slathered the jam on to the scones before applying a more than generous dollop of the cream.

As he took in the picture of serenity before him, Selitto thought ahead to the journey he would soon be making on the little ferry, and his gaze shifted to the ruin of St Saviour's Chapel which dominated the skyline above Polruan. Woons wanted to meet at 7.30 p.m. and would be sitting at one of the bench tables located close to the National CoastWatch Institute look-out station situated on the top of St Saviour's

Hill. This little outpost of the UK's coastguard system overlooks a sea area from Lizard Point in the west to the Eddystone Lighthouse in the east as well as having a commanding view over Fowey Harbour.

Selitto had parked in the Caffa Mill car park at the eastern end of the town which would afford him quick access to the road taking him out of Fowey following his meeting. He had had a leisurely walk along the street which connects the car park with the centre of the town, stopping to look in the windows of shops selling nautical clothing, yachting equipment, framed seascape paintings, and anything else connected with the sea. He had come across The Olde Quay Hotel by accident, and had suffered a jaw-dropping moment when he was shown out onto the terrace and found himself sitting at a table with the sound of small waves gently lapping at the sea wall around him.

However, time was now marching on and he needed to find his way to the rendezvous point. As a creature of habit, he always liked to reconnoitre a new meeting place in advance so he decided to set off early. From where he was sitting, he could see where the Polruan Ferry docked so he made his way back through the hotel to pay for his tea and then out onto the street. Heading west past more shops and a few restaurants, he soon took a left and found himself in a small square surrounded by the Royal British Legion Club on one side and The King of Prussia pub on another. He made his way over to the steps which led down to the sea and where the little ferry would dock. Continuing on to the sea wall, he looked out across the estuary and noted that the ferry was about halfway across on its inbound journey. He could do nothing more but wait for it.

Selitto stepped off the ferry and clambered up the stone steps leading from the landing stage on to the main quay at Polruan. Glancing at the map he had got up on his phone, he walked past The Lugger Inn where early evening drinkers were enjoying a few pints whilst sitting at the tables dotted around the quayside. A nice pint of Cornish ale would go down a treat at the moment, he thought.

Rounding a corner, he looked up as the road in front of him stretched ahead at an alarming angle. Did he really have to climb this hill in order to reach his intended destination? He consulted the map once more to check that he was actually on the right road. The map told him he should be on Fore Street. He turned to see that the road sign behind him read "Fore Street". So, there was no other option – he had to start climbing.

Eventually, after several stops and struggling for breath, Selitto finally arrived at the car park which nestled under the ruins of St Saviour's Chapel. Realising just how out of condition he was, and having again stopped to get his breath back, he climbed a grassy bank and plonked himself down on a stout wooden bench located just yards from the ruin. He gulped in lungfuls of the fresh sea air as he took in the spectacular scene laid out in front of him. The Fowey estuary stretched almost as far as the eye could see with the town of Fowey and its little harbour to his left and Polruan nestling below him with its working boatyard stretching round a bend in the river. The estuary was festooned with hundreds of sailing boats and other marine craft. It was a panoramic view the likes of which he could not recall having seen before.

Once his breathing had returned to somewhere near normal,

he turned to look up towards what remained of St Saviour's Chapel. Close up, it seemed to be no more than an obelisk of ancient stone. He noticed that there was an information board which had been attached to the wall of the ruin so he wandered over to take a look. The chapel itself had been built in the 8th century but had gradually fallen into disrepair over the centuries until its last rites had effectively been read as a result of Henry the Eighth's dissolution of the monasteries. Today, grasses and other vegetation were sprouting from the many gaps in the rubblestone, and Selitto thought that the ruin was looking a little sorry for itself.

Taking one last look at the fabulous view over the estuary, Selitto wandered on towards the tiny National Coastwatch Institution building. There was now a gentle breeze that was rustling the halyards of the maritime flag pole which was attached to one of the walls of the little building. The orange windsock close by was also starting to show signs of life. Skirting round a fenced-off children's play area, he arrived at the brow of the hill and found himself looking down a rolling grassy hillside which he presumed ended at a cliff edge as, in the distance, all he could see was an enormous expanse of water: the English Channel.

To his left were two bench tables similar to the ones outside some of the pubs back in Kent. This was presumably where Woons had suggested they meet so Selitto took time to take in details of his situation. It was certainly an exposed location although there were very few people about. In fact, he had only seen two walkers since he had been up there, and they had walked through at a frightening pace – as if they had a boat to catch!

He was still a bit early for their meeting so he sat at one of the tables and fired off a text message to Hunter to tell her that he was in position. He then laid his phone on the table and looked across the grassland to the sea beyond. There was a huge tanker making its way through the English Channel right on the horizon – it had a ghostly feel about it as it slipped silently across his field of vision. Closer in, he could see a couple of day boats returning to port, no doubt with some goodies for the local fish shop which he had passed earlier in the afternoon.

He was just thinking about whether he should make an overnight stop on the way home when his phone lit up with an incoming call. He swiped the screen to take the call.

'Is that you I can see at that table? Just picked your phone up?' Woons taunted. Selitto instinctively started looking around him to see where Woons was watching from. 'No need to bother looking, mate. You'll not see me from there. Now listen. If you look down the slope in front of you, can you see the path that's been trod down in the grass?'

Selitto looked for the path Woons was referring to. It was over to his right. 'Yes, I see it,' he replied.

'Okay!' continued Woons. 'I want you to follow that path down to what looks like an old look-out post used in the war. It's just a ruin now but if you get down the path, we can have a little chat. I'll be waiting there.' The call was disconnected.

Selitto scanned the area around him but couldn't see signs of anyone in the immediate vicinity. He was also out of the line of sight from the Coastwatch station. There was very little noise apart from the increasing thrashing of the halyards and the distant sound of the tide crashing onto the rocks somewhere beneath him. He crossed over to the path and started his descent towards the old look-out post. He stumbled and slipped a couple of times on the grass which was beginning to get damp as the evening dew started to form. Swearing profusely under his breath every time he felt his feet slipping, he was grateful when the path finally levelled out and he could more clearly see the ruin in front him.

The sound of the crashing waves was greater down here, providing an increasing crescendo of noise as they slammed onto the rocks below. Selitto climbed into what appeared to be a small concrete cockpit comprising an old battlement wall and the outcrop of rock which Woons had said had previously been some sort of look-out post. He scanned the area around him and noticed a figure leaning against a set of railings on the very edge of the cliff top looking out to sea.

'Billy Woons?' he called out. The figure pushed himself away from the railings and turned to face him.

'DS Selitto no doubt,' Woons replied. 'You got here then?' He walked over to the back of the ruin where there were a couple of old wooden benches. Woons sat down in the middle of one of the benches and beckoned Selitto over. 'Here, grab a seat!' Ideally, Selitto would have preferred to stand but he decided that it wouldn't do any harm to sit on the other bench.

'Okay, Mr Woons,' Selitto began as he sat down. 'I've come a long way to see you so what have you got for me?'

Woons gave him a sideways glance and then turned away to look out towards the sea. 'DS Selitto, the reason I wanted to see you here in Cornwall is because it is no longer safe for me to be anywhere near Kent. I could've gone north to Scotland or some such place but it's too fucking cold up there so I've come here to a place I knew when I was a nipper. I'll probably get some time here before they get to find out where I am and then they'll come for me.'

Selitto had a puzzled look on his face. 'And who are they?' he asked.

'Well now, Mr Selitto, you see that's just the problem.' Woons was looking at him now. 'I ain't got a fucking scooby do! I don't know if they're Bulgarians or Romanians. They might even be fucking Georgians for all I know. Or they could be any other nationality you care to mention! Do you know how many different nationalities get involved in trafficking people across the world?' Selitto shook his head. 'Lots! Lots and lots! And they all want their bit. They all want their share. And they're all as hard as fucking nails. Psychos the lot of them! But they can deliver good quality and I've never had a problem with any of the stuff they've got for me. Only problem is that the supply chain's been hijacked so now I don't know who I'm dealing with and, from what I've seen, the hijackers aren't taking any fucking prisoners. I'm sure you'll agree with that Mr Selitto – you must have seen some of their handiwork in those houses that have been wrecked. I mean, you've got to be fucking bonkers to do what those bastards have done to some of my best people.'

Selitto found himself subconsciously nodding his head in agreement. Some of what he had seen would certainly appear to have been the work of a psychologically deranged madman.

Woons looked away again, clearly dragging some recent memory to the forefront of his mind. 'The woman in that shoot up near Bedgebury,' he continued, 'she's got a twelve-year-old who'll never see her mummy again. Daddy fucked off years ago. She's all alone. You see, Mr Selitto, I've suddenly realised that I cannot go on any longer. When I started in this game, it was so much simpler. I provided the houses and staffed them up with people who knew their trade. I had a good pipeline for the supply of girls. I knew the traffickers well and everything worked tickety boo. But these fucking eastern Europeans have pissed all over the network which has been running successfully for years to the extent that I've got to get out before I'm blasted to kingdom come.'

Woons had got up from the bench and was now pacing. Eventually, he had returned to the railing which marked the edge of the cliff top on which the look-out post stood. 'So that's why I've come to you lot, DS Selitto,' he continued, 'because I reckon you guys would be interested in smashing an international people trafficking operation which focuses solely on the exploitation of young girls for the sex trade. There are some big players involved, and I know who they are and where the bodies are hidden. I can also tell you how it all works and where to find the sort of evidence you will need to nail these bastards.'

Woons had resumed his pacing around the extremities of the look-out post, and Selitto noticed that it was getting decidedly cooler. The light was also starting to fade as Woons continued talking about the connection to the people in a place called Kaspi – a town not far from Tbilisi in Georgia. He also referred to a Georgian Mr Fixit here in the UK. Selitto's ears certainly pricked up when Woons mentioned the name Vashlili.

'We understand that he's on the missing list, Mr Woons', Selitto interjected.

Woons was now pacing faster – backwards and forwards across the front of the look-out post. He grunted. 'That fucking bastard seems to be the cause of all my fucking problems. Fucked off and left me high and dry. Gave all the low down to the Bulgarians or Romanians or whoever they fucking are. Yeah, he's really dropped me and the others in it. Let's hope he's been cemented into the foundations of some new road building project somewhere in Europe. About all he's fucking good for.'

Backwards and forwards. Head down. Looking out to sea. The pacing continued. Eventually Woons came to a halt. He looked up to the sky as if searching for an answer to all his problems. Selitto had never taken his eyes off him as he had moved around the stone floor in the look-out post. Woons was now standing at the very edge of the structure, staring at the DS. Selitto studied him, waiting for another fusillade of invective about the people who were trying to hijack his world. Woons was becoming a silhouette against the sun as it got lower in the sky.

Which made it much easier to see the red dot that suddenly appeared on the left side of Woons' chest.

Selitto stared at the dot, its brightness fascinating him. His brain was in overdrive. He knew what he was looking at. But the context was all wrong. Surely not here on this remote cliff edge. It was as if his thought process had been paralysed. He managed to make a sweeping movement with his arms in a vain attempt to get Woons to move or duck or do whatever he needed to do to get rid of the red dot. But still it clung to the left side of his chest.

He was just about to shout a warning to Woons when he heard a muffled crack. He watched in horror as Woons' chest seemed to explode in slow motion, as his body was catapulted back onto the railings, as a fountain of dark red blood shot into the air between them. All life draining out of the body as it slowly slithered down the railings and crumpled into an untidy heap on the stone floor of the look-out post.

Selitto stared at the figure lying in front of him, finding it hard to believe what he had just witnessed. Then a sense of self-preservation kicked in and he threw himself behind the bench and lay there in the shadows watching and waiting for any sign of the assassin. He could see the lifeless body of Woons about five metres in front of him, a pool of blood spreading across the ground around the body. He waited as long as he dared but he knew that he had to get away from this place. Carefully, he eased himself upwards and clung onto the bench as he finally stood up. Instinctively, he now bent down and scuttled over to the body, making sure not to step into the pool of blood.

Working quickly, Selitto searched Woons' pockets for his phone which was thankfully tucked into his back pocket. He also found a SIM card and a couple of tickets in his trouser pocket which he decided to keep until he had time to see if they would lead him anywhere. He stuffed the phone, the SIM card and the tickets into his own jacket pocket and then sat back on his haunches, staring at the lifeless body in front of him.

The biggest problem was that he was operating on another Force's patch without authority, and now he had a body on his hands. So, he needed to get out of there as fast as possible. But was the assassin waiting for him to show himself or had he already gone – Billy Woons has been taken care of, job done! He shuffled over to the other side of the look-out post and saw that another grassy path led off into the distance behind what looked like a gorse hedge. As this seemed to offer some cover, Selitto crouched down and followed the path. He soon realised that he was walking uphill, and was mightily relieved when he eventually caught sight of the little Coastwatch station. The entire area was now floodlit and tentacles of light were stretching down towards the path. As he climbed to the top of the hill, he could see that lights were starting to glow along the estuary and he was able to pick out the warning beacons guarding the entrance to the harbour.

Cresting the brow of the hill, he followed the road back

down to the harbour and turned onto the quayside, only to see the ferry disappearing into the distance. 'Fuck!' he said loudly, drawing a stern look from one of the drinkers outside the Lugger. He walked on past the steps down to where the ferry would arrive in about ten minutes and on to the edge of the quay, well away from anyone else. He retrieved his phone from his shirt pocket and called Hunter.

She picked up almost immediately, and Selitto quickly filled her in on the events of the last couple of hours.

'Shit!' Hunter exclaimed after Selitto had finished his account of events. 'We're really fucked on this one! We certainly don't want the Devon & Cornwall boys to know that you've been on their patch so you'd better get the hell out of there. Hopefully, some poor unsuspecting tourist will find the body in the morning!'

'Afraid it's not that simple', replied Selitto. 'We weren't far from the Coastwatch Station which has a couple of CCTV cameras on it. May have picked something up.'

There was a pause at Hunter's end, and Selitto could picture her twisting strands of hair around her fingers as she gave some thought to the position they found themselves in. 'Well,' she eventually said, 'you've got to get away from wherever you are and get back across to Fowey without drawing any attention to yourself. Can't see that you've got any other choice.'

'OK, boss!' replied Selitto and disconnected the call. The light was definitely fading now so there was no time to lose in making his getaway. He also had a suspicion that the Polruan Ferry didn't operate much past the time that it got dark.

When the little boat finally arrived back at Polruan, he found that he was the only passenger for the journey over to Fowey so he tried to avoid doing anything which would give the ferryman cause to remember him after the journey was over – particularly as this was likely to be one of the last journeys of the day. Quite soon the ferry was pulling up at the main town quay in Fowey and Selitto exited the boat. He quickly walked up the steps and crossed the small square into the labyrinth of streets which made up the centre of the town.

Once he was on the main street, he headed east towards Caffa Mill where he had left his car some hours before. The shops were now mainly in darkness but the pubs, cafes and restaurants were doing brisk business. And there was quite a crowd of people thronging the street which enabled him to blend in easily as yet another tourist. Eventually the crowds thinned out as he passed the RNLI station, and he carried on round the bend in the road and down to the car park. To his right, he saw a small car ferry on its way over to the tiny hamlet of Bodinnick.

Wednesday 26 July

Jumping into his car, Selitto was just about to start the engine when he suddenly remembered the items he had retrieved from Woons' body in Polruan. He now removed these from his jacket pocket and stared at them in the fading light. The phone and the SIM card would have to wait until he got back to Tonbridge. Of more interest were the tickets which he now realised were for the Bodinnick Ferry which must be the vessel he had just seen mid-river. One of the tickets indicated that the bearer had purchased a single fare for a foot passenger available for the day of issue only. There was no date on the ticket but he noticed that it bore the number 04788.

Staring across the car park towards the slipway, Selitto contemplated the possibility that Woons had left his car in Bodinnick and travelled as a foot passenger over to Fowey before walking through the town and taking the ferry across to Polruan. Thinking that parking was probably severely limited in Bodinnick, Selitto decided to leave his car where it was and travel as a foot passenger over to the other side of the estuary to have a look around. Thankfully, the ferry had just docked so he walked across the car park, down the slipway and onto the gangplank. After a few minutes wait, the ferry got under way for its short journey across the river.

A man with a weather-beaten face and sporting an old dark waterproof jacket and leggings collected Selitto's fare and gave him a ticket – exactly the same ticket as he had found in Woons' pocket but with the number 04857 printed on it.

This meant that there had been sixty-nine foot passengers on the ferry since the original ticket had been issued and, as the ferry mainly carried road vehicles, Selitto concluded that it was more than likely that Woons had travelled across to Fowey earlier in the afternoon.

The crossing lasted for all of five minutes, and Selitto had three cars and two other foot passengers for company. On arrival at Bodinnick, he climbed up the steep slope from the water's edge and then stopped for breath at a fading red telephone box. There was no immediate sign of any car parking area. However, there were three cars parked beside the road in front of The Olde Ferry Inn although none of them looked as if they had just made the long journey from Kent. In fact, they didn't look as if they had made any journeys for quite some time! So, he walked on towards the pub which was lit up like a Christmas tree and obviously doing a roaring trade.

Trying to make himself as inconspicuous as possible, Selitto stepped into the pub and asked a couple sitting at a small table by the door about car parking in Bodinnick. 'Well, there's the pub car park up the hill yonder, but the Landlord makes sure that only people staying in the pub get to use it,' said the man taking a mouthful of a dark, syrupy-looking beer, 'or there's a small public car park round the corner on the road to Lanteglos.'

After making sure that he understood the directions being given to the car park, Selitto left the pub and walked back down toward the slipway before turning right and climbing up a steep incline directly parallel to the estuary below. He reached into his pocket for his LED torch and shone its beam on to the road surface to make sure of his footing. He also wanted to make sure that any oncoming motorists were aware of his presence.

The road wound upwards from the estuary and, after about 800 metres, he shone his torch onto a sign pointing out a car park immediately to his right. Climbing up into the car park area, he saw that there was room for about six cars and that only three of the spaces were taken. A red Renault Clio and a black Mini were parked next to each other in one corner of the car park, both looking as if they had been there for a few weeks as they were covered in leaves and twigs from the trees above.

But his eyes were immediately drawn to a gleaming white Mercedes E-class which was sitting in a bay just inside the car park. No doubt the vehicle of choice for someone like Woons, he thought. And, as he walked up into the parking area, he noticed that the trunk was not completely shut. He shone the torchlight through the windows of the car but there appeared to be nothing inside it, not even a road map although he could see the satnav facilities. He now moved to the back of the car and squatted down to take a closer look at the trunk. He could clearly see that the lid had not been properly closed, and his apprehension was suddenly raised a couple of notches when two flies flew out from the small gap under the lid. He pulled a pair of nitriles out of his jacket pocket and, after slipping them on, he took a deep breath before gently raising the lid.

Whatever he had been expecting to see in the trunk of the Mercedes, it probably wasn't the grotesque sight that greeted him. Dull sightless eyes stared out of sunken sockets, the red gash running from ear to ear giving the macabre impression of a raunchy red smile, the windpipe so clearly severed, a crater in the skull above the right ear, and dried blood caked on all the clothing. Limbs that had been broken in the attempt to get the body into the boot rested at improbable angles giving the impression that some sort of extra-terrestrial being had been packed into the car.

Selitto caught his breath. 'Who the fuck are you?' he whispered to himself, still not really taking in what he was looking at. As if in a trance, he took his phone out of his shirt pocket and started to photograph the body. He gingerly patted the loose-fitting jacket the man was wearing but there was nothing in the pockets – no phone. He desperately needed to get something from the body which could help with identification.

Shining his torch beam around him, he saw that the little car park had a cinder base. Pulling his notebook out of his jacket, he squatted down and rubbed some of the cinders onto one of the pages in the book. He then reached back into the boot of the Mercedes and took hold of the man's right hand. He gently rolled each finger onto the page before closing the book and pressing it tightly, just hoping that the crude fingerprints would be good enough to use back at the lab. He then brushed the light dusting of cinders off the fingers and let the hand drop back to where it had previously been resting. Taking one last look at the body and firing off another couple of shots on his phone, he pulled the lid of the trunk down.

As he walked back down the hill towards the ferry, Selitto tried to piece together what had occurred during the last two or three hours. Woons had clearly travelled to Cornwall with someone else, as yet unidentified. He had stopped in Bodinnick because of some family connection. It would be handy to have had a look at the house he had been staying at but Selitto knew that finding that house would attract far too much attention. Anyway, Woons had arranged their meeting in Polruan at which he had been taken out by an unknown sniper and, at the same time, his accomplice had been killed and his body dumped in the Mercedes. If this was a turf war, it was the most lethal that Selitto had ever experienced.

Arriving at the slipway, Selitto realised that not only was the ferry not at Bodinnick, it wasn't at Fowey either. Glancing up at a notice board hanging on the wall outside the Ferrymaster's office, he realised that the last ferry had departed some 15 minutes ago so he was stranded in Bodinnick.

Cursing his stupidity for not checking the time of the last ferry, Selitto took stock of his situation. Gazing up the narrow street to the bright lights of The Olde Ferry Inn, he suddenly felt hungry and tired in equal measure. What he would give for a plate of hot food and a bed for the night. However, he decided that he would draw far too much attention to himself by stopping for the night at the pub.

He was just wondering what to do when the door to the pub opened and two men wearing fluorescent yellow jackets, waterproof trousers and deck shoes barrelled out on to the street, laughing and shouting farewells to their friends who remained in the pub. They made their way towards the slipway, still laughing and joking with each other as they came alongside Selitto.

One of them stopped whilst his mate stumbled on down the slipway. He looked Selitto up and down. 'You look lost, mate!' he said, the smell of boozy breath washing over Selitto.

'Looks like I missed the last ferry,' Selitto replied. 'Bloody nuisance because my car's parked over there.' He pointed to the car park on the other side of the river. The yachtsman followed Selitto's gaze.

'Hmm! Shouldn't be a problem, mate!' the yachtsman laughed, slapping Selitto on the shoulder. 'We can give you a lift over there, can't we Kev?' The other yachtsman was at the water's edge taking his shoes off.

'Yeah! Whatever you say, Cap'n. Maisie should be here any sec,' whereupon Kev went back to the job of trying to balance on one leg to remove his other shoe. And, as if on cue, a small boat rounded the headland and headed towards the slipway.

'Looks like Maisie's on time tonight,' the Captain said as he also made his way down the slipway, beckoning to Selitto to follow. 'You'll have to get those shoes and socks off if you don't want to get them wet, and roll your trousers up to the knee.' Selitto did as he was told and all three of them eventually clambered into the small vessel.

Maisie took them across the river to the slipway at the car park where Selitto eased himself out of the boat and into the cold water which lapped up above his knees. He quickly made his way into the shallower water and turned to wave farewell to his rescuers, but they were already pootling up river to the yacht basin at Mixtow, roars of laughter gently floating on the night air – no doubt at his expense, thought Selitto.

He carefully made his way across the car park and sat on the tailgate of the Megane, drying his feet on an oily towel he kept in the car for emergencies. Although his trousers were wet from the knee down, his socks and shoes were at least dry so he got into the car, turned the heating up to full blast and phoned Hunter again. She answered straightaway.

'There's something wicked been going on down here,' he informed her. He then filled her in on the discovery of the body in the car and the fact that Woons was clearly not working on his own. Hunter suggested that he should get back as soon as possible. Was he going to get some shut eye? Selitto felt quite awake and had already decided to at least get some of the journey done before finding a quiet car park somewhere to have a rest. So, he ended the call and drove out of the car park, past the Fowey library and up the winding lane which took him to the main road out of Fowey from the east. Only another 260 miles to go!

Hunter put her phone down on the desk in front of her and stared at Stuart Crosby's crime wall. It was already becoming cluttered! Words had been linked together with arrows and lines, photos had been stuck on it with blue tac, and a whole raft of yellow post-it notes were scattered around it like confetti. She left her chair and went up to the board, picking up a white marker pen on her way. She wrote the word 'CORNWALL' in capital letters and put a wavy line underneath it. She then wrote the words 'Woons' and 'Mystery Man' before putting a diagonal line through both. She returned to her seat and sat staring at the board, elbows resting on the desk, cupping her face in her hands.

She had fielded a call from DCI Jack Pennington earlier in the evening. He was calling from the SOC in Maidstone, and wanted to fix up a time to come over for a briefing on the case. He hadn't sounded in any particular hurry and was at pains to explain that the unit was up to its eyeballs with the customary excuse of not having enough manpower to deal with all the referrals. He had seemed quite open about this which Hunter had found refreshing so her original negative feelings had been dissipated somewhat. In the end, she had managed to persuade Pennington that they were close to bringing the case to a conclusion so could she call him back early next week. That had seemed to fit in nicely with his schedule, and they had parted on amicable terms. Hunter had breathed a big sigh of relief.

Out of the corner of her eye, she caught sight of the office door opening as DC Carolyn Pennant and DS Grace Kendall entered the MIR.

'You two not got homes to go to?' Hunter said in a mocking tone. The detectives crossed the room and sat at two of the empty desks. Kendall was the first to speak.

'Carolyn and I have been reviewing some of the evidence which we've got from Meadowlands, and we think that there's more going on there than meets the eye.'

'Yes,' Pennant interjected whilst firing up the workstation on the desk in front of her. 'I've been down there three times now and each time I just feel that I'm being given the run around. It's also become quite clear to me that the staff are terrified of Dangerfield – and, with him not being there, they have said more than they perhaps might have done if he had been there. He seems to rule the place with a rod of iron, and doesn't come across as a particularly caring employer.'

Kendall continued. 'As I've mentioned before, he likes to travel and takes numerous short trips outside the UK. I've tried to do a bit more digging on him, and it seems that he had a run in with the Hungarian authorities in the past. You might recall that Hungary built a barrier on its border with Serbia & Croatia in 2015 during the European migrant crisis.' Hunter nodded slowly, wondering where this was going. 'This was to increase security and prevent illegal immigrants from entering the country other than through official checkpoints in order to claim asylum in Hungary in accordance with international and European law. As a result, the number of illegal entries to Hungary nosedived after the barrier was built as it effectively abolished access to asylum there.'

'Our Mr Dangerfield appears to have come to the notice of the authorities in Hungary because of the number of times he was crossing their borders with non-European nationals in tow. This was in the period immediately leading up to the construction of the barrier and, although we don't have any detailed information about where he was crossing from, logic dictates that he was probably coming through Croatia or Serbia. But the point is that he seems to have been involved in the trafficking of illegals in the past which makes me wonder if he is still involved and whether the hotel is somehow being used to facilitate the movement of illegals once they get to the UK.'

'How do you mean?' asked Hunter, very attentive now as she had long held a strong belief that Dangerfield was a key player in what they had gradually been uncovering.

'Well,' Grace began, 'we already know that the room at the hotel was a dead-letter drop between Vashlili and A N Other, and that someone was probably murdered there last week although we don't know who or why.'

Hunter interrupted her. 'Vashlili is definitely implicated in the whole thing. When Ted met Woons earlier, he talked about him doing the dirty on them and what he'd do if he got his hands on him. Unfortunately, Vashlili now won't have to worry about what our friend Woons might do to him as Woons won't be seeing another sunrise.'

Kendall's eyebrows shot up and she gaped, open-mouthed at Hunter. Pennant was similarly agog. 'Yes, Ted's just given me the news that Woons was taken out earlier this evening by an unknown assassin. Sniper's bullet we suspect. And right in front of poor old Ted! He also found the body of another man in the boot of Woons' Merc. No idea who it is but hopefully we'll be able to ID it when he gets back with the evidence that he's gathered.'

'Bloody hell!' exclaimed Kendall. 'What on earth are Devon & Cornwall going to say when they find that lot?'

'Let's wait and see if they come knocking at our door,' Hunter replied, not really wanting to get into a discussion about inter-force politics. 'The point is that it now looks as if Woons is or was the main man here, and that the two who were killed out at Bedgebury were also part of his gang. We can also probably safely say that the man in the boot of the Merc is in the mix. From what I can gather from Ted, it seems that Woons operated a number of outlets for the ultimate in sexual pleasure which was provided by girls who were sourced in Eastern Europe and trafficked to the UK where they were unmercifully exploited. They were held at different locations here in Kent and moved to these outlets when required. Vashlili seems to have been the link man between the traffickers and Woons, and he was responsible for sourcing the girls. It's likely that he was on the payroll of an international gang based in Georgia so he's more likely to have defected to another group from Romania or Bulgaria who seem to have been sniffing around Woons' patch for some time.'

Kendall and Pennant sat where they were, completely absorbed in what they were hearing, wanting to hear more from Hunter who let the silence float in the room. No one moved. Eventually, Pennant blew out her cheeks and shifted in her chair.

'If you don't mind me saying, ma'am', she began, 'I think that lighthouse needs to have a thorough going over. Each time I've been down there, I've just got the feeling that they'd rather that you didn't go down to the lake. When you mention anything to do with the lake, they give you such an obtuse answer that it makes you wonder if they are trying to deliberately put you off the scent.'

'Yes, I'm inclined to agree with you, Carolyn,' Hunter replied. 'But we would need to organise a formal search because, apart from anything else, we'd need to get a boat on the water.'

'No problem with a boat,' Pennant chided, 'there's already one there!' Hunter and Kendall stared at her.

Hunter looked confused. 'I thought Ted said that the boat on the lake had been sunk. So, I assumed that we'd have to get the marine boys in to help.'

'Well, on my last visit, I spotted a small rowing boat which looked as if it had been purposely hidden under the old jetty on the eastern side of the lake. I wasn't able to take a good look at it but it seemed to be seaworthy – if that's the right word for boating on a lake!'

Hunter smiled. She was thinking, her mind whirring through the options. The lengthy formal approach which she hated or the quick in-and-out solution – get in, take a look, get out. She much preferred the unconventional approach, and this situation seemed to be crying out for a surprise tactic.

There was more to come from Pennant. 'I also think I may have discovered another way of getting to the lake without going via the hotel. I've spent quite a bit of time on Google Earth looking at the lake and its surrounds, and I'm pretty sure that you can get to the top end by the weir along a track which cuts round the fields alongside. Let me show you.'

She accessed the Google Maps website and keyed in the location. Then she got the aerial shot of the location up on the screen. The other two gathered round.

Pointing to the screen with a pencil, Pennant drew their attention to the driveway from the main road to the hotel. 'You see here, this is the way into the hotel from the drive that links with the road. Here's the actual entrance to the hotel. But look back here, there's a track which leads eventually to a field immediately behind the lake. Then it looks as if there's a pathway that leads around the field and then into the woods by the top of the lake just here.' She tapped the pencil on the screen. 'That's the weir there and the jetty with the boat under it is just round here under the trees.' She tapped the screen again. 'If we could get a vehicle down to the corner of that field, I reckon we could easily access the lake and get across to the lighthouse using the boat.'

They all sat there looking at the picture of the lake, and the tracks and pathways that Pennant had pointed out. Each with their own thoughts. Each keen to move the investigation forward.

'Okaaaay,' Hunter elongated the word and let it hang in the silence of the room. 'I think we should take a look using Carolyn's suggested route in. I don't want the hotel to know that we have been there so we'll need to move quickly. What sort of time is it getting light in the mornings?'

Pennant accessed a 'Time & Date' website to get the information. 'It should be light enough to see where we're going at around 4.00 a.m. tomorrow morning. Sunrise is officially at 5.00 a.m.' she reported.

Hunter felt energised. 'Okay! Let's get this done!' she announced. 'Let's see - what will we need? Probably some sort of 4x4 vehicle or an off-roader for a start.'

'I can do that!' Kendall chimed in. 'My neighbour's got one and she's forever trying to get me to take it for a spin.'

So that was the vehicle sorted. Hunter was then keen to make sure that they had a plan which stood up to scrutiny. It was soon agreed that she and Pennant would row over to the lighthouse and take a look inside. Kendall would remain with her vehicle wherever they eventually decided to leave it, and she would be responsible for calling for back-up if she received a signal from the other two. Having spent about an hour discussing some of the details of the plan, and noticing that it was now pitch dark outside, they agreed to get home for a few hours' kip and to return to Pembury Road by 3.00 a.m. with Kendall in the 4x4.

98

Thursday 27 July

They had all reassembled slightly before 3.00 a.m. and were now on their way to Meadowlands in a rather ancient Volvo XC90. However, it purred along the dark, pot-holed roads of Kent and there was plenty of room to stretch one's legs inside the vehicle. Pennant sat in the front next to Kendall and gave her directions. There was very little traffic on the roads, and what vehicles they did see only served to arouse Hunter's suspicions about what they were doing out at this time of the night.

Hunter, herself, had had very little sleep. On returning home, she had suddenly remembered that her mother was arriving later that day. She had, therefore, charged around the house with the vacuum cleaner and had frantically changed the sheets on the bed only to then notice a voicemail on the house phone which told her that her mother's visit had been postponed by 24 hours! Was that okay? By the time she'd called her mother and had a quick bite to eat it was after midnight. And, when her head did eventually hit the pillow, she found that there was so much going on in her mind that sleep just wouldn't come.

They drove on in silence, each with their own thoughts. As the clock on the dashboard clicked on to 3.40 a.m, Pennant directed Kendall on to a narrow country lane which wound through a forest before telling her to slow down and look for the signpost to Meadowlands. Once off the country lane, they negotiated the long driveway to the hotel entrance before

Pennant indicated that they should turn off onto what, in the headlights, looked like a well-worn and uneven farm track. They bounced along the track which tunnelled through the forest surrounding the hotel. Each of them had a picture of the area in their minds from the briefing which Pennant had given them, but it was still difficult to marry it up with what they were actually seeing on the ground.

Eventually, the forest receded from the edges of the track and they came into what appeared to be a clearing. Pennant suggested that they stop here, and she got out of the Volvo to inspect the surrounding area. Her torch beam quickly picked out a pathway which led off into the trees in the direction of the lake. Hunter also got out of the vehicle and had a few words with Kendall about rendezvousing later. Pennant retrieved a small rucksack which she had placed in the trunk of the Volvo and strapped it onto her back. She then led the way into the forest. They soon came out of the trees and found themselves at the corner of a small field. It was just starting to get a bit lighter, and they could make out the area of the field with the path hugging the edge of the tree line. They followed the path round the field until Pennant suddenly put her arm out in front of Hunter indicating that they should stop.

'Hear that?' she asked. Hunter listened. 'A waterfall by the sound of it so we must be near the small weir. We need to be over there a bit more,' she said, pointing off to Hunter's right.' They walked on with Pennant leading. Quite soon, she stopped again and turned back to Hunter. 'Look! It's the boundary fence. Just a couple of wires which are nice and slack. We need to cross these and then get down on to the path. Once we're there I'll get my bearings for the jetty but we should be close. Shall I hold the wires down for you?' It wasn't really a question as Pennant was instinctively depressing the wires with her foot and Hunter had already crossed over into the grounds of Meadowlands.

Pennant followed and they both headed down to the path. The light was improving as the minutes went by, and they could now make out the edge of the lake which was enshrouded in an early morning mist. Once they were on the path, the giant obelisk which was the lighthouse reared up in front of them and sent a shiver down Hunter's spine. Pennant led the way as they turned towards where she remembered the jetty as being. They quickly found it whereupon Pennant stepped on to the wooden structure and dropped to her knees, her hands reaching under the boarding to get hold of the boat. After a good deal of tugging and not a little swearing, she finally managed to release the craft so that it floated alongside the jetty.

She instructed Hunter to get in and then hold on to the jetty whilst Pennant herself got into the boat. Thankfully, there were two oars stored under the seats so she fixed them into the rowlocks and edged out onto the mist-laden lake. She quickly realised that, although the water appeared calm, there was a current running towards the weir so she decided to row upstream and then more or less float down to the lighthouse. Using her oars to slow down her progress, she managed to bring the little boat alongside the landing jetty attached to the light-house which was where they encountered their first problem.

'All this wood looks pretty rotten to me,' Hunter whispered as both she and Pennant hung on to what was left of the jetty. Pennant could just see across the jetty and wondered if it was the same on the other side. So, she pushed away from the jetty and rowed round to the other side where she nudged into wooden boards which seemed much firmer. 'That's better!' she said under her breath. Hunter climbed onto the jetty and took the mooring rope which she held until Pennant had joined her. In the improving light, they found a mooring ring attached to the base of the lighthouse so they tied the boat up to it.

Taking care to avoid boards which looked as if they might give way and consign them to the water below, they crept over to the stone steps which led up to the door of the lighthouse. Standing in front of the steps and looking straight up the side walls of the structure, Hunter couldn't help being in awe of its sheer size and beauty. The mist lying on the water around it contributed to the mystical setting and also gave the building a certain eeriness.

Pennant had got to the door first where she stopped and then turned to Hunter, beckoning her to climb the stairs. 'Ma'am, look!' she whispered. 'The door's open! The padlock's hanging loose. And look! There's a light on inside!' Hunter looked to where she was pointing and then nodded. She agreed. It did look as if there was a thin sliver of weak light framing the unlocked door. Pennant shrugged her rucksack off her shoulders and delved into it, eventually pulling out a can of pepper spray for each of them. She also pulled out another heavy-duty torch which she gave to Hunter who thought it would probably make a better weapon than a means of lighting the way. Pennant still had her own torch and, feeding one arm through the rucksack straps so that it hung loosely on her shoulder, she gently pushed the door open and peered through the wider aperture she had created.

99

Thursday 29 July

As the door inched silently inwards, all Pennant could hear was a faint buzzing sound which reminded her of being in her kitchen at home. Light was drifting down from higher up in the structure and now cast a weak pall over the ground floor of the lighthouse. As she eased the door further open, a set of stairs came into view which hugged the rounded side of the structure, winding its way upwards. But what really caught her eye was a bank of freezers which took up most of the space around the entrance. She now realised what the buzzing was and tried to step aside to let Hunter take a look. But there wasn't really enough room for them both to stand on the same step so Pennant took the decision to launch herself into the lighthouse.

She pushed the door again but found that it wouldn't open any further. It seemed to have become wedged up against something which was lying behind it. There was, however, just enough room for her to squeeze through. Hunter quickly followed and they stood together in the limited space in front of the freezers. Pushing the door back to its original position, they noticed the reason why they couldn't open it further.

'That's a coracle!' Hunter whispered. 'Must mean that there's someone else in here.' She went over to the small, rounded craft which had been wedged between the door and the bottom of the staircase. Feeling the underside of the little craft, she indicated to Pennant that there was still water on it so there was every chance that it had been used very recently.

But Pennant was more interested in the freezers. She just couldn't imagine what they were being used for. Moving to the one nearest her, she tentatively tried to lift the lid. It wouldn't budge to start with but, after applying a bit more upward pressure, the suction was broken and the lid lifted up. Cold air spewed out of the appliance and condensed in the warmer air inside the lighthouse, momentarily obstructing Pennant's view of the freezer's contents. Once the cloud of condensed air had evaporated, she could see that it was packed to the gunwales with what looked like plastic bags full of meat. But what really caught Pennant's attention was the bag nestling on the top of the pile. The head of a young girl stared out of the bag, looking directly at Pennant, her long blond hair shoved carelessly into the bag, strands of it covering the lower part of her face. Pennant sucked in an audible breath which alerted Hunter who was still inspecting the coracle. She looked over and saw Pennant standing stock still, her eyes out on stalks, her mouth involuntarily open. Hunter quickly crossed the floor to look at what Pennant had discovered and now reached around her Detective Constable to push the freezer lid down. She pulled Pennant back towards the doorway and looked her in the eye.

'Carolyn, are you OK?' Hunter whispered. Pennant nodded but she was clearly still shocked by what she had just seen. Hunter got hold of Pennant's arms and gave her shoulders a shake. 'Come on, Carolyn, we need to nail these bastards. Be strong!' She looked deep into Pennant's eyes and felt her breathing returning to something like normality. Pennant let out a sigh and nodded her head.

'Right!' Hunter continued. 'We need to call this in before we go any further. I'll step outside and call Grace. You wait here and keep a look out in case anyone starts coming down the stairs.' And with that she slipped out of the door.

Pennant turned back to look at the bank of freezers, her shock turning to morbid fascination as she was drawn to one of the upright appliances. Moving towards it, she gingerly opened the door and was mightily relieved not to see a head staring out at her. The drawers were, however, packed with more of the plastic bags so she pulled one out to get a better look at its contents. Her inquisitiveness soon turned to horror when she realised that what she had picked up was an arm – just an arm as the hand had been removed. She threw the bag back onto the drawer, pushed it back into the freezer and closed the door. These freezers are full of body parts! she muttered to herself, shaking her head in disbelief. What the hell is going on here??

She was thinking of taking a look in another of the freezers when she felt a touch on her arm. Hunter looked at her and mouthed the word 'Okay?' Pennant nodded whereupon Hunter turned to face the stairway and pointed upwards with a questioning look. Pennant nodded again so they started climbing, Hunter leading. The steps were not particularly even, and the height of each one seemed to vary so progress was slow. But they were able to haul themselves up the stairs using the handrail, eventually reaching the next level where they stopped dead in their tracks.

Arranged around the circular wall were a number of what Hunter thought looked like the holding cells they had at the Tonbridge police station. But these were less sophisticated and weren't really much more than cages. Each cage adjoined the one next to it, thick metal bars rising about seven feet from the base, more bars crisscrossing the top of the cages. Big padlocks on the doors. Room enough inside for one person. They could see that most of the cages were empty but, in the dim light, Hunter could make out figures lying on the floor of two of the cages. Moving across to the two occupied cells, she crouched down and shone her torch on to one of the figures.

A young girl was sleeping on the floor of the cage, her knees pulled up to her chest, wearing a thin flimsy dress, her pretty face peering out from under a mop of hazel hair, eyes closed. Even as Hunter played the torch beam over her face, the eyes did not open. Was she in a deep sleep or had she been drugged? Pennant shone her torch beam onto the girl in the adjoining cage who was lying in a similar position. Again, there was no optical reaction.

The two detectives looked around them. Although the other cages were empty, there were discarded items of clothing lying on the floor in one of them. Hunter shone her torch into this cage and pointed to smears of blood on the bars surrounding the padlock and on the floor. The discarded dress was also covered in blood. She looked at Pennant and nodded her head upwards, a silent message that they should go on.

They returned to the stairs and climbed to the next floor, passing a window which had been boarded up. Hunter had been wondering how no one had seemed to have noticed that there was a light on in the building but then of course they wouldn't if all the windows had been boarded up. On reaching the next level, they found that it was much brighter here, presumably because they were closer to the source of the light which had been filtering down the stairwell since they first entered the lighthouse. They soon realised that there were more cages on this floor but, this time, each cage contained a young girl. The significant difference between these cages and the ones on the floor below was that these girls were all awake and staring at the two detectives with dull, sunken eyes. Each girl had a strip of duct tape across her mouth. Both hands had been cuffed to the bars at the side of the cage. They looked frightened and cold although the temperature in the room was reasonably warm.

'Oh, my God!' Hunter whispered under her breath. Pennant was frozen to the spot, having difficulty comprehending what she was looking at. She just stared, slowly playing her torch beam backwards and forwards across the semicircle of cages. Hunter tugged her arm to get her attention. She leaned over to whisper in Pennant's ear.

'I reckon the next floor is the top floor so if there's someone else in here then they're going to be up there. Let's take it slowly and see if we can get to them before they see us. Grace should be here with the cavalry soon but let's find out what goes on up there.' She looked into Pennant's eyes which were filled with a mixture of sadness and dread fear. 'You all right to go on, Carolyn?' Pennant nodded her head and licked her lips to get some moisture into her dry mouth. She nodded again and looked over to the staircase. Hunter let go of her arm and they both shuffled back past the cages and started to climb the last part of the staircase, Hunter in the lead.

On getting Hunter's call from the lighthouse, Kendall had called Selitto who was on the M25 just passing Godstone at Junction 6. Although he had managed a couple of uncomfortable hours shut-eye at Fleet Services on the M3, he still felt absolutely shattered. However, he said that he would divert off

639

at the next junction and get himself down to Meadowlands. He thought he would be able to find where Kendall had parked but he would call her once he was on the long driveway into the hotel.

In line with Hunter's instructions, she next rang the night desk to get DCI Iversen's emergency phone number. Hunter wanted him to authorise a raid on the lighthouse so that they could at least justify their actions. Iversen didn't sound too pleased to be awoken at four-thirty in the morning, but he was soon on the case once Kendall told him about the freezers.

'I suppose it's too much to ask that DI Hunter has waited for back up before going any further into the lighthouse?' he opined once Kendall had finished her account. He listened to Kendall's reply. 'Might have known it!' he sighed. 'Okay, Sergeant, tell DI Hunter that she has my blessing. I'll call the duty team leader now and get her to make contact with you directly. Hopefully, they'll be able to get this wrapped up without too much fuss. Keep me informed. I might as well get into the station now – not worth going back to bed – so call me there if you need me.'

Kendall was just about to leave the Volvo to recce the route to the lake when her personal mobile alerted her to an incoming text message. She pulled the phone out of her pocket and glanced at the screen, a wry smile crossing her lips -

Sorry, Darling. Can't make it back to your place. Too much on.

Maybe later. Can't wait to be back in your arms.

Dreaming of us. LYWAMH xxxxx

She continued smiling to herself as she stepped down from the vehicle and made her way towards the lake.

100

Thursday 27 July

The final staircase was a steel structure and was also much steeper than the ones they had climbed earlier so Pennant had to lag behind to avoid being kicked in the eye by Hunter's heels. As her head reached the level of the floor at the top of the lighthouse, Hunter stopped and carefully looked out across the lantern room, noticing that the lantern and its component parts had clearly been removed. She was, however, puzzled by the amount of equipment there was in the room, much of it resembling the sort of furnishings she was more used to seeing in Toby Swartzman's mortuary. She craned her neck to see what was round the corner of the stair wall, and then recoiled in horror, almost knocking Pennant back down the stairs. After a split second to regain her composure, she steeled herself for a second look.

Away to her right, she could see two stainless-steel gurneys, one with a body lying on it. Blood was dripping from the gurney on to the linoleum floor below, making little splashes as it hit the floor. Harsh lighting shone into the room from three portable LED floodlights which had been set up on stands around the gurneys. The reflections also provided additional lighting so that the whole of the lantern room was bathed in a stark clinical light. A huge man, with his back to Hunter, was bending over the table and Hunter could see the flash of a blade as he worked on the body. The man must have been over six-and-a-half feet tall with huge biceps and tree trunk legs. Hunter could see that he had a thick black beard and close-cropped black hair. His brown arms were covered in a luxuriant growth of black hair and, from where she was crouched, he looked as if he might have originated in a subtropical European country. She had another look across the floor but couldn't see that there was anyone else in the room so she assumed that the man was working alone.

No time to waste, she thought to herself. She turned to Pennant and gave a hand-signal to indicate that she should follow. She extracted the pepper spray from her pocket, gripped her torch in her right hand, and heaved herself up the remaining steps before leaping from her position on the staircase and launching herself at the man. Just as she was nearly on him, he turned from the table to select another instrument and caught sight of her out of the corner of his eye. He managed to raise one of his massive arms in time to deflect the torch as it arced down towards his head. With his other hand, he swatted Hunter away – a crunching blow to her upper body sending her skittering away across the linoleum. She slipped and slithered in the blood before crashing into the boarding which had been set up to block out all light from entering or leaving the lantern room. The pepper spray popped out of her hand and went flying across the bloodied floor of the room.

Pennant had followed her up the stairs and had grabbed hold of the second gurney. She was now taunting the man by pushing the gurney at him, similar to the way a Spanish matador would taunt a raging bull with a red cape. Although it was a tactic which was destined to only keep the man at bay for a very short period of time, it did allow Hunter an opportunity to get herself back together. Standing up again, pain coursing through her whole upper body, she looked around desperately for her pepper spray or anything else she could use as a weapon. At the same time, the man had tired of playing cat and mouse with Pennant and lifted the entire gurney into the air and flung it disdainfully in Hunter's direction. She dived to her right to avoid the flying gurney and crashed into a metal cabinet, ending up in a crumpled heap on the floor. The gurney smashed into the boarding which covered the windows, dislodging two of the wooden panels and allowing the merest hint of daylight into the room.

Pennant seized the opportunity to work her way across the blood-soaked floor to the workbench which she had spotted along one of the walls. This had an array of implements lying on it but her eyes were irresistibly drawn to the two hands which lay amongst the equipment. All thought of finding something to help contain this monster instantly went out of her head as she continued staring at her appalling discovery, and her general inertia gave the man the opportunity to catch up with her. He grabbed hold of her hair and violently yanked her back from the workbench. Pennant lashed out with her feet, trying to drive her heels into his shins but finding that she was too far away from him. She then fumbled in her pocket for the pepper spray and tried to hold it above her head so that she could spray it into his face. But before she had even managed to get as far as finding the button to release the spray, the man had smashed his fist into her hand and the cannister had gone flying. He then tightened his grip on her hair and started to drag her across the room. Where was Hunter, for God's sake, she thought.

Suddenly, she heard a dull thud and the grip on her hair loosened. Out of the corner of her eye, she saw that Hunter had managed to get hold of a piece of the board and had smashed it down on to the man's head. He now swung round in Hunter's direction and delivered what Pennant could only describe as a haymaker of a punch which cannoned into the side of Hunter's head. It knocked her sideways and she crashed into a small fridge which burst open disgorging hundreds of small glass phials and racks of test tubes. She collapsed onto the glass vessels as they rolled drunkenly across the floor, little shards of glass cutting her clothing and puncturing her skin. She was dazed and now had a searing pain in her ribs following the collision with the fridge.

Meanwhile, the man seemed to have tired of hanging on to Pennant's hair and, in one move, he jerked her towards him before sending her careering across the blood-soaked floor. She crashed into the other gurney and came face to face with the body of a young girl with limbs missing and a hole in her chest. The gurney caught the corner of the workbench and tipped over, the body sliding down Pennant's legs and onto the floor at her feet. Pennant had grabbed hold of the workbench to keep herself upright, and was again frantically looking for anything that she could use as a weapon. Suddenly, she heard a cry and spun round just in time to see the man standing over Hunter holding what looked like a claw hammer. Righting the gurney and kicking the body of the young girl out of the way, she took the only course of action she could think of and drove the metal trolley straight into the back of the man's legs. This made him totter sideways and he put his arms out to grab hold of something to stop himself falling over. But he only succeeded in crashing into one of the windows which had been exposed when the boarding had been removed.

Pennant drove the gurney at him again, this time catching him on the lower back as he struggled to regain his footing. Again, he crashed into the window but this time Pennant noticed that the window had moved and she suddenly realised that it was part of a door leading to the outside gallery. His weight had clearly smashed the locking system and, after years of being rotted by the weather, the wood surrounding the lock had obviously become loose so that the door was now being forced open. Her mind was racing, trying to work out how she could take advantage of this. But she wasn't quick enough. The man was back on his feet and had tossed the gurney to the far corner of the room. He lunged towards her but was having difficulty staying upright as he kept slipping on the phials and test tubes, and he soon crashed to the floor. Ribbons of blood immediately laced his fingers as he cut his hands on the smashed glass in his desperation to get back on his feet. But he was up quickly and now turned his attention back to Hunter who was limping around the wall of the room towards the workbench.

Hunter was almost up to the door leading on to the gallery when the man made another lunge towards her. She froze, anticipating the worst, unable to persuade her body to dart out of the way, her eyes closed waiting for the impact. But, at the same time, hearing a loud crack followed by an extended series of clicks. She wrenched her eyes open and stared as the huge man suddenly leapt past her, smashing through the door and barrelling out onto the gallery which ran around the outside of the lantern room. With her brain still not functioning properly, Hunter looked back across the lantern room to where Pennant stood holding what looked like a toy gun with wispy wires hanging from it. Both women stared wide-eyed at each other for what seemed like an eternity but was no more than a couple of seconds, unspoken words flying between them.

Hunter quickly pushed herself along the wall, wondering if she would have the strength to pull the door shut and leave the man outside. That might buy them precious seconds in which to try and make an escape. The dawn was starting to break, and she could see the man leaning on the railing, his body twitching as the last of the electricity drained away. She noticed that he had now started to stamp his feet as if to get the feeling back into his legs. Hunter looked down at his feet as he continued stamping on the wooden slats which made up the floor of the gallery. She suddenly realised that they were starting to come loose from the railings. She watched, fascinated and horrified in equal measure, as three or four of the slats suddenly pinged out of their sockets and plunged down the side of the tower.

The man was still leaning over the railing, seemingly oblivious to the fact that the gallery floor was breaking up underneath him. Hunter was transfixed, watching as the man finally realised what was happening. He suddenly pushed himself off the rail just as there was the dull clunk of corroded metal twisting apart. Hunter stared, hardly daring to blink, as the railing buckled before completely snapping away from the wooden slats. With nothing to hold them up, the slats collapsed and the man slid off the gallery floor. As he started to fall, Hunter noticed that the wispy wires from Pennant's taser became taut and almost pulled the handset out of her hand. But, just as quickly, they became flaccid again as the electrodes burst out of the man's back as he hurtled towards the jetty some 100 feet below. Both Hunter and Pennant heard the sickening thud as the body smashed into the rotting boards of the little landing stage.

Hunter was the first to come to her senses, pushing herself into the doorway. Peering out into the abyss now lit by early morning shafts of sunlight, she could see that the wooden boardwalk which stretched around the gallery had rotted over the years and had now given way under the man's weight. Holding on to the doorframe, she leaned out and could see his body spread-eagled on the landing stage, his head and one arm hanging over the side caressing the water.

She heard rather than saw Pennant making her way across all the broken glass on the floor, and she too peered out through the open doorway. With difficulty, and in a lot of pain, Sarah Hunter put her arm round Pennant, and rested her badly swollen face on her shoulder. 'Thank you,' she whispered.

Carolyn Pennant felt herself welling up but knew that now was not the time for emotional release. That could come later. So, she simply put her arms around Hunter and embraced her as she continued to rest her head on Pennant's shoulder. They still had to get out of this place and it was up to Pennant to get her boss safely back to the shore of the lake. So, she gently untangled herself from Hunter's embrace.

'We need to get out of here and leave it to the others to sort out,' she said to Hunter who was now doubled over, hands on knees. Resting.

'Okay, Carolyn,' Hunter said as she drew herself upright, 'you lead the way because I'll be a bit slow!' With that, they started off down the steep metal staircase with Pennant frequently turning to make sure her boss was still behind her.

Once on the floor below the lantern room, they quickly

eyeballed the cages and saw a sense of anticipation on the faces of the girls in the cages. Pennant gave them a weak smile. There was still no movement from the girls in the cages on the next floor down, and Pennant wondered if they would ever see another sunrise.

By now, Hunter was struggling and was taking one step at a time. She was clearly in a lot of pain and kept holding her side. Pennant was relieved when they eventually arrived back at the ground floor. Hunter, however, had noticed that the door to the landing stage was now shut which she found surprising as she had deliberately left it slightly ajar after she had made her call to Grace Kendall. She tugged at Pennant's arm. 'I left that door open when I came back in!' she whispered in Carolyn's ear. The DC frowned and turned back to look at the door. A new sense of fear started worming its way into her stomach as she realised that the door was indeed closed. Could it have blown shut when the door in the lantern room had been opened?

She was still trying to get to grips with this conundrum when the door suddenly opened and a figure slipped into the dimly lit entry hall. Fully expecting it to be one of the team from Tonbridge which would have been mobilised by now, Hunter was rendered speechless when the figure turned and stepped into a pool of light, a gun pointed at both of them.

Dangerfield.

101

Thursday 27 July

Selitto and Kendall had been keeping a watch on the lighthouse from the small jetty, well hidden from view. They had been joined by DI Andrea Ironside who was in charge of the SWAT Team which had been organised by DCI Iversen. However, he had omitted to let Ironside know that they would need at least one marine craft in order to reach the lighthouse so she was now awaiting the arrival of a dinghy.

Before DI Ironside had arrived, and as the mist was still hanging on the lake, Selitto and Kendall had caught sight of a small rounded coracle making its way along the far side of the lake. Selitto had trained the binoculars on the craft but was unable to make out who was paddling the small vessel through the mist. Kendall had also had a look but, as she had never actually met anyone from Meadowlands, she couldn't throw any light on who it might be. They had watched as the coracle had eventually been moored to the far side of the landing stage. The mystery sculler had then clambered onto the jetty. Through the binoculars, Selitto had seen what looked like a man with a cap pulled right down to his eyes and a dark windcheater with the neck pulled up and over his chin. The man had made his way into the lighthouse but then, almost immediately, had returned to the coracle.

Although it had been at that difficult time when daylight starts to take over from the darkness of night, their attention had soon been drawn to a panel of light which suddenly appeared in the lantern room at the top of the lighthouse.

Training the binoculars on to this strip of light, Selitto had been able to make out shadows moving about inside the room and had to assume that Hunter and Pennant were now up there.

They had both stared open-mouthed when a huge man barrelled out of the room onto the boardwalk around the gallery, and Selitto had just managed to get the binoculars trained on him before the wooden slats started to give way. He watched as the man tumbled off the gallery and had now passed the binoculars to Kendall who was looking at the body which had come to rest on the edge of the landing stage. It looked as if the jetty had virtually collapsed into the water due to the sheer weight of the man.

Ironside took a call on her mobile and indicated to the others that a couple of dinghies would be there in about twenty minutes. In the meantime, there was little they could all do apart from watch and wait.

They were wondering what was going to happen next when the mystery sculler suddenly leapt out of the coracle and slunk across the landing stage to inspect the body before mounting the stone steps and pushing the door open to enter the light-house. Grabbing the binoculars, Selitto wasn't quick enough to get another sighting of the man, but he didn't have to wait long before the door at the foot of the structure was opened and he saw DI Hunter being propelled out of the lighthouse. He watched in horror as she missed her footing on the first of the stone steps and fell headlong onto the jetty where she lay still. DC Pennant was similarly thrown out of the building and, although she managed to take the stone steps in her stride, she tripped at the bottom and went sprawling onto the wooden boarding of the landing stage. She almost landed on top of

Hunter who had still not moved, but managed to roll away as a figure came down the steps towards her.

'Bloody hell! That's Dangerfield!' Selitto whispered to Kendall and Ironside. Hardly daring to breathe, he trained the glasses on the man. 'Oh my God! He's got a fucking gun!'

Kendall grabbed the binoculars and watched as Pennant tried to sit up but Dangerfield was too quick for her and they all winced as he pistol-whipped Pennant across the face. Her high-pitched scream echoed across the calm waters of the lake, the torrent of water pouring through the weir being the only other sound. They all felt helpless.

Meanwhile, Hunter had still not moved. Dangerfield was now standing over her, pointing the gun at the prone figure, seemingly saying something but no one could hear him from the shore. He viciously kicked her lower back but still she didn't move. He walked round the body and kicked her again in the stomach. The gun was wavering between Hunter and Pennant, and Dangerfield still seemed to be talking to them both.

Selitto noticed that, despite the pistol-whipping, Pennant looked as if she still had plenty of fight left in her, and she had soon struggled back into a sitting position. She appeared to be saying something to Dangerfield who clearly didn't like what he was hearing and was now slowly raising the gun so that it was pointing directly at her. Hunter still hadn't moved.

Suddenly, everything stopped as a loud crack split the air and the birds around the lake took to the heavens, squawking warnings of danger to each other.

Selitto watched as Dangerfield's head blew apart, blood and brains and bits of gristle flying into the air, the rest of his body involuntarily tottering across the small landing stage before crashing over the side into the lake. Everything seemed to happen in slow motion, and Selitto found that he was still focusing on the empty space where Dangerfield had been standing.

He quickly grabbed the binoculars and now focused on Pennant. She was covered in a sheen of bloody detritus which had until recently been part of Dangerfield's head. He could see that she was completely overwrought, shaking her head, crying out, huge convulsive sobs. After what seemed like an age but was probably only a matter of seconds, Selitto watched as Pennant crawled over to Hunter's body and lifted up one of her arms, trying to get her into a more comfortable position, leaning into her to see how else she could help. Hunter looked like a dead weight to Selitto, and he was getting more and more concerned until he noticed that Pennant was talking to her.

Before the echo of the shot had receded, DI Ironside had leapt into action, screaming orders into her waveband radio as she disappeared to mobilise her team. Boat or no boat, they had a sniper to find. Selitto and Kendall remained where they were at the jetty, simply staring across the water towards their two colleagues, momentarily powerless to help them in their struggle to come to terms with their sickening ordeal.

102

Thursday 3 August

It had been a busy week for all who had been involved in what had become one of Kent County Constabulary's biggest criminal investigations since the force was set up in 1857. The Murder Investigation Team at Tonbridge had been supplemented by detectives from Canterbury and Folkestone who were able to help with their experience of dealing with illegal immigration and the trafficking of people from all over the world.

The case had attracted huge media attention both in the UK and further afield, and the Public Relations people at Maidstone had been rushed off their feet arranging press conferences at almost every hour of the day – and sometimes well into the night. The Chief Constable had regularly been on television news programmes, and huge white vans with antennae pointing to the heavens were a permanent sight in the streets around Police Headquarters annoying the hell out of the neighbours.

DI Sarah Hunter had spent much of the week in Pembury Hospital recovering from two cracked ribs, a badly sprained ankle, a fractured shoulder, extensive bruising, concussion and a nasty gash across her forehead. When the rescue team had finally got to her on the landing jetty at the lighthouse, she had lapsed into unconsciousness which had created problems for transferring her to a waiting ambulance in the adjoining field. The decision had, therefore, been taken to get her transported directly from the jetty straight to Pembury Hospital, and a Coast Guard rescue helicopter had been summoned.

Once at Pembury, she had been moved into the intensive care department where she was under the watchful eyes of the ICU staff. After a couple of days, she was able to get out of bed but was still having trouble with her vision and bouts of dizziness. Members of the team had been ferrying her mother to and from the hospital on a daily basis as Carol Hunter had stayed on after visiting her friend, Gracie, and was looking after Hunter's house in her absence. After five days at Pembury, Hunter had been allowed to go home – and that was when the pampering had really started!

DC Carolyn Pennant had also required hospital treatment to her severely bruised and swollen face, and to various minor cuts and abrasions she had suffered in the lantern room. There was also a worry that her jaw may have been fractured but, after extensive X-rays were studied, it was decided that she probably had only suffered a hairline crack. The Orthopaedic Consultant assigned to her case said that he would keep her condition under review and, in the meantime, had suggested that she should wear a neck brace which she was now doing under duress. At least Pennant's hair was long enough so she could let it hang loosely around her shoulders. This meant that it covered some of the livid bruising which had spread across her face. She had wanted to get back to the MIR as soon as she could but was suffering from sleepless nights with the memories of her ordeal fresh in her mind, the head of the girl in the plastic bag swimming in and out of her consciousness at all hours of the day and night.

Pennant had also attended a number of meetings with Professional Standards following her deployment of the taser in the lantern room of the lighthouse. She had been trained in the use of tasers whilst she was in Traffic, and had managed to persuade a former colleague to provide her with a taser which was 'on loan' for the night of the visit to the lighthouse. She had only taken it with her in case of what she always referred to as "the nuclear option". Sure enough, on this occasion, use of the taser appeared to be the last option she and Hunter had to save themselves against a ferocious enemy. Whilst most of these meetings were in respect of the reporting required when a taser is discharged, there had been a couple of uncomfortable encounters with the Professional Standards people which Pennant could have done without. But she had been able to give a good account of her decision-making in the heat of the action which had impressed those who sought to question her motives.

Although the team had been missing their leader, DCI Alan Iversen had stepped into the breach whilst Hunter was recovering from her injuries. If truth be known, Iversen was thoroughly enjoying being back in the thick of an investigation which got him away from tedious meetings with the top brass in Maidstone or Canterbury, and the team had responded well to his style of management.

At the moment, Iversen was in discussion with DS Ted Selitto and DS Grace Kendall who had almost lived in the MIR for the last seven days. The dark grey areas under Kendall's normally sparkling blue eyes told the tale of late nights and early mornings as she analysed and digested the endless flow of information that the case had generated. It had also been made more complicated by the heavy reliance on getting information from Europol and other local police forces in countries as far afield as Georgia, Romania and Bulgaria.

At first, the team had been faced with so much evidence that it had taken a few days to bring all the strands together and build a picture of what had been going on. There had, however, been two breakthrough moments which had enabled them to give much more focus to their investigation. The first had been the discovery of Woons's portacabin just outside Bidborough. Thankfully, the Techies had been able to triangulate its location by using the mobile phone which Selitto had taken off Woons's body at Polruan. And, although the portacabin hadn't in itself provided a huge amount of information, it had allowed the MIT to identify all the other houses which Woons had set up. These had now been closed down which had caused a massive headache for the team due to the number of illegal immigrants they had had to process. Thankfully, most of the girls could be accommodated at centres normally used for those detained at the ports and the Eurotunnel terminal. The women who were actually running the houses were processed at Maidstone and released on bail whilst the investigation continued.

The second breakthrough had come when Dr Toby Swartzman had been able to tentatively identify that body parts belonging to Tamaz Vashlili were amongst those stored in the freezers at the lighthouse. Fingerprints matched those found in the Crocus Room at Meadowlands, but the DNA was not a match to that found in the bathroom. So, it seemed that Vashlili had been killed elsewhere and that his body was then taken to the lighthouse to be carved up in the lantern room. Interestingly, the CSI team had been unable to find a head which matched Vashlili's torso. This revived the vexed question of the black rubbish sack which Selitto had seen one afternoon, but it was eventually agreed that this was probably a bit of a red herring. Having fed the prints through the Europol system, they had received notice of a match in Georgia with the Georgian police reporting a historical arrest for assault. This linked Vashlili with the town of Kaspi and it wasn't long before the authorities there had identified the Tsiklauri gang. And, after sifting through records until the early hours one morning, DC Elaine Jennings had made the connection with Woons when she discovered that Tsiklauri's right hand man, Irakli, had a brother called Zurab who had shared a cell with Woons at Maidstone in the mid-1980s.

Although they now knew that the trafficking operation was being controlled from Georgia, they were having difficulty in understanding why all the girls they had rounded up were Bulgarian. They also knew that all the girls who had been killed were Bulgarian including the two which Hunter and Pennant had discovered in cages in the lighthouse. And, as if to make matters worse, the bodies of another nine girls had been discovered in weighted-down body bags at the bottom of the lake at Meadowlands. All were Bulgarian. On a more positive note, the girl discovered by DC Mishraz on the floor of the cellar at the house in Roger's Rough Road was responding well to treatment at Maidstone Hospital and would eventually be processed by the UK Border Force before being repatriated to her family back home in Bulgaria. A small positive result in an ocean of misery.

Another question mark hung over a recent trip which Woons had made to Georgia. Whilst there was a record of him going through Passport Control on the way into Tbilisi, there was no record of him leaving. However, after calling in just about all the favours she had ever accumulated, Grace Kendall had obtained a passenger list for an Air Baltic flight from Tbilisi to Riga in Latvia which showed Woons as having a seat in the last row at the back of the aircraft. From there, she was able to place him on a connecting flight to Gatwick. So, the question was what was he doing in Georgia and was there now a connection with Latvia?

The Georgian Police had, in fact, been extremely helpful and Kendall had been impressed with the availability of information which they were happy to share. Through CCTV, they had managed to discover that Woons had been collected at Tbilisi Airport by two men but they had been unable to identify who these men were. Kendall had been dealing with Police Officer Nozadze of the National Security Department who had said that, unfortunately, they had been unable to follow Woons' progress from the airport. He did, however, mention an incident later that day when there appeared to have been a gang fight at a remote location off the main motorway linking Tbilisi with the Black Sea coast.

The Police had recovered the bodies of two Romanian citizens but had also found some blood in the vehicle which was not compatible with either of the two Romanians. At this, an idea had formed in Kendall's mind and she asked if they could either obtain a sample of the blood or DNA for comparison. Police Officer Nozadze had said that he would see what he could do and, the following day, Kendall had received the data requested. The Police Officer had also attached a set of prints which they had taken from the area around the blood and which did not match those of the two Romanians. Unfortunately, Woons's body was still in Cornwall but Forensics had managed to get a partial match on the prints from the desk at the portacabin.

This potentially put Woons in a vehicle with two Romanians and this, in turn, had given the MIT another major headache.

They had further cause to investigate a connection with Romania when the huge man who fell from the lantern room at the lighthouse was identified as Dracul Lazaresku. According to the Romanian Security Services, he was wanted for many crimes in respect of trafficking and murder, and was considered to be an extremely dangerous man. Notwithstanding his size, it seemed that he was able to move about with impunity and had avoided arrest over many years. This news had sent a shiver down DC Carolyn Pennant's spine. Just remembering her ordeal at the hands of this man was also contributing to her sleepless nights.

DC Stuart Crosby and DC Azzar Mishraz had been almost permanently stationed at the lighthouse, trying to work out how such an operation could have been set up without anyone at Meadowlands being aware of what was going on right under their noses. They started by trying to establish how all the equipment had been installed in the lighthouse in the first place. They quickly discovered that Dangerfield was very likely to have been involved in this, probably with the assistance of Vashlili and some of his cronies. They found out that, about a year ago, Dangerfield had suddenly ordered some repair work to be undertaken on the lighthouse. As far as anyone could recall, he had informed the staff that the work had been authorised by the owners and that everyone had to keep away from the lake on health & safety grounds. The gates onto the lakeside walk had been padlocked shut, and 'No Entry' signs had been posted at all points of entry. If any guests asked what was going on, they were to be told that the area had been closed off due to work taking place on an unsound structure. The detectives had also learned that a mobile crane had been positioned close to the lake which was presumably used to transfer materials to the lighthouse.

DC Mishraz had also discovered that the freezers in the kitchens had suddenly been replaced on the orders of Dangerfield even though they had only been about a year old at the time. The Head Chef had been able to identify the freezers in the lighthouse as being the ones which had been replaced so it seemed that Dangerfield had managed to get them transported to the lake whereupon they were craned over to the lighthouse – presumably under the cover of darkness. The crane would also have been used to transfer the cages and all the equipment which Hunter and Pennant had found in the lantern room. They also had to assume that Vashlili had organised a small workforce to install all this equipment.

There had also been a question as to how the lighthouse was powered but this was solved when the marine team had started searching the bottom of the lake and discovered a power cable which ran from the base of the structure to the edge of the lake just under the weir. The ground search teams eventually found a small generator housed in a wooden shed hidden in undergrowth not far from where the weir emptied out so that the sound of the cascading water virtually drowned out the noise of the generator. The shed also had some soundproofing which further reduced the chances of anyone hearing the machine. There was plenty of fuel stored in the shed so no doubt the generator was kept well topped-up.

Meanwhile, down at Tunbridge Wells, Dr Toby Swartzman and his team had spent most of their waking hours trying to piece together limbs, torsos, hands, feet and heads to try to make sense of the macabre contents of the freezers. He'd had to call in the help of two Pathologists from outside Kent. In addition, Norman Partington had had to miss a couple of golf days and even Professor Ilona Jenkyns had been persuaded to make the journey from London for a couple of days in Kent. The mortuary was full to bursting with corpses, body parts and pathologists, and it had been a measure of the professionalism of all concerned that they had managed to make real progress during the week.

103

Thursday 3 August

Over the last seven days, the MIT had held meetings two or three times a day to make sure that all the information which was coming in almost by the minute was processed. This meant that they could at least get a handle on the complexity of the crimes they were investigating. The clock was now ticking up to 6.00 p.m. on the Thursday following the incident at the lighthouse, and everyone was assembled in the MIR. The room was packed for the meeting as DCI Iversen called them together.

'Okay, everyone!' he began. 'Just a thank you from me for all your continuing hard work, and your commitment during this very tough investigation. We're joined this evening by DCI Jack Pennington from SOC. Jack's been keeping an eye on how we've been progressing, and I thought it would be a good idea for him to meet up with you this evening so that he can get an idea of where we're at with the investigation.'

'Yes, thanks Alan and hello everyone.' Pennington certainly had a presence about him; he commanded attention. A little over six feet tall, he was a swarthy handsome man with dark close-cropped hair and a set of very white teeth. He was dressed in a tailored dark suit with an open-necked white shirt, the cuffs of which protruded from under the sleeves of the jacket. He spoke in measured tones, and explained the role of SOC in Kent. He told the MIT about the heavy workload caused by the continuing trafficking problem which Kent suffered from, and he thanked them for all their hard work which had saved him having to try and find officers from his own team to assign to this investigation. When he had finished, Iversen asked DS Selitto to give an update on where they were.

Selitto moved to the front of the room and was just about to start when the door to the MIR opened and DI Sarah Hunter hobbled into the room, leaning on a hospital crutch to take the weight off her ankle. The team erupted when they realised that their leader was back, and started clapping and banging on desks. She stood there looking surprised and rather sheepish before making her way to the chair which DC Stuart Crosby had vacated and was now offering to her. She walked with a pronounced limp and the plaster round one of her ankles bore testament to the painful injury she had suffered when tripping down the steps at the lighthouse. Her left arm was in a sling and a huge yellowy black bruise covered the left side of her face. Her left eye was bloodshot and there was a gash across her forehead which still had traces of the sutures which had been used to close the wound up. She smiled at everyone as best she could, and then turned towards Selitto who was looking ever so slightly emotional. Eventually, the noise quietened down.

'It's great to have you back, boss,' he said, keeping a degree of formality in his voice, 'and I'm sure you'd like to know what we've been up to!'

'That's why I'm here, Sergeant!' she said with a wry smile, teasing him. There was a ripple of laughter in the room. Everyone was at the top of their game.

Selitto then proceeded to give them a rundown of the current thinking.

Woons had been introduced to the Georgian gang a long time ago after meeting one of its members in Maidstone Prison.

They had persuaded him to help them open up a series of private houses in Kent which were to be used by top end high rollers for no-holds-barred sex and more with young girls who were to be provided by the Georgians. The MIT had yet to finally establish ownership of the properties but it was likely to have been the Georgians who put up a lot of the funding to start with and then Woons could have bought more properties once he was financially established. What they had found was that ownership of the properties had been well hidden which meant they were now having to consider the likelihood that these houses were owned by offshore shell companies. But they had also decided that this wasn't a priority in the circumstances.

For some reason, the girls were all sourced from Bulgaria and were probably prepared for their new life in the back streets of Sofia. The actual trafficking was, therefore, from Bulgaria so could not be traced back to Georgia. The middle man between the Georgians and Woons was a guy called Tamaz Vashlili who organised the final leg of the journey across or under the Channel and who had created holding centres in the Kent countryside. Vashlili was a very clever operator who managed to get in and out of the UK with ease. And, although he was no doubt well paid by the Georgians, he seemed to have lately been lured by another gang which was probably offering more money or some other lucrative deal.'

He looked at his notes. 'It is likely that Vashlili set up the operation in the lighthouse with the co-operation of Dangerfield. He had to have a means of disposing of bodies and, judging by the numbers we have found in and around the lighthouse, it seems that girls were regularly subjected to such degradation that they either died as a result of depraved sexual activity or they took their own lives. Whatever was the cause of death, Vashlili was the one who would be summoned to take the bodies to the lighthouse.'

Selitto was now into his stride. 'We think that Vashlili had been in discussion with a gang of traffickers from Romania, and had been gradually shifting his allegiances to his new masters over the last few months. This was, however, the start of his downfall because those planning the takeover were a bunch of utterly ruthless criminals led by a man going under the name of Borislav Zlatkov. We have a number of conflicting reports about Mr Zlatkov although most point to the fact that he doesn't travel very far from his base in the suburbs of Bucharest. Instead, he employs a number of lookalikes, and we think that one of these was used to communicate with Vashlili by means of a dead-letter-box at Meadowlands. We suspect that Vashlili had never actually met Zlatkov so he thought that he was dealing with the real thing when one of the lookalikes turned up at the door of his hotel room and was welcomed in like a long-lost friend.'

'As you know, we've still been unable to establish exactly what occurred in the Crocus room at Meadowlands, and our best guess now is that the destruction in the room was an elaborate hoax to make us believe that Vashlili had been killed there. However, apart from the fact that his fingerprints were found in the room, we have eventually had to conclude that there was little other evidence to show that he was killed in that room. So, the mystery of who, if anyone, was killed in the bathroom remains, and the CSIs are now urgently reviewing all the evidence to see if they can shed any new light on what happened there. What we do know is that there is solid evidence to indicate that Vashlili was well in with his new masters as he was clearly passing detailed information to them based on the evidence we found in the room. But, soon after, it was likely that Vashlili had served his purpose in that he had given the Romanians all the information he had available to him. So, it's more than likely that he was eliminated and his body taken to the lighthouse for disposal, or he might even have been killed whilst visiting the lighthouse. Meanwhile, the real Zlatkov had ordered the destruction of the Georgians' UK operation and the kidnapping of the girls which represented real value as they could be put to use elsewhere in his own organisation.'

'Once Woons discovered that his empire was under attack, he seems to have jetted off to Georgia to see his masters and find out what they were going to do about the Romanians. And this is where it gets a bit sketchy because it's been difficult to get enough intel. We think that he actually met with the Romanians because his blood was left in a SUV alongside the bodies of two Romanians who were gangsters known to the Georgian Police. They had been killed in an ambush so the inference has to be that Woons was rescued by the gang from Kaspi. He was then spirited out of the country on an Air Baltic flight to Riga in Latvia before flying straight on to Gatwick. Here, he was picked up by his faithful right-hand man, Trigger Harding, who has a long record for thieving and had known Woons for years. We have CCTV footage of Harding picking Woons up at the Gatwick Hilton before they drove off to Cornwall. In the meantime, two of Woons' other acolytes, Richard Spink and Emma White, were shot dead by person or persons unknown in an ambush near Bedgebury. The lack of forensic evidence at the site of the shooting seems to indicate that the assassin may have been inside a vehicle which was blocking the road. If all the spent casings had been jettisoned inside the vehicle, that would account for the lack of evidence around the site of the killing.'

'Anyway, the shooting of Spink and White really put the wind up Woons who didn't seem to have the stomach for a fight which is why he fled to Cornwall. He then tried to do a plea-bargain deal with us which is why I went all the way to a tiny speck on the map called Polruan only to see him shot dead by a sniper's rifle – probably an execution. His side-kick Harding was also killed and crammed into the boot of Woons's Merc. So, that was effectively the end of the Woons gang. Devon & Cornwall didn't waste much time getting on to us when they had discovered the two bodies, and we have been able to maintain cordial relations with them throughout – thank goodness!'

Selitto shifted his stance and looked over towards Hunter. 'And, as you know, DI Hunter had long been suspicious about Peter Dangerfield, General Manager at Meadowlands. About a week ago, Grace got her hands on some useful intel about his involvement in trafficking Serbs and Croats through Hungary in 2015 before Hungary closed its borders. So, DI Hunter decided to investigate which eventually led to the discovery of the lighthouse full of horrors which you now know about, and one dead Romanian by the name of Dracul Lazaresku. We think that Lazaresku probably knew the fake Zlatkov and had been given use of the lighthouse to carry out his own depraved activities. One of our psychiatric advisers has suggested that Lazaresku was a... hold on, better get this right!' Selitto leafed through his notebook until he came to the note he had made. 'Yes, she said he was probably a necromutilomaniac which basically means that he got off on mutilating corpses. So, he cut up the bodies and kept a selection of limbs, torsos and heads in the freezers before consigning other parts to a watery grave in the lake. In view of his appearance at the lighthouse with a gun last Thursday, we have to presume that Dangerfield had some knowledge of these nefarious activities so he must have also been on the Romanian payroll – but not for long!'

Selitto looked up from his notes. 'As you know, Dangerfield was also executed via a sniper's bullet but we have been unable to trace who fired the shot, and it is very likely that that person would have left the country almost immediately. We have, however, just had some intel which the Techies have got from Dangerfield's phone. There's a note in the phone's diary which seems to indicate that he had a meeting with Vashlili and another man about ten months ago. This would seem to pretty much confirm his association with the Romanians, and he must have known what was going on in the lighthouse all along. No wonder he seemed pissed off when the Duty Manager had called us to report the original MisPer! And he certainly didn't like us taking walks around the lake!'

'So, that's about where we are, sir,' Selitto finished by turning to DCI Pennington. 'As you can see, there are some loose ends to tie up and a lot of interviewing to do with the people from the houses which the Romanians didn't get around to trashing. And there's a lot of referencing and cross-referencing work to do but the team are up for that – I think!' He looked around the sea of faces in front of him – most were smiling, all were looking exhausted.

Pennington pushed himself off the corner of the desk he had been perching on and moved into the middle of the room. 'Thank you, Sergeant. A very comprehensive account of the last few days. It seems to have been a terrific team effort and we in SOC are hugely grateful to you all for the hard work you have put in. Well done to all of you!' He looked over at Iversen. 'Now, I think that DCI Iversen has organised some refreshments for you all at the Vauxhall this evening so please do feel free to join in. Is that right, Alan?'

Iversen was nodding. 'Yes, everyone welcome! There's money behind the bar and some nibbles so let's have a night off and enjoy ourselves!' The team started to shuffle towards the door, the murmur of conversation growing in volume. They had worked hard so could afford to have a night off, even if there would be a few sore heads in the morning.

Pennington looked down at Hunter who was still sitting at a desk just to his left. She was concentrating on the screen but a sixth sense seemed to have alerted her to the fact that she was being watched. She looked up and smiled weakly at Pennington before turning her gaze back to the screen. He returned the smile even though she wasn't looking at him. So, this was the lady behind the voice he had spoken to on the phone, he thought. Suddenly, Kent didn't seem such a bad place after all.

104

Two Months Later

The flight from Riga had been uneventful and, after very little delay, Air Baltic flight BT651 touched down on the westerly runway at London Gatwick Airport. The eight-month-old Airbus A220-300 taxied to a gate in the South Terminal, and the passengers disembarked via the airbridge. They made their way along endless corridors, either using the travellators or slogging it out on foot. Round corners, down ramps and through doors until they eventually reached the Passport Control area. UK Citizens only, EU Countries, Non-EU Countries – so many signs, such a lot of choice!

The passenger from seat 10A on the Air Baltic flight wasn't sure which queue she should join. She stood there looking puzzled until a nice lady asked her where she was from. The lady had a badge on a lanyard round her neck which denoted that she was part of the 'UK Border Force'. She pointed the passenger to a short queue in front of a bank of desks, most of which were vacant. The passenger waited her turn and was then called forward to one of the desks where a friendly man took her passport and opened it at the page with her photograph on it. Smiling, he swiped the passport through a machine on his desk, and then handed it back to the passenger.

'Welcome to London, Miss Smirnova!'

THE END

ACKNOWLEDGEMENTS

I developed a love of crime fiction by reading books by Mari Hannah, Stuart MacBride, Ian Rankin, Mark Billingham, Alex Gray, James Oswald, Paul Finch, Lin Anderson and Peter James among others. Although I have never met any of them, they have collectively and individually inspired me throughout the long hours of writing until all my wild ideas had finally tumbled out of my teeming brain and become words on the page.

A huge thank-you to James Essinger for his unfailing enthusiasm, encouragement and belief in my book. Also, to all at The Conrad Press for their guidance through the vagaries of the publishing world about which I knew nothing. It has been an adventure in itself! I am also eternally grateful to my band of relatives, friends and colleagues who read the early drafts of the book and made so many constructive suggestions. In particular to Lindsay Crawford Jones, my dear sister and sternest critic. Also to Anne Eaves, Pauline Davies, Paul Hauff, Nicolas de Jong, Isobel Carver, Helen Gilmour, Julia Holland, Meriel Nye, Doug Cocker and Despina Koniordou. You have all been an incredible help to me!

I also owe a huge debt of gratitude to Elly Rees who was the inspiration for Eleonora. Your clever insight into how the character might worm her way into Woons' brain was inspiring, and was a turning point for the book. I am also indebted to George Cooper, my physical trainer and the sounding board every writer should have. Those early morning plot discussions in The Better Body Gym in Sevenoaks whilst trying to keep fit on cold winter mornings will live long in the memory!

And thank you to the beautiful county of Kent. What a lovely canvas on which to paint a story! Whilst all the characters and events are obviously a work of fiction, many of the locations are not and readers will, hopefully, be able to follow Sarah Hunter and Ted Selitto as they make their way around leafy country lanes, stopping for refreshment at some of the local pubs on the way!

Finally, a great big hug and lots of love for all my family who have been so supportive throughout. Not least to Barbara who has had to put up with me spending long hours at my desk rather than helping with household or gardening projects. Thank you for always being there to listen to all the crackpot ideas which I came up with along the way, and for your insightful comments when the first draft was completed. It has been quite a journey of discovery for both of us!

Robin Nye, July 2020